THE BLACK BREATH

BOOK 2 OF THE CHRONICLES OF TORGEIR

J. C. EYLER

GRIM
DRAGON
PUBLISHING

Cover art by Ryan Frederickson

First edition: June 2025

ISBN: 978-1-963717-13-6

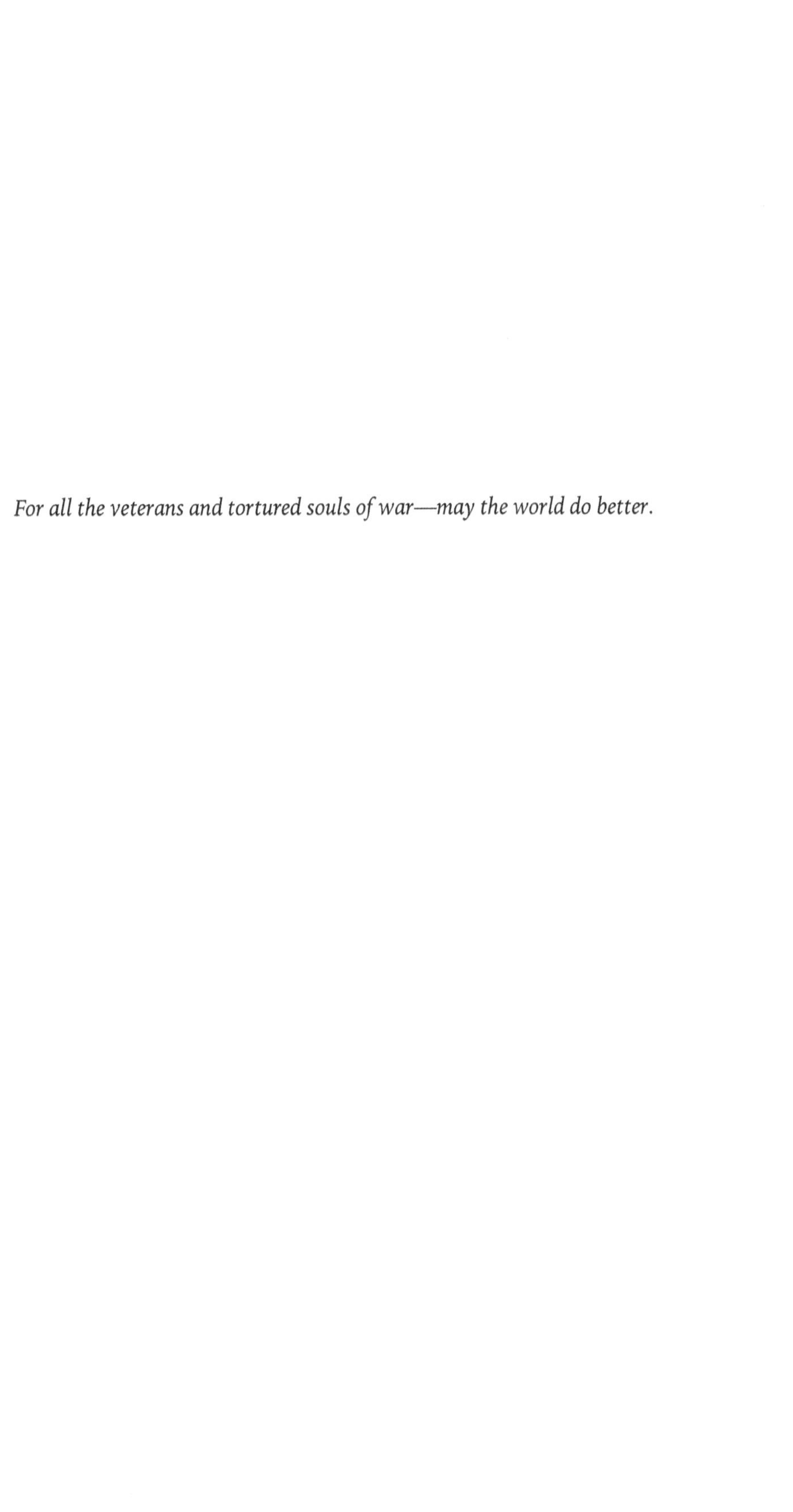

For all the veterans and tortured souls of war—may the world do better.

ACKNOWLEDGMENTS

Thank you to the Grim Dragon Team—Ryan Frederickson, Trevor Collins, Randy Seawright, Jason Holbrook, and Josh Branson—whose constant flow of memes and music keep my spirits high.

A special thanks to to Juan V. M. Mendoza, whose friendship has helped carry me throughout my life.

CONTENT WARNING

The Black Breath contains scenes with, but not limited to, the following:

- Torture
- Self harm
- Extreme suffering
- Sexual assault (off page)
- Prejudice

TORGEIR

TORGEIR
Blailon
Gorgosant
Wedilkind
Neuheim
Vestia
Bernward
Imutia
Aldbert
Horst
Birododoc
New Torgeir
Laira
Glaedia
Wbawee Forest
Onatah Forest
Nyalia
Serolle
Byrios
Ripanica
Orippe
Wbicbabpi Forest
Belachon
Meru'ut
Tanepauri
Castantor
Uleeri
Themsa
Estias
Silrin
Eno'olaa Forest
N
W
E
S
0
500
Miles

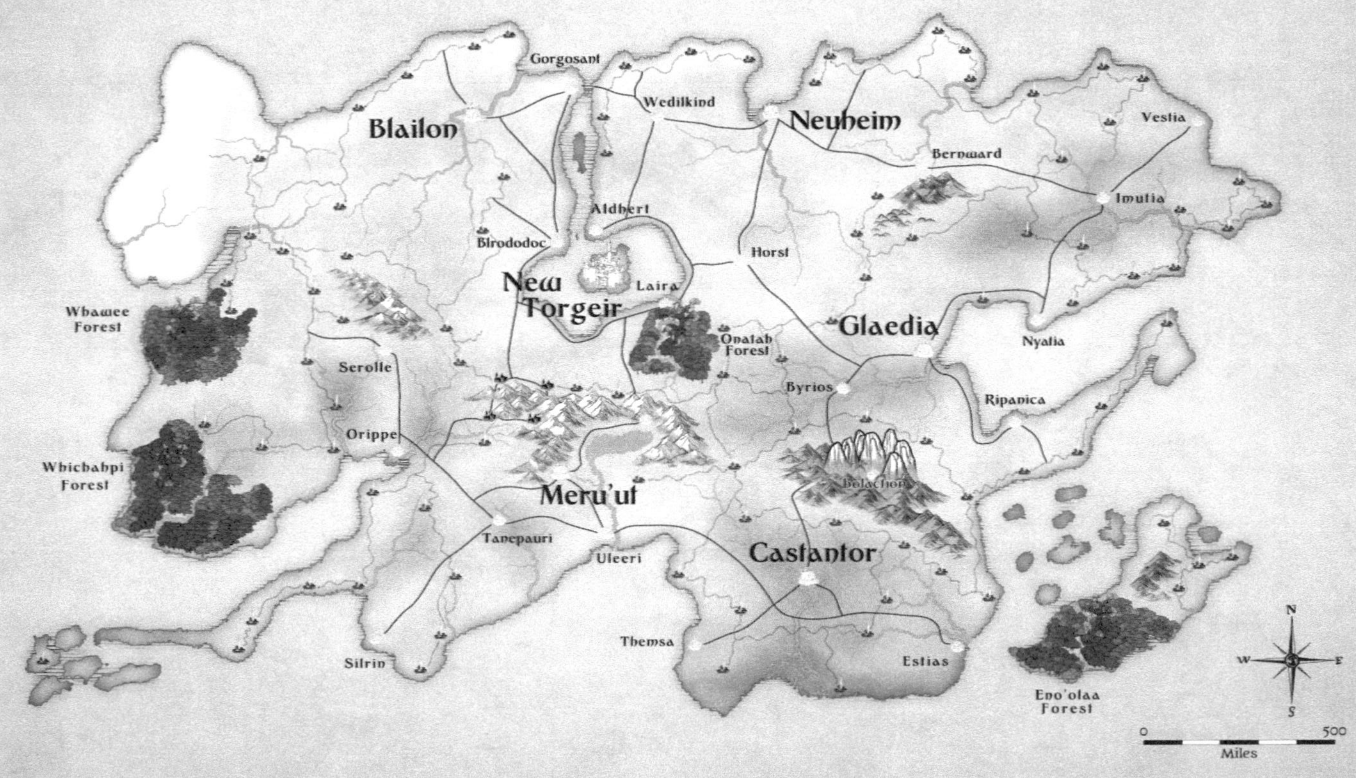

The Five Kingdoms of TORGEIR
Blailon
Neuheim
Glaedia
New Torgeir
Meru'ut
Castantor

PROLOGUE

Nilam leaned against the deck railing, focusing on the salty sea air and the hush of broken minds. The sound of crashing waves rumbled beneath squawking seagulls. He never thought he'd be happy to see those pestering birds, but he'd also never been at sea. His stomach heaved, but, as usual, there was nothing left to offer the wavers. The sailors' surety that the sickness would fade as soon as they saw land did little to comfort his spoiled stomach. They gazed at him with the blank look of the Faithful—those who had heard the Call of the Voice.

Nilam heaved again.

"Still sick?"

"Dear gods!" Nilam exclaimed, startling at the youthful voice.

Egan flinched, his disheveled blond hair fluttering in the wind. Their voyage seemed to have pulled more freckles across the boy's skin, not that anyone could see much past the grime.

And I'll be a terrentor's meal if he didn't grow two inches.

"You nearly scared the Light out of me," Nilam grumbled, rubbing his aching shoulder.

"I'm sorry," Egan said, ducking his head. His large brown eyes went wide, and he pointed, hopping from foot to foot. "Look! Shore!"

"And not a moment too soon," Nilam said, with a long stretch, his back and neck popping. "The sea has been as kind to these old bones as it has been to my stomach."

Egan wrinkled his nose. "Maybe if you washed, you wouldn't feel so bad?"

Nilam raised an eyebrow. "Have you looked at yourself lately?"

Egan folded his arms across his chest. "At least I swam with the sailors. You haven't touched a bath since…since forever."

Nilam chuckled at Egan's blissful innocence. "The light shines brightest within the darkness."

"I don't know what any of that has to do with the smell," Egan said.

Nilam ignored the boy's innocent remark, and he gestured to the shoreline and the town growing on the horizon. "Tell me what you see."

Egan's brow scrunched, and he shrugged. "I see Toliane, right? And a beach, and the waves, and birds. I love the way the ship sways, but I can't wait—"

Nilam raised a finger, and Egan flinched. Thankfully, it hadn't taken the boy long to learn proper respect for his elders. "I see darkness, Egan. Thousands upon thousands of our brothers and sisters living in darkness."

"You mean Phaerians!" Egan said, and flinched again. The child opened one eye. When Nilam's hand didn't strike, he opened the other and offered a weak smile.

Nilam pushed the offense to the back of his mind. He would wait to deal with the interruption and flinching until after they'd made shore. "So close to the shadow of the empire," he continued, gesturing to the town, "news of the Light has yet to reach them. That is the darkness I speak of."

Egan's lips trembled with a comment.

"What is it?"

"That's why we're here!" he said, his eyes brimming with hope. "To bring them out of darkness."

"That's why *I* am here," Nilam reminded him.

Egan's excitement wavered. "Right. You're the Voice. I'm just..." He scratched his head. "Why am I here?"

Nilam squeezed the boy's tiny shoulder. Eagan was still so young and innocent. Maybe that was why Nilam's power had no effect on him. Unlike the sailors, now obedient servants of the Light, Eagan seemed immune to the Voice.

"You're here," Nilam told the young boy, "because you're blessed by the Light. Chosen by our Radiance. You're divine."

Egan shuffled his foot and picked at the ship's railing. "I don't feel divine."

"How do you feel?"

"Bored," Egan mumbled, leaning over the railing to watch his spit fall into the sea.

"Enjoy that feeling," Nilam said, earning a confused look. "Soon enough, you'll wish to be bored."

Cool air cut through Aglia's drab Phaerian garb. Grabbing another dirty shirt from the pile of clothes, she tossed it in the cold washbasin and set to scrubbing. Craving warmth in the freezing fall air, she ignored her numb fingers drumming against the rough washboard, while beads of sweat chilled her brow. Aglia dismissed a flippant thought to ask Lady Maelly Bodiou for hot water. Her mistress might be light-handed with her Phaerians, but not her guard. Besides, the Lady never mentioned anything about asking one of her Vrath to warm the water in the washbasin.

Aglia's stomach growled for food, complaining about the measly breakfast she'd received. She risked a glance at the bucket of water and nu'food on the table—slagsticks, nu'cheese, nu'biscuits, and a too-sweet paste that was supposed to be strawberry jam, but tasted like sweet red goo. Even with the patina of dust coating the uncovered food, her mouth watered at the thought of filling her empty belly.

"And waste a perfectly clean towel?" Lady Maelly had said when

Aglia suggested covering the food. "It's still better than anything in Alduos, right?"

Alduos, but not home.

Memories of the idyllic village floated through Aglia's mind. The Square where everyone gathered for festivities, tables brimming with food—real food, not the nu'ofal Citizens called food—roasted pork braised in honied juices, buttery mashed potatoes, garlic fried into crispy treats, slabs of meat brushed with rosemary.

Maelly might be a sympathizer, but at her core, she was still a blasted Founder.

Even so, her cruelties paled compared to Aglia's former master, Lord Rodak. He'd told her Phlem didn't deserve to be so pretty, right before he tortured the beauty out of her. Day after day, she'd endured his heavy fists and adroit shaping. What little teeth she still had could hardly chew meat. Her crooked nose would always whistle when she breathed, and what remained of her wispy hair would forever stay dark and curly.

"Like Phaerians should be," Lady Maelly had said the day she bought Aglia and gave her that ridiculous name.

An ugly name for an ugly Phlem.

Aglia wrung the washed shirt, whipped it in the air a few times, and hung it on one of the yellow-tinted ropes of force Captain Gwyndril had shaped. Aglia grabbed another dirty shirt and scrubbed hard against the washboard, letting her pain overwhelm those terrible memories, before her thoughts drifted back to *him*.

Her vision watered, and still she scrubbed. Sweat trickled down her brow, her legs shook from the pain, and still she scrubbed. Sharp agony consumed her, and she collapsed to the ground, crying, nursing her bleeding hands.

A muffled curse startled her, and she stood, pretending to pick up something from the ground. She sighed in relief when Captain Gwyndril limped past the crates stacked beside Lady Maelly's trio of wagons. He grumbled at his jeering men before joining them at the campfire, and Aglia returned to the washbasin.

Lady Maelly poked her head up from her latest trench, one of the dozens snaking through her dig site. A silky ponytail of ruby-red hair draped down her back, swishing against her dusty tan jacket. She dragged her hand over her forehead, smearing a line of dirt on her alabaster-white skin. Not for the first time, Aglia wondered what Lady Maelly would have looked like without all the shaping. Had she been born with eyes so vibrant and green, or had they been dark like Aglia's? What tone had the Currents washed from her skin?

"Aglia," Lady Maelly said, waving her over. "I hate to admit it, but I think Jilsen was right. I think we're in the wrong spot. Maybe we should move closer to the Prus Ruins."

Aglia grabbed a towel-covered bucket of water from under the table, and set it where her master could reach. "In your defense, M'Lady, according to the Lady Jilsen, every dig site was a bad site."

Lady Maelly pulled back the towel and guzzled a ladle of water. "True," she said, dipping the ladle again. "You never have to ask Jilsen for her opinion, do you?"

"I would never dare ask, M'Lady."

"Best that you don't," Lady Maelly said, returning to ladle to the bucket. "Now, go back and finish the laundry. I swear, you take twice as long as your predecessor."

"Did she contend with a dust storm too?" Aglia said, immediately regretting the off-handed remark.

"I may be sympathetic to your kind's plight," Lady Maelly said, raising her brow. "I may even believe you are as Human as any other Citizen…Districters, obviously. But do not mistake my kindness for weakness, girl." She leveled a threatening gaze. "I'm still a Founder, and you're still a Phaerian. I think a couple of days without food will remind you of that."

Aglia's lip trembled, but she dared not cry. Tears would only prolong her days of famine. Lady Maelly expected her Phaerians to be as dispassionate as her research. Aglia gave obeisance, pressing her forehead to the ground to hide her trembling chin. "Thank you, M'Lady."

"Be glad I'm not Jilsen," Lady Maelly said. "She would have taken your tongue for an outburst like that, which is why I don't take you around people like her and Lord Rodak."

"Thank you, M'Lady."

Maelly grumbled, pulling herself out of the trench. She dusted off her hands and gave herself a quick look, sneering at the streaks of dirt in her clothes. "Oh, this will not do. Not at all." Her clothes rippled as if from an unfelt breeze, and the dust and grime sloughed to the ground. "Much better. Well, don't just stand there, Aglia. That laundry isn't going to wash itself. See me in my wagon when you're finished, and please, don't take all day like yesterday. You know how I abhor how lazy you people are." She tapped her chin. "I'll tell you what—finish washing the clothes before supper, and you can have my scraps. It's better than you deserve, but I'm nothing if not kind."

"Too kind, M'Lady," Aglia replied, plastering a wide smile. With less than an hour until dinner, Lady Maelly knew full well that Aglia could never finish all the laundry in time. Never mind that dust already covered the wet laundry hanging from the shaped lines, which meant Aglia would have to wash them again tomorrow. Lady Maelly, Captain Gwndril, and the other Vrath in her retinue could clean every shirt, trouser, dress, undergarment, and towel in the pile of laundry with a single thought, but they enjoyed watching Aglia perform menial tasks.

Her stomach twisted, begging for her to devour the dust-covered nu'food, but she dared not sneak a single bite. Two days without sustenance was bad enough without giving Lady Maelly a reason to extend the torture to a week. Ignoring her pains, Aglia grabbed another shirt and set to scrubbing. Shirt finished, she draped it with the others. Five more and she'd start on the pile of trousers, then the dresses, towels, socks, and undergarments.

The sun dipped over the horizon by the time she finished, the sky a medley of colors she'd once thought beautiful. Lord Rodak had taken that from her as well. She ran her tongue over her sparse teeth and empty gums, her anger growing with memories of her previous master. He'd murdered everyone—her friends, her family, everyone she'd ever loved. He'd only kept her because of her connection with...

with *him*. All her torment—every punch, every slap, every choke, and vicious pattern—done because of *him*. The man she'd once loved.

Smoldering with rage, she staggered to the rinse basins and peeled off her clothes. At least the water didn't smell too bad. She gazed at her reflection. Thin, lifeless hair curled from her scalp. Her nose, swollen from all the breaks, leaned off center, and an angry scar drifted around her right eye. Bones, once hidden beneath supple, tantalizing curves, now stood proud on her emaciated frame, her thin skin riddled with scars and sores.

"I used to be beautiful," she said, twirling a lock of her now-black hair. Hair that used to cascade down her back like a waterfall of honey. The memory of orange blossoms and jasmine drifted through her mind.

My smell, she thought, recalling a picnic by a majestic lake.

"Before *he* left me," Aglia spat. Before he left Headwater to the whims of her former master.

A bright flash on the southern horizon caught her eyes, and she stared at a distant plume of smoke rising above the Alrynn Mountains. Tiny at such a distance, the smoke churned into a dark mushroom, while an invisible wave rolled over the land, swaying trees and tearing out bushes. Moments later, the wave washed buffeted Aglia with a loud crack.

Fear turned her legs to mush, and she fell to her knees, while Lady Maelly's soldiers and Vrath scrambled with their weapons, forming a protective wall around the Founder.

Aglia gawked at the dark, mushroom-shaped cloud rising behind the mountains. Only one being could have caused so much destruction—the man who had left her. The man she'd once loved.

Kael Aelastair, the godsdamned Light of Prophecy.

PART I

PATHS

That which once was shall be no more, and her name shall be the Light, and Death shall follow.

1

A NEW FACE

Ash stung L'Veyna's eyes, her hope as dead as her god.

Tálise's bone-white remnants powdered her olive skin, muting the thin braids woven down her left arm to her elbow, each strand a muted color of autumn. The ash dusted her long ears and green Keeper's wrap, its acrid stench tainting her breath, and coating her tongue with death. Her stomach clenched, and she doubled over, spilling thick bile onto the floor of Keeper Orenda's house-tree.

Her brother, Prack, handed her a cloth that smelled of blessed gardenia and lilac, not the ashen bones of their god. His long pointed ears, decorated with emerald jewelry, swept past his dusty hair. Unbraided autumnal locks that scorned their traditional braids draped down his back from a tail of vibrant purple, red, yellow, orange, and brown. He crouched before an ornate trunk, his dark leather riding coat creaking when he reached to open the lid.

L'Veyna fought off another wave of gloom, seeking the comfort of her ever-blossoming power. The source of her Keeper's gift radiated within her, like pedals forever shedding from a flower, waiting for her to ask. But not even that blessed warmth could banish the cold truth plaguing her heart. Prophecy had come for her people.

Just a few hours ago, she'd been with all the other saplings of Onatah, gathering flowers, and finishing the Effigy of Light in preparation for their Blossoming. Instead of entering Tálise's Grove and shedding the chains of the Saplings Curse, she'd watched her tree-god crumble to ash.

"Pack lots of clothes," Prack said, his voice firm. Gone was the happy-go-lucky brother who visited between adventures, his emerald eyes hard and calculating, not puffy like hers. After all, what did he have to worry about? His Blossoming happened over a century ago. He wasn't the one prophesied to slaughter their people.

"Are you listening to me?" he said. "Pack thick clothes. The Boorde Alliance gets cold."

"*Like your heart?*" L'Veyna clacked against her beltboard, her throat too tight to speak.

"Clothes," he said, jabbing his finger at a chest near the front door. "Now."

She opened the chest to find it full of similar clothes to her brother's—thick hempen shirts and pants, along with thick socks, and ridiculous undergarments that would cover more of her than her Keeper's wrap.

"I am not wearing these," she said, gesturing to the autumnal braids wrapping her left arm. "I refuse to re-ask my braid every time I need to change my clothes."

"You say that now," Prack replied, stuffing his pack with something from the chest.

"What was that?"

"Never mind," Prack said, moving to a wall of shelves filled with books.

L'Veyna sneered at her brother's back. She packed a thick shirt and trousers, just to stop his nagging, though she ignored the thick, long-sleeved undergarments. She could always ask some if she needed them, but how cold could it get in the plagued Boorde Alliance?

"I can't believe you're dragging me to that frozen wasteland."

"I'm not dragging you anywhere," Prack replied, lifting a black box out of another chest. Before she could ask about it, he shifted outside to the horses, returning a heartbeat later in a blur of motion. "You're going for your own safety."

"But why the Alliance? The Boorde hate our people."

"They do not," Prack replied.

"They don't call us leaf-eaters because they like us."

Her brother stood before her, and placed his hands on her shoulders, his emerald eyes brimming with the concern she'd longed to see since they left Tálise's Grove. "Our beloved home is about to become a battlefield, Little Sprout. I can't help the other saplings, but I'll be damned if I let anything happen to you."

L'Veyna swallowed back another wave of dread. Every sapling in the forest, other than her, still slept at the base of ta'Ajiilee. All of them gathered for a Blossoming Ceremony that would never happen.

"What do you think the Council will do to the saplings?" she asked.

"I don't know," Prack said. "And we're not waiting to find out."

"What about Mother and—" Her voice cracked, and she fell into her brother's arms.

Prack rubbed her back, soothing the pain that poured down her cheeks. "Mother and Father are still at home, probably just now awakening."

"*We can't leave them,*" she clacked, her throat too thick to speak.

Prack's heavy sigh confirmed her fears. Even for a Chi'indi like her brother, able to dash with blinding speed, the place L'Veyna had called home for the past thirteen years rested too high in ta'Ajiilee's branches.

She squeezed her brother, pressing her face into his dumb, stinky clothes. He rocked her, caressing her braided locks the way he did before he left to venture with his rotten Boorde friend. At least this time, she'd go with him instead of watching him leave.

"I am so sorry, Little Sprout. I wish Prophecy had come a day later, or not at all. I wish you could have lived your life in ignorance of the world outside the Sacred Forest." He patted her and stepped back.

"But such is not the case, and if we don't hurry, you won't have a life to live."

L'Veyna nodded, shivering from his blunt honesty. She followed him through the doorway by the kitchen and into a dark, windowless room. Lined from floor to ceiling with more shelves, each shelf was crammed with more jars of cured ha'ath, books, scrolls, and bottles.

Prack knelt before an ornate box with no apparent lid. Maneuvering a series of hidden latches and buttons, he opened the box, revealing a plush velvet lining and a pair of tubes that called to L'Veyna.

"What's that?" she asked.

"Never mind," he said, disappearing in a blur of motion.

L'Veyna grumbled and explored the windowless room. She peaked around a shelf stuffed with books worn with age, and her legs went weak. Draped on the wall was an ancient tapestry woven with an image of the Saplings Curse. Different from the image carved into Mh t'Pralab, the Wall of Prophecy, the tapestry depicted a wave of corpses crashing into a Sacred Forest, and saplings on rafts, floating down a river toward a black cloud. A detailed image of a familiar young man stood on the lead raft.

L'Veyna's breath caught.

Jouler!

There was no mistaking his brown, wavy hair and penetrating eyes. The figure on the tapestry even bore a round scar on his bare chest. Woven next to Jouler was a faceless figure with autumnal braids, green Keeper's wrap, and the youthful curves of a sapling girl.

Like me…

"What are you still doing in here?" Prack asked, startling her. "Are you all packed?"

"What is this?" L'Veyna asked, gesturing to the tapestry. "How long have you known about this?"

"Over a century," he said, his brow rising.

"What is it?" L'Veyna asked.

"Jouler's face. It's always been blank." Prack's emerald eyes fell from the tapestry to her Keeper's wrap. "Like the sapling standing next to him."

Hand trembling, she clacked, *"Is that me?"*

"I don't know," her brother replied. "But Orenda will want to know about it. Now hurry. Grab your pack. I mean to be long gone before Alerix's warriors swarm this place."

THE EARLY MORNING sun poked through the thick canopy of rustwoods, maples, oaks, and black walnut trees. Exhaustion soaked L'Veyna, her eyelids far too heavy to keep open.

The metallic tubes she'd seen in the mysterious box teased the back of her mind, along with another, familiar presence—Jouler, the Harbinger of Death, the man prophesied to lead her people to destruction and bring ruin to the land.

Today was supposed to be a cause for celebration, not the fulfillment of Prophecy. She and every other thirteen-year-old sapling should be awakening from their night of festivities, ready to add their torch to the burning Effigy of Light, then dreamwalk with Tálise, and shed the Saplings Curse. Just one more day and she would have been free. She would have known her role in life, like her brother and every other adult in the forest. Never again would Tálise guide her people. Never again would Prytha know their sacred role in life. L'Veyna's generation, and those to follow, would mindlessly wander the Sacred Forests—whatever was left of them at the end of Prophecy.

She jolted awake in her saddle and stretched, giving a silent curse to the rot-ridden beast beneath her. How her brother tolerated such smelly animals, she'd never understand. Whoever believed hard leather made for a good seat had obviously never actually sat in a saddle. Not twenty minutes had passed, and her back already complained. Prytha legs were meant for climbing trees and skirting the forest floor, not for straddling these massive beasts. It wasn't like they walked any faster. If anything, they slowed her down since she couldn't treewalk. She doubted even Keeper Orenda could ask a portal large enough for these stinky animals.

Lupine shook her head and whinnied, as if reading L'Veyna's mind.

You are, she thought, waiting to see if the horse reacted. *Nothing.*

She had to admit, horses were useful. They might not walk too fast, but they carried a lot, especially Poppy, Prack's beautiful golden mare. A palomino, he'd called it. The poor horse looked as miserable as she, laden with a chest full of ha'ath, books, and the metallic tubes with their incessant call. Compared to Poppy, L'Veyna's horse Lupine didn't have it so bad, only carrying a backpack, bedroll, scrolls, and a box of books.

"Lupine," she mused, more to help keep herself awake. Such a silly name for a horse without a speck of purple to her coat. With her black-and-white pattern, Prack should have named her Storm or Cloud or anything besides Lupine.

Her brother led two other horses laden with more boxes and stuffed packs. One horse was a sleek, dark-brown stallion, the other a brown-and-white mare. Without warning, he guided them off the trail and into the thick, deciduous forest.

"Isn't Tálise's Grove that way?" she asked, pointing in Jouler's direction.

"It is," Prack replied, two other horses tethered to his saddle. "But it takes us too close to ta'Ajiilee."

"Do you think the saplings know?" she asked, swaying in rhythm with the horse. "About Tálise, I mean."

Prack shook his head, his emerald-jeweled ears swishing. "They're probably just now stirring after last night's festivities, but you can be certain Marun and his sycophants know."

"What do you think they'll do?" she asked.

"I imagine they'll dangle the saplings from cages," Prack replied. "For now."

L'Veyna let her tired mind drift to the happy chirps of squeaks of forest animals greeting the dawn. She caught another rhythmic sound, like beating drums and the haunting call of a long, tubular paampus. "Is that…is that music?"

Prack clenched his jaw, his face drawn with sorrow. "Just keep riding. We'll be at the Grove soon enough."

"Why are they playing music?" she asked, focusing on the distant tune. It was *Oh My Sunshine*, a sapling favorite, though a little too juvenile for L'Veyna's taste.

She would have been there too, if not for Jouler, Pendric, and… whatever their friend's name was—Karl, or Kackle, or something strange like that. She would have been waking up alongside all the other saplings…

"Marun won't really dangle them in cages," L'Veyna said. "Will he? The Grove won't let him, right?"

"I hope that's all they let him do."

JOULER BRUSHED ASIDE HIS BROWN, wavy hair, releasing a puff of bone-white ash. The glowing mushroom in his hand cast a soft green glow across his dark skin, illuminating Mh t'Pralab, the Wall of Prophecy. At a dozen paces high, the giant slab spanned the ashen grove. One side of the Wall bore a masterful frieze depicting the cruel Prytha Prophecy, the Saplings Curse, with morbid scenes of war and death. The opposite side of the ancient wall bore ancient writings in the Prytha's lost language.

His jaws cracked a yawn, and he rubbed the weariness from his eyes. His body ached for him to join Pendric, his childhood friend, asleep by the arched entrance of the grove. The grueling journey had caught up to them—escaping Headwater's destruction, enduring a Sotouri's cruelties, and finding refuge in a Prytha Forest. Such tales graced the pages of books, not the lives of Phaerians from a backwoods village.

And yet, here we are, Pen. If only Kael were with us.

Jouler refused to believe Kael had died, no matter what reason told him. He'd watched his friend disappear into the trunk of a tree god. A moment later, that tree turned to ash, and Kael with it.

He's not dead. He can't be.

Jouler pushed away the dark thoughts, distracting his mind with the etched writings on the Wall of Prophecy. Unlike the geometric Human alphabet, the lost Prytha language swooped and twisted, with dots and slashes adorning its graceful lines. The script teased his thoughts, whispering at the edge of understanding.

He blew ash from the words, focusing on their shape, how each word danced to the next with a certain rhythm...a proper flow that hinted at a meaning, almost like knowledge, or....

"Know....follow...guide..." he mumbled, testing his newfound power. Not entirely right, the words danced around the truth. "Obey... Heed."

The last word clicked, like snapping a puzzle piece into place.

"Heed what, though?" He focused on the next word, letting his thoughts dance along the word's curves and dots. Nebulous sentiments floated through his mind, offering impressions of words. "Heed the... No. Heed my... Almost. Heed these words, for this is my Prophecy."

"What did you say?" Orenda asked with her sharp chopping accent. Unlike every other Prytha, Onatah's highest Keeper trimmed her long talons, and refused to wear her green hair in thin braids. Instead, loose waves cascaded to her bare feet. Long pointed ears drooped with age, sparkling with topaz jewelry that matched her eyes.

"I'm just thinking aloud," Jouler replied. From what he'd already deciphered from the frieze on the other side, the Prytha prophecies centered on M'Ljot, the Harbinger of Death, who would lead saplings into battle against their own people.

The so-called Saplings Curse.

"And you're certain it says *Facets* of Prophecy?" Orenda asked. "Not the *Aspects* of Prophecy, as we've believed? They are synonymous, and they sound alike..."

"Positive," Jouler said for the hundredth time since Prack and L'Veyna had left to fetch supplies. He drew a calming breath, reminding himself she'd just lost one of her gods. At least she didn't find out she was the Harbinger of Death.

Orenda gave him a curt nod, her topaz eyes still red and puffy from crying. She moved to the other side of the wall. "And these are all Facets?"

He knew she pointed to the five depictions of the Facets of Prophecy, etched above a carving of ta'Ajiilee, the Life Tree. "The figure holding the sword is me, M'Ljot, the Harbinger of Death. Kael is the one holding the scales. The Crier of Change."

"And the others?" Orenda asked. "Who are they?"

"I only gleaned their titles," Jouler replied. "The strange one holding the bones is the Emblem of Life. The figure made of light is the Incarnation of Light, and the one holding the flower is Prytha, obviously—the Warden of Preservation."

L'Veyna.

The thought came unbidden, her presence teasing the back of his mind. If he concentrated, he could almost point to her.

"Why have I never heard of them?" Orenda asked. "These Facets?"

"Maybe you couldn't see it any other way," Jouler said, moving to join her on the other side of the wall. "Because you were so certain you were right."

Orenda clicked her tongue. "Maybe I just forgot."

"How could you forget something like that?" Jouler asked, not bothering to hide his disbelief.

Orenda raised an eyebrow over a puffy, yellow eye. "Do you know how long we Prytha live?"

"A few hundred years, I imagine."

"On the imperial calendar," she said, "I was born mid seven hundred P.S."

"Post Sacrifice?" Jouler blurted. "But that's...that's almost a thousand years ago. I can't...that's..." He knew Prytha lived long, but he never could have guessed a thousand years. His mind rumbled with the possibilities of such an extended life. The things he could do, all the books he could read, and places he could see. Not to mention witnessing such a long passage of time. "What was it like back then?"

"I don't know," Orenda replied. "No memories last forever. Even the strongest fade into impressions and sentiments."

"That seems odd to me," Jouler said. "Not remembering your life."

"Memories are such fragile things in their inception, prone to be whisked away by a whimsical laugh or an intrusive thought. Those memories that do take root flourish into strong, vibrant, fruit-bearing trees from which we can pluck and enjoy again and again. But overtime, that fruit wanes in flavor, the branches wilt with age, and the tree crumbles to the ground. Nothing lasts forever. Especially not memories." Orenda's topaz eyes twinkled with amusement. "You're what...twenty?"

"Close enough," Jouler replied with a yawn.

"Tell me," Orenda said. "What you were doing on this day, three years ago?"

"That's a bit specific," Jouler said, stifling a yawn. "But, based on the time of year, I'd say...cleaning the tack room, or pulling weeds."

"But you don't actually remember," she said. "At best, all you have are impressions of that day, and that was only three years ago. What about ten years ago, or fifteen? Now, imagine trying to think back eight hundred years. The farthest back I can remember is...oh, maybe two hundred years. But those memories are just impressions, until they, too, fade, making room for fresh memories. We call it, Ynipy, a renewal of the mind."

Jouler ran his fingers over the masterful carvings of the Saplings Curse, and his mind danced with nebulous thoughts of war, death, and rebirth.

And me at the head of it all, he thought, not wanting to speak the words and feel the truth snap into place from his Gift of Prophecy, as he called it.

Orenda's jaw cracked with a yawn, her wrinkled face heavy with exhaustion.

"What about your friends and family?" Jouler asked. "Do you remember them?"

"Some," she said. "Those who are still alive. I know who my parents were, but they died over four-hundred years ago. All I have are their portraits. No actual memories. Who they were and what we did, I glean from journals."

"I'm sorry," Jouler replied, fighting back images of his mother's mangled corpse. Of his father, sliced open from neck to groin.

And my brothers…

Pendric ran toward them, gasping for breath, his fresh shirt and trousers already stained from food. Before the cursed Ul'Kral stole his breath, Pen could have sprinted a mile without being too winded. Well, maybe not that far, but he could outrun everyone in Headwater.

"I think," Pendric said between wheezing breaths, "I heard… some…explosions."

Orenda looked upward, and her eyes glazed. "Vrath!"

"Here?" Pendric wheezed, working the hem of his sleeve.

"A small scouting party," she said, her voice quick with urgency. "They'll never reach Onatah, but at least they'll delay Alerix." She peered at Pendric. "How about I make something for that wheeze while we wait for Prack and L'Veyna?"

"Can you…heal me?" Pendric asked.

"I can't break the Ul'Kral's nasty curse," Orenda said. "Those insufferable creatures wield a strange magic. But I think I can ease your lungs."

Her gaze went distant again, and small plants and bushes sprouted around her. She picked sprigs of grass, and a satchel grew in her hands. Next, she added leaves, flowers, and bark from the plants she'd asked, and set them inside the satchel. Grinning at Pendric's wide-eyed amazement, she held her hand out, and a steaming sphere of water formed over her palm.

"Just a pinch of herbs from the satchel," she said, demonstrating. "Let it steep until the water looks like tea."

"Is that for me?" Pendric asked.

Orenda chuckled, passing him the sphere. "Of course it is, dear."

"You used your magic, didn't you?" he said, marveling at the ball of tea and woven grass satchel. "Asking, right?" He sniffed the sphere of steeping tea. "Can I drink it now?"

"It's still hot," she replied. "Count to a hundred, then you can drink it."

Pendric's shoulders dropped. "Can't I just wait until it's not so hot?"

Orenda's weary chuckles faded to the rumbled of hooves announcing Prack and L'Veyna. They rode through the arched entrance, a pair of familiar horses tethered to Prack's saddle horn.

"Smoke!" Pendric chirped, dashing to his horse. The sleek, brown stallion bobbed its head with excitement, while Cloud, Kael's horse, nuzzled him for attention.

A familiar sensation called to him from a pack strapped to Prack's golden horse. *More tubes?* he thought, finding the same call from the tubes in the pack Kael had left before disappearing to gods-knew-where.

L'Veyna sat well in her saddle, swaying with her horse's gait, though she gripped the reins too tight. Ash still powdered her hair, muting the thin autumnal braids woven down her left arm to her elbow. Jouler hoped she packed warm clothes. Her hempen wrap, green like fresh grass, might be enough to keep her warm during Onatah's mild winters, but the thin garment would do no more than draw lascivious gazes.

A wave of familiarity hit him, as if he'd known her from some distant past. The same familiarity he'd felt when he'd first met Kael.

Could it be?

"Do all Human stare?" L'Veyna said, her accent sharper than Orenda's. She clacked her fingertalons on a strip of wood at her belt, and her brother rolled his eyes.

"They do *not* all think that," Prack said, draped in a dark leather riding coat. Unlike his sister, Prack sat with a practice ease that would make Pendric's father Tied seem clumsy. "And to be clear, you stare just as much. Maybe more."

"I do not!" L'Veyna said, stealing furtive glances at Jouler.

Jouler turned his attention to the Wall of Prophecy where her ancient familiarity wouldn't tease his gaze. His eyes trailed across the scenes of life and happiness carved on the left half of the wall, to the depiction of death and misery that ruined the right half. Separating the two was a carving of ta'Ajiilee, so detailed its leaves seemed to flutter in an unfelt breeze. Above the Life Tree were the five Facets of Prophecy. Kael, the Crier of Change, held scales, while Jouler, the Harbinger of Death, held a sword. Next to his carved figure was the Prytha, the Facet holding the flower. Her name called to him, demanding him to speak it.

"L'Veyna," he whispered to himself. "She's a Facet of Prophecy. She's the Warden of Preservation."

The words snapped into place like pieces of a puzzle.

2

FRIED POTATOES

oonlight kissed the sacred forest, casting gentle rays through the thick canopy of rustwood, oak, fir, and maple. Croaking frogs and buzzing insects filled the night, broken by an occasional hoot. L'Veyna breathed deeply, savoring the smell of damp moss and fallen leaves, the crisp scent of pine, and the pleasant tannin of oak, but not even the comforting aroma of the night-kissed forest could assuage her conflicted heart. A full day ride behind her, all the saplings of Onatah, people she'd called friends, likely dangled from ta'Ajiilee's high branches, locked inside cages, while she rode away in safety.

I didn't even get to say goodbye.

The stiff, uncomfortable saddle seemed a fitting punishment for not trying to save anyone. For not even sounding an alarm. She'd slinked past the helpless saplings in the cover of darkness, and left her friends to their fate. Soon, their land, their people, their culture, everything it meant to be Prytha, would die under Prophecy's merciless hand. She let go of her reins and hugged herself, suddenly feeling very alone and lost in a forest she'd called home.

Her horse, Lupine, snorted and shook its head, yanking the reins free from her hand. She scrambled to pick them up before the foul beast decided to kick her off and bolt into the night.

Her gaze wandered to her brother, riding at the front of their ragged band, his golden mare laden with packs—one of which called to her like the tubes in Jouler's pack. He'd asked to see them soon after she and Prack returned to the grove, comparing the metallic tubes to the pair in his pack. According to Jouler, his tubes carried text from the original Human Prophecy. Not that he would know, since he refused to open them. Besides, if they carried the Human Prophecy, why did L'Veyna feel their call?

Maybe because Alnazet inspired their Prophecy too, she mused, shifting in her saddle. After all, her brother said the plague-ridden empire invented their gods. Not like Prytha, who worshipped the true gods. Her gaze drew to the remnants of ash still clinging to her wrap.

Dead gods.

Not even they were safe from the deadly chains of Prophecy.

Behind her, Pendric sat atop Smoke without a care in the world, like he'd been riding these beasts his whole life. Even with his wheezing breath, he looked comfortable enough to fall asleep, as if pain didn't radiate through his rear and back.

Jouler rode beside her, draped in his dark leather riding coat, his breath misting in the moonlit air. His familiarity washed over her again, pulling her gaze across his moon-washed face. Such links normally faded a few minutes after a healing, an hour at most, but never an entire day.

Maybe I'm just attracted to him, she thought. He did carry himself with a rugged confidence that stirred her curiosity, and he was kind enough on the eyes, but that seemed too hollow to explain the familiarity. Even if she could get past his wormy fingers and tiny, round ears, the sensation swelled with something far deeper than attraction.

Her horse whinnied and shook its head, startling her.

"Loosen your reins," Jouler said.

"Easy for you to say," L'Veyna said, certain the beast would run the moment she eased her grip. Her horse shook its head and snorted. "Look at her. She's just waiting to bolt."

"She's not going to bolt," Jouler said, dropping his reins. Behind his saddle, the tubes in his pack called to her, urging her to take them.

"The only reason Lupine is acting like that is because you're holding the reins too tight. Imagine if someone was constantly yanking your head back."

"I'm not yanking," L'Veyna mumbled, but after pointed looks from Jouler and her brother, she gave her reins some slack. She readied an asking a thick bed of moss to catch her in case Lupine bolted, but the horse only snorted as if in relief. Ignoring the call from the tubes in Jouler's pack, L'Veyna released her reins a little more until they drooped like his.

"Why don't the horses run?" L'Veyna asked. "If I was strapped with all this gear, I would bolt the first chance I had."

Jouler rubbed his eyes, his body drooping with exhaustion. "I guess it's a good thing we didn't strap you down with gear."

"Oh, I don't know," Prack said, turning to glare at her. "It might shut her yapper. We're still too close to Onatah, for my comfort."

"We'd be further," L'Veyna said, shifting in her saddle again, "without these rotten beasts."

"Keep your voice down," her brother said, turning in his saddle to glare at her.

"*I wouldn't have to talk*," L'Veyna clacked on her beltboard, "*if the stupid Humans spoke Talontongue.*"

"*But they don't,*" Prack replied, with a curious look to Jouler. The ever-curious Human tapped his wormy finger on his saddle, as if trying to tap their words. Prack grinned, and clacked, "*Not yet, at least.*"

"Are you trying to tap our language?" L'Veyna asked, the thud of his wormy fingers sounding odd in her ears.

Jouler blinked and looked down at his hand. "I suppose I was."

"Well, that's not how you do it," she replied.

"Then teach me," Jouler said.

L'Veyna shook her head, stifling a yawn. "I'm too tired. Maybe tomorrow."

"Why didn't Orenda come with us?" Pendric asked.

"She can't leave Onatah," L'Veyna replied.

Pendric's eyes widened, and he whispered, "Because she'll die?"

"What? No," L'Veyna replied. "Because she's the Chosen of

Alnazet. The Mother of all Keepers. She'll defend ta'Ajiilee to her very last breath. Speaking of which, Pen—how do you feel?"

"Better," Pendric replied. He patted the pouch Keeper Orenda had asked for him, woven from a single blade of grass. "But I still feel like I can't catch a full breath."

"And it's only going to get worse," Jouler said, sharing a concerned look with Prack. "Maybe we should head closer to the Hills until we figure out how to get your breath back."

"And go where?" Pendric asked. "Headwater is gone, and my da is gods know where. Reylan is in Nubidae. If there's anyone who knows what to do about those blasted Ul'Kral, it's him. Grim said I could make it…probably."

L'Veyna scoffed. "You think this Reylan, a Human, is going to know what Keeper Orenda does not?"

"It's quite possible," Jouler said. "He is a great healer. Maybe not as great as Orenda, but if she had once known a cure for the Ul'Kral's curse, those memories have obviously long-since faded to Ynipy, or she would have healed him. Why don't you try?"

"Me?" L'Veyna said, thick with incredulity. "I might be the youngest Bud to earn the wrap, but I'm still a Bud. She's the Chosen of Alnazet."

"Maybe you'll notice something she didn't," he said, somehow guiding his horse around an adolescent elm without so much as a tug on his reins.

Show off.

"Poor Pen," Prack said, shaking his head with dramatic aplomb. "If he's depending upon my sister noticing something…we might as well send him back to Alerix."

L'Veyna rolled her eyes, earning a quiet chuckle from her brother. After all the chaos, watching their god Tálise crumble to ash, then scrambling to fetch horses, pack supplies, and sneak through the Sacred Forest, her brother's return to normalcy warmed her like a ray of sunshine on a dreary day.

The day I learned the Saplings Curse is about me.

Maybe it was all a lie. After all, her people's interpretation of the

Aspects of Light had been wrong. Maybe they were all wrong about the Saplings Curse. Maybe the scenes depicting Prytha children slaying adults and standing on mounds of corpses actually portrayed something else…

Like what?

The language on the other side of the wall may have been lost to the Ensnarement, but there was no mistaking the meaning behind the Wall of Prophecy's images of pestilence, war, and death. Or the tapestry in Keeper Orenda's housetree. The one with Jouler in masterful detail, and the sapling girl woven beside him. Her gaze wandered over Jouler's handsome features—his skin, a lighter shade of brown to her own; his hair, soft, curly, and darker than the healthiest soil.

M'Ljot, she thought, struggling to see how someone so nice and gentle could harbor such a gruesome fate. His deep brown eyes raced with sharp cunning, but a good, caring heart beat in his chest. He cringed at the thought of harming animals and hurting feelings—hardly the type of person to rouse children into slaughtering their families.

Unless harm threatened his friends.

Maybe that was why she felt such a strong connection to him. It was his pack-like mentality, playing with her emotions.

"Tell me, Pen," Prack said, cracking the heavy silence with his soft voice. "What did you do all day in that village of yours?"

"Oh, sure," L'Veyna said. "It's okay for everyone else to talk?"

"Everyone else doesn't shout," Prack retorted, holding a finger to his lips. "As you were saying, Pen?"

"I didn't do much back in Headwater." Pendric shrugged. "Sometimes I helped my da with tanning, but mostly I made my own phaery tales."

"*You* wrote books?" L'Veyna asked.

"Of course not," Pendric said, tapping the side of his head. "All in my mind."

"Sounds…fun?" L'Veyna joked, but Pendric didn't seem to notice.

"It was!" he chirped. "Saving princesses and slaying hordes of

Sotouri." He blinked and lowered his gaze, his smile drooping into a frown. "I always…I always thought it would be different. I never thought…" He wiped his eyes and sniffled. "I thought it would be easy, you know? Because Sotouri are evil? I thought…"

"He's still alive," Jouler said.

"Who's still alive?" L'Veyna asked, then clacked to her brother, *"Who are they talking about?"*

"Sush," her brother clacked.

"But is he really alive?" Pendric said.

"Who are you talking about?" she asked.

"It's nothing," Pendric said, dragging a sleeve across his eyes.

Prack's talons clacked on his beltboard. *"Leave it be."*

"But I want to know who," she replied.

"Leave. It. Be."

"Sometimes I hate you," she clacked, and let her mind wander to the clop of hooves, chirps of crickets, and croaks of frogs. The symphony of night seemed louder than usual, as if the creatures knew Prophecy had reared its ugly head.

Prack stopped his horse and held up his hand for silence. He cocked his head, listening, his hands resting on the pair of needle-like tsah sheathed at his hip.

"What is it?" she clacked on her beltboard, still not trusting herself to speak.

"Listen."

Other than an occasional owl hooting through the chirps and croaks, and her horse's loud breathing, there was nothing… Then she heard it—distant screams flitting through the nocturnal symphony.

"Saplings?" she clacked, and her brother nodded.

"Sounds like they're heading this way," Jouler said, tapping his finger on his saddle horn as if trying to say 'saplings.' Without talons, he'd always have that dull, thudding accent, but after the second attempt, his fingers adroitly thudded *saplings.*

Impressive, L'Veyna thought. "That means saplings."

Pendric worked his finger in his ear and cocked his head. "I don't hear them."

Jouler tapped the word on his saddle horn, his brow creased in thought.

"Are they coming after us?" Pendric asked, working the hem of his sleeve.

"Running away from something more like," Jouler replied.

"Or someone." Prack gave L'Veyna a somber look, and clacked, "*Marun.*"

"It sounds like they're being chased," Jouler replied. "We need to help them."

"Stay here, and keep quiet," Prack said, drawing his tsah, the needle-like blades twinkling in the moonlight. He slid off his saddle and shifted into the thick forest in a blur of motion.

"Gods!" Pendric chirped and clamped his hands over his mouth. L'Veyna glared at him, and he whispered, "Sorry. How'd he move so fast like that?"

"He's a Chi'indi," L'Veyna whispered, brimming with pride.

"Oh…" Pendric said, nodding. "What's that?"

"Hush, you two," Jouler whispered, sliding off his horse, and motioning for her and Pendric to follow.

L'Veyna never thought planting her feet on the ground could feel so good, although she'd never get the stink out of her wrap without asking. They followed Jouler to a bed of ferns overlooking a game trail. The distant sound of snapping twigs and whimpered cries drew toward them, silencing creatures of the night. Moments later, a group of saplings, still dressed in their loose hempen ceremonial robe, leaped over a fallen log, and dashed down the game trail. L'Veyna counted seven…eight…nine of them, panic bright in their gem-colored eyes.

Below L'Veyna's perch, a familiar figure treewalked out of a rust-wood, her vivid-green Bud's wrap visible beneath her loose ny'tier blouse.

Breya.

The saplings skidded to a halt, screaming and pleading with L'Vey-na's once friend to let them go. Breya responded with asked vines, binding the saplings in place, and dragging them to their knees. Four more figures emerged from trees, one wrapped in a chestnut-brown wrap, the other three in barkarmor and armed with deadly chk'das.

L'Veyna entered the Posture of Root, sitting with her legs crossed, her hands on her knees. Before she could form an asking in her mind, a blur of motion darted between the Prytha, and moonlit sprays of blood misted the air. Breya and her four armored comrades collapsed, and the blur of motion stopped. Breathless, Prack stood amid the shaken and confused saplings, his needle-like tsah dripping onto the forest floor.

Breya's vines wilted to the ground, and saplings dispersed, screaming into the dark forest.

"Let them go," Prack said when Jouler moved to follow.

"We can't just leave them," he said.

"We have more pressing matters," Prack replied. "More of Marun's people will be here shortly."

L'Veyna's once friend stared with empty eyes into the night, blood oozing from a small hole in the back of her head. L'Veyna's head swam, her heart pounding in her chest, her lungs sucking in air. Her stomach clenched, and she doubled over, vomit spewing from her mouth. A hand rubbed her back, and Pendric offered her a handkerchief, his dark eyes brimming with compassion.

"Thank you," she mumbled, wiping her mouth with trembling hands. Body still shaking, her gaze seemed fused to Breya. She looked fake now, like a life-sized doll devoid of anything resembling life, her bloodstone eyes empty and staring, her evergreen skin as still as stone.

"It's nothing like it seems in the stories," he said, jerking his head to the corpses. "Is it?"

Jouler stirred the sizzling potatoes, onions, and peppers L'Veyna had asked, while the others warmed themselves against the morning chill. Exhaustion still hung heavy on everyone's face, belying their restless sleep. Especially L'Veyna, who hadn't seemed to sleep at all. He still hadn't told her, or anyone else, that she was a Facet of Prophecy. It seemed prudent given everything she'd been through, between watching her once-friend die, seeing her god crumble to ash, and the impending Saplings Curse, L'Veyna had enough on her mind without piling Facets on top.

His concern wandered toward Pendric's wheezing breath. Until Jouler found the Black Breath—whatever that was—his oldest friend would remain tied to those foul creatures and their blasted vial. Pendric's lungs already strained, never seeming to fill, and there were still so many leagues to travel. Jouler told himself Reylan would know what to do. He'd fix Pendric.

We just have to hope that he makes it.

Prack returned from relieving himself and sat beside his sister. She leaned her head on his shoulder, firelight twinkling in the jeweled emeralds along her long, pointed ears. She breathed a heavy sigh, and Prack draped his arm over her.

"What does Chi'indi mean?" Jouler asked, hoping to distract her from her dark thoughts.

"It means ghost," Prack replied.

"Because of how you move?" Pendric asked, and Prack nodded.

"It also means Sotouri hunter," L'Veyna mumbled, staring into the crackling cook fire.

She reminded Jouler of Dilna, both innocent to the world outside their home, stubborn as a tree root, and shoved into a dark, cold world. A sudden pang of guilt tightened his chest. He wracked his mind for something kind to lift her spirits, but what could he possibly tell her to allay such pain?

"But how do you do it?" Pendric asked, sipping on a cup of Orenda's tea. "How do you move so fast?"

Prack shrugged. "How do you flex a muscle?"

"Like this," Pendric replied, curling his arm.

"But *how* did you do that?" Prack asked.

"I just moved my arm like this," Pendric replied, demonstrating again. "And I just...do it."

"That's how I shift," Prack said. "It's like flexing a muscle. I just do it."

"I wish I had that muscle," Pendric said, his eyes wide and glazed with the workings of a phaery tale. "Is the food done?"

Jouler tested a diced potato, poking it with his fork. "Perfect."

Pendric shot to his feet, startling L'Veyna. "S-sorry. It's just…" His eyes widened when Jouler handed him a wooden plate steaming with potatoes. "They're so good. You'll see. Wait till you try them."

Pendric plopped a scoop of potatoes into his mouth. His eyes went wide, and he sucked in air. "Hot!"

"Almost like it was cooked with fire," Jouler said, earning a soft chuckle from L'Veyna. He'd watched the same innocence fade from Pendric after he stabbed Grim.

Except Breya had been L'Veyna's friend, not a blasted Sotouri.

Jouler handed two plates to Prack, who passed one to his sister.

"Smells good, doesn't it?" Prack said, nudging L'Veyna. She shrugged, and his brow drew with concern.

"Where do we go from here?" Pendric asked, blowing on his potatoes.

Prack pointed west. "We should reach the edge of the forest by noon, and Onti is a day's ride from there. However," he said, scooping a mouthful of potatoes. "Alnazet's blessing. These are amazing."

"Told you," Pendric said with a knowing smile.

"Have some," Prack told his sister, and she pushed around a piece of potato with her fork. "As I was saying, once we clear the forest, we'll have to cross the busiest stretch of imperial causeway in the empire."

"Wouldn't it be better to avoid any imperial towns?" Jouler asked, savoring his first bite of breakfast. The succulent flavors of potatoes, onions, and peppers invoked fond memories of Headwater.

"No one is going to recognize you," Prack said over a mouthful of food. "It would normally be best to avoid Onti, but we're meeting a friend of mine."

"Diou?" L'Veyna asked, a bit of life sparkling in her emerald eyes.

"The same." Prack scooped the rest of his breakfast into his mouth, drawing a chuckle from his sister. He clacked his talons on his beltboard in a happy rhythm, and she rolled her eyes at him, the corner of her lip teasing a smile.

"Jo makes the best potatoes," Pendric said, sighing at his empty plate. "But they're better with butter."

"Butter doesn't travel well," Jouler said.

"Yeah, but L'Veyna can ask for some?" Pendric asked.

"First of all," she said, holding up a long, taloned finger, "it's not ask for some butter. It's ask some butter, like churn some butter. And second, yes, I can, but Prytha can only eat things that grow from the land. You know, like fruits and vegetables."

"Will you die?" Pendric asked, eyes wide.

"No," Prack said, chuckling. "It makes us sick. Gives us stomach cramps."

"What about honey?" Pendric asked, and she shook her head.

"That's basically bee vomit, so...no."

"It is?" Pendric said. "Then what do you use to sweeten my tea?"

"Nectar from fruits and flowers," she said.

"Oh! That must be why it's *so* good." Pendric held his empty cup upside down and flashed her a toothy smile. "Can you ask for one for me? I mean, can you for ask some..." He cleared his throat. "Can you ask one for..." He tossed his hands up. "Can I have another cup of tea?"

L'Veyna brightened under a flurry of giggles, and Jouler's laden heart lightened. "I'll do one better," she said, forming a steaming orb in her hand. She pinched some tea into the orb and handed it to Pendric.

"I love these spheres," he said, marveling at the steeping ball of tea.

"Who is Diou?" Jouler asked, glad to see L'Veyna's mood lighten, even if she still only stirred her food.

"He's my Boorde friend," Prack replied.

"Friend?" L'Veyna said, her lifted eyebrow and half smile hinting at a deeper relationship between her brother and Diou.

Pendric's eyes glazed. "I can't believe I'm going to meet a Boorde."

Prack gave him a playful nudge. "We *are* going to the Boorde Alliance."

"Well, yeah," Pendric replied. "I just...I don't know. I never really thought I'd actually meet one."

"But," L'Veyna said, her brow tight with confusion, "we're *going* to the Boorde Alliance."

"I mean back in Headwater," Pendric said. "When I was young."

"You are young," L'Veyna said, giggling. She plopped a piece of potato into her mouth, and her eyes went wide, a slow smile splitting her face. "Alnazet's blessing. This is amazing!"

3

CONCUBINES

The coach swayed and bounced with a chaotic rhythm, mirroring Freja's scattered thoughts. She should be happy and exuberant, bubbling with glee. The emperor already had a horde of concubines, each as lovely as a sunrise if the stories about them were true. Not that Freja didn't think they were beautiful, just not as pretty as a sunrise, and not as beautiful as she.

That was why the emperor had chosen her. At least, that was what she kept telling herself, to keep from overthinking. Far more rode on this opportunity than leaving Eio's Upper Bronze District. She took out the letter he'd sent her, the folds loose and weak.

My Dearest Freja,

You occupy my mind as the sun occupies my day. Sleep has evaded me since the moment I left Eio. I am tortured by our distance. I fear the only restitution for my damaged heart is for you to join me in the capital.

Emperor Thjodoft
Seal of New Torgeir
Sovereign of the Five Kingdoms

FOR THE THOUSANDTH time since receiving the letter, Freja wondered about the hidden meanings behind its immaculate script. The emperor had likely practiced each stroke a hundred times, but such were the ways of the Founders scrutinizing every word and stroke for subtle implications.

Implications and arrogance, Freja thought, scrolling through her memories for a Founder who had impressed her. Rodak had been such a person until he blundered his attack against Makayla's Army of Light. In the end, he'd proven as arrogant as the rest. Now, rumors of uprisings trickled in from Neuheim despite the king's efforts to quell his Phaerians. He should have spent less time with his menagerie and more time securing his towns.

Who in their right mind keeps a pod of terrentors?

Freja folded her letter from the emperor and tucked it into one of the hidden pattern-forged pockets in her dress. Unlike the wavy nu'silk dresses that were the current rave among Eio's nobility, Freja wore a style popular among the Lower Tiers, though she wouldn't deign to wear nu'fabric. Real cotton draped over her shoulders from thin straps, the dress flowed in the wind like whispered mist, the sunflower-yellow color complementing her olive skin. Deidan told her it reminded him of a warm spring day, but the grizzled Sotouri always flowered his words with her.

Unlike Auntie Inga, she mused, wishing her old handmaid had traveled with her. Freja grinned at the thought of her Auntie's tongue, lashing at the coach driver with every bump and jostle.

The sound of a whip cracked the air, drawing Freja to the coach window. They drew closer to Laira's harbor, the city's Shining Wall looming less than a mile away. Lord Breinir undoubtedly watched for her arrival, safe within the heights of the city's Gold District. Once Freja won the emperor's hand, no tier or law would save the lecherous Gold Lord from her wrath.

Crammed between the harbor and Shining Wall was a haphazard conglomerate of tents and shanties. The decrepit hovels gave an odd sense of impermanence to the thousand-year-old Phaerian community. Freja lifted her pattern-forged sachet to her nose, warding off the stench wafting from the encampment with the sweet aroma of flowers and spices.

Wishing she could shape the Currents of Power like her father to clear the coach of the retched stench, she reached for her pack to distract herself from the malodor. A small trove of notebooks waited for her inspection.

Forty-eight notebooks, to be exact.

Emperor Thjodoft, Hrodny Bjorndin, Grim, King and Queen Ofiegsson...every piece of information written in a script she'd invented at eight. Not that she needed them with every note carved into her mind, every word, sketch, and diagram committed to memory.

"Most little girls learn other languages," Deidan had told her after he'd discovered her cryptic notebooks. "Not inventing their own."

"Most little girls aren't raised by the Sotouri's Master of Whispers." The fond memory warmed Freja's chest, and she pulled out the thickest notebook—Hrodny Bjorndin. Freja had more notes on Hrodny than anyone else in the empire, but petty childhood rivalries seemed to have that effect.

Petty in our youth, she thought. Gone were the days of foiled muggings and poisoned meals—nothing deadly...for the most part. Unfortunately, their machinations grew into devious ploys to bring ruin to each other's house, but at least they helped keep Freja's mind sharp.

The stench of rotted fish and misery grew to intolerable as they neared the harbor. She reached for her pattern-forged sachet, but the stench clung to the back of her tongue, forcing a gag. Citizens blamed the Phaerian encampment for the putrid smell, but poverty bred the same festering odor, be it a Phaerian shanty or the Workers' District.

A series of long breakwaters protected the harbor from the infamous storms that lurked the Serpent's Eye. Stretching from the shore were wide piers crammed with brick buildings, and bristling with hundreds of ships. Crude cargo ships with short, wide masts, and long oars loomed beside pristine luxury schooners with their massive sails, while bulbous military galleons with its rows of cannons bobbed next to small fishing vessels.

The harbor's loud din poured through the coach window with raucous shouts, laughter, and cries. She'd forgotten how loud the empire's busiest harbor could get. Thankfully, a summons to the imperial court came with an imperial escort to clear her path to the harbor.

The coach slowed to a stopped, and Freja stashed her notebook on Hrodny before stepping into the loud harbor. A troop of soldiers and Vrath held the bustling throng of Phaerians and Districters at bay away, giving the rest of Eio's concubines-in-waiting more than enough room for their inflated senses of self worth. Freja ignored their scorned looks of beautiful maidens and captivating men. Some had likely waited on her for hours, as they should. Gyrd Vestgeir, Asleif Jarnskeg, Tonna Birning, Jorulf Hlenni, and, of course, Hrodny... Twenty-three ladies beside herself, and thirteen men, each draped in unimaginative nu-silk waves of the latest fashion. All but Gudrin Freyling, the only Founder in the group, and Jorulf, the son of the wealthiest Gold Lord in Meru'ut. Gudrin's green dress shimmered the same vibrant green as her eyes, while the Jorulf's dress was black to make a new moon seem bright. Everything to look as far removed from a Phaerian as possible.

They could have their vibrant eyes, whitened skin, and colorful, silky hair. Freja rather liked her bronze skin, deep brown eyes, and the way her tight, dark curls bounced on her shoulders or coiled around her finger. Her hair and skin were bold, like her, and untouched by shaping. Well, barring her Shield and frequent healings due to her brothers' abuses or Hrodny's schemes, as well as whatever her father and Deidan had done to her when she was born. Some secret of the Sotouri they refused to reveal, no matter how cute she acted, or how violent her outburst.

A secret is only a secret, she thought, recalling her father's favorite words, *so long as it's not shared.*

The three other people in the group from the Bronze District stood out worse than a Phaerian in court. Valgred and her twin brother, Thurnjald, siblings of a semi-successful jeweler and an influential Weaver, which explained their excessive pattern-forgings. Freja's reports on the two were as thin as the wavy frills running down their nu'silk garments. Freja's only interesting lead on them had taken her to an apothecary in the Makers District. Valgred had purchased a tasty concoction the shop owner had sworn would lift a person's mood and make them a little dizzy. At least, that had been Freja's experience.

The third Bronze Lady, Svala Brynja, looked stiff and awkward among her betters, laughing and scoffing a little too hard at their stories. Eschewing frills, tassels draped in a spiral down her slate-blue nu'silk dress.

Poor girl, Freja thought, recalling what few notes she had on the concubine. Only recently raised from the Steel District, Svala's mother had won the attention of a wealthy Bronze merchant. Rumors had fluttered through Eio's Upper Tiers, implicating her mother in the death of the merchant's previous wife, but the truth was far darker. Svala's mother was his sixth wife. They'd all been lowborn, so the guards hadn't bothered to investigate their deaths. Svala had to know he'd kill her mother… Maybe the tall, skinny noble with long chestnut hair had left Eio hoping to return for her after she established herself in the imperial capital.

No…Freja recognized the look of resignation and the tight set to Svala's shoulders. The alluring Lower Bronze Lady knew of her new stepfather's macabre past. She knew her mother's fate and was never going home.

Freja applauded her tenacity. Such a woman could prove to be a potent ally…maybe more. Freja didn't shy from enticing thoughts of Svala's long legs twined with hers, her plump lips caressing Freja's skin.

"It's lovely to see you, Freja," Gudrin said, shattering Freja's fantasy. The Founder held out an alabaster-white hand adorned with pattern-forged rings, earrings, and bracelets. According to Freja's notes, the Gudrin's thin silver tiara would keep her complex braid of

Imperial-red hair perfect in a minor storm, while the pearl adorning her ears helped her hear nearby whispers.

The other ladies waited to see how Freja would react to Gudrin's extended hand. The implication was obvious—Gudrin may have waited for her, but Freja was still her lesser.

Freja wore an innocent smile, her father's voice echoing in her mind as she kissed the back of Gudrin's hand.

Let the high and mighty have their petty obeisance. Toppling giants is far easier when they believe you're a tiny mouse.

Against Gudrin's alabaster-white skin, Freja's hand looked almost as dark as a Castantorian bogman. "It's great to see you again, Gudrin."

Valgred sucked her teeth and peered at her sparkling pink fingernails. "Stunning as usual, Freja. I think I saw a dress like that in the Workers District." Her eyebrows rose with mock appreciation. "Though, definitely not made of such high quality nu'cotton as yours."

Thurnjald and Valgred snickered beside the Silver Lady.

"*Real* cotton," Freja corrected, with practiced disinterest. "From Glaedia, of course. I'm surprised, Valgred. I didn't take you for someone who frequented the District. I thought you and your brother only dipped as low as Steel."

Color warmed on the sibling's white cheeks, but, to their credit, they held their tongue.

"Not that I blame you," Freja continued, hoping to fan the flames with an ostentatious wink. "Watching soldiers on the practice field could warm a blizzard."

Svala smirked at the Bronze siblings in a clumsy show of annoyance, like a newborn foal to the intricacies of the Noble Game. Of course, a few well-placed suggestions would change all of that.

"Just watching, Freja?" Hrodny mused. "Is that as close as the soldiers will let you get to them?"

"Please," Freja said with a dismissive wave. "Everyone knows the best things to come from Steel are its women."

Svala dipped her head, her cheeks dimpling with a coy smile.

Murmurs rustled among the ladies and men in waiting, their

bright, colorful eyes darting to a sullen figure in drab Phaerian wool, apologizing her way through the throng. A large pack poked above her curly black hair, her skin a shade darker than Freja's. A wide, toothy smile split the Phaerian's kind, wrinkled face when she saw Freja. "Ah, here you are, My Lady."

The other concubines buzzed with disapproval, though none dared raise an alarm. They all recognized the symbol etched onto the Phaerian's forehead—a bright red circle struck through by a straight line—the symbol of an Auntie.

"Auntie Inga!" Freja beamed until her cheeks hurt, not caring about the rumors already dancing in the other concubines' eyes. "I thought you were staying in Eio."

Auntie Inga held up a hand, imploring patience while she caught her breath, her clothes wet with sweat. She dropped the sacks, set the pack on the ground, and bowed to Freja, right hand on left knee, thumb lifted. "It's great to see you, My Lady. Deidan sends his regards." Without waiting for a response, Inga rose and bowed, then hefted the burdensome luggage. "I will return to fetch your things, My Lady."

Freja watched her Auntie head toward the emperor's luxury barge, though her mind swarmed over Deidan's hidden message.

Your Sotouri are in place.

4

HOUSE NITH'IIL

Katima Nith'Iil walked down the tall labyrinthine hallways of her House, her black firedancer dress swishing with each stride. Her djohai, the traditional weapon of her ancient profession, bounced against her hip. The rhythmic tap of the dart dangling from its coiled rope helped ease her troubled mind. Today, it reminded her of the debt she owed her firedancer instructor for her lack of attendance these past two weeks, but some causes were worth the punishment.

Like these lemon bars, she thought, plopping the last delicious morsel into her mouth. *Chef Vyssara's sharp tongue is worth every bite.*

She passed a small group of brightly clothed Humans gawking between House Nith'Iil's vaulted stained-glass ceiling and its mirrored reflection on the glossy black floor. Everburning sconces reflected into infinity on smooth black walls, interspersed between black banners decorated with House Nith'Iil's Emerald Heron, along with weapons and armor claimed throughout the centuries of battle.

After one hundred and twenty-four years, these halls still sparked Katima's pride. Most Boorde felt a strange affiliation with their house symbol. House Brinnin was wise like a raven, House Fiorial as devious as a spider, while House Skelsav was as stubborn as a bull. Were they born with those traits, or did they feel obligated to act like their House Symbol? Katima doubted she'd ever feel like a heron, no matter how graceful she got. No feathers graced her snow-white skin, her silky hair as black as night like every other Boorde in the empire.

Except our skin and hair are natural, Katima noted, smirking at the Founder stalking the halls. All but the blessed half-Boorde, anyway, their skin almost as black as their hair, their diamond-shaped irises gray, not the color of fire like the rest of her people.

Color is meant for nature and art, not shirts and pants.

Housekeepers bowed as she passed, their smooth black hair cut too short to tie into a topknot, as befit their station. Dressed in a traditional Boorde garments, the black clothes were a soothing reprieve to the striking color in the Humans' hair and clothes.

The housekeepers' dark clothes sparked a pang of jealousy in Katima. An emerald heron marred their black ry'kus and ydus, but the spot of color was far less offensive than the strip marring traditional firedancers' dresses. Meant to shimmer like fire, the strip ran up the length of her dress, rippling as she walked.

Maybe it wouldn't be so terrible to be the first firedancer to remove the strip of color and sport an all-black dress. She'd lose face, of course...a *lot* of face, not to mention the shame it would bring to her House, but at least she wouldn't have a strip of color poking into her peripheral.

Katima headed into another series of hallways riddled with various turns and doors meant to confuse potential intruders. Of course, none had dared challenge House Nith'Iil for over millennia, so the mirror-like floors were more a source of entertainment from mesmerized visitors. Like the two Upper-Tier idiots arguing over which turns to make.

At least the pair of Phaerians her brother had brought home seemed tolerable. Especially the little girl with smooth, dark hair. She had potential. A shame such a bright flame had ignited inside a Human, and a Phaerian at that.

Honor cared not for status, Katima reminded herself, wondering what plans her brother had for the Human girl.

Katima paused at the House Library, second only to the Everburning Library in Micoé. Noonday light filtered through the stained-glass ceiling, dripping color down the library's five floors. The beautiful artwork splashed House Nith'Iil's emerald heron over the tables, chairs, and couches in the study area, the color raking Katima's sensibilities. As always, Boorde and Human scholars, philosophers, and strategists poured over books and scrolls, while an army of librarians hunted shelves for misplaced and forgotten tomes.

"Ah, there you are."

Katima flinched at her firedancer instructor's voice. "I am honored to see you."

"Are you now?" il'Olina replied, her smooth alabaster-white face tight with impatience. Masters who bore the affix 'il' hardly needed long hair to demand respect, but she could at least grow hers longer than the servants.

Katima dipped her head in a bow, her long dark hair whispering against her lower back. "I did not intend to miss so many days, il'Olina. But there are pressing matters that—"

"That are handled by those who are not my student." il'Olina met Katima's gaze, challenging her student to speak. Age may have dulled il'Olina's diamond-shaped, fire-colored pupils, but not her tongue or her grace. She motioned to follow, gliding on slippered feet with an elegance that belied her eight hundred years of life.

Graceful, but slow, and I'm already late.

Then again, Mother knew how much il'Olina loved to talk, and Katima couldn't dishonor her instructor by refusing the chance encounter, or the ensuing lecture. If nothing else, it was an honorable excuse for being tardy.

"I expect to see you on the morrow," il'Olina said, navigating the hallways toward Matron Nith'Iil's office. "Two hours before first meal. As you have used my time for personal motives..." Il'Olina waited for a housekeeper direct a ra'Vrath to the library before turning her annoyance back at Katima. "Then I will use yours for mine. Maybe this will teach you to manage your time better."

"Yes, il'Olina."

Her instructor stopped before her mother's waiting room, ignoring the two il'Spada, weapons masters, guarding the door. The two guards shifted when they saw the shrewd firedancer, undoubtedly glad to see il'Olina's infamously sharp attention aimed at Katima. "You are the Heiress Apparent to the most powerful House in the Alliance, and one of the most skilled firedancer I've trained. More so than your mother at your age."

"I'll tell her you said that," Katima joked.

"I dare you," il'Olina replied, then dismissed herself with a deep bow.

Hoping no one else occupied the waiting room, Katima motioned for the guards to open the doors. Four plush chairs and a pair of tufted sofas, each black with emerald buttons, occupied the large waiting room, though Katima knew better than to sit.

Not when I'm this late.

Thankfully, only two other il'Spada waited in the room, both standing by the tall black-iron doors to Mother's office. Gifted to House Nith'Iil after the Great Uprising, the imposing doors stretched to the vaulted stained-glass ceiling, and were inlaid with a giant heron comprising countless twinkling emeralds.

Colorful light from the stained-glass ceiling danced on the guards' black scale armor, their pale Boorde skin and fire-diamond eyes barely visible behind the slits in their helmets. Their only adornments were the five small emeralds set beneath the heron carved into their chest piece, marking them il'Spada of the highest order. Both held a short spear, with a sidaiyo their belt, the thin curved swords asleep in their scabbard. Dangling alongside the thin blades were a pair of maces, and small hand crossbows set with a poison-tipped bolt. Daggers and knives also poked from the various sheaths strapped to their legs, arms, and chest.

A small flame burst into life on the floor, forming a flickering image of her mother. "Come in, dear," the image said. "We must talk."

"Yes, Mother," Katima said with a deep bow, amazed at her mother's skill at harmonizing. Not so much as a spark of her mother's influence fed the flame. Katima might be more advanced than her mother had been at a hundred and twenty-four years of age, but

Matron Nith'Iil had been harmonizing for seven centuries longer than that.

The guards opened the tall black-iron doors and bowed as she entered Matron Nith'Iil's spacious office. Inlaid into the center of the black floor was a massive map of Torgeir Pre-Sacrifice, the Lost Kingdom of Astrakane seeming to shout warnings from the dead. Around the map, black tufted chairs and sofas with emerald buttons waited for her councilors. Paintings of past Matrons hung between tapestries baring the House colors. Flickering light from heron-shaped, everburning sconces stretched up the dark walls, the light brushing the vaulted ceiling.

Matron Nith'Iil waved for Katima, not bothering to look up from the mountain of papers and books on her wide obsidian desk. Eschewing the trend of elegance, her mother's hair fell loose from a simple topknot adorned with an emerald pin in the shape of a heron.

"You're late," she growled, the wide sleeve of her black ydu waving with her arm. "A growing habit of yours, from what I hear."

Katima's slippered feet whispered across the smooth marble floor, her coiled djohai bumping against her hip in rhythm to her pounding heart. Next to the obsidian desk, her mother's ceremonial mourning dress draped over a form, everburning sconces warming its snow-white fabric. In Katima's life, her mother wore that garb only twice—the day they gave Katima's grandfather to the flames, and the day Mother lost her firstborn.

My older sister, Shyran, the rightful Heiress Apparent of House Nith'Iil.

"Good morning, mother," Katima said with a deep bow, her gaze flashing to the white mourning dress.

"Don't mind that," Matron Nith'Iil said with a flippant wave. "I'm just airing it out."

"Of course, Mother," Katima replied, ignoring the obvious lie.

Who does she expect to die?

Matron Nith'Iil scowled at one of the reports on her desk, then turned her disappointed gaze back to Katima. For a Boorde well into her seventh century, her fire-diamond eyes still blazed bright.

"What has occupied your time that you ignore your lessons?" She gestured to Katima's djohai. "You may be more skilled than I was at your age, but you still have a lot to learn. Especially if you are to become Matron. How are you supposed to manage your House, when you can't even manage your time?"

"Il'Olina said much the same," Katima said, letting her mother know the old instructor had delayed her. Her mother tilted her head in acknowledgement, and Katima continued. "To answer your question—given the impending war between the Army of Light and the empire, I decided my time would be better spent pouring over imperial treatises and law."

Matron Nith'Iil leaned back in her tall velvet chair, and steepled her fingers over her chest. "Presumably so that I would let you champion our cause to the Five Kingdoms?"

"Yes," Katima said, and her mother shook her head.

"I need you here, now more than ever."

Katima swallowed a sharp retort about having traveled the entire empire before taking the Matron's mantle. "What about Diou? Don't you need him too?"

"Your older brother," Matron Nith'Iil said, peering at Katima, "isn't the Heiress Apparent. As skilled as he is, our House wouldn't fall if an assassin's blade found him. Losing you would embroil me in decades of bureaucracy while I begged for the Council to approve the birth of another Heiress. Don't let your feelings for your brother cloud your duty to your House. He's a male, and as expendable as any other tool at your disposal."

A tool like me to you? Katima thought, her gaze flickering to her mother's white dress.

"Your brother is not why I summoned you." Matron Nith'Iil breathed a heavy sigh and gestured to the chairs in front of her desk.

Katima sat, her heart surging with alarm at her mother's brazen display of emotion. "What happened?"

"Serolle has fallen."

Katima blinked, her mind slow to absorb her mother's words. "Serolle? The city? But...how? Even Boorde steel chips against the Shining Walls. Did Makayla discover a new power?"

"Not a new power," Matron Nith'Iil said, handing Katima a thin strip of paper. "Whispers from Serolle's Founders District mention a figure of light on the battlefield right before the explosion. The Shining Wall collapsed against the city."

"What of the inhabitants?" Katima asked.

Her mother raised an eyebrow at the question, her aged fire-diamond pupils flickering with annoyance. "Except for the Bronze District, most of the Lower Tiers were crushed. Thankfully, the Upper Tiers went unharmed."

"Thankfully," Katima repeated, and her mother slid a folded piece of paper. "What is this?"

"The reason you're sitting down."

Katima took the paper and sat back in the black velvet chair. Unfolding the paper, she read the brief message aloud. "Glaedia and Meru'ut march on Onatah." She turned the paper over, making sure she had missed nothing. "Why would they do that? Alnazet's Wreath…"

Katima's mouth went dry as the Stages of Boorde Prophecy fluttered in her mind. First came the Union, when the Alliance finally united under a single banner. The Proving, the longest Stage, came next, when her people drove war and pestilence from the land; thus inviting the Time of Plenty. It all started with a single sign—the First Sign. The day all Boorde lived to see, begging the Eternal Flame for the honor of ushering in Prophecy.

"Alnazet's Wreath has fallen," she whispered.

A wide smile split her mother's face. "And yea, the Sacred Wreath shall cry from the grave, and all shall bear witness to the glory of the Boorde, for the Dawn is nigh."

5

AMBUSHED

Perched atop a tall rustwood, Alerix Sagehaven gazed over Onatah Forest. Hempen straps wove through his long, thin braids, binding them in a tail. The promise of winter already kissed his hair, lightening its rich, green color. He shaded his eyes from the morning sun, glaring at the swaths of cleared land where the empire had invaded. In three short days, the empire's advancement already cut deep into the Sacred Forest on three fronts, once slicing southward from Laira, the other two stabbing from the east. Instead of leaving the forest be, the godsdamned imperials cleared the land as they advanced, felling trees that had seen the turn of a millennium, slaughtering animals, and obliterating the forest's delicate balance. At this rate, they'd reach Onatah City in a month or two.

All to feed their insatiable lust for power.

He descended from his perch, using his talons to claw his way down the rustwood's thick bark to its lowest branch. Running down the branch, he leaped onto the old black walnut tree where Tai'Enth waited with his squad. The walnut tree creaked with glee at his return, quivering in the wind, and shedding some of its autumnal leaves.

Tai'Enth welcomed him with a knowing frown, her apatite-blue eyes somber in the diffused evening light. Despite Alerix's pleas, she only wore her ochre Keeper's wrap, but at least she'd asked varying shades of yellow to help her blend into the foliage. She ran her talons along his green beard, drawing his attention downward toward the crunch of leaves and twigs.

On the forest floor, seven imperial soldiers crept as quietly as a bear in rut. None of their shoulders bore the telltale cord of a d'Tormena, but that didn't mean they deserved Alnazet's mercy.

"Scouts," he rapped against his chk'da's haft, noting how much better armed these imperials were than the platoon they had sent to Alnazet yesterday. Each soldier bore a spear, a buckler, two swords, an array of knives, and a pair of small crossbows.

"They never think to look up," Tai'Enth clacked, her lips tight with a familiar hatred.

Alerix tempered his well-guarded battle lust, and searched the nearby forest, looking for offset plants with twisted or broken limbs, the sudden movement of animals, squirrels yapping, birds warning, *any* sign of other imperial patrols. He found nothing but a forest dawning its autumnal clothes, and the oblivious squad of soldiers passing by the walnut tree.

The Human scouts crouched behind a family of ferns, presumably planning an assault the way they whispered and pointed.

"Let's get this over with," Alerix clacked.

"Wait!" Tai'Enth pointed ahead of the imperials.

Alerix followed her gaze, and he cursed under his breath. A few hundred paces from the imperials was a small group of saplings resting on a bed of leaves. *"Where did they come from?"* he clacked, then waved off the superfluous question. Cupping his hands to his mouth, he blew pigeon sounds to alert the other two squads. Ma'Tsoka and Ahskii replied in kind, their calls fluttering from a nearby oak and maple.

"Take your squads," Alerix clacked, *"and capture the saplings. My squad will handle the scouts."*

"We shouldn't be capturing saplings," Tai'Enth whispered.

"And risk the Saplings Curse?" Alerix replied.

"You know what Marun has planned for them."

"Better to be locked in cages," Alerix said, "than subject our people to Prophecy."

"Tell that to the saplings," Tai'Enth said.

"*We can talk about that later,*" Alerix clacked, gesturing to the soldiers below them. Seven imperial scouts to his squad of five—six, with Tai'Enth. He loathed risking the life of the woman who held his heart, but he had a better chance of defeating the soldiers by himself as he did of dissuading her.

Alerix met the eyes of his warriors, then nodded to Tai'Enth.

She pressed a hand to the trunk, and a treewalk portal rippled the bark of the ancient black walnut.

"*Now!*" Alerix clacked, letting his squad go first before he stepped into the thick honey-like portal. His vision turned black as his self stretched to the bottom of the tree. He stepped out of the portal and into chaos. Two of his warriors lay dead by the tree, their skin blackened around the shaft of a small crossbow bolt. The other lay at the feet of half a dozen hard-faced imperials.

Six? But there were seven of them.

A spearhead flashed at Alerix, his reflexes lifting his chk'da and deflecting the mortal blow. The spear pierced his barkarmor, biting into his side, and he rolled as the seventh scout charged through the space where he'd stood.

The Human spun, leveling his spear at Alerix. "Come on then, little fella. Let's see what you got."

Alerix's burning wound ignited his battle lust, consuming his sorrow for his warriors with the challenge of a skilled opponent. He slid past the scout's jab, and swung his chk'da, the spike stabbing into the human's calf. In a fluid motion, Alerix released his weapon, and spun with his talons, ripping out the screaming human's throat.

The other scouts recovered from their shock, half leveling spears while the other three drew their sword. With practiced grace, they maneuvered around Alerix, trying to corner him against the old walnut tree.

The dead scout's blood fueled Alerix's lust, his talons aching for more crimson warmth. He gave in to his inner beast, sucking in a deep breath and releasing his sacred gift. Time slowed to a silent crawl, almost stopping as Alerix dashed between the Humans, each motion draining the air from his lungs. Blood trailed from his talons, torn throats leaving six frozen streaks of crimson through the air.

Alerix stared at the Humans, their eyes still glimmering with life, unaware they'd already died. Lungs burning, he contained his sacred gift and crashed into a world of sound and motion. Corpses collapsed and frozen streaks of blood splashed to the ground.

Alerix reveled in the victory, thrilled by the warmth dripping down his hands, while his lungs begged for air.

"Alnazet's mercy," Tai'Enth said, stepping from the treewalk portal. She ran to the dead warriors, tears welling in her apatite-blue eyes. "What happened?"

Her pained expression calmed his lust, his hands cooling in the autumnal air. "They were ready for us," he said, holding onto his anger. He would mourn his friends once he got the other two squads back to safety. Them and the saplings. "I underestimated them."

"You can't blame yourself."

"I can, and I will," Alerix said, pressing a hand to his side. "Humans are smarter and a lot more skilled than I thought."

"You're injured," Tai'Enth said.

"I walked right into their trap," he said, wincing from her prodding fingers.

"You're not supposed to stop spears with your side." Tai'Enth leveled a pointed look at him, her cheeks glistening in the morning light. She caressed his cheek and her healing warmth spread across his wound, while warm water washed the blood from his hands, taming the remnants of his inner beast.

"Thank you," he said, touching his forehead to hers.

A moment later, Ma'Tsoka tree stepped from a nearby oak, her mouth agape at her slaughtered friends. "Li'Tohna, Chandan…"

"Did you secure the saplings?" Alerix asked, but she didn't seem to hear. "Ma'Tsoka!"

Dressed in her purple Keeper's wrap, she squeezed her ruby-colored eyes shut, tears dripping down her moss-green face. "The saplings were already gone. It was like they knew we were coming."

"Plagued lands," Alerix cursed, forcing his thoughts away from his fallen friends. The Saplings Curse promised far more death if the saplings weren't all captured. They didn't need to die, as some of Marun's sycophants claimed, but the Prophecies were clear about the danger they posed. For the preservation of his people, they *had* to be captured.

They had to…

"Light of my life," Alerix said. "Will you commit our friends to the land?"

Tai'Enth dipped her head and set to the morbid task.

"Where's Ahskii?" Alerix asked.

"*Tracking the saplings*," Ma'Tsoka clacked.

"Good," Alerix said, scratching his beard.

Ma'Tsoka's ruby eyes tightened with hatred. "What are your orders, High Rose?"

"We find those saplings," Alerix replied, watching asked vines pull his friends into the ground. "And then we prepare for war."

6

ONTI

Somber quietude permeated the edge of the Sacred Forest. Jouler motioned for Pendric to stay back with him and the horses, to give Prack and L'Veyna time to absorb the devastating scene. The ashen remnants of Alnazet's Wreath, the thick barrier of vines and bramble that had protected Onatah, cut a wide, sinuous wide line along the edge of the Sacred Forest, slicing through branches and vines that had stretched over the Wreath.

Prack wrapped his armed around L'Veyna, her shoulders shaking with sobs. His talons clacked against his beltboard, and she shook her head. Prack patted her back, and she shrugged off his embrace. Cheeks wet with tears, she stalked back to her horse and halted, emerald-green eyes raging with anger.

"Why?" she demanded.

"Sister…" Prack said, but she turned her glare on him.

"This is all *his* fault!" she said, jabbing a finger at Jouler. "He's M'Ljot. You saw it on the tapestry. Orenda even said it herself."

And you're the Warden, Jouler thought. *Whatever that is.*

L'Veyna marched back to the wide ashen line edging the forest. "This is what he'll bring. I saw it in a vision when I healed him. And don't tell me I'm wrong, Prack. The Prophecies foretell it."

"But Jo didn't do it," Pendric said, shifting in his saddle.

"His friend did," L'Veyna replied. "Your friend too."

"So now Pen is to blame?" Prack leveled a pointed look at his sister. "It's all right to hurt and be angry. But you can't drag innocents into your rage."

"It's fine," Pendric said, sympathy soft in his voice. "I know what it's like to lose your home."

The anger knotting L'Veyna's brow eased, and she wiped her eyes.

"Kael didn't kill Tálise," Prack said. "Prophecy set us on this path."

"Can gods even die?" Pendric mumbled under his wheezing breath.

"I doubt it," Jouler replied. "And if they can, I imagine it would take the power of a god to do it."

Prack squeezed his sister in a side hug, and she leaned into him. "I'm sorry you never got to meet Him."

"We're sorry too," Pendric said.

L'Veyna sniffled and gave him a confused look.

"If we'd arrived one day later," he explained, "you would have had your Blooming Festival."

"Blossoming," Jouler corrected.

"Then you wouldn't be a sapling," Pendric continued, "and you wouldn't be part of the stupid Curse."

"You're wrong," Jouler said, drawing surprised looks. "Whether she'd completed the ritual or not, every Prytha is involved in the Saplings Curse."

L'Veyna's brow drew in anger. "There's a big difference between playing the slayer in Prophecy, and playing the slayed. Prack isn't destined to burn our forests. *I* am!"

"And *I'm* supposed to lead you." Jouler gestured to himself. "Do you really believe *I* am going to lead an army of saplings to slaughter their families? Me, an average-sized Phaerian with no powers like shaping or asking?"

"It's what the prophecies say," L'Veyna replied with a stubborn set to her jaw.

"Sister," Prack said, squeezing her shoulders. "If there's one thing

I've learned about the Prophecies, it's that we can't trust them at face value. Look at how badly we misinterpreted the Aspects."

L'Veyna nodded, dragging her arm across her eyes.

"We'll find a way to break the Curse," Jouler promised. "I wish I'd had more time to read the Wall of Prophecy." He jerked his chin at the small chest strapped to Prack's horse. "Isn't it written in one of Orenda's books?"

"It's forbidden," Prack replied.

"It's such a dumb law," she said, folding her arms. "Maybe you're right. Maybe we were as wrong about the Saplings Curse as we were about the Aspects."

Jouler hated to douse her blossomed hope, so he kept the whisperings of his gift to himself. Prytha scholars were wrong about the Aspects, but Prytha adults would die at the hands of saplings. That much he'd gleaned from the Wall of Prophecy before they left. "We still don't know how or why the Curse is supposed to happen. Until we know what's written on Mh t'Pralab, all we have is speculation."

"And if we knew how and why," L'Veyna said, her lips curling into a smile, "maybe we can stop it."

Struck again by her natural beauty, Jouler marveled at the way the sun kissed her not-quite-brown, not-quite-green skin. Her long, pointed ears, sparkling with emeralds, poked back from a sea of thin braids, each braid a different color of autumn. Strips of purple, red, orange, yellow, and brown woven into a sleeve down her upper-left arm. No makeup accented her features, her body wrapped by a simple strip of green hempen cloth, her beauty effortless as a setting sun painting the sky.

She deserves better than her blasted Prophecy.

"I'll do everything in my power," he promised, "to prevent the Curse. Do the Boorde prophecies mention it?"

Prack shook his head. "Theirs mostly speak of events post prophecy. The Time of Plenty, when no one shall want for food, and peace shall reign over the land."

"That sounds…amazing," Pendric said with a shy smile.

"Sounds like a world free from the empire," Jouler said, earning an appreciative smile from L'Veyna.

"Of all the Prophecies," Prack said, "the Boorde's is the most beautiful."

Jouler's mind spun with ideas, which all pointed him to the Boorde Alliance. Their libraries were legendary, and Reylan might know where Kael went.

"We should get moving," Prack said, still staring at the line of ash snaking around the edge of the forest.

L'Veyna's shoulders slumped, and she made no move toward her horse.

"We can walk the horses for a bit," Jouler offered.

"After we cross the causeway," Prack said. "I want to put as much distance from that thing as we can before we dismount. Unfortunately, our options for crossing aren't great. There's a reason this stretch of road is called the Sotouri Strip. Not only does it carry their vile filth to and from the imperial capital, it's also one of the most traveled sections of causeway in the empire. Our first option," he said, nodding to the length of ash ahead of them, "is to continue straight ahead. The causeway crosses over a ravine that we can pass beneath unseen. It's called Gyda's Crossing. It's a common route for Phaerians smuggling Prytha goods into Onti, although who Gyda was is anyone's guess."

"Sounds good to me." L'Veyna moved to her horse and climbing onto her saddle. "Let's go."

"*However*," Prack said, "imperial soldiers like to ambush said smugglers, and, right now, we can be certain there will be a squad watching the crossing. And if there happens to be a Soutori in their midst, some of us will die."

"What's option two?" Pendric asked.

Prack climbed onto his golden palomino. "We ride north for a day and then head west."

"North of the forest are open plains," Jouler said. "And flat, from what I remember."

"So flat," Prack said, "you can see someone from miles away. And the few trees we'll find—more like glorified bushes—wouldn't hide a fox."

"What's so good about that option?" Pendric asked.

"If they can see us," Jouler surmised, "we can see them. And, if the empire's busiest causeway happens to be clear of traffic for long enough, we could reach Onti without running into a soul." It seemed unlikely, but the other route sounded like a definite trap. Prack's apprehension told Jouler there was more to the story. "What aren't you telling us?"

"Astute as usual," Prack said. "The Sotouri use the lands west of the Sotouri Strip to run their war games."

"Of course they do," Jouler said, guiding his horse to the edge of the forest. "On the one hand, we ride through a ravine and into a trap. On the other hand, we ride straight into the Sotouri's war games."

Prack bobbed his head. "Potentially."

"Isn't there another way?" Pendric asked, wheezing.

"Not without sailing," Prack replied. "Causeways split the middle of Torgeir from the Serpent Sea to Uleeri on the southern coast."

"Doesn't sound like much of a choice," Jouler said.

"North it is," Pendric said.

"What? No," Jouler said.

"But option one is a smuggler's route," Pendric mumbled, rubbing his chest. "I think I need some more tea before we head out."

A small, steaming orb formed over L'Veyna's palm. She pinched some herbs from a pouch at her belt, and sprinkled them in the orb, then handed it to Pendric.

"Is it hot?" he asked, blowing on it.

"Warm," she said. "It's just steaming because it's cold outside."

Pendric sipped on the orb and smiled. "Perfect."

"Do imperials take bribes?" Jouler asked.

"Imperials always take bribes," Prack said. "The problem is getting them to listen in the first place. Or honoring the bribe at all, for that matter."

Pendric slurped his tea sphere, his gaze lingering on Prack's lithe form. Pendric blinked, as if realizing he'd been staring. He slurped his tea, hiding his warmed cheeks.

"I…" L'Veyna hugged herself, her autumnal eyebrows drawn, eyes welling. "I don't know. I… I'm scared."

Prack edged his horse next to his sister's, his emerald eyes soft with compassion. "I was scared the first time I left the forest too."

L'Veyna sniffled and rolled her eyes. "You were not."

"I was," Prack replied. "Onatah was all I'd known, and the world outside is so big. But as soon as I crossed the Wreath, all I wanted was to see more."

"Hence why you rarely come back," L'Veyna said with a pointed look.

"Jo, you lead," Prack said, slipping off his dark riding coat and tucking it behind his saddle. "Sister, I want you between him and Pen."

L'Veyna nodded, her olive-skinned cheeks wet with fear.

"No matter what happens," Prack said, sliding back off his horse, "stay on the path."

"What about you?" Pendric asked.

"I'm going to set a trap of my own," Prack replied, handing his reins to Pendric. "Keep Poppy safe."

Jouler turned in his saddle to give L'Veyna a reassuring smile. "Are you ready?"

L'Veyna turned her head northward, and she gave a hesitant nod.

"Remember, not too tight," Pendric said, lifting his reins with his free hand. "Just pretend you're a pretty little bird."

L'Veyna's fear twisted into confusion. "A what?"

"You know," Pendric said, flapping his arms. "Because birds don't have hands, so they can't grab the reins too tight."

L'Veyna stared at Pendric, then rumbled with an infectious laugh. "Because it has no hands!"

Jouler laughed with her, his cheeks cramping.

"Alnazet's blessing," L'Veyna said, adjusting her wrap and braid-sleeve. "That was funny, Pen." Her emerald gaze caught Jouler's, her kind smile warming his heart. "Now I'm ready."

Jouler nudged Cloud forward, wondering how much of Pendric's antics were innocent. A clear blue sky greeted them outside the forest, the sun blazing over a vast wide plain. It was easy to see why imperials had chosen this spot for an ambush. The causeway spanned a steep ravine, providing smugglers an opportunity to cross the road without tripping its patterns.

Jouler led them down the soft slope to the bottom of the ravine, gazing up at the causeway as they passed beneath. Far too thin to hold its own weight, pattern-forging must keep the elegant bridge from collapsing. As with the causeway he'd passed with Grim, no alarms rang, nor did any bursts of light flash in the air above them.

"Filthy thing," L'Veyna said, sneering at the bridge. "I can feel it, draining life from the land like a d'Tormena." She shivered. "It's a wonder grass grows near the plagued thing."

Jouler scanned the ravine, noting a worn path down the northern slope. "They'll come from there."

L'Veyna pulled her horse beside his, and she peered at the ridge. "Do you think they're watching us?"

"Without a doubt," Jouler replied. "We'll take it slow."

Pendric worked the hem of his sleeve, his gaze fixated on the northern slope. "Shouldn't we, you know…gallop?"

"If there's a Vrath with them—"

"D'Tormena," L'Veyna interrupted.

"If there's a d'Tormena," Jouler corrected, "we could gallop right into an invisible barrier."

"How invisible?" L'Veyna asked, peering down the well-worn trail snaking through the bottom of the ravine. "The horses would sense them, right—the traps?"

"Completely and totally invisible," Pendric said. "And no, our horses would run right into them."

"Completely and totally mean the same thing," Jouler said, scanning the slope. The darker patches of soil betrayed a recent descent. Less than an hour passed by the look of it. The churned soil also held another clue. "There's no d'Tormena with them."

"How can you be so sure?" L'Veyna asked.

"A shaper would have cleaned up their tracks."

As suspected, a group of mounted soldiers pulled up to the northern ridge. In the span of a breath, a blur of motion raced through their ranks. Blood misted the air, and they collapsed from their saddles. Prack's blurred form stopped before the twitching corpses hit the ground.

"ANYTHING?" Pendric wheezed, his breathing more labored since they'd headed south toward Onti and the Eio Mountains.

"Huh?" L'Veyna mumbled over a tight knot of frustration. She'd scanned Pendric's lungs, his heart, his brain, every part of him, down to his toes, but there wasn't so much as a whisper of anything wrong with him. "It makes no sense."

"I know," Pendric said, and slumped in his saddle. "You should have seen how small the vial was."

"The what?" L'Veyna said. "No, I mean, there's nothing wrong with you."

"I beg to differ," he said, drawing a wheezing breath.

"I mean, there's no sign of the Oo'Kral's magic."

"*Ul'*Kral," Pendric corrected.

"Whatever. Don't you get what I'm saying? When Keepers ask and d'Tormena shape, they leave a residue, like a slug. Well, shaping is like that. Like a dark, necrotic slug. Asking residue is more like the aroma of a flower."

"Shaping is like slugs," Pendric said. "Asking is like a flower. Got it."

"But with you," she continued, "there's no slug trail or sweet aroma. Just…you."

Pendric puffed out his chest, pride pulling a sharp nod. "Yes, I am."

L'Veyna giggled, and asking him a warm ball of water for tea. Of the two Humans, Pen was her favorite. Jouler could be pleasant too, when he wasn't acting like a know-it-all. It was strange that her connection from the healing hadn't faded. Not for her, at least, though

Jouler didn't seem to feel anything, or he would have said something about it.

Wouldn't he?

He seemed to live in his thoughts, probably worrying over his morbid role in Prophecy. His kind, understanding patience spoke of someone who would try to mend her people, not bury them in the annals of history. Then again, the fondness he and Pendric spoke about Kael made him seem far from the man who killed her god and cursed her to her fate.

"How do you ask?" Pendric's curious tone pulled her from her dark thoughts. "Like, how did you ask for—" Pendric cleared his throat, and held up his tea sphere. "I mean, how did you *ask* this ball of water?" He nodded to himself, pride gleaming in his brown eyes. "With shaping, you use your will to mold a pattern with the Currents, and then..." He punched out his fist. "Fireball!"

L'Veyna bubbled with a soft chuckle, her mind frolicking with a playful image of Pendric fumbling over balls of fire. Pushing those images away, she recalled her mentor's lessons. "Inside each living being is an ever-blossoming power. It's what gives us life."

"Inside me too?" Pendric asked, looking down at his chest.

"Inside you too," L'Veyna replied. "Keepers are able to tap into that power, but only if Alnazet permits it."

"You're not going to take mine, are you?"

"No," L'Veyna chuckled. "Keepers can't do that. Besides, it's ever blossoming. It never runs out."

"Do you shape it, like Humans?" Jouler asked.

"No," L'Veyna replied. "Every asking starts with a Posture," L'Veyna said. "The first being the Posture of Root." Balancing on her saddle, she folded her legs and placed her hands on her knees, her thumbs and middle fingers forming a hoop. "Normally, we'd be on the ground, so you'd be able to—"

"Like this?" Pendric said, assuming the pose with ease.

Prack chuckled behind them, and L'Veyna sniffed at her impetuous brother. "Ignore him, Pen. He never takes anything serious."

"That's why I like him," Pendric said with a bashful smile.

L'Veyna ignored her brother's toothy grin. If only she could ignore her growing curiosity over the shiny tubes in his and Jouler's pack. The tubes begged her to open them, pleading for release...

"What purpose do the Postures serve?" Jouler asked, staring at the looming mountain range before them.

"If you'd waited one second," L'Veyna replied with a pointed look, "I was just about to explain that. Each Posture helps align a Keeper's spirit to prepare for an asking, and before you interrupt again, Jo, there are five Postures. The Root, which Pendric is showing, is the first and easiest Posture to learn. It's also the most difficult to master. The second Posture is Trunk, then Branch, Tree, and Sun."

Pendric unfolded his legs. "But you don't always do the Posture."

"They only *help* to align the spirit," L'Veyna said. "With enough practice, Keepers can assume a Posture without twitching a muscle. The second part of asking is the image. You have to form an image of your desired outcome."

"Like a mended wound?" Jouler said.

"Exactly," L'Veyna replied. "When I healed you, I formed an imagine of a healed wound. At first, it's like the image doesn't want to come into focus, and you have to fight to keep it from fading, but then the image just locks into place, which is when Alnazet accepts your asking."

Pendric's eyes sparkled with amazement. "It must be so wonderful. Just fold your legs, think of something, and...and you know." He wiggled his wormy fingers. "Vines!"

"It's a bit more complicated than that," she replied, chuckling.

"Not for you, I bet." Pendric sputtered his lips. "To me, asking is like wiggling my ears. No matter how many times people tell me how, I just can't do it. Maybe I don't have ear-wiggling muscles." His eyes went wide. "What if shapers and Keepers have special brain muscles, and *that's* how they can shape and ask?"

"Actually," Jouler mused. "That makes sense. Not an actual brain muscle, mind you. More like a part of the brain that allows them to use magic." He pointed at the back of his head. "Somewhere around here, I imagine. At least for shapers. Pen, remind me to ask Reylan about it when we see him."

"Like you'd forget," Pendric said, his face brightening with excitement. "I can't wait to see him, Jo."

"What's he like?" L'Veyna asked.

"Old," Prack said. "Even for a shaper. But he's funnier than a back-alley urchin, and he loves ha'ath like a Prytha."

"What's a back-alley urchin?" L'Veyna asked, and Pendric shrugged.

"You'll love him," Prack said with a soft chuckle. "It's the Boorde I'm worried about."

"What's so bad about them?" Jouler asked.

"Meat," L'Veyna said, gagging. "It's all they eat. They even have candied meats. *Candied*. Like, sweet meat."

"You've never even tried it," Prack said, then gave her a somber look. "And trust me, you don't want to. Made me sick for a week."

"Why would you eat meat?" she said, surprised at her brother. "You're lucky it didn't kill you."

"You never know until you try," Prack said.

"Famous last words," L'Veyna replied, wrinkling her nose from an acrid odor. "Bleh! What's that smell?"

"Onti," Prack said, pointing ahead of them.

L'Veyna shielded her eyes against the setting sun, but she still couldn't see the town. The acrid smell worsened as they rode toward the base of a towering mountain range, and the town finally took shape. Instead of the clusters of domed houses found in Prytha communities, Onti boasted conglomerates of buildings all made of a strange ruddy material. The crammed masses of houses bubbled high above the pathetic little wall surrounding the town, as if the inhabitants vied to pack as many houses as possible into the small area.

"Why not expand outward?" she asked with a sweeping gesture to the open plains and majestic mountains. "It's not like there's no room."

"The empire won't let them," Prack said.

Churning from some of the ruddy clusters, plumes of thick, black smoke hung over the town, forming the dark cloud she'd seen from a distance. A soft breeze carried the smoke's acrid smell, along with a pungent odor that clung to L'Veyna's nostrils.

"Bleh," she gagged, spitting out the foul taste. "Humans live here? Like…willingly?"

Jouler nodded, holding the back of his hand to his nose.

"Why does it smell like that?" she asked. "It's so bad."

"Some smell worse," Prack said without a hint of sarcasm.

L'Veyna prepared an asking, letting her mind drift to the power within her. She formed an image of a small hempen draw bag filled with lavender, cloves, cinnamon, and orange zest. The image wavered, offering little resistance before locking into place. She held the small pouch to her nose, welcoming the pleasant aroma.

"Speaking of which," Prack told her, "you'll need to ask some gold and silver nuggets."

"For what?" she asked, gagging at the stench.

"Humans love them," Prack said. "They'll do just about anything for gold and silver."

"Like, for jewelry?" L'Veyna asked, running her finger along her long bejeweled ears.

"That too," Jouler said. "But mostly to build wealth and power."

"But, how?" L'Veyna asked. "It's gold and silver. They're just pretty, like emeralds."

"We're weird," Jouler replied.

"Obviously." L'Veyna gestured to the disgusting town.

"Humans use gold and silver for currency," Prack said. "That, and copper, bronze, and steel."

"What if you don't have any?" L'Veyna asked.

"You starve," Pendric replied.

"They just let people die?" L'Veyna's mouth fell open. "Are you serious?"

"Sometimes," Pendric said. "I mean, sometimes people die. Townsborn, mind you. Not skirters, like me and Jo. We don't care about no gold or silver…unless we're heading to town, but that's only so we can trade at the market."

"I...what?" L'Veyna replied, reeling in confusion.

Jouler chuckled, explaining the difference between Phaerians born in towns and those born in villages like Headwater. "We mostly just filled a need to keep the village functioning. My family grew cotton and fruit. Pen's father tanned leather. Reylan made ales and liqueurs. We had a blacksmith, an inn with a tavern, and a Town Square for special occasions. We just all worked together."

"Sounds like our platforms," L'Veyna said. "Like normal life, with normal people who don't let others starve from not having any gold."

"Towns and cities are too big to function like that," Prack said.

"Bigger than Onatah?" L'Veyna gave him a pointed look, and he had the gall to smirk.

The wall engulfing Onti stretched higher than she'd expected, reaching higher than a full-grown elm. A line of miserable Humans shuffled out the gate, chains linking them together, their drab clothes more filth than fabric. Four other Humans in shining armor, their temple shimmering with a strange red symbol, led the chained Humans away from the town.

"Slaves," Prack explained. "Likely bound for New Torgeir."

"I am *not* going in there," L'Veyna said, pressing her pouch to her nose. "We're not even inside, and I can barely stand the smell."

"You'll be fine," Prack said.

"What about the horses?" Jouler asked. "A pair of Prytha with horses might not raise any brows, but two Phaerians with horses as nice as these will."

Prack clicked hit tongue. "Not a pair of Prytha with two horses each. You and Pen will act as our Phaerians."

"Why can't I wait out here?" L'Veyna said.

Prack cast a lazy wave to the mountains behind Onti. "Those slopes are crawling with soldiers and Sotouri trainees."

L'Veyna grumbled, her voice muffled behind her pouch. "How are we even going to find Diou in that mess? The plagued town is bigger than Onatah. Way bigger."

"That's easy," Prack said, halting his golden palomino. "There's only one place non-Humans are allowed in Onti—the Twisted Promise Inn. The Sotouri like to keep us corralled."

"This close to Eio," Jouler said, rubbing his stubbled chin, "I imagine the inn will have a few Sotouri Masks mingled within the crowd."

"And the staff," Prack said. "If there are fewer than a dozen Sotouri in the common room, I'd fear something was amiss. Masks use Onti as a type of proving grounds to cut their teeth."

"Why would they cut their teeth?" Pendric asked, working the hem of his sleeve. "Can't Diou come to us?"

"And how might we tell him?" Prack asked. "He's expecting us at the inn, not out here."

"Then you go get him," L'Veyna said. "The rest of us will wait here."

"Yeah!" Pendric chirped. "I'll pitch a tent, and L'Veyna can ask some potatoes for Jo to cook…"

"What if a Citizen stumbles upon us?" Jouler said with a sweeping gesture to the open plains. "There's nowhere to hide."

Prack sidled his horse next to Pendric's, and he laid a hand on Pen's shoulder. "I would never bring you there if I thought you'd be in danger. I would never let them hurt you."

Pendric nodded, returning Prack's smile.

L'Veyna shook her head, grumbling. "I can't believe you're dragging me into that rotted town."

OTHER THAN THE large number of Shielded temples Jouler glanced in the streets, Onti seemed no different from Alduos and Iaroca. The same loud drone filled the air, along with the familiar stench of unwashed bodies, vomit, waste, and rivulets of gray water. Stacks of unfinished brick buildings cast the same perpetual shadows over muddy streets pack with the same feral cats and mangy mutts. Towns-born still wore dull, patch-worked Phaerian garb, and looked as filthy as any in Alduos, yet, somehow, the town felt off.

As Jouler had imagined, Prack and L'Veyna stood out amid the drab sea. Their bright autumnal hair and long, emerald-jeweled ears catching gazes and halted steps. Some townsborn gawked at the Prytha, their eyes swimming in lust, while other Phaerians seemed nonplused by the colorful siblings.

Jouler shifted his pack, ignoring the persistent call of the tubes, and focused on a young man with a stern face, black curly hair, and a malformed hand. The townsborn carried himself a little taller than the others, his eyes sharp and searching, not dull and forlorn. His grime seemed different too. Fresher, like he'd just smeared it, not built up over the years.

Sotouri.

The realization churned Jouler's stomach and turned his limbs to mush. He saw them everywhere, now, their gaits and stances oozing with tempered confidence that no townsborn could fake. With a single glance, Jouler counted eight, sticking out worse than a bull in a chicken coop.

The townsborn had to see them too. They couldn't be that obtuse, and yet, they carried on as though their streets weren't filled with Sotouri, Vrath, soldiers, and Citizens. Somehow, the townsborns' lack of response made it all seem worse.

A hand gripped his wrist, and he startled, swinging his elbow. Prack ducked and gave Jouler a threatening look.

"Sorry," Jouler said. "You startled me."

"You need to calm down," Prack mumbled. Poppy nuzzled him for attention, and he patted her neck. "Trust me, you're almost too much of a skirter to pass as a townsborn, much less a Sotouri."

"I wasn't trying to pass as a Sotouri," Jouler replied, pulling his gaze away from the thick flow of townsborn.

"Then stop acting like one," Prack said.

"I do not miss this," Pendric said, holding his hand over his nose.

"And you," Prack said, pulling Pendric's hand down. "Stop that. You're supposed to be a townsborn."

"She's doing it," Pendric said, jerking his thumb to L'Veyna clutching her stomach and pressing her snuff bag to her nose.

"She's Prytha," Prack said. "It's expected of her." He turned a worried frown for his sister. "Are you all right, Little Sprout?"

"I feel sick," she replied with a wince. "It's this place. I knew I shouldn't have come."

"It's the shaping," Prack said. "It makes Keepers sick."

"Why?" Pendric asked.

"Because their power is rotten," L'Veyna grumbled.

"Try and push it from your mind," Prack said. "Focus on something good."

"You focus," L'Veyna snapped.

"Take my hand and walk behind me," Prack said, and she hesitated. "So you don't have to look at the filth."

After another wince she took his hand and followed in his footsteps.

Clever, Jouler noted, letting Pen walk in front of him. Prack's subtle manipulation reminded Jouler of they ways he would get his little brothers to help with chores.

After trudging through Onti's putrid streets, ignoring all the Sotouri and Citizens, Jouler breathed a sigh of relief when they walked into the Twisted Promise Inn. Unlike the clamor permeating the streets, a gentle din of conversation floated through the inn's large common room. Jouler gawked at the patrons, unable to contain his surprise at the number of Prytha cloistered around tables, their long, pointed ears bejeweled with precious stones to match their eyes. Their light green and autumnal braids added welcomed splashes of color to the drab inn. Like Prack, they'd eschewed traditional Prytha clothing for trousers, thick coats, blouses, boots, and hooded cloaks.

Jouler's heart skipped when his eyes passed a tall figure with impossibly black hair and skin as white as snow. Rodak had such skin and hair, but he didn't have diamond-shaped irises the color of fire, or elongated canines.

Boorde!

A full head taller than any Human Jouler had seen, the Boorde sat alone, sipping a chestnut-brown liquor from a snifter. A long, curved sword lay sheathed on the table.

Prack cleared his throat and shook his head. "That's not Diou."

Jouler recovered from his shock enough to notice townsborn sprinkled throughout the common room. Only a handful wore their oppression as if they'd grown up in Onti. The others tried to emulate that misery, but hard, calculating eyes belied their insidious nature.

They're studying Phaerians.

The Sotouri weren't here to sniff out skirters or catch enemies of the empire. They were here to learn how to be Phaerian. That was why Onti felt off. It wasn't just a town. It was a huge classroom for Masks.

"You're not from around here," a man said from the bar. A white sash adorned with rusted steel filigree hung across the man's bright red coat, both too small for his round frame. Likewise, his dark blue pants cried for someone much thinner. He drained his mug of ale, and pushed his plate of half-eaten slagsticks, nu'biscuits, and what could have been brown scrambled nu'eggs or mashed nu'potatoes.

"Was it the long, pointed ears that gave us away?" Prack asked.

"Good one, friend Prytha. Name's Osrod Ipero." The man's eyes lingered on L'Veyna, and she tugged at her green Keeper's wrap, shrinking behind her brother. Osrod's lips curled, and he gestured to the back of the common room, where the haze of smoke was thick and the light dim. "You all look like you've been on the road a while. Please, let me buy you all a round of drinks, maybe a plate of food?"

Pendric opened his mouth to speak, and Jouler kicked him in the shin. "Ouch, Jo! That hurt. Why do you always do that? It's not like I was going to tell him we're—ouch! Stop that, Jo!"

"Thank you, Osrod," Prack said. "But we're waiting for someone."

"No sense in waiting on an empty stomach," Osrod replied, gesturing again to the dim corner.

"We mean no offense," Jouler said, jerking a thumb to his pack. "It's been a long day. We just want to get cleaned and rested."

"Osrod!" a man greeted with a thundering voice. The short newcomer clapped the lecherous-eyed man on the back. Dressed in pristine Phaerian drab, the newcomer's well-used apron wrapped twice around his thin frame.

"Ah, Emril," Prack said, shaking the newcomer's hand.

Emril glared at Osrod until the round, brightly clothed man sneered and returned to his seat at the bar. A seat no one had dared to fill, the portly man's half-eaten food still waiting for him. In a town full of empty bellies, everyone seemed to know better than to take Osrod's things.

"It's good to see you, Prack," Emril said.

"And you," Prack replied. "Is Diou here yet?"

Emril shook his head and turned to L'Veyna. "This must be your sister. It's so great to finally meet you."

"You know about me?" she asked, cringing back from his extended hand.

"You're all your brother talks about," Emril said, and turned to Jouler. "And you are..."

"Jouler," he said, shaking the innkeeper's hand. "Pleasure to meet you."

"Any friend of Prack's is a welcomed guest at the Twisted Promise." Emril turned to Pendric and a fond smile split his face. Emril clapped him on the shoulder. "Pendric Loyalton."

Pendric shifted on his feet. "Do I know you?"

"By the gods, I should say not!" Emril replied. "But I'd recognize that face from a town away." He leaned to whisper. "I wouldn't be here if it weren't for your father."

"Is he here?" Pendric wheezed.

"I wish," Emril said, and jerked his chin at Osrod. "That worthless Shield-licker wouldn't be found within a league of Onti if Tied were here."

"My da never mentioned you," Pendric mumbled.

"And I'm glad he didn't." Emril blinked and shook his head as if awakening from a deep thought. "Gods forgive me, you all must be exhausted. Please, this way. I have rooms for you, of course."

Emril led them up two flights of stairs and down a long, dim hall lined with doors. Mounted above each door were tiny glowglobes the size of a thumbnail, illuminating the room number.

"Where are the children?" Pendric asked.

Emril blinked. "The who?"

"The children," Pendric said. "The orphaned children from the streets. I didn't see any in the common room."

Emril shook his head with an easy chuckle. "Now you're talking crazy, son. My inn is already filthy enough without those mangy little leeches."

"Oh…"

"Wait." Emril stopped and rubbed his head. "You thought inns were where urchins go to get fed?"

"That's how Mistress Symmonds runs the Honeyed Ale," Pendric said. "Her and Chas, back in Alduos. There's children in there all the time, laughing, playing, eating her wonderful mushroom soup. It's the best. You don't happen to have any here, do you? Any mushroom soup?"

Emril shook his head and continued down the hall. "That's not how the rest of the world functions, son."

The doors grew farther apart, suggesting larger rooms, until there were no small glowglobes to light their way. When they reached the end of the corridor, Emril pressed his hand against the wall, and a door-sized portion slid away with a creak.

"Da has a secret door, too!" Pendric said, slipping past Emril into the clandestine suite. "Tolrik's beard! Jo, get in here. This is amazing!"

Jouler followed Emril through the door and found an opulent room furnished with plush chairs and two sofas. In a dark corner of the room was a plush red leather chair lined with brass studs, and a small, round table. On the other side of the room, a crystal chandelier illuminated a heavy dining table and long benches, but most impressive were the shelves of books. Lots of books, wall to wall, floor to ceiling, wherever space allowed.

"Isn't it great?" Pendric said, plopping onto a sofa.

"I could live here," Jouler whispered.

"There are no windows," L'Veyna said, crossing her arms. "No windows. No sunlight."

"I'm afraid not," Emril replied. "It's too dangerous."

"Diou shouldn't be long," Prack said. "We'll only be here a few days at most."

"Days, not hours?" L'Veyna wilted, and shuffled to sit beside Pendric on the sofa. "At least my belly stopped aching."

"There's a washroom in the back," Emril said, "with a hot waterbox for baths. Please use it. All of you."

Prack chuckled and walked Emril to the secret entrance. After exchanging whispered words, Emril wished them a good day before closing the door behind him.

"What am I going to do, Prack?" L'Veyna whined. "I can't go that long without feeling the sun on my skin."

"Every winter, the sky is overcast for weeks." Prack gave her a pointed look. "You'll be fine."

"That's different," L'Veyna replied. "It's still outside when it's cloudy. This is more like a cave."

"Or a dungeon," Pendric said, his eyes glimmering with a phaery tale.

Prack shook his head with a chuckle. "You two need to get out more if you think this is what a cave or a dungeon look like.

Pendric nudged L'Veyna. "I understood what you meant."

Jouler perused book titles, searching for historical books, or books on prophecy. The types of tomes Reylan had forbidden. One wall of shelves seemed dedicated to adventure books, though it lacked *Two Ferns for Ebron* and *Flight of a Finch*. He pulled a few titles that sparked his interest and continued his search, passing more adventure books, shipping records, and building plans.

"Here we go," he said, sliding out a thick, leather-bound book with no title, a familiar figure embossed on its spine and cover—the figure from the Wall of Prophecy, holding the sword. "That can't be a coincidence."

Prack's gaze rested on the book, and he clicked his tongue. "I almost forgot about that."

"What is it?" Pendric asked, following Jouler to the dining table.

L'Veyna joined them, sitting next to Jouler. Her head jerked back when she saw the figure of the Harbinger. "M'Ljot?" she said, curiosity sharp in her voice. She gazed at him as if searching, her smile twinkling in her emerald eyes. "You're right. You don't seem like a Harbinger of Death."

Pendric tossed his arms up. "That's what I've been saying! There's got to be something wrong with that name."

Jouler shook his head, pushing back the call of the tubes. "Of that, I'm certain. Kael is the Crier of Change, and I'm the Harbinger." The words felt right, like puzzle pieces snapping together. He opened the book cover, and a wave of fear washed over him.

L'Veyna's mouth fell open. "Prack!"

"I already know," her brother replied.

"No, come here. Look!"

"I know."

"I can't read," Pendric said, working the hem of his sleeve. "What's it say?"

Prack pulled a long drag from his pipe and filled the room with the sharp smell of ha'ath. *"How the Dark Defeats the Light: Volume One, The Harbinger of Death."*

7

SCHEMATICS

Iruviaa Taniria glared at her ruined forge-sling. Smoke twisted from the exploded steel tube, curling inside the force dome, and licking around the chunks and bits of steel embedded in the invisible barrier. This time, some of the thinner slivers had come close to piercing through the dome.

Maybe less power…not more, she thought, phantom pain lancing up her missing arm. She rubbed her knobby elbow, wishing her body understood what gone meant.

"Gone, like this schematic," she mumbled, pressing her pattern-forged ring to the crumpled parchment on her workbench. Pressing the ring with her thumb, she activated the pattern-forging, and the schematic curled with flame. She brushed the burning parchment onto the floor, revealing the well-charred spot on her workbench where countless other schematics had met a similar fate. But such were the ways of pattern-forging. Weavers like her didn't simply invent new gadgets; they discovered thousands of different ways on how *not* to invent said gadgets.

Like this blasted forge-sling.

The concept seemed simple enough—projectiles like arrows and shot balls needed force and direction. The steel tube provided the latter, giving the lead shot a straight path, but something needed to be done about the force. Too much power and the tube exploded; too little, and the shot just rolled out of the tube.

She released the force dome's pattern, letting the tainted Currents drift away, releasing the trapped smoke into the spacious workroom. She longed for an open meadow in the middle of nowhere, or maybe a quaint cabin by a lake. Anywhere but this blasted island.

Flashes of lightning splashed through the workshop's glass ceiling, drowning the soft light cast by the sconces, while claps of thunder rumbled the myriad tools and gadgets hanging on the stone walls. The storms of the Tempest's Embrace never relented, perpetually drowning the island. It was no wonder the Cabal had set up their headquarters here.

"I told you it'd blow up," Kyndraeth said, coughing and swishing the air.

She rounded on the Half-Boorde, and he clamped his mouth shut. Not as tall as the enigmatic race, Kyndraeth still stood a full head above her. He dragged a hand over his bald scalp, light from the sconces casting a gentle glow on his coal-black skin. Not a hair poked from that toned body, his tantalizing form hidden beneath a thick black shirt with wide sleeves, and his loose black trousers.

"Not a word," she warned, reading the mischief behind his gray diamond-shaped irises

"The tube was too thin," he said.

She whipped out a dagger and threw it at his head.

He let the dagger fly past him with effortless grace, watching the weapon clatter to the ground. "Not even close," he said, gliding to the target she'd setup for her forge-sling. He pointed to the steel ball embedded near the top edge of the thick wood. "But your forge-sling worked…sort of. You're almost there."

"Almost there?" Iruviaa scoffed. "The tube exploded, and I almost missed the target."

"But you didn't."

"It's less than two paces from the forge-sling!"

"Not for a baby."

Iruviaa lunged for Kyndraeth, swiping and kicking, though she might as well have tried hitting a fly as the nimble man. Still, she continued her barrage, letting the physical exertion liberate her pent up rage. It wasn't like the blasted man would give her the release she wanted. Men rarely would with scars and a face like hers. Especially not Human men. Boorde could see past the ugly, but they were so rare to come by, and as much as she'd love to bed a Prytha, they hated shapers. Those leaf-eating bastards would rake her to death with those claws before she got their clothes off.

But it sure would be fun.

Unlike trying to land a blow on Kyndraeth. The damned Half-Boorde slipped by her kicks and slapped her hands away. The edge of her fist brushed against his cheek, and she shouted in triumph, "I got you!"

Chuckling, Kyndraeth used her momentum to spin her, then landed a series of light blows on her back that hinted of a massage.

"Oh, yeah…more of that," she moaned, and he obliged. Breathless and dripping with sweat, she leaned into his massaging pats and claps.

"That was a quick scuffle," Kyndraeth mused, no more winded than before her outburst. He worked her neck and kneaded a tight spot below her shoulder blade. Clapping her on the shoulders, he signaled the end to the impromptu massage, and she collapsed onto her cool leather couch.

"Long night," Iruviaa explained, a towel landing on her face. Wiping off her sweat, she sat back up. "Why won't the projectile fly straight? I aimed right in the middle of the board."

"Maybe the tube is also too short," Kyndraeth said. "Too thin, and too short."

Iruviaa pushed herself to her feet and snatched one of the lead balls from her charred workbench. "Do you think it's the shape?" she asked, holding up the metal sphere. "Sling shot hardly flies straight to begin with. Arrows do, but it's not like I can put some fins on something that shoots from a tube."

"Hmmm…" Kyndraeth tilted his head, brow furrowed the way he

did when a novel idea crossed his mind. "You might be on to something with the shape."

Her workroom door opened with a slam, and she startled, dropping the projectile, pain shooting up her missing limb.

Thannel the Mark strode into her room, a grin on the once Sotouri Spade's gruff face. Dark for a South Blailonian, his scruffy hair and beard were as unkempt as his timeworn shirt and pants. His gaze fell on the wooden target and exploded tube, and he lifted an eyebrow.

"Don't say a godsdamn thing," Iruviaa warned, rubbing her nubby elbow.

"Not a word," Thannel said with a sweeping bow. "Besides, I'm sure Kyndraeth already beat me to it."

"Did you come here to yap?" Iruviaa said. "Or do you have something useful to say?"

Thannel's lips slid into a dark grin. "I have a new mark."

"Gods, it's about time," Iruviaa said, happy to finally leave this dreadful island and all its people.

"Who is it?" Kyndraeth asked.

"An old friend of mine," Thannel replied.

Kyndraeth's mirth fell, and a twinge of dread tainted Iruviaa's excitement. For all the decades she'd served alongside Thannel the Mark, he'd only called one person his friend.

"Reylan Svaldenson."

8

THE OLD WORLD

Not a speck of life glowed in Xi'Tslna's mind. Last winter had claimed the hatchlings and the oldest of her brood. This winter promised to claim far more.

At least they'll have one less mouth to feed.

She retracted her death sense and continued toward the sound of tumbling water. A howling wind rushed down the mountainside and through the pines, whipping the tails of her thick leather coat around her legs. Fashioned to accommodate the spikes along her spine, the brown coat didn't quite reach as far down her calf as it had last year.

Darkness preserve me, I thought I'd finished growing.

Following the soft rumble of water, she skirted around a steep spur and gazed upon her crystalline prize. A gentle stream tumbled down the moss-covered cliff side, pouring into a wide pool rimmed by tall pines.

She laid her pack on a flat rock by the water, then leaned her spear against a tree, unslung her bow, and unhooked her quiver from her belt. Peeling off her heavy leather coat, she carefully folded it and set it on her pack. Next came her pants and shirt, each folded with equal care and placed on her coat. Free from its woolen confine, her necklace of shadow cat claws clacked against her scaled chest. She flexed her taloned fingers, still feeling the two that had been bitten off by the same cat.

Naked, she stood before the pond and looked at her reflection. She rather liked the coloration of her scales. They weren't flamboyantly blue or yellow like some in her brood, or muted brown like her all of her fathers. She'd taken after one of her mothers, their green outer scales shimmering like butterfly wings under the sun. Four old scars ran along her side, marring the cream scales on her belly and under her chin.

As with other mancers, the mane running down the back of her head and spine had turned white when she came into her abilities. According to grandfather Xi'Tlys, it had happened far too early, but that was no cause to leave the city and ban her from the dark arts.

Try to ban me, she corrected.

Her brood couldn't stop her from scribbling skemata on her slate pads while she hunted, or keep her from finding old bones for practice. A golem, or better yet, a reanimated wolf pack could have saved her fingers, but her elders would have thrown her into the Light Tank for a week.

If I was lucky.

Deep into the mountains and far from incriminating eyes, Xi'Tslna reached out with her death sense, finding small bones from rodents and birds, but nothing large enough to hold the simplest skema. Later, she'd sense for something large enough to scribe a mancer's torch, but for now…

She waded into the pristine pool, digging her clawed feet into its sandy bottom. She kicked up sand and wriggled, exfoliating between her scales. After a gentle scrub, she swam to deeper water to shake the sand free from under her scales.

Darkness forsake me, that feels so good.

With a deep breath, she closed her transparent eyelids and plunged to the bottom of the pool. Beams of light danced through the water, refracted by the hypnotic surface high above. Swaddled within the cool depths, she closed her opaque outer eyelids and let the constant grumble of water wash her mind clear.

After Darkness knew how many minutes had passed, burning lungs awoke her from her bliss. She kicked off the rocky bottom and swam to shore. She shivered from the water, the crisp autumn air washing over her scales. Ignoring the angry gray sky, she slipped into her clothes and rummaged through her backpack, hoping to find a lost morsel of dried fruit or meat. Rope, blanket, bandages, flint, cotton, knife, and a change of clothes, but no food.

Gathering her things, her heart choked, gripped by the hard realization she'd never again visit her swimming hole. If what her grandfather said was true, once Xi'Tslna joined the Grand Armada, she might never see Sati again. She pushed back a wave of loss and set off for De'h'larka, determined to make the city by morning.

Following the trail up the mountainside would be grueling, but the view at the pass always stole her heart, especially at sunset, which she could still make if she stopped dawdling. Thoughts of wandering through the city tamped her anger, fueling her steps. Once she joined the Grand Armada, she'd finally learn the secrets of her powers from the world's leading scholars, and her people would honor her as a living symbol of Death.

And the food!

She'd ignore the grub vendors, of course, but if her elders' descriptions of the markets were any indication, she'd lose herself in all the different fruits and vegetables, not to mention all the amazing bone-tech. Autocarts and trolleys to whisk people down streets. Small curriers—chests with numerous short bone legs—scuttling down sidewalks to deliver precious goods and important messages. Abacuses etched with skemata to solve mathematical equations.

The city wouldn't all be fruits and flowers, of course. Once she joined the Grand Armada, they would cram her on a ship with Darkness knew how many other people. That aspect of her new life wouldn't be much different from life with her brood, but she'd have the freedom to be herself—her true self—and the Armada would honor her for it.

Halfway up the trail, the entire valley she'd called home for the past twenty-one years spread below her. Smoke from her broodhome, tiny in the distance, curled above a thick forest in the throes of autumn. North of the painted forest, in the evergreen mountains, sparkled the small lake where she'd lost her fingers.

Xi'Tslna halted, cursing her luck. Before her was a wide span of mountainside that had fallen, taking the trail with it. Backtracking around the other side would set her back an entire day, but what choice did she have?

Her long back spikes shivered with the sensation of death, stealing her thoughts. She set her spear down and nocked an arrow, listening to the unnatural silence draped over the mountains. The sensation drew her gaze to a large hole at the base of the recently fallen slope.

A cave?

At least twice her height, the mouth of the cave looked too purposeful, too perfectly round to be natural. Maybe it had been some ancient Human burial ground from thousands of years ago, before her people banished them from Sati.

Curiosity returned her arrow to its quiver. After unstringing her bow and strapping her spear to her back, she pulled her rope from her pack, tied it around a young pine, and clawed footholds down the soft cliff side. The shiver in her spine spikes increased as she drew closer to the cave, her senses heavy with death.

A wide ledge littered with bone protruded from the mouth of the cave. Old bones, pale with age, without a speck of rotted flesh or marrow—perfect for bone-tek. Bird bones, shadow cats, wolves, deer, rodents—every type of creature in the forest. Even a dragon tooth, dulled with age, lay among the pile. But not a single bone lay inside the cave. None that she could see, at least.

She yipped, and her voice echoed down the deep cave, fading into the darkness. Grabbing a long bone, she checked for whatever invisible barrier had kept the animals out—the type of barrier Humans were said to have made with their strange magic. If the remnants of the Bowl were any measure, they'd wielded far more power than any mancer could hope to possess.

Enough to form a crater hundreds of miles wide.

Oh, to have seen Humans in their glory, but none had roamed Sati for over three millennia. Not since Sze't'kha'atsu, the Awakening, when her people rose from ignorance and drowned the Humans in the sea. So said the stories, at least, but what if they were wrong? What if humanity had survived the Endless Sea?

With a quick prayer to Qi'k'krasz, the Dark, she tossed the bone into the cave, and it clattered to the ground. No flash of light or burst of flame. Just a hollow clatter, echoing down the deep cave. Cringing, she stretched her arm out, waiting for her hand to burn, or for a bolt to strike, or...

She opened her eyes, her arm well past the line of bones.

With a sigh of relief, she let her arm drop to her side. At least she wouldn't die out here like all these creatures, but the question still remained—what had kept them out of the cave?

Shaking the nerves from her hands, she grabbed a femur bone large enough to hold skemata for a mancer's torch. Her death sense connected to the bone, impressing a faded impression of the deer's final pain-filled moments, after being driven here by an insatiable longing, only to die of starvation.

Curious, Xi'Tslna thought, grabbing another bone. A bear, driven here by the same insatiable desire, also dead from starvation. Every bone told the same morbid tale—animal after animal, driven by an urge they could not deny. She peered at the dragon tooth. More sentient than the other beasts of the land, a dragon should give her a clearer impression of what had brought it here to die.

She grabbed the tooth, ignoring the rumbles of thunder and tiny patters of rain that urged her to take shelter, and her death sense connected with the dragon. She soared over Sati, flying through mountainous crags and valleys. Fiery spittle dripped from her powerful jaws, igniting brushfires on dried plains and forests. A single urge obliterated the dragon's mind, overwhelming the hunger ravaging her belly. It was the same urge that had led animals to their death.

The Light's call.

Xi'Tslna recoiled from the unholy power, dropping the tooth. As proven by this graveyard, Na'n'khi, God of Light, feigned benevolence while She threatened to consume the land in fire. Each animal had been driven here by the Light, and they'd all starved.

She fished out another femur, slipped her mancer's nail over her finger, and etched the skema for a torch that would activate on command. Reaching into the well of darkness within her soul, she infused the skema with the spark of unlife and uttered her chosen command.

"Ksra."

The lines of the skema glowed sky blue, the holy color of Qi'k'krasz, and blue flames flickered down the length of bone. As always, the heatless fire licked her hand, mesmerizing her with the sensation of feeling no heat from the dancing flames.

She stepped over the piled up line of bones and gasped. Not a hint of death tingled her spine spikes—not even from her manced femur, though blue flames still flickered over the bone. She spun around and saw nothing had changed outside the cave. Bones were still piled near the entrance, with the painted valley far below. Nothing but her death-sense had changed.

Can I still mance?

Panicked, she stepped outside into the heavy rain, and her back spikes tingled with her death sense once more. Breathing a sigh of relief, she stepped back into the dry shelter of the cave. She entertained the idea of mancing a small golem from the bones outside, but the process would carry her well into the night. Swallowing her unease, she flexed her mangled hand and headed into the dark depths of the cave.

Blue light from her bone-tech torch flickered along tall stalagmites rising from the floor, stretching to meet its stalactite mate. She maneuvered around thick columns, marveling at how long it would have taken for them to form—hundreds of thousands of years, if not over a million, long before A'a'nxil or Humans roamed the land. The ancient cave continued straight, like a giant shaft bored into the mountainside by a massive screw.

Or a god.

The rough floor of the cave ended in a sharp line that poured into replete darkness. She held up her torch. Holy blue light danced up the cave walls and across its dripping ceiling, but it wouldn't pierce the darkness beyond. Maybe it was a portal to Qi'k'krasz's realm.

She yipped again, and her voice faded into the void. She held the torch over the sharp line, and her arm didn't pass into some other realm. The cave simply ended as though cleaved. She tossed a small rock and was surprised when it landed with a sharp, reverberating snap.

Like rocks on an icy lake.

Xi'Tslna crouched and laid her torch on the invisible ground. The torch seemed to float in the darkness, the floor drinking in the flickering blue light. She pressed her hand on the impossibly smooth ground. Cool to the touch, it felt as solid as marble, her slap sending the same reverberating waves across its surface.

Before she could change her mind, she stepped forward, and her foot found purchase. A sensation washed over her, like stepping through a gentle waterfall. Shivers coursed down her scales, her toeclaws clicking on the smooth floor.

"Death's embrace," she whispered, almost dropping the torch. She dared another step. The darkness swallowed the holy blue light of the flames.

She took another step, and another, looking back over her shoulder to make sure she could still see the hint of light at the mouth of the cave. Deeper into the darkness, glints of another blue light hinted at objects. She pressed forward, finally making out three humanoid statues carved with immaculate care and detail. The statues sagged as if melted by an intense heat. One was an A'a'nxil, its spine spikes drooping against its back. Another statue looked as Human as any sketches Xi'Tslna had seen, while the third statue looked like no species she'd read about. Shorter than the Human, it bore talons on its fingers, its long melted ears drooping against its shoulders. All three statues appeared to be protecting the melted remains of what had to have been a fourth statue.

Melted by what?

The cave was far too small for a dragon, and based on the pile of bones outside, no other creature had entered the cave. Yet something, or someone, had destroyed the center statue.

She looked at them again, at how they surrounded the rubble, the hard expressions carved into their features, the strain etched on their brow, the weight of duty pressing on their shoulders.

They hadn't been protecting the crumbled statue. They'd kept it imprisoned.

But why?

She touched the melted pile of rubble, and pain consumed her mind, stealing her breath. In some distant reality, her mancer's torch clattered to the floor. Unable to move, bright cerulean power licked up her arm and seeped into her chest. Blue tendrils stretched toward her heart, promising sweet release.

See…

The voice in her head was both hers and not.

Open your eyes…

The Dark's blessed power enveloped her heart, and her pain evaporated. Expecting to find a necrotic limb, she breathed a sigh of relief when she found her arm whole.

Know the truth…

A sparkle on her arm caught her eyes. She lifted her sleeve and swelled with pride. Between her scales, her skin shimmered the same sky blue as the fire on her mancer's torch, the holy color of Qi'k'krasz.

"What's this?" The strange voice echoed through the darkness.

Startled, Xi'Tslna reached for her bow and nocked an arrow. "Astsna," she whispered, activating the bone-tech. Skemata etched into the bones lining the edges of her bow glowed blue, and she drew the string with no effort.

From the darkness, the warm light of an oil torch drew toward her.

Xi'Tslna released a guttural warning, but the wavering flame still advanced. She aimed her bow, guessing at the individual's torso. "Stop, or I'll loose. I said—"

A figure materialized from the darkness, and Xi'Tslna's mouth fell open. Her arms fell to her side, her bow falling to the floor.

A Human!

Taller than Xi'Tslna, he lacked the glorious mane she'd seen in sketches. Wisps of hair cupped the back of the human's head, his bald pate glistening in the torchlight.

"Statues?" the man mused, as if neither seeing nor hearing her.

This must be a vision from the Dark, which would explain why the blue light from the mancer's torch didn't touch the human's red cheeks and sand-colored hair, or his drab, well-worn clothes.

Xi'Tslna followed the human's gaze to the statues. No longer melted, their sharp, defined features looked freshly carved. The statue in the center stood head and shoulders above the others, but bore no more detail than feminine curves. In front of it, a ball of purest white light sparkled beneath a dome that swirled with unholy light.

"Yes," the Human said. Eyes glazed, he fell to his knees before the dome. "Yes, show me. Give me your power!" He reached out, touching the dome, and the unholy surface shattered with a violent crack. Bursting from the broken dome, the ball of light slammed into the tall feminine statue. The statue bulged, leaking sparkles of its bright prisoner until it exploded in a violent shower of sparks.

Xi'Tslna's spine spikes tingled as the ball of light hovered over the melted remains of the statue, radiating a familiar power.

The Human spread his arms, and the holy power of Qi'k'krasz soaked into his being.

9

SWORDS AND STAVES

Confined in Emril's cloistered hidden suite, L'Veyna lounged in the deep copper tub, and soaked in the warm water, her worries drifting on the fragrant aroma of herbs and flower petals. Worries like being cooped in their luxurious quarters for three—no, *four* days! She'd sit and sleep on the hard floor until Diou arrived, if she could just bask in glorious sunlight for a minute. As if sunlight could pierce the toxic, black cloud blanketing this rotted town.

So much for not thinking about my worries.

She drew a deep breath, and imagined her intrusive thoughts lifting from the calm bathwater on a trail of steam, and then dissipating in the air until her mind drifted in tranquility. Nothing but relaxing warm water and the peaceful, calm aroma. If every day could be like this moment, maybe staying here wouldn't be so bad.

Pendric's muffled voice leaked through the door. "What's this word?"

"Could," Prack replied.

"Why's it spelled like that? Why isn't it spelled like good? Who made this language?"

"Humans," Prack mumbled.

"Well, it's stupid," Pendric mumbled, and L'Veyna couldn't help but chuckle.

I guess not every good moment has to be calm and serene.

"See!" Pendric chirped. "This is why no one likes to read and write."

"Plenty of people like to read and write," Jouler said, likely engrossed in his own book. That's all he'd done since they'd arrived—scour through every book of Prophecy he could find. L'Veyna pictured him in his quaint little corner, sitting in his plush chair, ankle over his knee, peering at Pendric over his book with those dark, penetrating eyes. That or practicing his Talontongue…or, Fingernail-tongue, since Humans had no talons. Just short, disgusting, wormy fingers.

The ancient familiarity she felt from Jouler swelled in her chest, along with the calls from the strange metallic tubes.

Open, open, open…

"Shut up," she growled, splashing the bathwater with a heavy sigh. It seemed neither Jouler nor the tubes would let her bathe in peace.

Stepping out of the bathtub, she pictured water wicking from her skin and hair, leaving the subtle aroma of irises, and then she asked. Her skin and braids dried, water coalescing into an undulating sphere. The last drop floated from her body, and the ball splashed onto the slatted floor.

Her long Keeper's wrap lay draped over the only chair in the spacious bathroom. The hand-width strip of green hempen fabric seemed brighter than normal next to the drab clothing her brother had chosen for her. Forming an image in her mind, she asked again, and her wrap slithered around her nudity. Next came the drab blouse and trousers, which, she had to admit, would keep her a lot warmer on their travels than her thin wrap. That, along with her fur-lined boots and cloak, should keep her warm and cozy in the Boorde Alliance, no matter what her brother said.

"You going to spend all day in there?" Prack teased, knocking on the door.

"You'd like that," L'Veyna called back, then swung the door open with dramatic aplomb. "Wouldn't you?"

Pendric startled with a yelp, then chuckled and sniffed the air. "You smell good."

"Iris?" Prack asked, peering at her. "Interesting choice…"

"Yeah, that's it," Pendric replied. "One of Jo's favorites."

"Is it?" L'Veyna said, hoping she at least sounded sincere. Thankfully, Jouler seemed too engrossed in his book to hear anything, or notice anyone, for that matter. He didn't even look up, or wave, or grunt. He just sat there, staring at those plagued pages, tapping out words like sapling, rustwood, lavender…

Not bad, she thought, even with his thudding accent.

A sudden pang of hunger drove her to the dining table, and an uninviting plate of nu'biscuits, mushroom soup, and pitcher of water. Someone had placed a bowl over a second plate, which almost piqued her curiosity.

Looks like I'm asking breakfast again.

Thankfully, Jo's favorite food was easy to ask. Not that she would ask it because it was his favorite. Who didn't like potatoes, onions, peppers, and spices? It was filling, it tasted good, especially the way he cooked it…

"Mine's roses," Pendric said, plopping in the chair across from her. "In case you're choosing favorites. For your perfume, I mean." He jerked his chin at the covered plate, his eyes dripping with desire. "Go ahead. Look what's underneath."

L'Veyna removed the bowl, revealing two spiraled rolls oozing with promised delight. The sweet aroma of cinnamon reignited her hunger, spittle dribbling from the corner of her lip. "Alnazet's mercy," she said, wiping her mouth. "This smells amazing."

"They're called cinnamon rolls," Pendric said, licking his lips. "They're my new favorite food."

"They're dangerous," Prack said, sprawled on a sofa. "Dangerous, but worth it."

"I won't tell you how many there were," Pendric said with a sheepish grin. "Jo stopped us."

Oh, he did, did he? L'Veyna thought, unable to hide her smile.

She peeled a roll from the plate and licked a dollop of the gooey glaze before it fell to the floor. "Ooo, that's good."

"Try the roll," Pendric said, squirming with anticipation. "You have to save the center for last. It's the best part."

L'Veyna obliged, and sweet, delicious, cinnamon-spice flavor caressed her tongue. "Alnazet's mercy, how are these this good?" She took another bite, rocking in delight. "Have the other one, Pen."

Pendric licked his lips and shook his head. "No…you should have them. I had plenty."

"Thank you, Pen," L'Veyna said, dancing in her chair. Imagining her scent as rose, she asked.

Wheezing, Pendric sniffed, and a slow smile split his face. "You changed your perfume!"

"I did," she replied. "Just for you."

"Perfumed or not," Jouler mumbled, eyes still focused on his book, "L'Veyna always smells like happiness." He blinked, as if surprised by his words. "I mean…I think…" He grumbled under his breath and hid his flushed face behind his book. "You always smell good."

Prack barked a laugh. "Gods, man. I'd love to see you at our Festival of Light."

"Stop it," L'Veyna said, holding back a laugh at the thought of Jouler around hundreds of naked Prytha basking in the sun and moonlight. "That's the nicest thing anyone has ever told me. Thank you, Jouler."

"Um, I beg to differ," Pendric said, pressing a hand to his chest with feigned insult. "You said I could have the other cinnamon roll, and I said no."

"True," L'Veyna said, tearing off a morsel and plopping it into her mouth. "But I still insist you have the other."

"Well, if you insist…" Bouncing on his chair, Pendric peeled the other roll from the plate. "And that," he said, taking a big bite, "was the second best thing anyone has ever said to me."

"Second best?" L'Veyna said, returning feigned shock.

"Emril said I could have as many rolls as I wanted."

"He's bringing more?" L'Veyna said, her brow climbing her forehead.

"Yep," Pendric said, plopping the rest of his roll into his mouth. After wiping his hands clean, he returned to his spot on the sofa next to Prack, and picked up the faded red book Jouler had given him. "What's T-H-R-O-U-G-H-O-U-T?"

"Throughout," Prack replied.

Pendric snapped the book shut and sputtered his lips. "How'd you read this thing so fast, Jo?"

Jouler shrugged. "How far are you? Has Coleton won the Hero's Hunt yet?"

"I'm still on the first chapter," Pendric said. "I think maybe I need a different book. This one's too hard."

"Let me find something else," Prack said, standing with a grunt. "So many rolls."

L'Veyna finished her roll, saving the plump center for last like Pendric suggested. "Alnazet's mercy, that's so good. It's like a fluffy pillow filled with gooey cinnamon perfection, and slathered with nectar of the gods."

"Come now, sister," Prack said, picking a few books from the shelves. "Nectar of the gods never tasted that good."

After licking her fingers, L'Veyna wiped her hands clean, and moved into the common room, pouring herself into the plush chaise. "When's Diou going to get here?"

Pendric held up *Two Ferns for Ebron*. "You should read. Your time will go faster. I can't believe we've already been here for five days."

"It's been four," Jouler said.

"Only four?" Pendric said, dropping his hands in his lap. "Emperor's ass! When are we going to leave?"

"Today," Prack said, pulling a fifth book from the shelf. He flipped through its pages and gave a curt nod. "These should do."

"How's the book, Jo?" L'Veyna clacked to test him.

Jouler's brow furrowed, and he tapped out, *"Can talk it you again?"*

"Can you say it again?" she corrected.

Jouler nodded, tapping the question again and again until it flowed almost as natural as any Prytha.

Gods, he learns so quick, she thought, then clacked her question again. *"How's the book?"*

Jouler closed his eyes, his brow drawing in concentration. *"The book is…information."* He shook his head. *"No, not information. In…informative, yes?"*

"Yes," L'Veyna said, turning to Prack. "Did you teach him that?"

Her brother shook his head. "He's been doing that all morning."

A quick series of knocks rapped on the door.

"That's him," Prack said, leaping to his feet, joy brightening his face.

Pendric's eyes widened. "Or maybe it's Emril with more cinnamon rolls."

The familiar series of muffled clicks and scraping levers sounded from the wall, and the door swung open. A tall, pale figure ducked under the doorway, his too-black topknot almost brushing the ceiling, his snow-white skin bright against his loose faded-black clothes.

L'Veyna's breath caught, and she stared at his iconic eyes, his diamond-shaped pupils like gems of fire.

"Diou?" she said, not sure if she should embrace the Boorde her brother called family, or keep her distance. Only a fool felt safe around a Boorde, or so the saying went. That and the only thing more dangerous than a hungry terrentor was a hungry Boorde, but that just seemed ridiculous. Diou might be tall, and he might even be as skilled as her brother claimed, but he was still just a Boorde.

"It is an honor to finally meet you," Diou said, his rolling accent thick in his deep voice. He bowed at the waist, his wide sleeve swallowing his clasped hands.

"Forgive my dishonor," Jouler said, also bowing, "but I have no meat to offer."

Diou's eyebrows climbed his forehead. "Your honor is bright in my eyes, Jouler Davinin." He offered Jouler the same bow. "I am Diou of House Nith'Iil."

"Watch out for that one," Prack said, embracing Diou. "He's smarter than an owl."

"I should hope so," Diou said, wrapping L'Veyna's brother in a warm hug. "Owls aren't particularly smart compared to Humans."

Prack untangled himself from Diou and gestured to Pendric. "This is Pendric."

"Everyone just calls me Pen. Well, not everyone. Some people don't even know my name, so how could they know..." Pendric gulped and gave a shaky chuckle. "Are all Boorde so...so tall?"

Diou dropped to a knee and bowed. "It is a true honor to meet you, Pendric Loyalton, son of Tied Loyalton."

"*You* know my father?" Pendric asked, beaming. "I mean, of course you do. He's famous, you know. My father, I mean. Wow, you have long teeth. Like a dog's—not that you're a dog. If anything, you'd be a wolf. Is it true Boorde drink blood?"

"No," Diou replied with a chuckle. He turned on his knee to face L'Veyna. Still taller than she, a thin smile cracked his chiseled features, exposing his iconic canines. "I have a gift for you." He reached inside a small pouch at his waist and proffered a masterful silver ring crafted to look like a cluster of elm leaves. Specks of emerald and fire opal sparkled throughout.

L'Veyna stammered, gazing at the beautiful jewelry. "It's... It's..."

"Gorgeous?" Prack offered. "Pretty?"

Pendric shook his head.

"You're right, Pen." Prack lips turned a sagacious frown. "It's too pretty to just be pretty."

L'Veyna sneered at her brother, then looked up at Diou. *Alnazet's mercy. He's so tall.* He didn't act like the Boorde from the tales adults would tell at night. He had yet to tear off strips of her flesh, or sink his long Boorde canines into her neck to drink her blood.

"It's beautiful," she said, admiring the craftsmanship of the ring. "I didn't think to bring anything for you. But I can ask—"

"There is no need," Diou said, pressing a hand to his heart. "Gifts bearing expectations are no gifts at all. They're obligations. Besides," he said, rising to his feet, "your brother had it commissioned before he left Nubidae."

"I did not," Prack said, feigning insult. "Don't listen to him, sister."

Diou raised an eyebrow. "He also told me not to tell you."

"I would never…" Prack's huff oozed with sarcasm. "Who are you going to believe, dear, kind, lovely sister—your brother, or some stinky Boorde?"

L'Veyna lifted an eyebrow, imitating Diou. "If anyone stinks, dear brother, it's you."

Prack leaned toward Jouler and Pendric. "So much for the unbreakable bonds of family."

"Forgive me," Diou said, his deep, stoic voice dispersing their mirth. "But I'm afraid I must sour this joyful union. The destruction of Serolle has made the empire…shall we say, on edge?"

"That's putting it mildly," Prack mumbled.

"Good!" L'Veyna said. "Let's see how they like it. I hope whatever destroyed that city destroys them all."

"Do we know what happened?" Prack said. "A thousand shapers couldn't take down a Shining Wall."

"Kael happened," Jouler replied.

"The Dawn," Diou said with a nod. "Or, the Light, as he's known in your Prophecies. Reylan said the same."

"Does he know where Kael is?" Jouler asked, and Diou shook his head.

"From all reports," the Boorde said, his rolling accent thick with remorse, "no one on the battlefield survived the blast."

Jouler stumbled into his chair, his face ashen. "He's not dead."

"Reylan said the same," Diou replied. "The question remains— where is the Light?"

Jouler dry-washed his face. "There is no Light."

"Of course there's a Light," Diou said, face drawn in confusion. "The Prophecies—"

"Are wrong," Jouler interrupted.

Prack clapped Diou's back. "Come help me pack. There's a lot I have to tell you."

A STRANGE QUIETUDE blanketed the forested foothills south of Onti. Despite the thick pine groves and underbrush, no birds chirped among the trees, no deer pranced through the woods, no squirrels squeaked warnings to the other creatures of the forest. Only the sounds of muffled hoofbeats over pine needles drifted on the bitter wind, as though the land itself feared the Sotouri Spades that roamed these foothills.

Jouler shivered despite his thick coat and the warm evening sun, an uneasy weight settling in his gut. The Harbinger book hadn't offered any clues to the Black Breath. Few parts had snapped with the truth, just like the rest of the Prophecies the empire had butchered. Some of those broken truths seemed to contradict each other. How could betraying the Light lead to the Dark's defeat, and why would he ever return the Dark's glory?

"It's so cold," L'Veyna said, pulling her fur-lined cloak tight around her shoulders.

"Can I have another tea sphere?" Pendric asked, his wheeze heavy in his voice.

L'Veyna's gaze went distant, and a steaming sphere formed above her palm. It was the second sphere she'd asked since they'd left Onti, when one cup in Onatah had lasted well into the evening.

How much farther can you go, my friend?

"I'm fine," Pendric insisted, as if reading Jouler's thoughts. "It's just cold, like L'Veyna said. Besides, it tastes good."

Ahead of their small troupe, Prack's golden palomino looked tiny next to Diou's black destrier. Prack pointed through the thick forest of pines climbing the mountainside, and Diou shook his head, tapping the spear nestled in a special sheath attached to his saddle.

"It's written on your face, Jo." Pendric leveled a pointed look. "I can say that, now that I can read. It's actually not that hard once you get the hang of it."

"I knew you'd enjoy it," Jouler said.

"I mean, I'm not as good at it as you." Pendric offered him a sip of his tea sphere, and Jouler waved away the offer. Pendric shrugged and sipped his sphere. "I don't know how you read so fast. It's like, here, read this book, Jo, and you just hand it right back because you're already done."

"I wish I read that fast," Jouler said, bubbling with a chuckle. "How many books did you bring?"

"Three," Pendic replied. *The Broken Thorn, Memory of Sorrow,* and *The Gardens of Fortune.* What about you?"

"Just the one," Jouler said. "I'm hoping to find its sister volumes in Nubidae."

"Just the Harbinger book?" Pendric asked. "Haven't you read it like a dozen times?"

"I wish," Jouler replied, ignoring the call of the tubes. Two pairs, one in his pack, the other in Prack's, both begging for release. "More like three times."

"What's it say?" L'Veyna asked, her gaze drifting to his pack.

"Books don't say anything," he joked, earning an emerald-eyed sneer. "The book is like a roadmap of Prophecy, detailing how the Harbinger can affect the Dark's victory. But it's all just conjecture—someone's ideas."

But nothing on the Black Breath, Jouler thought, not wanting to ruin Pendric's joyful mood.

"Then why'd you take it?" Pendric asked.

"Because it contains the Prophecies," Jouler said. "The parts that pertain to me. Some of them, at least."

"Anything interesting?" Pendric asked, slurping his tea.

"Yes," Jouler said, twisting in his saddle to fish the book from his pack. He flipped to his bookmark. "For example, here, it reads, 'And the Light shall rise, bearing the fist of youth. Darkness shall the land know, her people laid to rest.' The only part that feels true is '…shall rise, bearing the fist of youth.' The rest feels…wrong, like bad synonyms."

"Mmm…cinnamon rolls," Pendric said.

L'Veyna slouched in her saddle. "I'm still angry we didn't wait for more."

"I promise to make you some in Nubidae," Diou said from atop his large destrier, his snow-white appearance reminding Jouler of the Boorde he'd seen in Emril's inn. With features so similar, the two Boorde could have been siblings, lending to the sentiment that they all looked the same. Both with the same white skin, their jet-black hair pulled to a topknot. Doth dressed in similar black clothes—a wide-sleeved blouse, held closed by a cloth belt, with slippered feet poking beneath wide trousers.

Diou caught Jouler's attention with his fire-diamond gaze. "You can sense the truth?"

"Only about Prophecy," Jouler said. "Words and phrases that are true feel right the way a puzzle piece feels right when it snaps into place."

Diou shared a look with Prack. "When we reach the Alliance," the Boorde said, resting his fire-diamond gaze on Jouler, "tell no one of your gift."

"I thought the Alliance was safe," L'Veyna said.

"Not for the most dangerous man in the empire," Diou said. The subtle heat in his rolling voice washed over Jouler with a wave of dread.

"Jouler's not dangerous," Pendric said, sputtering his lips.

"The empire is founded on a lie," Diou replied, turning to Jouler. "Your gift threatens that lie. Let me ask you, if you are the most dangerous threat to the empire, what would that make the Matron who held you captive?"

"The most powerful person in the empire," Jouler replied, understanding the implications.

"You and the other Facets pose such a threat," Diou said. "So says Prophecy."

"Me and Kael," Jouler said, keeping his gaze from L'Veyna.

"The man Reylan believes to be the Light," Diou said.

"The old man is going to be so disappointed," Prack said with a mischievous grin. "I can't wait to tell him."

"I doubt Reylan will be disappointed," Diou said. "I suspect he'll be at least as curious as I. What more can you tell me of the Facets, young Harbinger?"

"Nothing we didn't say at the inn," Jouler replied, over the sharp call of the tubes. "I'm the Harbinger of Death. Kael is the Crier of Change. The other three are called the Emblem of Life, the Incarnation of Light, and the Warden of Preservation."

L'Veyna looked up, a curious glint in her emerald eyes.

Yes, it's you, Jouler thought. *You're the Warden.*

She'd seemed so morose in Onti, subjected to a sunless fate as she'd called it, Jouler had wanted to wait until they'd left to break the news about her role as a Facet. Now seemed even worse after Diou's warning.

What am I supposed to tell her? Hey, I know you just lost home, but you're also going to be one of the most hunted people in the world—hope that helps!

Diou sucked an elongated canine, his stoic gaze as readable as a clear sky. "Does your gift allow you to derive the truth from a lie?"

"It doesn't work like that," Jouler said. "When I looked at the Wall of Prophecy, I felt notes of the truth. Like smelling blueberries baking in the oven, and guessing between a pie, cakes, and muffins. But if there's no truth to discern..."

"There's nothing baking in the oven," Prack said.

"Sometimes knowing a lie," Diou said, "can be as valuable as the truth."

"Are all Boorde so white?" Pendric asked.

"Almost all," Diou said, seeming unaffected by the cold despite his thin clothes. "Half Boorde—the rare result of a child born from a Human and Boorde coupling—they have dark skin."

"Rare?" Prack said, his breath clouding before him. "House Nith'Iil hasn't seen one in centuries."

"Thank you," Diou replied, his deep, monotone voice matching his stoic expression, "for giving an accurate example of rare."

"You need to use a stronger word," Prack said. "That's all I'm saying."

"Are you two always like this?" L'Veyna asked.

"No," Diou admitted. "Usually, your brother is much worse."

"I am too," Prack said, his scowl dripping with humor.

A quiet chuckle rumbled Diou's chest, a faint smile cracking his stoic face. "That one always cracks me up."

Jouler scanned the forested mountainside. Patches of yellow, orange, and red bubbled among the thick, green canopy of pines. Not a sign of life among the trees and bushes, yet Jouler's skin crawled from unseen gazes.

"That was you cracking up?" L'Veyna asked.

"A veritable knee slap for Diou," Prack replied. He pointed up the hill again, and Diou shook his head.

"What do you two keep pointing at?" Jouler asked, peering up the foothills.

"We're looking for something," Prack said.

"Looking for what?" L'Veyna asked, following Jouler's gaze.

"It's called an eila," Diou said. "E-I-L-A. Eila."

"What's it look like?" Pendric asked.

"That's the thing, young Pendric," Diou said. "No one has ever seen one."

Jouler hid his smile behind a cough. Eila, spelled backwards, was alie…a lie.

"That doesn't make any sense," L'Veyna said. "How do you know they exist if no one has seen them?"

"If you listen," Prack said, cupping a long pointed ear with his taloned hand, "you can hear them."

"I don't hear anything," L'Veyna said.

"Listen harder," her brother replied.

"Speaking of which," Pendric said. "I've been meaning to ask you, Lord Diou—"

"Just Diou is fine."

"Okay, Just Diou," Pendric said, earning a quiet chuckle from the Boorde. "Where's your sword?"

"I don't carry a sword," Diou replied, tapping the black haft of his spear.

"But...you're Boorde," Pendric replied. "There's even a sword named after your people. The Boorde sword." His brow furrowed and his mouth quirked to the side. "That sounds weird, now that I said it aloud."

"Humans call them Boorde-style blades," Diou corrected, his accent rolling over the words. "We call them sidaiyo."

"But why don't you have one?" Pendric asked.

"Because our light-skinned friend here," Prack said, "doesn't believe in swords."

"Of course I believe in them," Diou droned. "They exist. It's a fact. I don't like using them."

"Why?" Pendric wheezed.

L'Veyna nudged her horse beside his and produced another steaming ball of tea.

"Thank you," Pendric said, dancing in his saddle.

"Spears are superior to swords," Diou said, "in almost every way. Besides, swords were designed for a single purpose—to kill people. A spear can be used to hunt game, while a dagger and knife dress it. Axes are primarily used outside of combat, as are bows. The only thing a sword is good for—"

"Here we go," Prack mumbled, rolling his eyes and drawing a rumble of chuckles.

"—is killing other people," Diou said with a sidelong look. "And it's not even the best weapon for that. Maces, especially spiked, are better against an armored foe, and against opponents of equal skill, a spear or staff beats the sword every time."

"Then why do so many people use swords?" Pendric asked, sipping his tea.

"Because swords possess an undeniable beauty that every other weapon lacks. Forging a sword eschews utility, blending art with science. The dance of swords is a dance like no other, unabashed and unmistakable in its purpose. The true dance of death."

"It sounds like you admire them," Jouler said.

"I do," Diou replied. "For its art and discipline. But it is not my weapon of choice."

"Aren't you worried the haft will break?" Jouler asked, gesturing to the black spear.

"That's not normal wood," Prack said.

"It's…" L'Veyna's gaze went distant, and she hissed. "It's heartwood, from an iron tree."

"The tree is made of iron?" Pendric wondered.

"No," L'Veyna said with a giggle. "That's just the name because the wood is so hard."

"The haft was forged by Prytha woodsmiths." Diou hefted the black spear, and the edges of its long blade glowed like smoldering embers. "A shaft made of steel would chip and break before this."

Pendric's jaw dropped. "That's…that… How does it do that?"

"Boorde steel," Diou explained, handing the spear to Pendric.

Eyes wide, Pendric grabbed the weapon, almost dropping it. "It's heavy," he said, and the glow dissipated from the blade. "What happened?"

"You haven't harmonized your inner flame," Diou said, returning the spear to its saddle sheath.

"The haft is old," L'Veyna said, her voice soft and reverent. "Ancient. Who forged it?"

"That depends on which historian you question," Diou replied. "It's been handed down through generations of Nith'Iil il'Spada."

"Il'Spada?" Pendric gulped the last of his sphere tea.

"It translates to weapons master," Diou said.

"Not blademaster?" Pendric asked.

"Not all weapons have blades," Diou replied.

"Like which?" Pendric said.

"The staff," Diou replied. "Hands, rods, chained rods, maces, clubs."

"Hammers," Prack offered. "Whips, chains, harsh words, angry glares, scowls."

"Poor humor," Diou said.

"You said Boorde weird," Prack replied.

The call of the tubes wormed into Jouler's mind, souring the easy mood with reminders of his morbid destiny. Scouring the book about the Harbinger had only added to his worries, confirming his fears that so many people would die at his hands. Words of Prophecy peeled from his memories, flashing images of crushed cities, burning forests, and death…so much death. He tried to focus on the breeze whispering through the towering pines, the crisp smell of winter teasing the air, but the call of the tubes rang too loud in his mind.

Death belongs to that one.

The Ul'Krals warning drummed from his past, resonating with the guilt that fueled his steps. Without the Black Breath, Pendric would forever remain cursed by those vile creatures. Emril's clandestine library hadn't offered a clue about the mysterious artifact, but it only contained excerpts from the Human Prophecy. If any of the three Prophecies mentioned the Black Breath, it would be the Prytha's.

"Who taut you the sword, Jouler?" Diou asked, pulling Jouler from his thoughts.

"H-How did you know I learned the sword?"

"You carry yourself like you've been trained in the Basic Forms."

"You can see that?" Pendric asked.

"I can," Diou replied. "You also mentioned Jouler had a Boorde-style blade back at the inn. So, Jouler Davinin, Phaerian of Headwater—who trained you?"

"Grim," Jouler replied, and Diou grunted. "Do you know him?"

"Every Boorde knows about Grim," Diou replied. "Is that why you do not wish to continue with the sword?"

"It's because I'm the Harbinger," Jouler replied, feeling the truth of his words. "Death is already my calling."

"Very good," Diou said, sucking his teeth. "L'Veyna?"

"Y-Yes?" she stammered, blinking awake from her daze, staring at Prack's pack.

"Be a dear, and ask a staff for our friend?" Diou slid from his saddle, and bade Jouler follow. "As long and thin as my spear, please."

"Ooo!" Pendric chirped with a wheeze. "Can I have one too?"

"If L'Veyna would be so kind?" Diou said, his smile exposing his long canines.

"Of course," L'Veyna said. "But why?"

"To teach the Harbinger a path other than death."

JOULER ADDED another log to the campfire, sending an army of bright orange dancers into the night. Beneath the crackling logs, embers swirled with heat, breathing with their own type of life. Sore from his lessons with Diou, he sat down between L'Veyna and Pendric on the fallen tree, and watched the graceful Boorde slide through the Staff Basic Forms with the effortless grace of a bird in flight. The staff L'Veyna had asked for Jouler whirred in the Boorde's alabaster hands, wide swoops buffeting the air, while overhead chops slammed into the ground. Jouler measured each movement, cataloguing the Forms, and absently replaying them in the back of his mind.

"You really don't feel hot and cold?" Pendric asked Diou.

"Do you feel the planet spinning around the sun?" Diou bowed, ending the first Basic Form for the staff. "Boorde know hot and cold exist. We know that without meat in our belly, we will perish in extreme temperatures. But we don't *feel* those temperatures."

"Does it hurt when you're burned?" Jouler asked Diou, also tapping the words to practice his Talontongue.

"*Almost,*" L'Veyna clacked against the log. "*You tapped out 'when your burned'. Not you're.*"

"We still feel pain," Diou replied, slipping into the Second Form. "It just takes a lot more for us to feel it. For us, pain is there, and then gone, and always dull no matter how sharp the blade."

Prack nudged Pendric. "It's how them blasted carnivores are able to walk on a broken leg."

"You can?" Pendric wheezed, his brow raising.

"It's how we're able to *set* a broken leg," Diou corrected, flowing through sweeps, jabs, and blocks. "Not walk on it."

"That's still impressive," Jouler said. "How long does a break take to mend?"

"Take to mend," L'Veyna tapped. *"You said 'heal'."*

"With enough meat and rest," Diou said, sweeping the staff in a wide arc, "I'd be limping on a broken leg in a few days, and sprinting by the end of the week. Superficial bruises heal in about an hour," he continued, flowing into the third Form. "A deep bruise in the morning will be healed by supper."

"Gods!" Jouler breathed. It was no wonder Boorde reigned as Torgeir's elite warriors. Besides being so tall, anything less than a mortal wound would only make them angrier.

Pendric gawked as Diou spun in the air and slammed the staff in to the ground when he landed. "How does he do that? It's like he's not even trying." Pendric's eyes glazed in another phaery tale. "Like he's an emotionless assassin, cutting through crazed imperials."

"Been reading *The Gardens of Fortune?*" Prack asked, and Pendric nodded. "I figured you'd start with that one. Don't let Diou's grave exterior fool you. On the inside, he's all soft and cuddly."

Diou halted at the end of a powerful swing, his black topknot drinking in the firelight. "Soft and cuddly are, in fact, an accurate description of my internal organs."

Pendric's face scrunched with confusion. "Was that supposed to be Boorde humor?"

"Not at all," Diou said, flowing into his graceful dance. "There's nothing funny about getting cuddly with my internal organs." He finished the Third Form, stamping his staff into the ground. "Now *that* was Boorde humor."

Pendric shrugged, looking to Jouler for help. "I don't get it."

"Don't worry, Pen," Prack said, nudging him. "No one does."

"Is this all we're going to do?" L'Veyna mumbled, shivering against Jouler. Thankfully, the chilling weather had forced her to ask thicker clothes, although her scent, the pleasant aroma of morning dew on dried grass, demanded a deep breath.

That's my favorite smell.

Not that he could tell her without invoking some sort of mischievous banter for the next few weeks. It just reminded him of home, a place he could only visit to in his memories.

"We've been here all day," L'Veyna grumbled.

"And night," Prack said.

She mumbled under her breath, and peered up at Jouler, her emerald-green eyes calling his gaze worse than the tubes in his pack.

Knowing she'd only tease him more if he continued to ignore her, he held open his cloak, and she leaned into him. Startling from a jab to his side, he pleaded with her to stop.

"You're no fun," she mumbled, firelight warming her olive skin and setting her autumnal braids aglow. "Can you actually learn something from just watching Diou?"

"Not really," Pendric wheezed. "Jo probably can, but he can do anything. I mean, look at Diou! How does he twirl the staff so fast?" Pendric froze the way he did when a grandiose idea crept into his thoughts. He looked at Prack, then Diou, and back to Prack. "What if you and Diou fought, but not for real? Like for practice, but real practice."

"We spar all the time," Prack said, chuckling.

"No, but like..." Pendric's mouth quirked to the side. "Like you were really fighting, but you wouldn't hurt each other."

"Exactly."

"But do you shift?" Pendric asked, and Prack nodded. "But...how? You move so fast, and Diou is just, well...he's just a Boorde."

"They can see the future," Prack said.

Pendric's mouth fell open. "You can?"

"Don't listen to him, young Pendric." Diou shot Prack an exhaustive look. "No one can see the future, but we do possess a certain battle prescience. Not that I need it against someone I've sparred with a thousand times."

"We have not sparred that many times," Prack said.

"Not with blades," Diou said, winking at the end of a dramatic sweep.

"Well, in that case," Prack said with a coy smile. "I'd say you greatly underestimated."

"Ack," L'Veyna said, gagging. She cast a worried gaze at the night-cloaked forest behind them. "Do you think Citizens can see our fire?"

"Not if they're blind," Prack said, and L'Veyna sneered at him. He directed her gaze away from the foothills, to the moon-soaked plains below. Tiny lights from hundreds of campfires flickered across the Sotouri's massive training field. "If we can see them...they can see us."

"Aren't you worried they'll come get us?" she asked, and Prack shook his head. "You're infuriating."

"They're too far away," Jouler said. "It'd take them at least two days to get to us."

"Even if they did," Pendric wheezed, chopping his hand, "Diou and Prack would fight them off."

"Maybe if Jouler helped," Diou said, restarting the First Basic Form.

"Me?" Jouler said with a chuckle. "I'm just a farmer."

"Says M'Ljot," L'Veyna mumbled, the name soaking into Jouler's concentration. "Like Diou said—you're the most dangerous man in the world."

"In the empire," Jouler corrected.

"Same thing," L'Veyna mumbled, poking his side. She gestured to the book on his pack. "Learn anything new?"

"I did," Jouler sighed, shrugging off a sudden call from the tubes.

"That doesn't sound promising," L'Veyna said.

"Is there anything good about the Prophecies?" Jouler said.

"Good point." L'Veyna yawned and snuggled against Jouler's side.

"In his voice, truth," Jouler quoted from the book. "For the Harbinger is come, and his wake is Death."

10

THE VOICE

The Banner of Light rippled over Tilaine's Guard Tower. Inspired by female Boorde who had heard the Voice, Nilam Fonth had replaced the blasphemous sky-blue Rising Sun for a more natural color. A warm yellow sun now graced the pristine field of white. Pride swelled within in him, pulling a deep breath and wide smile. Soon, every tower and soaring roof would fly the holy banner.

"My banner," he grumbled. "Not that blundering child's. She who'd led her people—*my* people to the slaughter."

Far below, on the tower green, Tolaine's garrison gazed up at him with the fanatic devotion of the Faithful. His voice, the Voice blessed to him by the Light, had spread faster than he could have hoped, turning even the most stalwart Citizens into loyal followers. His folly in Wandius had taught him a truth about the Light that seemed so obvious now. Tolrik and the Light were benevolent and compassionate deities. Hatred and cruelty belonged to Dra'Nahl and His decrepit followers. But to any who turned toward the Tolrik and Light, be they odious Citizens or wayward Phaerians.

The weaker the mind; the stronger the devotion.

Unlike stubborn Egan, below in their room, kneeling on the Penitent Rocks. The next time the insolent child decided to wear pretentious jewelry, maybe the blood and scabs on his knees and legs would remind him of his humility.

"For the Light shall raise the meek and humble," he quoted, imagining the little boy rolling his eyes at him. Almost twenty days had passed, and Egan still resisted his voice. On the voyage, Nilam had assumed the boy's youth or innocence had shielded him from the voice, but plenty of Toliane's children gaped at Nilam with the same glazed adoration as the soldiers on the green.

The boy's youth, however, did explain why he thought an iron ring would ever be appropriate for one of the Faithful. Even with the Rising Sun stamped on it, the iron would better serve as knives, forks, or anything other than a useless bauble. Such trinkets could not buy the Faithful. They heard the Voice and heeded the Call.

Like now, he thought, listening to the chant from the green.

"...hear Her Voice...heed Her Call...hear Her Voice...heed Her Call..."

"It's not *Makayla's* voice," Nilam said. The power of Nilam's voice had come from the Light, not that harlot. She'd been a vessel, a tool of the Light to pass Its power onto Nilam. *He* would free their people. *He* would fulfill the Prophecies, and destroy the empire. *He* would do what *she* could not.

"And still, they'll praise her," he said, pulling Egan's iron ring from a pouch at his belt. He rolled the simple trinket between his fingers, noting its imperfections. Scratches and rusting pocks marred its surface, and its not-so-square face showed the Rising Sun stamped off center.

Look at me, the ring cried, feigning humility with its simple design. *Look at my faith. See how I believe.*

Squeezing the ring in his fist, he recited a line from the Hymns of Tolrik. "The Light shall cry truth upon every creature under the sun."

Except, not everyone could hear the Call. What about the deaf? Tolrik wouldn't abandon those unfortunate souls. He would provide a way for them to still heed the Call.

Nilam opened his hand, the Rising Sun imprinted on his palm.

Like a humble ring, baring the Light's holy symbol.

Shame pulled at Nilam's shoulders. It seemed even he, the most faithful, could blind himself with pride. He tucked the ring back in his pouch and descended the tower stairs to his chambers.

Once the elegant home of the guard captain, Nilam's simple furnishing replaced the trappings of opulence. His bare feet slapped against the cold marble floor, echoing against bare walls. With five more oversized rooms, the captain's quarters could have accommodated three or four families, not just an old man and his willful charge. Even if that old man spoke with the Voice of the Light, he didn't need so much space.

Happiness, joy, prosperity—those were the fleeting moments people chased through the agony of life. Suffering purged the soul of temptation, bringing it closer to the Light.

"…hear Her Voice…heed Her Call…"

In the eyes of the Faithful, Makayla would forever remain infallible and beyond reproach, the embodiment of everything good and holy. They revered her, invoking her name, and praising her as if she were a god.

Nilam scoffed at the blasphemy. Gods didn't die by mortal hands, and she'd hardly liberated her people. She was no Light. In the end, she'd proven herself to be as Human as the rest of her people. Just a pesky little tool, like Egan and his stubborn little mind.

On the far side of the long room, the young boy knelt on his Penitent Rocks, small puddles of blood below his knees.

"That's enough for today," Nilam said.

Egan hesitated. "But the candle only burned four notches."

An hour…

It was far less than the boy deserved for his pride, but Egan had more important matters to attend. "You can finish your penance tonight."

Egan's shoulders drooped and he nodded. Wincing, he lifted himself from the pad and stood on quivering legs. Rocks stuck to his bony knees, blood streaking down his shins.

"Would you forgive a man his debt," Nilam asked, "if he couldn't settle it with a single payment?"

Gaze on the floor, Egan shook his head.

"Precisely," Nilam said. "Why, then, would you deny the Light the suffering you owe for your blasphemy?"

Again Egan shook his head, tears dripping from his cheeks.

"Now, tell me," Nilam said, holding the iron ring in his palm. "Who gave this to you?"

"No one," Egan said, shrugging.

"The ring just appeared out of nowhere?"

"No," Egan mumbled. "I mean, it wasn't anyone special. I just saw a bunch of people wearing it, and I liked it. I thought, maybe if I wore it, I wouldn't get in trouble all the time. I thought, maybe…" he shrugged again. "I don't know."

"You thought maybe you could hear the Call?" Nilam offered, and Egan nodded. He offered the ring to the young boy. "Take this to the person who gave it to you. Tell them the Voice of the Light wants every Faithful to wear one."

Egan took the ring, his eyes wide with glee. "You do?"

"Yes, now be off," Nilam said, ashamed at having judged the boy so quickly. Pride, it seemed, could fester in the holiest of souls. He waited for Eagan to shut the door behind him before walking to the pad of rocks next to Egan's. Nilam hiked up his trousers, his knees and shins a medley of wounds, bruises, and scars.

11

A BUDDING KEEPER

The moon's silver light pierced the forest canopy, illuminating the soft mist gliding over beds of moss and ferns. Armies of crickets and frogs filled the darkness with a soothing cadence, challenging the silent denizens of the night. Tucked into a perch within a middle-aged maple, Alerix breathed in the gentle aroma of bark and autumnal leaves. Blanketed in such serenity, he could almost forget the past two weeks.

Almost.

Not only had Tálise abandoned His people, He'd also taken the Blossoming, the roots of Prytha culture. The damned god had all but ensured saplings would wander the forests with no purpose. Like the ones he'd tracked all day, not fifty paces away, nestled in the arms of an elderly oak.

Tai'Enth stepped from a treewalk portal in the trunk of the maple, her ochre wrap and autumnal braids muted under the moonlight. The unhappy clouds roiling behind her apatite-colored eyes drew his attention away from her seductively long ears.

"The Grove has ordered us to return," she said.

"Which grovemember was it, this time?" Alerix mumbled.

"All of them," Tai'Enth replied. "Even the Eldest."

"What do we do with the saplings?" Alerix asked, gesturing to the old oak. "We can't just leave them out here."

"And Taking them to Marun would be better?" Tai'Enth asked. "He wants to put them in cages like they're filthy d'Tormena."

"It's not that I agree with him," Alerix said. "But he's a grovemember, and I'm the High Rose. Besides, rounding up the saplings until the Prophecies have passed isn't a bad idea."

"You sound like the Grove," Tai'Enth said. "At least the Eldest remembers what it means to be a Keeper."

"They endorsed the plan to lock them in cages."

"Not the Eldest," Tai'Enth countered.

"Then what do you propose we do?" he asked again. "You know how unkind Prophecy is to our people."

"And you think cages will stop that?" She gave him a derisive snort. "You think Prophecy—the same power that bound Alnazet and Dra'Nahl—can be thwarted by a few cages dangling from a platform?" Tai'Enth's gaze lingered on the old oak that cradled the saplings. "What if it's all wrong?"

"All what?" Alerix mumbled.

"The Prophecies," she said, tugging on his arm. "Pay attention. I think I'm on to something."

"Forgive me. Please, continue."

"No one knows what Mh t'Pralab says." Tai'Enth held up her finger when he tried to respond. "The empire took our language during the Ensnarement, when they slaughtered anyone old enough to ask or wield a chk'da, so no one knows what the Saplings Curse is actually about. Even the name is suspect."

"We can't read one side of the Wall," Alerix said. "But the other side clearly shows young Prytha standing on a bed of very dead adults. Not on just one Mh t'Pralab, but every…single…one."

Tai'Enth lifted an eyebrow the way she did when he talked himself into her rhetorical trap. "That must be why there's no debate over Mh t'Pralab's one and only interpretation."

Alerix's argument vanished behind gleaming eyes and the aroma of dew-kissed dry meadows. He thought about all the books he owned on the Saplings Curse, each book disagreeing with the next about the symbolism etched throughout the wall. For all their disputes, most scholars agreed that saplings would bring an end to their people.

Alerix dropped his gaze from her long sparkling ears, down the maple leaves of her namesake woven into the braids across her chest and down her left arm, to the flakes of apatite etched into her sharp talons.

Sharp like her mind.

He ripped his attention back to their predicament, following her gaze to the saplings.

Tai'Enth's eyes went wide, and she gripped his arm. "The Ensnarement!"

Alerix blinked, confusion fumbling his tongue.

"The Saplings Curse," Tai'Enth said, making even less sense. "Sorry, I know I'm all over the place. During the Ensnarement, the empire slaughtered every Prytha old enough to ask or wield a chk'da, right?"

"Everyone but the saplings," Alerix said, grasping at her branch of logic.

"Saplings who stood on the corpses of their parents," Tai'Enth said. "What if the Curse already happened?"

"How? If Keeper Orenda is to be believed, then M'Ljot is over a thousand years too late."

"The saplings on Mh t'Pralab are symbolic," Tai'Enth said. "What if they're meant to represent us—everyone who came after the Ensnarement, after all the adults died?"

"You make a lot of sense," Alerix said, unable to keep the doubt from his voice.

"Just...think about it while we decide what to do with these saplings."

"We could take them to Keeper Orenda," Alerix said, cringing at his own idea.

"*You* want to take them to *her*," Tai'Enth replied. "Everyone knows she'd sooner rip off your limbs than lend you aid."

"Exactly," Alerix replied. "Who better to hide them from Marun?"

The corner of Tai'Enth's lip curled, and Alerix cupped his hands to his mouth, releasing a flurry of dove calls to summon Ma'Tsoka, Steward Yara, and the rest of his warriors. "Let's go wake up some saplings."

ALERIX WATCHED the small group of saplings sleep while his warriors settled upon neighboring branches. Still dressed in their too-long Blossoming shirt, the four saplings lay huddled together, sharing warmth under a blanket of leaves. A fifth sapling, presumably on guard, slept against the trunk of the old oak, a chk'da laid across his lap.

Alerix reached for the weapon, and vines wrapped up his legs, binding his arms against his sides. Grunts and startled yelps sprouted throughout the tree from his warriors, belying their own entangling vines.

Giggles bubbled from the saplings as they rose from their feigned slumber, hatred darkening their gem-colored eyes. The guard with the chk'da, a young boy with short evergreen hair, stood in front of the other saplings. Pride lifted his chin, his evergreen braids falling over rose-quartz eyes.

"Why would you ever think we'd let you capture us so easily?" The other saplings chuckled, and the chk'da-wielding guard gestured to the branches above. "Don't worry about your warriors. They're all bound, just like you."

"You did this?" Alerix asked, not hiding his disbelief.

The boy puffed his chest. "I'm the only Keeper here."

"Good to know," Alerix said.

The giant oak writhed under the clustered saplings, and a treewalk portal opened beneath them, pulling them into the old oak. The asked vines holding Alerix wilted, and he clawed his way down the oak to meet Tai'Enth and the rest of his team. His warriors descended from the branches and surrounded the frightened saplings at the base of the tree. Only the budding Keeper bore vines around his wrists and ankles.

Alerix nodded his thanks to Tai'Enth, then motioned for his steward.

"Yes, High Rose," Steward Yara replied, pulling away from her squad. Thin evergreen braids draped down the back of her barkarmor, the onyx gemstones in her ears as invisible in the night as her eyes.

"Go tell Ma'Tsoka I need her," he said. "We're heading back to Onatah."

Yara pressed her hand over her heart in salute and headed into the dark forest.

"How did you ask?" Tai'Enth demanded of the young boy.

"Let me go, and I'll show you," he replied, pulling at his bonds.

Tai'Enth crossed her arms, her finger tapping her shoulder. "You're too young to ask."

"Apparently not," he said.

"Just like the Elmhand girl," Tai'Enth mused.

"L'Veyna?" the boy said, and the other saplings perked at the name. "She's a hero."

"A hero? How?" Alerix asked, and saplings erupted in a flurry of disjointed stories. "Stop, stop," he said, waving his hands. "One sapling at a time. You," he said, pointing to the boy who could ask. "What's your name?"

"V'Nahuu Oakmind," the boy replied, pride lifting his chin.

"Tell us about L'Veyna," Tai'Enth said, "and I'll think about freeing you."

V'Nahuu unfolded the harrowing tale of his flight from Onatah with the other saplings. "I cried so hard when Tálise died," he said, tears welling in his eyes. "I didn't know what was happening, and…"

"If it wasn't for V'Nahuu," a little boy said, "we'd all be in cages too."

"Or dead," a little girl mumbled.

The vines binding V'Nahuu slithered back into the ground. He climbed to his feet, and rubbed his wrists, flinching from Tai'Enth's stern gaze.

"If I so much as sense you asking," she warned, "I'll rip out your eyes and cut off your fingers so you can never ask again."

V'Nahuu stumbled back a step.

"What you did was impressive for a Bud," Tai'Enth said, motioning for him to take her outstretched hands. "Wrapping four warriors is no small feat."

V'Nahuu hesitated before resting his hands on hers, and the marks on his wrists and ankles healed. "You pulled all of us through a single portal."

Tai'Enth clicked her tongue. "I said impressive for a Bud."

"What are you going to do to us?" V'Nahuu asked.

Tai'Enth gestured to Alerix. "You tell them. It's your idea."

V'Nahuu stepped back from Tai'Enth. "Where are you taking us?"

Alerix took a deep breath, preparing himself for the onslaught of shouts and cries. "We're taking you to Keeper Orenda."

"What? No, you can't!" V'Nahuu said amid the clamoring saplings.

"She'll keep you safe," Alerix insisted over a fresh wave of protests about sapling stew. "No, she won't make into stew. The stories about her are just that—stories."

"She's still Prytha," Tai'Enth said. "Prytha can't eat meat."

The saplings cast doubtful looks between her and Alerix, until a new treewalk portal opened in the oak, startling them.

Ma'Tsoka stepped from the oak, her purple wrap slithering up moss-green skin. Her light-green eyebrows lifted at the saplings, her ruby eyes twinkling with an unspoken question.

"Report," Alerix said. "What of the imperial forces?"

"The Second Branch holds in the north," Ma'Tsoka replied. "But our eastern fronts need reinforcements."

"Treewalk back to Onatah," Alerix said, his mind coursing with plans to bolster his eastern forces. "Have the Fifth gear up."

"Me?" Ma'Tsoka asked.

"Did I stutter?"

"No, High Rose." Ma'Tsoka's worried gaze rested on the saplings, her jaw clenching. "Forgive me, but I must ask. Where are you going to do to the saplings? You're not taking them to Marun, are you?"

"No," Alerix said. "I'm taking them to Keeper Orenda."

Ma'Tsoka jerked as if slapped. "But...she hates you."

12

SHADES OF EVIL

L'Veyna huddled around a crackling fire at the edge of a small meadow. Squeezed between Pendric and her brother, she fanned her hands, glad for the heat during the morning twilight. The sun took far too long to warm these frozen foothills. She cringed from a knot in her back, doubting anything would strip her of her pain, not even time.

On the meadow, Jouler faced Diou, each holding a recently asked staff. At the rate they broke the plagued things, L'Veyna would ask a dozen more before they reached Nubidae. Shirtless, Jouler's soft-brown skin glistened and steamed into the morning air, his corded muscles rippling, chest sucking in air and spraying sweat with each exhale. After the beating he'd just endured, L'Veyna doubted he'd drop his stance to wipe his face again, no matter how distracted Diou seemed.

Unlike Jouler, not a drop of moisture glistened the Boorde's face, even though far more steam rose from his snow-white skin. Diou lowered his staff, his face as stoic and calm as ever, as if he hadn't sparred with Jouler all morning.

Must be nice not to sweat, L'Veyna thought, scooting a little closer to the fire. *Must be even nicer to never feel hot or cold.*

"Ready?" Diou asked, each breath clouding the air before him as if an actual forge burned in his belly.

Jouler stretched his wounded side and nodded, shifting his stance. For as much as he claimed to have never used a staff, L'Veyna would never believe him. Even Diou seemed dubious…although, it was hard to tell with the Boorde. Calm, upset, stoic, doubtful—his expressions all looked the same on Diou's chiseled features.

"How long until breakfast?" she asked, her stomach begging for food.

Her words faded under another flurry of clacks. Diou pressed his attack, Jouler's staff raising just in time to block each strike. Within moments, Jouler's face no longer twisted in concentration. He flowed between movements, not as effortless as Diou, but far more graceful than any Human had a right to be. His staff cut the air in a powerful arc and met Diou's with a loud crack.

"Great," L'Veyna grumbled. "You broke another one. You know, it might not seem like much, but asking takes its toll."

Diou's head tilted. "Do you not recover between askings?"

"Well, yeah, but…" She shivered and pulled her coat tight. "But that's not the point. The point is, it's freezing, and I'm hungry. How long are you two going to practice?"

Diou considered his shivering companions, steam billowing from his nostrils with each breath. "It might be prudent for us to stop for the morning."

Jouler sagged with relief and dashed to fetch his clothes. Shivering, teeth chattering, he crouched by the fire, and draped his coat over his shoulders. "Gods, I feel like the mountain suddenly sucked out all my heat."

"I smell snow on the wind," Diou said, "and the lower races aren't known for enduring the cold that well. Obviously."

L'Veyna's jaw dropped. "Did you say lower races?"

"That is what I said," Diou replied, tossing his broken staff into the fire. "The Boorde Alliance resides at a higher elevation than any other settlement. Even Bolaction, the highest imperial city, sits a few hundred yards below Jubhax, the Alliance's lowest city. As far as handling the cold," he said, fishing a large strip of jerked meat from his pack. "I could survive naked in a blizzard for a whole day with this strip of meat."

"Please don't demonstrate," L'Veyna mumbled.

"No, please do," Prack said, nudging Pendric. "The Boorde body is a sight to behold, my friends."

"Like Prytha," Pendric said.

"Not quite," Prack replied. "Each Prytha looks different. Our skin, our eyes, our facial structure. Boorde, on the other hand... Well, you know the saying—if you've seen one, you've seen them all."

"I've never heard that before," Pendric said.

"We do not all look the same," Diou mumbled.

"Same snow-white skin," Prack said. "Same black-upon-black hair. You all wear black..."

"It's not all black," Diou said, pointing to the sun-faded heron embroidered on his chest. "This part used to be green."

"Same fire-diamond pupils," Prack continued. "You're all tall."

"Some are taller than others," Diou said. "And we do not have the same pupils. Your untrained eyes can't see the difference. Like the colors in your hair, and how they differ from your sister's."

"No, they don't," Pendric said, glancing between her and Prack.

"They're a *little* different," Jouler said, peering between her and her brother.

He noticed... L'Veyna thought, a smile tugging her lips. "My hair is prettier."

"That's debatable," Diou said, and Prack rumbled with laughter. "Please, do not get offended, young L'Veyna. I simply meant beauty is subjective. What one finds attractive, another might find abhorrent. Most Boorde see color as a thing meant for art and nature, not clothing. Such things distract from the quality of the person behind ostentatious adornments."

"What about sunsets?" Pendric wheezed. "The really pretty ones. I don't think anyone would call those ugly."

"That's nature," Diou pointed out.

L'Veyna offered to ask Pendric a tea sphere, and he beamed in delight. "Just a small one. I don't want to stop a hundred times to make water."

"Diou, my good friend," Prack intoned in a snooty, singing voice. "Do us lower races a favor and chop up some more wood for the fire?"

"I'll come with you," Pendric said, taking the fist-sized tea sphere L'Veyna asked for him.

"That is honorable, Pendric," Diou said, dipping his head in a bow. "But it is best if you stay here to help guard the camp."

Pendric nodded, a phaery tale sparkling behind his mischievous brown eyes.

Diou fetched a black hatchet from his pack, the edge of the blade glowing like the embers in the campfire. He walked to a fallen tree and hacked, the hatchet slicing through thick branches in a single swing.

"Knowing Diou," Prack said, fetching the cook pot, "he'll have enough wood for two nights before breakfast is finished."

"Challenge accepted," Jouler replied, standing with a stretch.

His dark eyes caught L'Veyna's, and his warm familiarity swelled in her chest.

Alnazet's mercy, he's so....

"Gods it's chilly." Jouler blew into his hands and rubbed them together. "How does soup sound?"

"Handsome," L'Veyna replied, a wave of dread following her words. "Have some. Let's have some soup. Sounds good to me!"

L'VEYNA PULLED her coat tight, cursing the bitter afternoon wind. Fashion, not utility, dictated the cut of her people's coats and jackets. The pine-scented air might be a fresh change from the vibrant smells of the Sacred Forest, but she'd never get used to the bone-chilling cold. At least the trees here allowed more sunlight between their branches. Not that she felt it through all the layers of thick clothing covering her skin.

Alnazet's mercy, what a frustrating existence, trapped in a land ripe with sunlight, yet too cold to bask in its glory. Maybe the summers were nice, especially in this dry climate. No muggy heat or molding clothes soggy with sweat, just crisp, clean pine summers.

At the edge of her vision, she caught Jouler gazing at her from his saddle. Not in lust, as the Humans in Onti had looked at her. Concern seemed a permanent feature on his stubbled face, his eyes sunken by the weight of his dark fate.

And mine.

Besides worrying over the Saplings Curse, he probably struggled over how to tell her she was the Warden of Preservation. Shadows danced across his light-brown skin, shading his dark eyes and graceful jawline. All those smarts, and he didn't realize she already knew her prophetic role.

As always when her mind rambled around Prophecy, the call from the tubes teased her from the two packs as if confirming her suspicion. Not that she needed their confirmation. Why else would her powers develop so early? Before her, no Prytha could ask before their Blossoming, and Keeper Orenda said she'd be the most powerful Keeper in history.

It just makes sense I'd be a Facet..

L'Veyna's mind drifted with possibilities. Of hidden powers she might develop, like Jouler had. Maybe she'd learn things at a glance too, or develop shifting like her brother. Her mind filled with thoughts racing beside her brother, weaving through forests and bounding over rolling hills.

L'Veyna shifted on her saddle, and, for the thousandth time, wondered why people made them so hard. A soft cushioned seat would ride just as well, if not better, than these stiff contraptions.

"How much farther do we have to go?" she asked.

Pendric turned in his saddle and shrugged. "Diou doesn't even know."

"That's not what I said," Diou called over his shoulder. "I said we'll get there when we get there."

Pendric put a hand to the side of his mouth and whispered, "Which is just a fancy way of saying he doesn't know."

"I can hear you," Diou said, and Pendric squeaked in surprise.

"It's not fair," Pendric mumbled. "Prytha and Boorde can hear like hawks."

"Don't you mean bats?" Jouler asked.

"No, not bats," Pendric wheezed. "Boorde. Prytha and Boorde. Compared to them…Humans are just…so boring. We can't do…anything special."

"Humans can shape," Diou said. "That's an amazing trait."

"It's disgusting," L'Veyna said.

"Yeah, see!" Pendric wheezed. "Shaping is bad…and besides…I can't shape. Every Prytha hears well. Well…except for…the ones who can't hear. And you're all so…so beautiful. It's not fair."

Prack clicked his tongue. "I don't think you remember what Orenda and the Eldest look like."

Pendric chuckled, sucking in breaths that didn't quite catch.

L'Veyna guided her horse beside Pendric's, and she asked him a tea sphere.

"Thank you," he said, sipping the tea. "I feel like…I just had one."

"You did," L'Veyna said. "A couple hours ago."

"No wonder I have to make water again." Pendric called for a halt, slid off his horse, and disappeared behind a thick sugar pine.

"Maybe we should turn back," Jouler said. "Your breathing is only going to get worse the farther we go."

"And go where?" Pendric called from the other side of the tree. "Maybe Reylan knows where…the Black Breath is."

"What is the Black Breath?" Diou asked.

"We don't know," Jouler replied. "It's something the Ul'Kral told me."

"Cute little creatures," Pendric said, climbing back into his saddle. "Mean, but cute."

"You could die, Pen." Jouler's sorrow draped over L'Veyna, weighing on her heart. "We don't even know how far you can go. All we have are the words of a Sotouri. What if…what if the next step takes all your breath away? Or the one after that? What if some careless Ul'Kral breaks your vial?" Jouler's jaw clenched, his dark brown eyes watering. "I can't lose you, Pen."

Pendric sputtered with feigned bravado, blinking to hide his tears. "You think a little thing like losing my breath is going to stop me? I've been with you since Headwater. Well...except for when Kael and I were in those cages, but you were right above us. Right, L'Veyna?"

She nodded, her heart stabbed by a sharp pang of guilt. While she mourned the future tragedy of her people, Jouler had already lost his family and the only home he'd ever known. L'Veyna still had her brother, and Pendric still had his father, wherever Tied might be. Jouler had no one but Pen.

"Besides," Pendric said, his wheeze softened after the tea sphere. "It's not much farther to the Alliance. Right, Diou?"

"That is correct," Diou said.

Jouler sniffled, his lips pressing into a tight line. "And you promise to tell me when it gets too hard to breathe?"

"Quiet," Diou said.

Pendric leaned to L'Veyna, and whispered, "I think someone—"

Diou's sharp glare snapped Pendric's mouth shut.

Soft laughter cut through the chill afternoon air.

"Imperials," Diou whispered.

"Platoon, at least," Prack said. "Headed straight for us."

Fear soaked into L'Veyna's limbs, turning her body to mush. "Can't we run?"

"They're too close," Diou said, "their direction of travel too intentional. They know we're here."

Pendric's wormy fingers worked the hem of his sleeve. "But isn't that *why* we should run?"

"Just stay quiet," Prack said, his firm voice demanding a nod from Pendric. "Let Diou and I do the talking."

"*What about me?*" L'Veyna clacked on her beltboard.

"*You stay quiet too,*" Prack replied against the rising sound of hooves and chatter. "*And stay close to Jo and Pen.*"

Jouler nodded, sidling his horse closer to Lupine as a mass of imperials crested the rise, their lances crackling with the perverted power of pattern-forging. Fifty soldiers, at least, each draped in armor made of small metal rings, an irrationally large sword strapped to their saddle.

L'Veyna pressed a hand to her belly, her stomach bubbling like she'd eaten rotten food.

"*Shaping,*" she clacked on her beltboard.

The lead imperial pointed at them and barked a command. The other soldiers fanned out, jeering and whistling at L'Veyna.

"At ease," the leader said, quieting his soldiers.

"Oh, come on, sergeant," one soldier said. "We're just having fun."

"I said at ease, Tulian." The sergeant mumbled under his breath, and turned to Diou. "You keep strange company, friend Boorde."

"As you well know," Diou said, holding out his hands. "All are welcome in the Alliance, sergeant."

"Why are you here?" the sergeant asked. "The causeways are just down the hill?"

"Simple," Diou replied. "The causeways are crawling with imperial squads. Traveling with pairs of Phaerians and Prytha, I'd be stopped every half hour to answer these exact questions."

The sergeant peered at Diou. "I didn't catch your name, friend."

"I never offered it," Diou replied.

Annoyance flashed across the sergeant's face. "Listen here, Boorde."

"Please forgive my friend," Prack interrupted, the patience in his voice suggesting he'd made the same plea on countless other occasions. "His race can be infuriatingly logical."

The sergeant craned his neck, issuing a series of pops. "All right, then. What's your name, Boorde?"

The corners of Diou's lips twitched. "I am Diou Nith'Iil, Second-born of House Nith'Iil."

The sergeant's face turned white, and murmurs rippled through his soldiers. "I–I didn't know, M'Lord." The platoon shifted in their saddle, hands twitching to oversized swords. The sergeant waved for them to lower their hands, his eyes darting to Diou's spear. "Please, forgive me, M'Lord. I didn't recognize you, of course."

"Of course," Diou said. "What brings you this far out, sergeant? As you said, the causeways are right down there."

"I'm sure you heard about Serolle, M'Lord?" Diou nodded, and the sergeant jerked his chin at Jouler and Pendric. "We're looking for runaway Phlem."

Diou leaned forward, his low voice rumbling with deadly promise. "Do not use that term again. I will not condone such foul language."

The sergeant licked his lips, his horse shifting on its hooves. He took a calming breath and plastered a toothy smile. "I spoke out of turn, M'Lord. We're just looking for runaway Phaerians, which yours are not. Obviously."

"Obviously," Jouler said, crossing his arms.

The platoon grumbled with half-spoken threats, nudging their horses forward a step. Some soldiers lowered crackling lances, while others drew their oversized swords, somehow able to hold the large blades in one hand.

Fear pounded in L'Veyna's chest, smothering her mind. There were so many soldiers and not a woman among them, their gaze lingering on her. She tried not to think of what those looks promised, fighting through her crippling fear, and pulling her legs into the Posture of Root.

"I'm sorry," the sergeant said, his hand settling on his sword hilt. "What did you say…Phlem?"

Jouler slipped his staff from its holster, his steeled gaze devoid of emotion.

L'Veyna's mind bled with a thousand images of her fate. She squeezed her eyes shut, willing the intrusive thoughts to leave, but she may as well have tried pushing away the wind. She conjured an image of vines wrapping up the soldiers, but the image vanished in her maelstrom of fear.

Alnazet, please help me.

L'Veyna fought to bring the image into focus, pleading with her goddess to accept her asking.

Please…

Horrifying thoughts swarmed her mind, consuming her attempts to reform the image.

I don't want to die…

Ancient familiarity blossomed within her chest, its comforting warmth chasing her fears and slowing the maelstrom of dark thoughts.

Jouler…

L'Veyna opened her eyes, her watery gaze resting upon him. No anger touched his brow. No fear darted in his eyes. He sat in placid indifference while the fuming sergeant glared at him.

At M'Ljot.

A slow realization melted her fear. What were a few dozen Humans to the man prophesied to drown the land in blood?

"Sergeant!" The voice cut through her thoughts.

Tulian, the soldier who'd jeered at her, sheathed his oversized sword, and advanced in front of the platoon. He removed his helmet, revealing a youthful face framed by brown hair matted with sweat. His temple shimmered in the afternoon sunlight.

"Let's just move on," Tulian offered, his eyes darting to Diou and Prack.

"And let that Phl—" The sergeant cleared his throat, and swallowed the insult. "You know the law, Tulian."

"Blast the law," Tulian swore. "We're in the middle of nowhere, and that's… Emperor's ass, sergeant, that's Diou!" Tulian sidled his horse beside his sergeant. "How many of us are you willing to sacrifice for your pride?" Hesitation flashed across the sergeant's anger, and Tulian stiffened his back. "This whole thing is my fault, anyway."

The sergeant blinked, relief sagging his shoulders.

"I offended the young miss," Tulian continued. "Lord Diou's honor demanded he defend her."

"Yes…" the sergeant said, resting his hands on his saddle horn. "Yes, you did." He barked for the platoon to sheathe their weapons and get back into formation, then bowed to Diou. "Forgive my brash subordinate, M'Lord. I'll make sure Tulian is properly reprimanded."

"See that he is," Diou said. "It would have been a shame to have killed you."

The sergeant's already light skin drained of color. "Y-Y-Yes, M'Lord. Thank you."

"What is your name, sergeant?

"Sv-Svafar, M'Lord," the grizzled man replied. "Sergeant Svafar Durmisson, Third Platoon, Alpha Troop, Tenth Cavalry."

"Tales of the Tenth's deeds shine bright in my eyes, Sergeant Durmisson." Diou's gaze found Tulian. "Some deeds more so than others."

"Thank you, again, M'Lord." Svafar gave a sharp whistle, and his platoon maneuvered their horses into two columns, crackling lances held upright, oversized weapons resting in their sheath.

Their muffled hoofbeats and grumble conversations faded down the slope, and L'Veyna breathed a sigh. A bubble of relief stirred a giggle, and a comforting wave of joy flooded her body.

Alnazet's mercy, they're gone.

"You're okay," Jouler said, moving his horse beside hers.

"I know," she said, her voice shaking for some reason. Her chin quivered and her chest cramped. "I'm all right. Really, I'm fine. I'm..." Her voice caught, her fear returning in force. No, not coming back. It had never left. It welled in her eyes and thickened her throat. Her frail facade cracked, and a surge of emotions flooded down her cheeks, tightening her chest, and draining her strength.

"Breathe," her brother said, rubbing her back.

How'd I get on the ground? she wondered, wishing the world would stop swimming.

"In through the nose," Prack said, breathing with her. "Out through the mouth. That's it, breathe, Little Sprout."

L'Veyna focused on her brother, his gentle voice slowing the maelstrom raging inside her. Her tension eased, her tears faded, the plagued cold demanding a shiver.

"I'll start a fire," Diou said.

"But it's still early." L'Veyna sniffled and leaned into her brother.

"Sometimes taking a break," Diou said, "takes us farther than trudging forward."

Pendric's head jerked back in confusion. "That makes no sense. If I stop and rest, I won't go anywhere."

Diou chuckled and fetched his Boorde-steel hatchet, while Jouler and Pendric set to scrubbing the horses.

"I'll fetch your pack and bedroll," Prack said, patting her shoulders.

L'Veyna pulled her knees to her chest and pulled her coat over her legs. Exhaustion soaked into the void left by her evaporated fear, weighing her eyelids.

A loud crash startled her, and she realized she'd dozed.

"Forgive me," Diou said, setting down the other armload of logs and sticks. After chopping some kindling, a few strikes from his flint and steel ignited the tinder, and in moments sparks from a crackling fire fluttered into the air. Diou settled by the fire, and pulled a strip of dried meat from his pouch, his diamond-shaped irises dancing with the flames.

Prack draped a blanket around L'Veyna's shoulders and unfurled her bedroll by the fire. Warmth soaked into her muscles, her eyelids laden with comfort.

Pendric plopped next to her, startling her awake. "How many more days till we get to the Boorde Kingdom?"

"Boorde Alliance," Prack corrected, sitting beside him. "I'd say three more days."

"Sounds about right," Diou said, poking the fire.

"You know what sounds about right?" Pendric flashed L'Veyna that mischievous smile that always tugged at her lips. "Jouler's famous potatoes."

A soft chuckle shook her chest. She wanted to tell him that Jo's potatoes sounded perfect right now, but speaking seemed like so much work, and the fire was so warm.

A familiar presence sat beside, and Jouler's voice rumbled in her ears. "I'll tell you what, Pen. Chop up the potatoes, onions, and garlic, and I'll cook us some food."

Comforted by their ancient bond, L'Veyna leaned against Jouler, and let her mind fade to the crackling fire.

13

THE CHOSEN OF ALNAZET

Alerix kept his gaze away from Keeper Orenda's wormy fingers, focusing on her topaz-colored eyes. As if sensing his discomfort, she ran her fingers through her evergreen hair, highlighting her loose, unbraided locks. He swallowed the retort bubbling at the back of his throat, reminding himself he hadn't come to remind her about tradition. He'd come to throw it to the wind.

Maybe not every *tradition*, he thought, forcing a smile when she allowed V'Nahuu and the other saplings to stay in the sitting room while adults discussed matters of the forest. The younglings stared at the infamous Keeper from across the room, likely wondering when she'd turn them into trees or chop them into stew.

"Do you know how long I've studied our Prophecies?" Keeper Orenda said, returning a jar of ha'ath buds to its place on a shelf full of more jars. For someone who carried herself in such disarray, twigs and bits of leaves stuck in her unkempt hair, her loose robes long faded of whatever color they'd once possessed, Keeper Orenda kept a tidy housetree. Shelves covered the walls, every book, scroll, and jar placed just so, while drying herbs hung from the ceiling.

She shambled back into the common room and sat on her pillow with a heavy thud, her topaz eyes leveling on Tai'Enth. "I've studied them longer than your parents have been alive, and you just traipse in here with a group of saplings, and with a single comment," she said, wiping her face, "you throw it all into the fire. Do you realize how infuriating that is? Maybe I should cook *you* into stew." Keeper Orenda's brow bobbed at the uneasy saplings, loosening a few giggles. "What do you all think? Huh? Should I make Alerix and Tai'Enth into stew?"

Giggles bounced through the saplings, cracking the tense air, and Alerix released a heavy sigh. Alnazet's mercy, after three hundred years, the infamous Keeper still made him feel like a youngling.

"Tai'Enth," Keeper Orenda said. "Would you be so kinda as to fetch us some tea?"

Tai'Enth bowed her head. "Of course, Chosen."

"Cups for the young ones too," Keeper Orenda chimed, smiling at the saplings. "Little cups."

"But," Tai'Enth said, sniffing the kettle, "this is ha'ath tea."

"With lavender," Keeper Orenda noted.

"Blossoming or not, they're still saplings," Alerix growled, meeting her unnerving gaze. "Are your hair and talons not enough of an affront to our culture without—"

"How many summers had you known," Keeper Orenda said, " when you first sipped ha'ath tea?"

Her question sliced through Alerix's outrage, and he sat back on his pillow. All the saplings save the young girl were older than he when he first snuck some of his older sister's tea.

"That was over six hundred years ago," he said. "Times were different back then."

"How would you know?" Tai'Enth chuckled, carrying a tray piping with small teacups. "According to my journals," she said, adding dollops of honey to the cups, and handing them out, "I was eight."

V'Nahuu spurted, spilling his tea.

"It's quite impolite," Keeper Orenda said in a singing voice, "to waste good ha'ath. Tai'Enth, be a dear, and refill the young prodigy's cup? After you serve the Rose, of course."

"Of course," Tai'Enth replied, lowering the tray for Alerix. The promising smile gracing her lips soothed his wounded pride.

"Thank you," he said, taking one of the three large cups.

"No honey?" Keeper Orenda asked.

"Not for him," Tai'Enth replied, her coy smile heating his blood. "He likes it raw."

After refilling V'Nahuu's cup, and adding honey to her own, she finally brought the tray to Keeper Orenda. The adherence to guests' rights seemed odd for someone who spat at every other tradition.

"Two dollops, please," Keeper Orenda said, her topaz gaze lingering on V'Nahuu. "Do you know how many Keepers have ever been able to ask before their Blossoming?" Alerix shook his head, and she held up two fingers. "This young sapling, and the Elmhand girl."

"L'Veyna," V'Nahuu said, puffing his chest.

"But what does it mean?" Tai'Enth asked.

"There are far too many what ifs loaded into that question," Keeper Orenda said, finishing her tea. She produced a thin pipe from under her robe, her gaze flickering to the only curtained doorway in the housetree. "And far too little ha'ath."

Taking the hint, Alerix offered her his ha'ath pouch, and she returned in kind—another tradition strangely kept. Sweet floral fragrance wafted from the aged Keeper's pouch, demanding a deep sniff. "This is ha'ath?" He took a bulbous cluster and handed the pouch to Tai'Enth.

"Alnazet's mercy!" she said, drawing curious looks from the saplings.

"Oh, come on," Keeper Orenda said, waving them over. "Come smell."

Tai'Enth held the pouch for them to smell, smacking a reaching hand, and igniting a flurry of giggles.

"Now shoo," Keeper Orenda said. "Go find some sapling trouble to be at." She pointed to the doorway covered by drawn curtains. "I'm sure there's something in there to keep you entertained. Don't forget to leave your cups by the sink."

The saplings scurried to the kitchen, then through the curtains with a flurry of gasps and awes.

"What's in there?" Alerix asked, crumbling the ha'ath cluster and packing his pipe.

"Things I've collected throughout my life," Keeper Orenda replied, a thread of smoke curling above her pipe. After a deep pull, she blew a thick plume and smacked her lips. "Tasty. Did you grow this?"

"I did," Alerix replied. "What do we do about Marun and the empire?"

Keeper Orenda tilted her head, apparently waiting for him to keep to the simple tradition and smoke from his pipe before they discussed matters of business.

"We don't have time for—"

Her raised eyebrow cut his words short, fueling his frustrations. "Plague your guests' rites," he growled, drawing a hiss from Tai'Enth. "An imperial army is about to wipe out our people while Marun plans on wiping out our saplings. Are you going to tell them all to wait until we've exchanged pleasantries?"

Silence dangled over the housetree. A frightened sapling peeked through the curtains, and shut it under rumbling murmurs.

Chiding himself for his outburst, Alerix begged forgiveness from the Chosen and held his pipe to his lips. An asked ember flared in the bowl, and he pulled a deep drag. Sweet floral smoke swirled past his tongue and into his lungs. He released a thick plume, surprised by the flavor. A familiar calm seeped into his body, easing his tension, kneading his worried mind.

"The small things in life," Keeper Orenda said, tapping her pipe clean, "are always the most significant."

Tai'Enth blew a thick plume of smoke that curled Keeper Orenda's lips. "What is this? I've never tasted anything like it."

"One of my favorite strains," Keeper Orenda said. "I crossbred it with a fern."

"A fern?" Tai'Enth said, thick with disbelief. She smacked her lips, smoke leaking from her nostrils. "It's like... It's what you'd get if ha'ath was a sweet flower. It's amazing!"

"Alnazet, preserve me," Alerix grumbled, his patience tattered by the inane banter. "If we don't figure something out, or do something, or...I don't know, something. Anything!" He pressed his talons into his palms, the sharp stabs numbing his frustrations. "I can't just sit here."

"We are doing something," Tai'Enth said.

"But we aren't!" Alerix squeezed his hands again, savoring a pain he could understand. "We're just sitting here, following traditions from her, of all people. Gods, I should have known coming here would be a waste of time."

Keeper Orenda repacked her pipe and waved from him to continue. "Well? Keep going. Give us all these ideas of yours."

"If I knew what to do," he growled, "I wouldn't be ranting like a madman."

"You know exactly what do to," Keeper Orenda said, pulling another long drag. "You just don't want to do it. You'd rather sit here and complain about traditions, instead of doing what you must."

"And what would that be?"

An excited cry came from the curtained room. "Look, it's L'Veyna!"

Confusion pulled Keeper Orenda's brow, and Alerix leaped to his feet. In four quick strides, he crossed the common room and swiped the curtain aside. More shelves lined the sizable room, each shelf filled with a strange assortment of objects. Small figurines, carvings, candles, copper mugs, dice...all of which the saplings ignored, their excitement aimed at a tapestry dangling from the wall. The masterful tapestry depicted a wave of corpses crashing into a Sacred Forest, while cages of Prytha, both young and old, floated down a river toward a black cloud.

Amazed at the masterful craftsmanship, Alerix could have sworn one face looked like his. The depiction of M'Ljot stole his breath. It showed the Human who Tai'Enth had brought to the Sun Branch, down to his dark wavy hair, brown eyes, and the puckered scar where an imperial arrow had pierced his chest.

Excited saplings hopped and pointed to a figure beside M'Ljot, to a deciduous sapling girl with bright emerald eyes and elm leaves woven into the autumnal braids of her short Keeper's sleeve.

"L'Veyna," V'Nahuu said, beaming with pride.

Keeper Orenda stalked into the room, Tai'Enth close behind. "What is this talk of…" The ancient Keeper's voice trailed when her topaz gaze rested on the tapestry.

"What is it?" Tai'Enth peered over Keeper Orenda's shoulder, and she gasped.

"There are only three of its kind," Keeper Orenda said, her shaking voice stilling the sapling's excitement. "The Wu o'Pralab—the Living Weaves of Prophecy. One here, one in Eno'olaa, and the last, only Alnazet knows. This morning, it only showed M'Ljot's face."

"And now it shows L'Veyna?" Alerix asked, a haunting chill dragging his gaze to a corpse with a familiar face.

My face, and Tai'Enth's…

Keeper Orenda stumbled back, gaping at the tapestry. "It shows everyone."

14

A WARM FIRE

Jouler sat on a rock outcropping high within the Haldr Mountains, the blazing sun casting the last of its light over the sky. To the north, the glow from New Torgeir warmed an angry horizon. A vast storm raged over the sea surrounding the infamous island city, dark clouds flashing with bolts of lightning. The dark clouds stretched south over the vast plains far below, where Sotouri still played at war games.

Currently, two large armies maneuvered against each other in mock combat, like groups of ants from Jouler's vantage. Near the sparring forces were four well-organized bivouacs grouped into tents of red, blue, green, and orange. Presumably orange and green battled on the field, their campfires smoldering while the others flickered with life. Fireballs soared over the battlefield, lightning cracked with jagged bolts, and swaths of soldiers halted their combat where the shaped illusions landed. Wedges of cavalry charged at blocks of infantry, while archers streaked the sky with illusory arrows.

"Ruthless," Diou said, startling Jouler. "Aren't they?"

"Gods, you scared the Light out of me!" Jouler pressed a hand to his pounding chest. "I've heard shadows louder than you."

"What is impressive," Diou said, sitting beside him, "is that you can hear shadows at all. It appears the orange army will beat the green this year. That's…surprising."

"You can see their guidons from here?" Jouler asked, and Diou nodded.

"Green is always much stronger than orange," the Boorde said, his breath clouding the cold mountain air. "The red and blue armies are more evenly matched, although red is always a little stronger."

"What's the point of that?" Jouler asked. "Shouldn't they be more evenly matched?"

"War is never fair and even," Diou said. "It doesn't care about rules or moral struggles. War is ruthless, like the Sotouri Blades leading those armies."

"I take it the green army is losing all the soldiers?" Jouler asked, mesmerized by a wave of sparkling bursts showering groups of tiny soldiers.

"It would seem that way," the Boorde replied. "But you have to remember a key factor—Sotouri don't look at people as living beings with feelings, dreams, and loved ones." He gestured to the swaths of ant-like soldiers walking off the field. "They don't care how many people they have to kill to accomplish their mission."

The Boorde's words ignited terrifying memories of Grim. The way he'd used Pendric to keep Kael and Jouler in line. How the blasted Sotouri had pushed them all to their limits, and then pushed them even more, just to show them limits were something to conquer. In a way, he'd been Jouler's greatest teacher, though Grim's methods precluded him from any manner of praise.

Jouler turned his attention back to the armies far below, noting a large platoon of cavalry pulling away from their rear forces, leaving the archers exposed. The cavalry formed a wedge and charged toward the main battle.

Except they're swinging too wide, Jouler thought. Unless the cavalry changed the direction of their charge, they'd skim the battle at best. He analyzed the war games, gaging the pockets of sparring soldiers and shaped illusions, and the battle unfolded in his mind.

"The exposed archers," he said, pointing, "are luring the green forces, while the wedge of cavalry charges around the main battle to take out the green army's command tent."

"We shall see," Diou said, sucking an elongated canine.

As predicted, the green army deployed their reserves to overwhelm the battlefield. Illusory patterns burst through the tangled mess of soldiers. The orange army's front line caved, and infantrymen charged up the hill toward the exposed archers. Phantom explosions rippled down the slope from the orange army's archers, consuming the charging infantrymen. The illusory eruptions continued forward, through the broken front, and into the ranks of the green army.

A bright light shot into the air, bursting over the battle field in a shower of orange sparkles. The battling soldiers halted, and moments later, a deep boom rumbled over Jouler. Northeast of the battle, the orange army's stray cavalry hoisted a large green flag.

"How'd you know they'd win?" Jouler asked.

"The same way you did," Diou replied.

"You saw it way before me," Jouler said. "And until you said something, I thought the orange army was going to lose."

"That's only because you haven't watched a thousand battles. In fact," Diou said, fixing Jouler with his unnerving fire-diamond gaze, "I'd say this was the first battle you'd witnessed, real or not."

The Boorde's snow-white skin seemed far too smooth for him to have seen a dozen battles, much less a thousand. Not a single wrinkle creased his skin, not a gray hair streaked his too-black hair. Only his faded black clothes and the strap of worn leather holding up his topknot bore any sign of age.

"Don't take this the wrong way," Jouler said, "but how old are you?"

Diou's eyebrows rose. "Is there some other way to take the question, other than as an inquiry about my age?"

"I only ask because Humans can get offended by the question."

Diou chuckled, and adjusted the cloth belt holding his shirt closed. "It was a joke. To answer your question—I am two hundred and forty-eight."

Jouler whistled in astonishment. "I knew Boorde lived long, but you don't look a day over twenty."

"Nor will I," Diou replied. "We don't age like the lower races. Instead of wrinkles and white hair…" He pointed to his fire-diamond eyes. "Our pupils lose their color."

"Do you go blind?"

"My eyesight will never fade," Diou said. "My bones will never creak or ache, and I will be able to hear a whisper for as long as I draw breath."

"That's amazing!" Jouler said, wondering why the gods had slighted Humans. No extended life, unless they could shape, no amazing hearing, or ageless senses, just plain Human.

A rustle of leaves and a clicked tongue announced Prack. "Don't let Diou fool you," he said, sitting on the other side of Jouler. "Boorde are far from perfect. For one, they're Boorde. Not that I need anymore example, but I'll also add, they don't feel pain—"

"We do to feel pain," Diou mumbled.

"—so forget about crying on their shoulder," Prack continued, dripping with sarcasm. "Or any sort of sympathy, or happy birthday, or good morning."

"Isn't there a tree that needs tending?" Diou grumbled. "Maybe a garden that needs tilling?"

"Undoubtedly," Prack replied, matching the Boorde's dour look with a toothy smile. "But I'm a Chi'indi, not a Keeper. Tree and gardens grow far too slow to keep my attention."

Jouler chuckled through their exchange, the playful banter whispering of their love.

Diou looked over his shoulder into the pine-strewn mountainside. "Where's your sister and Pendric?"

Prack offered a flippant wave. "L'Veyna is trying to soak all the warmth from the campfire. Pen is reading his book."

"Perfect," Diou said. "I wanted to talk to young Jouler about serious matters."

"Ooo," Prack said, nudging Jouler. "This sounds serious."

"Blessed Flame burn me," Diou grumbled, then turned his unnerving gaze on Jouler. "What answers do you seek from your book?"

The question tangled Jouler's mind, and he fumbled over a response. "I, uh...I..." He cleared his throat, gathering his thoughts. "Sorry, your question caught me off guard. I refuse to believe that there's no way around the Saplings Curse. That all my Paths lead to some blasted war between Prytha children and their elders." He jerked his chin at the rock ledge and the ground far below. "If I jumped now, there'd be no Harbinger of Death to lead the saplings. No Curse to unfold."

"And here I was," Prack said, clapping Jouler on the back, "worried you'd have no solution."

"Ignore the idiot," Diou said. "Fortunately—or unfortunately, depending on your point of view—I do not believe Prophecy can be so easily thwarted by jumping off a cliff. More likely, someone else will be chosen to fill your mantle, or the Curse would continue without you to guide it."

"Who am I to lead an army?" Jouler asked. "I'm a farmer from a backwoods village."

"For someone who had never watched a battle until today," Diou said, gesturing to the ant-sized armies filing off the battlefield, "you read it quite well. You take to things easily, young Jouler. Not even Boorde learn the Basic Forms so quickly."

"Story of my life," Jouler replied with a dismissive wave.

"The gods have truly blessed you," Diou said.

"Is that what it is?" Jouler said. "Aren't gifts supposed to be good? Mine comes with a depressing title."

"Titles do not make a person," Diou said. "Someone like you could mean the difference between a leader who cares for his soldiers..." He gestured to the muddy field far below. "And a leader who sees them as tools."

Diou's words settled on Jouler's mind, giving him a new perspective on his dark fate. Just like a good farmer could save more crops from a plague, Jouler could save more saplings from the Curse.

Assuming there really is no way around it.

"What does the book say about it?" Prack asked.

"Nothing useful," Jouler replied with a derisive sniff. "Not about the Saplings Curse, anyway. Based on the author's descriptions, she'd seen Mh t'Pralab, which means she wasn't a shaper. However, all her interpretations about the Wall are wrong."

"Too wrong for your gift to clarity?" Prack asked.

"Everything except the obvious," Jouler said. "The part about me leading an army of saplings to war."

The words snapped into place in his mind, his gift confirming the prophetic truth. He turned his gaze to the ombre sky, twilight cloaking the muddy battlefield in jagged shadows from Haldr's sharp peaks. Hesitant chirps and clicks of nocturnal creatures called to the encroaching night, begging it to banish the painted glow above the mountains.

"You said the interpretations about the Wall of Prophecy were wrong," Diou mused. "What did the author get right?"

"She wrote about a Path," Jouler replied, then corrected, "*multiple* Paths the Harbinger can take that lead to the Dark's victory over the Light."

"That's…disappointing," Diou said. "But far from useless."

"It's not even the worst part," Jouler said, wishing he'd thought to bring his waterskin. "Within the Human Prophecies, there are more Paths for me that lead to the Dark's victory, than there are for the Light's."

The words snapped into place, ringing with truth.

"I'd say that's a little more than disappointing," Prack said.

"It gets even worse," Jouler said.

"Oh, great!" Prack chuckled. "There's more."

"Would you please take this serious?" Diou said. "Your quips do not help the others."

Prack dipped his head. "Forgive me, Sun of My Sky. I shall refrain from uttering my impulsive thoughts."

"No you won't," Diou said. "Please, Jouler, continue about the Dark Paths."

"In all the Paths that lead to the Light's victory," Jouler said before doubt held his tongue, "I kill the Facets. All of us."

The words snapped into place.

"Alnazet's mercy," Prack said, then clacked on the stone outcropping, *"I'm so sorry, Jo."*

"Why do you kill them?" Diou asked. "There must be a reason. You would not kill your friends. That much about you is obvious."

A shrill cry pierced through the snapping words.

"L'Veyna!" Prack cried and shifted away in a blur.

THE FADING sun retreated behind the jagged Haldr Mountains, chased by chirping crickets and the encroaching blanket of night. L'Veyna sat by the campfire, basking in its crackling warmth. The wind shifted, blowing acrid smoke in her face, burning her eyes and her lungs. She coughed, waving her hand at the smoke, her eyes welling, tears dripping down her cheeks.

"Smoke follows beauty," Pendric said from the other side of the fire, his eyes fixated on his book. He sat in his shirt and pants, his blanket forgotten around his shoulders. The staff she'd asked for him lay across his lap, his free hand tapping it while he read. "Something my mother always said."

"Must be why it never follows my brother," she said, muttering a curse at a sudden breeze. Cold cut through her blanket and thick layers of clothing and clawed at her back. Wishing she sat between two fires, she pulled her blanket tight and scooted a little closer to the flickering heat.

A warm bath in Emril's copper tub sounded perfect. Even if it meant not seeing the sun for a few days, at least she wouldn't be so plagedly cold.

"Do you really think it'll get worse than this in the Alliance?" she asked. "The cold, I mean. Prack makes it sound like ice."

"Gods, I hope not," Pendric wheezed. "That'd be slippery. I'd be falling all the time. Probably break my arm." He finally looked up from his book, and a curious look skewed his face. "No wonder you're so cold. You can't pull your blanket so tight. Open it up, like mine."

L'Veyna rolled her eyes at the ridiculous prank. If anything, she needed more blankets.

"It's true," Pendric wheezed, gesturing to himself. "Try it. What's the worst that can happen?"

"I could freeze to death," she grumbled, and he tilted his head in disbelief. "It's true."

"You won't freeze," Pendric said.

"Prytha and Humans are different, Pen."

"Like this," he said, fanning his blanket like a cape. "Catch all the heat."

Giggling, she rolled her eyes at him and sat up straight. "Fine," she said, deciding to indulge him, if for no other reason than to tell him she'd told him so. "But when I freeze, you better roll me into the fire to defrost."

"Deal," Pendric said, closing his book with a snap.

L'Veyna cracked open her blanket, and as suspected, cold rushed in. "I told you!"

"It'll be a little cold at first," Pendric said. "But trust me."

"Alnazet's mercy, fine." She let the blanket fall open, and the rush of cold dissipated under the fire's heat. She opened the blanket a little more, and warmth raced around her frozen back.

"It'll still get cold when there's a breeze," Pendric warned. "But life's never perfect, you know?"

"Tell me about it," L'Veyna grumbled.

"Your ears are pretty," Pendric said.

"That's…" L'Veyna flushed and cleared her throat.

"What?" Pendric said. "They are pretty, and really long. I think they're longer than Prack's."

"Alnazet's mercy, stop," L'Veyna implored, her face heating from the sensual compliments. "Ears are…um…" She pulled her blanket over her head, and cleared her throat. "That's something my father would say to my mother, to…uh…you know, tell her she's sexy."

Pendric spurted, his eyes wide. "What? No! I…I didn't

mean....gods, I was just..." He released a heavy sigh. "I'm never looking at your ears again."

L'Veyna's embarassment fled under a rush of laughter, and she gave Pendric a playful nudge.

"You know I didn't mean it like that, right?" Pendric said.

"Of course," L'Veyna replied, turning her chuckles in to a mischievous grin. "But you should definitely tell that to my brother."

Pendric's eyes went wide again, his light-brown face turning red. "I wouldn't—I mean..." He cleared his throat and dug the toe of his boot into the ground. "What...what would he do?"

"Probably get at least as embarassed as you," L'Veyna replied. "Which would be a nice for a change. Wouldn't you say?"

Pendric offered a sagacious frown and nodded. "I do say."

L'Veyna chuckled and opened her soul to Alnazet, forming an image she'd asked countless times over the past week. The tea sphere should have locked into place without effort, but it resisted her will, shaking until she forced it to lock into place. Her soul, the ever-blossoming power within her, swelled, and a tea sphere formed over her palm.

"Whew," she said, rubbing the back of her neck. It seemed Pendric's breath wasn't the only thing that grew more difficult as they climbed these rotten mountains. "That one took a lot out of me."

"Thank you," Pendric wheezed, scooting to taking the steaming sphere. He sipped and slumped with a relaxed sigh. "Much better."

"You should have asked me sooner," L'Veyna said, tugging the blanket back over her shoulder.

"I didn't want to bother you." He took a long sip and smacked his lips. "I can tell it isn't so easy anymore."

"It's the elevation." Her gaze floated up the mountain peaks, to the alps high above the ring of life, where the Boorde reigned. "But keeping you alive is never a bother, Pen."

His soft brown cheeks flushed, and he slurped the last of his tea.

"In the morning, I'll ask you some dried herbs for tea," she said. "Just in case it's too difficult to ask up there. Can you add more wood to the fire?"

"Not too much," Pendric warned. "You don't want to summon a southwestern snow cobbler."

L'Veyna poured her doubt through her smirk. "You just made that up."

"No, they're real," Pendric said, without a hint of sarcasm. "They're big, twice as tall as a man, and covered in long white fur, so you can't see them in the snow. You just never heard of them because it never snows in Onatah. My pa told me about them."

"Even if there was such a thing," L'Veyna said, "what would it eat? There's nothing up here except pines and squirrels."

"Lots of critters live in the mountains. My pa also told me about goats that walk up sheer cliffs."

L'Veyna sputtered at the ridiculous notion. "Now I know you're making it all up. Goats climbing rocks? What do they do, grab hold with their hooves?"

Pendric shrugged, hurt rumbling in his forced chuckle. "It's just something my pa said, and he wouldn't lie." He yawned, sucking in his breath, but never getting enough. "I'm getting tired." He put his book down, and curled on his bedroll, his back to the fire.

His back to me.

She shouldn't have made fun of his stories, but it was hard not to laugh at wall-climbing goats and southwestern whatevers. Still, Pendric didn't deserve to be laughed at. The young Human embodied sincerity in a way no Prytha could hope, his heart offered in every action and fanciful tale. He had a pure soul, which was nothing to poke fun at.

"Pen, I'm sorry. I shouldn't have laughed." She waited, but he didn't respond. He'd probably fallen asleep. Understandable considering the exhaustion seeping into her bones, but she wanted—no, *needed* to apologize. "Pendric, are you asleep? Pen?" A sudden chill pierced through the warmth of the fire. "Pen—" Fear clenched her throat, sucking the moisture from her mouth. Voice shaking, she called to him. "Pendric!"

He grumbled, and she breathed a sigh of relief.

Alnazet be praised! I thought…well, never mind that.

"Pen, I'm so sorry. I didn't mean to—" Her stomach churned, and invisible bands wrapped around her, holding her fast. She opened her mouth to speak, her stomach churned again, and invisible hands snapped her mouth shut.

"What have we here?" a woman said from the shadows of the forest.

A familiar figure stepped into the firelight, accompanied by a stout woman who could have been Pendric's cousin. Tulian's Shield poked from beneath his wool cap, his oversized sword replaced by a crackling spear. A dark cloak draped around his shoulders, hiding whatever weapons lay beneath.

L'Veyna should have expected as much from an imperial, but the sharp pang of betrayal still made her want to shout.

"That's one of them," Tulian said, peering into the darkness. "But the other one is the one you want. He's far more dangerous."

The woman beside him considered L'Veyna. Warm firelight danced across her dark features, highlighting the mud and grime smeared across her face and drab clothes. Matted, curly brown hair poked from under the hood of her thick, patch-worked cloak, her stench soiling the crisp pine breeze.

L'Veyna opened her soul to Alnazet, and formed an image of vines wrapping around the intruders and ripping them apart, but the image shattered under a wave of fear.

"The other one can't be far," the woman said, kneeling in front of L'Veyna. "You didn't say she was *this* beautiful."

"I told you there weren't any words," Tulian replied.

L'Veyna's mind grasped for askings, begging the images to lock into place, though she may as well have asked the sun to rise in the north.

"It's a good thing you kept your filthy platoon away from her. Then again," the woman mumbled, standing to fan herself before the fire. "Considering what she's about to endure…"

L'Veyna pleaded with Alnazet, watching image after image shatter.

"What about the Phaerian?" Tulian asked. "I'm telling you, he's one of the three Lord Rodak is looking for. The three that disappeared into Onatah, and, if I'm not mistaken," he said, dripping with sarcasm, "she is a Prytha."

"Your tone is not appreciated," the woman said.

"My apologies," Tulian said with an uneasy chuckle. "It won't happen again."

"No," the woman replied. "It won't happen a third time. You are, however, correct about one thing. He is one of Lord Rodak's Phlem. The question is, how far away is the other?"

"I say, let the Prytha scream a little," Tulian said. "Trust me. He'll come running."

The woman's lips curled into a cruel smile. "Oh, how she'll scream."

Desperation clambered over L'Veyna, stealing her thoughts, and sapping her strength. Arms and legs like mush, she pleaded with Alnazet to help her, to save her most precious Keeper.

The dark woman caressed L'Veyna's braids, her brown eyes glimmering with demented glee, her temple bereft of Shield.

Sotouri!

"Ah," the woman said, rubbing her naked temple. "You noticed." The Sotouri shook her head in disbelief. "Emperor's ass, but you're so beautiful. Your hair, it's…" Her fingers slid down the braids around L'Veyna's arm. "It's beautiful. You know, we don't really know much about your culture." She caressed L'Veyna's cheek. "But we're about to, aren't we, my dear?"

Yes…

L'Veyna forced a shaky image.

You…

The image resisted L'Veyna's asking, threatening to shatter.

Will!

L'Veyna forced her will onto the image, and it locked into place.

Vines and roots shot from the ground, snaking up Tulian's and the woman's legs. Tulian released a shrill cry before roots pierced him and burst from his chest and mouth, but the Sotouri's foul magic sliced through the vines aimed at her.

The invisible hands holding L'Veyna squeezed around her body, forcing the breath from her lungs. L'Veyna's askings popped from her mind, and the vines withered into the ground. Her lungs cried for air and her vision darkened under the inexorable squeeze. In a sudden rush, air filled her lungs, her dry throat burning. She coughed and hacked as Pendric struggled on the ground beside her.

"I...can't...breathe," Pendric wheezed.

"Pen!" L'Veyna cried, and a moment later her bonds vanished. She scrambled to her feet, and saw her brother in front of the Sotouri with the tips of his tsah jabbed at her throat. "L'Veyna, heal Pen. Ask him some tea. Do something. Anything!"

"Chi'indi..." the Sotouri cooed, and L'Veyna's stomach soured. Prack's eyes widened, and she stepped back from his frozen figure. "Well, this is my lucky day. You didn't really think I'd let you kill me, did you?"

"Of course not," Prack replied with that confident ease that always melted L'Veyna's fears. "I mean, we're quick, but nothing is quicker than thought. I had to do something. Lazy Boorde can't run as fast as Chi'indi."

Diou rushed toward Prack, the Boorde's faded-black ry'ku whipping behind him. The Sotouri leaped back as Diou's glowing spearhead sliced through the spot where she'd been standing. He tapped Prack with the butt of his spear, and the dark shaft flared with fiery runes. A sound like shattered glass pierced the air, and Prack shivered from his invisible bonds.

"I hate being the bait," Prack mumbled.

"Don't run so fast," Diou said, setting his feet as a ball of fire slammed into his chest, throwing him back. The Boorde hit the ground, rolled to his feet, and tossed away his shirt in a single motion. Snow-white chest singed, he twirled his spear, a sadistic grin exposing his long canines.

Diou leaped at the Sotouri, and Prack became a blur of motion. The Boorde's black spear whirred in his hands, shattering the woman's flow of filthy patterns, while Prack stabbed at her with blinding speed.

Sweat dripped down the woman's dark face, melting her confident smirk. Armed only with her mind, the Sotouri fell back, and Diou shifted his attacks. No longer a graceful dance, the Boorde's powerful swings crashed against the Sotouri's invisible barriers.

"Pen!" Jouler shouted, his staff in hand.

The Sotouri's gaze flashed toward Jouler as Diou's spear slipped through her invisible barrier with a shattered crash. The woman slouched on his weapon, the glowing spearhead sticking from her back, while her essence poured onto the ground.

L'Veyna shook on her knees, her limbs too weak to stand. Her gaze drifting to Tulian's mangled body, bloody shoots sprouting from his ripped-open face, his skull split in two. Her stomach clenched, and vomit warmed her chest.

L'Veyna huddled in her saddle, glad to be away from the bloody scene, even if exhaustion weighed on her body. Darkness settled over the land, creeping into her mind with images of Tulian's mangled corpse.

I asked the vines. I ripped him apart. I…I…

"The cave isn't too far," Prack called from somewhere up ahead. "It's not much, but it'll keep us warm."

L'Veyna's eyes welled, her cheeks too numb to feel the tears.

"I still don't get how you're not cold," Pendric told Diou.

The shirtless Boorde chewed on a strip of jerked meat atop his massive black destrier. Instead of blackened and melted flesh, an angry burn reddened his chest where the fireball had hit him. The Boorde's pale skin glowed under the moonlight, accentuating his lean, corded muscles, his breath clouding beneath his nose.

"I simply do not feel it," Diou said, biting off another strip of meat.

Memories of Tulian's ripped face stole L'Veyna's breath, and she swallowed back the bile rising to her throat.

"Are you okay?" Jouler asked, sidling his horse beside hers.

"Where were you?" L'Veyna snapped, her anger latching on to Jouler's flinch. "You just wandered off. Just left me and Pen."

"I'm sorry, I..."

"We almost died!" His reply faltered under her glare. She knew he couldn't have done anything against the Sotouri. M'Ljot or not, he would have gotten himself killed if he'd tried, but she couldn't stop her bitter tirade. "You just stood there, watching that woman wrap her filthy magic around me."

"That's enough," Prack called from the darkness ahead.

"You're worthless," she whispered, and Jouler winced.

"I'm sorry," he mumbled.

"Yes, you are," she said, clinging to her anger. The pain furrowing his brow stabbed her heart, but stopping meant drowning in a pit of misery.

"I said that's enough!" Prack's shout echoed down the mountainside.

Jouler stiffened his back and faced forward in his saddle, his kind dark eyes brimming with anguish. His warm familiarity called to her, threatening to crack her angry shell, and drown her in Tulian's memory. She steeled her mettle and pushed Jouler from her mind. Like he could ever know how she felt. He'd never taken someone's life.

L'Veyna squeezed her watering eyes to shut out the world.

Jouler called for a halt, and something heavy and warm draped over her shoulders.

When she looked, his coat hugged her. His tender smile shattered her shell, and the guilt she'd so feared to accept flooded through her, wracking her with sobs.

"I killed him."

The crunch of hooves on snow drew near, and her brother's voice drifted through her torment. "There, there, Little Sprout. Let it out. The cave isn't far. Stay here with Jouler and Pendric, while Diou and I start a fire."

"No," she blubbered, reaching for her brother. "Don't...leave... me."

"I'll find the cave," Diou said. "Stay with your sister."

L'Veyna curled into a wailing ball of misery, not caring if she fell from her saddle. Maybe then, her head would bash on a rock and end her suffering. Or the horse's hoof, or anything just to end it.

Please, I don't want to feel like this anymore…

Strong hands braced her in her saddle and rubbed her back until her sobs eased to sniffles. She opened her puffy eyes and found Jouler with his blanket wrapped around her shoulders.

Pendric offered her a handkerchief, his face drooping with concern.

Throat sore and hoarse, she croaked a thank you, and blew her nose. "Where's my brother?" she asked, noting Poppy's empty saddle.

"He shifted to the cave," Jouler said, his gaze cast upward. Moonlight kissed his soft brown face, his dark eyes sparkling like the stars high above. "It's all a bit confusing, isn't it?"

"I mean…yeah!" Pendric peered at the night sky. "It *is* the universe."

"That's not what I meant," he replied, bobbing his head toward L'Veyna.

"Ah," Pendric said. "I guess, but maybe if we were Prytha, changing hair color wouldn't be so confusing."

"I think he meant…what I did," L'Veyna said, too numb to care about the fresh well of tears. "I don't even know why I'm so upset. They were evil."

"They were," Jouler agreed, dark memories furrowing his brow. "But death isn't easy, even when they deserve it."

"But why do I feel this way?"

"It's because you're a good person," Pendric replied, still gazing at the stars. His eyes widened. "A shooting star! Did you see that? Headed in the direction we're taking, no less. Which, as we all know, is a good omen." His gaze dropped, and he dipped his head with an abashed smile. "Sorry, I saw a…well, anyway. I also did what you did to someone who really deserved it. He was *so* evil, but it still hurt. So, Kael—mine and Jo's best friend—told me it hurt so much because I was good. And being good takes courage. He said that too."

"He sounds like a good person," L'Veyna said. "Even if he's d'Tormena."

"You're going to love him, isn't she, Jo?"

"I'd be surprised if she didn't," Jouler said, his smile carrying the warm familiarity.

"How long did it take to go away?" L'Veyna asked.

"What, the pain?" Pendric replied. "Never. You just get used to it."

15

NUBIDAE

Jouler peered up the trail, his thin black eye wrap dulling the bright snow. He checked L'Veyna's reigns around his saddle horn before continuing up the twisting trail. Another bend led to another steep climb to another bend... Back and forth, they snaked up the mountain, the bright sun gleaming off the pristine white landscape. Face numb, he cast his gaze down the sheer cliff, marveling at the height they'd traveled. Somewhere far below, well beneath the narrow trail winding up the cliff side where vegetation still grew, was the cave they'd shared on that dreadful night.

L'Veyna rode behind him, her reins wrapped around his saddle horn. Three thick blankets wrapped around her, hiding even her face. Balanced on her saddle with her legs pulled into the Posture of Root, she looked more like a chrysalis than a shivering sapling. But at least she wouldn't freeze.

Diou had promised they'd reach Nubidae by noon, which couldn't come soon enough. Three nights on these frozen trails were hard enough on Jouler, and he'd grown up in a climate that snowed most winters. L'Veyna had never needed more clothing than her hempen Keeper's wrap, and now she wore every article of clothing she'd brought, and Jouler's as well.

Riding in front of him, Pendric slouched in his saddle, his breath too weak for him to talk. Prack rode beside Pen, seeming unconcerned that his palomino's hooves landed inches from the edge of the narrow trail.

After a brief stop for a round of warm tea spheres to help open their lungs, they continued up the precarious, winding path, enduring the never-ending wind and biting chill. They stopped twice more before the trail crested between two granite slabs shaped like large gray talons.

At the head of their frozen group, Diou halted between the granite talons. "My friends," he said with a sweeping gesture. "I present to you, the Boorde Alliance."

The trail poured into an enormous bowl large enough to engulf Alduos ten times over, and surrounded by jagged peaks. Massive black compounds, like small towns made of obsidian, dappled the snowy bowl. Large estates filled each compound, all made from the same glossy black material. Wide, covered avenues connected the isolated compounds, large braziers lining either side of the lanes.

"It's beautiful," Jouler said.

"It's freezing," L'Veyna replied, her muffled voice barely audible beneath the blankets.

Diou led them to the largest compound in the massive bowl, steering them away from the main entrance. "Fewer eyes," he explained, guiding them along the tall, black outer wall to a small, arched entrance.

A dozen Boorde stood guard, each armored in black ring mail. A curved sidaiyo hung at their belt, while black spears leaned against the wall. Jouler wanted to believe the rumors unfounded, but guards all could have been Diou's brothers and sisters, each tall and striking, with the same snow-white skin, chiseled features, and too-black hair. One guard disappeared through the arched entrance.

"Diou," a stoic Boorde said, slapping palm to breast in salute. A wave of slapped chests spread through the other guards, their fire-diamond eyes measuring Jouler and his companions. "Had I known you were coming, I would have prepared some cottlewomp stew."

"I'm never living that down, am I?" Diou said with an affable grin.

"Not while my flame burns," the guard replied.

"It's great to see you, Eldri." Diou dismounted his large destrier and clapped the guard in a warm hug. "I'm glad il'Yluran is finally putting your talents to good use."

Eldri chuckled. "It takes a special type of someone to guard the Pointless Post."

"Pointless Post?" Prack said, sliding off his horse to clap Eldri in a hug. "But Diou and I use it all the time."

"As I said," Eldri replied, with a somber nod. "Pointless."

"Could be worse," Diou said, motioning for everyone else to dismount. "You could be throwing your weight around the training yard again."

The guard winced and clapped Diou's shoulder. "It's good to see you, my friend."

"You as well, Eldri," Diou replied, scooping Pendric into his arms.

"What's wrong with the boy?" Eldri asked.

"His lungs are weaker than most," Diou replied, and Eldri bowed his head.

"Fythlin," the guard said, and another stoic Boorde slapped palm to chest. "Make haste for some tea for Diou's companion."

"Stay, Fythlin," Diou said, halting the guard. Diou gestured to the ball of blankets still mounted on her horse. "We have a Prytha Keeper."

Eldri's fire-diamond eyes widened. "By the Flame, Diou!" he cursed, gesturing them through the entrance. "Stop wasting time chatting about the snow and get them some warmth."

Diou chuckled, shifting Pendric in his arms, and headed into the compound.

"You can pass too, Prack," Eldri mumbled, his lips curling with a smile. "I'll be seeing you later, I hope."

"Yes you will," Prack promised, and clicked his tongue.

Jouler helped L'Veyna off her horse, then guided her and their mounts through the entrance. He ran his hand along the wall's smooth black surface. It couldn't be obsidian. Maybe black marble or granite polished to a mirror-like surface. His mind reeled at the amount needed to construct a single compound, much less the dozens that dotted the massive, frozen bowl.

The arched entrance opened to a vast courtyard centered upon a peculiar fountain. Instead of water, streams of liquid fire splashed over a tall emerald heron in flight. At the edge of the courtyard were dozens of racks filled with myriad wooden weapons. Swords of all styles and lengths, shields, bucklers, spears with different blades, daggers, clubs, as well as strange, unconventional weapons—a fist-sized ball at the end of a long, thin rope. Two or three short sticks held together by a chain. Scythes, sickles, gauntlets fashioned into claws, and fans tipped with blades. Long archery yards stretched alongside the outer walls, with targets set at varying distances. Racks of unstrung bows, some longer than Jouler was tall, waited at each shooting station, along with barrels that bristled with arrows.

A long cobbled path lined with fiery braziers led from the majestic, emerald-heron fountain to a massive building made of the same black stone as the outer wall. Five stories high, the dark building boasted dramatic curves and spires that epitomized Boorde's beautiful and deadly nature. An immense stained-glass window glowed above the tall, arched doors of the compound's main entrance. The round window depicted the same emerald heron as the fountain, set against a field made to look like dancing flames.

Wheezing in Diou's arms, Pendric gaped at the stained-glass window. "How does it...do that?" he asked between breaths. "It's not...really on fire, right?"

"No," Diou replied. "The technique of making the glass causes the fire to dance as you move."

"Everything's made of stone," L'Veyna grumbled, her face poking from under the hood of her blankets.

"Not the...practice weapons," Pendric wheezed.

"Wood is too precious to use for buildings," Diou said. "Nothing grows at these heights."

"Thank you...for carrying me," Pendric said, patting Diou.

"It is my honor," Diou said. "All the lower races suffer in the

Boorde heights. Inside the house, we have similar tea to the tea L'Veyna asks for you. So she won't have to ask all the time."

"I don't mind," she replied, her voice muffled by blankets. "Maybe my tea tastes better."

Diou bypassed the glorious main entrance and took them to the blessedly warm stables. A handful of liveried Boorde grooms bowed to Diou, their too-black hair draping past their eyes like an upside-down bowl. Men and women alike wore an outfit similar to Diou's, with a skirt instead of flowing trousers. Unlike Diou's faded ry'ku, the grooms' clothes looked new, the emerald heron bright on their too-black breast.

Out of the freezing weather, L'Veyna peeled off her blankets, looking like a stuffed doll with her multiple layers of clothing.

"Everything here is so tall," Pendric wheezed as Diou put him down. Jouler's childhood friend slouched, breathing hard, never quite catching his breath. He cast sunken eyes to the high, arched stained-glass ceiling. Colorful rays of light beamed from masterful depictions of horses grazing on flowered meadows and prancing on rolling hills. "It's *so* pretty."

"And blessedly warm," L'Veyna said, stripping her coat and a few layers of clothing.

Another bowl-haired servant dashed into the stables and bowed to Diou. "Matron Nith'Iil requests your immediate presence."

"As soon as I see to my guests—"

"Your *immediate* presence," the servant reiterated.

"Very well," Diou grumbled. "Prack, you know where to take everyone."

"Forgive me," the servant said. "But, I was told—"

"You were told to take me to my mother," Diou said, and the servant stiffened.

"Of course." The servant snapped another bow and led Diou from the stables.

"Is he in trouble?" Pendric asked, working the hem of his sleeve.

"No," Prack said. "Or, at least, I hope not. Come on. Let's head to the guest wing. Someone's been waiting to see you."

L'Veyna followed her brother, having lost all sense of direction in the mirrored black-marble labyrinth of House Nith'Iil. She'd seen oak branches less twisted than these halls and corridors.

And so many herons!

The House symbol decorated each entryway, door, column, bench, chair, and table in the manor. Liveried servants bowed as they passed, their strange bowl-shaped hair falling past their eyes. Other than guards, who all wore the same black armor made of interlaced rings, Boorde only wore two styles of clothes. Most men wore ry'kus, clothes similar to Diou's, with loose buttonless shirts held closed by a belt, and wide flowing trousers, while most women donned a tight dress that fell to their ankles, long flowing sleeves draping from their blouse, and a wide cloth belt wrapping their torso. Although, she'd also seen a handful of women in ry'kus, and a few men in dresses.

"Why do Boorde hate color?" L'Veyna asked, watching a tall, beautiful Boorde woman glide with impossible grace over the glassy floor. She wore a different type of dress than the other women, tight around the bodice, and a loose skirt. A single strip of flame-colored cloth ran up the side of the too-black dress.

"Obviously they don't hate color," Prack said, gesturing to the majestic stained-glass ceiling depicting a sun setting behind a mountain range, the sky painted in gold, purple, red, and orange. "Just not in clothes."

"No wonder they don't like us," L'Veyna said, imagining Boorde wandering through Onatah, gawking in disbelief at the vibrant clothing her people preferred. Or lack thereof, considering how little skin Boorde showed.

"They like us just fine," Prack said. "They're just subject to the same prejudices every race holds.

"I do not—"

"Humans are impatient," Prack said, holding up a finger.

"Which is true," L'Veyna replied.

"Boorde are emotionless killers," Prack said, holding up another finger.

L'Veyna gestured to the stoic-faced servants, bowing as they passed. "Well…maybe not *all* of them are killers."

"Prytha exist in their emotions," Prack said, holding up a third finger.

"And Phaerians are dumb and dirty," Pendric wheezed.

"We're Human," Jouler said.

"Well, yeah, but…" Pendric shrugged. "You know what I mean."

"My point is," Prack said, rushing them through spectacular hallways with amazing stained-glass windows and high vaulted ceilings. "Boorde don't hate Prytha. Although they do think we're weak."

"That's so much better," L'Veyna mumbled.

"Wouldn't you feel that way too?" Jouler asked. "Look at them. They're all tall and fit, like Diou, and he's a lot stronger than all of us."

"There's a lot more to strength than muscles," L'Veyna replied.

"They're also the brightest philosophers," Prack said.

"Oh, wow. Thinking is so hard. I'd like to see a single Boorde grow a sprig of grass."

"They're art…is pretty," Pendric wheezed, gawking between the glossy black floor and the stained-glass ceiling.

"It's all right," L'Veyna mumbled, and her brother chuckled.

"Admitting a culture is beautiful," Prack quoted, "does not lessen the beauty of another culture."

L'Veyna rolled her eyes. "I suppose a Boorde said that?"

"Keeper Orenda," Prack said, clicking his tongue. He led them to a spacious, heron-infested room with black velvet sofas and chairs set with marble buttons, black tables decorated with the House symbol, and elegant crystal chandeliers.

"This way," Prack said, opening one of the twenty doors lining the glossy walls. He led them down more majestic hallways, and into another large room splashed with color. An old Phaerian in dark red robes rocked in a creaking wooden chair, a curved pipe in his mouth.

Smoke blew from his crooked nose, adding to the layers of haze that drifted throughout the room.

Ha'ath! L'Veyna thought, breathing in the comforting aroma.

The old Phaerian had darker skin than Jouler and Pendric. Especially compared to the breathtaking Boorde, sitting on a sofa next to a little Phaerian girl with silky black hair.

"Dilna?" Jouler fell to his knees.

The young girl's eyes widened, and she ran into his arms.

Pendric bubbled a laugh, tears streaming down his cheeks, and he wrapped them both in a tight hug, squeezing until she yelped for air.

"Gods, it's good to see you boys," Reylan said, earning a squeak from Pendric.

"Reylan!"

The old Phaerian wrapped them all in a hug, igniting a rumble of sobs.

"Your breath," Dilna said, eyes wet with tears.

"I'm fine," Pendric wheezed, his sunken eyes belying his health. "I sound worse...than I feel."

Reylan stepped back and wiped his eyes with the sleeve of his dark robe. "Gods bless me, I'm so happy you're here."

L'Veyna watched the touching reunion with a pang of jealousy. Not over Dilna, of course. Pretty for a Human, she looked younger than L'Veyna, though notably taller, and with hair almost as smooth and black as a Boorde's.

"Who is she?" L'Veyna asked, and her brother gave her a knowing smirk. "I'm not jealous. I just...where'd she even come from? Did you know she was here the whole time?"

"I did," Prack said, raising his hands to implore patience. "Reylan swore me to secrecy. He wanted it to be a surprise for Jo and Pen."

"I just don't know why you couldn't tell me," L'Veyna mumbled.

"L'Veyna!" Jouler called, his excitement chasing away the awkwardness in her gut. "Come here. Come meet Dilna and Reylan. L'Veyna, this is Dilna and this is Reylan." He ruffled Dilna's silky hair, and she swiped at his arm. "She's the little sister Pen and I never had."

A confusing wave of relief washed over L'Veyna. Sure, his rugged, handsome features were pleasant to look at, but he was still Human. Regardless of Jouler's warm familiarity, she didn't think of him as anything but a friend. She just didn't know why he never told her about his 'little sister'.

"And I," Reylan said, bowing to L'Veyna, "am their grandfather."

L'Veyna jerked in surprise. Even without the man's much darker skin, he looked nothing like Pen and Jo.

"Not by blood," Reylan said.

"More like the village grandfather," Pendric said.

"Dilna..." Jouler's gaze found L'Veyna's, and his breath caught. A warm smile softened his features into something more than a smile, something deeper...something more than the ancient familiarity flaring inside her. "L'Veyna..." He blinked and cleared his throat. "This is...this is L'Veyna."

"Gods, you're so pretty!" Dilna said, wrapping L'Veyna in a tight hug. "I love your hair! Just...wow! It looks like autumn." She giggled and took L'Veyna's hands in hers. The young human's warm affection melted L'Veyna's hesitation, while the mischief twinkling behind Dilna's eyes promised fun and excitement.

Prack put a hand to the side of his mouth and whispered, "You're supposed to say thank you."

She elbowed her brother and giggled alongside Dilna. "Thank you," L'Veyna said, offering Dilna a sweeping bow. "You're beautiful too."

"Why, thank you," Dilna replied, imitating L'Veyna's exaggerated bow.

Prack rolled his eyes. "I can already tell you two are going to be fast friends.

L'Veyna shared a mischievous look with Dilna, and they both bowed to Prack and said, "Why, thank you."

L'Veyna and her newfound friend burst into laughter, as the tall Boorde woman glided across the floor, her long too-black hair pulled to a long tail that fell past her waist. Tight around the bodice, her black dress flowed around her legs, matching her grace with silent waves. A single strip of fire-colored cloth shimmered up the side of the dress. She bore the same snow-white features as every other Boorde, with the same fire-diamond pupils and elongated canines, yet she caught every eye in the room.

"It's my pleasure to introduce," Prack said with a sweeping bow, "Katima Nith'Iil, daughter of Matron Nith'Iil, Heiress Apparent of House Nith'Iil, and, most importantly…Diou's sister."

Katima gave a derisive grunt, her hands falling to her sides. She gave Prack a pointed look. "Are you always like this?"

"Sometimes he's even worse," L'Veyna said.

"You must be L'Veyna," Katima said, kneeling and pulling her into a hug. Gods, she even smelled pretty. "It's so great to finally meet you. Your insufferable brother has—surprisingly for him—spoken well about you."

L'Veyna's heart swelled, and she poked at her brother. "I knew you loved me."

"I didn't mean it," Prack joked, rubbing his side.

"I am so sorry about your home," Katima said, stealing the soft mood.

"Thank you," L'Veyna mumbled.

"Sister," Diou said, motioning for her to draw near.

"What?" Katima asked, and he whispered to her. Katima's eyebrows climbed her head, and she turned to L'Veyna. "I am so sorry. I should not have reminded you about the destruction of the Wreath. I'm sure it only reminded you of—"

"Sister," Diou said, shaking his head again.

Katima drew a slow breath and bowed to L'Veyna, then offered her a small yellow orb. "Forgive me," the tall Boorde said.

"What is it?" L'Veyna asked.

"It is a lemon candy," Katima said. "To save face for my wandering tongue."

"Ooo!" Dilna squeaked, holding out her hand. "Me too, please." The mischief dancing in her eyes chipped at L'Veyna's gloom, demanding a smile, and Dilna nudged her with her shoulder. "They're so good."

"Can I have one?" Pendric asked, peering at the sweet. "I don't know…how to save your face—it doesn't look like…it's going anywhere, but I can help you…find your tongue, maybe."

"Pendric Loyalton," Katima said, dropping a lemon candy in his hand. "You are exactly how Reylan described."

L'Veyna waited for him to plop the sweet into his mouth, his wide-eyed surprise almost enough to banish the unpleasant thoughts of home.

"It's so good," Pendric said, rolling the candy in his mouth.

Ignoring the banter floating around Jouler about Prophecy, L'Veyna plopped her into her mouth and the sweet taste of lemon, basil, and ginger coated her tongue. "Alnazet's mercy, that's *so* good."

"Told you," Dilna said with a wink.

"How did Kael get to Serolle?" Reylan asked, packing his curved pipe. A sour pit churned in L'Veyna's stomach, and smoke curled from Reylan's pipe. "Sorry, dear. I forgot you can ask." She offered him a confused look, and he blew a thick plume of smoke, the smell of ha'ath easing her belly. "Shaping. It'll sour your stomach, dear."

"After we made it to Onatah," Jouler said. "Me, Kael, and Pendric, Kael entered Tálise to dreamwalk, and…" Jouler looked to L'Veyna, and she nodded for him to finish the morbid story. "And the tree turned to ash."

Reylan's brow drew, and he blew another plume of comforting ha'ath.

"Also," Jouler mumbled, taking a slow breath. "I'm the Harbinger of Death."

"Yes, I know," Reylan said. "Any news on Onatah?"

"The empire is already invading," Prack replied.

Reylan shook his head, his dark eyes tight with thought. "This is terrible."

"Wait," Jouler said. "What do you mean, you knew I'm the Harbinger?"

Reylan rubbed his crooked nose. "Why do you think I'm here, son?"

"You knew this whole time?" Jouler said, a confluence of emotions tangling his words.

"No," the old Phaerian replied. "Although I had my suspicions."

"Well," L'Veyna said. "Did you know I'm the Warden of Preservation?"

"The what?" Reylan took a deep breath, his smoking pipe forgotten in his hand.

"You knew?" Jouler asked, his familiarity swelling inside her.

"Of course I did," L'Veyna replied, savoring the confusion twisting his face. "How could I not?"

"Slow down," Reylan said. "What's going on?"

"It appears my sister," Prack said, the pain on his face twisting her fleeting joy, "is a Facet of Prophecy."

"A Facet of…" Reylan dry-washed his face. "A what?"

"The Prophecies are wrong," Jouler said. "There is no Light. Not how we believed, anyway."

Reylan searched Jouler's eyes. "Tolrik's beard, it's true, isn't it?"

"Every word," Prack said.

Reylan fell into a chair and repacked his pipe. "I'm going to need more ha'ath."

Katima raised an eyebrow. "I'll get the wine."

Reylan motioned for everyone to sit, then struck a sulphurstick and lit his pipe. Pulling a long drag, he blew a thick plume of smoke. "Now…start from the beginning. What's a Facet of Prophecy?"

REFRESHED after a night in the most comfortable bed Jouler had ever slept, he followed Reylan down majestic black hallways polished to shine like glass. An army of liveried servants scoured the estate, hunting motes of dust, smeared fingerprints, and tracks of mud, while soldiers, guards, and iconic firedancers trained outside.

"Is it always so busy here?" Jouler asked, sipping Boorde tea to ease the altitude sickness. His sleep may have refreshed him, but he still hadn't recovered from seeing Reylan again. Jouler, the Harbinger of Death, had crossed half the empire, was kidnapped by a Sotouri, endured the infamous Kralnach Hills, and Reylan still made him feel like a child.

"Busy, yes," Reylan replied, his robes swishing along the mirror-like black floor. "But not like this. Serolle's fall has the entire empire on edge. Tolrik's beard, son, if what you said about Facets is true…" The old man rubbed his crooked nose, and gave Jouler a sidelong look. "Do you have any idea how much work your revelation has piled on me? Do you realize how long I've studied the blasted Prophecies?"

"It does make a lot more sense," Jouler said. "Didn't you ever think it a little…inconsistent that the Light was supposed to be both the god who created the universe *and* a lowly Human who saved it? And why a Human? There are far more competent races than us."

"You obviously haven't read *Sacred Paradox: Contemplating the Unity of the Light.*"

"How would I have read that?" Jouler retorted. "All you'd let me read were adventure books and notes on plants."

"Which," Reylan said, turning down another corridor, "you undoubtedly found useful during your travels."

"I absolutely did *not*," Jouler replied, passing a Boorde woman dressed in a traditional male ry'ku. "Between running from Rodak's men, losing Pendric's breath, and being dragged to Onatah by a blasted Sotouri, I didn't have much of an opportunity to point out the differences between wild garlic and death camas."

"You probably wouldn't have liked it anyway," Reylan said with a dismissive wave.

"Where are you taking me?" Jouler said, stopping in his tracks. "And why couldn't L'Veyna come? She's a Facet too."

"What makes you think this has to do with Prophecy?"

"I'm not a child," Jouler replied, moving for a tall Boorde servant carrying a small stack of books. "Everything you do is tied to Prophecy."

"That obvious, huh?" Reylan said, continuing down the hallway.

Curiosity pulled Jouler behind the old Phaerian, but his worried thoughts drifted to L'Veyna. While he'd struggled with revealing her troubling role in Prophecy, she'd already figured it out. Mostly, he'd felt a fool for doubting she'd be able to do it.

She's young, not stupid.

"Where are you taking me?" he asked again, his gaze catching on another female Boorde dressed in male clothing. A thin, curved sidaiyo nestled in its scabbard at her left hip, along with another, smaller blade.

"Eidraael," Reylan explained, grinning at Jouler's confusion. "Boorde culture is far more complex than their outward appearance. More...fluid, shall we say."

"Do men also wear dresses?" Jouler asked, curious about the strange culture.

"Of course not," Reylan replied. "Neither do women wear men's clothing. Boorde honor would never allow it."

"But, I just saw—"

"A man," Reylan said.

"But she had..." Jouler grabbed his chest, his face heating under the old man's chuckle.

"Breasts?" Reylan said, and Jouler nodded. "Boorde don't see gender like the lower races. It's not so much what you have as it is who you are. Think of it more like roles. In Boorde society, men fight in battles, women rule and oversee House affairs, while eidraael walk both worlds."

"Eidraael?" Jouler asked. "They're both male and female?"

"Or neither," Reylan replied.

"But...how?"

Reylan stopped and fixed Jouler with an inquisitive look. "You tell me how. You're a man, right?"

"I just am," Jouler said, realizing he'd never thought about it. "I can...you know, make babies."

"Not me," Reylan said. "Never could. Am I not a man?"

"Of course you are," Jouler replied, trying to wrap his mind around the Boorde's complex culture. In Headwater, men were men and women were women. Sure, most families shared chores, but men hunted and did all the heavy lifting, while women cooked and tended to the children.

Well, except for the outposts with mock-families trained by Harold. Come to think of it, Nalla, Harold's wife, could best most men in a scuffle, while Livia's father did most of the cleaning in the house. The Hilltops, the Tinsnips, the Loyaltons...it seemed only Jouler's family had stuck to men being men and women being women. But, in such a small community as Headwater, it made sense that everyone helped. Maybe Alduos had different customs, not that Jouler would have noticed. All townsborn dressed in similar drab shirts and trousers, and Jouler had seen his fair share of women in Alduos beating metal on an anvil.

"Confusing, is it?" Reylan asked with a knowing smile. "Most people walk through life assuming truths instead of questioning them. They believe themselves normal, while ignoring that same truth in others. But then, crazy people also believe they are normal... Who's to say how I feel and how I see the world isn't wrong?"

"That's a lot to take in," Jouler admitted.

"The truth is," Reylan said, "no matter how well we know someone, no matter how long we've spent with them, no one can know any other perspective but their own." He gestured to a male Boorde in an ydu dress, dusting a suit of armor displayed on the wall. "All we can do is trust when people tell us how they feel. Eidraael are blessed among the Boorde, able to experience aspects of life forbidden to everyone else."

"But what if they're lying?" Jouler asked, and Reylan chuckled.

"Thankfully for us," Reylan said, "for the Boorde, finding one's true path, their ris'wahri, is highly honorable. It's a lesson we could all learn."

He followed Reylan down another black-marbled hallway, passing countless servants and guards, even a few visitors from other Houses and a handful of Citizens. "Where are you taking me?"

Reylan opened the door to a sizable room with black plush chairs adorned with emeralds. He pointed to a pair of tall doors guarded by a pair of imposing guards. A large, blue-flamed diamond split down the middle of the iron doors. Sunlight painted the stained-glass ceiling on the floor, mirroring the masterful artwork of lush farms, verdant forests, vibrant meadows, and peaceful gatherings of the three races of Torgeir.

"I'm taking you here," Reylan said.

"Here where?"

"House Nith'Iil's Seers," Reylan said.

"To do what?" Jouler asked, his mind reeling with questions.

"Seers are connected to the Currents of Power like no other people on Torgeir. They give people glimpses into Prophecy."

"And you believe they'll show me my Path," Jouler said, and Reylan nodded. "Why isn't L'Veyna with us? I feel like she should be here too."

"Every Prytha who's tried has lost their mind. Like snapping for shapers. Besides," Reylan said with a fond smile, "I doubt her and Dilna will wake up anytime soon."

"True," Jouler said, happy the two had become fast friends. After hearing the pair laughing in the common room until the sun rose, he doubted either would be up and about in time for lunch. "I can only imagine the trouble those two will brew."

Jouler chuckled at the thought of L'Veyna and Dilna roaming the House halls, pushing the limits of their hosts. His unease dissipated under his growing curiosity, and he gestured to the ornate doors leading to the Seers' Chamber. "What are the diamonds blue? Boorde irises are like fire."

"It mimics the Seers' eyes," Reylan said. "No one really knows why their irises are blue, but I'll be happy to show you some books on the subject *after* you learn your Path."

"I already know my Path," Jouler said.

"Do you?" he said, nodding for the two Boorde guards to open the doors.

Curiosity pulled Jouler into the long room, and the doors closed behind him. Warm light from dozens of everburning torches flickered along the walls of the large black-marble chamber. At the far side of the vaulted room, three small Boorde waited in black thrones atop a tall dais.

"Be welcome, Jouler Davinin," the Seers said in unison. "Harbinger of Death, Facet of Prophecy."

Jouler crossed the long floor, noting stark differences in the Seers from the other Boorde. Still porcelain white, their long, soot-black hair fell past their waist in gentle waves, not strands of silk. Almost as small as children, they bore a depth of wisdom in their eyes, their fire-diamond irises blue like a clear sky.

"We have waited for you," they said in unison, their voices too old for their small frames. "Tamer of the Black Breath. That is why you have come, is it not?"

"What is the Black Breath?" Jouler asked.

"A fine line you walk, Harbinger. Between life and death, your heart dangles. Between Light and Dark, your soul wanders."

"What does that mean?"

"Come closer," they intoned, stretching their hands toward him. "Let us show you your truth."

Jouler climbed the dais and knelt before them, the glossy floor cold on his knees.

"Close your eyes," they said, and his lids obeyed their deep, soothing voice. "Take a deep breath…and release."

The gentle weight of their hands settled on his head, and then they were gone, his knees no longer pressing the hard floor. Wind buffeted him, whipping his clothes and rushing past his ears. Panic slammed against his chest. He opened his eyes, expecting to fall through the air, and was surprised to find himself on a lifeless white desert stretching to the horizon.

The Blasted Lands? he wondered, noting the sun's absence in the clear sky.

Dry wind blew in his face, sucking the moisture from his eyes. He turned to put the wind to his back, but it always blew at his front, pushing against him no matter which way he faced. With no way to tell north, he headed straight, his steps releasing small puffs of lifeless white dust that settled almost as soon as they rose, defying the strong wind.

It's almost like the wind is trying to stop me.

His legs grew weary, his body heavy, his feet sore as if he'd walked for days. He pressed forward against the wind until his leg gave out, and he fell to the ground. Exhaustion clouded his mind and soaked into his limbs, tempting him with blissful slumber.

A dark speck on the horizon caught his attention, igniting enough curiosity to pull him back to his feet. As with the wind, the speck stayed in front of him, no matter which way he turned. He pushed through his fatigue, forced one foot in front of the other, his strength ebbing with each step, but the speck never drew closer.

Jouler fell to his knees again, and the Blasted Lands vanished along with his fatigue. He knelt on the rough floor of a massive cavern. Light from some unknown source cast long shadows along the ground and impossibly high, jagged ceiling.

The light is coming from me, he realized, watching the shadows dance as he walked.

In the center of the cavern was a tall column. Stairs wound up the column, the top hewn flat as if by a massive blade. There, swirling above a bowl-like pedestal, was a black cloud so dark it made the cavern seem bright.

The Black Breath.

"Take it," L'Veyna urged, suddenly by his side, clutching his arm, urging him toward the column. "Alnazet's mercy, Jo! Take it!"

Jouler ran to the column and climbed the stairs, his light dimming with each step. When he reached the top, only a flicker of his light remained.

No…this isn't right.

"Jo…help me." Pendric's faint voice warbled through the darkness. "Hurry…"

The Black Breath swirled with whispered promises of power. Not the insufferable meddling of shapers, Keepers, and firedancers, nor the laughable influence of the Seers—*true* power. The power to end the empire once and for all. The power to end all wars and suffering, to usher in a time of peace and bounty…if he but let the darkness in.

"And if I refuse?" Jouler asked, and found himself floating high above the clouds, a ruined empire spread far below. Blackened trees poked from the charred remnants of the Prytha forests, while a vast pool of magma drowned the Boorde Alliance. Darkness crept across the land, swallowing imperial cities and Phaerian towns, until only the stench of death remained.

This doesn't have to be your fate, Harbinger of Death.

The deep, ancient voice tumbled in Jouler's mind, and he found himself back in the cavern. The Black Breath churned before him.

Take my power. Forge a different fate. A kinder fate.

Jouler plunged his hand into the darkness and found himself in a small village that tugged at his heart—*Headwater*. Citizens, Phaerians, Prytha, Boorde, and a strange lizard-like creature all celebrated in the Town Square, cheering the Light's victory.

"If this is my Path," he said, and the words snapped into place. "Then why does it feel wrong?"

His feet fell on something too soft to be grass. Instead of a vibrant, green field, countless corpses lay across the land. Blood dripped from his fingers, splashing on the dead bodies. He wiped his hands, but the blood still poured onto the ground.

"I don't understand."

No matter which Path you forge, the voice rumbled in his mind, *Light or Dark, you will always be the Harbinger of Death.*

PART II

FORKS

Caste low, to be elevated upon high; bred a hound, the den of traitors defeat.

16

WHISPERS FROM THE PAST

Weeks after the explosion, ash still darkened the slopes of the Alrynn Mountains. Not a drop of rain or flake of snow had fallen, as though the land itself refused to let that terrible memory fade. It had to be worse along the south side of the mountains facing Serolle, but Makayla never wanted to see that city again.

Or the crater Kael and I caused.

Memories swarmed her of the moment their powers touched—Kael's, the power of the Light, hers, the power of the Dark. They'd left Serolle a ruined mess. Its once Shining Wall fallen against the conical city, her army, hundreds of thousands of Phaerians, vaporized in the explosion.

I should have listened to Rammond.

Makayla's sigh misted the brisk morning air. Her gaze drifted down the mountain, past the rolling foothills, to the bustling Phaerian town Lurant. Foundries, smithies, and mills churned thick, black smoke into the air, draping the town in filth. She dreaded returning to the Phaerian town, but the ashen mountains still bore no food. Each visit to the town stabbed her pride, each unrecognized glance from towns-born sending a bitter-sweet pang of loss, reminding her she *had* been someone. Now, to her people, she was just another miserable little wretch begging for food.

I deserve no less, she thought with a guilt-laden sniff. *No…I deserve far worse.*

Kael would still gripe and moan to her about getting caught in the town. Then she'd ask what they were going to eat, and he'd complain about being bedridden again and wishing he could help her.

At least he can still shape.

An empty space still lingered in her soul where her power had resided. A foul void in her self corrupted by the Dark. Every time her will brushed through that void, her stomach churned, sickened by the knowledge of where that power had come from. At times, she grasped for it without thinking, reminding her how much she'd relied upon her power for mundane tasks, like lighting fires and cleaning clothes.

I should have known it was the Dark's.

The evidence had glared at her from behind a ball of blue energy swirling above the neck of the Sotouri she'd killed. Laa and Tolrik never would have given her the ability to create headless. Such a power could only come from Dra'Nahl.

Despite its profane source, Makayla still mourned its loss. She'd never felt more alive than she when she'd swam in its sweet embrace. It was a power more seductive than a lover's kiss, more intoxicating than a ruler's throne, and more liberating than death's embrace.

Her attention caught on a patrol of imperials heading north along the roadway from Lurant. They looked like tiny little ants on a tiny little path, joining the dozens of other ant patrols searching for her and Kael. East beyond the roadway, armies battled on rolling plains that stretched to the giant Serpent Sea. At night, the horizon glowed from New Torgeir's perpetual light, especially when clouds covered the sea.

Makayla pictured the infamous Island City swarming with a sea of alabaster skin, shimmering red temples, and tables piled with mounds of delicious food. Maybe not in the Workers District, if New Torgeir even had one. From what Kael said, life in the District seemed as miserable as any Phaerian town.

Almost.

As poor as Kael had been, he'd spent the first twenty years of his life behind the shelter of the Imperial Paradigm. He'd never wanted for food, and as rancid as his streets had been, the mud in the District wasn't composed of equal parts waste and refuse. He'd never scavenged through dumpyards, hoping to find working parts to fix his nu'oven. He'd never feared his home being inspected by imperial soldiers, or watched a man's tongue being ripped from his mouth over some imagined insult. No one had ever beaten him and left him for dead just for being born on the wrong side of a blasted wall. Kael had lived beneath the umbrella of evil, while she'd faced it.

Our lives couldn't be more different…and yet, I was the one who'd embraced the Dark.

Shivering against a biting wind, she stepped back inside the cave. She crossed the protective ward Kael had shaped, and a sensation washed over her, like walking through a gentle shower. Anyone else would have alerted Kael, the Crier of Change, the strongest shaper the world had ever known. A ward to incinerate flesh from bones would have been a better deterrent, but, as Kael had pointed out, it would have left a mess.

Best leave the shaping to someone who can still shape.

Kael insisted she hadn't snapped, and that the presence of a void suggested he should be able to repair the damage, but she dare not hope. That had died with Rammond, Hurian, and everyone else her pride had slaughtered. They'd all still be alive if Kael hadn't shown up. They would have swarmed over Rodak's army and taken Serolle.

A cold pang of truth washed over the lies. Rodak's forces, armed with pattern-forged weapons and armor, would have rolled over her army if Kael hadn't shown up and turned into the Light of Prophecy. Without him, her followers would have been subjected to the mercy of a Founder who had none. Without him, the Dark would still plague her soul.

Kael didn't kill my people. I did the moment I took that filthy power.

With a heavy sigh, Makayla wiped her watering eyes and continued to the back of the cave. The walls twisted around a couple of bends before opening to a wide chamber. A small, woodless fire warmed the room, fluttering above a pile of rocks, the flames shaped by the only person who still cared about her.

Even if I don't deserve it.

"Let me guess," Kael said, warming his gaunt hands by the fire. He might look like a skeleton with skin in rags, but at least he could walk. "There's nothing outside but ash and imperial patrols."

Makayla crouched next to him, and he dragged a blanket over their shoulders. The nu'clothes he'd shaped from grass and leaves looked and *almost* felt like cotton—thick and sturdy, though not as soft. "There's rain to the south again."

"Is it headed this way at least?"

"I wish," she mumbled, staring into the woodless fire. "What are we going to do? We can't stay here, unless you want me to keep making trips into Lurant?"

Kael grumbled and shook his head. "No, you're right. We can't stay. But where are we going to go?"

"Somewhere—anywhere!" She leaned her head on his shoulder. "You can take me to Onatah. I can finally meet Jouler and Pendric. Maybe we can all find some skirter village like Headwater."

His stories of the rustic village were her favorites. They seemed straight out of a book Rammond would have read to her, like the one about a boy and his dogs.

"You ever get the feeling," Kael said, his gaze lost on the fire, "that no matter how hard you try, no matter how good your intentions, everything you do turns out wrong in the worst way?"

"I wish I didn't know that feeling," she said. "At least you can still shape."

"You're not snapped," he said, and his ancient familiarity comforted her broken soul. "I can still sense the ability in you. Or, more specifically, the *lack* of ability."

"That makes no sense," she said.

"But it does," Kael replied. "It's too bad Jouler wasn't here. He'd explain it better." Kael rubbed his chin, and started to speak three times before saying, "It's like tracks in mud. They show a pocket in the ground where something had passed. You have such a pocket. People who snap do not." He grumbled, rubbing his face. "Who knows? Maybe if I become that figure of light again, I'll be able to give you your power back."

"Well, if you're going to do that," she said with a measured look. "You're going to have to put some meat on those bones, or you'll burn up like a sulphurstick."

"I just wish I could do something right for a change."

"We're alive. You got that right. Come on." Makayla stood and tugged him to his feet. "Some fresh air will do you good."

He grabbed the curved wooden pipe he'd shaped from an oak branch, plopped it in his mouth, and gave it a few pulls. He never smoked anything out of it, but he never left it out of his sight. "We could go to Nubidae," he said. "Reylan is there. No one knows the Prophecies like him. He'll know what we should do."

"And, for the tenth time," Makayla said, "how are we supposed to get there? Even if you were strong enough to make the journey, the Boorde Alliance is likely crawling with imperials, same as the roads. Why would Reylan even go there in the first place?"

"The Alliance is neutral," Kael replied. "They don't allow conflicts between Citizens and Phaerians within its borders."

"But why not go to some other Cabal outpost?"

"We can ask him when we see him," Kael said with a playful nudge. Outside the cave, he took a deep breath, smelling the morning air, and he frowned. "Still stinks like char. One more reason to leave, I guess." He looked back at the cave, then cast a thought-filled gaze down the mountainside. "I guess today is as good as any?"

"It's not like it's going to rain," Makayla said, sneering at the distant rain clouds on the southern horizon.

Kael's knee gave, and he almost fell to the ground.

"Easy," Makayla said, slipping an arm under his shoulder. "Can you make it to Nubidae?"

"It's closer than Onatah," he replied, shifting his gaze to the tall Boorde peaks. "We'll skirt far enough north of Lurant that no one will see us." He pointed to an intersection in the roadway where an old, overgrown path lead over rolling hills to what appeared to be an enormous pile of rubble. "We'll just follow that until no one can see us from the road, then head south to Nubidae. Just like that."

"Just like that," Makayla repeated, oozing doubt. "And, uh...*how* exactly are you getting there? You look like a strong wind would carry you away."

"That's not a bad idea." Kael looked down the mountainside with a contemplative frown. "But I think I might get stuck in one of the trees."

"Funny," she replied. "What do we do if we run into imperials?"

"You let me worry about the imperials."

"Ugh, why do men do that?" Makayla grumbled, savoring the confused look on his face. She deepened her voice and said, "Don't worry, helpless little girl. A man has arrived."

"That's not what I meant," Kael said.

"No?" Makayla said. "Then what, exactly, did you mean?"

"I just meant..." Kael chewed on a thought. "I meant, like, obviously I'll take care of the imperials because I can shape."

"Obviously," Makayla said. "That's the key word. Obviously. Do you think I needed another reminder that I'm helpless? Do you think I need some storybook hero to sweep me off my feet?" Come to think of it, that would have been nice right about now. A ruggedly handsome type who always said the right thing, even if it was wrong.

Especially when it was wrong.

Silence clung to the acrid morning air.

"I'm sorry." Kael pulled her into a side hug, and she squeezed his hand.

"Were you serious?"

"Of course," Kael replied. "You're right. I shouldn't have treated you like—"

"No," she said with a lazy wave to the foothills far below. "I mean, about leaving."

Kael took a deep breath, nodded as if to himself, and with a word, headed downhill. His knee gave, and he fell, rolling down the hill a few paces before sliding to a stop. He lifted his head, dusty ash covering his face.

"I'm alright," he said, waving, and Makayla burst into laughter.

Kael might not be a storybook hero. No bulging muscles would ever fill his skinny frame, and his unassuming dishwater-blond hair was far too matted and dirty to wave in any amount of wind. In every book Rammond had read to her, Kael would have been an unnamed character mentioned in passing, and yet, there he stumbled, covered in ash, as graceful as a two-legged dog—a true hero.

My hero.

"I'm sorry," he said, wiping his face with the inside of his shirt. "I get it, and I'm sorry.

"Sorry for what?" Makayla asked, sliding down the path he'd cleared.

"For the whole, don't worry, Little Lady, I'll save you."

"You're still thinking of that?"

"Of course," Kael said, continuing down the slope. "I offended you, and…and I'm sorry."

"I feel like you're going to ruin this with a 'but'."

"*However*," he said, nudging her, "I disagree that you're helpless."

She waited for his sarcastic remark, or witty joke, but when none came, she asked, "What do you mean?"

"You're a Facet of Prophecy," he replied, and her hope deflated.

"A powerless Facet," she said, unable to keep the bite from her voice. "You talk about not being able to do anything right, but *I* can't do anything. Me! I'm a fifteen-year-old townsborn, Kael. What am I supposed to do, pinch the Dark to death? Whatever plan Prophecy had for me died along with my power."

"You're wrong," Kael said, the ancient familiarity settling over Makayla. "You are the Facet, not your power. Jouler can't shape either. For all we know, I'm the only Facet born with any magical abilities." He rested his hands on her shoulders, and his kind gray eyes eased her anger. "You're important because of who you are. Your Path can still change the outcome of Prophecy."

Makayla offered him a weak smile, wishing she could believe him. "I still don't really understand this whole Facet and Path thing."

"You and me both," Kael replied. Not the response she'd been hoping. "But the more I think about it, the more sense it makes. Jouler would be proud of me."

"For what—thinking?"

"For being able to…" Kael paused, and he gave her a sharp nod. "Actually, yes, for thinking."

Makayla rummaged through her inner darkness for a laugh and settled for a weak smile.

Kael returned the dour look and helped her down a steep decline. "It helps to envision your Path of Prophecy as a literal path that you walk on. One path leads to the Light's victory over the Dark. The other leads to the Dark's."

"But, how do we know which Path we're on?" she asked. "I mean, I know which one I'm on now, but I was convinced I was on the Path of Light from the start. The power inside me didn't feel evil. It felt like power, like sweet, succulent invincibility coursing through my veins."

"Isn't that the way of evil?" Kael said. "Disguising itself behind a veil of righteousness, or a Shining Wall? The righteousness of our veil was seeing the empire for the evil it is. Slaughtering the Citizens of Serolle was the evil behind our veil."

"And what about everything they've done to us?" Makayla snapped, resisting the urge to send him sprawling down the slope.

"What about average, everyday Citizens like my parents? What about the children? What have they done, other than having been born on the wrong side of a wall? There has to be a way to topple the empire without killing everyone."

"Gods, you're so frustrating," Makayla growled, wishing he didn't make so much sense. "Aren't you the Facet who's supposed to guide us to the Path of Light, not drag us down into the depths of despair?"

"I'm sorry. I'm terrible at this," Kael said with a forced a smile. "Jouler would be able to explain it better."

Makayla chided herself for dragging the mood down again. At least Kael was trying to bring a little joy to their miserable existence, even if he tended to shove his feet in his mouth. "Jouler sounds like Rammond."

"In a lot of ways, he is," Kael said, bracing himself against a tree to catch his breath. "But Jo's not nearly as big. He's about my height, but from what you've said about Rammond, Jo's just as kind and gentle." Kael chuckled as if from a fond memory and continued down the ashen slope. "Pendric used to joke about how hard it was to get Jouler to fish, much less hunt."

Makayla followed Kael, sticking to the paths he cleared in the ash. His loyalty and fondness for his friends always tugged at her heart. Jouler, so smart and reasonable, and Pendric, whose love for food rivaled his childish heart. The image of Pendric's infectious laughter and Jouler's knowing smile warmed her against the stubborn gloom.

"Come on," Kael said, hopping over a log. "I'll bet we can make the foothills by dark."

"I don't know about you," Makayla said, hopping over the log and sliding past him. "But I'll make it."

THE GOLDEN SUN splashed the wispy sky in vibrant purple, pink, and red. Tall pines and beds of ferns swarmed over the Alrynn Foothills, waiting for a strong breeze or rain to rid them of the choking ash. Kael gave a fleeting thought to shape much-needed wind to clear the forest and restoring the land. Even if he could muster the strength, such a display of power would summon every Sotouri and Vrath within a hundred miles.

"You need some proper food," Makayla said, as if reading his mind. "A deer would be nice, or a nice juicy boar. What was your favorite food in Headwater?"

"Everything," he replied, pangs of hunger consuming the void in his self left by his missing Shield. "Food there was always good. Best I've ever had."

"Oh, come on," Makayla said, doubt lifting an eyebrow. "You had to have eaten some glorious meals at the Citadel."

"Until I landed in Headwater," Kael Replied, "I'd only eaten real food on rare-*rare* occasions. Like…both of them." She scoffed, and he told her it was true. "Even in the Citadel, I only ate nu'food. The first time I had food that wasn't made from a nu'oven was at a friend's house."

"What was it?" she asked.

"Tea and cake," Kael said, retelling his day at Tylel's estate in the Silver District. "Everything there looked so delicate. Like glass statues, of…weird shapes, I guess? I don't know what they were supposed to be. They looked so breakable, I was afraid to breathe in their direction."

Makayla's laughter flitted past the weakness gnawing at his limbs, and a smile pulled on his lips.

"No, really," Kael said. "The whole time I was there, I kept my head down and breathed through my nose."

"You didn't say anything?"

"Barely," he said, and she laughed again. His heart glowed at her joy, savoring those fleeting moments. He wanted to help ease her pain, but every time he tried, he seemed to make things worse for her. So, he endured his hunger and pain, and pushed through his exhaustion to make his little quips. "It was more like incoherent blabber than actual words."

Makayla smirked and rolled her eyes at him.

"In Headwater," Kael continued, "we ate a lot of potatoes."

"That's what we eat too," Makayla said. "Well, my family mostly turnips, but Father had a secret little plot of potatoes. Not many, but they were so yummy."

"You'll have to try Jouler's garlic butter-fried potatoes," Kael said. "It's especially good when he tops it with cheese and bacon crumble."

Makayla moaned and wiped her mouth. "Gods, that sounds so perfect right now."

"They also made this special liqueur," he said, remembering a picnic on a lakeshore, and a cherished kiss shared between two hearts. He swallowed back the painful memory before Livia's image ripped open his chest. "It's made from special peaches and roses."

"Sounds tasty," Makayla said. "But not as good as those potatoes."

"Or a big fat boar," Kael said.

He followed a winding game trail through the foothills, skimming through a thick grove of naked white birch and into a thicket of pines and ferns. A bushy fir had fallen over a tall granite boulder, the pine's branches still thick with needles.

"We'll stop here for the night." Kael pushed past the fatigue numbing his mind and submitted his will to the Currents. Scanning far and wide for the telltale ripple of pattern-forged gear, he waited to the count of a hundred before trickling a whisper of power. A tiny fluid pattern formed, its undulating twists and turns carrying the essence of blades made of force. With the speed of thought, he sliced into the branches of the fallen pine, creating a large pocket beneath the trunk. He shaped again, laying the branches to form a shelter to hide their fire. Before he could finish, exhaustion buckled his knees, and he crumbled to the ground.

"I'm fine," he said, waving off Makayla's concern. "I just need a little rest."

"Well, then just sit tight," Makayla said, helping him to sit against a large rock. "I'll setup our little shelter."

Kael rested his head back and released a weary sigh.

Sit tight, he mused. *What an odd idiom.*

A hand on his shoulder startled him, his soggy mind slow to understand the night sky and chirping symphony.

I fell asleep.

"Hey..." Makayla stirred him, nodding toward the shelter. "Come on. It's ready."

He crawled through a thick layer of branches and pine needles, and into their little shelter. A small crackling fire greeted him with the smell of burning pine.

"This is amazing," he said, continuing to a thick bed of fern fronds.

Makayla pulled branches over the opening, and she sat beside him. "Do you like it?"

"It's amazing," he said, pushing through his hunger to give her a wry smile. "But...where are you going to sleep?"

"Funny," she said. The small fire warmed her olive skin, her dark curly hair a far cry from the smooth black locks from his dreams. She leaned her head on his shoulder, as she'd done every night since that terrible day.

Kael fought against the exhaustion ravaging his body, refusing to lie down and fall asleep until her jaw cracked with a yawn.

Patting his hand, she lay on the bed of fern fronds and pulled him down beside her. "How is someone so skinny, so warm?"

"Luck?" he mumbled.

"Don't worry," she mumbled, her voice drifting through Kael's fading mind. "We'll find you some food in the morning."

MAKAYLA ROLLED from under Kael's arm, his gaunt body surprisingly warm through the night. Sunlight peeked through branches and pine needles, piercing their shelter with thin rays. Grabbing a stick, she poked the muted remains of their fire, scattering the ash to uncover what little heat remained. A handful of dry pine needles, a few puffs of breath, and soon, a tiny flame flickered to life. She stacked more needles and added small sticks until a small fire crackled warmth into the shelter.

After checking Kael's pulse, she crawled through the wall to scavenge for food. The brisk chill scattered what little remained of her sleep, and her breath caught on the majesty of the forest. A diaphanous morning mist covered the forest floor, glowing where rays of sunlight leaked through the pine tops. Ferns poked through the mist, dew beading on their fronds, while high above, birds chirped and sang from the branches.

She headed into the forest, keeping the warm sun at her face. Rammond would have loved it here. So would Kael, but he needed his rest more than he needed a beautiful sight. He also needed food. Some meat would be nice, though she had no idea how she would fell a skittish deer, much less a charging boar. Maybe she'd stumble into a patch of berries, or better yet, a grove of fruit, or...

She froze, her ravenous belly growling with glee. "Pears!"

Vision watering, she clambered around the base of the tall trees, searching for fallen fruit. Most had rotted, adding an overly-sweet aroma to the brisk morning air, but more than a few promised a tasty delight. She bit into a pear, and sweet, glorious juice exploded in her mouth, dripping down her chin. She devoured three more pears before scooping some in her shirt for Kael. Mouth and fingers sticky, and a belly full of fruit, she made her way back to the shelter.

Squeezing through the outer branches, she displayed her treasure to Kael. His blubbering cry yanked at her heart, and she promised him she'd already eaten her fill.

"I probably ate too many," she said, holding a hand to her churning belly.

"Did you see any game?" he asked.

"None. But, there are a lot more pears. Maybe you can dry some with your power, now that you aren't going to whither away and die."

His gaze grew distant for a few breaths, undoubtedly searching for Vrath and Sotouri. After the count of a hundred, he smiled, and their shelter sliced open to the brisk morning air. He shivered, rubbing his hands together. "Let's go find some more pears."

THE SUN DIPPED WELL past its zenith, promising a couple more hours of light. Kael crouched behind a bush on a large mound, watching an imperial foot patrol heading south from Lurant to Gasolde, both towns hidden beyond the horizon.

"How much longer are we going to sit here and watch?" Makayla sputtered her lips.

"You said there were a handful of patrols," Kael said.

"There are."

"Dozens aren't a handful." Kael grabbed some dried pears, wishing they'd discovered another grove on their way down.

"Maybe reinforcements arrived?" Makayla said.

Kael lifted his finger to his lips.

Less than twenty paces away, the patrol heading north passed by their mound. Across the road from Kael, the old roadway he'd spotted drew the soldiers' attention, the path barely visible beneath all the grass and bushes.

Kael waited until he could no longer hear their raucous laughter, then led Makayla down the hill.

"How do you feel?" Makayla asked.

"Better, after all those pears," Kael replied, patting his pouch full of dried fruit. He itched to let his will gorge on the Currents, to let that sweet power course through him, but he didn't dare submit his will this close to so many roving patrols. "What I really crave is meat. A thick juicy slab of meat sounds perfect. Or a whole cow, even. I think I'd actually be back to normal after that."

"Normal will be nice for a change," Makayla said.

"You say that now." Kael pointed across the road to a distant patch of bushes. "We'll stop there."

"That's a little far, don't you think?" Makayla asked.

"Not if we run."

Makayla's lips curled with a wry smile. "Do you think you can make it?"

"Just try to keep up," Kael said, nudging her off balance before taking off.

"Hey!" Makayla chirped, waving her arms to regain her balance.

Kael's strength waned, his legs and lungs begging for relief. Makayla ran past him with a giggle, her long, curly hair bouncing. Kael looked behind him, casting his gaze up and down the barren roadway. Side splitting by the time he reached the bush, he collapsed, gulping for air.

"Gods," Makayla said, handing him a waterskin. "You have a terrentor crawling in your stomach."

Kael pressed a hand to his raging belly and reached into his pouch. "Blast!"

"All gone?" Makayla asked. "Me too. Doesn't a slab of roasted cottlewomp sound good?" She giggled at his cringe. "What? It's good! Pendric would like it."

"Pendric likes everything," Kael replied, warmed by her familiarity with his friends.

"Have you ever thought about what you'll do when this is all over?"

Kael's heart dropped, and he pushed himself to his feet. "Come on. The roadway is still clear."

"You don't believe we have a future," Makayla said, walking beside him. "Do you?"

He shook his head, unable to tell her Tálise had told him as much. *Step through that door*, the god had said, *and happiness will remain forever beyond your reach.*

"It doesn't matter—"

"Maybe not to you," Makayla growled.

"What I meant to say," Kael replied, chiding himself for spoiling the mood. Tálise said *he* wouldn't find happiness, not everyone else. Besides, right now, they could both use a bit of hope. "What I *should* have said was that I try not to think about the end of Prophecy. I don't know what our future holds, but I know what Prophecy says about the future if we don't succeed."

Makayla sighed and gave him a playful bump. "Well, I plan on finding a nice plot of land far from the empire. Maybe I'll plant some potatoes and convince Jouler to cook me some of those butter-fried potatoes you're always talking about."

"So, Jouler is there too?" Kael asked, a cool breeze chilling his sweat-soaked clothes. He'd shape some thicker nu'clothes as soon as they were far enough away from prying shapers.

"Why not?" she said with a shrug. "We can all live there. You, me, Pendric, Jouler...whoever."

"Your own little Cabal outpost," Kael said, his grimy trousers swishing in the dried grass.

"No," Makayla said. "After this, I want nothing to do with the Cabal or the empire or Prophecy. Nothing. Just a quiet place, far away from everything."

"That sounds perfect," Kael said, fatigue seeping into his legs and chest. He ensured Makayla that he could at least make it to the other side of the hillock, even as his body begged him to stop and lay down, here and now. His resolve drained with each step up the steady climb, his will teetering on collapse. His head pounded, his pack like a mountain on his back. He spared another glance over his shoulder, and a flutter of hope lightened his feet. Not a hint of a patrol marred the distant roadway.

Makayla reached the top of the hillock and froze.

"No, keep going," Kael called between breaths. "They'll see you."

He reached her side, and a hard tug at the back of his mind dragged him to his knees. A mindtrap formed around his will, blocking him from the Currents. Three Vrath raced up the other side of the hillock, two in black chainmail trimmed in orange, the third in an officer's jacket. Behind them, a platoon of soldiers marched beside three large, ornate coaches lacquered in red and green.

"Phlem," one of the do'Vrath snarled, as bands of force lifted Kael and Makayla off the ground.

The other do'Vrath lifted an eyebrow, a single lieutenant's knot tied on his black-and-orange cord. "Don't let Lady Maelly hear you say that."

The first do'Vrath rolled his eyes, his hungry gaze resting on Makayla. "What a fine catch."

The third Vrath bore captain's knots on the green-and-yellow cord dangling around his shoulder. He stroked his grizzled beard, measuring Kael and Makayla under a hard, calculating gaze. "Isol," the captain barked, and the do'Vrath with hungry eyes snapped right fist to left shoulder in salute. "Report to Sergeant Arnith. Tell him…" The captain mulled over a thought. "Tell him I hope his grandchildren are doing well."

"Captain?" Isol said, finding no help in the lieutenant's flat stare.

"Did I stutter?" the captain asked.

"No, Sir." Isol cleared his throat. "I am to report to Sergeant Arnith, and tell him you hope his grandchildren are doing well."

The captain lifted an eyebrow. "Dismissed."

Isol snapped a salute and marched back to camp.

"Lieutenant Baelorin," the captain said, turning back to Kael and Makayla. "Tell me what you see?"

"Phaerians, Sir." Baelorin turned his young, rosy-cheeked smirk on Kael.

The captain sighed, mumbling and rubbing the bridge of his nose. "Look a little deeper, lieutenant."

Baelorin's confident smirk cracked, and he cleared his throat. "Um…they can both shape? Otherwise, the mindtraps wouldn't have worked."

Hope pierced through the fear, wrinkling Makayla's brow.

"Very good," the captain said, his dispassionate tone saying otherwise. "Go tell our fine Founder we caught a pair of Cabalists."

"Yes, Sir." The lieutenant scowled at Kael before heading toward the coaches.

"Now," the captain said, addressing Kael and Makayla. "Where might two Cabalists be headed? There aren't any villages within a dozen leagues of here."

A distant shout pulled the captain's attention to Lieutenant Baelorin waving at him at him from camp. The captain put his head in his hand and sighed. Without warning, Kael and Makayla lifted in their bonds and floated down the slope behind him.

"Captain," the lieutenant said, saluting again. "Lady Maelly wants to see the prisoners."

"You don't say?" the captain mumbled, walking past the lieutenant to the middle coach. The captain sighed as though preparing for some unsavory task, then he knocked on the door. "I'm here with the prisoners, My Lady."

Kael's invisible bonds vanished. His knees buckled under his own weight, and he crumbled to the ground.

The door to the coach opened, and an alabaster-skinned Founder stepped out, her ruby-red hair blazing in the sunlight. "Captain Gwyndril," she said, her voice dripping with condescension. "Why was…" She offered a dismissive wave. "Oh, I'm so bad with names. Why did you have one of your men detained?"

The captain nodded to Makayla.

"I see," the ruby-haired Founder said, icy rage drawing her brow. "Feed him a chain."

"Of course, My Lady." Captain Gwyndril tilted his head in a nod before dismissing himself.

"Disgusting," the Founder mumbled as if to herself, stroking her shining red hair. Her face softened, and she pulled Makayla away from Kael. "Do not worry, dear," she said, scowling at him. "I'll keep you safe. My name is Lady Maelly. What's yours, dear?"

Panic washed over Makayla's face, her hands shaking. "Ma... Mandy."

"Hmmm..." Maelly frowned and shook her head. "No. I think Eglona suits you better, don't you?" Makayla looked to Kael for help, but the Founder stepped in front of her. "You do *not* have to ask him for approval anymore, child. You don't have to ask any man for anything, yes?"

Makayla nodded, then shook her head, her chin quivering.

"Oh, poor thing." Maelly's too-green eyes smoldered at Kael, and she draped a protective arm over Makayla. She called over her shoulder, "Aglia! Are you sure this is him?"

A wretched, emaciated soul peaked out the coach door. Thin black hair curled from her scalp, the lifeless locks falling on her Phaerian drab blouse. Her nose, swollen and off center from too many breaks, whistled with each breath. She winced when she saw Kael, and she shied back into the shadows of the coach.

"That's him!" she shouted.

The unforgettable voice ripped Kael's breath from his lungs. "Livia?"

"That's the bastard that killed Lord Rodak's child."

17

NEW TORGEIR

A low din rumbled through the spacious palace room from dozens of concubines in waiting lounged on plush white sofas, chairs, and chases. White drapes stretched from tall walls, reaching the pristine marble floor. Pattern-forged chandeliers floated among the high ceilings, casting warm light over the expansive room.

White... Freja thought, maintaining her dispassionate mask while she cringed inside. *Everything is so blastedly white.*

The only color in the room radiated from the concubines' clothes, jewelry, and hair, although most of them pandered with imperial red. Other than Freja in a simple lavender dress, bare at the shoulders with a slit running halfway up her thigh, only a handful of concubines dared express any personality. That, or their tastes were as bland as their fair skin.

Far more woman than men filled the large room. One hundred and two to the men's fifty-six, to be exact, bringing the current total to one hundred and fifty eight. The number had fallen from one hundred and sixty-eight, but accidents were prone to happen, especially around the precarious heights found in New Torgeir. She doubted her Sotouri would take out a Founder, but, so far, most of Freja's serious threats to win the emperor's hand had met an untimely end. Which meant

Hrodny wasn't a serious threat. It seemed the blasted woman would pester Freja to her dying day.

Seated on a plush chair, and surrounded by a pathetic group of ladies, Hrodny almost seemed competent. To her credit, she'd amassed more allies than Freja had expected, even attracting the notice of a couple Gold Ladies—Milehnez from Blailon, and Lyfennia from Castantor. Not that any of it would matter. The emperor might bed all as his concubines, only one could be the Imperial Consort and bear imperial heirs.

We're all after the same prize. Well…most of us.

The beautiful men in the room longed for a life of luxury and power.

"Still here, Freja?" Valgred said with a measured look. Much like the woman, her imperial-red gown tried too hard to be noticed. Loose waves of fabric struck down the length of her gown, washing onto the white marble floor. Her gaze flitted over Freja's tight curly hair and bronze skin, and she mouthed, *Phlem-tone whore.*

Sugrid, Valgred's cute little button of a shadow, sneered at Freja. The insipid Silver Lady's pattern-forged shawl and dress wavered with different colors. Pearls and polished bits of abalone shell decorated braids that swam in green, purple, and blue.

At least she has some taste.

"Standing in the back, as usual," Sugrid said, her purple lips curling with an empty smile. "Away from your betters."

Taste, Freja thought, *but not class.*

She blinked with feigned innocence. "But, then…what does that say about the two of you standing here with me?"

Valgred sniffed and turned away with Sugrid lapping her heels to sit with the rest of the low-hanging fruit.

"Such a lively group," Svala said, handing Freja a tulip glass brimming with the emperor's favorite peach liqueur. The young Bronze Lady seemed content to live in Freja's shadow, acting more like a lady-in-waiting than a contender for the emperor's hand. Svala's long silver hair fell past the elegant straps of her sapphire-blue dress, the tips of her locks swishing the small of her exposed back.

"At least the drink is good," she said, tapping her glass to Freja's.

Freja glided her finger up Svala's arm, watching bumps trail her touch. She leaned in to whisper, and their cheeks brushed, Slava's inviting aroma twisting Freja's thoughts. "And the company."

Freja sipped the silky liqueur, savoring the rush of peach that warmed her throat, and the notes of rose that lingered on her tongue. Imitations of the liqueur came close, but nothing tasted quite like the real thing, which made this occasion quite special. If Deidan's last message was true, this glass of the emperor's favorite drink could very well be the last she sipped. Apparently, Lord Rodak Toren had unknowingly blasted the land that had given the liqueur's peaches their unique flavor, but no one wanted to tell the emperor.

Least of all me, she thought with another sip.

Svala squeezed Freja's wrist, warning of an approaching Sotouri. The young Bronze Lady bit her lip when Taloran walked past, her hungry gaze following him to the back wall. "He looks like he would be...fun. Tall, dark, and dangerous." Svala shivered. "*So* much fun."

"And about as interesting as granite," Freja said, using another one of her father's play on words. Granite, it turned out, was quite fascinating. Granite formed Yrsa's tallest peaks, could dull the sharpest blade, and could be polished to shine like marble.

"You say that about every Sotouri. And it's not like I'm not trying to talk to them. In fact, it's a little better when they don't."

"I don't say that about Sotouri women."

"True," Svala admitted. "You call them blank sheets of paper."

Also fascinating, Freja thought. The words they carried could destroy a kingdom or portray the crude musings of a curious little mind.

"See the Silver Lady standing behind Hrodny? The one being as conspicuous with her eavesdropping as a District whore."

"Madya Laiy," Svala said with a chuckle.

"Go compliment her hair."

"But it's..."

"As flamboyantly uninteresting as the others?" Freja said of the gregarious hairstyles. "When everyone is extravagant..."

"No one is extravagant," Svala finished, caressing her silky smooth locks. "Then why would I compliment her hair?"

"Because she's a talker," Freja replied, and Svala dipped her head.

"And *that* is why you'll be the emperor's Consort," she said, her hand lingering on Freja's. "They're all playing Foxes and Hares, while you're playing at Kings and Castles."

I'll be the emperor's Consort, Freja thought, following Svala's enticing stride as the succulent woman waded into the crowd. *And you'll be mine.*

"She's right," Taloran said, startling Freja.

She slapped the Sotouri's shoulder. "You should try sneaking up on Svala some time. Preferably in her bedroom."

"I have my eyes on sweeter fruit," Taloran replied, his gaze darting about the room.

"Well, then…" Freja said, handing him her empty tulip glass. "I recommend the emperor's liqueur."

Taloran chuckled and offered a sweeping bow. "It's great to see you, Little Mouse."

"Can you believe this?" Freja said, jerking her chin at the other concubines. "Serolle was destroyed, and the emperor is gathering men and women from across the empire to satiate his imperial needs." Freja took a settling breath. "What about Blailon's northern towns?"

"Blet and Toliane both fly the Banner of Light."

"Damn, that was fast."

"Very," Taloran said. "Not only did Rodak *not* end the uprising, as he claims, but apparently, not a finger has been lifted to stop this Voice person."

"That's impossible," Freja said, a flash of worry biting at her stoic mask. "But, the town guard—"

"All wear the Voice's colors," Taloran said. "They stuck a hot poker to their Shields."

"Why would they…" Freja shook the disturbing image of melted temples from her mind. "Does the emperor know? What's he doing about it?"

"Like you said…" Taloran gestured to the concubines.

"Meanwhile, two towns fly some crazed man's banner," Freja said. "Any news from Blailon? Isn't a Phaerian rebellion the very thing that rouses King Ashtur's loins?"

"Nothing yet," Taloran mumbled, "but I doubt he wants news of his incompetence to spread."

"Speaking of incompetence," Freja said, filing the Sotouri's news for later. "The emperor is supposed to be here, right?"

"Any moment."

"And you're sure he'll choose me?"

Taloran's smirk dripped with hunger. "Positive."

The door opened, and a young blond harpist strummed into the room. The emperor's Founder-white crier followed, her melodic voice as beautiful and seductive as her curves. She put a fist to her mouth and cleared her throat, her gossamer white dress swishing around her ankles.

"Emperor Orn Thjodoft IV," the crier announced, "last of his name, Seal of New Torgeir, Sovereign of the Five Kingdoms."

Silence draped over the room, and an almost handsome man walked in, his smooth hair almost as white as his skin. A diaphanous sheet looped around his body and draped from his arm, his sizable manhood dangling between legs as bereft of definition as the rest of his body. Concubines coughed and shifted in their seat, undoubtedly disappointed by the man who looked so different from his busts and portraits. Their looks seemed lost on the emperor, who floated above the opinions of his lessers, drifting in a realm of pleasure while his empire crumbled around him.

His gaze drifted over his precious little treasures, lust glimmering in his eyes until his gaze fell upon Freja. His empty smile fell, his lust dissipating into awe, and the other concubines wilted.

Freja swallowed her disgust, trying not to think about the future she would have to endure. She tilted her head, acknowledging the emperor.

It won't be your empire for long.

18

VIDIMIR

Jouler soared in his dream, high above a wide tundra speckled in red, orange, and yellow. Far below, a herd of cottlewomp grazed on the colorful fields. Like cows with fluffy wool, the cottlewomp seemed oblivious of the causeway or the wagons and coaches speeding toward a massive, conical city with an imposing wall.

A Shining Wall.

Jouler flipped through his memories of imperial cities situated on the empire's northern seas. Only two cities endured Torgeir's frozen coastline, but neither matched the land spread before him. Neuheim rose beside a large bay which this coastline lacked, and the horn Gorgosant rested upon pointed east not north.

The city called to Jouler, begging him to come back home. His heart yearned for its Shining Walls and familiar smells—plowed fields, ripe peach orchards, and dew on warming grass.

No, that's not right.

Those memories had come from Headwater, his real home, not this monstrosity...hadn't they? Imperial cities couldn't accommodate such rustic experiences, and yet, his chest swelled like a man coming home after a lifelong journey.

But, coming home to where?

Sharp pain lanced the back of his head, and he found himself beside the causeway. A long coach with red-lacquered walls, led by a majestic team of six black mares, careened past a simple cart and its draft horse. Elaborate yellow and orange scrollwork trimmed the wagon's black edging, and a complex geometric symbol graced the smooth black roof. The driver, in matching red-and-black long coat, cracked the reins with a sharp shout, and the geometric symbol flared on the coach's roof, speeding the coach toward the mysterious city.

The aged driver of the simple cart waved as the coach raced down the causeway. Drawn by a single horse as weathered as the driver, the cart brimmed with baskets full of cottlewomp wool. Jouler waved at him, but the man didn't seem to notice. That, or he didn't care about a lone stranger standing beside a causeway in the middle of a tundra.

The poor fellow had to be a Districter, like Kael, or the lacquered coach would have stopped. No lord would deign allow a Phaerian to travel on their precious causeway. The old man's drab clothes with their myriad patches cried townsborn, yet his confidence cried Citizen. He turned his kind, wrinkled face to the sky, and drew in a long breath, his temple—his very dirty, very *naked* temple—dull in the afternoon sun.

He's Phaerian?

Jouler rolled awake in his bed, struggling between dream and reality. Soft, warm light flickered from a pair of candles melting on a desk at the far side of a large room. Black, polished walls reflected the candlelight, reminding him of his room inside House Nith'Iil while his mind clung to the memory of a home that had never been his.

Kael had spoken of such dreams that felt like more than dreams, though his had been about an alabaster-skinned girl, not an old Phaerian traveling an imperial causeway, or a city that didn't exist on any maps Jouler had seen.

Muffled laughter drifted from the floor vents, heating his room. The soft, rumbling joy from Dilna and L'Veyna sparked curious thoughts about the mischief they must be planning. They hadn't left each other's side since they'd arrived, and they already had half the House staff watching for them.

Dilna's sharp cackle ignited a flurry of muffled laughter, drumming a chuckle in Jouler's chest. He flipped his pillow, curled under his blanket, and let his mind drift to the joy of mischievous youth.

L'Veyna stalked the halls of House Nith'Iil, trying to ignore her sour stomach. According to Reylan's experiments, it took at least a dozen pattern forgings to give her an ignorable ache, like shaping a tiny-tiny flame. That wouldn't have been so bad, but every part of this plagued building seemed pattern forged—walls, floors, the rotten glowtiles that gave the illusion of sunlight beaming through stained glass ceilings. Like the majestic scene above her on the bottom floor, depicting a broken landscape laden with mystery. Boorde were supposed to be heartless killers, ruled by fits of dispassionate logic, not masterful artisans, craftsmen, and cooks. What they did to the fruits and vegetables she asked, she had no clue, but it had to involve some sort of magic despite whatever her brother and Reylan claimed. Even Pendric agreed that food shouldn't taste so good. Not that he seemed to mind. He'd filled out over the past two weeks, no longer as emaciated as a townsborn.

And Jouler...

She hadn't exactly avoided him these past few weeks. He just spent all his time in places she'd rather not be. Like the training yard with Eldri, or rummaging through the library, collecting books with Reylan. Besides, Jouler rarely visited her little garden, so why should she go visit him? Not that she *needed* him to see it, but a little time with her plants would do him good, especially in this lifeless landscape. Pendric and Dilna visited her tiny garden all the time, and without having to beg. Especially not Pendric, who found it easier to breathe among the plants. Dilna almost spent as much time in the garden as L'Veyna, but their souls grew from the same soil.

My Human twin.

L'Veyna's chest warmed, hoping to find Dilna in the garden. If not for chancing upon that dotard Reylan, she'd be with Dilna, searching this plagedly beautiful labyrinth the Boorde called a house for hidden rooms and passages. Diou and Katima had promised her these walls held as many secrets as their mother, Matron Nith'Iil, but after a few weeks, Dilna and L'Veyna had only stumbled upon two very nondescript rooms with no furnishings.

L'Veyna cast her gaze to the mirror-like floor, watching her feet meet their reflection as she walked, mesmerized by the stained-glass ceiling painted across the polished black floor. Instead of more emerald herons, depictions of verdant, bountiful lands graced the ceiling in this part of the massive house. It showed the Time of Plenty, the era following Alnazet's victory over Dra'Nahl, when none would want or cry for war.

Of all the races in this plagued world, the battle-hungry Boorde got the peaceful Prophecy, while fate condemned her people, the race that cherished life, to death and devastation.

And I'll be at the head of it all. Me, Jouler, and an army of saplings.

For all the time that man spent in the library, Jouler hadn't discovered much more about the Saplings Curse. Maybe if he spent less time in the training yard, and more time meditating in the garden, he'd figure out how to save her people. Instead, he wasted countless hours twirling a staff, and pouring over books that, according to him, held more lies than truths. Then again, how much did she expect him to find without copies or sketches of Mh t'Pralab to study? If her people hadn't retreated from the rest of the world, maybe a Boorde scholar could have uncovered the mysteries of the Saplings Curse.

Too many ifs, Jouler would say. She deepened her voice in her best impression of the astute Phaerian, and she mumbled, "Focus on solutions before you if yourself off a cliff."

Her voice trailed under penetrating fire-diamond gazes from Boorde passing her in the halls. They always seemed so…self important. It didn't help that her head hardly rose above their waist, so they *had* to look down at her, but they could at least show a hint of emotion.

And I thought Diou was bad.

She grinned at the tall, statuesque Boorde, amazed at their undeniable beauty. Men, women, and eidraael—a beautiful concept of people who flowed between genders that the Prytha should have adopted long ago—every Boorde was as captivating as a sunrise in black and white. After a time, the subtle differences in their features grew more apparent to L'Veyna's untrained eyes. Katima's lips, for example, were a little fuller than other Boorde's, her cheekbones slightly higher, her...her *everything* was just better, and it seemed to run in her blood. Where Katima carried the grace of the gods, Diou bore their wrath, his unflinching gaze devoid of emotion when he entered that deadly dance. It reminded her of Jouler, the way he carried himself in the training yard, as if every emotion had fled from his heart, and he floated on a sea of apathy.

L'Veyna followed a route she took multiple times a day, winding through the labyrinthine halls to her garden. Reylan's urgency nagged at her as she walked through the visitor's wing of House Nith'Iil, past the Human and Prytha quarters, to her garden. Well, the Keepers' Garden to be precise, but no other visiting Keeper had maintained more than a small patch of moss.

So...it's mine!

She opened the garden door, welcoming the wave of relief as her sour stomach abated. Light from glowing crystals meant to mimic the sun filled the quaint room during the day, and twinkled with mock-starlight at night, while vents blew warm breezes. Soft beds of moss now blanketed the floor and climbed its walls. The wooden bench she'd asked waited for her alongside one wall, with a thriving fern on either side. A colorful island grew from the center of the room, bristling with clusters of aster flowers, their petals like purple needles bristling from a bright yellow ball, stalks of white-capped yarrow, and blanket flowers, with bursts of red and orange edged in yellow.

She could have stayed here the rest of the day, asking food and tea, soaking in Alnazet's glory, but Reylan's demand that she fetch Jouler and the others nagged at her mind.

"And for the Light's sake, hurry," he'd said.

My garden is on the way to the library...sort of.

Growling over the seed of guilt growing in her belly, she asked nutrients into the garden. Her ever-blossoming power flared, and tiny prickles stippled the back of her head. The nebulous image locked into place, and gentle beads of dew kissed the garden. She'd endure the sharp discomfort every time to see life flourish in these frozen heights. Rubbing her neck, she bid the plants a good morning and headed for the library, where she prayed she might happen upon Dilna and everyone else. Heatless everburning sconces flickered up the five floors of House Nith'Iil's massive library. In the center of the tall room, light from a giant stained-glass ceiling splashed an emerald heron over the people in the circular reading area.

"Can I help you, My Lady?" a librarian asked.

L'Veyna craned her neck, entrapped by the tall Boorde's lustrous eyes. They might not be as colorful as gems, but their almond shape and fiery tone never ceased to catch her breath. "I...no. I mean yes. Yes, you can help me. I hope. Have you seen—" As soon as the words left her mouth, she saw Dilna at one of the tables. "Never mind, I see her. Have you seen my brother?"

"He left a moment ago," the librarian said, dipping her head.

"Thank you," L'Veyna replied, remembering to bow. For a race as emotionless as their black-marble buildings, Boorde were quite sensitive about their honor.

Who needs forty-something ways to say the plagued word? And gods forbid I use the wrong word, or offer the wrong bow, or bow when I shouldn't have...

"Where have you been?" Dilna asked, banishing L'Veyna's nagging thoughts with a warm hug. "Your brother and Pen were just here. They went to go find Reylan."

"Of course they did," L'Veyna grumbled. "That old curmudgeon has me running around looking for everyone. He's got some news he's all excited about."

Dilna's giggle fluttered through L'Veyna's chest. "I can already see him rubbing his nose," Dilna said, her infectious giggle fluttering through L'Veyna's chest. Neither could laugh without the other joining. Dilna frowned and deepened her voice. "Hurry now, lass. This is important."

"It's almost like you know him," L'Veyna said.

"You should see him on a horse," Dilna said, rolling her eyes.

"What's he got you doing?" L'Veyna asked.

Dilna gestured to the three books on the table. "He wanted all the books that mention the Black Breath."

"Three, that's it?" L'Veyna asked, her gaze drifting over the library's countless shelves, bristling with books.

"The librarians are still looking." Dilna scooped the books into a cloth satchel, then she took L'Veyna's hand. "Come on, let's go get Jo."

"He's in the training yard, isn't he?" L'Veyna asked, letting Dilna pull her out of the library. "I didn't want to be cold today. Let's go grab our coats, I guess."

Sweat soaked Jouler's shirt, the afternoon sun glaring at him from a pristine blue sky. Ignoring the clamor infesting the training yard, he dipped his staff, inviting his opponent to attack. Only a few years older than he, Banvith stood a whole head taller than Jouler, the Boorde's too-black ry'ku stark against his snow-white skin.

Banvith lunged, and Jouler twisted past the attack, letting the Boorde's staff slide off his own. Banvith entered a familiar stance, his feet together, staff clutched in his arm and pointed at the ground. In the space of a thought, Jouler's mind flickered through strategies against the Third Basic Form, some feeling more right than others. Guided by his Gift of Prophecy, Jouler struck, his movements feeling right the way true words of Prophecy snapped into place when he spoke.

Banvith held against Jouler's whirlwind attack, but the Boorde's juvenile battle prescience couldn't match Jouler's Gift. In a fluid motion, Jouler slid toward his opponent, angling his staff to block Banvith's swooping attack and pulling the Boorde's leg off balance.

"Flames!" Banvith cursed, toppling to his back.

Onlookers clapped and murmured in their all-black clothes, their fire-diamond pupils focused on Jouler.

"I almost had you," Banvith said, the eidraael's feminine voice and figure still jolting Jouler's sensibilities. Their entire culture seemed composed of opposites—philosophy and war, too-black hair and snow-white skin, their domain frozen while a fire raged within them. Only eidraaels danced between both extremes, courting roles and customs forbidden to men and women.

Balance, Jouler realized. Eidraael existed in a realm of harmony, balanced between the Boorde extremes.

"One of these days," Banvith said, "you'll have to show me how you got so good so quickly."

"Diou taught him," another Boorde said, a curved sidaiyo stuck through the belt of his too-black ry'ku. His fire-diamond pupils were almost as brilliant as Banvith's, belying an age closer to Katima's—a little over a century. After a couple of weeks in the Alliance, Jouler still struggled to discern their subtle age differences. Even the oldest Boorde looked no older than Jouler, and could still outrun him. Other than their eyes, nothing faded with time, not their hearing, not their strength, not their endurance. Even their mind stayed crisp throughout the centuries. So close to perfection, it was no wonder Boorde looked so similar.

Banvith bowed to the newcomer. "Ansis. It is always an honor to see you."

"And you," Ansis replied, his thick accent rolling over the words. He turned to Jouler, and gestured to the tall, white onlookers draped in too-black clothes. "They're calling you Vidimir."

"What does it mean?" Jouler asked, feigning ignorance of the Boorde language. Diou's warning about his mother, Matron Nith'Iil, still chilled Jouler's nerves. She could not learn about his Gift of Prophecy.

"Just so," Ansis said, bowing his head in a show of respect. "Your mastery of our weapons has some of us believing the Dawn of Prophecy has come. However," Ansis said, his tone belying how little he thought of the believers, "rational minds believe you are a prodigy, much like another Human who passed through here."

"Grim did not pass through the Alliance," Banvith said. "He tore through it like a blizzard."

Jouler's mouth went dry with memories of that evil man and his endless lessons, dragging Jouler, Kael, and Pendric through the Shattered Plains, pushing them through their exhaustion.

"And what would you know of him?" Ansis asked, his thick accent.

Jouler almost replied before Banvith said, "And how old were you when Grim dragged his taint through our land?"

"That matters not," Ansis replied.

"You were a swaddling ember when he left," Banvith said.

"I was old enough to walk," Ansis said, "and to remember every time my father took me to watch him."

"What was he like?" Jouler asked, donning his thick leather coat lined with soft cottlewomp wool.

"Very...Human," Ansis replied. "Talented, but it still took him years to learn what you seem to have picked up in a few weeks. I wonder if you could learn to harmonize your inner flame. Grim never could, but you... Boorde steel might actually glow in your hands, Vidimir."

"You should learn the sidaiyo with me," Banvith said.

"Like I've told everyone else," Jouler said, switching his sweat-soaked eye wrap before it froze to his face. "I don't like swords."

"How do you know, unless you try?" Banvith offered.

"I don't have to eat putrid food," Jouler replied, "to know I won't like it."

"Ah," Ansis said, holding up a finger, "but you do have to smell it, or see it. You need to experience it on some level to know you won't like it."

"I've already trained with the sidaiyo," Jouler said, spotting two pairs of familiar eyes among the sea of fire-diamond pupils—one set of eyes as dark as his, the other set sparkling like emeralds.

Wrapped in a bundle of furs, L'Veyna motioned for him to hurry, while Dilna waved hello.

"One should not make such claims," Ansis said, the threat in his voice sharpening Jouler's attention. "Not unless you are prepared to defend them. I am not sure how you Humans comport your affairs, but Boorde hold honor above all."

Banvith backed away, bowing, and Jouler cursed himself for being so careless with his words.

"I don't have a sword," Jouler said, his gaze resting on Ansis' curved sidaiyo.

L'Veyna shook her head, and motioned again for him to hurry, while more onlookers gathered for the challenge. As if summoned, a young Boorde pulled away from the thick cluster, his black robes swishing, a pair of wooden practice sidaiyo clutched in his snow-white arms.

Jouler looked from Banvith retreating into the crowd to the sly smile pulling the corners of Ansis' lips, and the sour pang of betrayal roiled his anger. They'd both planned this—the sparring, the casual conversation, the feigned friendship, and offer to train.

"Get him, Jo!" Dilna shouted, igniting a flurry of chuckles.

A rumble of commotion crept up through the crowd, following Diou into the circular clearing. "What is this?"

Ansis faltered, bending at the waist in a deep bow. "The Human claims to have trained with the sidaiyo, and—"

"He has," Diou said, cutting off Ansis. "Unless you care to challenge my claim?"

Ansis bowed again and again with emphatic assertions of Diou's impeccable honor, while the onlookers dissipated throughout the training yard.

"Skills with a blade," Diou told Ansis, "does not the truth make."

Ansis bowed again, thanking Diou for his wisdom. "If I may ask," he said, waiting for Diou's permission. "Did you train him on the sidaiyo?"

"You know I did not," Diou said, impatience hot on his breath. He waved for L'Veyna and Dilna. "If you could not tell by Jouler's gait, Ansis, I am afraid I will need to speak to il'Grivlys about your training."

Ansis's bow came after a slight hesitation. He turned on his heels, and walked away, motioning to the Boorde child, who scampered beside him, still clutching the practice swords.

Diou watched them leave, his face as unreadable as a freshly snowed field. "Problems stir for you on the horizons, young Jouler. Ansis would not have noticed, but any of the dozens of il'Spada in the crowd would have recognized Grim's mark on your style. Once word gets out, it will be a matter of days until someone comes to avenge their loved one's honor."

"On me?" Jouler said, his stomach roiling with fear, anger, confusion...revulsion.

"Grim has a particular taste for Astasi—apprentices," Diou said. "There are several il'Spada in every House that hold an honor debt with that man."

"But I was never his apprentice," Jouler said. "He forced me to train."

"Nevertheless," Diou said. "To them, your skills would only confirm their truth."

"Can we talk about this inside, where it's warm?" L'Veyna mumbled, all but her face hidden by her thick coat.

"Don't be mean," Dilna said. "People want to kill Jouler."

"And being cold won't change that," L'Veyna said.

"I concede to your wisdom, Keeper," Diou said, starting toward the estate's majestic front entrance. Colorful stained-glass windows framed the giant black-iron doors. A heron made of countless emeralds stretched across the surface, the gems sparkling as the doors swung open.

"Boorde honor is as malleable as our iconic blades," Diou said. "Make no mistake, Jouler. You will be challenged before long."

"How long?" Jouler asked, worry cramping his stomach.

"After that unfortunate exchange," Diou replied. "I'd say no more than a couple of days. Ansis will tell il'Grivlys, who will send a formal letter to me, demanding a match between you and his pupil. Honor will not allow Jouler to deny the challenge."

"What if he's not here?" Dilna offered, and Diou smiled. "That's why you came to get us, isn't it?"

Diou's head tilted in acknowledgement. "Very good, young Dilna."

"We're leaving?" L'Veyna chirped with unconfined excitement. "Thank Alnazet!"

"L'Veyna, that's mean," Dilna said, nudging the Prytha.

"Where are we going?" Jouler asked.

"Does it matter?" L'Veyna said, stripping off another layer of clothing. Still covered in a thick, long-sleeved blouse and trousers, she draped the stripped layers over her arm. "Anywhere would be better than…" Dilna cleared her throat, and L'Veyna offered Diou a sheepish grin. "Than a terrentor's stomach?"

"It's all right," Diou said, patting L'Veyna's head. "I'm quite aware of the Alliance's inhospitable climate. Your brother refuses to let a day pass without reminding me. As for where we are going—currently, we are meeting Reylan in the Visitor's Wing. That's all I know."

19

SEVERED TIES

Katima strode through the famed mirrored halls of her House towards her mother's office. For once, she disagreed with the Vote of Flame and the Assembly's refusal to march in Onatah's defense. Despite Boorde prejudices, the Council of Flame should have sided with the Prytha. After all, their forests and culture were threatened, not the empire's.

Unfortunately, her people's resentment for the Prytha's languid lives and sensual nature had overruled the Assembly of Matron's reasoning. No philosopher had ever condoned the eradication of the lower races. They'd argued just the opposite. Every culture, even the Prytha's, added immeasurable value to the whole of the empire. Nevertheless, the Assembly had voted to hide amid the Boorde's frozen heights while the Torgeirian Empire ravaged the Prytha. After all, how could the Boorde usher in the Time of Plenty without the destruction of the Sacred Forests? One could not happen without the other, so said the Prophecies, and yet, Katima marched to her mother's office to demand she change her vote. The Prytha might be an inferior race, but the same could be said of Humans, even those who could shape. At least, until Jouler had come to the Alliance. Not only had he drawn crowds in the training yard, Katima had met plenty of Citizens, both Vrath and Founders alike, whose mind would shadow under Jouler's.

The most dangerous mind in the empire.

Diou had done well to keep the human's gift a secret, but Mother would find out soon. Not a secret in the Alliance passed lips without Matron Nith'Iil's permission.

Well…everyone except the Spider, Katima mused. *I guess there are always exceptions to the rule…*

Like L'Veyna, for example, who seemed more powerful than any Keeper who'd graced House Nith'Iil's halls. She grew, or asked, vegetation where every other Keeper had failed. Even young Dilna seemed more adroit than most Humans her age. She almost reminded Katima of Grim, if Grim had an endearing smile, fierce loyalty, and a sparkling inner flame.

Katima didn't wait for her mother's guards to introduce her, daring them to bar her entry.

"Good, you're here," her mother said when the doors opened. "We have much to discuss."

"We do," Katima said, crossing the long room, noting her mother's white mourning dress, still draped beside her desk. "What happened during the assembly? The Spider's never voted with you."

"Not in your lifetime," her mother said. "Not in centuries."

"Why now?" Katima demanded, earning a raised eyebrow warning of a line she'd almost crossed. "What would make the Spider vote with you, Mother?"

"Matron Fiorial understands a simple truth," her mother said. "Preserving the Alliance is far more important than a simple forest."

"Even at the cost of an entire culture?"

"Even at the cost of every culture," her mother said, standing from her desk. She moved to a shelf against a wall, and she removed a long roll of paper, then unfurled it on her desk, revealing an ancient map of Torgeir.

Pre-Sacrifice, Katima noted.

Her mother pointed to the Lost Kingdom of Astrakene, sank

during the Sacrifice to bring an end to the Uprising. A kingdom lost in order to keep the rest of the empire whole.

"This is the result when the Alliance fractures," Matron Nith'Iil said. "When one of the Great Houses secedes. Far more lives perished that day than resided in Onatah and all the Sacred Forests. Since that terrible blemish in our history, the Alliance has remained united, maintaining the delicate balance between the five remaining kingdoms, and I will not see that balance disrupted. Not by this House. Not while I'm Matron."

"Do you think the empire will stop with the Prytha?" Katima asked. "Once they claim the Sacred Forests, what's to stop them from claiming the Alliance?"

"No force on Yrsa can withstand a united Alliance."

"And what's keeping the Spider from betraying you again?"

"Promises," Matron Nith'Iil said, eying the ceremonial white dress still displayed by her desk.

The doors opened and four familiar figures walked into the room—Vaelithrae, Thalrion, Nyrr'kas, and their leader, the infamous Ishariel Tungie, her mother's most honored Ascended. Eyes not as faded as her mother's, they'd all seen well over half a millennium, and bore the marks to match their deadly trade. A scar sliced down the side of Vaelithrae's face, his missing eye replaced by polished onyx set with a tiny emerald heron, while melted scars covered half of Ishariel's scalp, her infamous djohai reflecting the fiery strip in her firedancer dress.

"The Heiress Apparent isn't feeling well," Matron Nith'Iil said, her pale-diamond gaze burning into Katima. "She must have gotten some leaves in her meat. Take her to her quarters and see that she is not disturbed until I call on her."

Katima stood and curtsied, a common display in the company of Citizens.

"We shall speak on this later, daughter." Her mother's gaze shifted to the white mourning dress, her eyes sparking with muted rage.

No, Katima thought, stalking past the Ascended. *We won't.*

Katima's djohai twirled around her limbs, shooting and twisting in harmony with her dance. Fire licked down the thin chain, reaching the bladed top with a violent explosion. She altered her rhythm, and the djohai swirled around her, engulfing her in a fiery bubble. A quick jerk sent the tip screaming outward, fire channeling down the weapon in a roaring jet. Finishing her set with a sweeping wave of flames, she coiled her djohai in a smooth motion, and hung it from her belt.

With a calming breath, she gazed at her reflection in the tall, wide mirror. Set in the only wall allowed on a traditional firedancer stage, the mirror reflected a churning sky. The wind already tasted of snow, while the clouds promised righteous lightning. Scorch marks from her more violent dances pocked the otherwise polished black-marble floor. In time, her sky stage would have become as blemished as those of the other masters of her craft. Now, Katima doubted a week would pass before her mother had the stage resurfaced for the new Heiress Apparent.

Her mother wouldn't have an official marriage contract until Katima met an untimely fate, but that hadn't stopped Matron Nith'Iil from unveiling a dress reserved for mourning the death of a loved one.

You will not shame my House, her mother had said. *Not* our *House.*

Katima pressed a hand against the knot tightening in her stomach. Since the Uprising, House Nith'Iil had reigned as the most powerful of the Great Houses, and no Matron had ruled as long as her mother.

How far would she go to maintain that power?

Gusting winds whipped her dress against her legs, tossing her long hair.

What really happened to my oldest sister?

Lightning flashed in the churning clouds, thunder rumbling a few seconds later.

I finally understand, brother.

She unsheathed the knife at her belt and sliced through the leather cord that had never left her topknot. The cord tumbled to the floor, and she gathered her hair in a tail.

I understand why you shun tradition.

The blade sliced through her hair with little effort, the long strands fading into the black floor.

You forged your own path.

She sheathed her knife and wiggled her fingers, sparking a gentle flame that swarmed over her hand.

And I will forge mine.

With a sharp pang of loss, she passed her fiery hand over her scalp, singing off the rest of her hair.

For I am Houseless.

Wind caressed bare skin where thick hair had tugged at her scalp. She extinguished the flame, and ran her hand over her bald scalp, the curious new sensation distracting her from her deep loss.

Diou would be gathering the others by now—Reylan, Prack, Jouler, Pendric, L'Veyna, and that popping ember Dilna. Katima checked the small pouch at her waist, stuffed with enough jerked meat to firedance for a few days straight.

Or get me through a torrential blizzard, she thought, eying the ominous clouds.

She pulled a thin strip of meat, letting it smoldered in her stomach. It was far more than enough energy for the dance she intended, but with Mother's Ascended guarding her quarters, she might need the reserves.

Squeezing her eyes shut, she pushed out thoughts of her mother and the Prytha's inexorable slaughter. Her body swayed to the silent tune of a haunting melody, matching the ebb and flow of the energy that smoldered in her belly. Harmonized, she snapped her finger, and a messenger flame sprouted before her, taking upon her brother's form.

"Sister?" Diou said, his face hardening. "What's... Your hair! Katima, what happened?"

"It's Mother..." Katima took an even breath, her heart slamming against her chest. She'd only seen her mother's snow-white ceremonial dress two other times—after Father died, and the day House Fiorial's assassins killed Mother's firstborn daughter, the rightful heir of House Nith'Iil.

I will not allow you to shame my House. Katima's mind tumbled with her mother's threat. *Am I to follow my sister's fate?*

"Where are you?" Diou asked, concern knitting his brow.

"My sky stage," Katima said. "Ishariel and her team are guarding my door."

"Get your gear ready," Diou said, rage flaring in his eyes. "Prack and I will be there soon."

20

THE POINTLESS POST

Jouler opened the door to Reylan's quarters, letting Dilna and L'Veyna inside. Stacks of books filled each table of the common room, making it seem more like a study, the couches and chairs pushed against the walls to make room for the six large slate boards, each board scribbled with lines of Prophecy and notes. Pendric cast a lazy wave from a plush chair, a half-eaten tea bar in his hand.

Reylan poked his head from behind a slate board. "Ah, good," he said, his pipe bobbing in his mouth. "You're finally here."

Dilna dumped the three books she'd taken from the library into Reylan's waiting hands. "No thanks to Diou," she said, then skipped to sit on a plush couch beside L'Veyna.

"Where is he?" Reylan asked. "Him and Prack."

"Diou got a message from his sister," Jouler said. "Sounded urgent, so they ran off."

Reylan rubbed his crooked nose, his gaze lingering on the door.

"What's going on?" Jouler asked, skimming over the notes on the slate boards. Most bore Diou's immaculate handwriting, while Reylan's and Prack's chicken scratch poked about the boards. The lines of Prophecy bore Jouler's translations, along with various interpretations of their cryptic meaning. One line in particular bore far more notes than others.

Oh Light, return the Dark Its glory. Betray the Light, send the glory back whence it came, lest He be devoured, Your faith restored. Oh, Harbinger, break free the Serpent's Eye; break free, tradition crushed under heel, the bounty reborn.

Dark—void, black, colorless, empty, without light.

Glory—praise, worship, majesty, victory, triumph.

He (capitalized?)—Light, Dark, Facet, Kael, Jouler.

"Any luck finding references to the Black Breath?" Jouler asked.

"Nothing but speculation," Reylan said, setting the books Dilna brought onto a clustered table. More to himself, the old Phaerian mumbled, "Three blasted weeks, and all we have are three blasted books. That'll have to do."

"Due for what?" Jouler asked. "Reylan, you're not making sense."

"Best sit, son," Reylan said, gesturing to an empty chair. He waited for Jouler, then took a deep breath. "Cabalist spies have located Kael."

Jouler tried to ask where, but the sudden lump in his throat caught the word.

He's alive!

Jouler had hoped. He'd told everyone, even himself, that he knew Kael lived, but a tiny seed of doubt had always festered in the back of his mind.

"Kael!" Pendric cried, shooting to his feet, tears welling in his eyes.

"I knew the whole time," Dilna said, nudging L'Veyna. "Not about the spies. That he's alive. He is the Light, after all."

"The reports," Reylan continued, his voice thick, "place Kael and two other Phaerians among a Founder's caravan. Not Rodak," he said, before Jouler could ask. "Maelly Bodiou, not that her name means anything to any of you. She's a well-known sympathizer—Citizens who promote Phaerian humanity—which bodes well for their treatment."

"Who are the others?" Pendric asked at the same time Jouler said, "Where are they heading?"

"Two girls," Reylan said. "That's all I know about them. As far as where? They were heading south from the Prus Ruins, likely on their way to Eio."

"Eio?" Pendric wheezed, pouring himself a cup of Boorde tea. "That's where the Sotouri are."

"And Rodak," Reylan said. "Along with half the Founders of Torgeir. They're all gathered for the Ceremony. The induction of new Sotouri."

"Then we have to get Kael before he gets to Eio." Jouler stood and paced, recalling a map of Torgeir. "The Prus Ruins aren't far from here."

"The report was over a week old," Reylan said.

"So, we rescue Kael," Pendric wheezed, sipping his tea. "Then we head to the Blasted Lands for the Black Breath."

"Just like that," Reylan said, and Pendric nodded. "If only it was that easy." Reylan glanced at the front door again, a hint of impatience in his breath. "Jo, take the girls and pack your bags."

"Pack?" L'Veyna jumped off the couch, excitement lifting her brow. "We're leaving right now?"

"As soon as your brother and Diou return," Reylan said, nudging them toward the door.

Jouler headed to his room, while Dilna and L'Veyna disappeared into theirs. He walked into his room, and the tubes sang to him from his pack, begging for release.

Once we save Kael, he promised, wondering what plans Reylan had already devised to save Kael. *We'll all open them together. Me, Kael, and L'Veyna. Maybe they'll point us to the other two Facets.*

He stuffed as many clothes as his pack would hold, adding a supple pair of leather boots better suited for warmer weather. After a brief consideration, he left the dense book he'd taken from Emril's hidden room. As with everything else tainted by the empire, lies had filled most of its pages. He gave the room one last look before meeting the girls back in Reylan's room.

"Still no word on Prack and Diou?" Jouler asked, and Reylan shook his head, his eyes deep in thought. "How are we going to save Kael?" Again, the old man shook his head. Jouler swallowed a lump of frustration, and he focused on what he knew. "This Founder, Maelly Bodiou—she's heading to Eio for the Ceremony, which is the induction for new Sotouri?"

Reylan nodded. "It happens every four years. This one came almost a year early, presumably to send the new recruits to handle the troubles in North Blailon."

"The Voice," Pendric mumbled.

"I imagine Maelly," Jouler continued, an idea forming as he spoke, "will follow the roadway we skirted to get here. The one connecting Elpa and Onti. Ideally, we'd want to save Kael along that route, before he reaches Eio, but imperials are crawling all over the roadways."

"Not to mention," Reylan said, rubbing his crooked nose, "the Sotouri are still holding their war games. Those plains will be full of spectators."

Reylan's door burst open, and a blur of motion rushed into the room. Prack stopped, gulping for air, sweat pouring from his face. "Good, you're all packed." He guzzled from a pitcher of water and dragged a sleeve across his mouth. "We have to get out of here. Katima's mother is trying to kill her."

JOULER FOLLOWED Katima and Diou down a dark, hidden passage. Their only light, a small flame dancing over Katima's palm, reflected into infinity in the polished walls, ceiling, and floor.

Like floating among the stars.

"What happened?" Jouler asked, trying not to stare at Katima's bald, snow-white scalp.

"My sister," Diou said, bowing his head to Katima in a show of respect, "said, no."

Katima rubbed her scalp, her eyes burning with anger. "The Assembly of Matrons voted against sending aid to help defend Onatah."

"I...I didn't..." L'Veyna cleared her throat, her voice hoarse with pain. "I didn't realize your people cared."

"They don't," Katima replied. "That's why they voted no, including my mother."

"But some still voted yes, didn't they?" L'Veyna asked. "Maybe one of those Houses—"

"They won't help," Katima said with cold finality.

Jouler tempered an urge to snap at Katima, reminding himself she'd just denounced her people, and her mother wanted her dead.

I'd be on edge too.

"Why does your mother want to…" Jouler's voice trailed.

"Why does she want to kill me?" Katima said, wiping her scalp, her face as readable as the flame hovering above her palm. "Of that, I can only speculate. However, there is one thing I am certain—she knows you are a Child of Prophecy."

"What about L'Veyna?" Jouler asked.

Katima shook her head, assuaging his worry. "Like Humans and Prytha," she said, "we, too, believed the Prophecies foretold a single person."

"Then she believes I'm the Dawn," Jouler said.

"That is the logical conclusion," Diou said, halting them at an unlit sconce set on the wall. "We're inside the outer wall. This hidden door-way, empties right next to Eldri's so-called Pointless Post." He crouched and pressed a hidden button in the wall, and a small cubby opened, revealing a small handle.

"Stay here," he said, giving his sister's scalp a blank look. She folded her arms, and he held up his hands, imploring calm. "I applaud your courage, sister, but your timing is poor."

"I can regrow it," Reylan offered, and Katima rounded on him.

"You will do no such thing, old man." Her fire-diamond eyes flashed in the darkness, and Reylan stepped back.

"It was only a suggestion."

"Then I suggest we hurry," Diou said. "As soon as Mother's Ascended realize we're gone, she'll send her entire army after us."

"No, she won't." Katima's brow drew in confusion. "She might release all her Ascended, but not…" She blinked, her lips pressing a line. "Sarcasm, I take it? You spend too much time with Prack."

"We want to avoid bloodshed," Diou told everyone. "But we also can't allow the guards to send warning to our mother."

L'Veyna raised her hand. "I can—"

"You can stay here," Diou interrupted, and she snapped her mouth shut. He pulled the hidden lever in the cubby, and a section of wall slid inward. The cold, angry night poured through the hidden doorway, spilling into the corridor. Spear in hand, Diou slipped outside.

"Diou," Eldri said, his voice floating into the hidden passage. "Please, stop. Our Matron sent word this morning that you are not to leave."

Jouler shivered, gripping his staff, waiting by the doorway with Katima. Above, snow drifted from a threatening sky, while bursts of wind rumbled with thunder.

Prack shifted to stand beside Diou, his colorful autumnal hair bright next to the black-and-white Boorde.

Eldri and three other guards faced them, their spears lowered. "Lay down your weapons, and—"

His words ended with a strangled gasp, four shocked gazes fused to Katima's bald scalp. Cloaked in regal dignity, she strode from the hidden doorway, her face chiseled with pride, snow-white scalp steaming in the freezing night. "There is no honor in dying tonight."

Jouler felt a tap on his shoulder.

L'Veyna looked up at him and winked. She clacked on her belt-board, *Stand back*.

"Heiress..." Eldri's gaze darted between Katima's scalp and Diou's spear. "Though I know you would both strike us down, my honor will not permit—"

Vines burst from the ground, slithering around Eldri and his companions, gagging them, and wrapping them in a tight cocoon.

Diou and Katima stumbled back a step, and gaped at L'Veyna.

"As I was saying," she said, pulling on her thick furry jacket, "I think I have a solution."

FREEZING darkness bit through L'Veyna's thick, fur-lined coat, prickling her skin with shivers. The blizzard Diou predicted raged around them, howling through the night. Waves of Katima's fire warmed the falling sheets of snow as she cleared the path ahead of them.

Dilna shouted next to L'Veyna, but the storm devoured her words. She tugged on the straps to her hood, motioning for L'Veyna to pull her hood closed. In ways, she seemed older than L'Veyna, rather than a couple years her younger.

L'Veyna reached into her memories, and filled her mind with happier, warmer times—skittering with Dilna through House Nith'I-il's glorious labyrinth of halls, snatching up lemon candies and tarts, inventing book names and trying to find them in the library. Her Human hall, as Pendric called her, always came up with the funnest ideas—adding hot spices to Jouler's food, freezing Reylan's undergarments, sneaking into the kitchen at night. That girl might even teach Diou a thing or two about walking like a shadow.

Cold misery chipped at her warm memories, her throat freezing with every breath. A harsh wind stabbed her eyes, forcing her gaze down. Not that there was anything to see beyond Katima's waves of fire.

She trudged ahead, walking in Jouler's footprints while Dilna followed Pendric. Time ebbed with each miserable step, while the biting cold soaked through L'Veyna's layers. She cursed the timing of the howling storm. She cursed every moment in her life that had brought her to this freezing moment. Hands numb beneath her worthless gloves, she contemplated pulling her arms inside her coat, but then her pack would fall off her back.

Her foot slipped, and Dilna caught her before she fell. "Thank you!" L'Veyna shouted, though she doubted Dilna heard her over the raging storm.

L'Veyna's stomach soured, and she turned to see a streaking ball of fire explode against an invisible barrier. Her stomach clenched, threatening to relieve her lunch, and the ground rumbled. Jouler threw himself over her, while Pendric dragged Dilna to the ground. Darkness enveloped the world, the roar of the storm muffled. L'Veyna's stomach twisted again, and she vomited into the snow. A powerful crack sounded from deep inside the mountain. The ground shook and rolled with terrible force. Again her stomach clenched, but she had nothing left to offer, and the shaking ebbed to the muffled shrieks of the storm.

Jouler lifted himself, his whispered apology floating in replete darkness.

"Get off me, Pen," Dilna mumbled.

A tiny flame flickered to life, chasing the darkness away. The dancing flame danced over Katima's hand, her face and scalp glowing in the light. She wiggled a finger, and the flame grew, its warmth gleaming against their large, dome-shaped tomb.

"What happened?" Pendric wheezed, working the hem of his sleeve.

With a heavy sigh, Reylan let his pack slip to the snowy ground. He pulled his hood down and wiped sweat from his dark pate. "Ascended," he explained, proffering his pipe from beneath his coat. "I collapsed the trail around them."

"Along with half the mountainside," Katima said.

"At least we're safe," Prack replied. "We can wait out the storm in here."

"In the snow and mud?" L'Veyna asked, gesturing to the ground.

"Of course not," Katima said. She pointed to the ceiling, and a stream of liquid fire bored a hole through their tomb. Next, jets of fire shoot from her fingertips, melting the snow on the ground. Steam leaked from the drying ground, and funneled through the bored hole. Warmth radiated from her flames, filling the large dome, forcing everyone to peal off layers. Then she danced a small campfire in the middle of the round floor.

"Are you all right?" Dilna asked, handing L'Veyna a rag.

"It's the shaping," she said. She wiped her mouth, no longer seeing a frail old Human in Reylan. As kind as he'd been, a glaring truth stripped away the kindness in his gentle smile—*he's still d'Tormena.* A d'Tormena that had just saved her life. "It makes me sick."

"I'm sorry, dear," Reylan said, lighting his pipe with a sulphurstick, and filling the dome with the soothing aroma of ha'ath. "But I had no choice."

"Do all Keepers get sick?" Jouler asked.

"Not *that* sick," Prack replied, handing L'Veyna a waterskin.

Reylan handed Prack his pipe and squatted by the fire. "They've likely never been exposed to that much power."

L'Veyna swished her mouth and spat at the edge of the dome, then joined everyone by the fires.

"What do we do now?" Pendric wheezed, his face drooping with exhaustion.

"We wait for the storm to pass," Reylan said.

"Mother will send more Ascended," Diou said, taking a pull from Reylan's pipe before returning it to the old man.

"Not in this weather," Katima retorted. "There's nothing we can do but wait."

"We may as well get comfy," Reylan said.

"What are Ascended?" Pendric wheezed, crouching by the fire.

"Elite warriors," Katima said. "Il'Spada and firedancers chosen for their exceptional skills, power, and—most importantly—loyalty to their House."

"Officially," Diou added, "Ascended scour the land looking for books."

Pendric's head jerked in confusion. "Books? You send the best of the best to look for books?"

"Books contain everything about us," Diou said, gesturing to the group. "Our histories, our cultures, our discoveries, everything. Is there anything more important?"

"Food?" Pendric replied with a shrug.

Diou chuckled, breaking the tight air. He sat cross-legged, towering between Prack and Reylan. Prack handed him the pipe, and he pulled a crackling drag, plumes of smoke billowing from his nostrils.

"What do they do unofficially?" L'Veyna asked. "The Ascended, I mean."

"They're assassins," Jouler said.

"More like specialized treasure hunters," Prack said, earning a sharp look from Katima.

"They are not treasure hunters," Katima said.

"Deadly treasure hunters?" Prack offered.

"Deadly to you, Chi'indi," Katima said, her fire-diamond eyes flashing.

"This isn't helping," Reylan said. The bowl of his pipe flared from a long drag, and he blew a thick plume of smoke into the dome. "We're all tired. Let's get some rest. There's nothing we can do until this storm passes, anyway."

"You're wrong, old man," L'Veyna said, knowing just the thing to lift spirits. "There *is* something we can do." She formed an image in her mind and asked, ignoring the sharp stipples along the back of her head and neck. After a little coercion, the imaged locked into place, and a steaming tea sphere materialized over her palm. "We can have tea."

21

CHAINS

Kael forced one raw foot in front of the other, his tattered trousers stuck to the weeping scabs on his thighs and knees. His bare back and shoulders blistered beneath another evening sun, his skin a medley of colorful bruises. Agony raged with each step, but stopping only made everything worse. The pattern-forging in the shackles around his wrists kept his will wrapped in a mindtrap, blocking him from the Currents of Power, while the heavy chain connecting him to Lady Maelly's rear wagon kept him from trailing too far. Blood ran down his hands and crooked, broken fingers, and dripped onto the clinking chains. Lieutenant Baelorin would break them again once they stopped for the night.

When the real torment begins.

It wouldn't be too long before Aglia and Lieutenant Baelorin found new ways to make him scream. Crimson already painted the clouds along the eastern sky, a tiny sliver of the golden sun glowing on the horizon. Sometimes such sights sparked memories of a happy little village with a young, curly-haired boy. They were delusions from a tortured mind, no doubt. They had to be. How could such joy exist in a world consumed by maddening pain? Maybe those happy memories leaked into his mind from a past life. It had to be why that girl seemed so familiar. The one who was always with Aglia, even if he couldn't place her pretty face. She hated him, that much he knew. Every time her eyes fell on him, she glared, seeming almost as angry as Aglia.

Almost, he thought, chuckling at the ridiculous notion. No one hated him more than Aglia, the conductor of his symphony of pain.

Is she wrong to hate? a voice asked in his head. *You left her to die.*

He pressed his broken fingers against his leg, and screamed, sharp pain drowning the awful voice and shattering delicate memories of honey-colored locks. His heel met a sharp rock, and he fell to the ground. Splintering pain radiated from his broken ribs. In an instant, his chains went taut, and the coach dragged him despite his desperate cries. A divot in the ground bumped him over, raking his sunburned back across the rocky ground.

His shrieks pierced the air until his throat cracked. He flapped and floundered on the ground, desperate to flip over. His blistered shoulder dug into the rocks and fiery pain ignited along his side. He pulled against the chains cutting into his wrists and swung his legs forward. Rocks cut through his shredded trousers, lancing his rear before he could shove his heels into the ground and force himself to his feet.

His body begged him to curl up and weep through the pain, but he dared not stop. Again, he forced each raw foot in front of the other. He would greet the next stabbing rock with agonizing glee.

Anything but falling.

A deep voice called a stop from the front of the caravan, and renewed fear draped over his pain.

Almost anything.

Kael existed in his throbbing pain while Lady Maelly's soldiers dismounted and began setting up camp. A familiar soldier with a bucket made his way to Kael, the soldier's name evaporating in Kael's pain-addled mind. The soldier's grizzled brown beard and calculating gaze spoke of a seasoned veteran. Knots in the yellow-and-green cord marked him an officer, while his light skin belied an upbringing in the Maker or Bronze District.

The soldier set the bucket down, water sloshing over the handle of a ladle. He rested his hands on Kael's head, and a sensation like ice water coursed down Kael's body. Screams ripped from his throat as broken bones shifted back into place, his fingers straightening, while bruises, cuts, and burns healed. In a rush, his daze mind cleared, and his pain washed away, flooding him with memories of the torture he'd suffered—the torture he *would* suffer as soon as the soldiers finished setting up camp.

Kael fell to his knees, sobbing in terror.

"Tonight's your lucky night," Captain Gwyndril said, holding the ladle for Kael to drink. "No torture for you. Isol passed his ball this afternoon."

Isol…Isol…

Kael stumbled through his memories, searching for the familiar name, but his mind still stumbled over the past few days.

Isol…lewd comments…the captain's granddaughter.

"He—" Kael coughed, his throat still parched. The captain scooped another ladle, and Kael swallowed the cool, refreshing water. "Isol, he…he did something to your granddaughter?"

Confusion knit Gwyndril's brow, and he peered into Kael's eyes.

No, Kael thought, pushing through his exhaustion. *The lewd comments were about…Makayla!*

"Lady Maelly fed Isol a ball and chain," Kael said, recalling the lewd comments Isol made toward Makayla—no, Eglona. Calling her Makayla would see her on her own torture rack.

"You remember," Gwyndril said, a flash of relief crossing his face. He scooped another ladle of water for Kael. "Not all Citizens are monsters. You, of all people, should know that."

Says the man who keeps me alive through the tortures.

If not for Captain Gwyndril and Lieutenant Finndras, Maelly's other tii'Vrath, Kael would have entered that sweet eternal bliss the day they'd found Kael and Makayla.

"How is Eglona?" he asked.

"She's well," Gwyndril replied, his steel gaze hardening. He dropped the ladle in the bucket, splashing water on Kael's feet. "Why did you take her power? *How* did you take it? She's not snapped. She's…"

"I did it to keep her safe," Kael lied. "From people like you. I thought, maybe if she couldn't shape, the empire would ignore her, but I couldn't snap her." He squeezed his eyes against the memory of his power meeting Makayla's. "I don't know what I did. I just…I did it out of desperation."

"To save her," Gwyndril said, more to himself, his brow tightening. "You didn't just take her power. You took a part of her soul."

"I kept her alive. If she could still shape when you found us, she'd be in chains alongside me."

I know what she would have done to you, he thought, recalling her tentacles of blue light shredding imperial platoons.

Captain Gwyndril pressed his lips in a line and unhooked Kael's shackles from the chain. "Come with me."

Kael pushed through his exhaustion and rose to his feet. He followed the captain while soldiers rushed to set up Kael's tent, carrying canvass, poles, two chairs, and a table..

No torture rack…

Kael tried tamping down his hopes that the rest of the night would go so well, but his healed wounds felt too good not to germinate expectations. He flexed his fingers, happy to see them straight again, and not immediately re-broken as had happened over the past week. Perhaps he would get whole food instead of the mush the soldiers chewed and spat onto a plate.

Captain Gwyndril shaped a ball of light and led Kael into a field where two wooden posts had been driven into the ground. One post bore a wench and crank, the other a metal hook. With a disappointed frown, the captain turned the crank, and the wench lurked with each rotation.

"She's going to kill Isol?" Kael asked, understanding what the captain had meant when he said Isol had passed his ball.

"All Founders are a bit…out of touch, shall we say?" Captain Gwyndril said with a note of disgust. "Lady Maelly is peculiar when it comes to little girls. Hence why she's encouraged your torture."

"But Isol was just rude," Kael said.

"Like I said," Captain Gwyndril replied. "A bit out of touch. I'm surprised you care."

"I don't," Kael said. "Just surprised."

"To the Founders," the captain said, "we're all just tools for their entertainment."

After the soldiers finished erecting their sleeping tents, they gathered around the posts. Draped in repulsive delight, Lieutenant Baelorin pulled a naked Isol by a long, thin chain that dangled out of the doomed man's mouth. The other end of the chain hung from Isol's hand, the links trailing into his rectum. Baelorin handed Kael the long portion of the chain trailing from Isol's mouth. Then the lieutenant attached the balled end to the hooked post.

Isol's teeth chattered, his lips turning blue from the frosty night air, his eyes puffy and crazed.

A heavy shiver rolled through Kael, reminding him of his own nakedness. Something soft and warm settled over his back, and he startled from the touch.

"Easy," Gwyndril said, adjusting the heavy cloak over Kael's shoulders. "Can't have you freezing to death."

No, Kael thought, telling himself it was just another ploy to get under his skin, but the comforting warmth of the cloak melted his resolve. Baelorin also hadn't hit me when he handed Kael the chain. The Lieutenant had never missed an opportunity to leave Kael with a medley of bruises, cuts, or broken bones. Not once had Baelorin refrained until now.

Had Makayla won Maelly's favor and pleaded for Kael's life? Maybe Livia...no Aglia—*Aglia*. Maybe she'd forgiven him for bringing Rodak's vengeance to Headwater. Had aiding in Kael's tortures cracked the woman who had once loved him?

Dare I hope?

Minutes stretched into the night, the sun's crepuscule glow withering into darkness. Captain Gwyndril's men stood in silence, dark long coats draped around them, breath freezing in the light of shaped glowglobes. Not even the nighttime critters dared break the somber mood.

Lady Maelly's coach door clicked, the sound sharp in the still air. Isol groaned, spittle leaking down the chain coming from his mouth. The ruby-haired Founder stepped from her coach, drifting down the steps, dark satisfaction pulling the corners of her lips. Makay—no, *Eglona* and Aglia followed close behind, their virulent gaze finding Kael.

At times, he wondered how much of Makayla's act she faked. Like Gwyndril said, Kael had taken a part of her soul. His actions had destroyed her army and killed the people she'd loved. How could she *not* hate him?

And yet, he thought, clinging to a whisper of hope, *she'd cared for me in the cave.*

She could have left him to die in the cold. Instead, she'd hauled him up a mountainside and nursed him back to health. Her glares *had* to be an act.

Aglia, on the other hand, delighted in his pain. Whatever torment she'd endured under Rodak had taught her things that had even surprised Baelorin. Her wispy strands of hair fluttered in the breeze, where thick locks had once poured past her shoulders like waves of honey. Her dark brown eyes, once sharp with intellect and compassionate, now raged with demented rage.

And why shouldn't they?

Kael could have saved Headwater and ended Rodak's brutal reign. As the figure of light, he could have turned the Founder and his Vrath to ash. Olan didn't have to die, Pendric needn't have lost his mother, and Livia never should have become the tortured soul glaring at him now.

Maybe if I'd taken the Prophecies seriously…

"Look at this wretch," Lady Maelly said with dramatic aplomb, pointing at Isol. "The lowest of Humans. A filthy predator who hunts our most vulnerable." She dragged her gaze across the gathered soldiers. "Some might say, 'But Eglona is just a Phlem'—a word that I *abhor*, and will not tolerate. I cannot…" She put an alabaster hand to her chest and sighed. "No, I *will* not abide such ignorance. Filthy predators like Isol have no place on Yrsa."

Fear poured down Isol's face, his eyes wide with panic, his body quivering in the frosty night.

"Attach the chain," Captain Gwyndril mumbled to Kael. "And don't look away from Isol when you crank. Lady Maelly wants you to watch."

Kael obeyed, telling himself Isol deserved his fate. How many lives had he already destroyed? How many Makaylas had the man preyed upon? But no amount of reasoning quelled the festering ache in his gut.

He turned the crank, each tick running up his arm and settling in a pit of misery. The wench clicked through a rotation, and the slack in the chain tightened.

Isol deserves it.

Strangled groans reverberated from Isol's chest, thick spittle oozing off the taut links pulling from his mouth.

He deserves it. He…

Kael turned the crank again and again, forcing himself to watch the chain draw from Isol's mouth. Isol's groans sharpened into desperate shrieks, his body flailing and convulsing against his invisible bonds of force. Blood mixed with the viscous spittle on the thin chain, along with small chunks of viscera.

Kael's stomach clenched and heaved, bile spilling on the ground.

Isol's convulsions slowed, his terror-filled shrieks fading into gurgles, and then he went slack against invisible bonds.

Still, Kael turned, cranking gears ringing in the silent night air.

"Don't stop until the chain breaks," Lady Maelly said, before heading back to her coach.

Without a word, Gwyndril and his men retreated to a large fire near the coaches.

Kael continued to turn the crank, ignoring the stench from the chunks of shredded viscera tumbling from Isol's mouth. Kael heaved a dozen more times before the chain snapped. Numb, he worked his way to the large tent the soldiers setup for him every night. He opened the flap, stepped inside, and activated the glowglobe.

Aglia's peccant smile brought him to his knees. Behind her, Baelorin unbuckled his belt and dropped his trousers.

"You *really* thought tonight would be different?" Baelorin said.

Invisible bonds lifted the captain's cloak from Kael's shoulders, ripped off his tattered pants, and bent him over his torture table.

"My Lady said I finally get to have a turn with you." Aglia lifted a razor. "After the lieutenant is finished with his fun, of course."

AGLIA REVELED in Kael's misery, savoring every painful shriek. Lieutenant Baelorin buckled his belt, and shot her a wicked smile that promised she'd be next. Rodak and his only child, Lokir, had taught her that such depraved acts weren't about lust or desire. After all, who could desire such a miserable wretch like her? No, what Baelorin had done to Kael ran far deeper than any physical trauma. It was all about power, about ripping someone's innocence, and watching it fade in their eyes. Never again would Kael feel whole. Never again would a touch be just a touch. Never again would promises be more than empty words.

Aglia strapped him to the table, tying his wrists and ankles to the table legs. She grabbed her kit of blades and tools, and set it on the table with a heavy thud where Kael could see it. Untying the leather straps, she unrolled the kit, displaying saws, knives, files, pliers, and needles of various sizes.

"I know what you're thinking," Aglia said, caressing her kit. "Lieutenant Baelorin doesn't have so many toys. Well, as you know, Kael, I can't shape, which means I can't heal you." Drawing one of the longer, thicker needles, she moved to Kael's side, and let the tip of the needle poke his back.

He flinched and cried, his blubbering pleas exciting her with euphoric shudders. Without warning, she pressed the needle through his back until it stuck into the table, reveling in his desperate flops and shrieks. Once he lay breathless and groaning, she drew another needle and placed the tip against his back. "One for every tear I wept." She eased the second needle through his back. "One for every life you left in that monster's hands." She grabbed her thickest needle, jabbed it into his thigh, and shoved it through his leg. Blood warmed her hands, his anguish quickening her heart.

She ran her tongue over her empty gums, each tooth wrenched from her mouth by her own hands.

A needle pierced through his cheeks and tongue.

"I hate you!" she screamed, wading through her tormented memories. She ripped off her shirt, exposing the scars where her breasts had been. "Look at me!" She grabbed the wood file and dragged over his back. "Look at what you did!"

Hatred poured from her eyes as Kael twisted and wailed beneath her deft hands. She set aside the file for a pair of pliers and ripped off a toenail.

The so-called Light.

"Where are your Prophecies now?"

MAKAYLA SCREAMED into her pillow and pounded her fists against her thighs, but nothing assuaged the guilt ripping through her heart. While she lived in relative luxury, riding in a coach with Aglia, eating better food than she had in Pegrans, all for the price of washing clothes, Kael lived in perpetual agony.

I won't leave you. I'll get us out of this, Kael.

Aglia had sparked the wretched idea to let him believe his suffering had ended. Apparently, Lord Rodak loved fewer things more than watching his victim's hope drain into terror. If a sliver of the things Aglia said were true, he deserved to scream worse than Kael for the rest of his life.

Makayla buried her face in her pillow again, hating herself for finding any pity for Aglia. That wretched creature was a far cry from the loving person Kael had described. She guided his torture, instructing Baelorin's every move, and then describing it to Makayla in sickening detail. Those awful stories helped fuel Makayla's mask of fury. The more she appeared to hate Kael, the safer they would be. She just hoped he could somehow see past her mask.

I don't hate you, Kael. I hate her.

Makayla's will stretched to that place within her that had once churned with power, finding a pocket in her soul still lined in the Dark's slick corruption. Ironic that something so evil could be used for something so good. Her power had healed blasted areas. She'd Awakened hundreds of her people and liberated countless more. Had she listened to Rammond and not overstepped her advance, she'd still be fighting the empire instead of riding in a coach while Kael cried in torment.

Makayla's comfort would come to an abrupt halt once they reached Eio. Lady Maelly didn't recognize her, but Rodak would the moment he saw her. Thankfully, Lady Maelly's hatred for roads and causeways gave Makayla more time to devise an escape. Unfortunately, without shaping, all of her ideas fizzled as soon as they sparked.

It didn't help that Aglia only left her side to torture Kael. Not to mention the obstacle Kael's health posed. Even if they managed to escape, Kael wouldn't make it a hundred paces before his strength gave.

A soft knock came at her door.

"It's me," Captain Gwyndril said.

Makayla wiped her face dry and settled on her cushioned bench. "Come in."

Tall, with peppered hair and a hard, grizzled face, the captain dipped his head when he entered. "Rough night," he said, sitting across from her on Aglia's bench, his shimmering Shield glaring at her from his temple.

"Rougher for some," Makayla said, and the captain released a heavy sigh.

"I agree with Lady Maelly," Gwyndril said. "People like Isol have no place on Yrsa. But neither does that method of punishment."

Makayla's anger stirred from the captain's empty words. He might fancy himself a sympathizer like his matron, but for all of his purported equality, he never squirmed from Kael's cries. The captain and that bastard Finndras kept Kael alive to be tortured over and over.

"I came to check on you," Gwyndril said, breaking the heavy silence. "And to give you this." He held up a hand-carved wooden horse. "I made it for you. I know it's…" He looked at the wooden statue in his hand and snorted. "It's stupid, I'm sorry."

"No," Makayla said, swallowing her anger. She took the wooden horse, running her fingers over its rough-carved features, wishing it could carry her and Kael away from this awful place. "Did you carve it yourself?"

Gwyndril nodded and ran a hand through his peppered hair. "You…you remind me of my granddaughter." He held up his hands when she leaned away. "Please, be at ease. I wasn't that kind of grandfather. I wasn't like Isol, or I never would have lasted in Lady Maelly's retinue. Obviously."

Makayla forced a soft expression, quelling her thoughts of raking the captain's face and gouging his eyes. He was a monster, a tii'Vrath, not some kind and broken-hearted grandfather. "You have a granddaughter?"

Pain closed the captain's eyes, and a fleeting smile crossed his lips. "She was a little younger than you when she died. She was so beautiful. Like a puffy little cloud of joy."

"What happened to her?"

Gwyndril's eyes glimmered, and he shook his head. "That's not a story I wish to tell. Neither should such precious ears as yours be made to hear it." He cleared his throat. "Then again, you've probably been through worse than any of my soldiers."

His tender words invited memories of Rammond, when she'd sit with the large man into the late of night, listening to his stories, and confess her fears. A sob burst from her lips, and Gwyndril's brow creased, his eyes brimming. He sat next to her and patted her back. Her mask cracked, she poured her pain into his smelly shirt, hating herself as she cried in his arms. The captain stroked her hair, telling her to let it all out and that everything would be all right, his soothing words juxtaposed by Kael's screams.

"Don't worry," he said, his deep voice rumbling in his chest. "It'll all be over soon enough."

"What do you mean?" she asked, pulling away from the captain as another scream ripped the air. Gwyndril's Shield shimmered in the faint light, reminding her this grandfather's kindness bore claws.

"At the rate we're traveling," Gwyndril said, reaching as if to pet Makayla's head. His hand froze, a memory stealing his gaze. Lips pressed into a line, he shook his head and dropped his hand. "We shouldn't take more than ten days to reach Eio. Yes...ten days at the most. Then..." Gwyndril stood and moved to the door. His soft smile cried of sympathy, while Kael's cries swore of his cruelty. "Then, hopefully, we'll be done with this mess, and things will get back to normal." Another wail made the captain wince. Shoulders drooping from with the weight of duty, he breathed a heavy sigh, and opened the door. "Maybe we can get back to digging ruins."

Makayla waited for the door to close behind him before she grabbed her pillow and mashed it over her face. Her hate-filled screams rolled into sobs, and she curled on her bench, haunted by Kael's shrieks. If she still had her power, she would have saved him and torn their captors to shreds, especially Maelly and that blasted Aglia. Of course, with if she still had her power, they never would have gotten caught. Maybe if she'd paid more attention to Rammond and read some of his books, she could have figured out how to save Kael and escape.

But I didn't, and I can't. I'm worthless.

"I'm so sorry," she cried. Tears soaked into the cushion until she had no more to give, her body numb and drained, her eyelids so heavy...

A loud bang startled her awake, her groggy mind fighting to make sense of the disfigured face at the door.

"Eglona, wake up!" Aglia grinned from ear to ear, blood soaking her dress. "You should have seen his face!"

22

SCOUTING AHEAD

Jouler soared in his dreams again, the mysterious city calling him from the tundra far below. Unlike the pleasant scenes of grazing cottlewomp and Phaerians traveling causeways from his previous dream, war ravaged the land. Smoke from a raging wildfire streaked across the sky, promising inexorable doom, while imperial armies clashed. Vrath launched explosive patterns at each other, and pattern-forged weapons and armor met with deafening booms and cracks.

The call from the city yanked at his heart, begging for salvation.

A mass of soldiers flying Blailon's colors, a crimson bull on an ocher field, swarmed over the city's main body. Bearing a lilac banner with a blue snake coiled around a chalice, the defenders' line broke and a thread of crimson-and-ochre leaked into their ranks. Unless a few thousand soldiers hid in waiting, Blailon would seize the city before the sun finished its descent.

Jouler's heart yearned for him to take action, to do *something* to save his home.

No, he thought, rubbing his temples. *Headwater is my home.*

A loud war horn pierced his malaise. Jouler followed the sound to a dark mass of soldiers, their unmistakable snow-white skin stark against their too-black topknot.

Boorde.

Groups of il'Spada and firedancers pealed away from the sea of black, and filtered into Blailon's forces. The blades, glowing like fire, smashed through Vrath patterns and sliced through imperial armor, while firedancers melted Blailon's ranks.

Jouler slacked with relief, pride welling in his eyes at the sound of Blailonian horns trumpeting retreat. The Boorde chased the fleeing soldiers while cheers erupted throughout the defenders.

The city's Shining Gate slid into the ground, and a procession of imperials filed out, their lilac banners held high, the deep-blue snake and a silver chalice whipping in the wind. Riding at the head of the procession on a sleek gray horse was a homely woman with alabaster skin and long silver hair. A dark-red cloak draped behind her, pouring over the rear of her horse like velvet wine.

Jouler's attention slid off the silver-haired Founder, his heart yearning for the city—for home.

No, he thought, his mind fading into the oblivion of sleep. *Headwater is my home.*

JOULER PLODDED over the soft snowpack, glad for the snowshoes L'Veyna had asked for everyone. Adjusting his pack, he glanced back at their trail of churned snow leading up the blanketed mountain pass. Between the Boorde Alliance's towering peaks and the forested slopes of Haldr's Bowl, the pass poured into a pristine white meadow dappled with pine tips. No other tracks marred the frozen landscape, but only a day had passed since Reylan sent Matron Nith'Iil's Ascended down the mountain along with half the cliff side.

Jouler scratched at the thick stubble on his neck, promising himself a shave when he didn't wake up inside a frozen shelter. Katima's fire had been far too small to keep them warm, but, in her defense, Boorde weren't the best at understanding how much heat Humans and Prytha needed.

"How much farther?" Dilna whined, her snowshoes crunching the snow behind him. "Aren't you getting tired, Pen?"

Walking next to her, Pendric nodded and slumped to his knees, sinking in the soft snow, breathing as though he'd sprinted all morning. Until Jouler retrieved the Black Breath, Pendric would forever be at the Ul'Kral's mercy, forever bound to a tiny, delicate little vial. Jouler could only imagine how those pesky creatures might keep it safe—maybe clutched in a web of branches, or nestled in a bed of leaves. However, they stored the vial, they could never keep it as safe as Kael could with the Currents.

"I…need…rest." Pendric wheezed.

Katima stared down at him with a frown of disappointment, her firedancer dress rippling around her ankles in the gentle breeze. A twitch of her finger ignited a small fire on the ground close to Pendric.

"Bigger," Dilna said, holding her arms in a circle. "Like, this big."

"Of course," Katima said, the corner of lips curling. She twitched her finger again, and the fire grew.

Reylan shivered beneath his thick coat, and let his pack fall. "For Pen's sake," he said, crouching beside Pendric near the fire, "we dare not head much farther west. Or south, for that matter."

"Can't you do something for Pen?" L'Veyna asked, falling back into the thick snow. She crawled out of her pack and scooted to the fire.

"I can," Reylan said. "Once we get to calmer lands. The Currents here are too turbulent to risk such a delicate pattern." He pointed to the southeastern slopes of Haldr's Bowl. "Merru'ut capital is on the other side of those mountains. The Currents will be calm as a pond by the city, but those mountains are also crawling with soldiers and Sotouri trainees."

Diou jerked his chin to the flat plains far below the rolling foothills. "Those plains aren't too far south, and they aren't crawling with imperials."

"That's not a bad idea," Reylan said, fishing out his pipe. "We'll have to cross a couple causeways and ford Skogsnár River, but we'll have a clear path north to Eio."

"Clearer," Prack corrected, letting his backpack fall to the ground. "I'll run ahead and scout out the causeway."

"I'm going with you," Jouler said, setting his pack next to Pendric.

"I'm going too," L'Veyna said, getting to her feet. "Dilna, you coming?"

Dilna shivered, spreading her hands to the fire. "You go. I want to rest and warm up a little."

Jouler hefted the staff L'Veyna had asked him, and took off after Prack, L'Veyna's crunching footsteps close behind. She offered him a coy smile, her pleasant aroma caressing his senses. It never changed, no matter how hard they traveled, or how hot the weather, she always smelled of flowers mixed with the soft scent of grass and soil after a rain.

Unlike me, he thought, already aware of his souring odor. He forced his gaze away from her, focusing on Prack's autumnal hair falling in a tail down his back, but L'Veyna's captivating beauty demanded his attention. Their ancient bond didn't help, either. It especially didn't help that beauty captivated him wherever he saw it. Be it a sunset, a pristine meadow, a stunning woman, or an impressive man, Jouler's eyes craved beauty. Like Katima, who somehow seemed to stand out among a race that all looked sculpted from the same vein of snow-white marble. She had the same alabaster skin, the same lissome figure, and the same flame-colored pupils, yet she captured every gaze that crossed her elegant form. Even her bald scalp seemed to add to her beauty.

Jouler dismissed the thought that Katima might be a Facet as soon as it blossomed. The burgeoning silence from his gift belied the truth. He'd never felt an ancient kinship with her, like he had with Kael and L'Veyna. Of course, not every oddity had to be connected to Prophecy. Maybe, after all these centuries, change had finally come to their race.

"Why does it feel this way?" L'Veyna asked, scooting to catch up to him. "The Facet feeling."

"The familiarity?" Jouler said, amused by her choice of words. "The feeling like I've known you for longer than I've been alive. Longer than anything."

"The same," L'Veyna replied.

"I don't know why we feel it," Jouler said. "But I felt the same for Kael. My guess is that we'll feel the same connection for all the Facets."

"Oh," she said, and Jouler couldn't help but think he'd said something wrong. She pasted an empty smile and sped up to walk beside her brother.

"Speaking of Prophecy," Prack said. "Please tell me you learned something new from the Nith'Iil library?"

A flutter of hope crossed L'Veyna's brow, forming a lump of guilt in Jouler's gut. "The Boorde prophecies were the most difficult to interpret," he said. "I think because they're not set in stone, so to speak. The feelings I got from them were more nebulous. They're more like a conglomeration of dreams compiled from thousands of different people over thousands of years. The Boorde Prophecy of Dawn is true, for example, but in a very general sense. Assuming Alnazet is victorious," he said, his gift snapping with truth as he spoke, "the Emblem of Life, whoever that is, will usher in the Time of Plenty."

"Reylan believes the Emblem is Boorde," Prack said, following a low spot in the snow between two gentle slopes.

"That seems to make sense, right?" Jouler replied. "Five Facets. Boorde, Prytha, Citizen, Phaerian, and a fifth, which somehow represents every race. Or maybe none? At least, that's what Reylan believes."

"But not you," Prack said. "It's as clear on your face as…well, your face."

"My gift only stirs when I say it," Jouler said. "Like it's only partially true." He paused to catch his breath, the soft snow sapping his strength. "The Human Prophecy mostly talks about Kael's Path, the Crier of Change, with a handful of references about me, the Harbinger."

"Ack," L'Veyna gagged. "He's d'Tormena."

"He's a Facet, like you," Jouler said. "Our Paths are bound, whether we like it or not."

"Definitely not," L'Veyna mumbled, asking a round of tea spheres. "What about *our* Prophecies, Jo? What about the Curse?"

Prack gestured up a snowy slope. "That should give us a good view of the causeway."

"There is one thing that stood out," Jouler said, using his staff to help him up the hillock. He sipped his tea sphere, savoring the sweet floral flavor and warmth ebbing into his chest. "A few lines speak a bit of the Harbinger's…of *my* role at the end of prophecy. They read—*Oh Harbinger, return the Dark Its glory. Betray the Light, send the glory back whence it came, lest He be devoured, Thy faith restored. Oh Harbinger, break free the Serpent's Eye; break free tradition crushed under heel, the bounty reborn.*"

"That was on Reylan's slate boards," L'Veyna said, beaming at Jouler's surprise. "I can read."

"I know that, I was just…" Jouler shook his head, and made a mental note about L'Veyna's apparent aloofness. It seemed she paid far more attention than she led people to believe.

"But what does it mean?" Prack asked.

"Unfortunately," Jouler said, "my gift has been less than forthcoming with this particular section."

"Maybe the passage is wrong?" L'Veyna offered, and Jouler shook his head.

"Every word of it is true," Jouler said. "But that's all my gift will reveal."

Prack clicked his tongue. "Well, that's annoying. Have you asked nicely?"

"I have not," Jouler admitted. "Even when I mull over potential interpretations to see if one feels right, I get nothing. Why would I betray the Light in the first place, much less return the Dark's glory? Assuming I want the Light to win, wouldn't I try to *prevent* the Dark from regaining its glory? The only thing I'm fairly certain about is the Serpent's Eye. It has to be a reference to the empire. The island capital sits in the Serpent Sea."

They reached the top of a hill offering a clear view of the causeway a league south, cutting through wide rolling plains. Two coaches sped along the causeway at amazing speeds. Faster than an unburdened horse, thanks to horseshoes and coaches pattern-forged to use the special roads.

Legs burning, Jouler looked back at Pendric and the others. Prack had taken them a lot farther than Jouler had imagined. Even farther behind them, a too-black mass of Boorde crept down the mountain pass. Fifty strong at least, less than a mile from the others.

"Prack," he said, pointing.

Prack turned and cursed, drawing his sister's gaze to the Boorde. He released a sharp, shrill whistle, then one more. In the distance, Diou stood and turned toward the approaching Boorde. Katima scooped up Dilna while Diou lifted Pendric into his arms, and they dashed toward the forested slopes of Haldr's Bowl. Reylan trailed behind them.

He'll never make it, Jouler thought, starting toward the old man.

"We're too far away," Prack said, grabbing Jouler's arm. "And we have nowhere to hide in this blastedly barren landscape."

L'Veyna crept closer to her brother, fear dripping from her eyes. "Dilna…"

"We have to help them," Jouler said, alarmed at the approaching Boorde's speed.

"Reylan and Diou can take care of themselves," Prack said.

"Against fifty-odd Boorde?" Jouler replied.

"Not fifty," Prack said as half of the dark mass broke away and headed toward them. Prack spun, taking in their surroundings. "There. We'll head for that lowland." He pointed south and set a fast pace toward a winding line of snow-dusted trees.

"What's there?" L'Veyna asked, falling in step beside her brother.

"Water," Prack replied. "A good-sized stream, by the look of those trees."

"Ah," L'Veyna said with a wicked smile.

"I don't understand," Jouler said, struggling to keep up in his cumbersome snowshoes.

"Water amplifies my powers," L'Veyna said, hardly a strain to her breath despite the quick pace.

Jouler glanced over his shoulder. The Boorde seemed to gain on them with each long step. Sweat stung his eyes, his legs burned, his chest heaved for breath. Sharp pain lanced his side with each desperate inhale, muscles cramping, body begging him to stop.

"You have to keep up, Jo," Prack said, picking up his pace, his breathing no more labored than if he'd been on a casual stroll.

The words floated over the pain coursing through Jouler, desperation fueling his numb legs, while Prack and L'Veyna pulled farther ahead. A ball of fire exploded behind Jouler, heat rolling up his backside. He fell hard to the ground, the pungent odor of singed hair filling his nose.

"Jo!" L'Veyna screamed, struggling against her brother's tight grip around her waist. The world blurred, the landscape speeding by as Prack shifted away from the Boorde. She leveraged her feet against his side, tears streaming back across her temples, and she pushed.

Weightless, the world spun around her, her stomach lurching as she flew through the air. She crashed hard onto the snowy ground, dull thumps and sharp pains riddling her as she tumbled to a stop.

"That was stupid!" her brother shouted above the ringing in her ears. "Alnazet's mercy, L'Veyna, you could have killed yourself."

Head dazed, L'Veyna pushed her brother away, and looked for... someone. Someone important... If only the plagued world would stop spinning enough for her to form a thought. She spotted a familiar Human in the distance surrounded by rows of black figures, though his name refused to form in her muddled mind. She pushed herself to her feet, but her knees refused to work, and she found herself on the ground again.

The snow isn't so thick, she thought, her hand settling on a small rock.

Prack peered into her eyes and cursed. "Gods damn it, L'Veyna, you're concussed. This is the last thing we need." He turned his gaze to the black figures. "It appears Jo was the Boorde's target. Not us. At least, not yet."

Jouler!

Ancient familiarity wormed through her muddled mind, but her memories of the person popped as soon as they formed. Her stomach churned, and her mouth watered. "I think I'm going to be sick."

Prack rubbed her back, casting a mournful gaze to the rows of black figures. "Next time I shift with you," he told her with a pointed look, "don't jump off."

"What are you talking about?" L'Veyna grumbled, clutching her head through waves of pain. "I'd never do that. I'm not that dumb."

"I CAN'T BELIEVE I jumped off," L'Veyna mumbled over her cracking headache and the fear gripping her over Jouler's safety. "What was I thinking?"

"I don't think you were." Prack added another log to their fire, sending bright embers into the ancient chestnut tree. The rush of a nearby stream drowned his mumbled curse, though L'Veyna read it on his lips.

Damned child.

Guilt tightened her chest, matching the darkening sky. "What are we going to do? We have to help Jouler."

"Well..." Prack stabbed the fire again. "The Boorde have half a day on us. Thankfully, their captive is Human, so they'll actually have to stop to rest and sleep, otherwise we'd never catch them."

"What's the other bad news?" L'Veyna asked, knowing her brother too well to believe that would be it.

"It looks like they're headed for Urna. It's a Phaerian town on the Caelya Bay, three...maybe four days from here."

"Why would they take him there?" L'Veyna asked, already missing the comfort of Jouler's familiarity.

Prack rubbed his face with a weary sigh. "It makes no sense. It's far quicker to walk back to the Alliance than to sail."

L'Veyna shut her eyes, breathing as evenly as possible, but nothing seemed to help her pounding head.

"Feeling any better?" Prack asked.

"A little," she replied, wincing. "I'll be fine in the morning."

"Let's hope so," Prack said, lifting an eyebrow. "You're not trying to ask, are you?"

"No," she promised, her gaze mesmerized by the crackling flames. "My head still hurts too much."

"Good." Prack added another stick to the fire, sending orange sparks int to air. "Remember that next time—"

"I decide to jump off while you're shifting." L'Veyna fixed him with a pointed stare. "Yeah, I got it the first hundred times. I get it. I messed up. I'm sorry, okay?"

"Well, that makes it all better, doesn't it?"

"What do you want from me?" L'Veyna asked over the lump in her throat. "You don't think I feel bad enough? I said I get it. It's all my fault Jouler's captured." Her heart cramped over the thought of Jouler in the hands of those crazed Boorde. "If I'd stayed with Dilna, I wouldn't have been here to mess everything up. You would have already saved him by now, but here we are, in the middle of nowhere, and it's all my fault." The agony in her heart swelled, and her vision watered. "How am I supposed to be a Facet, when all I ever do is get in the way? I'm not a hero. I'm just a little girl."

A sob choked her voice, and she fell into Prack's arms.

"There it is, let it out," her brother said, his soft voice tugging more sobs. "But, sister?"

She looked up at him, his wry grin wavering through her tears. "What?"

"Who said you were a hero?" Prack said, his humor cutting through her misery.

"You know what I mean," she mumbled, slapping his arm.

"I do." Prack used his shirt to wipe her eyes. "But I don't think you do. Climbing a mountain can be overwhelming when you're standing at the bottom. But all you have to do is take it one step at a time. Don't think about the Prophecies as a whole. Don't think of them at all. Prophecy can take care of Itself. Trust me." He squeezed her in his arms, his emerald-green eyes sparkling with pride. "True, you're only thirteen, Little Sprout, but you've done more than any sapling I've ever known. Even me. You traveled to the Boorde Alliance, and not many adults can say that, much less any saplings."

"Yeah, but I didn't do anything,"she mumbled. "I was just following you and everyone else. You all did the hard work."

"And I guess you'd say your askings are child's play?"

"That's different," she said, entranced by the embers, how they wavered and pulsed with heat.

"Is it different?" Prack asked in that voice that dared her to say yes. "Do you think Jouler feels like the M'Ljot?"

"I don't see why not," L'Veyna said. "The rotten man can do anything. He picked up Talontongue on our way to Nubidae, and he learned Boordish in a couple weeks."

"But he can't ask," Prack said. "He can't shape, or firedance, or shift. He's just a farm boy from a tiny little village, just trying to do what he believes is right."

L'Veyna shrugged, snuggling into her brother's arms. Perhaps it was the crackling fire, or Prack's comforting voice, but her eyes wanted nothing more than to shut.

"Go ahead and get some sleep, Little Sprout. Just so you know, I'll be waking you throughout the night."

"Why?" she asked, letting her brother lay her by the warm fire. "You have a plan, right, brother?" He always had a plan.

Her brother stared into the fire, his face devoid of emotion.

"Prack, you have a plan, right?"

His emerald eyes, normally filled with such casual confidence as to make any doubt flee in terror, now glistened with doubt. "No...I don't."

23

PILLARS OF FIRE

Katima scooped Dilna and tossed the small child over her shoulder, then she ate a chunk of meat from her pouch, bolstering her inner flame. Diou ran beside her, Pendric bouncing in his arms, while Mother's Ascended maneuvered down the snow-packed pass.

"To the mountains!" Reylan shouted, falling behind, dragging Jouler's pack.

"No!" Dilna cried, slapping Katima's back. "Stop! We have to help Reylan."

"He can take care of himself," Diou said, leading them into the dense pine forest prickling the slopes of Haldr's Bowl. He pointed to a bushy ledge overlooking the encroaching Ascended. "We'll wait for him there, and set up a defense."

Katima deposited Dilna into a plump mound of snow, ignoring the child's complaints while she entered a simple defensive stance, her djohai dangling from her hand. Expecting to find a few dozen Ascended on their heels, she jerked in surprise when she saw only Reylan huffing up the hill, his dark skin glistening with sweat.

"Where are the Ascended?" Katima asked.

Reylan dumped Jouler's pack and held up his hand, begging for a moment while he caught his breath. "Apparently," he said, his hands on his knees, "there are a lot of deep holes in the ground. One just appeared and gobbled them right up. Just like that."

"You buried them?" Katima asked.

"Of course not." Reylan stood up straight. "I'm not that powerful. But let's not dally. The hole isn't terribly deep. It won't take them all day to climb out. Go on," he said, pressing his fist against his lower back. "I'll hide our tracks. Can someone take Jouler's pack?"

"What about the others?" Dilna demanded. "We can't just leave them."

"They'll have to fend for themselves," Diou said, grabbing Jouler's pack and heading deeper into the forested mountains.

"We have to trust them to stay alive," Reylan said, their footsteps filling with snow as he walked. "Just like they have to trust us."

"Which won't happen," Katima noted, her spine tingling from his pattern, "if we don't put more distance between us and Mother's Ascended. How deep was that hole, old man?"

"Old?" Reylan huffed. "You're not much younger than me."

Katima measured the old man, wondering how much help he would provide once the Ascended caught up with them. A single team would have been difficult enough without having to worry about two children and an aged Phaerian. Katima devoured a large strip of meat from her pouch and her inner flame raged inside her, begging for release.

"I will live for another seven or eight centuries," she told Reylan. "You, on the other hand, will be lucky to squeeze out a couple more decades at best."

"Ouch," Diou said, chuckling over his own strip of meat.

"Did I say something wrong?" Katima asked, noting the offense in Reylan's mumbles. "Are you not relatively close to the end of your—"

"Sister," Diou said, cutting her off.

His blatant insult shouldn't have surprised Katima, given the inordinate amount of time he spent with Prytha and Humans. "You forget yourself, brother. I am still Heiress Apparent of our House."

"You *were* Heiress Apparent," Diou said, the truth of his words brushing over her bald scalp. He cast a casual wave to their forested surroundings. "Out here, you're just prey. You're not in the Alliance anymore, dear sister. For all we know, those Ascended aren't here to bring us back home."

"Mother wouldn't dare," Katima said, while her mind flashed with memories of the white mourning dress.

Diou fixed her with a gaze that said he knew she didn't believe it anymore than he did.

"What about…" Pendric wheezed, slumping to his knees. "What about…Jo and L'Veyna? How will we meet—" He coughed, his face turning red as he fought for air.

Reylan ran to his side. The old Phaerians eyes went distant, Katima's shaping sense rippled down her spine, and Pendric's breathing eased.

"That will help for a while," Reylan said, clapping Pendric's back. "I think you were going to ask how we're going to meet up with Jouler?"

A toothy smile split Pendric's face, and he squeezed Reylan in a tight hug.

"Okay, okay," the old man chuckled. "We need to get going. I should have shaped a deeper hole for those Boorde."

"We disagree," a voice sounded from the deep shadows of the forest. In the darkness, flames licked down a djohai, the warm light flickering off a single strip of flame-colored cloth. Three more djohai licked with flames, and a dozen il'Spada stepped from the shadows. Armed with spears, sidaiyo, and maces, they spread out with practiced grace. The first firedancer stepped into the light, a flash of shock crossing her placid features. "I can't say your mother will be disappointed by your scalp. She might not even have to worry about wearing that ridiculous dress."

Reylan breathed a heavy sigh. "I really should have shaped a deeper hole."

Katima's shaping sense rippled down her back, and three pines exploded, jagged slivers rippling through all but one of the firedancers. Molted darts whistled through the air, piercing a handful of il'Spada, while shards of obsidian shot from the ground, piercing the legs and groin of two others.

Katima slid into a dance, her graceful swoops and twists matching her twirling djohai. The firedancer Ascended entered a rhythmic dance, disrupting Katima and launching a jet of fire. Katima's spine rippled and a slab of rock burst from the ground, dispersing the jet.

Without breaking stride, the firedancer shifted her dance, and whips of liquid flame lashed at Katima and Reylan. Katima twirled her djohai, catching the whips, and sliding into a new rhythm. She let her djohai twist around her, a ball of liquid flame forming around the bladed tip. Twisting with a shout, she launched the djohai. Her spine rippled from Reylan's shaping, and the firedancer's foot slipped. Katima's fiery djohai slammed into the firedancer's chest and liquid fire splashed out her back.

Diou stood still as stone, his spear held low, blade dripping blood. A pair of il'Spada circled him, their steps synchronized, moonlight glinting along their sidaiyo.

Dilna ran for him, dagger clutched in her tiny fist.

"Get back here," Katima growled, grabbing Dilna before she got herself killed. At least Pendric seemed to know better than to get in the way, even if he cowered behind a thick sugar pine.

Katima's back rippled again, and a shower of sparks burst in front of the Ascended.

Diou dashed through the sparks, his spear severing the Boorde's hands. A spinning stab pierced the il'Spada's chest while blocking the other's strike. The dead Ascended crumbled to the ground, and as if by some unspoken agreement, Diou relaxed, and the il'Spada sheathed his sidaiyo.

"What is he doing?" Dilna asked.

"My brother honors him with the Myr'koth," Katima replied. "The Final Duel."

Reylan shook his head, his face drenched in sorrow. "I should have shaped a deeper hole."

KATIMA WATCHED her brother and the il'Spada walk into the serene meadow, the promise of night creeping on the horizon. Dilna's chattering teeth rumbled through Katima's mind. "Where is your coat, child? And your gloves?"

"You and D-D-D-Diou don't ha-have any," Dilna replied.

"We're Boorde," Katima said, wriggling her finger to dance warmth around the girl. "We feel neither hot nor cold."

"I know," Dilna said, drooping her shoulders. "I just wanted to be tough like you."

"Standing in the freezing cold without a coat isn't being tough," Katima said. "Keep watching my brother. Stick by his side. He'll make you tougher than terrentor hide."

"You think I can get that good?" Dilna asked, gripping the hilt of the dagger Diou had given her. She'd never make the Boorde steel glow, but it would serve the fiery little girl well, as long as she didn't try to run before she could crawl.

"You will never get that good," Katima said before she could stop herself. Humans needed gentle persuasions, not blunt honesty. "What I mean is that it's not fair to compare yourself to any Boorde, because you'll never develop our battle prescience, and, unfortunately, a human's life is a blink to a Boorde's. My brother has already trained longer than even your shapers live, and his eyes still have a lot of centuries before they pale."

"So it's pointless," Dilna mumbled, her dagger sagging in her loose grip.

"No, that's not..." Katima sighed, wondering how Diou maneuvered these conversations with such ease. "You are special, because you are the only you in the world. It doesn't matter if you're as skilled with a blade as my brother. Just be the best you that you can be."

"Gods, now you sound like Reylan," Dilna said, which the old man didn't seem to hear.

Reylan stood beside Pendric, their gaze following Diou and the Ascended.

"Why didn't Diou just cut him down?" Dilna asked.

"Honor," Pendric replied, and Katima gave him a nod of approval.

"Just so," she said. "My brother honors the il'Spada with the Myr'koth."

"But Diou could die," Dilna said. "I don't get it. He hates swords."

"My brother will teach you," Katima said, pressing a finger to her lips for silence.

Diou and the il'Spada faced each other on the snowy meadow, their breaths aglow in the soft moonlight. They bowed in unison and drew their sidaiyo. Diou swung his foot back into a wide stance, the blade he'd taken from a fallen Ascended pointed behind him and parallel with the ground. The Ascended rolled his shoulders and lowered the point of his curved sword. Poised like statues on the moonlit field of white, they waited for the unspoken signal.

In a blink, they moved, dashing toward each other, ry'ku whipping behind them. The il'Spada chopped, his blade bouncing off Diou's as they passed. They halted after the strike and stood up straight. The il'Spada dropped his sword, blood spurting from his neck. He fell to his knees and disappeared under the thick snow.

"Gods' mercy," Dilna whispered, gawking at Diou. She looked down at the dagger clutched in her hand, and she sheathed it, embarrassment burning her cheeks.

Katima crouched in front of her, demanding her gaze. "I was wrong about you. I can see that now."

Dilna blinked, and the fire rekindled in her eyes.

"You're only a couple of years older than my brother was when he started training, but you have something Diou never had, and he never will."

Doubt pulled at Dilna's lips. "I do?"

Katima nodded and pointed to her brother. "You get to be trained by the legendary Diou Nith'Iil, the Boorde who single-handedly slayed an Aandari."

"What's an Aandari?"

"Prytha call them the Scourge," Katima said. "But to Humans, they're called headless."

Dilna shivered, a thought twinkling in her eyes. "So...they're real? Kael really was stabbed by a...by a headless?"

"Did his skin look shattered?" Katima asked, and Dilna nodded. "Then yes, he was stabbed by a headless. Come on, Little Sister," she said, leading Dilna onto the meadow.

"Where are we going?"

"To commit the Ascended's souls to the Flame."

BENEATH A PALE HALF-MOON, Dilna accepted the cold, like Diou taught her, letting it pass through her, channeling the pain into pleasure…

Nope! she thought, shivers wracking her body. *I'm still Human, and it's still freezing.*

Footsteps crunched the snow behind her, and she focused on the sound, noting the person's short stride. Something dragged over the snow…a cloth, like a robe.

Reylan.

"I know it's you, old man," she said, peering over her shoulder.

"I wasn't trying to sneak," he said, holding up her coat and gloves. "I just thought you might like these."

"Thank you," she said, slipping on the clothes. Warmth radiated from the fabric, as if warmed by a campfire.

"Weavers aren't the only ones who can pattern-forge." Reylan bobbed his eyebrows. "The gloves should feel nice too."

She slipped them on her hands, and soft warmth melted her aching cold. "Gods, they feel great. Thank you. How's Pendric?"

"He's fine," Reylan replied, puffing on his curved pipe. "He's asleep by the campfire."

Dilna's gaze drifted to the Boorde corpses atop a large pyre. Twelve Ascended, the world's finest warriors, slain in moments. "I thought they were supposed to be, well, you know…the best?"

Reylan frowned, the bowl of his pipe flaring. "They are."

"But, you and Diou just…" Dilna dragged a finger across her throat.

Smoke plumed from Reylan's nostrils, filling the air with the pungent smell of ha'ath. "Everyone has their weaknesses, dear. Remember that." The old man put a finger to his lips and gestured to the pyre. "Boorde honor demands our silence."

Dilna snapped her mouth shut and pulled her warm coat tight against the biting cold.

Katima, strong and elegant, stood in front of the pyre, her firedancer dress rippling in an unfelt breeze. Her hips swayed, slowly at first, pulling her torso back and forth. She slid her arms over her head, and they moved with the rhythmic flow of her dance, swaying faster and faster.

Like fire, Dilna realized.

Katima stopped, stomping her foot, and the pyre ignited into white flames. The fire grew, rising into four intertwining pillars that twisted into the sky.

Dilna shielded her eyes from the light, watching Katima's shadow continue the mesmerizing dance while the radiant Boorde stood still and statuesque. Reylan squeezed her shoulder and gestured to the latticed pillar of fire. He must have shaped, because the light didn't burn her eyes when she looked. Now *he* was a master. For all of Kael's power, Reylan shaped with an ease that made Kael seem like a little baby.

Across the burning pillar from Katima, Diou stood as still as stone, his fists at his sides. A living legend, the only Boorde to single-handedly slay a headless. No wonder he'd handled the Ascended with such ease.

Katima's arms fell to her sides, and the winding pillars of fire dissipated into the twinkling night sky. "I commit your souls to the Flame."

Reylan walked to meet them in the meadow, three masters discussing the things of heroes.

I truly am a child among giants, Dilna thought. *At least I have Pen.*

24

SEEDS

L'Veyna's legs begged her to stop, but her brother insisted on staying *ahead* of the plagued Boorde. The sun glared at her in the clear afternoon sky, demanding beads of sweat. Maybe she didn't need so many layers anymore. The autumn in this part of Torgeir almost reminded her of Onatah, though not so humid and without so many trees.

Or any trees! she thought, gazing over the small oaks, olives, and pines. *Not* actual *trees. More like glorified shrubs.*

L'Veyna meandered down a dry riverbed, imagining what it would look like after a season of spring showers, bushes bursting with color along the riverbanks. It was a far better image than the smooth gray rocks clacking under her feet, the steep banks of the riverbed brown and dry with a smattering of dead, frazzled bushes.

As always, when her brother left to scout ahead, her heart yearned for Dilna's company and Pendric's banter. They'd always stayed with her whenever the adults ran off to play hero. Now her friends were gods knew where, running away from Boorde, while L'Veyna and her stupid brother ran toward them.

Not just any Boorde. Godsrotten Ascended!

Prack's blurred form sped toward her up the riverbank, splashing rocks with each shifted step. He stopped beside her and doubled over, sucking in air, sweat pouring down his face and soaking his shirt.

She formed an image of a large sphere of sparkling water and asked. At least that was easy, now that they'd descended to life-baring lands.

"Thank you," he said, splashing the sphere over his head.

L'Veyna offered him a pointed look, and asked him another sphere, adding the same tea she made for Pendric. "Go ahead and splash this one," she warned, handing him the tea. "What did you see?"

"More of the same," Prack said, slurping his sphere. "Thirty two Ascended and one Jouler, all heading to Urna. They've slowed their pace, at least."

"They have *not* slowed their pace," L'Veyna said, asking a tea sphere for herself. Her lungs opened with the first sip, her fatigue fading with each breath. If only she knew of a tea that would sooth her aching muscles. "How are we going to save Jo? There's thirty of them, and two of us."

Her brother's face hardened, and he shook his head. "I still don't know. It doesn't help that the Ascended aren't making any sense. They know we're tracking them, but they make no attempt to stop us."

"The rustwood cares not about the other trees of the forest," L'Veyna said, recalling a quote from her mentor.

Prack clicked his tongue. "Ineom's words have never felt more fitting."

"Maybe the Ascended are bringing Jouler to the empire. To Rodak."

Prack shook his head. "Rodak is in Eio. Even by ship, it would take them far longer than having headed straight there after they captured Jo."

"So...what?" L'Veyna said. "We add that to the list of things to figure out before we rescue Jo?"

"Of course not," Prack said. "But we can't just rush in and grab him. Even if Reylan, Diou, and Katima were here, we'd be hard-pressed to save him against that many Ascended." His brow drew.

"We're missing something. Let's start from the beginning. What does Matron Nith'Iil know about Jouler?"

L'Veyna finished her tea sphere, clacking on her beltboard, "She *probably knows everything you and I know, and more. She's a Matron. She has spies. And a bunch of hidden rooms. Dilna and I only found two.*"

"And an army of librarians to do research," Prack mused. "We have to assume she knows Jouler is M'Ljot, and that she knows about his gift. If so, she undoubtedly believes him to be their Dawn."

"But why not take me with him?" L'Veyna said, smooth river rocks clacking under her feet.

"Because she doesn't know you're a Facet," Prack asked. "She probably still thinks Prophecy is led by a single person. To her, you're nothing more than a refugee from Onatah."

"Well, that's comforting," L'Veyna mumbled.

"Would it make you feel better if she'd sent Ascended after you too?"

"Well, no, I just…"

"Matron Nith'Iil knows Jouler's Path of Prophecy, as he calls it, because her Seers tell her everything they see. My guess is, they told her about the Black Breath, and she plans to use him."

"She wants to use M'Ljot?" L'Veyna asked, not hiding her disbelief at such a senseless idea. As if anyone could control Prophecy.

"Such are the ways of leaders," Prack replied.

"To use the Harbinger of Death," L'Veyna said, reiterating her incredulity.

"The same," her brother said. "You have to admit, it would be a lot easier to expand your borders if Death itself fought alongside you."

"And the Matron expects him to what—just kneel and obey?"

"I expect not," Prack said. "But Matron Nith'Iil is as smart and insidious as they come. If she gets her hands on Jouler, he'll do her bidding, and he'll believe it was his idea the whole time."

"But why put Jo on a ship?" L'Veyna asked. "Why not take him back to Nubidae?"

"Because she doesn't need him in Nubidae," Prack replied, brow furrowing. "But why Urna? Why…" He clicked his tongue and looked toward what had to be Jouler and the Boorde. "Because they're taking Jouler to the Blasted Lands."

CRICKETS, mosquitoes, and bats sang to the night, while sauntering clouds leaked beams of moonlight onto the ground. For the thousandth time since morning, L'Veyna wished for an actual tree, not the glorified bushes dotting the rocky landscape. A tall, needly pine would be nice, or a scraggly naked elm. Jouler liked oaks, the gnarlier the better, but not even those graced this part of the land. Even grasses seemed scarce, popping out of the ground in clusters.

At least we're out of the plagued snow.

From her perch between two large boulders, L'Veyna could barely make out the Ascended's camp in the soft moonlight. Over thirty Boorde, surrounding Jouler, their bedrolls splayed around him like rays of a black sun.

For two days they'd tracked him and his captors, and for two days the Ascended hadn't deviated from their routine. As always, four Boorde stood around Jouler—three il'Spada and one firedancer. The guards would change in half an hour, their replacements seeming to awaken of their own accord, and always ten minutes before their shift. No more. No less. Always standing around Jouler in cardinal positions with the firedancer always in the east. Far beyond their camp, the Phaerian town Urna glowed against the dark of night.

Prack sat on the ground below her perch, his gaze fixated on the Boorde camp. L'Veyna tossed a pebble at him, somehow missing. "I don't understand why you can't just shift into their camp, take out the guards, toss Jo over your shoulder, and shift out?"

"Battle prescience," Prack said. "Boorde see actions before they happen. It's what makes them so dangerous, even to Chi'indi. That's why it was so impressive that Jouler beat a Boorde in the training yard." Her brother jerked his chin to the Boorde camp. "Those are il'Spada. Weapons masters, not sixteen-year-old children. I'd be lucky to get two down before they killed me."

L'Veyna clicked her tongue, not liking this reserved version of her brother who acted as if he hadn't slain half a dozen imperials within the beat of a heart. Boorde couldn't be *that* prescient, no matter what Prack said. Besides, L'Veyna was far from helpless.

If my brother won't save Jo, I will.

Prack rocked on his feet, the soles of his boots scraping on the rocky ground. "There, did you see that?"

"See what?" L'Veyna said, cracking a yawn.

"The guard. Did you see it?"

"Just tell me what it was," she said. Regardless of the tea she'd asked to help her recover, her body still demanded sleep after the Boorde's grueling pace. "Those godsrotten Ascended make Alerix seem relaxed."

Prack clicked his tongue, and the corner of his lip curled. "He's falling asleep."

"Who?" L'Veyna asked, her weariness dissipating from a flash of hope.

"The il'Spada in the southern position. I saw his head bob." Prack clicked his tongue. "He did it again."

"You can see that from here?" L'Veyna said, peering at the Boorde camp. "I thought you said they were elite."

"Even Diou gets tired," Prack said with a wink.

"You have a plan," she said, catching the first note of confidence in his voice in two days.

"Just the seeds. For now, at least." Prack settled back against a tall slab of rock, his emerald gaze lost in thought. "There's nothing we can do, for now. Let's get some sleep."

"I'll ask us some tea," L'Veyna said, forming the image.

"Not so strong this time." Prack stood and yawned into a stretch. "I don't want to be groggy in the morning."

"Like we are now?" L'Veyna said.

There might be nothing you *can do,* she thought, handing her brother his tea sphere. *But I'm a Facet. I have the power of Prophecy on my side.*

L'Veyna jerked awake on the cold slab of rock, her dream fading beneath the starry sky. She ignored her body's protests to return to sleep, and she sat up with a silent curse to the Boorde. If not for them, she'd be back with Dilna and Pendric, and her body wouldn't ache so much. Her brother still slept curled on his side, his breathing too deep and relaxed to be faked. The extra bit of lavender and chamomile she'd asked in his tea helped a bit too. He would have just tied her up if he knew her plans, anyway. Besides, once he saw her with Jouler, he'd thank her for the sleep.

L'Veyna stood, her body demanding a stretch, arms reaching toward a clear night sky. The moon, not quite full, draped its soft glow over the rocky landscape. A beautiful sight, if not for the Boorde camp.

Prack snorted and smacked his lips, then he rolled to his other side.

L'Veyna waited for the count of twenty before sneaking away. There might be nothing *he* could do to save Jouler, but she was the strongest Bud in Onatah.

And the youngest, she thought, a note of pride singing through her frayed nerves.

She looked back at her brother, still asleep on his rock, and a part of her wished he'd awaken and save her from this foolhardy plan. He would scold her again, call her immature, and tell her to grow up.

Instead, I'm scrambling through the night to save a wormy-fingered Human from Ascended.

Obscured in the darkness, she edged toward a large domed rock for a better look at the Boorde. As always, Jouler slept on a bedroll, with four Ascended standing around him at cardinal positions. The rest of his captors slept around them, forming rings blacker than night.

Alnazet's mercy, thirty-two seems far more in person…

L'Veyna's chest tightened at the sight of Jouler, alone in the middle of his captors. He seemed unharmed, though she couldn't see much beneath the growing clouds. Sudden fear soaked her limbs, her heart pounding in her chest. What if they'd drugged him? What if she entwined Jouler's guards, and he couldn't walk? She'd have to ask vines to carry him away and hope the other Ascended didn't awaken.

L'Veyna pushed her intrusive thoughts away. Doubt would kill her as certain as a Boorde's glowing blade. Her plan was good. She'd ask clouds to block the moonlight, wrap the Boorde in vines, and sneak away with Jouler under the cover of night.

L'Veyna gazed up at the twinkling night sky, and imagined a pocket of cold air high above the Ascended, forming small clouds. Hardly abstract, her asking gave no resistance.

It's easier to ask a tree from a seed than to ask it from nothing.

Her mentor's words pulled a smile to her lips. The air chilled around her, drawing a shiver, and a gentle breeze stirred.

The seeds of my plan, she thought.

The wind picked up, funneling air upward to feed her voracious asking.

No…no! I wanted seeds, not strong wind!

Jouler's captors lifted their gaze to the clouds forming high above them, obscuring the moon. The clouds spread across the sky, growing larger and faster than she'd intended. The Ascended scanned the darkness while sleeping Boorde awoke and grabbed their weapons.

Churning clouds soon dominated the sky, grumbling and flashing in anger. The wind howled, robbing the air of what little warmth remained in the night. L'Veyna shivered, pulling her coat against the plummeting cold. A light drizzle sprinkled over the camp and soaked into her hair. Lightning cracked the night, stabbing the land with deafening blows, as sheets of rain rolled over the land.

Boorde searched through pouring rain, fiery djohai and glowing blades sizzling in the night. Grumbling clouds drenched the land, forming large pools and frenzied riverbeds. A bolt of lightning shattered the air, washing the Boorde camp, and ringing her ears. A purple line snaked across her vision, tracing the lightning's jagged path. In the camp, six bodies smoldered where the bolt had struck, while the other Ascended covered their eyes and stumbled about. Jouler lay in the middle of it all, curled in a ball, and covering his head.

L'Veyna ignored the numbness spreading up her arms and legs, and she focused on Jouler balled up against the howling wind. She imagined him carried away on vines, but the image crumbled, her mind too numb to ask. She fell to the boulder, and curled up like Jouler, shaking, her hands and feet numb, mind sluggish.

Someone grabbed her and slung her over their shoulder. Eyelids too heavy to open, she drifted to the sudden rush of howling wind. Too frozen to care, she drifted in and out of consciousness. The gushing wind died, the angry storm replaced by a crackling fire and heavy breathing. Light tapped at her eyelids, inviting them to open. Dancing flames flickered above a pile of snapped branches set against a wide slab of rock.

"Gods, that was stupid. Stupid stupid stupid." Her brother glared at her, daring her to speak.

He shifted me away, she realized, recognizing the howl she'd heard.

Prack squeezed his fists, anger crackling in his eyes. He drew a slow, shaking breath, and his face softened with a sigh. "Warming up is going to hurt, Little Sprout. Let's get you out of those wet clothes."

He draped his coat over her naked skin and helped her to lie beside the fire. As promised, the crackling heat melted her frozen skin, and countless hot needles seared her arms and legs down to the tips of her fingers and toes. Her screams tore through the night, the hot pain stabbing into her soul. After an eternity of agony, the searing needles faded, and her body throbbed in rhythm with her heart.

"Why did you do that?" Prack asked, adding more wood to the fire. "Why didn't you tell me?"

Anger stirred within her, rising above her fatigue. "Because you would have just said no."

"And for good reason." Prack clicked his tongue. "Wouldn't you say?"

"It would have worked if you would have helped."

"And what would we have done if it had?" he asked, his question stealing her anger. "Let's say we whisked Jouler away like heroes in some adventure book. What next?" He glared at her, anger welling in his eyes. "What would we have done with thirty-two Ascended on our trail? Or did you expect me to be your little assassin and kill them all while they slept?"

L'Veyna turned her gaze to the crackling fire, unable to meet his eyes.

"I'm tired of reminding you to grow up," Prack said, jabbing a stick into the fire. "One of these days, you're going to get someone killed."

25

ONLY SO MUCH

Kael watched one foot step in front of the other…or was that a memory? The creaking wheels and ever-present dust told him he walked, but he'd also just seen Olan's pleading face, so he couldn't be awake…could he?

Something slammed into him, his tortured mind struggling to make sense of the sharp points jabbing his back.

I'm on my back, he realized, panic swallowing his mind. *Dear gods, no!*

The chains connecting him to the coach went taught, and darkness enveloped him.

Freezing water coursed down his body. His head jerked back, and a misshapen face filled his vision. Dark, uneven eyes stared at him, blood smeared across her forehead. Fire lanced across his belly, his throat too hoarse to cry. He looked down, and saw a pile of…something, spill from his gut and steam at his feet—

One raw foot in front of the other, blades slicing his body, a glaring sun scorching his blistered back, white-hot pokers burning his skin, chains dragging him over rocks, dragging, and dragging—

A man's voice fluttered through his torment. "…an't stop now… ave to keep going."

The woman with the misshapen face rounded on a man with blond hair and a shimmering temple. The woman jabbed a finger at Kael. "Do you want to turn this over to Rodak? Gwyndril and Finndras are both having a hard time healing his mind."

The voice, so familiar… Distant memories struggled for life, while Kael's mind crawled toward oblivion. Cold water washed down his body, igniting a sparkle of clarity, and a name floated from his lips.

"Livia."

The woman with the misshapen face peered at him with her dark, troubled eyes. "He needs a break," she mumbled. "*I* need a break."

The raging man's lip curled in a snarl, and something tightened over Kael's throat.

"Release him," the misshapen girl with Livia's voice demanded. Aglia…her name was Aglia. "Now!"

The band over Kael's neck disappeared, and air flooded back into his lungs, his broken ribs cracking with each breath. The man with the shimmering temple stood before him, his crazed blue eyes clenching Kael's stomach with fear.

"He remembers who I am," the man said, slamming a fist into Kael's gut. "Enough to fear me, at least."

Blood spewed from Kael's mouth.

"Touch him one more time," the broken woman warned, and the man took a threatening stride toward her. "Go ahead," she said with a chuckle. "Lay a finger on me, and you'll be swallowing Isol's ball and chain. Now, be a good little boy and fetch your captain before I decide to ask Lady Maelly for a more competent apprentice."

The man looked down at her, considering, then he scowled and strode from the tent into the dark of night.

"Blasted fool," the woman cursed, peering into Kael's eyes.

"Thank you." Kael vomited blood again, covering the front of her blouse.

The woman gripped his hair and slammed it back against the rack. "Let me make myself clear. I stopped him from killing you because I know what Lord Rodak will do to *me* if we handed him a blithering idiot. That, and you haven't suffered nearly enough, oh Light of Prophecy." She spat in his face. "I want you to suffer for what you did.

Headwater would still be there. My family would still be alive. Lord Rodak never would have turned me into this…this thing."

She let go of his hair, and his head fell forward.

Icy water splashed over his body again, shocking his mind clear. *Not water…a healing.* His gaze drifted to the misshapen woman.

Aglia, not Livia.

Standing beside her, a young man measured him, his rosy cheeks and red hair tingling Kael's memories. "Emperor's ass," the man cursed, his green eyes flashing with fear. "I thought you said you knew what you were doing."

"Baelorin, he—"

"I will speak to *Lieutenant* Baelorin," the man said, and Aglia dipped her head.

Finndras, that's his name.

The tii'Vrath placed his hands on either side of Kael's head. "This won't feel good," he said, his deep voice rumbling with sympathy.

Icy talons gripped Kael's mind, and a sound like rushing wind filled his ears. Body rigid, his guts writhed, and dark excrement poured down his legs. His stomach heaved again, and gooey clumps of coagulated blood spilled from his mouth. He dangled from his bonds, his strength sapped by the sudden relief from his pains.

"No more for tonight," Finndras said, rolling up the sleeves of his simple blouse.

"I told Baelorin as much," Aglia replied. "He almost killed him."

"I know."

"If Lord Rodak—"

"*I know,*" Finndras said, pinching the bridge of his nose. "Baelorin is a good soldier. Loyal to the empire, unlike this filth." The tii'Vrath waved a dismissive hand at Kael. "He deserves everything Lord Rodak is going to do to him. Baelorin knows that too. He's passionate, but his heart is in the right place."

"With all respect, Captain Finndras," Aglia said, bowing her head. "The lieutenant's heart lies in watching the life fade from his victim's eyes. A dangerous trait in a torturer, according to Lord Rodak."

"And do you not seek this man's death?" Finndras asked.

"Wanting to see him suffer for allowing this to happen…" She pointed to her face, and ripped open her blouse, exposing the two ugly scars where her breasts had been. "That's not the same thing as being aroused by torture. Not even Lord Rodak is that perverse."

Finndras put his hands on either side of Kael's head, releasing another wave of healing energy. Breathless, the captain stepped back, his green eyes drooping with fatigue. "That's all the healing you're getting tonight, I'm afraid."

Strength ebbed back into Kael's limbs, his mind refreshed and keen once more. Knowing better than to meet Finndras's eyes, Kael kept his gaze on the floor. His shredded pants, little more than strips of cloth dangling from a waistband, dripped with his blood, his legs and feet glistening red on the muddy ground.

Finndras held a hand to his nose. "But there *is* something I can do about your smell."

Freezing water, *actual* water this time, splashed and coursed around him, scrubbing his body clean, and ripping off what little remained of his pants. Teeth chattering and naked, Kael convulsed from the cold, his wrists and ankles straining against his bonds.

Sudden warmth blossomed in within Kael's chest, spreading to his arms and his legs. Welcomed needles pierced his numbed fingers and toes as sensation crept up his limbs. Free from pain and blanketed in comfort, Kael sagged again, hardly noticing his sharp pang of hunger. Sleep pulled his eyes closed, and a sharp pain in his cheek brought them open again.

Aglia shook her hand. "Eat first."

Confused by the fresh shirt and trousers covering his body, he sat up and swung his legs off his bed. Before he could ask how he got in bed, the smell of meat awakened his raging belly, devoured his thoughts.

"Sit," Aglia commanded, her glare as sharp as her tone. She stood by a small round table with three large plates piled with meat, beans, and potatoes, and a tall pitcher of water. "You will eat it all."

The pang in Kael's belly assured him that it wouldn't be a problem, but even Pendric would struggle to finish a single plate, let alone all three. Kael sat in the rickety stool, a spoon his only utensil. Grabbing a slab of meat, he ripped off a chunk with his teeth, warm juices dribbling down his chin. His jaw ached from the tough cut, while his stomach demanded more. A gulp of water helped wash the meat down, and he gobbled spoonfuls of beans and potatoes spiced with pepper and garlic.

By the time he'd eaten half the first plate, his stomach protested against more. A knowing smile crossed Aglia's face, and she unsheathed the blade she'd so deftly used on him these past few days...weeks maybe?

Gods, how long has it been?

Aglia sat across from him, toying with the knife. What was left of her wispy hair, once like thick waves of honey, fell lifeless to her bony shoulders, her thick shirt and pants doing little to hide her emaciated form. Her dark eyes, once so full of life and love, sat uneven on her scarred face. Her gaze hardened with disdain.

She slammed a fist on the table, shaking the pitcher of water. "Eat!"

Kael forced another spoonful of beans, then another until the plate was empty. Stomach distended and warning to stop, he pushed the empty plate aside. His insides gurgled and bloated with gas.

"Baelorin added a little pattern to your food," Aglia said, her smile widening, displaying what few teeth remained on the one side of her mouth. Kael's bowels rumbled again, and she lifted an eyebrow. "Something to help you pass your food a little faster." She frowned and put a finger to her lips. "Or was it a *lot* faster? I forget."

Pressure built inside him, his bowels demanding release. He looked for a bucket or bag or *anything*. He stood, and Aglia stabbed her knife into the table.

"Sit!"

"Aglia, I—"

"You will sit," she said, wiggling the point of her dagger out of the table. "And you will eat."

Unable to contain himself any longer, he grimaced and relaxed. His stomach reeled from the disgusting warmth soiling his new clothes.

Aglia tilted her head, seeming unaffected by the stench of partially digested food, if she could smell at all through her misshapen nose. She nudged the last two plates of food toward him. "Now, finish your food," she said, and moved to the torture rack, "so I can put you to bed. I know Finndras said no more fun, but I just can't bear the thought of leaving without hearing you scream a little more."

AGLIA DRAPED a strip of damp cloth over Kael's wounds, his back rising and falling with slumber. She'd rip the strips off in the morning like she had in Headwater, when she'd cared for the pathetic coward. How hard she'd worked to win over the villagers, conspiring with Jo and Pen to keep him safe, only to watch him walk away and leave the person he said he loved. The so-called Light prophesied to save her people, not abandon them to Lord Rodak.

You told him to leave, a voice chimed in her mind. *You forced him to go.*

"He didn't have to," Aglia growled, cleaning the blood from her knife. He couldn't see the pattern she'd etched into his back, mirroring the shattered-glass scars on his belly. She laid the last damp bandage over the thin blue scar where the headless had run him through. "He could have saved us."

Laughter cackled in her mind, and she dragged her knife over her thigh, silencing the voice with a deep cut. Soothing pain leaked from the wound and dribbled down her leg.

She considered awakening Kael with a cut. He deserved far worse. Of course, nothing she did could ever compare to Lord Rodak. He would teach Kael to a higher understanding of pain.

She scored her leg again, and moaned, warmth dripping down her thigh.

But he wouldn't show Kael the pleasure hidden behind the burning pain. The realm of blissful agony even the mighty Lord Rodak dared not tread.

Aglia reached between her legs, rubbing herself while she scored her thigh again. She squeezed the cuts, riding the waves of pain into a wash of ecstasy. Timing her release, she pressed her fingers into the cuts and cried out, shuddering with each euphoric pulse.

Kael didn't twitch, far too exhausted to awaken from her excitement.

Taken by the moment of painful bliss, memories of happier times stirred in Aglia's mind. Times when she hadn't found Kael's dishwater-blond hair so repulsive. When his gray eyes stirred her heart, not her rage. When she'd taken him to a special spot on a lake shore...

No! she thought, squeezing her cuts and forcing her mind toward the moment he left. She let that awful day wrap her in a hot blanket of fury. Maybe one day, she'd be able to think about him and not want to rip out his throat, but that day was not today. He'd thrown away every excuse for sympathy the moment he turned his back on Headwater.

The moment you *turned him away.*

"Shut up!" Aglia shouted, pounding her palm against the side of her head.

She strode out of Kael's tent, the voice cackling in her mind.

A cricket-filled night welcomed her outside, the stars bright in the moonless sky. She sucked in the crisp air, letting the icy wind shock her mind clear. It shouldn't take too much longer to reach Eio. A week, maybe two at the most, and then she'd be done with him. Lord Rodak would take him, and she would venture off to whatever wind caught Lady Maelly's fancy.

You know what he'll do, the voice said.

"Kael deserves no less."

Does he?

Aglia stomped the ground with her injured leg, washing the voice from her mind as she headed toward her wagon. Maybe she'd skip retelling the events to Eglona. As much as the girl resented Kael, Aglia knew she only pretended to enjoy his torture.

She's a pure soul, the voice said. *Unlike the rest of us.*

The thoughts halted her steps, and she squeezed her eyes shut. Freezing darkness blew around her, fluttering her thin blouse and skirt. Prickles washed over her skin, burning through her myriad scars, and stabbing into her fresh cuts.

Sucking in a deep breath, she opened her eyes, and Baelorin's face filled her vision. Startled, she yelped, and stepped back, her heart slamming with dread.

"Lieutenant," she said, her mouth dry. "You startled…"

Baelorin's wicked half smile stole her words, the perverse hunger in his eyes reminding her of how alone they were. Emptiness surrounded them, the wagons well over a hundred paces away, the soldiers all asleep in their cots.

"Lady Maelly will know—"

"That you tried to escape," Baelorin said, his calm voice drifting on a gentle breeze. "And that I stopped you."

"I could shout."

Invisible bands clamped over her mouth and held her fast. A blade flashed in the moonlight, Baelorin's lips crooked in a sinister smile.

"Can you?"

KAEL'S second set of screams had been brief. Makayla wiped her eyes dry and blew her nose, guilt tearing her inside. Any moment, Aglia would burst through the door, eager to regale her with Kael's torment, and Makayla would have to pretend to enjoy every disgusting detail.

Makayla pushed those thoughts aside and focused on finding a way out of this godsforsaken situation. However they escaped, it would have to be after Gwyndril or Finndras healed Kael for the night. Then again, she and Kael wouldn't get too far with his will trapped.

Other than Baelorin and Gwyndril, the soldiers and Vrath didn't seem fond of Lady Maelly, often making disparaging remarks about Founders and their unrealistic expectations. Though they couldn't hate her too much. As much as they complained about her and grumbled about their brother-in-arms being murdered over a Phlem, not one of them had requested to leave Maelly's retinue.

And why would they?

Sure, traveling over rough, untouched land was frustrating when a perfectly good causeway stood a few hundred paces away, but none of

Maelly's soldiers or Vrath had to face an army of Phaerian rebels, or spend their life trapped behind a Shining Wall. Her soldiers ventured throughout Torgeir, joking and laughing all day, ate hot meals, drank dark ale, and slept in warm comfort.

Makayla rubbed her eyes, wondering why she always waited until sleep weighed on her body before she started planning their escape.

Because Aglia is always with me, she thought, shaking herself awake. Between washing laundry and listening to Maelly's incessant ramblings about wearing proper colors for the different seasons—as if Phaerians could ever consider such a pointless "rule"—Aglia only left her side to torture Kael.

Speaking of which, where is she?

She'd never taken this long to return to their coach. Maybe Captain Gwyndril had stopped her for a chat after he healed Kael. Given the captain's disdain for Aglia, it seemed impossible, but stranger things had happened.

Makayla fiddled with the horse figurine Gwyndril had carved for her, its contours smoothed by the oils in her fingers. The blanket he'd shaped for her draped over her shoulders, weighing her with guilt. Kael existed in nudity, his bare skin exposed to the encroaching winter, his desperate screams trailing behind her coach when they traveled, while she sat in comfort.

Makayla steeled her nerves, wiping the tears from her eye. Crying over Kael would only get them killed. For their sake, she had to play her part, no matter how much it clawed at her heart. Swallowing a lump of shame, she focused on Captain Gwyndril's good qualities. The man was hard, but fair, for a Citizen. More importantly, Makayla reminded him of his granddaughter.

Which is exactly how we'll escape.

The captain had already condemned one of his men in order to protect her, but that didn't mean he'd defy a Founder's orders, throw away his career, and abandon his life just because he reminded him of his granddaughter.

Rammond would have known what to do. Not that I would have listened.

She groaned and flopped back to lie on her cushioned bench.

Gods, where was Aglia?

Probably still washing off Kael's blood and grime. Maybe this torture session had been so gruesome that she needed to beg Lady Maelly for new clothes. The weighted silence pressed dark thoughts into her mind.

What if they'd gone too far? What if they finally killed him?

A knock at the door startled a squeak from her lips. Only Gwyndril waited for an invitation. "Come in, Captain."

The door creaked open, and Captain Gwyndril stuck his head inside. "Aglia or Baelorin aren't here, are they?"

Makayla raised an eyebrow, gesturing to the small space inside the coach.

"Has either stopped by?" he asked.

Makayla shook her head, and he pressed his lips into a fine line. "I'm surprised you're worried about Aglia."

"I'm not." Gwyndril scowled. "That woman is pure evil, but I can't retire for the night until I find her."

"She's not with..." Makayla squeezed her eyes shut, hiding her grief under a mask of rage.

The captain's heavy boots fell on the coach floorboards, and the door clicked shut. He sat beside her and rested his hand on her back. "She was...kind to him tonight. If such a thing can be said for what she does." A tear dripped from her nose, and the captain leaned back, his steel burdened by a heavy weight. "Makes you wonder about the things Rodak did to her. Well, it makes *me* wonder." He dry washed his face. "Blessed empire, whatever that woman was before, she's pure evil now."

"Kael told me she used to be beautiful," Makayla said, daring to let a hint of sympathy float on her voice.

"That's hard to believe," Gwyndril replied, and his grizzled features softened. "It's okay to mourn him."

Makayla's heart skipped. Had she heard him right? Dare she hope Tolrik had heard her supplications? Had the captain finally broken?

"I...no, I hate him," she said, the lie clear in her voice.

"It's fine," Gwyndril said, his deep voice rumbling in the camped space. He pinched the brim of his nose and released a heavy sigh. "Emperor's ass, even I feel sorry for the poor lout. There's only so many times a man can hear those screams before it breaks him. You know?"

Makayla nodded, not daring to shatter the delicate tension with a fumbled response. If Kael's pain-filled cries had worn at the captain, maybe some of his soldiers felt the same. They couldn't all be like that bastard Baelorin. Given time and the right type of prodding, and Makayla might start another, much smaller uprising.

Gwyndril cleared his throat, his back stiffening. "I shouldn't be saying this." He moved to stand, but Makayla grabbed his hand, and he settled back on the bench. He opened his mouth to speak, then shook his head. "As much as my heart bleeds for Lord Rodak's loss…" Gwyndril's gaze dropped, and he cleared his throat again. "I wish we'd never run in to you and that man."

Hope fluttered in Makayla's chest, her tongue too clumsy for words.

Gwyndril looked at her and chuckled. "Don't think this conversation ends with me helping you escape." He breathed a heavy sigh and shook his head. "In another life, I would have already swept you away from that evil woman." He gave a derisive sniff. "In another life, I never would have accepted this blasted position in the first place. It's a coward's post."

"Why did you take it?" Makayla asked, holding onto her hope that he'd help her, despite what he'd said.

"Founders always get what they want," Gwyndril replied, his gaze lost on a distant memory. "Damn them all. Did you know I earned the Medal of the Golden Flame? It's a high honor among the Boorde."

"How'd you earn it?"

"Saved a dignitary's family from a pod of terrentors."

"A pod?" Makayla said in disbelief.

"It sounds a lot more impressive than it was. It's what caught Lady Maelly's attention." He blinked, as if remembering where he was, and he smiled down at her. "You remind me so much of her. Of my granddaughter. She was beautiful too. Her hair was a bit curlier than yours, and dark as night, but she had the same defiant spark of life in her eyes."

"She was Phaerian?"

"That's how I knew you and Kael were skirters." He held up his hands. "It's okay. I'm not here to weasel out the location of a hidden village. I just, I see her when I look at you, and I..." He patted her hand again, and stood. "Well, I'll never get any sleep, at this rate."

Makayla's heart wrenched for Gwyndril, but she couldn't let him go when he was so close to breaking. "What was her name?" she asked, blurting the first thing to pop into her mind. He froze with his hand on the doorknob, and her chest squeezed with fear.

I pushed him too far.

"Forgive me," she said, her mind scrambling for something to pull on his sympathies. "I just... I thought maybe her name could live on."

Gwyndril opened the door and paused. "Enid—," he said, his voice cracking. He cleared his throat. "Her name was Enidwyn. Enidwyn Mistfall."

Without looking back, the captain climbed down the steps and shut the door behind him.

Makayla's mind raced over her broken heart. She had her crack in Maelly's armor. Tomorrow, she'd make sure Gwyndril saw her as much as possible to remind him of whatever tragedy had befallen his granddaughter. No doubt, it had something to do with Founders, maybe even Maelly, but would it be enough to convince him to betray the Founder?

Would Kael survive that long?

A man's scream broke the silence, followed by shouts and the commotion of booted feet.

"Finndras!" someone shouted.

"What's going on?" Maelly's shouted. "No, no, no! Why?"

Makayla's chest pounded, hands shaking, as a single thought ripped through her mind—*Aglia killed Kael.* That was why Gwyndril couldn't find her or Baelorin. She'd killed Kael, and they all knew what awaited them in Eio.

Makayla's chin quivered, the reality of her situation seeping into her chest.

Kael's...dead.

The coach doorknob turned, the door creaked open, and Aglia climbed inside. Eyes wide with shock, she sat on her bench, seeming oblivious to the blood soaking her torn blouse and dripping from her hands. Her gaze fell on the trail of blood she'd trailed across the floor, confusion wrinkling her brow.

"Whose blood is that?" Makayla asked.

Aglia shook her head, wiping her hands on her tattered blouse and skirt. Panic filled her eyes, her scrubbing growing more frantic.

Makayla reached out, and Aglia flinched from her hand. "It's okay," Makayla said, settling her fingers on Aglia's shoulder. The terrified woman shivered beneath her touch.

Aglia blubbered, scraping at the blood on her hands. "I can't...it won't...come off."

Makayla unbuckled Aglia's blood-soaked belt and set it by the door. Then she pulled the woman's blouse over her head. As always, the sight of her naked body stole Makayla's breath. She tried to see past the two large scars on Aglia's chest and the burns streaking her torso. Fresh cuts leaked down her thigh, soaking more blood into her tattered skirt. Despite Makayla's loathing for the cruel woman, empathy wormed into her heart. It didn't excuse what Aglia had done to Kael anymore than Makayla's misery excused her for all the death she'd caused in her quest to free her people. The pain just made it understandable.

Makayla tossed Aglia's sopping shirt onto the floor, covering the trail of blood. Grabbing their pitcher of water, she helped Aglia wash her hands, then she draped a blanket over the tortured woman's back.

"Thank you," Aglia mumbled, pulling the blanket to cover her mangled skin.

Makayla returned to her bench and grabbed a blanket for herself. "What happened? Where have you been?"

"I don't know. I just..." Aglia squeezed her eyes closed and drew a shuddering breath. "He wouldn't stop. He was going to kill me."

"Who wouldn't stop?" Makayla asked. "You're not making any sense."

"Baelorin, found me, and he…" Aglia pulled her knees to her chest, her frenzied gaze made worse by the blood still smearing her face. "Gwyndril found us. He…he killed Baelorin, and then he—" She squeezed her eyes shut. "He slit his own throat."

"He what?" Makayla said, suspicion swarming around her heart. "That makes no sense. Why would he…" Her gaze fell to Aglia's precious knife. Did the blood seem brighter and thicker than usual? "Aglia…what did you do?"

Aglia wiped her eyes and blew her nose onto the floor. Her panic melted, her face a cold, placid lake. She spoke slowly, her gaze daring Makayla to challenger her. "He slit his throat."

Maelly's shouts filtered through their coach walls. "Aglia? Aglia!"

"It was late," Aglia continued, ignoring the shouts. "You came to check on me, and you saw the good captain slit his throat in a fit of despair."

Makayla listened in shock, Aglia's words drowning her hopes of escape.

Their door flung open, and Maelly's ruby-red hair and alabaster-white face poked inside the coach. "Aglia! What did you do?"

Aglia flinched back into her traumatized character, blubbering an unintelligible reply.

"Damn it, woman," Maelly said. "Make sense."

"It was Baelorin, My Lady," Makayla said, a new plan of escape germinating in her mind. "He was going to kill Aglia, and the captain saved her. He…he killed Baelorin."

Maelly loosed her rage on Makayla. "Why is my captain dead?"

"He took his own life," Makayla replied, and Maelly's face contorted in confusion. "He said a name right before he did."

"A name?" Maelly asked. "What name?"

"Enidwyn," Makayla said, and Maelly slipped down a step and caught herself on the doorframe, her pale face frozen with shock. "Are you all right, My Lady?"

"Of course," Maelly said, her brow wrinkling over her too-green eyes. "Yes, well…" Her gaze fell to the floorboards, and she cast a lazy wave to Aglia's blood-soaked clothes. "Toss these rags out, Eglona, and wash your face, Aglia. You know I loath blood."

Maelly walked back to her coach, and Makayla grabbed the empty pitcher. "I'll get more water," she said, kicking the sopping clothes out the door.

"Thank you," Aglia said, soft and meek.

Makayla raised an eyebrow, and Aglia's gaze lowered.

That's right, Makayla thought. *You owe me, and you're going to help us escape.*

MAKAYLA STOOD BESIDE AGLIA, away from the formation of soldiers. Armored in shining chainmail, swords hanging in their sheath, the soldiers faced a stout barrel-chested man with three sergeants' knots dangling from his left shoulder. Blood still shimmered on Sergeant Arinth's black leather armor, spots of red tinging his greying beard and temples. He stared forward, his steel-gray gaze laden with duty. Behind him, Captain Gwyndril's sword stuck up from the ground, his boots on either side of the blade, yellow-and-green cord dangling from the hilt.

"Corporal Gormlach!" Sergeant Arinth's deep voice shattered the morbid silence.

"Here, Sergeant!" someone shouted from the formation of soldiers.

"Lieutenant Caelitha!"

"Here, Sergeant!" a woman called over a quivering chin.

"Swordsman Neryslyn!"

"Here—" The soldier cleared his throat. "Here, Sergeant!"

Arinth squeezed his fists, his jaw clenching. He drew in a slow breath, his voice hoarse when he called out, "Captain Gwyndril!"

The name hung in the silence.

"Captain Gwyndril!"

Backs stiffened in the formation.

"Capt—" Arinth's voice cracked, his cheeks glistening in the morning sun. "Captain Gwyndril!"

The peal of a trumpet pierced the air, its morbid melody stabbing Makayla's heart. One by one, soldier and Vrath marched to the captain's memorial and rendered salute, then turned on their heels and marched back into formation.

Aglia sniffled and wiped her cheeks, her eyes red and puffy. "Gods, I hated him. I still hate him." Tears leaked from her eyes. "I *want* to hate him. He deserves it, Eglona. You know that, right? Kael deserves it all and more."

Who are you trying to convince? Makayla thought, fighting the rage boiling within her. Since their capture, Kael's torment had awakened him in the morning, and chased him to sleep at night. They dragged him behind the convoy when he couldn't walk and made him stand naked under the blistering sun when Maelly stopped for a break. Every morning and night, Aglia returned to their coach covered in his blood, her lips curled in ecstasy.

"Of course he deserves it," Makayla said, sick with self-loathing.

Despite Maelly's assurances, no one believed Aglia's story that the captain had taken his own life.

Aglia whispered, "How did you know Gwyndril's granddaughter's name?"

"The captain told you her name?" Makayla asked, wondering why he would ever impart such a precious thing to Aglia, of all people. Enidwyn Mistfall, the Phaerian Gwyndril had seemed to love more than life. Aglia's putrid mind needn't spoil such a beautiful memory.

"He said she looked like you," the broken woman said.

"He told you about her?"

"No," Aglia said. "I overheard him gloating about her to Sergeant Arinth." Aglia motioned for Makayla to follow. "Let's get the laundry hung."

They walked in silence to the small piles of clothes waiting next to large washbasins and shaped clotheslines. Aglia tossed the white laundry into one of the steaming basins and stirred it with a paddle.

"You going to sit there and watch?" Aglia said. "Or don't you want to eat today?"

Makayla grabbed the pile of linens and tossed them into another steaming basin. For a Founder, Maelly hadn't been as cruel as Makayla had envisioned. Well, except for the Founder's expectation that every article of clothing, towel, sheet, blanket, and handkerchief remain pristine. Of course, tying their meals to the cleanliness of the laundry had proven to be a powerful motivator, although Makayla doubted she'd ever understand why Maelly didn't shape everything clean.

Founders always get what they want.

The captain's words haunted her thoughts. She grabbed the other paddle and stirred the linens, wrinkling her nose at the odor of grimy garments mixed with soap.

"He killed her," Aglia said, scrubbing at a stain in a handkerchief. "Gwyndril killed his granddaughter when she turned twelve."

"What? That's ridiculous." Makayla stole a glance at Aglia's somber face, and her heart dropped. "You're serious."

"It was Lady Maelly who'd convinced him."

"How?" Makayla asked, not wanting to believe the truth she heard in Aglia's voice.

"Gwyndril's granddaughter could shape," Aglia replied, churning the whites with her paddle. "According to Lady Maelly, she'd convinced him it would be a mercy for him to kill Enidwyn, rather than take her to the Citadel."

Aglia wrung out a white blouse and draped it on the shaped clothesline. "Oh, don't look so surprised. Lady Maelly told me, not him. Gwyndril never trusted me from the moment we met."

Makayla grunted to hide her relief. The captain may have been a filthy Citizen, but he'd been a decent man. Maybe filthy Citizen was too harsh…

Misguided, she thought. *Like Kael.*

"What's on your mind?" Aglia asked.

"Why didn't Lady Maelly do it?" Makayla lied, blurting the first thing to come to mind. "I mean, obviously she wasn't going to let Enidwyn go. But why make him do it?"

Aglia mouthed, *She's evil*, then she said, "I don't know. Why don't we ever take the causeway? Why do we wash clothes, when a shaper can clean them much faster and much better? Why do Founders do anything they do? Because they're Founders, and they can." Aglia held Makayla's gaze and mouthed, *Because they like to watch people suffer.*

Makayla looked around, as if expecting to find Maelly or her Vrath spying on them, but they all sat around the blazing campfire, drinking ale, draped in doleful silence.

She can hear everything, Aglia mouthed. She seemed at the point of breaking, but would she want to help them escape? As much as Aglia hated Kael, Makayla doubted the woman had a pinch of forgiveness in her heart.

"Let's hurry and finish these clothes," Aglia said with a heavy sigh. "I'm getting hungry, and tonight promises to be a feast. I'd hate to miss the captain's celebration of life over a stain."

AGLIA WATCHED the slow rise and fall of Kael's chest, his face so calm, the gentle waves in his dishwater-blond hair falling past his naked temple. She traced her finger along the angular scars on his belly where the headless' blade had shattered his skin. So consumed by anger, she hadn't thought to ask about Jo or Pen. Where were they? *How* were they? Did Pendric know about his mother?

What about the tubes? the voice in her mind asked.

"No," she said, smacking her palm against the side of her head.

Humming to quiet the voice, she gathered the rags sopped with Kael's blood, and placed them around him on the table. Stepping back, she admired his crimson aura and its dripping melody.

Drip…drip-drip, drip.

"That's who you are," she said, folding her arms. "That's the real you—a man bathed in blood. Only this time, it's your own."

You sent him away, the voice said.

Drip…drip-drip, drip.

"No!" she shouted, rubbing her temples to keep those memories locked away. "He ran! He could have stayed."

Kael stirred, his slate-gray eyes fluttering beneath his eyelids. A moment later, his dream passed, and he returned to the void of sleep. He looked peaceful, laid on the table, his blood dribbling to the floor.

Drip…drip-drip…drip.

Like in the sick house, the voice whispered.

He'd been even paler back then, his skin never having seen the sun. Now, a hint of ruddy brown touched his skin, making the blue lines on his shattered belly seem brighter.

Drip…drip…drip.

He'd been struck dumb by her beauty when he first saw her. Now all he saw was Aglia.

Because that's who I am.

Drip…drip.

Livia had been beautiful and full of life. That woman had loved Kael, and had believed he was the Light, but she'd died in Headwater.

Drip…drip.

Livia had to die. She'd been weak. She never could have lived through Rodak's twisted teachings. Livia never would have found the deep pleasures hidden behind the pain.

But Aglia could, the voice said, guiding her hand to her knife. *Aglia did.*

She caressed the scars streaking her legs, hating herself for yearning to feel that burning pain and depraved release.

Drip…

Vision watering, she drew the knife across her leg and shuddered in ecstasy. She drew another red line on her leg, self-loathing tumbling down her cheeks.

Drip…

What have I done?

A third score choked her with a sob.

…drip.

"Dear gods…what have I done?"

26

URNA

The putrescence of unwashed bodies, stale urine, and misery clung to Jouler's nostrils and pasted to his tongue. Not enough time had passed since he'd last walked the congested streets of a Phaerian town. Never again would be fine with him. The malodor didn't seem to bother his Boorde captors, who hadn't spoken a word since they'd taken him.

Yesterday, after a fiery message from the group of Ascended who had chased Reylan and the others, most of Jouler's captors had left to hunt them. Sixteen Boorde surrounded him now, four firedancers and twelve il'Spada, their snow-white skin and too-black clothing stark in the drab town. Their leader, a tall firedancer with a burn scar on the side of her head, strode at the head of the head of the towering Boorde. Townsborn scurried to clear their path, while marveled gazes followed them down the streets. Even the imperial guards at the gate had feigned being busy when they'd entered the town.

"Do not cry for help," a brute of an il'Spada warned, his thick Boorde accent rolling through his deep, rumbling voice. "Or we'll carve our way through this wretched town."

Jouler fought against rolling his eyes at the pointless threat. Even without his spear tipped with a long curved blade, the scars raking down the right side of his face carried enough threat do dissuade anyone but a Sotouri or Vrath from approaching. That and the smooth onyx replacing his missing eye, an emerald heron set into the stone. Besides, what aid could townsborn offer against sixteen of the Alliance's deadliest Boorde? He'd witnessed their morbid grace the night L'Veyna had asked that freezing storm, the Ascended's slinking black forms caught in the flashes of lightning. They'd moved like true masters, warriors who'd trained for centuries, not a single action wasted.

Like Diou, Jouler thought, wondering how these Ascended would stand against the famous Boorde.

"That's very good," another il'Spada said. Unlike the others who favored the spear or trademark sidaiyo, he carried a pair of daggers. He was shorter than the other, though still a head taller than Jouler, and bore a thin scar on his cheek.

"Your gait," the Ascended explained. "It's almost natural."

"I hadn't realized I was doing it."

"Put a few more years behind your eyes," the il'Spada said, "and you could pass as a Sotouri Blade. Almost."

"Why almost?" Jouler said, now awkwardly aware of his stride.

The Ascended smirked as if to say, "That's why."

"Where are you taking me?" Jouler asked.

The statuesque firedancer leading the group glared at the much shorter il'Spada. An old scar covered one side of her head, the skin melted from a terrible burn. White streaked her hair from the scar, the tail streaming from her simple topknot falling to the small of her back. Coiled at her waist, her djohai swayed in rhythm to her strides. The fiery strip in her too-black dress shimmered in the town's poor light, the color bright against the monochrome group.

"*Why are you speaking to him?*" she asked in Boordish.

Jouler wore a confused mask, pretending to not understand the rolling language.

The short il'Spada dipped his head. "*Our orders were to remain silent until we reached Urna. We're here, so I'm talking to him.*"

"Careful what you say around him, Kherlyn," she said, and his brow drew in confusion.

"Even if he understood us," the il'Spada said, *"What could I say that would matter? You know where we're headed, Ishariel. Look at him. He's harmless."*

"I'd hardly call the Vidimir harmless," another Boorde said.

"He bested a child," Kherlyn replied. *"Like I said—he's harmless."*

Jouler feigned disinterest, while he searched for anything he could use to leave a clue for Prack and L'Veyna. The town's muck would instantly consume any torn clothing, and no townsborn would approach close enough to whisper. Not with the loud drone saturating the town. Every time he so much as took a step out of place or let his gaze linger too long on anything but Kherlyn's back, his captors growled and nudged him.

They continued in silence down Urna's bustling streets until the stench of rotting fish overwhelmed his senses. Jouler gagged and covered his nose and mouth with his sleeve. Even a few of the Ascended wrinkled their nose at the stench. The street emptied into Urna's bustling harbor. Tall-masted galleons, caravels, and frigates loomed over cogs, longships, and knarrs, while an army of dock-workers hurried with cargo.

A skinny townsborn in ragged, drab clothing waved to the Ascended, his frazzled black hair dancing in the salty breeze.

"Finally," Kherlyn mumbled, then leaned to whisper to Jouler. "We'll chat once we're on the boat."

Ishariel gave Kherlyn a sidelong glance before meeting the skinny townsborn. After a brief exchange, the Phaerian wiped his brow and gestured for Ishariel to follow.

The skinny man led them to a large frigate that swarmed with dockworkers, loading large crates and barrels. "Here we are, Ma'am," the townsborn said, dry washing his hands. "The Charred Leech."

"Sounds more like a tavern," Kherlyn mumbled before returning to Boordish. *"Ask him how long to Cowine?"* The firedancer's eyes flashed with anger, and he held his hands up, motioning for calm. *"Easy...he can't understand us."*

Cowine? Jouler thought, no longer needing to pretend to be confused. He drew up a mental map of Blailon, and he understood. *They're taking me to the Blasted Lands.*

Ishariel stepped close to Kherlyn, her anger dripping down at Kherlyn. *"I don't care how your team operates. I am the lead Ascended. You will do as I say."* She raised an eyebrow, her arms falling to her sides. *"Unless you'd like to challenge me?"*

Kherlyn's jaw clenched, and he lifted his chin, exposing his neck. *"I am yours to command, of course."*

"To Cowine it is," Ishariel said, and Kherlyn scoffed.

"So much for keeping it a secret."

Ishariel headed up the plank to the Charred Leech. *"If you think he hasn't understood every word we've spoken, you're more a fool than I thought."* She laid her hot gaze on Jouler. *"Isn't that right, Vidimir?"*

Kherlyn scoffed. "He can't speak Boordish."

"Forced or willing," Ishariel said, her fiery gaze burning into Jouler, *"you will do as I say. The choice is yours."*

Jouler looked to the lapping water below, questioning the types of creatures that might lurk in its thick, putrid depths. Even if he jumped, Ishariel would turn him to ash before he touched the water.

Jouler dipped his head. *"To Cowine it is."*

L'Veyna fought back the desire to rip off the thin band of cloth wrapped around her head, to free her ears and let them breathe. Not that she *wanted* them breathing this foul air, but it'd be better than stuffing her ears under a plague-be-gotten cloth. The dingy clothes her brother had insisted they wear were bad enough.

And did we really have to color our hair black?

Sure, their autumnal locks would have shone as bright as the sun in the Phaerian sea of brown and gray, but there was no hiding their emerald Elmhand eyes or their Prytha grace. Besides, all the Humans here already stared at them. Well, more staring at her, it seemed, though her brother caught plenty of gazes.

"Put your arm down," Prack said above the loud din.

"It stinks," L'Veyna mumbled behind her hand.

"You're drawing attention."

"Everyone's already staring at us," she said.

"No," Prack said. "They're staring at you because you stick out like an iris in a mud pit."

L'Veyna kicked a clump of muck from her boot. "You got the mud part right."

"Just keep your head low and stay close."

Prack pulled her past a small group of children no older than her. They surrounded a decrepit old man, teasing him and threatening violence. Such behavior never would have been allowed in Onatah. It never would have crossed a sapling's mind, for that matter. Stifling an urge to wrap the petulant children in vines, she sloshed behind her brother through the cramped town.

"Tavern Row," Prack said, gesturing to the congested street ahead. More people than usual packed this part of Urna, the loud din bouncing off tall stacks of raucous buildings.

She pointed to a balcony with scantily clothed women and men on display. "It's nice to see *some* Humans with some sense of style. What are they doing?"

"Enticing would-be patrons," Prack said, guiding her around two men squabbling over who Ilsna loved more. "Not *all* the buildings in Taverns Row are taverns."

"Are they all like this?"

"What?" Prack called over his shoulder. "You have to speak up, Sprout."

"Phaerian towns," she said, scooting to walk beside him. "Are they really all like this?" Her brother nodded. "But...why? It's not like there isn't enough food and fabric to go around."

"That's not the point," Prack said. "Having more makes Humans feel like they're better than everyone else."

"But that's...that's ridiculous," L'Veyna replied. "Having more things just means you're selfish and you have no friends."

Prack clicked his tongue. "That's surprisingly accurate."

"But...why?" L'Veyna asked, still not understanding why so many Humans lived like this. "Is it like this in the cities?"

"Only at the bottom," Prack said, leading her down a tunnel of houses to another congested street that looked no different from all the others.

"Do you even know where you're going?" she asked.

"Of course I do," Prack replied with that smirk that made her question everything he said.

The stench of rotting fish grew until it drowned the town's other odors, and the street opened to a loud, bustling harbor. Countless boats and ships, the butchered remains of trees, bobbed at the end of long piers. Just one of the larger vessels would have required a large grove to construct, and dozens of the monstrosities filled the harbor.

Her vision watered, her heart breaking at the thought of so much murder. "How could they? Humans are so...so...vile!"

Her brother gave a heavy sigh and draped his arm over her shoulders. "The first time I saw a ship, I cried too."

L'Veyna gaped at the floating graveyard, and a quick breeze coated her tongue with the harbor's putrescence. She gagged, her stomach clenched, and the bitter taste of vomit added to her revulsion.

"I did that too," Prack said, handing her a rag. "Come on, Little Sprout. There's nothing we can do for our fallen brethren, but we can still save Jo."

"Can we?" L'Veyna asked. Since Jouler's abduction, they'd done nothing but fail—*she'd* done nothing but fail. If not for Prack, the firedancers would have turned her to ash. Without her to botch everything, her brother could have shifted Jouler to safety. If she'd just stayed with Dilna, Jo would be here with Prack, searching for a corpse-vessel to sail.

I never should have left Onatah, she thought, and her knees hit the congested dock.

Humans cursed and jostled her as they passed.

Prack hurriedly lifted her to her feet and shuffled her away from the grumbling crowd.

"What was I thinking?" she asked, out of breath for some reason, her heart slamming in her chest. "I hardly ever left the Canopy. What made me think I could be a hero like you and Diou? I'm thirteen." She pressed her hands to her churning stomach. "Alnazet's mercy, I'm only thirteen! I should be back home, breaking in my new pipe and sipping tea." She slouched, drained, as if she'd spent the whole day asking. "I'm no hero, and I'm certainly no Facet."

Prack led her to the edge of the dock, and he sat, letting his legs dangle. She sat beside him, too numb to care about the bustling noise or stench of the harbor. Resting her head on her brother's shoulder, she let her legs sway over the harbor's murky depths.

Why is the water so thick and grey?

"You're right," Prack said. "You're far too young for this. I was almost fifty when I first left Onatah, and I still felt too young."

L'Veyna grunted. "Is that supposed to make me feel better?"

"Yes," Prack replied without a hint of sarcasm, his eyes sparkling with compassion. "Do you think I felt any less lost than you do at thirteen? The first time I saw a harbor, I wept for days."

"You did not," L'Veyna said, huffing. "Not days."

"Cried myself to sleep the first night. Then it was on and off for a while. Took me two weeks to work up the courage to come back to the harbor to find my contact."

"Was it Diou?" L'Veyna asked.

Prack chuckled and shook his head. "It was a dock boss. They're the greasy men shouting at dockworkers."

"What did you do?" she asked. "To work up the courage to go back to the graveyar—the harbor?"

Prack clicked his tongue. "Graveyard...I like it."

"Floating graveyard," she specified.

"I like it even more," her brother said. "It's more fitting than you realize."

L'Veyna lifted her brow. "Oh?"

"Graveyards are meant to honor the dead, just like these ships honor the trees that made them."

"Honor?" L'Veyna clacked, her anger flaring. *"They slaughter our cousins and trample over their corpses, and you call it honor?"*

"I do," Prack replied. "Yes, they chop down thousands of trees to make just one of these terrentorous ships, but Humans can't ask, and Prytha haven't offered their services for thousands of years. Did you know the empire plants groves specifically to use for shipbuilding? In fact, they've never chopped down a single naturally grown tree to build a ship."

L'Veyna jerked her head, surprised that the cursed empire would show such benevolence. "That still doesn't make it right. Those trees could have grown into a thriving community. How'd they like it if we harvested Human babies for…for fertilizer?"

"That's not the same," Prack said. "Tii'Vrath use the Currents to help entire groves grow to full size in just a few years, and they replant with seeds from previous grows."

"That doesn't give them the right. Trees feel. You know that."

"Not like us," Prack replied, lifting an eyebrow. "And you know that."

L'Veyna crossed her arms. "It's still murder."

"Look closer," Prack said, pointing to a large vessel. "Look at the craftsmanship. See how they use ships to fish and transport goods that would otherwise be unattainable. Can you think of a better way to honor a grove's sacrifice than to use it to sustain life? Isn't that the ultimate purpose of a tree?"

She offered a begrudging nod. "The purpose of life in general."

"Did you know sailors treat their ship like a living thing?" Prack clicked his tongue, the sound sharp over the harbor's dull drone. "And they're all women."

"The sailors?" L'Veyna asked, noting a significant lack of ladies.

"The ships," Prack corrected. "The ocean too, for that matter."

"Well, that makes sense," L'Veyna said. "The ocean is water, and water is life."

"Humans have a different reason," Prack said, "but yours makes a lot more sense."

"What do they call it?" L'Veyna asked.

"It doesn't matter," her brother replied with a flippant wave.

L'Veyna dragged her languid gaze across a smaller ship, only the size of a large house. Her brother was right. Every inch of the monstrosity sang with beauty. Each tall pole that held a massive canvass, the rails, the stairs, and decking, it all looked crafted with love.

"Is that where the driver stands?" she asked, pointing to the elegant, spoked wheel.

"Captain," Prack corrected with a chuckle. "And yes. It's where the Captain or First Mate navigates the ship."

L'Veyna's face scrunched in confusion. "What if the Captain hasn't mated?"

Her brother's chuckle rolled into a laugh. "Not that type of mate. It's just what Humans call their second-in-command."

"I see..."

"But only for ships," Prack said. "On land, the lowest ranking Human does the navigating, and captains are more like glorified supervisors."

L'Veyna clicked her tongue. "I do not see."

Prack shrugged. "Humans are weird."

"Especially their fingers," she said with a shudder.

Her brother gave her a sidelong glance. "You don't seem to mind Jouler's anymore."

"That's different," she said. "We share a special bond. You wouldn't understand."

"Oh?" Prack said. "Special, like the bond Diou and I share?"

"Ew, we're not lovers," L'Veyna said, nudging him.

"That's not what I meant," Prack said, chuckling. "Feeling better, Little Sprout?"

She nodded and released a heavy sigh. "But I still don't feel like a Facet."

"And maybe you never will," Prack said. "For all my confidence and bravado, I don't feel like the hero our people have made me to be. It's why I always make it a point to come home to visit you."

"So I can pester you?" she said with a playful nudge.

"Because you make me feel like a hero."

Her chest warmed, her vision watering once more. "I do?"

"Of course," he said. "How could I not? The way you talk about me while I'm gone, and how you look up to me. It's almost enough to make me believe I really am that person."

"Almost?"

He graced her with that smile that meant everything would be okay. Then he groaned to his feet and held out his hand to help her up. "Let's go find out where our friend went."

"But how?" L'Veyna asked with a tinge of hope.

"If you think *we* stick out in this crowd," he said, glaring at another creepy old man who'd been staring at her, "imagine a bunch of statuesque Boorde."

A wide grin split her face.

Of course!

She'd been so consumed by her guilt that she'd missed the obvious. Every person in this floating graveyard could probably tell them which ship Jouler had boarded. As sure as Alnazet's glory rose in the east, the first dock boss Prack questioned shouted the name of the ship.

"The Charred Leech," the rotund man said, then he shouted to a dockworker rolling a barrel down a long plank. The dock boss's ample belly poked beneath the man's patchwork shirt, draping over trousers meant for someone far skinner than he. "Hurry, gods damn you!" Shorter than Prack, the dock boss half-spoke to them, his eyes never leaving his workers. "Boarded the Charred Leech, they did. Two days ago. Caused quite a stir, as you can imagine with those type. Them Boorde don't have no soul, they don't."

"Charred Leech?" Prack said. "Sounds more like a tavern."

"That's what—hey! You!" the dock boss shouted at another worker. "Yeah, you! Laa burn you. If you drop that cargo in the bay, you'll jump in and fetch it." He half-turned to Prack. "My apologies, M'Lord. What was I...ah, yes, the Charred Leech. Everyone says the same thing. Sounds like a tavern, it does." He chuckled, his gaze falling on L'Veyna. "My, you're a beauty, you are. Same eyes as your father too. Never seen'em so green like that. Pardon, M'Lord, but you're both so…" His gaze fell to their taloned hands, and his brow rose. "Prytha? We don't see much of your kind around here."

L'Veyna slid behind her brother, and away from the grimy man's hungry gaze.

"She's my sister," Prack corrected, folding his arms. "And I'm no lord. We're just simple travelers, looking for our friend."

The dock boss pulled his gaze from L'Veyna. "Huh? Oh, yes, your friend. Boorde, you said? Yeah, they was here. Gone to Cowine." His eyes darted to L'Veyna again. "Not too many ships making that trip this time of year, though. Not with the storms, and all…"

Prack opened the pouch and poured some of the gold and silver nuggets she'd asked this morning.

The dock boss licked his lips, his gaze glued to the shining ore. She hadn't believed her brother when he said Humans lusted after the metal, but the crazed look on the dock boss's face spoke truth to her brother's words. L'Veyna had no doubt the man would have traded the entire dock for those nuggets.

Prack dumped the nuggets back into the pouch, and the dock boss snatched it from his hand. Weighing it, the round man's brow rose in surprise before he stashed the pouch under his drab shirt.

"Thankfully," the dock boss said, "I know just the Captain."

"*I don't trust him,*" L'Veyna clacked on her talonboard.

"*Neither do I,*" Prack clacked in response.

"*Then why are we following him? He's probably trying to sell us to slavers.*"

"*He's* definitely *trying to sell us to slavers.*"

"What?" L'Veyna said, halting.

The dock boss turned, confusion scrunching his face. "Did you say something, young miss?"

"Forgive my sister." Prack nudged her forward. "She's never sailed. She's a bit nervous."

"Ah," the dock boss said. "There's nothing to worry about, lass. Captain Halstokk and the crew of the Scarlet Kiss will take good care of you. They'll get you to Cowine, they will, or my name isn't Gromir Viklund."

"Thank you, Gromir," her brother said, gesturing for the man to carry on. *"Definitely not his name,"* he clacked, winking at her with that confident smirk.

Hope burgeoned in her chest.

My brother has a plan.

27

EIO

K ael's heavy, pattern-forged shackles dug at his wrists. Their familiar pain was a constant reminder of the mindtrap wrapped around his will. Linked to Makayla's coach, his chain clinked and swayed in rhythm to his steps. His feet and legs begged him to stop, but he dared not push Maelly's newfound kindness. Not only did new clothes grace his body, nu'leather boots covered his feet, and it had been days since they'd dragged him. Not since Gwyndril murdered Baelorin before he turned his knife on himself.

Assuming Aglia hadn't lied about the whole thing.

To his right, lenticular clouds hovered over Haldr's Bowl like upside down saucers. Their destination, and Kael's fate, waited on the other side of those towering peaks. At the base of the famous mountain range, dozens of mounted patrols meandered the roadway connecting Onti and Elpa. To his left, the flat expanse of land rolled into the horizon, the soil churned from a recent battle in the Soutouri's famous war games. In Kael's childhood dreams, he'd led a heroic charge in those games, astounding Founders and high lords with his vast powers. But those dreams belonged to another person, someone he'd left behind along with a part of his self. He raised his fingers to his temple, his chains clinking in his sunburned ear. No raised skin met his fingers, his temple as smooth as any other Phaerian's. Only, none of them felt a void in their self, reminding him he'd never be whole.

I would have kept the blasted thing, if I'd known it felt like this.

It had to get better, or at least more bearable, like his captivity. Reylan had never spoken about the terrible emptiness, but then, he'd never had a chance. As soon as the old man had confided in Kael about his shaping, Rodak's son had upended their life.

Kael lifted his gaze to Aglia's coach. *Especially her life.*

No one had suffered more for Kael's actions on that terrible day. No one had more right to hate him, other than Rodak...maybe. Did the loss of a son warrant the lives the Founder destroyed? Could it excuse what he'd done to Aglia, to turn her into such a broken creature?

Kael's stomach churned from the memory of the torment he'd endured from Baelorin. Aglia had been right—every kind touch, every warm memory, and every pleasant dream, tainted by that man's thrusts and throbbing groans. It could never compare to the horrors Aglia had suffered, but he understood the hatred roiling behind her dark eyes, just as he knew the joy she'd feel watching him die. It was the same joy Kael had felt after he learned Baelorin's fate.

Maybe I'm more like Aglia that I'd like to admit.

The command to stop rippled down the convoy, the noonday sun high in the clear cerulean sky.

"You're getting stronger," Finndras said, startling Kael. The tii'Vrath chuckled and slid off his chestnut stallion. "Did you forget I was here?"

"Yes," Kael said through gritted teeth.

Concern pressed the tii'Vrath's lips into a line. He pulled back Kael's eyelids, peered into his eyes, then clapped his hands in front of Kael's face. Kael flinched, and Finndras nodded as if to himself. He gestured for Kael to kneel. "Nothing a quick healing won't fix."

Kael obeyed, his knees splashing in the freezing mud. Finndras laid a hand on Kael's head, and an icy wave coursed down Kael's body. The raw lines on his wrist mended, burned skin sloughing from his body, sensation needling his numbed feet.

"It's a shame," Finndras said, helping Kael to stand and unhooking the chain from the rear coach. "Your power would have made you the greatest tii'Vrath in history. You obviously love Phaerians. You could have done so much good for them."

"I can't heal," Kael said, following Finndras to a stake driven into the ground. "Not well, anyway. I can shape a gravity ball while charging on horseback, but a second-year cadet can heal better than me."

"The gravity ball is a Forbidden Pattern," Finndras said. "You know that, right?"

"What are you going to do, torture me?"

Finndras snorted and hooked Kael's chain to the stake. "*Why* can't you heal? That's what I want to know. Even ra'Vrath are adept at it."

Kael shrugged. Not that he would have told the blasted man.

"So much power...wasted." Finndras shook his head. "You could have been raised to the Gold, cavorting with Founders, and you gave it all away to become a...a Phaerian? Why?"

Kael gave a derisive snort, noting the Seals on the Vrath's Shield. A minor Bronze District lord, presumably from the lower half of the tier. The half that sat below the rim of the Shining Wall, filled with lords who acted like they understood Districters because they shared the same obstructed view. They also slept in rooms larger than Kael's house, ate real food, and breathed filtered air.

"You really think they would have allowed a Districter to climb so high?" he asked.

"I...well, I mean..." Finndras swallowed his words and shrugged. "You never know."

"Districters only become rich in novels," Kael said, with a pointed look. "And it's always the same story—poor lout discovers they're a powerful shaper, and they become a Sotouri. If they're a Spade, they single-handedly obliterate Cabal Headquarters, and if they're a Mask, they save the empire from a dastardly Cabal plot."

"And always in the nick of time."

"That too," Kael admitted. "I, of course, had always imagined myself as one of those heroes. I even earned the crimson cord. But such are the dreams of children." He gestured to his naked self chained to a stake. "I'm an adult in a nightmare."

"That you are," Finndras said, and left Kael to join the other soldiers.

The door to the rear coach opened, and Aglia stepped down the stairs. Makayla followed, casting a quick glance at Kael. Her coal-black hair looked good on her, but he still preferred her natural locks brushed with a ruddy tint. Shading her eyes with her hand, she squinted against the afternoon sun. Her eyes caught Kael's, and a flash of relief curled her lips.

At least she's doing well, Kael thought, his burdens easing, if only a little.

As if sensing their shared look, Aglia turned and followed Makayla's gaze. Rage, guilt, pain, and a dozen other feelings twisted Aglia's scarred face. A memory twinkled in her dark eyes, and she lifted a hand to her wispy locks. Something had snapped in her the night Gwyndril and Baelorin died. She still awakened Kael with pain, and his screams still followed him to blissful unconsciousness, but her crazed, hate-filled passion had fled. In rare moments, when she hesitated with her knife, Kael thought he caught glimpses of her former self. Then again, maybe that was just his tortured mind clinging to hope.

Makayla and Aglia took their spot around the cook pot, but not before Aglia stole one last glance at Kael.

This time, a single emotion dominated her marred complexion—fear.

A FADING sun streaked the sky pink and gold, while mist blanketed the churned fields where Sotouri played at war. Crisp air bit through Makayla's thick wool shirt, her breath freezing before her. Maelly's soldiers and Vrath warmed themselves by the campfire, their usual late-night grumbling mixed with relief that they'd reach Eio by tomorrow afternoon. Untouched by the soldier's glares, Aglia's distant stare stretched up the steep causeway that would take them to Rodak, the man who'd turned her into that monster.

"Are you all right?" Makayla asked, placing a hand on Aglia's arm.

The broken woman startled, her confusion fading under a scowl. "You must be happy."

"Me?" Makayla said. "I'm a Phaerian heading to the home of the Sotouri. Why would I be happy?"

"To finally be rid of Kael." Aglia studied Makayla, then she mouthed, *Can you read?*

Alarm prickled Makayla's skin, and a voice in her warned against admitting the truth. As much as Aglia had changed since Gwyndril's death, Kael's screams still shattered the air every morning and night.

Every day except today. Maybe she had *changed.*

Did it matter? Makayla may have fooled Aglia and everyone else in Maelly's retinue, but Rodak would recognize her the moment he laid eyes on her—black hair or not. By this time tomorrow, she'd be on a ship to Blailon to face King Ashtur's judgment. Or worse, she'd be stuck in a cell with Kael. At least she'd get to see the look on Maelly's smug face when Rodak revealed Makayla's true identity—the girl who'd almost toppled Blailon.

"Well?" Aglia asked, drawing looks from some soldiers.

Makayla nodded.

Aglia shivered and jerked her head to their coach. "Let's get out of this cold."

Makayla closed the door behind them and sat on her bench.

Aglia raised a finger to her lips and pulled out a slate board and a stick of chalk. *We need to save Kael,* she wrote with handwriting far more elegant than anything Makayla could manage.

Makayla ignored the warnings crashing through her mind, telling her not to trust the woman. *How?* She mouthed, and Aglia shrugged. Makayla snatched the slate and charcoal. Painfully aware of her awkward letters, she wrote, *Why didn't you torture him this morning?*

Aglia wiped the board clean and wrote, *Not important. Kael is all that matters. Kael is the Light.* She looked at Makayla as if waiting for a response. "You already know."

It's complicated, Makayla mouthed, then wrote, *I'll tell you once we get out of here.*

Aglia circled *get out of here,* then she wrote *HOW???*

"I just asked you that," Makayla growled.

Aglia's arm whipped, the back of her hand crashing against Makayla's cheek. "We don't have time for your snide remarks."

Rubbing her swelling cheek, Makayla spat, her blood splashing on Aglia's boots. "Do that again," she warned, meeting Aglia's hard glare, "and I'll make up another story about how you killed yourself."

Their coach door flung open, and Finndras stuck his head in. "We're packing up..." His gaze fell on the slate board, and invisible bands wrapped around Makayla. Aglia grunted, her eyes wide with fear. Finndras closed the door behind him and snatched the slate board. "What have we here?"

"Finndras, I—" Aglia's mouth snapped shut.

"The Light?" Finndras whistled, his eyebrows climbing his forehead. "Isn't that interesting?"

BANDS OF FORCE held Kael to Gwyndril's horse, forcing him to endure the rough ride, speeding along the causeway. Compared to the torture he'd endured over the past...however many days, or weeks, the ache running up his back was a welcomed relief. Freezing air rushed past his ears, carrying the thunder of hoofbeats and rumble of coach wheels. Coat flapping behind him, the nu'clothes Finndras had shaped did little to ward against the cold, but it was better than riding naked.

Vestrund Pass sped by in a blur of snow, granite, and pines. Above him, the famous crags he'd read about so many times drifted by with hardly a glance. Finndras had been quiet today, distracted, his gaze drifting to Kael with curious intent.

Maelly must have admonished the Vrath for being too nice to Kael this morning. But then, if that was the case, why had Aglia awoken him so peacefully? No stabbing dagger or burning poker. No broken femur or disembowelment for Finndras to heal. She'd helped Kael to the small round table for breakfast, and had watched in silence as he ate, a haunted look on her broken face. When she left, two solemn words had floated from her lips—*I'm sorry.*

Her words hung in his mind, dangling over every thought, stirring the darkness that had plagued him since the first day of his torture. That seductive voice in his mind that promised to end his suffering. It called to him now, caressing him with macabre thoughts, begging him to break the bands of force holding him to the saddle, to jump and bash his head on a rock, to bring an end to his suffering—

Maelly's caravan crested the mountain pass, and piercing sunlight burned Kael's eyes, stealing his thoughts as they entered Haldr's Bowl. Eio's pristine Shining Wall loomed to his left, glowing bright in the late afternoon sun. As if grown from the granite mountainside, the city stretched to the shore of the famed Lake Skjold, the massive body of water that filled Haldr's Bowl, its distant shores lost over the horizon.

Maelly's convoy stopped short of the Shining Wall. The tall Founder stepped out of her coach, her ruby hair whipping in the cold wind. Eschewing her normal rugged clothes, the frills of her yellow dress fought with the fur lining her pearlescent jacket. She strode up to the Wall and pressed a hand to its smooth surface. A moment later, a sharp crack sounded, and a large portion of the Shining Wall slid into the ground.

"Must be strange," Finndras said to Kael, nudging his horse forward. "I bet you never imagined coming here as a prisoner."

Kael grunted, recalling his welcome into Onatah, and dangling in those blasted cages. "Story of my life."

MAKAYLA LOOKED over the rail of the wide platform, speeding up Eio's tiers. Far below, muddy streets snaked through a chaotic mess of buildings made from the same brick-and-mortar found in Phaerian towns. No parks or trees decorated the Workers District, only unfinished hovels packed so closely together that it was impossible to distinguish one house from another. She'd been right not to believe Kael's claims that life in the Workers District was worse than life as a townsborn.

This was far worse, she thought, staggering at the enormity of the ruddy sea splayed out below. Pegrans would have fit ten times over inside the District, and the town hadn't smelled half as bad.

At least townsborn could see past the pathetic excuse of a wall surrounding their towns, and the sky didn't look like vaporized vomit. The only view Districters had was the Shining Wall, which may explain the lack of windows in their hovels. That and the thick, murky air aglow from the Wall's light.

No wonder Kael had never returned.

He stood on the other side of the wide platform, surrounded by Finndras and three other Vrath. Brow wrinkled in thought, Kael seemed oddly perplexed for a man speeding toward inscrutable torture. At least he had clothes now. Makayla couldn't imagine the looks they would have received if he'd been naked when they'd entered this cursed city.

Draped in yellow and self-importance, Maelly stood alone in the center of the platform, her languid gaze staring into the distance.

Aglia nudged Makayla and nodded toward Finndras. Like the other three Vrath, he stood with his back straight, hands clasped behind his back, gaze steeled on some distant spot. Makayla doubted he'd divulged what he'd read on Aglia's slate board, or else they'd have their own guards. Other than stiff backs and formalities, no one acted as if they'd been told about the note, but why would Finndras keep such a secret? Maybe he sought to gain some favor with Rodak. Maybe Finndras spied for the devious Founder.

I may as well hope he's a Cabalist for all the good hoping will do.

The wide platform continued up Eio's second tier, the Makers District. Markets and lush parks dotted this noticeably cleaner section of the city. No mud tracked over its straight, cobbled streets. Even the air, while still rank, smelled far better than below.

Not as thick and oily, Makayla noted.

Gone were the conglomerates of cramped hovels, replaced by artful stacks of sizable residencies, each stack painted a different bright color. Juxtaposed against the colorful buildings was a massive granite fortress shaped like an Imperial Shield, its parapets painted the same sickening red.

"The Citadel," Aglia mumbled, sneering at the building.

Without the Citadel, without shaping, the empire would crumble in a day, while Phaerians would prosper all across Torgeir. Maybe that was how she and the other Facets were supposed to topple the empire, by somehow ending its ability to shape. She gripped the railing, knuckles white, wishing hatred alone could burn the blasted building.

And then what?

Vrath hardly needed a building in order to shape, but watching it crumble sure would feel good.

Aglia pointed to another enormous building. Built to resemble a giant loom, rows of flowers lined its roof and walls, apparently representing threads of fabric.

"What a strange building," Makayla mumbled.

"Pattern Weavers Guild," Aglia explained with a note of resentment. "Cowards."

Rising to the next tier, the Steel District, Makayla's hatred for the Citadel smoldered under the thunderous beat of countless soldiers marching in cadence. Gods, there were so many, their stomps and shouts echoing down row after row of tall barracks.

Tens of thousands of armored men and women filled a parade field half the size of Pegrans. Their perfectly lined formations summoned painful images of Ramond, nodding in approval at such a display. *Now those,* he would have said, *are well-trained soldiers.* Borig would have mumbled some curse, while Hurian would have ranted for weeks about the squalid Workers District. The formations blurred, and she took a slow breath, stilling her watering vision.

Her guilt and sorrow tumbled into anxiety as the platform sped up the conical city toward her inexorable doom. Maybe Rodak wouldn't recognize her. He might see no one else with Kael standing there.

Who am I kidding? she thought, pressing a hand to her souring stomach. Rodak didn't seem like a man who forgot a face. Especially not the face of the woman who had threatened to overthrow Blailon.

The Steel District gave way to the Bronze, half of which sat below the Shining Wall. Wealth resonated throughout the fourth tier, with hints of superfluous beauty. Ornamental lights floated above pristine cobbled streets. Organized communities filled this part of the Bronze District, consisting of proper houses with small yards, lush parks, and colorful markets. Bundled for the weather, lords and ladies meandered the immaculate streets, their loud monochrome clothes bright beside their black-liveried Phaerian slaves.

The top of the Shining Wall passed below her, and her breath caught. Haldr's Bowl spread before her, the jagged, snowcapped mountain range aglow in the evening light. As much as she hated the people meandering those entitled streets, with a view like this, it was obvious why Upper Tiersmen believed they were better than everyone.

The Bronze District gave way to the Silver, where sharp hedges, far too green to be natural, lined meticulous cobbled streets. Instead of fenced houses, stairs rose from the streets to squat floating islands with lavish estates, lush gardens, and manicured trees.

More liveried Phaerians walked the streets here, their skin almost black next to their Silver Lords. Makayla also noticed the rare Citizen seeming to serve Silver Lords or Ladies like a Phaerian.

"Wards from the Bronze District," Aglia whispered. "In return for loyalty, Bronze Lords send their children to serve as wards. Glorified Phaerians, more like, but don't tell them that. Silver Lords do the same for Gold Lords, and Gold Lords for Founders."

"So the whole empire is built around slavery?"

"The lordlings aren't slaves," Aglia corrected. "They're wards."

Makayla pointed to a young man in loud Bronze District colors, struggling to carry a chest for a pair of lords in matching yellow suits. "Giving it a different name doesn't make it different."

"Of course it does," Aglia said, gesturing to the yellow-suited lords and their Citizen servant. "Switch Bonze with Gold and the ward is suddenly in charge of his masters."

"That's different from changing a name," Makayla said.

"True," Aglia replied. "Responsibilities change with titles. Changing your name changes everything about you."

THE GOLD DISTRICT was exactly as Kael had expected from his books. Liveried wards, not Phaerians, maneuvered the famed marble streets that coiled through the district. Ornate wooden stairs and bridges led to squat floating islands wide enough to hold Headwater. Each floating island boasted an enormous manor constructed in some garish shape—a cluster of leaves here, a flower there, or some other stretch of the imagination. Without shaping, those manors would collapse in a heartbeat. The entire city would crumble, and its Citizens with it.

They deserve no less, Kael thought, imagining the devastation if the city's nodestone failed. *I may as well expect the sun to rise in the north.*

Makayla seemed nonplussed by the sight, shaking her head at the ostentatious platforms. "People *choose* to live there? Like, on purpose? Trees don't look like that. Everything is so…fake."

Aglia shrugged, her brow wrinkled in thought.

The platform sped past the Gold District to the city's final tier— the infamous Founders District, closed to all but the residents and their servants. They docked at a landing surrounded by towering white marble walls. Well over twenty paces high, the walls blocked any view but the long flight of stairs leading to the Archon's Palace. Any Citizen could make their plea to their king or archon, but only Districters had to climb the Petitioner's Penance. Everyone else could afford to pay the pale-skinned porter in a stark white suit, waiting by dozens of pattern-forged lifts at the base of the infamous stairway.

Gods, is everything *here white?* Kael mused.

A door-sized section of the towering wall slid into the ground, issuing a skinny man with alabaster-white skin. Silky blue hair fell past the man's shoulders, complimenting the wisps of color shimmering through his slate-blue dress.

"I thought you were studying the Prus Ruins," the Founder said, greeting Maelly with a kiss to each cheek. "It's so good to see you." He took in her yellow dress and pearlescent jacket, and he offered her a nod of approval. "You'll be the crave of the Ceremony, my dear."

"Bjartur," Maelly cooed. "It's so good to see you too."

His ice-blue gaze settled on Kael, and he stepped back, pressing a gloved hand to his chest. "You found him?"

"I did," Maelly replied with a satisfied smile. "I'm surprised you're attending the Ceremony."

Bjartur rolled his eyes. "Trust me, it wasn't my choice."

"Oh, stop," Maelly said with a playful slap to his arm. "You know you love seeing the newly inducted Sotouri as much as I."

"All those incredibly fit, naked bodies..." Bjartur shivered with a grin. "Better than the rabble you have to look at now." He bowed his head to Maelly. "I'll not waste more of your time. Give Lord Rodak my regards."

Maelly gave him a knowing smile. "Good travels, Lord Bjartur."

"Good travels, Lady Maelly." Bjartur shaped a black cane made of force, and his slate-blue dress rippled into a charcoal-grey suit, with a shimmering turquoise shirt, and black leather shoes. Shaking his now black hair, he stepped onto the platform Kael and the others had left. "I do so abhor the ravel below."

Maelly nodded, and Finndras shoved Kael toward one of the porter's lifts. As depicted in the books Kael had read, the meandering curve of the stairs and towering white walls blocked his view inside the Founders District. Did they have floating islands like in the Silver and Gold Districts? Was it rustic and wooded, like Glaedia's famous Hunting Lodges? Why were Founders so secretive? What were they hiding?

The winding climb gave Kael's mind too much time to imagine the pain Rodak would inflict. Only Aglia knew for certain, and deep lines of worry had creased her brow since morning. Jaw clenching, she pressed a hand to her belly and looked like she might vomit. She knew what Kael faced, and it must be eating her inside.

Makayla's gaze fixated on Kael, her jaw quivering, hands shaking. She knew she'd join him in his misery as soon as Rodak saw her. The poor child, born into misery by no fault of her own, manipulated by Dra'Nahl and tainted by His power. Kael had done what Tálise had told him; what Alnazet had expected of him. He'd freed Makayla from the Dark's grip, and set her on the Path of Light. He'd listened to the gods, and they'd abandoned them. Now, Rodak would torture Makayla with him, and he could do nothing to stop it.

Not without becoming the figure of light.

Even if he knew how, he'd been healthy and hale the last time tapped into his Power of Prophecy, and it had almost sucked his life dry.

Unsurprisingly, the massive Archon Palace glowed white in the waning sunlight, its massive columns stretching hundreds of paces. Countless balconies poked from the enormous building, some decorated with glowing white trees or bushes. As expected, the same monochrome pallet continued inside the palace. White spanned glossy floors, plush furniture, and high vaulted ceilings. The enormous building seemed carved from a mountain of pure white marble.

Just like in the books.

A young, Gold Tier ward guided them through the palace, her skin almost as white as Maelly's. Dressed in imperial-red livery, her bright orange hair fell in smooth locks to her waist. Unlike the books Kael had read, the upcoming Ceremony seemed to have robbed the palace of its notorious crowds. A few lords and ladies wandered the immense building, but these halls were said to bustle with nobles maneuvering for position in some complicated game with rules only they seemed to understand.

Or care about.

Not once had Kael heard bakers in the Workers District scheme to unseat another baker or sabotage a batch of dough. Between working all day and raising a family, Districters didn't have time to make such devious plans. Like townsborn, they barely had time for life.

The Gold Tier ward turned down a long hallway to tall white doors. She pressed a delicate hand to the doors, and they swung open without a sound. "Lady Maelly Bodiou of Blrododok," she announced with a deep bow.

At the end of a long great room, Rodak sat on an obsidian throne, his alabaster skin bright against his jet-black suit. "Took your time as usual, Maelly," he said, waving for them to enter.

"One of these days," Maelly said, gliding over the marble floor, "I'll convince you to take the unbeaten path."

Rodak waved a casual dismissal, his black-eyed gaze resting on Kael. "You've done me, and the empire, a great service, Lady Maelly. For that, you have my thanks, and," he said, pulling a letter from his black coat, "the emperor's as well."

"An invitation?" she asked.

Rodak dipped his head in acknowledgement. Eyes like coal drifted over Kael and Makayla. "My, my, you truly *have* brought me a treat. They'll have to wait in the dungeons for now. I won't have time to deal with them until after the Ceremony. But, I suppose, the darkness will provide its own delightful suffering. If nothing else, it'll give them time to fatten up for my pleasure. We can't have them whither away before justice has been served, can we?"

"Them?" Maelly asked, confusion flashing across her porcelain skin.

Aglia's broken face drained of color, fear quivering her chin.

Rodak lifted an eyebrow. "Do you not know who stands beside you?"

Maelly's confusion drifted to Kael. "The man who took your son's life?

"Not him, you fool!" Rodak roared, quivering with rage. "The girl."

"Eglona?"

"Is that what you call her?" Rodak cocked his head. "You really have no idea. Why am I not surprised?"

Maelly fixed him with a sweet smile. "Not all of us live with our head up the empire's ass."

"Well then," Rodak said, his voice dripping with arrogance. "Lady

Maelly, it is my honor to introduce you to none other than Makayla Penfrost, the Terror of Blailon, Slayer of Serolle. The child who sparked the Second Uprising." Rodak eased back in his obsidian throne. "Does any of that ring a bell?"

Maelly looked at Makayla, fear flashing across the Founder's composed features.

"Emperor's ass, woman." Rodak slapped the arm of his chair, and Maelly flinched. "You really are as daft as the ruins you study."

Aglia's face twisted with relief and confusion. "I trusted you," she said, stepping back from Makayla. "I can't believe, I…"

"Aglia, I can expl—"

The back of Aglia's hand cut her words short.

They squeaked, both of them frozen in place by invisible bands.

"It amazes me," Rodak said, "how quickly your slaves forget their place. Isn't that right, Aglia?"

Aglia squeezed her eyes shut and nodded, tears dripping down her cheeks. "Yes, My Lord Rodak."

Maelly tilted her head, and the Vrath beside Finndras slapped mindtrap cuffs around the tii'Vrath's wrists.

Wide eyed, Finndras yanked at his metal cuffs. "What is this? Release me!"

"As aloof as I am," Maelly said, batting her eyes at Rodak, "*somehow*, I managed to not only bring you your son's murderer *and* Makayla Penfrost, I also happened to uncover one of the Cabal's lead operatives. Didn't…" Maelly pressed a finger to her cheek with feigned shock. "Didn't *you* recommend Finndras to me?"

"Stop with your games, Maelly." Rodak jabbed a finger at her. "Tell me who his handler is, and be done with it. I have a Ceremony to conduct."

"Of course, My Lord," Maelly said, bowing her head. "From what I hear, his handler is one of your friends. Apparently, the two of you are very close. Again, from what I hear. But," she said, lifting a finger, "I am as daft as my ruins, so…" She nudged Finndras with her elbow. "Go ahead. Lord Rodak is dying for you to tell him."

Finndras squeezed his eyes shut, his jaw clenching.

Maelly whispered in his ear, and the tii'Vrath crumbled to the floor.

"How did you know?" Finndras asked, tears streaming down his face.

"Well?" Rodak barked. "Who is it? Who's your handler?"

Finndras breathed a heavy sigh. "Grim."

Rodak barked a laugh and fell back into his obsidian throne. "That's almost as ridiculous as accusing me."

"Almost," Maelly noted, her voice dripping with implications. One of her Vrath handed her a black velvet pouch. "Grim will be here for the Ceremony, yes? Ask him yourself."

Rodak steepled his fingers over his chest. "Very well. We will address your inane accusations after the Ceremony."

"Until then…" Maelly opened the pouch and pulled out a small metallic ball connected to a thin chain. She patted Finndras' cheek. "Be a good boy," she said, handing him the ball. "Swallow this."

28

RAZE THE FIELDS

Alerix looked through the documents T'Ktchoee, his second in command, had left for his signature. As always, he read the battle reports first, and, as always, their losses reminded him just how unprepared they'd been to combat the empire. No amount of drills, skirmishes, or duels could have prepared them for such a ruthless foe.

Who could have imagined the empire would clear the forest with their advance? It made no sense. Just one Sacred Forest could feed the entire empire. Why waste so many resources? Maybe the emperor accepted such a sacrifice if for no other reason than to show the fate of the other Forests should they resist like Onatah.

Alerix fell back in his chair under a wave of despair and tossed the documents onto his desk. Keeper Orenda was right—the empire was too vast to stop, but they could still save the saplings and a piece of Onatah with them.

Alerix took in his large office, wishing he was back in the forest, embraced by all of Alnazet's glory. Instead of lush trees and vibrant flowers, he got to look at a huge desk piled with reports. Rather than swinging through trees and hunting imperials, he met with his officers at the long table in the middle of the spacious room. At least the office windows offered a glorious view of ta'Ajiilee's expansive branches.

A soft clap came from the curtain to his office.

"Enter," Alerix said, and his second in command parted the curtain.

"Is this a good time?" T'Kchowee asked, her andradite-colored eyes sparkling with excitement.

"As good a time as any," Alerix replied, gesturing to the pair of chairs on the other side of his desk. "Besides, I could use some good news."

"The imperials are running," she said.

Alerix shot up from his chair, searching T'Kchowee for a hint of sarcasm. Her fingers twitched with glee, and he breathed a sigh of relief. After a month of losing ground, watching the empire deepen Onatah's scars, he'd wondered if Alnazet had abandoned her people. He cleared his reports, uncovering the living map set into the desktop. Three long scars from the empire's advance cut into the forest, almost reaching halfway into Onatah.

T'Kchowee tapped a talon on the scar stretching south from the imperial city of Laira. "The Lairan advance has fallen. Their forces are running scared."

"And the Glaedian forces?" Alerix asked, pointing to the other two scars in the east.

"Still advancing," she said. "I've already directed our western flank to augment our forces."

"Excellent," Alerix said, his mind swimming with plans. With an entire front fallen, they might save their forest. "Tell Keeper L'Apu to have his Keepers focus on creating more Sentinels. They should be able to double their number by the time they reach the eastern fronts."

Light-green eyes sparkling with joy, T'Kchowee paused at the curtain. "We may not have to raze the fields, after all."

"Alnazet be praised," Alerix said, making the sign of the tree to hide the chill coursing down his spine. Raze the fields—a disgusting term adopted by Marun's sycophants. Something he never thought to hear from T'Kchowee, whose own saplings sat in cages high above Alerix's office.

He waited for her footsteps to fade before he dropped his fake smile. If Marun had gotten to her, it didn't bode well for the rest of Alerix's warriors.

"Fear is an insidious whore," he mumbled.

"That it is," Tai'Enth said, startling Alerix as she stepped from her treewalk portal.

"Alnazet rot you!" Alerix cursed, pressing a hand to his pounding chest. "You scared the life out of me."

"What did T'Kchowee have to say?" she asked, smirking at his glare. Sunlight splashed her light-green skin, warming her ochre Wrap. Apatite and sapphire sparkled along her finely sculpted ears, matching her blue eyes.

"Marun has gotten to her," Alerix said.

"But T'Kchowee has saplings," Tai'Enth said, shaking her head. "Are you certain?"

"She came to me with news about the northern front." Alerix pointed to the map. "Apparently, the Lairan forces are retreating."

Tai'Enth peered at him, suspicion floating in her voice. "That's... good news."

"It was," Alerix said, "right up until the point she said we may not have to raze the fields, after all."

Tai'Enth slouched with defeat. "If he's gotten to her..."

"The rest of our forces can't be far behind." The northern scar on his map grabbing his attention. Something about the empire's retreat didn't sit right. Four weeks of heavy losses, and suddenly his forces repelled one of the empire's three advancing bodies. "It makes no sense."

"Fear, like you said," Tai'Enth replied.

"What?" Alerix said, realizing she was talking about T'Kchowee. "Not her. The empire's retreat. They had every reason *not* to fall back."

"It could be a trap," Tai'Enth offered.

"Doubtful," Alerix mumbled. "The few battles we have won feel less like victories and more like insults to all the battles we've lost. We're like rats, trying to stop hungry bears."

"What would make a bear leave its meal over some pesky rats?"

"Maybe the bears aren't as united as we thought," Alerix said. "The northern forces fly Meru'ut's banner. The eastern forces fly Glaedia's. Onatah sits on the border of both kingdoms."

Tai'Enth gave a slow nod of understanding. "They were in a race to claim Onatah."

"Exactly," Alerix said. "It wasn't us, the rats who stopped Meru'ut. They realized the other bears would beat it to the meal."

"Do you think we can stop them?" Tai'Enth asked.

"With only two fronts to fight…" Alerix shrugged, avoiding the painful truth that plagued his heart—Onatah was doomed. "We were spread too thin with Meru'ut's forces. Maybe now we actually have a chance."

Tai'Enth measured him, her blue eyes reaching into his soul where he hid the truth. "How much time do we have?"

"I never could hide anything from you," he mumbled.

"Makes me wonder why you still try," she said in that comforting tone that always felt like a hug.

"Without Meru'ut to thin out our forces…" Alerix eyed the scars on the map. "I'd say, a month and a half, two at the most."

Tai'Enth moved to the window, gazing up at the dangling cages. She pressed a hand to her stomach. "Alnazet's mercy, those poor saplings."

"What of the Grove?" Alerix asked. "Has Marun infected any more?"

"It's as bad as Keeper Orenda says. She, the Eldest, and two other grove members are all that stand against Marun. N'Lahu folded this morning."

Alerix cursed under his breath.

"Marun has infected our army," Tai'Enth said. "He's infected the Grove and at least half the Keepers. Alnazet's mercy, Alerix. We have to free those saplings now. Tonight, if we can."

"And have half the forest chasing us?" Alerix shook his head. "No, we stick to the plan. Once the empire reaches Onatah, we'll sneak the saplings out amidst the chaos. We just have to keep them alive until then."

"Gives a new meaning to raze the fields and start anew." Tai'Enth clicked her tongue. "Maybe the Saplings Curse isn't so bad, after all."

29

INNER FLAMES

Katima hiked up the mountainside, happy to let her brother take the lead through the thick pine forest. It gave her a chance to watch Diou teach Dilna the Basic Forms for the dagger. It said a lot about the young Human that Diou would start her with such an advanced weapon. Boorde learned half a dozen other blades before touching a dagger.

Gasping for breath, Pendric trudged beside her, his longing gaze fixated on Dilna's training.

"Did you want to walk with them?" she asked. "I'm sure Diou would train you as well."

"It's okay," he wheezed, using the staff L'Veyna had asked to help him up the slope.

"Diou can carry you on his back," Katima offered, wondering why Humans lied when they wore their emotions for all to witness. Even if Pendric's lungs wouldn't allow the strain, he clearly wished to train alongside Dilna.

"I don't need Diou to carry me," Pendric said between breaths. "Besides, maybe I want to walk with you."

Why do Humans bother lying about such inane matters?

Perhaps, to them, being carried was shameful. But then, what did they do when their injuries prevented them from walking? She reached into her pack and retrieved one of the wooden cups L'Veyna had asked. Packing it with snow, she danced heat to melt it into steaming water, then added some Boorde tea, and offered it to Pen.

"Thank you!" He sipped the tea and jerked his head back. "Hot! It's very hot."

"Forgive me," Katima said, finding an appropriate-sized morsel of jerked meat to atone for her loss of face.

"No, it's fine," Pendric said, waving off her gift. He scooped a small ball of snow and dropped it in the tea. "Just, maybe, not *so* hot next time?"

Katima bit off a sharp retort, reminding herself Pendric didn't understand Boorde customs like Reylan. "I know you didn't mean it," she said, "but in my culture, refusing a gift meant to restore one's honor is a deep insult."

Pendric sputtered over his words, spilling a bit of tea. Hissing, he shook his hand and accepted her gift. "I'm sorry," he said, plopping the morsel into his mouth. He bit down, and his eyes widened. "It's so —" Drool dribbled from his mouth, and he wiped his chin. "It's so good!"

A chuckle rumbled Katima's chest. "I figured you for an orange-honey-glaze pork type of man."

"That I am," Pendric said, seeming pleased, as though she'd somehow praised him. "I like savory foods too. One of these days, you'll have to try Jouler's garlic and butter-fried potatoes. He crumbles bacon on top."

"That does sound tempting," she said. "Have you tried lavender-honey-glazed bacon?"

"You know…before you gave me that piece of meat, I would have said that sounds disgusting."

"And now?" Katima asked.

"I bet it's delicious." Pendric tested his tea with a gentle sip, then guzzled it, chewing on the bits of tea.

"You know you're not supposed to eat that, right?"

"I know." Pendric shrugged, still wheezing. "But, I figure, this way, I'll get *all* the effects."

"Especially if the indigestible bits of leaf shred your intestines."

"The what shred what?" he said, spitting the tea out.

"I jest," Katima said. "Obviously you can eat it, otherwise Humans wouldn't stuff it under their lip."

"They do?" Pendric said, peering into the pouch at his belt filled with the tea L'Veyna always asked for him.

"You don't *have* to make tea from it," Katima said. "You know that, right?"

"Yeah," Pendric replied, though his tone said otherwise. He pinched a large clump of L'Veyna's tea between his finger and thumb, and showed it to Katima.

"Less," she said. "Maybe half. Now, stick it under your lip…no, the lower lip. Here," she said, pinching a small bunch of tea from his pouch, and tucking it under her lip. "Like this."

"Oh," Pendric said, following her example. "Like Pirate Tea."

"What?"

"Well, you see," Pendric said. "Pirates can't drink tea when they're manning the sails."

"I'm not sure pirates man sails," Katima said.

"Especially not when the seas are rough," he continued, as if she hadn't spoken. "It gets too wavy to drink tea."

"They don't seek shelter in raging storms?"

"Nope," Pendric said, with all the confidence of youth. "They pinch tea under their lip. Like this."

"You just made that up," Katima said. "Didn't you?"

Pendric shrugged. "Maybe."

Katima chuckled, enjoying young Pendric's antics. Maybe that was why her brother spent so much time among Humans. Sure, they lived a fraction of a Boorde's lifespan, but what a life to live, bouncing through emotions, without a care beyond their few decades of life. Maybe that was the real reason her brother enjoyed Humans—far more than Prytha and Boorde, Humans enjoyed the moment. They somehow lived in the present, forming bonds that rivaled an Ascended's loyalty to their House. Humans seemed to enjoy life, whereas Boorde and Prytha suffered its passage.

Like Pendric, who had struggled through far more hardship in his tiny life than Katima had in a hundred and twenty-four years. Even with his stolen breath, he continued forward, brightening an otherwise dull trek up a mountainside.

He was a true hero, the type that changed history without even knowing it.

Katima offered Pendric a piece of candied lemon, which he plopped into his mouth.

His face puckered. "So sour… Now it's so sweet! It was just…but now…" He closed his eyes, chewing on the candied lemon. "Gods, you have good treats."

Katima caught her brother's attention, and gestured for him to wait. "Now's your chance to catch up, Pen."

"Thank you," Pendric said, moaning over his treat as he scurried to catch up to Dilna and Diou.

Reylan's shuffling footsteps drew Katima's attention away from her brother.

"That was kind of you," Reylan said, returning from relieving himself behind a tree.

"What can I say?" Katima replied. "Pendric grew on me."

"He does that," Reylan said, his dark pate gleaming in the sunlight. "Dilna too."

"She's a popping little ember," Katima said, watching the young girl slide through the first few steps of the First Form with an uncanny grace, her smooth black hair flaring behind her. "My brother believes she has Boorde ancestry."

"But not you," Reylan said, proffering his curved pipe from beneath his long coat.

"That phaery tale is older than the Alliance," Katima said. "My brother chased it his whole life, and all he found were more phaery tales. You know why? Boorde seed can't quicken a human's womb, and even if half Boorde weren't sterile, her skin is far too light to carry that blood. More likely her great grandmother had birthed a Founder's child."

"But what if?" Reylan mused, puffing on his pipe.

"That," Katima said, offering him a candied lemon, "would be amazing."

"Thank you," Reylan said, eating the treat. He shivered, his face puckering worse than Pendric's. "Ooo, I love how it makes the back of the mouth tight."

"That's my favorite part too," she said. "And the sweet part. Actually…" She plopped one into her mouth. Her tongue curled, the sharp jab of sour tightening the back of her jaw before she bit into the chewy candy, releasing a burst of sweet lemon syrup. "I like everything about it." The hem of her dress caught on a twig. "Unlike my dress."

Reylan chuckled, snatching the twig. "I've always said firedancers should wear more practical clothing. Your djohai might be able to shatter patterns, but your dress won't help you against an arrow or knife."

Katima's hackles roe at the insult to firedancer tradition. Which, of course, made no sense. It hadn't been that long ago since she'd complained about the traditional strip of flame-colored cloth in the dress, and yet, she couldn't deny the insult. After all, what could a short-lived Human know of tradition?

"Firedancers," she said, keeping her voice neutral, "have used this dress for millennia."

"That doesn't mean it's a good idea," Reylan said, as if plucking the argument from her past. He gestured to her bald scalp. "Breaking tradition is never easy, and no matter how necessary it is, you can't help but feel like you're betraying all those who came before you."

Katima gawked at the old human's poignant sapience. If not for her shaping sense, she would have sworn he'd somehow shaped the thoughts from her mind. Bowing her head in respect, she doubted the profound wisdom she found in such a short-lived race would ever cease to amaze her.

"You speak from experience, I take it?" she said. It was another admirable trait humanity had embraced. Unlike Prytha and Boorde, who both stuck to their respective domains, Humans—at least Citizens and cabalists—traveled the empire, gathering experiences the way philosophers gathered knowledge.

"I come from a long line of shapers," Reylan replied. "Ra'Vrath, to be precise. My father was a ra'Vrath, and his mother, and his mother's mother, and her father, and so on."

"But you're Phaerian," Katima said, noting his naked temple.

"That's a story for another day." Reylan rubbed his crooked nose. "Suffice it to say, it wasn't easy for me to become the man you see today. It took a lot of soul-searching, or stoking your inner flame, as Boorde say it."

Katima dipped her head in acknowledgment, storing her questions about Reylan's past for another day. "If I might ask—what were you searching for that led to such a tradition-soaked ra'Vrath to join the Cabal?"

"I imagine the same thing as you," he replied. "The truth."

His words resonated with the doubt chilling inside her. She wiped her shaved scalp, still relishing the smooth texture. Compared to that, wearing something other than a firedancer's dress seemed trivial, and yet, a pang of betrayal still settled in her gut, stirring her predilection for a topknot and long streaming tail.

"When you start to doubt," Reylan said, with a knowing smile, "keep this in mind. Your ancestors may spite you for turning your back on them, but your progeny will forever praise your defiance."

"Assuming I'm on the right path," she added.

"In all my studies," Reylan said, "though my years be short to Boorde and Prytha, I've learned one thing to be true." His gaze fell on Pendric, who practiced beside Dilna, using a stick for a dagger. "History looks kindly on those who defend the weak. But for those who break oppressive traditions…history calls those people heroes."

Katima ran her hand over her scalp again with a newfound appreciation, and the weight of her decision eased. "Thank you," she said, fishing out another lemon sweet. "It seems I have a lot more to learn about your perplexing race."

"No, thank you," Reylan said with childish glee. He plopped the sweet in his mouth, giggling over his puckered face.

"On the matter of understanding Humans," Katima said. "Why wouldn't Pendric admit he wanted to practice with Dilna?"

Reylan chuckled, as if she'd said something funny. "Generally speaking," he said, accepting her proffered hand to help him up a tall step, "Human men are annoyingly...male. Especially the young ones."

"That makes no sense."

"Human men are proud creatures," Reylan said.

"You're not," Katima noted, and Reylan laughed as if she'd told a joke.

"I just hide it better," he said.

"But...why are Humans so proud when it comes to being helped?"

"Well," Reylan said, rubbing his crooked nose. "I'd say, compared to Boorde and Prytha, Humans are a relatively weak race. Even shapers live and die before Boorde are considered old enough to birth children. We break easier, we're not as rugged, we can't hear as well... Without shaping, we're not that impressive, but we're proud of who we are. Our flaws, as you see them, make us stronger. Our bones break easier than yours, but that doesn't stop Sotouri Blades from training with your il'Spadas. We don't thrive in the Alliance's harsh climate, but that doesn't stop Humans from visiting its peaks. We don't live nearly as long as Boorde and Prytha, but we do far more with the few decades we have than Boorde or Prytha in that same amount of time. Mix all that with our propensity for charged emotions, and you get a very proud creature."

"But not you," she said, helping him up another tall step.

Reylan patted her arm. "Humans also care less about the opinions of others as we age."

"That seems backwards," Katima said, convinced she'd never understand them. "Shouldn't you care more toward the end, so people remember you well?"

"Yes," Reylan said, taking a moment to catch his breath. "But, when you get old, all your joints ache, and all your efforts to pass on your wisdom fall on the same type of deaf ears you had when you were young…it gets a little difficult to care. Besides, what you do with your life is how people will ultimately judge you, not whether you took a beautiful woman's arm."

"That depends on what you mean by take," Katima said, her wink drawing a chuckle.

"That it does, My Lady."

"Thank you for talking to me," she said, finding an appropriate strip of jerked meat. "You seem like a peppered meat kind of man."

"You got anything with some spice."

"How much spice?" she asked.

Reylan raised an eyebrow. "Have you ever heard of the Castantorian viper chili?"

Katima's lips curled with a smile. "A man after my heart."

KATIMA SAT ON A FALLEN PINE, glad for a moment of solitude after a day filled with chatter. High in the mountain pass, she gazed at the famed Lake Skjold, its placid surface reflecting the moonlit sky and jagged mountain peaks. In Nubidae, when the drain from being around others smoldered her inner flame, she had her firedancer stage to rekindle that fire.

I also didn't have to sleep next to a living rockslide.

There had to be something Reylan could do about his snoring. No matter how impossible he claimed it was to shape on one's self, there had to be *something* he could do. L'Veyna could have helped, maybe opened up the old human's lungs like he did for Pendric, but Flames only knew the young Keeper's fate. Mother's Ascended had to be after Jouler, which didn't bode well for L'Veyna and Prack.

Katima closed her eyes, ignoring her intrusive thoughts, and focusing on her inner flame. Thanks to the bear her brother had hunted, the source of her firedancer power burned white-hot at her core. It purged her emotions, singing her thoughts as they formed, until she floated in blessed harmony.

"Hi Katima!" Pendric said, startling her from her tranquil solitude.

Next to him, Dilna offered a sheepish wave.

"You two scared the flame out of me," Katima said, cursing under her breath.

So much for my alone time.

Pendric nudged Dilna. "Told you I could be quiet."

"You *just* blew your cover," she said.

"I mean…right *now* I did," Pendric replied. "But up until then, I didn't."

"Why are you two here?" Katima asked, their splash of surprise reminding her to be less direct with these Humans. Pendric and Dilna were children with simple upbringings, not the Vrath and Upper Tiersmen who meandered the halls of House Nith'Iil.

"What I meant to say," she said, remembering to sound happy, "was, what brings you out here?" Pendric worked the hem of his sleeve, and she raised an eyebrow at him. "You wanted to see if you could sneak up on me, didn't you?"

"Pendric did," Dilna said. "I already knew I could."

"Well then," Katima said, bowing her head to Pendric. "You succeeded."

Pendric's hand dropped from his sleeve, and he straightened his back. "Thank you."

At times, Katima envied simple Human courtesies. No ritualistic exchanges of meat or candied fruits, no time wasted on determining the right size morsel to dole, just a simple expression of gratitude.

She dipped her head to Dilna. "And what brings you out here, Little Sister?"

Dilna gestured to the shimmering lake cradled in the jagged bowl. "The view."

"Just the view?" Katima asked.

"I wanted to see our route," Dilna said, jerking her chin to the lake.

"As if you can see that far," Pendric said, peering into the night.

"I can," Dilna replied, bumping him with her shoulder. "Look," she said, pointing for him. "See where the lake pours into the Skogsnár River?" Pendric nodded, and she shifted her hand. "All along there, it's mostly grass." She pointed to the mountains along the eastern lip of Haldr's Bowl. "It's all rocky and barren over there."

"Oh!" Pendric said. "I guess I *can* see. I thought that was blurry—" He snapped his mouth shut. "Never mind, I see it now."

Despite Katima's best efforts to maintain her inner calm around the children, a smile pulled her cheeks. She doubted even her mother could maintain a straight face around Pendric.

The corner of his lips curled with satisfaction at cracking her composure.

Not just at cracking it, she thought, seeing the joy filling his brown cheeks. It hadn't been a simple challenge to break her calm exterior. Surprising her had accomplished as much. Pendric had wanted to see her smile. He'd connived and wormed his cute way into her heart because he wanted her to be happy.

That's all he ever wants, she realized.

"You are a pure soul, Pendric Loyalton."

"I know," he mumbled, and pointed to his chest. "It's what the Ul'Kral said before they took my breath."

"No they didn't," Dilna said with a playful slap. Hair almost as straight and black as a Boorde's hung past Dilna's shoulders, while a brown mess of curls tumbled from Pendric's head. Her skin, fairer than Pendric's, invoked thoughts of the Boorde myth Diou had chased his entire life, which Katima dismissed for a more practical explanation. Dilna, or her mother, was an Upper Tiersman's bastard. That person likely drove the poor child's family to risk the perils of life outside the empire. It was a shame Dilna's family had died, although the greater shame would have been to let such a beautiful flame as hers to sputter away on a tiny little farm in the middle of nowhere.

She's so bright with potential, Katima thought, wondering if—no, *when* her brother would take her on as his Astasi.

"What those vile little Ul'Kral said," Dilna continued, "was that your breath wasn't tainted."

"Same thing," Pendric replied, and sucked in a shallow breath.

Katina stood behind the two of them and rested her hands on their shoulder. They looked up at her, their dark-brown eyes, so very Human, so full of trust, tugging at Katima with a string of familiarity.

Pendric picked up a rock and aimed. "I bet I could hit the lake from here,"

"Put it down, Pendric," Katima said, amused by his innocent bravado. He wasn't a savant like Dilna, whose skills would undoubtedly shake history. He didn't have Diou's insatiable hunger to be the best at everything he did. Neither did he have any magical powers or gifts like her and Reylan. In a world rife with people trying to leave their mark, Pendric seemed content with being himself. Just a simple life with one simple goal—to see people smile.

And yet, she thought, savoring the sensation of her hand dragging over her bald scalp, *there is no denying how important Pendric's role is in Prophecy.*

He and Dilna, as tangled in Its convoluted weave as the Dawn—or, rather, the Facets of Prophecy.

Dilna's mouth pursed to one side. "You look…perplexed."

"I was thinking about you and young Pendric."

"You were?" Pendric chimed. "You weren't wondering how good we'd taste, roasting over a fire…were you?"

Katima chuckled and patted his back. "And you say you don't understand Boorde humor. I was thinking about how important the both of you are to Prophecy."

Pendric's brow drew. "Was that more Boorde humor?"

"Not at all," Katima replied. "Your inner flame burns hot with the power of Prophecy."

"How can you tell?" Dilna asked.

"All firedancers have an affinity with Prophecy," Katima said. "The more powerful the firedancer; the stronger the affinity."

"Is that what makes a Seer?" Dilna asked. "Having too much power?"

"Very good." Katima said, the young girl's bashful grin tugging on that string of familiarity again. "We don't know how strong a firedancer can be, but at some point, the gift becomes a burden."

Pendric patted her hand. "I'll bet you're as strong as anyone can be."

And there goes Pendric, tugging on a different type of string.

A part of Katima wondered how much of his endearing heart was an act, but she ignored that petty voice, and focused on the moment... on being happy.

"I'LL BET Ascended are still hunting us," Pendric said, huffing.

"No, they aren't," Dilna replied, peering back the way they'd come. The western rim of Haldr's Bowl rose above the horizon, while the distant Skogsnár River poured down Meru'ut's grassy plains, eventually dumping into the sea. Unlike the jagged mountains that gave Haldr's Bowl its name, a tall plateau dominated the southern lip of the bowl. The rocky terrain atop the plateau didn't seem to offer any place to hide, and yet she saw no sign of Diou or Katima.

It hadn't been *too* long since they'd left in search of trailing Ascended. Once Dilna learned the dagger's Basic Forms, maybe Diou would let her scout beside him, instead of babysitting an old shaper who was more than capable of caring for himself.

"If you're not worried about Ascended," Pendric wheezed, nudging her, "then why do you keep looking back?"

"I'm trying to find Diou and Katima," she said, measuring the afternoon sun. Shielding her eyes, she looked at their path ahead, spotting Reylan a few hundred paces ahead, making his way toward the bouldered slopes of the Bowl's eastern rim.

"You might find Katima," Pendric said, "but you're never going to find Diou, unless he wants you to find him. He's a master at everything he does, including hiding from annoying little girls."

"I'm not annoying," she said, kicking the back of Pen's foot as he walked.

He recovered from his stumble, and turned, spreading his arms as if to say, "You just were!"

"I found them," Dilna said, squinting at what she thought had been a Boorde. "Never mind. It's just the shadow of a rock."

"Come on," Pendric mumbled, motioning for her to quicken her pace. "Reylan is already way ahead of us."

"He's a hundred and seventy-something years old," she said, skipping to catch up. "How much farther ahead do you think he's going to get?"

"He's not that old." Pendric snorted a laugh. "He's like...seventy. Maybe seventy-five."

Not a hint of sarcasm trailed his voice, his eyes reflecting his usual innocence. "You really believe that."

"Why wouldn't I?" he said. Look at him.

"You know shapers age slower than non-shapers...right?"

"Yeah." Pendric scoffed. "Everyone knows that."

"Then, how could he look seventy-five, and also be seventy-five?"

Pendric frowned. "Is he really that old?"

"Would I lie?" she joked, poking his ribs for a wheezing laugh. "How are you holding up?"

He sucked in a weak breath. "About the same? It's hard to tell. I miss L'Veyna."

"Me too," Dilna said, her chest constricting with heartsick, fear, and worry for her dear friend. "I miss her every day."

"Don't worry," Pendric said, taking her hand. "We'll see her again. Jo and Prack too."

Despite Pendric's weak lungs, it didn't take them long to catch up with Reylan. The old man waved at them from atop a flat rock, his curly white hair frizzled around his dark pate sun.

"Did you find them?" Reylan asked, rubbing his crooked nose.

"Of course not," Pendric said, as Diou and Katima walked out from behind the large, flat rock Reylan stood upon. Pendric sputtered, his eyes wide. "It's you! But, when did...how did you get in front of us?"

"Isn't it obvious?" Dilna said, hiding her mirth under a somber mask. "He didn't want us to see him."

Pendric's shoulders drooped, and he gave her a pointed look. "Funny."

"Nevertheless, true," Diou said.

"Ha!" Pendric barked, sneering at Dilna. "So I was right."

"Now that we're all here," Katima said, addressing the group. "We have good news and bad."

"Bad first!" Pendric blurted, earning a stern look from Reylan.

"Bad it is," Diou said. "We found no sign of pursuit."

"How is that bad?" Dilna asked.

Diou raised an eyebrow, signaling her to either ask a better question or answer her own.

She wracked her brain for a reason it would be bad if they did*n't* find any tracks. "Because…there should be tracks?"

Katima cast an accusatory look at Diou, and he held up his hands. "You don't have to tell me," he said. "I've known she's special. You're the one showing up late to the campfire."

"Then why am I the one trying to convince you to do the right thing?"

"I know what I have to do," Diou said. "That doesn't mean I have to like it."

"Don't have to like what?" Pendric asked, saying the words Dilna could not.

Diou doesn't want me to be his apprentice.

Dilna fumbled for something to do with her hands, somewhere to look, somewhere to hide her warming cheeks. He only trained her to pass the time, not because she had any actual skill with a blade. He probably thought it was cute, watching her stumble through the Forms.

"What about the Ascended?" Reylan asked, pulling out his pipe.

"They must be keeping their distance," Katima said.

"Or waiting for backup," Reylan offered.

"Other than finding defensible ground," Diou replied, scanning the way ahead, "there's not much we can do."

Dilna swallowed the awkwardness lumped in her throat. Diou could loath the thought of training her all he wanted. She'd just show him how wrong he was. "What about Kael? How are we going to rescue him from Eio?"

"I think I have a plan," Katima said, her fire-diamond eyes sparkling with amusement. "One to get us inside the city, at least, which is the good news."

Diou sucked his teeth, exposing his elongated canines. "I still don't like it."

A sparkle of hope shone through Dilna's dejection. He wasn't talking about accepting her as his Astasi. He didn't want to go inside Eio. Not that Dilna blamed him. It was the last place on Yrsa she'd ever want to go. Well, maybe besides New Torgeir…maybe.

"Oh?" Reylan pulled a long drag from his pipe, his thick plume of smoke dissipating in the gentle breeze. "What's this plan of yours?"

"I will attend the Sotouri Ceremony as Heiress Apparent of House Nith'Iil."

Reylan frowned over his pipe, his gaze settling on her bald scalp. "You're not the Heiress Apparent."

"A fact that Mother needs to keep secret," Katima said. "Hence why she sent her Ascended to silence me."

"And the rest of us," Diou said. "Matron Nith'Iil can't risk the knowledge of my sister's perfidy to reach the wrong ears."

"But, if you attend the Ceremony," Dilna said, "won't the Ascended know where to get you?"

Diou scowled, while Katima wore a smile of amusement. "That's the beauty of it all," she said. "The Ascended won't be able to touch me while I'm in the city. Too many prying eyes, especially in the home of the Sotuori. My mother's only hope is to get to us before we reach Eio."

Reylan chuckled, smoke leaking from his nose. "Well played, my dear."

"Don't encourage her, old man," Diou said, shaking his head. "You haven't heard the whole plan."

Pendric lifted a finger. "I'm confused. Who played what?"

"You see," Reylan said, pointing with his pipe. "As long as Katima plays her part as Heiress Apparent, the Ascended won't be able to go near her without drowning the empire in rumors that Katima has denounced House Nith'Iil—her perfidy. Her…treachery."

"Oh!" Pendric said. "That makes way more sense. I thought perfidy had something to do with being so pretty."

"But what about your hair?" Dilna asked, and Katima wiped her snow-white scalp.

Reylan tapped his pipe against his palm and repacked the bowl with ha'ath. "I guess that's where I fit into the plan."

"What about me?" Pendric asked. "Where do I fit?"

"You will stay here with Reylan," Diou replied, and Pendric's shoulders slumped. "Did you *want* to go into the home of the Sotouri?"

"Well, I...I mean, no," he said, working his toe into the ground. "I guess not."

"I guess that means I'm staying too," Dilna said.

Diou and Katima shared a look, their infuriating Boorde face devoid of emotion. Katima shrugged. "Unless you have a better idea, brother?"

Diou turned his dismal frown at Dilna. "You will come with me as my apprentice. My Astasi."

Dilna's excitement warred with the obvious disapproval chiseled on Diou's hard face.

"Now hold on," Reylan grumbled, moving to Dilna's side. He draped a protective hand over her, the smell of campfire and ha'ath invoking pleasant memories of their journey to the Boorde Alliance. "What about Grim?"

"Who's Grim?" Dilna asked.

"He's the embodiment of evil," Diou said. "A Sotouri Blade raised in the Boorde Alliance."

"Grim used to be Boorde?" Pendric asked.

"What?" Diou said, shaking his head. "No, that's not how... No, he came to us as an infant. His father was an ambassador from Themsia, in Castantor."

"What does he have to do with me?" Dilna asked, washing Reylan and the Boorde in silence.

Diou took a deep breath. "He has vowed to kill my Astasi."

"He what?" Dilna said, her excitement drowned under an icy wave of fear. No wonder Diou looked so upset.

Pendric worked the hem of his sleeve, concern washing his eyes. "Then don't make her your Astasi. Why does she even need to go? She can stay here with me and Reylan. Or…or, *I* can go. I can pretend to be your Astasi."

"You could not," Diou said, his hard gaze settling on Dilna. "And she would not be pretending."

Hope opened a pocket of clarity in Dilna's confusion. Diou hadn't been upset with her. He wanted her to be his Astasi. He just didn't want her to die at the hands of some crazed Sotouri.

"But why does she have to go?" Pendric said, chin quivering.

"She's going to find Kael," Katima said.

"Me?" Dilna squeaked. "How am I supposed to find him? I'm just a little girl. I can't shape, and I'm no il'Spada."

"Exactly," Diou said, kneeling in front of her. "We do not know where Kael is being held, and it's a big city. My sister and I will have to maintain our guise as Heiress Apparent and her First Blade. We'll have too many eyes on us to snoop about."

"But a Phaerian can," Dilna concluded.

"An *Astasi* can," Diou corrected. "A Phaerian, especially a skirter like yourself, wouldn't make it past the Shining Gate."

"She wouldn't make it to the Wall," Reylan grumbled.

"But an Astasi," Diou continued, "would be free to carry out her Shai'jan's errands, and talk to people we cannot. People like, say…the servants who bring Kael his food?"

The mischievous plan pulled the corners of Dilna's lips into a smile. She looked at her hands and grimy clothes. "But, I look like a Phaerian."

"I assume," Reylan said, "that's where I come in again?"

"Just so," Katima said.

Reylan huffed a sigh and squeezed Dilna's shoulders. "I don't like this plan," he grumbled, rubbing his crooked nose. "Not one bit. Maybe, given more time, I'd devise a better plan. If we hadn't been separated, Jouler could have gone in place of Dee, but…"

"But there really is no one else," Dilna said, buffeted by a confluence of emotions.

Reylan slouched with a heavy sigh and motioned for Diou and Katima to walk with him.

Pendric sniffled, snaking his fingers between hers, his face wracked with worry. "Do you have to go?"

Dilna squeezed his hand and nodded over the lump forming in her throat.

"But…" Pendric sniffled and dragged his free arm across his nose. "But you'll come back, right?"

She nodded again, not trusting her voice.

"Promise me," Pendric said, chin quivering. "If you ever see someone with dark skin and a crooked nose…run. Run as fast as you can and don't ever look back."

Dilna frowned. "But…that's Reylan. Dark skin, crooked nose."

Pendric blinked. "No, that's—" He peered at Reylan, and his eyes widened. "That's Reylan, too! It's Grim *and* Reylan." Pendric loosened his hand from hers, and he smacked his forehead. "They both have the same broken nose, but Reylan is *way* older, and Grim…" Pendric shuddered. "He's evil, Dee. He's the man who took us from you. Like Diou said, he looked like the in-body-mint of evil."

"Embodiment," Dilna chuckled, poking at Pendric's ribs. "Embodiment of evil."

"That's what I said," he squealed, slapping at her hands. Pendric grinned at her, then pulled her into a tight hug. "At least this time, I get to say goodbye."

Dilna's voice cracked from the lump in the back of her throat. "I… I'll bring you a surprise from Eio."

"You will?" he said, stepping back, tears dripping down his cheeks.

"Something special," she said, poking him again. "I promise."

"We're not leaving just yet," Diou said. "Katima and I must prepare for the bonding ritual."

Butterflies returned to Dilna's stomach, fluttering amid her festering apprehension. Did Diou believe she could be his Astasi, or was this all a ruse to find Kael? Would she still be Diou's apprentice once they freed Kael, or would he dismiss her once they were out of danger?

"You know what that means?" Reylan said, the soft joy in his eyes melting away her concerns. He plopped his pipe in his mouth and draped his arms over her and Pendric. "We have time to share one last meal."

~

DIOU GUIDED Dilna across a grassy field toward the area he and Katima had prepared for the binding ceremony. The evening sun warmed Dilna's face, pride straightening her back. Folded and tucked under her arm was the ry'ku Reylan had shaped out of extra clothes from Jouler's pack, her daggers sheathed at her sides.

"This path," Diou said, tugging at the blouse of his faded ry'ku. "The path of an Astasi. It is not an easy path, even for a Boorde. At the end of this path lies the sacred title—il'Spada. However, this situation is…unconventional, to say the least. Normally, you would have had a few decades of training before I even considered you as a candidate. The relationship between a Shai'jan and their Astasi is as unyielding as it is unbreakable."

The gravity in his tone melted the humorous quip bubbling through her thoughts. She rested her free hand on one of her daggers. A year ago, no one had trusted her to hold a knife, much less an actual weapon. But that Dilna had been weak. That Dilna had been a helpless wretch.

Drawing strength from the dagger, she recalled the lessons Diou had already taught her—Vis'Mar and Tezrel, the first two Basic Forms. She thought about Reylan, who'd saved her from being trampled at Iaroca and had taught her to read and write. Pendric, of course, acted more like her older—or maybe younger?—brother.

Bigger. He's definitely bigger.

He also made everything better in a very Pendrickian way. Reylan had a similar effect, but more like a loving grandfather.

"We will see them again, right?" she asked, gazing back up the hill at Pendric and Reylan. They waved, and she waved back. "Why do I feel like that was goodbye? Like, goodbye-goodbye."

"Farewells are strange creatures," Diou mused. "When we don't get to say them, we're haunted by the thought of being robbed of that opportunity. When we do get to say them, we're haunted by the prospect of it being the last."

"Was that supposed to be comforting?" Dilna asked, wondering what Pendric would have said.

Of course you'll see us! You're not blind, are you?

"It was the truth," Diou said.

Were Boorde parents like this to their children—all reason and no heart?

Gods' blessed mercy, what a strange life that would be. No comforting, *Of course we'll see your friends again,* or, *We'll be back before you know it.* Just cold, uncaring facts.

Facts don't have feelings, she thought, imagining Diou's deep, rolling voice.

Maybe Boorde had it right. Their strict and confusing code of honor had always seemed heartless, and as appealing as the life as a townsborn with all its rules, but maybe it wasn't so bad after all. Every Boorde had a place within their House. There were no poor within the Alliance. No Boorde went without food. Every profession held a place of honor. House keepers, cooks, soldiers, blacksmiths— every member of the Alliance mattered, not just its leaders.

Katima waited for them, standing beside a tray with a steaming teakettle, a clay bowl, a wooden whisk, and a traditional Boorde tea cup, which had always seemed more like a deep saucer to Dilna. Katima bowed to her, the Boorde's long locks of too-black hair falling from her topknot past her waist.

"Dilna Freeman," Katima said, her tone stiff and formal. "Do you choose to wear the mantle of Astasi?"

Dilna hesitated, doubt worming through her excitement. She was just a little girl, barely eleven years old, not a tall, strong Boorde like Katima or Diou.

"What do you think I should do?" she asked, looking up at the statuesque Boorde.

"We cannot tell you," Diou said. "It is a decision only you can make. It's not too late to change your mind, but once the ritual is performed, you'll be bound by threads stronger than any magic."

"But what about saving Kael?" Dilna asked. "Who will talk to the servants if I don't come?"

"We can find another way," Katima said.

Insecurities boiled back to the surface of Dilna's thoughts, reminding her of her fragility, and the very real fact that a maniacal Sotouri Blade would hunt her down the moment he learned of her.

"I'm just a girl," she said, doubt trembling her voice. "I don't heal like a Boorde. I'm not as tall, or as strong, and I never will be. I don't have any special powers…I'm just me."

"You're right," Diou said, kneeling in front of her, his fire-diamond eyes soft and warm. "Lucky for you, becoming an il'Spada doesn't require special powers." He tapped her chest. "It takes heart, and yours is stronger than any I've seen."

An il'Spada, she thought, pride burning through her doubt. *Me, little Dee, an il'Spada!*

"Do you really think I can do it?" she asked, and Diou nodded. "What about you, Katima?"

A warm smile cracked her somber features. "Who do you think convinced him to take you on?"

Dilna beamed a toothy smile. "Then I accept."

"Very well." Katima dipped her head in a bow, then patted Dilna's shoulders. "Let's get you dressed."

Draped in serene reverence, Dilna sat back on her heels, facing west as instructed. Sitting on the other side of the ceremonial tea set was *the* Diou Nith'Iil, whose very name commanded respect across all Torgeir, and fear from any who would challenge him. A year ago, childish fancies had filled her life, and now the most famous il'Spada in history wanted to be her Shai'jan.

Dilna's heart twisted from a fond memory of her mother, singing to herself while she cooked, her smooth black hair glistening in the sun. She would have been so proud of her little Dee. Dilna blinked against the painful memory and cleared her mind of her past.

Wait in silence, Katima had instructed, while she'd dressed Dilna in the ry'ku Reylan had shaped.

The thick, buttonless blouse fit snug around the torso, held closed by a long belt that wrapped twice around her waist before being tied in a special knot. Standing, the loose trousers fell to her feet, covering her new slippers. Chill wind nipped at her bare skin, whipping her topknot. Even without a coat, her ry'ku kept her warm, the slippers sturdy despite their thin sole. Reylan must have pattern-forged the fabric to keep her comfy.

As with everything in Boorde culture, Katima had said, her fire-diamond eyes flickering with pride, *the tea ceremony is rooted in honor.*

Without a word, Diou bowed to the clay bowl that held the powdered tea, then he heaped two tiny spoonfuls into the squat teacup. He bowed again, this time to the teacup before pouring two small dashes of steaming water.

Each bow gives honor and shows respect.

Diou dipped the whisk in the teacup.

Even the whisk? Dilna had asked.

Within Boorde culture, Katima had said, *even the modest tool has its place of honor.*

Diou bowed to the splintered wood, then whisked the tea.

When an il'Spada becomes a Shai'jan…

Diou handed Dilna the cup, then bowed to her, pressing his forehead to the ground three times.

…they bind their inner flame to their Astasi.

Dilna held the teacup in her left palm.

When someone becomes an Astasi…

Dilna bowed to the cup, and turned it once to honor Diou's bond to her, once more to honor her bond to him, and again to honor their bond to the Sacred Flame.

…they bind their inner flame to their Shai'jan.

Dilna drank the tea in three measured sips, one to accept Diou as her Shai'jan, one to become his Astasi, and one to seal the ceremony under the Sacred Flame.

No bond is stronger than a Shai'jan and their Astasi...

Dilna set the teacup on the ground and bowed three times to Diou.

...not a mother's, nor father's, nor sibling's.

Katima approached Diou, her silky firedancer dress whipping in the wind. One of his daggers rested on her palms, the weapon's worn black hilt sticking from an equally worn, black wooden scabbard.

In a traditional ceremony, Katima had told Dilna, *Diou would have presented you with one of his sidaiyo...*

Diou bowed to her, and she placed the sheathed dagger on his outstretched palms.

...but this is hardly a traditional ceremony, and you are far from a traditional Astasi.

He presented the weapon to Dilna with another bow, and she accepted it likewise.

Swelling with pride, Dilna resisted the temptation to clutch the dagger—*her* dagger—to her chest.

Mark my words, young Human, Katima had said right before the ceremony had started. *Bards will praise your name....*

Dilna bowed to il'Diou three times.

...while the empire trembles at your passing.

30

A STILL NIGHT

The setting sun splashed Alnazet's glory across an impossibly large sky, painting fluffy clouds in vibrant red, pink, yellow, and purple. The colorful scene did little to settle L'Veyna's stomach. It clenched again, threatening to relieve what little remained in her belly. Two days had come and gone, and she still paled from the churning ocean. Wearing the ridiculous cloth to cover her ears didn't help, either, but her infuriating brother wouldn't let her remove it. That or the plagued gloves to hide their talons.

Her stomach clenched again.

"It gets better," Captain Halstokk said, his rasping voice chafing her ears. Dressed in a loose shirt that exposed the man's ample chest hair, his lingering gazes made her want to scrub her skin clean.

Him and half his crew, she thought, shivering to think what would happen if the other half stopped treating her like a little sister.

"Give it a month or two," the Captain continued, "and the waves will feel more like home than land ever did."

"That's how long it takes to get to Cowine?" she asked, watching how the sailors glided across the deck, not once having to flap their arms to keep balance.

Captain Halstokk frowned, then nodded as if remembering something. "Right, Cowine. It all depends on the weather, lass. Could take longer if we catch a storm around the Fingers. Meru'utian waters are far from delicate this time of year."

"Couldn't we sail farther out and avoid it altogether?"

Captain Halstokk grinned, displaying what few teeth remained in his wide mouth. "Already thinking like a sailor." He folded his arms and leaned on the rail. "An inexperienced sailor, but your mind is in the right direction. Always avoid rougher waters, if you can. Which is why we can't sail around the types of storms Laa brews in the deep sea." He slid his arm over her shoulders and pointed up at the crow's nest. "Imagine waves twice as high as the nest, crashing down on us."

The stench of stale sweat and rancid breath upended L'Veyna's already empty stomach. She heaved again and again, drooling thick spittle. Out of breath, she leaned against the rail, whimper-groaning.

"There, there," the Captain said, patting her back with his greasy, wormy hand. "I'm still hoping you and your brother will stay on. The boys work harder with you two on deck."

L'Veyna endured another spasm and wiped thick spittle from her mouth. A ladle of water appeared in front of her, and she jumped back with a yelp.

An older, barrel-chested man dipped his head in apology, his peppered curly hair fluttering around a dark bald pate. "Sorry, Little Miss," he said, using the term the more protective sailors had taken to calling her. His hard gaze pushed the Captain aside.

"As you were," Captain Halstokk said, excusing himself to bark commands at a young deckhand with dark, curly hair.

L'Veyna sipped from the proffered ladle, swished her mouth, and spat into the dreadful ocean. "Thank you."

The burly man rested his elbows on the rail. "We're not all bad." He glanced over his shoulder and shook his head. "Most of us are bad, but not all of us."

She pressed a hand to her sour stomach, wishing it was all due to the ever-present rock of the ocean.

"I know being cooped in the captain's quarters isn't ideal," the barrel-chested man said, casting his gaze across the unending horizon.

"But it sure would do me good if you'd stay in there with your bother."

"I like the feel of the sun on my face," L'Veyna replied, wishing she could tear off her bulky clothes and truly bask in Alnazet's glory.

"Yes, well, that speaks of my concerns, young miss." The barrel-chested man cleared his throat. "It's just that, well, you see..." He dry-washed his hands, his gaze flitting between her and the ocean. "The boys, they..." He pressed his lips into a thin line. "You've too pretty a face to be out here."

L'Veyna spared a glance around the deck, surprised to see everyone busy about their work instead of stealing looks. "Having you nearby seems to keep everyone in line."

The man's face reddened, and he pushed himself back from the rail. "Unfortunately, I have a ship to feed."

"You're the cook?"

He dipped his head. "The only crew member the Captain truly fears." He dipped his head again. "I'll send a special tea to your quarters to help with your stomach. It's what I give all the legs."

"Legs?" she asked.

"New sailors who still haven't gotten their sea legs." He dipped his head again and headed below deck.

L'Veyna tuned out the Captain's grating shouts and focused on the crisp saltwater breeze, taking deep breaths in through her nose and out through her mouth.

Just like Jouler, she thought, welcoming the images his name conjured. She didn't dare tease the sailors like she'd teased him, but then, he'd never looked at her like a starved man at a feast. These rotted sailors wouldn't be so lewd with their glances with Jo around. Especially after they saw why the Boorde called him Vidimir, the way he whirled with his staff.

A staff he cherished because I made it.

Her chest warmed, her lips parting with a smile. Once they freed him, she'd have to ask him a new staff—a better staff. She pictured Jouler on the deck of his ship, watching the last bit of color fade from the horizon before she headed into the Captain's small room.

"How's your belly?" her brother asked, sitting on the edge of the bed. A small chair waited for her beside the captain's desk, where the promised tea steamed from a kettle.

"Horrible," she replied, settling into the chair.

"The cook just sent it up. Said it would help with the sour stomach."

"Why can't you be the one who's sick?" she growled.

Prack stood to pace with the same fluid grace as the sailors. "Because I already have my sea legs, and you're much more convincing at being sick."

"Because I am sick." L'Veyna put her head in her hands, groaning through another wave of nausea.

"Have some tea," Prack said. "It's good."

"You had some?" she asked, pouring a cup.

"Just a cup," he said with a wink. "Had to make sure it's not poisoned."

L'Veyna rolled her eyes, savoring the aroma of lemon, chamomile, mint, and ginger. She took a sip.

And just the right amount of honey.

"The cook is nice," she said, and her brother raised an eyebrow at her. "What? Don't give me that look. They're not all bad. Not him."

"Warm tea, does not a good man make."

She slurped another sip. "Sense, does not that make."

By the time she finished her second cup, Prack's chest rose and fell with sleep. Stifling a yawn, she poured a third and final cup and wondered what Jouler was doing. He wouldn't be in the captain's quarters, that was certain. The plagued Boorde probably forced him to sleep on the deck in the freezing nights.

Another yawn cracked her jaw, her body lumbering under a thick wave of sleep. She stood to go to bed, and her leg warbled. Eyes suddenly laden, she fell back into the chair. Exhaustion pulled at her limbs, her head heavy.

The tea!

The cup slipped from her gloved fingers, and the rattle of a doorknob followed her into darkness.

L'Veyna awoke to rough hands, sitting her upright. More hands wrapped rope around her, strapping her to a chair. Garbled voices filtered through the cloth wrapped around her head, her tongue thick in her mouth.

"Careful," came a familiar voice in the darkness.

The cook.

"But," came another voice, "Captain said—"

"The Captain's a fool," the cook growled. "Rough her up one more time, and you'll be eating soup the rest of your miserable life. *No* bruises. Put a damn cloth over her wrists. Blasted idiot."

Strange that her brother hadn't already sprung into action. The cook, his accomplices, and everyone else on the ship should be dead by now. Unable to lift her head, she forced an eyelid open. Rope wrapped around her chest and wrists, holding her to a chair.

The captain's chair, she thought, her mind as sluggish as her body. *Where's Prack?*

A hand pushed her head back, and she saw the pepper-bearded face of the man she'd dared trust.

"Did you drink it all?" The cook peered into the kettle, his brow drawing in confusion. "Sure did…"

L'Veyna peered toward the bed, searching for her brother among the crumpled blankets.

"Looking for your brother?" the cook mumbled. "We already carried him down. Are you laughing?"

L'Veyna tried to speak, but her words fumbled over her thick tongue.

"What's that?" The cook leaned close to listen. The door shattered, and warm blood spurted from the cook's neck and mouth.

"You're dead," L'veyna whispered, as the cook crumpled to the floor.

The cook's aide followed him to the ground, blood gurgling from his mouth.

"Still groggy?" her brother asked, his face filling her blurry vision. "That will not do. I need you to wake up."

Her brother dug his talon deep into the back of her hand, hot pain clearing her mind. Her ever-blossoming power burgeoned within her, augmented by the deep ocean and its potential for life. L'Veyna asked without thinking, images locking into place with the slightest compulsion. Within a heartbeat, a wooden fist grew from the floor, and slammed into Prack. He fell, rubbing his chest.

"Sorry," she said, turning her anger on the shouts from outside, the torchlight spilling beneath the door, the clang of a bell breaking the air.

Attuned with her goddess, L'Veyna's power swelled inside, her will contorting reality with a thought. A sudden boom shook the Charred Leech, and the world went still. No waves lapped the ship. No wind whipped its sails. Wrapped in sharp anger from the cook's betrayal, L'Veyna strode out of the captain's quarters, and into the placid night.

Dozens of sailors gawked at her, swords and knives forgotten in their hands.

"Magic, but how?" one of them asked. "We're over water!"

"That's shaping," Prack said, standing beside L'Veyna.

She pulled the cloth off her head, finally letting her braids and ears free. Infused with power, every image she asked locked into place the instant it came to mind. Orbs of water materialized over filthy heads, watery spikes piercing perverted hearts. Her brother's blurred form danced between sailors, leaving fountains of blood, while tentacles of water snaked into lungs.

A handful of sailors cried for mercy, their arms held high.

L'Veyna screamed, "Why should I?"

Her brother appeared by her side, breathing hard, bloody tsah dripping on the deck. "We need them, sister. We can't sail this ship alone."

"It weren't us, Little Miss," a large sailor said.

"Honest," another large sailor replied. "The cook, see, him and the Captain, they—"

"Where is he?" L'Veyna demanded.

"The cook, he—"

"The Captain!" she shouted, searching the small group of cowering sailors.

The large sailor winced, his blubbering pleas turning into sobs of mercy.

"He fell off," someone said. The young deckhand she'd seen earlier approached, his dark curls plastered to his face. "It was one of them tentacles what threw him off."

"What's your name?" Prack asked.

"H-Horgar," the boy stammered.

"I am your new captain," Prack said, his voice clear in the unnatural calm. "Horgar will be my new First Mate.

"What are you doing?" L'Veyna clacked.

"We need a crew," her brother replied.

"But Horgar is barely older than me," she clacked.

"He's the only one here we're saving."

The scratched words chilled her anger. *"What do you mean?"*

Prack's cold gaze floated over the knelt sailors, their cries and sniffles loud in the still night. *"You didn't think I was going to let them get away with what they did. Did you?"*

JOULER SOARED ONCE MORE, high over a war-torn land and a besieged city. His heart ached for a place he'd only seen in his dreams, its name bobbing at the edge of his memories, and yet, it felt as much like home as Headwater. Perhaps it was because this land had been as peaceful as the quaint village, its Phaerians and Citizens prospering without the constraints of the Imperial Paradigm.

It had been glorious, the thought both his own and not.

Murky memories of a life in that city high above those Shining Walls mingled with memories of Headwater, dragging him through confusing dreamscapes—picking Dralin's peaches on a floating island flashed to a scene depicting him seated on a glass chair in the middle of a cotton field.

Sounds of battle shattered his jumbled memories, throwing him into the middle of a clash. Soldiers in strange quilted armor bearing the Imperial Shield fought against soldiers with the Snake and Chalice of his home.

No, Headwater is my home, Jouler thought, fighting memories of vaulted wooden ceilings, walls made of windows, and the crisp aroma of dried pine needles over late-summer grass.

The sharp peal of retreat pierced the battle, and a wave of excitement rushed through the imperial soldiers.

"We've got her on the run!" an officer called from his imposing destrier.

"Hold the line!" came a deeper shout, pounding over the officer's words. The familiar voice filled Jouler with pride. Standing among the bowing line of Snake-and-Chalice soldiers was a stout man, his gruff, bearded face fitting his booming voice. Instead of a spear, he wielded an odd sword, the end-half of the blade curved like a crescent.

The soldiers shouted in unison and formed a shield wall, prickling the imperial assault with pattern-forged spears that sizzled with power. Behind them, rows of archers and support personnel funneled through the Shining Gate into the city.

"Hold the line!" the stout officer shouted, and Jouler shouted with him. "For honor! For Codoine!"

The imperial line folded under Jouler's assault, and his soldiers slaughtered the retreating forces.

No…that's not me. I'm not a soldier. I'm a farmer.

Deep rumbling laughter, like mountains shaking and cracking, shook Jouler's soul, and an ancient voice filled his head.

No matter which path you walk, you will always be the Harbinger of Death.

Jouler blinked awake, the dream fading to the lazy flap of sails. High above him, an empty crow's nest warbled amid a twinkling night sky. His stomach churned, and he sat up, the bitter taste of bile rising in his throat. Swallowing, hoping to quell his stomach, he breathed in the salty sea air and focused on the lap of waves against the ship's hull, the creek of lines, and soft flutter of sails—anything but the stillness permeating the Charred Leach. Even at this late hour, grumbles and laughter should have filled a ship like this, not dead silence.

Working his mind to more pleasant thoughts, he imagined L'Veyna staring at the same night sky, though not from such a depraved vessel as the Charred Leach. The macabre irony of the name conjured the vivid memories he'd tried to ignore, of desperate screams, mutilated bodies, and strips of flesh sizzling over a firedancer's flame.

Jouler's stomach clenched, his mind swarming over the ancient voice from his dreams.

No matter which path you walk, you will always be the Harbinger of Death.

PART III

DESTINY

Return, Daughter of Hollows, sundered gardens of old and salted land. Hope rises from ash, the Circle complete.

31

NEW WAVES

Xi'Tslna endured the ship's roll, regretting every decision that had brought her to this miserable point. Life at home had always seemed so monotonous—wake up, eat, check traps, return to a crowded home, eat, go to sleep, wake up... At least that life hadn't made her want to empty her stomach every time a group of waves rocked the ship.

Anchored at sea, awaiting the rest of the fleet was bad enough. She couldn't imagine sailing the deep seas in this Light cursed ship.

The loud din of the mess deck reminded her of lunch time with her brood, only a thousand times worse. Dozens of A'a'nxil sat at tables, clamoring about the long voyage ahead of them. Less than a year at the Academy, and her exceptional skills at mancing, had earned her a spot in the vanguard.

My skills and my blessing, she thought, the holy light of their god hidden beneath the sleeve of her officer's jacket.

"Afternoon, Priestess," the cook said, new sergeant stripes on the collar of his pristine uniform. An impressive rank for a male, especially considering the three broken spine spikes, numerous scars, and meaty fists that spoke of the man's short temper and penchant for brawling. He flashed a knowing smile and slopped a lump wriggling goo into her bowl.

Ugh, nothing but grubs until they returned to shore. However long that would be.

He could at least cook them. In the city, it hadn't taken long for her to fall in love with crispy grubs dipped in spicy caramel, or rolled in lemon salt, or dipped in spicy caramel *and* rolled in lemon salt. On the other hand, fresh, live squirming grubs…

The shorter, older cook jeered at her, the brown in his teeth matching his mottled scales. "Your favorite, as always, Priestess."

"Sir," she corrected the sergeant. "Or lieutenant. It'd be a shame to lose your stripes again, sergeant."

"Might be worth it," the cook said with a shrug, a guttural chuckle rumbling in his throat. "Lieutenant."

"Don't you think it strange that we adopted ranks from an ancient Human society—one we may have driven to extinction? No?" she asked, noting the sergeant's blank stare. "You don't think lieutenant and sergeant and captain are strange? What does sir even mean—is it just short for officer?"

"It's not strange if you knew our history," the cook mumbled.

"I know our history," Xi'Tslna said. "Better than you, it seems."

"Lighted Wilders," he grumbled.

Xi'Tslna leveled a hard gaze at the insufferable man. "What did you call me?"

He jabbed a claw at her claw necklace. "A Light cursed—" His eyes widened, and he snapped to attention. "Captain on the deck!"

"As you were," Captain S'ra'xkya said, waving down the other sailors before they scrambled to their feet. The captain's well-worn uniform fit her well, the faded red cloth complimenting her violet scales and glorious, long spine spikes.

"By all means, sergeant," the captain said. "Tell us what you called *Lieutenant* Tibit."

"I believe," Xi'Tslna said, "the sergeant called me a Light-cursedly good mancer."

"I, uh…" The cook's brow drew, and he spared a glance and Xi'Tslna. "It's true, sir. I heard she was at the top of her class. The lieutenant, I mean."

"I'm glad that's all you said," the captain replied. "I'd hate to rip off those stripes right after I gave them to you." The captain scowled at Xi'Tslna's bowl. "Leave your food, lieutenant."

"Officer meeting right now?" Xi'Tslna asked, handing her bowl to the cook.

"Right now," the captain replied, then turned to the cook. "And, sergeant?"

"Yes, captain."

"If a single member of my crew has to eat uncooked grubs for another meal, I'll throw you into the ocean myself. Spice it up too. Sweet, savory, hot… Do your damn job, or I'll promote someone who will."

The cook squeezed his meaty fists and dipped his brown-mottled head. "Yes, captain."

Xi'Tslna followed Captain S'ra'xkya onto the deck, the afternoon sun dipping port side. As always, her heart leaped at the sight of the Grand Armada. Hundreds of ships rocked in the waves, massive warships like hers, the Night's Embrace, along with frigates and supply barges, all pushed through the seas with bone-tech propellers.

"This way, lieutenant," the captain said, opening the door to her quarters.

Like Xi'Tslna, the captain favored simple, high-quality furnishings over the loud colors found in the city. A large woman with the white mane of a mancer sat at the captain's desk, admiral's knots affixed to the shoulders of her sharp black uniform.

"Admiral Za'Iri," Xi'Tslna said, snapping to attention.

"Relax, lieutenant," the admiral said. "Captain S'ra'xkya speaks highly of you."

Pride swelled in Xi'Tslna's chest, cramping her cheeks in a smile. "I am grateful to be under her command, sir,"

The admiral's gaze fell to Xi'Tslna's arm. "May I see it?"

Xi'Tslna pulled off her glove and raised her right sleeve, revealing the soft cerulean glow leaking beneath her scales.

"Then it's true," Admiral Za'Iri said, reaching for Xi'Tslna's arm but not daring to touch something so holy.

"I will admit," Admiral Za'Iri said, "I was skeptical of S'ra'xkya's choice of lieutenant."

"Because I'm a Wilder," Xi'Tslna said, unable to keep the bite from her voice.

"Precisely," Admiral Za'Iri said, pouring dark rum into three tumblers. "Civilized youth spend their days in school, learning etiquette and reading dense novels. You, on the other hand, learned to live off the land." She handed the tumblers of rum to Xi'Tslna and the captain. "And that is exactly why the Night's Embrace will be leading the invasion."

"The fleet is formed?" Xi'Tslna asked.

"We sail at night," the admiral said, lifting her tumbler. "To the Grand Armada!"

"To the Grand Armada!" Xi'Tslna drank her rum in a single gulp, her heart slamming with excitement. "Then it's true—humanity survived."

"They had to survive, lieutenant." The admiral chuckled and refilled Xi'Tslna's tumbler. "Our Prophecies foretell as much. The Seed of Aqel shall bear the Stolen Darkness," she recited. "Traitor to the land, for his holy name is Death. Reclaim the Holy Power, oh Child of Prophecy, lest the unholy seed infect the land with its cursed Light."

"Then it's true," Xi'Tslna said. "Prophecy has arrived."

"Glory be to the Dark," Captain S'ra'xkya said, raising her tumbler in salute.

"What do we do when we find the Humans?" Xi'Tslna asked.

"We rid that land of their filth."

32

ASPIRATIONS

Freja lounged in a bed large enough to sleep a small family, imperial-red silk sheets swishing against her skin. A dozen paces above the mattress, a deep purple canopy emblazoned with the Imperial Shield draped from thick mahogany posts. Light from a wall of glass filled the spacious bedroom, the clear wall reaching the high vaulted ceiling.

The Consort's Quarters.

For every concubine still in the palace, becoming the Imperial Consort had been the pinnacle of their dreams, but Freja's had only begun. Her belly fluttered with warm, fuzzy butterflies, demanding a stretch. She'd never doubted that the emperor would choose her to be his Consort. In a sea of immaculate bodies with skin the color of snow and hair to make silk feel rough, her natural olive tone, dark bulb of curled hair, and gentle imperfections had seduced the emperor with a type of beauty that shaped perfection could never attain. Her wardrobe had helped too, each piece hinting enough to entice the emperor's salacious curiosity.

On one side of her bed were ornate tapestries pattern-forged to weave various scenes of the empire's glory. Today, draping down the wall was the end of the Great Uprising, when Emperor Hrafnagud betrayed the

Prytha Keepers and elders. Prytha understandably referred to that day as the Ensnarement, while the empire, as usual, masked their evil deed under a kinder, gentler, and far more insidious name—the Deliverance.

Such are the ways of the empire, she thought, wondering if the tapestry would show the "Sacrifice" next. The word carried noble connotations —parents sacrificed for their children, soldiers for their kingdom—but sinking an entire kingdom and breaking an entire culture was nothing but an act of pure evil. Annihilation or Extermination would have been better names—something that invoked disgust and fear, not warm bubbles of pride.

When I'm empress, Freja thought, *I'll change those filthy names. I'll change everything.*

The door to her bedroom swung open, and the shimmering white emperor strode inside, naked but for a diaphanous robe. Without acknowledging her, he strode to her mirror, ruining her pristine view of the island city.

"Once I've tasted the rest of the concubines," he mumbled, twisting to look at his rear, "I'll send them off—as promised." As well-endowed as any man with funds to alter their manhood, he groped himself and giggled like a child. "Then you'll have this all to yourself."

Disgust shivered through Freja at the notion of his soft, glimmering-white body rubbing against hers. He lacked everything that made women like Svala crave Sotouri. Instead of a lean, chiseled body marked with scars, the emperor's flawless skin hid any hint of danger or definition.

Like a man who couldn't even be bothered to chew his own food

"How many concubines remain?" Freja slipped out of bed, and stretched, her sheer slip raising the emperor's attention.

"Fifty," he said.

"Fifty total?" She asked.

"Women," he admitted. "Are you really going to demand I give men up too? That hardly seems fair."

"And why not?" she asked. "Must I not commit to you, body and soul? Would my infidelity not send my head rolling from the chopping block? Must I not abstain the comfort of others for the rest of my life? How is *that* fair?"

"I can change the law," he said, excited about the apparent loophole he'd discovered.

"That's cheating," Freja said. "And hardly the type of change the empire needs."

"What's the point of being the most powerful man in the empire if you can't flex your muscles?"

Because you have no muscles to flex, Freja thought, before saying, "True strength, the type of strength that stirs loins, comes from forgetting about yourself, and choosing the hard right over the easy wrong. Why do you think men and women fawn over Sotouri? They do the unsavory deeds we cannot, and they do it from the shadows, unknown to all but their victims and their masters. Sotouri give up everything—a normal life with a family, high above a Shining Wall, with all the luxuries such a life entails—all to preserve the empire. *That* is true strength."

"More like perfect tools," the emperor said, gazing at his soft, shimmering body.

Freja skirted the glass wall, her shift swishing against her legs as she strode to the robe hanging by her armoire. The emperor's gaze fixated on her, desire rippling off his raised brow, his manhood stiffening.

Men could be so disgustingly simple, Freja thought, slipping on her thick, poppy-colored robe. *Especially this man-child.*

"Make me your wife," she said, savoring the disappointment in his eyes, "and my fruit is all yours."

"I already made you my official Consort," he said. "Your body is mine to do with as I please."

"Everyone is yours to do with as you please." Freja poured two glasses of a sweet Meru'utian gold and brought one to the man-child. "But is that what you truly want—a pair of legs like any other?" She sipped the sweet golden wine, savoring its sweet back notes of blueberry and oak. "Or do you want to conquer me? Do you want to command me to bed?" She leaned to whisper, her lips caressing his ear. "Or do you want me to beg for your touch?"

The emperor growled and reached for her, but she slipped away. Squeezing his fists, he took a deep, slow breath. "Right now, I have a mind to order you." He released a heavy sigh. "Which would be weak, according to you. But making you my wife? No emperor has even entertained taking a wife. The empire has been, and always will be, ruled by an emperor, not an empress."

"And it will continue to be so," Freja said. "I will just be your wife, no different from any other lord's spouse."

"And if I died?"

"Perish the thought," Freja said, setting a hand on his repulsive shoulder.

"But what if? Then you'd rule."

"Do you think the Founders would ever allow such treason?" she asked. "What about the Sotouri? They'll always defend the empire. They exist to keep it whole."

"True," the emperor mumbled, his gaze lost on his reflection in the tall mirror.

"All great emperors break the rules," Freja said, stoking the sparkles of glory flitting in his golden eyes. "*That* is what it means to be great."

His brow furrowed. "Didn't you just say I had to adhere to the law?"

"I said you shouldn't cheat to get me to bed you," she replied. "All the greatest figures in history chose the good of the empire over their own desires."

"But how would making you my empress help the empire?" He raised an eyebrow over a golden eye. "Seems there's a reason men have ruled for so long. Women just don't have the heart to make the hard decisions." He barked a laugh. "Could you imagine a woman leading an army?"

Far more than I can imagine you, she thought, imagining his head bursting when someone told him about all the female generals, Vrath, and Sotouri in the empire.

"Absolutely ridiculous." Freja caressed his smooth arm, swallowing her revulsion as she ducked under his lecherous reach once more. "Think about what our marriage would accomplish. For the first time in history, women across Torgeir would be able to themselves at the right hand of the emperor, as more than an object. You would set a new tradition to unite the empire like no other emperor before you. More than Emperor Hrafnagud. More than Emperor Droag himself."

The emperor's gaze drifted to his reflection, his golden eyes filled with delusions of grandeur.

"Make me your wife," she said, letting the length of her leg slip from under her robe. "Make me your empress, and usher in the Age of Orn Thjodoft."

"Yes, yes, and more yes." The emperor squinted at her and bit his lip. "If you only knew the things I'd do to you…you'd let me."

Freja swallowed a surge of disgust. "Then it's a good thing I don't know."

"Come on, just a taste," he said, caressing his manhood again.

"Just think about how amazing it will be when it finally happens."

"I'm trying not to," he joked. "If I do, it's all I'll think about for the rest of the day." He swaggered to her bed and flopped on the mattress. "Can't I have a peek?"

I'll have to have those sheets burned now, Freja thought. *Maybe the mattress too.*

"Don't you have meetings?" she asked. "Every northern town in Blailon has fallen to the Voice, including their garrison. Doesn't that have you worried?"

"Do you have to ruin every moment?" The emperor sat up, dangling his feet off the edge of the bed. "I have kings and counselors to deal with all that nonsense, so I can focus on what's really important."

"Nonsense?" Freja said, hiding her flash of anger behind a feigned cough. "Citizens loyal to the empire, *Sotouri* even, have all laid down their arms and joined this…this Voice, whoever he is."

The emperor scoffed. "He's a feeble old man."

"Old man or not, he's taken four towns, and no one has lifted a damn finger to stop him."

The emperor waved away her concern. "Exaggerated gossip. I'll handle the Voice like I handled that little whore…Marala."

"Makayla," Freja corrected. "And, in case you forgot, you lost Serolle."

"People still live there."

"Its Shining Wall was destroyed," Freja said, wishing she could express her pride for her Phaerian cousins. One day she would, but for now, she had a shimmering man-child to deal with. "The *indestructible* Shining Wall was destroyed. Doesn't that concern you?"

"Why should it?" the emperor asked, hopping to his feet. "Makila destroyed the city, not the Voice."

"Mak*ay*la," Freja said. "Ay, like pain."

"Whatever," the emperor said with a dismissive wave. "Makahla, Makula, it's doesn't matter. She's dead."

Unfortunately, Freja thought. Makayla would have made for a powerful ally. After all, their ultimate goals aligned—the downfall of the Torgeirian Empire.

"You act like this old man, this *Voice*," the emperor said, "is an actual threat. He's a Phaerian, not a Sotouri."

"Have you ever met a Phaerian?" she asked, wondering if he'd point to her.

"Why would I?" he asked. "I've seen them from afar, and that's close enough. Would they even understand me?"

"They speak Imperial," she said.

He snorted and rolled his eyes. "I guess they build their own towns too?" Without another word, he hopped off the bed and strode from the bedroom.

She listened for the outer door of the Concubine's Quarters to click shut, then she asked, "Is that the person you want leading the realm?"

Taloran and Auntie Inga materialized from the shadows beside her armoire. Dressed in pristine Phaerian drab clothes, undoubtedly sewn yesterday, Freja's Auntie chose a long, open-backed violet dress from the armoire.

"Slip this on, dear."

Auntie Inga exchanged a worried look with Taloran, and the brown-skinned Sotouri adjusted his plum shirt, his black suit seeming to fade into the shadows behind him. Dark eyes hard with anger, he poured himself a glass of wine, and drank it. Scowling, he poured himself another cup, and one for Auntie Inga.

"This is…disturbing," Taloran said.

"Disturbing?" Auntie Inga asked, waving off the offered glass of sweet Meru'utian gold. "Running out of wine and ale in a brothel is disturbing. This is…"

"Treason," Freja said, catching a twitch in Taloran's eye. "You disagree?"

The Sotouri sucked his teeth. "How can the emperor commit treason?"

"By letting the empire fall to a crazed Phaerian." Freja held Taloran's unreadable dark gaze, a spike of fear piercing her heart. The Sotouri could kill her now, and the empire would praise him as a hero. He dipped his head, and Freja kept herself from sighing.

"What of Onatah Forest?" she asked, moving to the glass wall and gazing at the large pillowy clouds. Like giant cottlewomps grazing on a cerulean field.

"Nyatia has sent reinforcements," Taloran said. "As per your request."

"And Meru'ut?" Freja asked.

"Focused on the Ceremony," Auntie Inga said. "Your father said to pass on how proud he is of you."

"And that he'd expected no less?" Freja said, earning a nod from her Auntie. He'd never say what he and Deidan had done to Freja, what patterns they'd woven over her.

But Deidan will.

He'd have to once she rid the empire of the emperor's filth and became empress.

Taloran stood beside her and shared the majestic view. "It's only a matter of time before the emperor finds out you've been sending orders behind his back."

"Someone has to run this empire," Freja said. "I'll be damned if I let it fall to the hands of some blasted townsborn calling himself the Voice. I refuse to let a shiny man-child destroy my empire."

Taloran shared another look with Auntie Inga. She nodded, and he scowled. "Are you sure, woman?"

Auntie Inga raised an eyebrow, and she knelt in front of Freja.

Taloran ran a hand along his stubbled chin, his brow tight.

"Remember your oath, Sotouri," Auntie Inga said, and Taloran scowled before kneeling beside her.

"Loyalty in Blood," they said in unison.

"Victory in Shadow," Freja replied, finishing the Sotouri's motto.

The emperor won't destroy the empire, she thought, sipping her wine. *Neither will the Voice. When Torgeir falls, it will be by my hands.*

33

TIDES OF CHANGE

Jouler curled under his blanket, unable to care about the ache gnawing at his belly. Some distant recess of his mind begged him to eat, but the monumental task seemed too much to kindle a spark of motivation—get up, pull his boots on, and walk all the way to the galley just for a bowl of sailor-meat stew.

No thanks.

It had been a dumb hope, thinking Prack and L'Veyna would catch up to the Charred Lizard and somehow free him. As talented as they both were, Prack was still just one man, L'Veyna a little girl. On the other hand, honed fighters had captured Jouler, the youngest being well over three hundred years old. Watching Ascended in action was to watch perfection. No wasted movements or fancy flourishes from the il'Spada like he'd seen in the training yard, while the grace of Ishariel and her firedancers made everyone, and everything, seem clumsy. They'd maneuvered through the ship as if of one mind, blending their attacks with one another, flowing between the Charred Lizard's sailors, blocking and striking without so much as a grimace of effort. Not one spoken command, and the entire crew had fallen save the ten they'd chained for food...now six. They almost made Grim seem kind.

Almost.

Jouler rolled over, wishing the lap of waves would lull him to sleep. That or his hunger would finally consume him. Then, at least he'd be with Olan and his brothers. Then, he wouldn't be alone.

The way I'll be when I die.

A knock came at the door, and Jouler rolled to his other side. Despite the Charred Leech's peculiar name, not a single mote of char blemished the Captain's immaculate quarters. Or the ship, for that matter. The crew kept every line, sail, and plank pristine, their love for the ship evident in its care.

Not anymore.

A few days ago, a storm had washed away the stench of rotting corpses. At least there was that. Too bad it hadn't washed away the screams of the living as well. If waiting to be chopped into stew, counted as living. Even now, their cries echoed through the ship.

The door opened, and Kherlyn ducked into the captain's quarters. "Get up! We made port." The statuesque Boorde scowled at Jouler. "Flames, man! You look horrible."

"We're in Cowine?" Jouler asked, recognizing the sharp clang of harbor bells ringing over the shouts of dockworkers.

Kherlyn kicked Jouler's boots to him. "Ishariel won't be happy when she sees you like this. Why didn't you eat?" He sucked his teeth, displaying his long canines. "There was more than enough food."

"Seasick," Jouler lied, pulling on his boots.

Kherlyn's eyes narrowed, his distrust palpable since Jouler revealed he could speak Boordish. After Jouler shrugged into a coat that seemed to have tripled in weight, Kherlyn gestured to the door. "Make sure you grab everything you want to keep."

"Where are we going?" Jouler asked, scanning the luxurious room. He rolled the Captain's detailed maps of Torgeir's western coastline, and stuffed them in a leather travel tube along with a gold-tipped quill. Kherlyn's raised eyebrow warned Ishariel might forbid those items along with everything else she'd forbidden—no packs or pouches, no rope or string, and nothing useable as a weapon.

Jouler held up the tube full of maps. "Burning these would be a mistake."

"She's been doing that a lot lately," Kherlyn grumbled.

Jouler feigned indifference while his mind roiled with implications. Since Urna, Kherlyn's defiance had grown from pursed lips to conspicuous complaints. Maybe all Kherlyn needed was a little push. Then again, maybe it was all an act. "You know she's always known I can speak your language."

Kherlyn scoffed and cursed under his breath. "You couldn't have been at Nith'Iil Manor for more than a couple of months, and you spent most of that time in the training yard. How'd you learn so fast?"

"*It's a gift,*" Jouler replied in Boordish, drawing another scowl.

"You don't even have a Human accent," Kherlyn said. "More like a Boorde who'd lived too long in a Human city." Suspicion flared in his fire-diamond eyes. "Ishariel was right. Even without a blade, you're a dangerous man, Vidimir."

Jouler gestured to his frail form. "It's been a week since I've eaten. How sharp could my mind possibly be?"

"Sharp enough to grab a quill and maps," Kherlyn said, grabbing the leather tube from Jouler. "Convenient tools to leave a note, perhaps?"

"Only if you know where you're going," Jouler said, wondering how upset Kherlyn would be if he knew Jouler had already figured out their destination. He cast a longing gaze across the captain's quarters, wishing he could take the ornate wooden chest, polished brass astrolabe, and gold-worked writing tray, its inkwell coiled by a winged serpent.

"I'm sorry I deceived you," he said, prodding the Boorde's wavering loyalties.

"I understand why you did it," Kherlyn said with a dismissive wave. "I'd have done the same thing. Actually, I take that back. I *never* would have revealed I could speak Boordish."

"But you *are* Boorde."

"*I didn't say it'd be easy,*" Kherlyn said in Boordish.

Ishariel and the other Ascended waited for them on the deck, along with a skinny, wispy-haired dock boss begging for the ship's manifest. Empty docks stretched over the harbor's thick, murky water. A large crowd of townsborn shouted and shoved their way down the only other dock, forcing their way aboard what few ships bobbed in the harbor. Some townsborn fell, screaming into the thick, murky water. The hungry water churned red, swallowing men, women, and children.

"If it please, M'Lady, uh, B-Boorde." The dock boss wiped a thin hand over his balding pate. "The manifest, M'Lady? If I could just grab it…"

"Why is everyone in a hurry to leave?" Ishariel asked.

"Rumor," the dock boss said, shrinking under her hard glare. "Rogue imperial unit, going from town to town, hunting Phaerians. Pardon, My Lady Boorde, but…" He wrung his hands. "You're not them, are you?"

Ishariel ignored the grimy dock boss and turned her glare on Jouler. "I'll not have you too weak to walk. You *will* eat."

"Just kill me already," Jouler said, meeting her gaze. "I'll not do whatever it is you expect of me, and don't bother threatening pain and torment," he said, and she tilted her head in interest. "At this point, I'm certain my body wouldn't handle much more than a slap to the face before it gave up. So, you may as well finish me now."

The dock boss's eyebrows climbed his forehead, and he scurried away down the gangplank.

"If that is your wish," Ishariel said, and without another word, the Ascended followed her off the ship.

Kherlyn measured Jouler for a breath, then sucked his long canines, and followed his comrades onto the dock.

Jouler's weary mind wallowed in suffering, the loud clamor of the harbor scrambling his thoughts. Legs heavy with exhaustion, he meandered to the gangplank, unsurprised to see expressionless Boorde staring up at him from the dock. Ishariel lifted an eyebrow, and the terrified screams of the six sailors still in the ship accompanied the soft smell of burning wood.

She set the ship on fire!

Dark smoke billowed from the floorboards. Crackling flames and popping wood drowned the sailors' throes. Jouler slumped in defeat, her message clear. She didn't need to threaten him with pain and suffering in order to get him to comply. The screams of others would do just fine.

A muffled explosion rocked the ship, and Jouler's resolve crumbled. Alarm bells peeled throughout the harbor, and dockworkers rushed for the Charred Leech. Jouler grunted at the irony of the ship's fate, and made his way down the gangplank, telling himself Ishariel would have destroyed the Charred Leech whether he'd obeyed.

"You may not feel it," Ishariel said once he'd reached the pier, "but your flame still burns too bright to be extinguished."

"Where are you taking me?" Jouler asked, her words sparking a glimmer of hope. If she thought his flame burned bright during his lowest, what would she see at his peak?

"To put some food in your belly." Ishariel lifted an eyebrow. "Kherlyn…" The Boorde stepped forward, head tilted, exposing his neck. "Take your team and hunt us some food. A cottlewomp sounds nice." She glanced around the harbor. "And find a funnel. A long one." She picked at Jouler's shirt. "The sooner we fatten him up, the sooner we can be on our way."

"Fatten me up for what?"

"We have a long road ahead of us," she said, measuring him. "And you'll never get there if you're too weak to walk."

As if banished by her words, Jouler's strength fled his legs, and he crumbled to the dock. "Where are you taking me?" he asked, as a pair of il'Spada hoisted him onto his feet.

Ishariel peered at him with a knowing smile. "Stop playing coy, Vidimir. You know damn well where we're going."

Jouler reached through his exhaustion to feed off his anger. He planted his feet on the dock and pushed the two il'Spada away.

"You're taking me to the Black Breath, but why?"

Ishariel's long canines poked beneath her smile. "Let's get you fed, shall we?"

SILENCE CLUNG to Cowine's harbor, dread creeping over L'Veyna from its empty docks. No people bustled here, its buildings as devoid of life as its streets.

"Where is everyone?" she asked, grabbing her brother's hand to help her out of the rowboat.

"I don't like it," Prack said, helping Horgar next.

The young pirate looked back to the Scarlet Kiss anchored beyond the docks, sorrow dripping into his dark-brown eyes.

"Let's go," Prack said, clapping Horgar on the shoulder. "This place is…wrong."

L'Veyna slid her arms through the hoops of her pack and followed her brother down the dock toward the empty town.

Horgar walked beside her, casting lingering glances back at his ship. "I'm never going to see it again, am I?" he asked, his voice thick with heartache. He sniffled, dragging an arm across his eyes. "It's just…that's the only home I ever had."

His words roused the loneliness creeping around L'Veyna's heart, and a fresh lump of guilt formed in her throat. They'd destroyed Horgar's home and slaughtered his family, no different from the cursed empire cutting through Onatah.

"We'll find someplace new," L'Veyna said, holding Horgar's hand. "Somewhere we can all call home."

Horgar blinked, tears tumbling down his cheeks. Chin quivering, he rubbed his eyes and drew a shuddering breath. "I don't know what—"

A blubbering sob swallowed his words, and Prack pulled him into a hug. "There, there, let it out," her brother said, rubbing Horgar's back. The sobbing young Human sagged, weeping in Prack's arms.

Horgar's pain stabbed at L'Veyna's heart, conflicting with the rage she still felt for the demised crew of the Scarlet Kiss. Her heart ached for Horgar's loss, but those sailors would have done terrible things to her and Prack.

A different type of misery dripped from Cowine's haphazard stacks of brick dwellings, putrescence oozing in its streets. Deeper into the town, they discovered the reason everyone had left. It seemed a massive wave of mud had inundated the town. Broken beams, chunks of brick wall, and twisted metal stuck from the deluge. A white stick poked from the mud, catching her eye. Curious, she looked closer, only to draw back with a hiss. A bone, not a stick, protruding from a mangled hunk of flesh.

"No wonder everyone's gone," Horgar said, holding a hand to his mouth.

"Vrath did this," Prack said, invoking dark thoughts of the armies threatening their home.

Would Onatah share the same morbid fate? L'Veyna tried pushing those thoughts away, but climbing over so much debris and sloshing through mud made it impossible to think of anything else. She reached out with her senses, expecting to find the town plagued with d'Tormena's foul magic. "I don't sense any taint."

"It's long faded by now," Prack said. "A few months back, Makayla's armies took Cowine. I heard the battle was fierce, but…"

"This is what the empire does," Horgar said, slipping up to his knee in mud. He cursed and held out his hand for Prack to help him out. "We're nothing but slaves to the empire. Less than Human, even."

"But you are Human," L'Veyna said.

"Not according to the empire," Prack said. "The Three Laws, specifically."

"And the blasted Paradigm," Horgar said.

"That too," Prack agreed, helping L'Veyna over a questionable slab of brick wall. "They state that Phaerians are a sub-Human species."

"But they're not," L'Veyna said, gesturing to Horgar. "Obviously."

"Obviously," Prack replied. "Why do you think the empire keeps its Citizens locked behind big Shining Walls?"

"But not all of them," L'Veyna said. "Soldiers, Vrath, those other d'Tormena…"

"Weavers," Prack said.

"Them." L'Veyna clicked her tongue. "They have to know."

"They do," Prack said. "They might tell themselves and everyone else that they don't, but deep down inside, they all know Phaerians are just as Human as they." He gestured to the dilapidated town. "They just don't want to lose all this."

"All what?" L'Veyna said, kicking a clump of mud from her boot.

"The power," Horgar said.

"The lie," Prack corrected. "The empire can't function without it. Almost every Phaerian lives and dies in this misery, without ever leaving town. All the townsborn, anyway."

"It's true," Horgar said. "Farmers live just outside town, and miners leave to mine, but sailors are the only ones who actually travel." He puffed his chest, holding up a beam for L'Veyna to pass beneath. "I've sailed as far east as Luticio, in Castantor, and Blet, in Blailon."

She crouched under the beam, careful not to get too close to Horgar's wormy fingers. "I don't know where those places are, but it sounds impressive."

"It is," Prack said. "What goods would you transport?"

"Transport?" Horgar asked with an awkward smile. "We, ah, *he*, the captain, would, uh… He would acquire different contracts to transport goods from one port to another, so there were a lot of different types of cargo."

"Pirates," Prack stated as a simple matter of fact.

"No!" Horgar said, his eyes darting to L'Veyna, color flushing his face. "We were honest, hard-working—"

"Pirates," Prack finished.

"What's a pirate?" L'Veyna asked.

"They sail up and down the coast," Prack said, "raiding and pillaging villages and other ships."

Horgar scoffed. "We did nothing of the sort."

L'Veyna clicked her tongue. "Your crew tried to do gods-know-what to us."

Horgar's mouth snapped shut, and his gaze fell.

"Not that we blame you," Prack said, glaring at her. He stopped them before a stack of houses leaning over the street. Debris crumbled from a crack along the width of the stack. Prack looked about. "We'll have to find another way."

"It's fine," Horgar said, ducking under a fallen building. A chunk of mortar hit him on the shoulder, and he yelped, scowling up at a large crack in the wall. "I'm fine. It's fine."

"Little Sprout," Prack clacked. *"Would you be a dear and make sure the building doesn't crush our swaggering little friend?"*

An image popped into her mind, her power flared, and the image locked into place as though anticipating her will. Thick wooden beams sprouted from the ground, bracing the crumbling stack of buildings. Horgar screamed, and scrambled back through the knee-high mud, while Prack cackled. The asked beams grew, thickening, and forming a tunnel beneath the crumbling building.

Curious, L'Veyna thought. Even the simplest asking needed a *little* coercion. It had to be her proximity to the ocean. That or Alnazet sensed her urgency to rescue Jouler.

Panting, Horgar scowled at Prack. "You could have warned me."

"Why are you blaming me?" Prack said, then he clacked on his beltboard. *"What's wrong, Little Sprout? You look troubled."*

"The image," she said, wondering if she'd imagined the whole thing. It wouldn't surprise her with everything going wrong in her life, fleeing home without so much as a goodbye to her parents, running across the empire, and losing Jouler to some crazed Boorde. "It locked into place on its own."

"That's good, right?" Prack asked, peering ahead. "Come on, I think we're almost through the mud."

A CRESCENT MOON dangled in the twinkling night sky, the bitter cold robbing the air of its chirping symphony. Jouler held his hands to the crackling fire, haunted by the memory of Cowine's mud-laden streets packed with broken homes, twisted corpses, and shattered hopes. Not that townsborn had much to hope for. Especially not the people who'd survived the deluge. Maybe, in some twisted way, the wave of mud had been a kindness to the tens of thousands of corpses, Phaerian and Citizen alike, littering the town's twisted streets.

Ishariel and her il'Spada, Vaelithrae with his polished onyx eye, Thalrion with his arsenal of swords, and the eidraael Nyrr'kas with his djohai and sidaiyo, stood guard around him, while the rest of the Ascended gathered around the spit and fire. Dressed in only a firedancer dress, Ishariel stared at him, her expression as unreadable as the djohai dangling from her waist. Unlike the other Ascended, her team remained as rigid as the day they'd captured Jouler, not even chatting among themselves while they guarded him. Kherlyn, on the other hand, talked and joked with Jouler, often dragging the other Ascended into some deep philosophical debate.

As expected, Ishariel hadn't divulged more information about their mission, leaving Jouler to struggle over why Matron Nith'Iil would order so many Ascended to force him on a journey he'd already planned on making. The Boorde Alliance's strongest Matron needed him. That much was clear, but to what end? Did she want the Black Breath? Would her Ascended kill him once he retrieved it, or did she want to use him as the Harbinger?

As if anyone could use Prophecy.

Jouler chewed off a piece of well-seasoned cottlewomp, wiping savory juices from his chin, the marbled slice of meat warm in his hand. He could cook his whole life and never hope to achieve Kherlyn's culinary mastery. Of course, it made sense that a four-hundred-year-old Ascended with a passion for cooking would be as skilled with a skillet as he was with his daggers.

Kherlyn spun the spit, mopping the cottlewomp with spices he'd mixed for the mission, while the other Ascended hovered, sniffing the air, and laughing over stories. Over the past few days, Kherlyn had become more brazen in his kindness toward Jouler, and more defiant toward Ishariel. Jouler entertained the thought of the short Boorde coming to his rescue and defeating Ishariel and her il'Spada in a glorious battle.

I might as well wish for the other Ascended to join the rebellion. With a grunt, he tore off another piece of meat and chewed the image from his mind.

After a while, Kherlyn and his team peeled away from the spit and approached Jouler.

"It's not your shift," Ishariel said.

"Everyone else is still eating." Kherlyn's mouth quirked, his fingers drumming the hilts of his daggers. "Surely you're not going to challenge me over something so trivial?"

Ishariel raised a hand at Vaelithrae, halting her First Blade before he lowered his spear.

Jouler froze, afraid to even breathe the delicate air. Had the gods heard him? After all this time, had they finally intervened?

Ishariel straightened to her full height and stared down at the much shorter Boorde. "Surely, I wouldn't waste my time on some*one* so trivial." With a sharp-toothed grin, she left Kherlyn to stew with the insult.

"I hate that woman." Kherlyn jerked his chin at Jouler's fire, and Quirr'Ik, his firedancer, made the flames larger.

"I think everyone hates her," Jouler dared to say. Kherlyn sucked his teeth and handed Jouler another slice of meat. Hot juices dripped down Jouler's hand, the meat succulent, smoky, and bursting with flavor. "Gods, this is amazing."

Kherlyn patted a pouch at his waist. "Never leave home without your spices."

"You take that everywhere?" Jouler asked.

"He makes a different batch for every mission," Quirr'Ik said, gathering her dress to sit on a log.

"You're welcome," Kherlyn said, sitting on a rock at the western position.

Zhyndor moved to the southern position. The eidraael tugged his too-black shirt, and sat with his legs folded, spear rested over his knee. "What about that batch you made for our mission to Castantor?"

Kherlyn turned a somber frown. "We agreed to never talk about the concoction that shall never be named."

"Isn't that giving it a name?" Jouler mused, dismissing an urge to leap for Zhyndor's spear. Even if he wrestled the spear away and slayed the Ascended, fifteen remained.

"Vidimir strikes again!" Tristian said from the northern position. Almost as tall as Ishariel, Tristian's skinny frame matched the slender sword and dagger at his side.

"Zhyndor," Quirr'Ik said. "Give him your spear. Let's see what he can do."

"Now you're just trying to get him killed," Zhyndor said, the eidraael's voice only slightly deeper than Quirr'Ik's. "Ishariel's eyes might be pale, but she's House Nith'Iil's First Ascended for a reason."

"Is that's why Matron Nith'Iil put her in charge?" Jouler asked, stoking the fire as the Boorde idiom went. "Because she knew no one would challenge her."

Kherlyn peered into the dancing flames and sucked his teeth.

"Diou would challenge her," Tristian said, and they all mumbled in agreement.

Jouler swallowed his excitement. With the right amount of nudging, these sparks of discontent could flare and melt Ishariel's hold on the group. Nudge too hard, and he'd smother the discontent, and lose all hopes of escape.

"Diou." Quirr'Ik scoffed. "You mean the traitor who'd turned his back on his Houses?"

"Katima too," Zhyndor said. "She shaved her head, according to Eldri."

Kherlyn's back stiffened. "What say you, Tristian the Wise?"

Tristian tapped the hilt of the needle-thin sword and dagger. "In six hundred and eighty-three years, I have never known a Boorde more honorable than Diou."

Jouler still marveled at Boorde agelessness. Almost seven hundred years and not a wrinkle or scar marred Tristian's skin, not a strand of grey protruded from his too-black topknot.

"I do not know the Heiress Apparent well enough to render judgement," Tristian continued, "but Diou's flight does not speak well for our Matron's hold on the House."

"Neither does this conversation bode well for Ishariel," Quirr'Ik said, sucking her teeth. "I can't believe she let that leafeater escape."

"A Chi'indi saved her," Zhyndor said.

Quirr'Ik hissed, her fire-colored pupils flaring. "All the more reason to have someone more competent in charge. If a single Chi'indi can thwart Ishariel, then I say she is unfit to lead."

"Who's going to challenge her?" Tristian asked, and the other Ascended hesitated. "Exactly. Like Zhyndor said, she's still the legendary Ishariel sa'Nith'Iil."

"Lyndara has been chatting with the other teams," Kherlyn said. "Seems we're not the only ones who're dissatisfied with our pale-eyed leader."

"Do you think she'll challenge Ishariel?" Zhyndor asked, and Quirr'Ik shook her head.

"Like Tristian said, Ishariel is still a legend." Quirr'Ik's fiery gaze drifted to the other Ascended, standing around the spit-roast.

"Someone has to do it," Zhyndor said, draping heavy silence over the team. "She's going to get us all killed, and for what—to carry some lowlander across the Blasted Lands?"

"He's not just some lowlander," Kherlyn said.

"He's the Dawn," Zhyndor replied with a flippant wave. "If you truly believe that, then *someone* has to challenge her. How long do you think a Human will last in the Blasted Lands? A few hours—a day at most?"

"He has to go there," Kherlyn said.

"Says who?" Zhyndor replied. "Ishariel? I don't remember reading anything in the Prophecies about the Dawn wielding a dark power, do you?" Silence weighed over them once more. "Does anyone?"

That power isn't part of your Prophecies, Jouler thought. *It's part of mine, and I'm not the Dawn.*

He stared at the danced fire, not wanting to break the delicate air. Offering to challenge Ishariel might push them all into action, not just Kherlyn's team—all of them. Then again, his obvious push might offer them a common enemy and rally their support behind Ishariel.

Kherlyn sucked his teeth and tapped the hilt of a dagger.

"Your words are...compelling," Tristian said.

"Someone has to start the avalanche." Zhyndor's thin lips pressed into a line, and he stood, gripping his spear.

"Stay your blade," Tristian said, getting to his feet and towering over the eidraael. "I am older. I will challenge her."

"No," Kherlyn said, shaking his head. "This death is my honor. Besides..." He tapped his daggers. "Ishariel's will hardly be the first firedancer's blood Wrath and Scorn have tasted. Isn't that right, Quirr'Ik?"

The firedancer's back stiffened, her jaw clenching.

Tristian's snow-white face drew, sorrow glistening in his eyes. Kherlyn pulled him into a hug, his head resting on Tristian's chest. The short Ascended looked up and whispered to Tristian, and the slender Boorde nodded, tears steaming down his cheeks.

Zhyndor and Quirr'Ik stood off to the side, draped in sorrow, watching the tender moment, and a dark understanding melted over Jouler.

They know he's going to die.

"Kherlyn..." Jouler's chest tightened, and he realized how much Kherlyn had come to mean to him. The short Ascended had sparked the fire, as they said, breaking their stern treatment of Jouler with acts of kindness. "No, stop. Please, you can't."

"This day is a long time coming." Kherlyn clasped Jouler on the shoulder, calm in the Ascended's fire-diamond eyes. "Sometimes, symbols are far stronger than a person could ever be. Remember that, Vidimir, Dawn of Prophecy."

A HAWK'S shrill cry pulled Jouler's gaze to the crisp blue sky. Shielding his eyes from the late afternoon sun, he spotted the raptor soaring high above. Far below the hawk, Kherlyn stood on a wide Blailonian tundra, sheathed daggers at his sides. Brisk wind ruffled his ry'ku, his alabaster skin fading against the snow-dusted landscape.

Ishariel stood twenty paces away from him, her firedancer dress fluttering against her lithe form, djohai swinging from her waist.

Myr'koth, Jouler thought, his Boorde captors towering beside him in dark solemnity.

Without a word, the two Ascended bowed in unison.

Kherlyn dashed at her with surprising speed, the sharpened edges of his daggers glowing like embers. He sliced, stabbed, and chopped, his blades tracing graceful orange lines in the air. Ishariel wove between his attacks, his daggers turned by simple twists and flicks of her wrist. Like a goddess among mortals, she danced with the il'Spada, his effortless movements seeming clumsy next to the famed firedancer.

"Sacred Flame, she's good," Tristian mumbled, shifting beside Jouler.

Kherlyn pressed his attack, kicking up a tuft of snow, breaking Ishariel's rhythm. A shark kick caught the firedancer's leg, and a jab sliced a hole in the side of her dress. Ishariel spun with Kherlyn's kick, catching his second stab with her foot. She stomped, and Kherlyn slid back, avoiding a crushed knee.

Ishariel unhooked her djohai. Instead of spinning it in graceful patterns as Jouler had seen in practice, the firedancer looped the thin chain between her hands, blocking and wrapping up Kherlyn's renewed strikes.

The il'Spada slid between Forms, breaking up his rhythm into a chaotic slew of attacks. Ishariel's dance complimented Kherlyn's discordant assault with an odd, sinister harmony. Kherlyn stepped behind her foot and stabbed at her side, but she twisted into the strike, slipping around Kherlyn, and slapping his back.

"Stop with your games!" Kherlyn shouted, lunging at her.

With the grace of a hawk in flight, she slipped past him, blocking his daggers with her looped chain, and tripping him.

Kherlyn rolled to his feet and spun with a kick, but Ishariel swiped under his leg, tripping him again. This time, Kherlyn fell to his back with a loud grunt. Ishariel danced away, and he leaped to his feet.

"Douse your flame, woman!" Kherlyn lunged at her again, but she pranced away from his attacks. "Fight me!"

A smirk turned Ishariel's lips. "Waiting on you."

Rage twisted Kherlyn's face. He lunged again, throwing his hand out as she passed.

Ishariel twisted with a grunt and stumbled away. She looked down, confused by the dagger sizzling in her side. Gripping the hilt, she yanked the blade out and stuck it in the ground with an angry shout.

Kherlyn's rage melted into calm, letting her know it had all been an act.

Pale eyes flaring with hatred, Ishariel let her djohai unravel to the ground. She undulated in a seductive dance, and the darted end of the djohai lifted. A slight shift in her graceful rhythm ignited flames down the length of the chain, the djohai lifting and swaying like a fiery serpent. Ishariel's dance shifted, and the dart struck.

Kherlyn leaped into a roll, hopping and slipping away from the djohai's searing bites.

Ishariel swung into a new lissom dance, its captivating flow enthralling Kherlyn for a breath. Her djohai coiled back, ready to strike, and a dozen more fiery serpents split from the weapon. Ishariel twirled, and thirteen molten fangs stabbed into Kherlyn's arms, legs, and torso. A sharp stomp dispelled the fire, and Ishariel's djohai shot through Kherlyn's chest.

The il'Spada crumbled to the ground, his blood steaming the chill air.

Vaelithrae, Ishariel's First Blade, rushed to her side, but she waved him away. "I'll be fine," she said, stooping to fetch Kherlyn's daggers and black-lacquered sheathes. She walked up to Jouler, the other Ascended, dropping to their knees in obeisance. She glared at him, heat radiating from her fire-diamond eyes. "Kherlyn would have wanted you to have these."

Fear, sorrow, and shock coursed through Jouler, his hands quivering as he took the daggers.

Ishariel scowled in pain and limped away. "Vaelithrae, see to Kherlyn's pyre."

"We'll do it," Tristian said, squeezing Jouler's shoulder.

Jouler nodded, unable to take his eyes off the sheathed daggers in his hands. Simple and elegant, the only difference in the weapons was the small red etching in the otherwise nondescript black wooden scabbards. Both in Boordish, one read Wrath, the other Scorn.

"Your sorrow honors him," Tristian said, awakening Jouler from his daze.

Jouler looked around, surprised to see everyone had left them. "Why did she give them to me?"

"Isn't it obvious?" Tristian jerked his chin to Kherlyn's corpse. "So you'll remember the only one of us who cared about you."

The words sank in Jouler's chest, the daggers heavy in his hands. "What about you, then? Why are you helping me?"

"I do it, not because I care about you," Trisian said, the sorrow in his voice stretching over centuries. Steaming tears dribbled down his cheeks. "I do it because I loved him. He was different. His flame burned brighter than anyone else's. He didn't just go on missions. He made sure they were memorable." Tristian sniffled, steaming tears dribbling down his cheeks. "This mission most of all, I suppose."

Jouler's breath caught from the Boorde's pain, and he offered the daggers to Tristian. "You should have these, not me."

"No," Tristian said, moving Kherlyn's corpse into a more dignified position—flat on his back with his hands by his sides. "Ishariel did not lie. He would have wanted you to have them. Especially now. He was the best of us, and he saw something in you. Something more than whatever skills Prophecy has bestowed upon you. Something worth dying for." He pressed the daggers to Jouler's chest. "I can think of no one better than the Dawn to carry his memory."

Jouler gave a sharp nod, not trusting his voice.

"Good," Tristian said, smiling over his tear-laced cheeks. "Now, where do you suppose we might find wood in this godsforsaken land?"

"I haven't seen a tree for leagues," Jouler said. "What about moss? Would that work?"

Tristian considered the idea and nodded. "We'll have to gather a lot."

Jouler tucked the sheathed daggers under his belt. "Then I supposed we'd better get to work."

34

SHARED FATES

"What do you mean I won't be able to ask in the Blasted Lands?" L'Veyna adjusted her pack she'd asked from grass sprigs, and pulled her thick coat tight against the bitter wind. Despite the clear sky, the early-morning sun offered little heat in this barren, godsforsaken tundra.

Not a single tree for days, she thought, noting the patches of red and yellow grasses dotting the snow-dusted land. At best, they passed small copses of glorified bushes Horgar called trees. Of course, he'd never seen a rustwood or the massive oaks that grew in Onatah, so he didn't know what an *actual* tree looked like.

"The Blasted Lands are just that—blasted," Prack said, leading them toward a thin trail of smoke leaking into the vast cerulean sky. "It has no potential for life, thus, no asking. Keepers have tried for centuries."

"Not this Keeper," L'Veyna said, bobbing her eyebrows.

Horgar's face twisted in confusion. "Why would we cross the Blasted Lands? The Boorde aren't actually taking Jouler there, are they?" Prack nodded, and Horgar halted. "That's...that's insane!"

"It's not insane," Prack said. "Insane is fighting naked against a pod of terrentors. Crossing the Blasted Lands...that's much worse."

"Well then," Horgar said, dashing to catch up. "We'll just have to rescue Jouler before they get there."

"We'd still have to cross the blasted Blasted Lands," Prack said, grinning at his not-so-witty humor.

"Wait...what?" Horgar said, gripping his dark curly hair. "Why?"

"Prophecy dictates Jouler's path," Prack said, eyeing L'Veyna, "as much as it does my sister's."

Horgar offered an uneasy chuckle. "You're not fanatics like those crazy Zealots of Laa, are you?"

"No," Prack said, holding up a finger. "But we are crazy."

"And we are bound by Prophecy," L'Veyna said. "Jouler and I are, anyway."

"You're serious, aren't you?" Horgar said.

"Do you not believe in Prophecy?" L'Veyna asked.

"Well, yeah," Horgar replied, rubbing his arm. "Everyone does, but..." He shrugged. "I don't know, it's one thing to believe in Prophecy, but you talk like...like It's here already. Like you're the Light."

"Don't be absurd," Prack said, dripping with sarcasm. "L'Veyna isn't *the* Light."

Horgar breathed a sigh of relief.

"She's *part* of the Light," Prack clarified.

"What?" Horgar clamored, tossing his arms up. "Part of the... But how? She's Prytha."

"Typical Human," L'Veyna replied, rolling her eyes at the young pirate. "Only they can be heroes. Why would Prophecy choose a tiny little Prytha when there are such big, strong Humans?"

"No, that's not what I meant," Horgar said. "I—"

"No?" L'Veyna said. "And why can't I be part of the Light?"

"Because..." Horgar dry washed his hands. "Because, don't Prytha have their own Prophecy with Prytha heroes?"

"We do," Prack said before L'Veyna could respond. "They speak of a Prytha hero. They also speak of a Human hero."

Horgar blinked. "They do?"

"We call him M'Ljot," Prack said. "In Imperial, he's called the Harbinger of Death."

Eyes wide, Horgar mouthed the name.

"But we just call him Jouler."

Horgar stumbled to a halt. "Jouler's the…the what? The Harbinger of, of Death? What's the Harbi…" His face drained, his olive skin like ash. "Blasted Lands? I'm not…I can't go to the Blasted…"

Prack helped him to sit, comforting him with soft words, urging him to relax. *"Help him,"* Prack clacked. *"Quick. He's having a panic attack."*

L'Veyna knelt beside Horgar, the memory still fresh in her mind of her own experience enduring Prophecy's crushing weight. Like Horgar said, it was one thing to believe in Prophecy, and another to live through its destruction. Stretching her senses, she felt the young pirate's rush of anxiety pounding through his veins, his lungs raging for breath. She Imagined Horgar relaxed, his breathing eased, his heart beating normal, calm soaking his body. Warmth blossomed in her chest and the image locked into place on its own.

Horgar shivered and stretched with a loud yawn. "Gods, I…" Eyes drooping, he released a heavy sigh and sank back into the snow-dusted ground. "I feel so light. So free."

"What did you do?" Prack clacked.

"Nothing, I…I asked without asking again."

Prack clicked his tongue. "How, exactly?" he asked, helping Horgar to his feet.

"How what?" Horgar asked, acting as if he'd smoked a whole pouch of ha'ath.

"Normally, when Keepers ask," L'Veyna explained, "the images resist the asking. We have to force them to lock into place, so to speak."

Horgar grunted, his red eyes half open. "I don't even know what any of that means, and that's okay, because *you* know what you're talking about." He jerked a thumb at himself. "I don't need to know."

"I barely formed the image," L'Veyna told her brother, ignoring the young Human, "and it just locked into place. I didn't even try."

"Nothing abnormal?" her brother asked, watching Horgar as they walked.

"Didn't you just hear me?" L'Veyna said. "I asked without asking."

"What image did you form?" Prack said.

"I pictured Horgar relaxed," she replied.

"Well then," Prack said, nodding to the young pirate, "I'd say you succeeded."

"Me too," the young pirate replied with a toothy grin.

"Alnazet's mercy," L'Veyna mumbled. "I can't believe I'm stuck with you two. How are we ever going to save Jo?"

"We can't, for now," Prack said.

"We could leave him here," L'Veyna said with a nod to Horgar.

"L'Veyna!" Prack said, draping a protective arm over the young Human. "I can't believe you said that."

"Not leave him with nothing," L'Veyna said, realizing how bad it sounded. "I would have asked him shelter and food."

"That doesn't make it better," Prack said. "Besides, we couldn't save Jo even if we left our young pirate behind."

"I'm *not* a pirate," Horgar said with a conspicuous wink.

"So we just leave Jouler with the Boorde?" L'Veyna asked.

"For now," Prack replied. "They seem intent on getting him to his destination. I say we let them. Besides, we still have to figure out how we're going to follow them through the Blasted Lands."

"Like this," Horgar said, peering at the ground and taking slow, intentional steps.

L'Veyna bubbled with a laugh. "Something like that."

"If only it was that easy," Prack mused, rubbing his jaw. "This would be so much easier if Reylan were here to show you. Let me see, how can I explain? The Blasted Lands are…well, see, they're blasted. No, hold on," he said, holding up his hands. "This is harder than it seems. You've never seen anything blasted. It's not just dead land. It's…nothing, and anything that touches it becomes part of that nothing, eventually."

"It'll blast us too?" L'Veyna said, working out the cryptic meaning.

"Eventually," Prack clarified.

"Like, how eventually?" L'Veyna asked. "Minutes, hours, days?"

"I don't know," Prack said. "It can't be minutes. It must be days… maybe? Like I said, if Reylan were here, he'd explain it better."

"Horgar could have explained it better."

Horgar shook his head and spread his hands. "I mean…no, but I could try."

"What about food and water?" L'Veyna asked, wishing Dilna could see what she had to put up with. Dilna would never believe half the stories L'Veyna would tell her. L'Veyna's chest fluttered at the thought of seeing the Human who had nestled in her heart. Knowing Little Dee, they'd both fill the day and night with fantastic stories until their sides hurt too much from laughing.

Alnazet's mercy, I miss her.

"If I can't ask," she explained to her brother, "how are we supposed to eat?"

"A wagon full of dirt," Prack said.

Horgar eyed Prack with a sidelong glance. "A wagon?"

"Full of dirt." Prack held up a finger.

"And how," L'Veyna asked, "is that supposed to help us cross the Blasted Lands?"

"In theory," Prack said, "if we keep the soil off the ground, it won't blast. Assuming we can find a horse in Pegrans to pull the cart."

L'Veyna gawked at her brother. "Oh, I can't wait to tell Jouler about your brilliant plan. How is that supposed to help us?"

"To be clear," Prack said. "This was Reylan's idea. The original idea was to help him and Kael shape while we crossed, but circumstances have changed. Basically, the Currents-rich soil, as Reylan called it, should allow you to ask."

"Asking doesn't come from the Currents," L'Veyna said, pressing a hand to her chest. "It comes from the heart, and from our connection with Alnazet."

"And yet," Prack said, "Keepers cannot ask in the Blasted Lands. You will be—you *are* a powerful Keeper, but you're still a Bud. I don't pretend to know all the secrets of your order, but I do know there is a lot more for you to learn."

L'Veyna clicked her tongue. She'd never heard of blasted lands affecting a Keeper's powers, but then, maybe Keeper Inoem hadn't gotten to that part of her training. Maybe she never thought to bring it up. After all, when was the last time a thirteen-year-old Keeper left the forest?

Then again, she mused. *When was the last time a Prytha could ask before their Blossoming?*

"We'll see if I can't ask," she said, raising a hand to stifle her brother's objection. "We'll still get your wagon full of dirt, even if I have to ask one."

"You can do that?" Horgar asked, his eyes twinkling with wonder. "Can you make a ship?"

"*Ask* a ship," L'Veyna corrected. "And yes…probably. With time. Not all at once, mind you. I'd have to ask the parts, and…" She clicked her tongue, a new idea sparking in her mind. "What about sailing? We already know where they're going. We could go back to Cowine, and just sail to the Blasted Lands."

"You can't sail those waters," Horgar said, chuckling as if she'd said up was down. "They don't call it the Lost Sea for nothing. Too choppy. Too shallow."

"Besides that," Prack said. "The Blasted Lands are vast. Hundreds of miles separate the Codoine Ruins in the north and the Kendene Ruins in the south, and we do not know where the Ascended are going. We have to follow them."

L'Veyna grumbled at his reasoning and cast her gaze at the barren landscape. Still nothing but the looming column of smoke adorned the flat horizon. She pulled her hood down, basking in the warmth of the morning sun. Hawks soared the clear sky, scanning for rabbits that looked like furry balls of snow. Off to her left, a herd of peculiar animals, like cows with thick wool, grazed on tufts of grass.

"Cottlewomp," Horgar said, scooting to walk beside L'Veyna.

"A cottle-what?"

"A cottlewomp," Horgar repeated. "They're like sheep cows…or, maybe cow sheep."

"They look so…fluffy," L'Veyna said, imagining herself lying on one of the creatures. "Are they gentle?"

"Nothing gentler in the empire," Horgar replied. "But you can forget about riding one. Not a wild cottlewomp, anyway. They're as cute as they are shy."

"But are they as fluffy as they look?" L'Veyna asked.

Horgar put a hand to the side of his mouth and whispered, "Fluffier."

L'Veyna squeezed herself. "Oh, I want to hug one."

"No!" Prack said, leading them farther away from the adorable creatures. "Terrentors use them as bait."

Fear chilled her glee and shivered down her spine, drawing her gaze across the horizon for a sign of Torgeir's apex predator.

"If a cottlewomp is attacked," Prack said, "or it thinks it's getting attacked by a strange Prytha wanting hugs, it releases a pheromone that drives the rest of the herd into flight."

"That's so sad," L'Veyna said, still wanting to lie in a bed of cottle-womp wool.

I bet it feels like a cloud.

"Terrentors," Prack continued, eyeing her with a pointed look, "can smell the pheromone from leagues away. They come and eat up the predator and prey."

"What do terrentors look like?" she asked, her wishes for a cottle-womp companion shattered by her brother's words.

"Big," Prack said. "Gray hide, two legs, four arms, two with huge pincers that can cleave a man in half."

L'Veyna shivered at the thought of meeting such a powerful beast, and she reached for the comfort of her warm power glowing within her.

"Can I tell you something?" Horgar asked her.

"Of course."

"I'm scared," he confessed.

"I think we're all scared now," L'Veyna said with an accusatory sneer for her brother.

"Not the terrentors," Horgar said. "Well, yes, that. But…" His gaze dropped, and he sniffled. "One day, I'm headed out to sea. The next…" He dragged a sleeve across his eyes. "I'm all alone."

"You're not," L'Veyna said.

"But I am. Everyone I ever knew died on that ship. I know they were bad, but…"

"They were all you had," Prack said, and Horgar nodded. Prack stopped and put his hands on the young pirate's shoulders. "I'm sorry, Horgar. I truly am."

Horgar nodded, his chin quivering.

Prack pulled him into a hug, and Horgar burst into sobs, weeping in his arms.

"There it is," Prack said, rocking Horgar. "It's okay, let it out."

Horgar's cries dwindled, and he sagged in Prack's arms.

L'Veyna asked a sphere of warm tea similar to the spheres she asked for Pendric. "We're your family now."

Horgar stared at her, confused by the steaming tea sphere balanced on her palm. Wiping tears from his eyes, he gawked at the sphere.

"It's tea," Prack said, nudging him.

Giggling, L'Veyna slipped the tea into Horgar's cupped hands.

"It's warm," he said, staring at the sphere. He hesitated, eyeing the tea before lifting it to his lips. With a loud slurp, his eyes went wide. "It's so good! Like…like, a bed of flowers, and fruit, and…and sweet joy."

Prack's brow lifted. "Sweet joy, you say? Sister dear, ask me one of those spheres. I need to know what joy tastes like."

L'Veyna rolled her eyes, but asked him a sphere just the same.

Prack slurped his tea and smacked his lips. "Yep. That's joy all right."

Curious, she asked one for herself and sipped. Glorious flavors ignited her tastebuds. Succulent melons, berries, and stone fruits mingled with vibrant floral notes. She giggled, unable to contain the warm joy coursing down her throat.

"Alnazet's mercy!" L'Veyna said as wide eyed as Horgar. "This is amazing!"

"Told you," Horgar mumbled, giggling through another slurp.

"I don't know what you did, Little Sprout," Prack said, waving them onward, toward the pillar of smoke. After another sip, he smacked his lips again. "But I like it."

"Me too," Horgar said, slipping in step beside Prack.

I wish I knew, L'Veyna mused, too happy to give it more thought.

Skipping on the other side of her brother from Horgar, she sipped through her tea, watching the pillar of smoke leak into the sky. "What do you think it is?"

"I already know what it is," Prack said. "There's only one thing that burns like that. A Boorde funeral pyre."

Fear flashed through L'Veyna's cloud of joy. "Jouler?"

"It's only for Boorde," he said, and she released a sigh of relief.

Her brother led them between two hillocks, to a wide meadow. L'Veyna's breath caught at the glorious pyre, her mind ablaze in awe. Four pillars of fire burned around a pile of ash, the flames twisting around each other, stretching high into the air. Ominous dark smoke churned from the latticed pillar, leaking into the pristine sky.

"The smoke honors the Boorde," Prack explained.

"How long will it burn?" Horgar asked.

"Until sunset," Prack replied, scanning the ground. He drew a sharp breath, his gaze darting around the area. "No…"

"No what?" L'Veyna asked, still happy from the tea's effect.

Prack pointed to the top of the hillock. "That's where the others watched."

"Watched what?" L'Veyna asked, bubbles of angst lifting through her joy.

"Myr'koth," Prack said. "The Final Duel."

"What's so important about that?" Horgar asked.

"Ascended don't duel each other," Prack said. "At least, not in the middle of a mission. This isn't normal."

"Do you think it was Jouler?"

"No," Prack said. "He's good, but Ascended are hundreds of years old."

"He beat that one Boorde at the training yard," L'Veyna said.

"A teen," Prack replied. "Not a four-hundred-year-old Boorde."

"Maybe you don't know Boorde as well as you think," she retorted.

Prack shot her an annoyed look and returned to scanning the ground. He spun around, then walked off, following a trail only his trained eyes could see. In a blur of motion, he shifted around the area, finally stopping near a patch of red moss. Breathless, he stooped to examine the moss, and he let out a whoop.

"What is it?" L'Veyna called, running to see what the red moss hid.

"Jouler, you sly fox." Prack pointed to footprints in the ground. "Those are Jouler's." Prack scooted to point to a tiny curved line cut into the patch of red moss.

Not a line, she realized. *A letter.*

"It's a C," she said, and Prack nodded.

"Codoine," he said. "They're headed to Codoine."

ICY WATER SHOCKED Jouler's mind, stabbing his flesh, ripping away his thoughts. He sucked in a sharp breath and swam deeper into the swimming hole. Too cold to think, he let his mind drift to the fading sunlight and the calm babble of the stream.

The sound of approaching footsteps spun him in the icy water, and he cursed under his breath.

Ishariel stopped at the edge of the crystalline pool and folded her arms. "Enjoying yourself?"

"I was." Teeth chattering, Jouler wondered how much she could see of his naked body.

Without a word, Ishariel pulled her firedancer dress over her head, her alabaster skin glowing in the twilight. Honed from centuries of dancing, her lithe body captivated Jouler, caressing his desires, while her myriad scars ignited a savage passion.

With a coy smile, she slid into the pool and waded toward Jouler, water rippling around her small bosom.

Aroused in ways no other woman had made him feel, Jouler ripped his gaze away from her beauty and stared at the twilight sky.

"I often forget," she said, dipping her head underwater. "You were raised in a prudish Cabal outpost."

"It's not prudish to be modest."

Able to stand in the pool, Ishariel stepped closer, and he swam away. She gave him a curious look. "Are you ashamed of your body? You shouldn't be. You're a very handsome young man."

Jouler knew he wasn't ugly, but she didn't have to lie to him with empty flattery. He swam closer to his clothes, wondering how fast he could grab them. With his luck, he'd break his ankle on the slick rocks, and she'd have to help him out of the water.

The thought of her toned body aroused his desires once more, pulling his gaze to her naked form.

She cocked her head, her fire-diamond eyes sparkling in the fading light. "Is it the Prytha Keeper who tried to save you? Does she hold your flame?"

"What? No," Jouler said. "I just don't think it's proper to stare."

"I can see why you like her," Ishariel said, ignoring his words. "What's her name?"

"I told you, I don't feel that way for her."

Ishariel regarded him, her long canines poking from her smile. "Is that so?"

"Yes," Jouler said, his conviction drained from his voice.

"Interesting," she replied. "Tristian says your training goes well. Almost too well. He says you learned the first Basic Form in a day."

"It wasn't a day," Jouler said, thinking through the complex Form for the twin daggers. "I learned it in the morning."

Ishariel's brow climbed her forehead. "Truly?" she asked, and he nodded. "How do Kherlyn's daggers feel in your hands?"

"Heavy," Jouler admitted.

"Good." Ishariel's gentle smile faded, and the mischievous twinkle in her eyes hardened into an icy stare. Steam rolled off her skin. "Kherlyn was the best of us. I warned him your mind was dangerous, but he believed in you. Mark my words, Vidimir." Fire licked around her eyes. "If you cause any more of my Ascended to claim Myr'koth,

I'll make you watch those pesky leafeaters die, then force you to cook them, and eat their flesh."

The hatred burning in her eyes dared him to say otherwise. She slipped closer to Jouler and his veins chilled, fear purging his modesty. Even without her powers, he'd never best the scarred firedancer. He waded toward shore, and a fiery serpent slithered to life on the rocks, keeping him in the cold water.

"You will leave when I say," Ishariel said, and the fiery serpent struck at him, forcing him back. "You will eat when I say. You will sleep when I say. Your life, your happiness, all your dreams…" A flame flickered above her palm. She clenched her fist, and the flame puffed into smoke. "They're all mine to take, if I so please. House Nith'Iil has reigned since the Sacrifice. We hardly need whatever power you may gain in the Blasted Lands."

The fiery serpent chased Jouler deeper into the water. It slithered around him, its flames licking his back and chest, forcing him to dip to his neck.

"Accidents happen," Ishariel said, and the serpent coiled closer. "People drown."

Slithering flames singed his hair, hot pain clearing his mind. He drew a deep breath and plunged beneath the surface, the rush of water soothing his fear. Ishariel couldn't firedance if she couldn't concentrate. He kicked off the bottom, spearing toward her snow-white legs.

Her firm hand clamped the back of his neck, shoving him down until his face hit the rocky bottom. Her arm wrapped around his neck, while she wrapped her legs around him.

Jouler struggled against her grip, but she wouldn't budge. His lungs burned, begging for air, as darkness crept into his vision. He kicked and jerked, desperate to break her hold. His chest convulsed, demanding a breath.

No, please! I can't die!

Frantic thoughts coursed toward L'Veyna and Prack, to Pendric, Dilna, Reylan, Kael, and every beloved face he'd never see again. Waves of heartache and regret swarmed around his fear, his face wracked in terror, his sobs carried away by the grumbling stream.

I don't want to die…

The fiery serpent shot into the water, and pain erupted in Jouler's eye.

His lungs forced a breath, sucking in freezing darkness.

JOULER DRIFTED among the clouds high above Codoine, a city that felt as much like home as…as… A name fluttered at the edge of his mind, stirring languid memories of a humble village, twin ponds serenaded by a chorus of frogs and crickets, and unbreakable bods of friendship. The hesitant name drifted into his mind.

Headwater.

Jouler reached for those warm memories, struggling to hold on to the name, but the strange sight below him stole his thoughts. Two rows of people stretched from the Baro Gulf in the south, across hundreds of miles, to the northern coast.

The Sacrifice, he thought, recognizing the day the empire blasted his beloved kingdom into the sea.

Astrakane's two majestic mountain ranges stretched west of the rows of people, the northern range squat and condensed, while the southern mountains curved down the center of the kingdom. South of the long mountain range, vast pine forests cover the land to its rocky coasts, while frozen tundras dominated the kingdom's northern boundaries.

Pain slammed in his chest, and intense light flared along the two rows of people, cutting north and south to either coast.

Pain crashed into his chest again, and a wave of maleficent energy spread west of the rows. The destructive wave swept over the majestic mountains and thick pine forests, turning Astrakane into lifeless white powder.

Pain ripped through him, consuming his mind.

WATER SPEWED from Jouler's lungs, his vision exploding with light. He sucked in life, choking and coughing more water. Vision dark and blurred, ears whining, he winced against the hot pain burning his left eye and stabbing his chest.

After a time, the whine in his ears merged with the rush of blood, the sound like wind raging through a deep tunnel, which then eased to a low hum, and finally faded to the familiar gurgle of the stream. Coughing up the last drops of water, he waited for the burning pain in his eye to ease, then he pushed himself upright. The freezing night air bit through his aching chest, reminding him of his nudity. Shaking from the cold, he crawled to his clothes and huddled under his thick coat, breathing into his numb hands.

Warmth blossomed, and he snapped his head up. Left eye swollen shut, he focused on a strange, narrow flame that shimmered within a too-black void.

Not a void, he realized, his mind clearing with his vision. *And not a flame.*

Hate yanked him to his feet, a pair of daggers clutched in his hands.

Ishariel's too-black firedancer dress stood out against the dark of the night, the shimmering strip of flame-colored cloth shimmering in the pale moonlight. Pain, lethargy, and the freezing wind sapped his strength, pulling him back down to his knees. Besides, what could he do that Kherlyn could not? The il'Spada had mastered his daggers over three hundred years before Jouler's birth, and he'd barely wounded the infamous firedancer.

"You drowned me," Jouler said.

Ishariel sucked an elongated canine. "I did far more than that."

Jouler put a hand to his burning eye, and his palm fell into an empty socket.

My eye!

"You deserve far worse," Ishariel said.

Rage burst through his pain and panic, robbing his senses. "I'll kill you," he growled, grabbing his daggers.

A fiery snake slithered to life above Ishariel's palm, and he halted. "Not yet, you won't."

The cold truth chilled his rage into a smoldering pit of anger. Naked and armed with a pair of daggers, he'd have a better chance of surviving a blizzard as killing the blasted woman.

"Get dressed," she said. He hesitated, and she cocked her head. "Get dressed, or I'll take your arm too."

Jouler winced into his clothes, his numb feet fighting against his boots. Sudden warmth swelled around him, easing the cold from his limbs.

"Better?" Ishariel asked, and he realized she'd danced the warmth.

Refusing to acknowledge her aid, he rubbed his feet, enduring the needling sensation prickling his skin until his feet returned to normal. Boots on, he shrugged into his heavy coat, and breathed in the crisp night air.

The sharp bite of the freezing tundra whipped across his face, cooling the burning pain in his eye socket. He needed a clear head. Emotions clouded the mind, coloring thoughts with beautiful lies. The truth walked a far harsher path, bereft of color and feelings. His truth was simple—nothing he, Prack, or L'Veyna did would save him from his captors.

Which might not be so terrible.

For whatever reason, right or wrong, Ishariel and her Ascended meant to take him to the Black Breath. They had a plan to get them through the Blasted Lands, though Ishariel had yet to divulge it to any but her team. It had been another point of contention Jouler had meant to exploit until Ishariel took his eye. For now, setting aside his anger seemed the quickest path toward vengeance.

"Come with me," she said, her too-black dress obvious in the darkness. Climbing the gentle slope of a hillock, she cast a sweeping gesture and asked him what he saw.

He took in the vast tundra, noting how the soft moonlight brushed the snowy plains. No birds chirped. No insects buzzed through the night. Nothing but the howling wind, twinkling night sky, and a landscape he'd once considered barren.

"It's beautiful," he said.

"Would you have thought that an hour ago?"

Jouler fought back a spark of annoyance, refusing to let Ishariel ruin this moment. "Is that why you took my eye and drowned me—so I'd appreciate a barren tundra?"

Ishariel shook her head, the white streak in her too-black tail swishing against her back. "I did that because I wanted to kill you."

"So why'd you bring me back?"

Ishariel sucked her teeth. "Because of Matron Nith'Iil's Seer vision."

"The one where I'm leading her House to glory and honor?"

"The same," Ishariel admitted. "What do you know of it?"

"Only what you've told me."

"For almost eight hundred years," Ishariel said, "every Boorde has learned about her vision. It's considered one of the Hallmarks of Prophecy. A sign we draw close to the Time of Plenty. Prytha call you M'Ljot, the Harbinger of Death—a fitting name, considering my Matron's vision."

Jouler's gift stirred at the mention of M'Ljot. He knew if he repeated Ishariel's words, they would snap with truth.

"But to us," Ishariel continued, "you are the Dawn, prophesied to usher in the Time of Plenty, and Matron Nith'Iil's vision promises as much. I want to squeeze the life from you for what you did to Kherlyn. I want to burn your other eye and rip off your limbs, but you cannot save the world if I satiate my pain."

"So, I am the Dawn," Jouler mumbled, testing the words. His gift fluttered around the statement, hinting at half truths.

Not me, he thought. *Or not only me.*

Maybe the Light and the Dawn were different names for the same thing—the five Facets. He mumbled as much, and it felt as wrong as it did right, like a truth hanging on a technicality.

"I will never forgive you," Ishariel said, her fire-diamond eyes glowing in the night. "Or myself for losing control. Without you, without the Dawn, nothing matters. Not Kherlyn's memory. Not my House. Not the empire. Nothing. For without you, there will be nothing. Kherlyn's inner flame saw that in you. He saw past his loyalties to the figure at the end of this mission. To you, the Dawn of Prophecy. He tried telling me, but my eyes were too pale to understand."

She grabbed the darted end of her djohai and scored a line down her forearm. Her steaming blood trickled onto the frozen ground.

"I vow to see you fulfill your destiny, Jouler Davinin, Dawn of Prophecy. Thus, shall I pay my debt to Kherlyn's honor. Thus shall I pay my debt to my House."

Jouler hesitated, never sure what to say in these awkward situations. Prophecy cried of his greatness, but inside, he'd always be a simple farmer from a backwoods village.

"Does this mean I'm no longer your prisoner?" he asked.

"Hardly," Ishariel replied, though the bite had vanished from her voice. Tall and beautiful, she looked down at Jouler, her streak of white hair glowing in the moonlight. "No one is safer than a prisoner. Especially one in my custody."

Jouler thought to remind her she'd just drowned him, but he didn't want to shatter the delicate mood.

Ishariel cleared her throat and turned her gaze to the tundra's subtle beauty. "I will, however, refrain from further abuse." She gave him a sidelong glance. "Assuming you don't warrant it."

"Fair enough," Jouler said with a curt nod. "What about my friends?"

"The leafeaters?" Ishariel said, clenching her jaw. "We'll take care of them, if they ever catch up. After all, it's only fair they follow Kherlyn's fate."

35

DARK SPACES

"So, tell me again," Makayla said amid the absolute darkness, drumming up any conversation to chase away her foreboding isolation. "How do you know the most terrifying Sotouri in history?"

"Grim isn't the worst," Kael replied from the adjacent cell. "Thannel the Mark is far more terrifying."

"Who?" Makayla asked, gliding her hand over the cold stone walls as she made her rounds, or squares, since each wall was almost ten lengths of her foot. "How can he be worse than Grim if I've never heard of him?"

"I've read almost every book about Thannel," Kael said with a note of regret. "All his harrowing adventures. Some say he's not even real. Just a myth the Sotouri invented."

"But not you?" she asked, waiting for a response. "Did you shake your head?"

"I did," Kael said, chuckling. "And no, I don't believe Thannel is just a myth. The stories I read were probably exaggerated, but—"

"Probably?" Makayla said.

"Definitely exaggerated," Kael amended. "But I think the man who inspired the stories is real."

"What if he isn't?" Makayla asked. "What if it's just some privileged Founder who's never stepped foot outside his precious district? Someone who'd always fancied himself as a powerful Sotouri, but in real life, he's short, flabby, and can't shape?"

"He's real," Aglia said from another cell. "Lord Rodak spoke of Thannel like he knew him. He said all the stories get Thannel wrong, but not because they exaggerate him. They tone him down. He's the only person Lord Rodak has ever feared. Other than Kael."

"You think he fears me?" Kael asked.

"He didn't when I saw him last," Aglia said. "But that was before you routed his army and destroyed Serolle. I'd never seen him afraid until we walked through that door."

"He seemed composed to me," Makayla said.

"That's because you don't know him like I do," Aglia replied, her voice faint in the darkness. "No one knows him like me. When I last saw him, nothing, not the Ceremony, not the emperor himself, would have stopped him from torturing every last scream from your throat. He *hates* you, Kael. You killed the last good thing in his life, and now he wants to take every good thing away from you."

"Aglia, I—"

"*Nothing,*" Aglia said over Kael's apology, "would have stopped the Rodak I knew from taking you to Imutia the day we arrived. Instead, he sent you here, and he hasn't visited since. He's not just afraid. He's terrified of you, Kael."

"Doesn't Rodak have another son?" Makayla asked. "The other good thing in his twisted life?"

"He does have another son," Aglia admitted. "But Lokir is as far from good as darkness is from light. You'll see soon enough."

"How do you know he'll come?" Makayla asked.

"Because I'm here," Aglia replied, draping the dungeon in silence.

Dark memories clawed at Makayla's mind, leaking vibrant visions of brutal soldiers, her dying father, and the power that had made her whole again. Her will dashed to the tainted void in her soul where her power had dwelt, and she wilted.

Not my power, she thought. *Dra'Nahl's power.*

"How long do you think we'll be down here?" she asked. "I feel like it's been here forever."

"Can't wait to get tortured?" Aglia said.

"No, I—"

"It was in jest," Aglia mumbled.

"The Ceremony takes a few days," Kael said. "I think it depends on how many candidates they have. The festivities, however, are said to last weeks."

"Festivities?" Makayla asked, counting her ninth circuit around her cramped cell.

"No, it's not," Kael mumbled, as if arguing with himself. "The Ceremony only happens once every *three* years. I know they sped it up, but it's *supposed* to be once every three years. Regardless, half the empire's Upper Tier nobles gather in Eio for the Ceremony, and you simply can't have that many self-important lords and ladies in a single place without showing off their riches. Yes, I know, but I can't shape."

"Know what?" Makayla asked. "What are you talking about?"

"All those lords and ladies," he mused. "I did it to Serolle. I could do it here…"

"Kael, you're scaring me."

"Huh?" Kael said over a yawn. "Sorry, I thought I was…"

"Do you think the Ceremony is already over?" Aglia asked.

"Maybe?" Kael replied. "I can't tell how long we've been down here. Aglia?"

"I don't know, either. That's part of the torture."

"At least we eat well down here," Makayla offered.

"Healthy victims last longer on the rack," Aglia said. "Enjoy it while it lasts. When Lord Rodak feeds you, he won't let you chew your own food." She barked a laugh. "Takes too long, he says. Easier to mash it all to goo, and force it down your gullet."

Days and nights passed in the thick darkness, time broken up by lucid dreams, circuits around the cramped cell, and servants bringing plates of nu'food. The entrance door to the dungeon creaked open, its loud hinges echoing down the long hall of cell doors. Booted feet clopped down the hall, not the hushed slippers worn by servants.

Makayla's heart slammed in her chest. Rodak had finally come for her.

Her thick, iron-wrought door swung open, and Makayla flinched from sharp torchlight. The pain abated, and her vision adjusted to the cold light cast by a glowglobe. A young man stood in the doorframe with two large guards looming behind him. Dressed in a black suit trimmed in gold, the young, alabaster-skinned lordling bore the same jet-black hair, dark eyes, and angular jawline as his father.

Lokir, Makayla thought, her will scrambling to the tainted void in her soul.

"*The* Makayla Penfrost," the lordling said, drumming the tips of his fingers together. "I thought you'd be…taller." Giggling, he grabbed a plate from one of his guards and tossed it on the floor, spilling beans, mushrooms, and a dense nu'biscuit.

Makayla stewed in her fear, Aglia's terrifying warning prickling her skin. Her stool pot flared in the corner of her cell, startling her with a brilliant flame, and choking the air with pungent fumes.

"I'll see you soon, my dear," Lokir promised, closing the door behind him.

Kael's door squeaked open and a grunt of pain sounded from his cell.

"Good morning, traitor. Or is it night? Guess it doesn't matter down here. Have the hallucinations started? Yes…no?"

Kael grunted in pain again.

"Ah, they have," Lokir said. "Do you see him in the darkness? Do you?"

Kael grunted.

"Do you see my brother? Do you?"

Kael grunted again.

"Do you see him, traitor?"

Kael's plate clattered to the ground, and he grunted over and over.

Makayla sunk to the floor. Her heart shattered once again by Kael's cries.

"I can't wait…" Lokir said, breathless, "…to take you…home and…hear your screams." Kael grunted in pain again. "I can't wait to hear your screams." Kael's door slammed shut, and Aglia's opened, framing Lokir. "And you…"

"Lord Lokir," Aglia gasped.

"I was so sad when my father gave you to that whore, Maelly. Father told me you wanted to leave."

"Lord Lokir, I…" Aglia said, her voice shaking.

"You wanted to leave me?"

Aglia sniffled. "I'm sorry."

"Well," Lokir said, his voice sharp. Aglia's plate scraped across the stone floor. "I'm so happy you're back."

"I'LL SEE YOU SOON, my dear," Lord Lokir told Eglona—*no*, Makayla.

Aglia's resentment still stirred whenever her thoughts strayed toward the sharp betrayal. She'd been honest with Makayla from the very first day. She'd taught her how to wash laundry. She'd confided in her, telling her all the horrible things Rodak had done. She'd *trusted* Makayla.

No, she thought. *I trusted Eglona.*

Aglia knew nothing about Makayla, if that was even her real name.

Hadn't you done the same? the voice said in her mind. *Gave Rodak a false name in case he found yours scribbled on one of Reylan's notes?*

"That's different," she mumbled. "I'm a Phaerian, not a Founder."

What name did you give Rodak?

"*Lord* Rodak," she whispered, shoving against a barrage of dark memories—.

Sittia, wasn't it?

Aglia dug her fingernails into her legs, wishing Rodak hadn't healed her cuts before throwing her into this dark pit. She pinched hard, savoring the sweet burn of pain as her nails pierced her skin.

Wasn't Sittia the name of Kael's little sister? the wicked voice asked.

Aglia pounded her palms against the sides of her head. She pulled her knees to her chest, rocking from side to side. Kael's door creaked open, and her heart swam with fear. The death of Lord Rodak's youngest son may have broken the lord, but it had shattered Lokir.

A grunt of pain sounded from Kael's cell, his groans creeping into Aglia's heart. In her mind, she saw Kael curled on the floor, his back a riddle of scars she'd inflicted.

"He deserved it," she mumbled. She'd seen the explosion he'd caused in Serolle. She'd heard the reports, how he'd annihilated two massive armies and crushed the city's Shining Wall.

Fifty Vrath—that was how many Lord Rodak had sent to raze Headwater. Kael could have killed them all without batting an eye.

You pushed him away, the petulant voice chimed.

"No," she whispered, fighting against a wave of agonizing memories—Reylan's empty house, a pair of metallic tubes, and the old man's standing order in case of emergency.

You knew the risk…

Aglia buried her head between her knees and rocked.

…and you did it, anyway.

An image pierced her mind of an evil man with dark intents, a bounty hunter with light streaming from his mouth and eyes.

Why? the voice asked, stirring her anguish. *Why did you send him away?*

"Because he's the Light of Prophecy," she admitted under a wave of guilt. She'd handed Kael to the very man she'd wanted to protect him from when she'd told Kael to leave.

That's not why…

She remembered the pain twisting his face, and the hurt in his voice. "…please, don't do this."

She'd pulled him into a gentle kiss, his body shaking in her arms, his cheeks wet with tears.

Aglia gritted her teeth and laced her fingers together to keep from pounding her head, letting her memories carry her down a tender path of picnics, promises, and shared hearts. They'd been so happy together, daring to dream of an idyllic life on the outskirts of Headwater, where Olan could visit, and Jouler could escape his father's wrath. A small little farm by the sick house, where she'd first met him, and had wanted nothing to do with him. Somewhere close to the lake where they'd first kissed.

Why did you send him away?

"Because I love him," she whispered.

"Good morning, traitor," Lokir said from Kael's cell, shattering Aglia's memories. "Or is it good night? Guess it doesn't matter down here. Have the hallucinations started? Yes...no?"

Kael grunted again.

"Ah, they have," Lokir said. "Do you see him in the darkness? Do you?"

Kael grunted and Aglia pressed her hands against her ears, humming to block out his cries.

You brought him here, the voice said, sharp and accusing. *You knew what fate awaited him.*

She steered her thoughts away from Lokir, but memories of the cruel youth and their time together clawed through her mind. The pain he'd explored on her body. The invisible scars dug into her soul.

Her cell door creaked open with blinding light. "And you..."

"Lord Lokir," Aglia gasped, feigning surprise the way the petty lord liked it.

Suited in all black with gold trim, Lokir's alabaster face drooped with empty sorrow. Like a smaller, weaker version of his father, Lokir didn't need the knife sheathed at his belt, but shaping couldn't satiate his depraved desires. "I was so sad when my father gave you to that whore Maelly. He said you wanted to leave."

"Lord Lokir, I..." Aglia's voice trailed, teasing him with timidity. Too much, and she'd stir the ravenous beast inside him. Too little, and he wouldn't quiet her guilt with the pain she sought.

"You *wanted* to leave me?"

She sniffled, squeezing more tears. "I'm sorry."

"Well," Lokir said, his voice sharp and chipper. Aglia's plate scraped across the stone floor. "I'm so happy you're back." He crouched and ran his alabaster finger through her wispy hair. "I just wish we had more time to catch up."

"What do you mean?" Aglia asked, flinching from his touch.

"Oh, not this, my dear," Lokir said, patting his knife. "My father told me I'm not to touch you." He leaned in and whispered, "I'm not supposed to touch Kael, either, but he provoked it. Besides, from the looks of him, you did far worse. Didn't you, my dear?"

Aglia didn't need to fake the fresh stream of tears. "Why—" Her voice caught, and she cleared the lump in her throat. "Why don't we have time? Aren't I going with you?"

Lokir stood, his white lips pressed into a thin line. "Unfortunately, no. Father says I need to learn to let go." He gestured to the tiny cell. "You are to live a long, healthy life down here."

Aglia knew him too well to believe his lie. She'd be lucky to live to see Kael and Makayla leave. "How much time do we have?"

Lokir lifted an eyebrow, his finger tapping the hilt of his knife. With a deep sigh, he crossed his arms. "A couple weeks…three, maybe a month." He shrugged. "Strip my Shield if I have to spend any longer in this blasted city than I have to. I swear, Aglia…" He rolled his eyes. "The people here aren't right. To make it worse, Father demands my presence during these blasted festivities.

"But don't worry," he said with a sweeping bow. The stool pot flared with a pungent odor. "I promise to visit you when I can."

He spun and left, slamming the cell door behind him.

Two weeks, maybe three, she thought, her door shutting her into darkness once more. *That's how long I have to right my wrong. That's how much time I have to save Kael.*

KAEL'S MIND drifted in the darkness of his cell, his stomach and back bruised from Lokir's kicks. Thankfully, the skinny lordling hadn't broken anything, although Kael wouldn't soon find a comfortable position. In a way, Lokir's rudimentary techniques were worse than Aglia's. As excruciating as hers had been, at least they'd ended in blissful unfeeling not throbbing pain. Writhing hatred burned within him. Lokir, Rodak, Maelly, and every other blasted Citizen deserved to die.

Soft whimpers from Makayla's cell rolled off his consciousness, filling him with images of her in the throes of a nightmare. His cell door creaked open, issuing a faint light, and Olan stepped inside, mist coiling around his feet, his neck pouring blood.

"You're my hero, Kael."

Guilt jolted him awake.

"That one sounded bad," Aglia said, her voice muffled through the doors.

"Those ones always are," Kael replied, wincing from his bruised side.

"It was of Headwater, wasn't it?"

"Olan," he replied, his voice hoarse.

"He…" Aglia's voice cracked. "He loved you."

The words seared Kael, tightening his throat and demanding his tears.

"You were his hero," she said, "and you let him die. You let us all die."

Oh gods, he groaned in his head, his throat too thick to speak. He punched the wall, welcoming the sharp, flaring pain in his hand. Anything but the torment clawing at his heart.

If he'd stayed in Headwater, maybe his desperation to save the village would have triggered his gift. After all, what were a few dozen Vrath when an entire army couldn't withstand his power?

You could have saved Headwater. You could have saved Olan.

He pressed his palms to his eyes, but Olan remained in the doorway, his curly hair matted with blood.

Your cowardice killed him.

The unbidden thought rang with truth. He'd known about Rodak's cruelties. He'd know nothing good could have come from that chance meeting on the road to Alduos. Deep down inside, Kael had known Olan would die, and he'd done nothing to save him. He'd done nothing to save any of them.

They're all dead because of you.

He'd led Rodak to Headwater, just as he'd led the archon's Vrath to Dilna's farm. His attempt to cleanse Makayla's dark power had instead stolen it from her and slaughtered her army.

Everything you touch turns to ash.

Kael curled on the ground, agony heavy on his chest, tears leaking down the side of this face.

You know it's true, the voice sang in his head.

Images flooded him of Headwater burning from Rodak's patterns, of Vrath ripping apart villagers, and terrentors crashing through the charred remains of his idyllic home.

"Kael!"

Aglia's sharp voice startled him awake.

Gods, he thought, rubbing his face, *I can't do this anymore. It hurts too much.*

Lokir—he was the key to ending Kael's suffering. The lordling always carried that knife. He'd have to be quick, but all he needed was a single jab to bleed the darkness from his heart. A single stab and his misery would finally end.

"You were having another nightmare," Aglia said, the concern in her voice assuaging his troubled mind.

"It's always the same blasted thing," Kael said, sitting upright, his back against the wall across from the cell door. "Nightmares filled with all my wrong choices."

"At least you didn't doom the world," she mumbled. "Hey, Aglia, why'd you hand the Light over to the empire? Well, you see, I was really angry because I told him to leave, and he did, so now the entire world gets to burn." She gave an uneasy laugh. "At least you aren't *that* person."

"It's a little more complicated than that," Kael said, heavy with regret. "I never should have left."

"No," Aglia said. "Don't you get what I'm trying to say? You're more than just a powerful shaper. You're the Light, the savior of our people, and vanquisher of evil."

"There is no Light," Kael said, explaining the Facets to her.

"Jouler too?" Aglia asked.

"Yep," Makayla said.

"You're awake," Kael replied.

"Have been." Makayla moaned as if stretching. "I think? It's hard to tell when I'm awake and when I dream."

"Start from the beginning, Kael," Aglia said, sounding more like Livia. "What happened after you left Headwater?"

Kael took a deep, calming breath, readying himself for an emotional onslaught. Then he told her every painful detail of his journey. How he'd led Vrath to Dilna's farm, and how they'd escaped into the Kralnach Hills. He described the leaf-winged Ul'Kral and Pendric's stolen breath. He choked through the moment Grim took them and abandoned Dilna in Iaroca, and he detailed their arduous trek through the Shattered Lands, how Pendric had pretended to befriend the Sotouri in order to trick Grim and saved them all. He told her about hanging in a cage in Onatah, the beautiful Prytha, and Tálise's grove.

"So, *now* the gods want to intervene?" Aglia said.

"I think he sacrificed Himself to help me," Kael replied. "Like he'd waited all those centuries for that moment. Gods, what a life. Imagine existing for a single moment, and knowing you'd die when that moment arrived. Nothing but a glorified tool."

Is that so different from your own life? a small voice chided in his mind. *Just another tool of Prophecy?*

"So…the son of Alnazet was a tree?" Agila asked.

"Not exactly," Kael replied. "The tree was more like a doorway to his realm."

"Interesting," Agila said, stirring an image of Livia contemplating a quandary. "And we know Alnazet as Tolrik?"

"Yes," Kael said.

"What about Da'Nahl, the Dark?" Aglia asked. "What's His real name?"

"It's the same," Kael said.

"Why change Alnazet to Tolrik?" Makayla asked.

"A world ruled by men," Aglia said, "can't have a universe created by a woman."

"Sounds like something Jouler would say," Kael said.

"Or Rammond," Makayla mumbled.

"Do gods even have a gender?" Aglia asked, invoking an image of Livia frowning in thought.

"Not according to Tálise," Kael said. "He appeared to me in a form that would soothe my mind."

"He looked like Reylan, didn't he?" Aglia asked, her voice toeing on amusement.

"Without the crooked nose," Kael replied. "He explained the Facets and the Paths of Prophecy."

"Paths?" Aglia asked. "As in plural?"

"Specifically Light and Dark," Kael replied. "My role as Crier of Change is to help the Facets walk the Path of Light."

"Or the Path of Dark, if you're so inclined?" Aglia asked.

"Yes," Kael replied, soaking in memories of Livia's inquisitive mind.

"Kael changed my Path," Makayla said.

"Wait, *you* were on the Path of Dark?"

"Not by choice," Makayla said. "I thought I was helping the Light."

"How could you believe that?" Aglia asked.

"It didn't seem evil," Makayla said. "We were fighting the empire. I freed our people. In Blailon, at least. If there was ever a path that felt like the Light's, I was on it. Anyway, I was about to assault Serolle when Kael appeared right in front of me. Out of nowhere. One moment it was just me and my army. I'd prepared this long speech I was going to shout at Serolle, and then, suddenly, there's Kael, the man who'd haunted my dreams, looking as confused as I'd felt."

"You dreamed of him?" Aglia asked, thick with doubt.

"We actually dreamed of each other," Kael said. "She was the alabaster-skinned girl in my nightmares."

"That was *her*?" Aglia said.

"I'll bet those dreams came from the Dark," Makayla said. "That's who gave me my power."

"Your power came from Dra'Nahl?" Algia blurted. "Why would you... How did... But you're so...so good. I mean, sure, you lied to me the whole time we were together, but I get it. I did the same thing when Rodak's men took me." Aglia cleared her throat. "Never mind that. Are you sure your power came from the Dark?"

"Positive," Makayla said. "I can feel his foul residue even now."

"From what I understand," Aglia said, "that shouldn't be possible. The Light and Dark are bound by Prophecy. They can no more directly influence events as the sun can rise in the north."

"You should probably tell that to Dra'Nahl," Makayla said.

"I believe you," Aglia replied, her voice bouncing with excitement. "I heard the stories about you. I'm saying your power *shouldn't* have been possible. And, yet…here you are. But what does that mean about the gods? Are their bonds breaking, or did the Dark find a way to subvert Prophecy?"

"I'm impressed," Kael said. "You know a lot more about Prophecy than I thought."

"Thanks," Aglia said, a bite in her voice. "It's almost like I apprenticed under Reylan."

"The Cabalist?" Makayla asked. "That's who we were trying to get to, right? At the Boorde Alliance? Him and Jouler and Pendric."

"*Maybe* Jouler and Pendric," Kael said. "Reylan was there months ago. Before I left Onatah. There's no telling where he is now."

"Wait," Aglia said. "Kael, how'd you get to Serolle? Why'd you leave Jo and Pen in Onatah?"

"Tálise gave me a choice," Kael said. "I chose my role in Prophecy."

"What was your other choice?" Aglia asked.

Kael swam in the sweet memory of Livia gathering berries, locks of honey cascading over her shoulders, a gentle smile tugging her lips. "To live out my life in peace and happiness with the woman I love."

After a long moment, Agila's whisper pierced the silence. "I'm glad you chose Prophecy. That woman died in Headwater."

36

PEGRANS

Sweat dripped from Jouler's nose despite the cold afternoon, his fingers numbing around the hilt of Wrath and Scorn, his twin daggers. Ishariel slipped to his left, taking advantage of the eye she'd taken. He let a spike of anger surge through him, imagining the foul energy dissipating into the ground, while he nestled in a sea of placid unfeeling.

Guided by his gift, he lunged at Ishariel, and, as expected, she twisted past his dagger. He feinted a kick at her knee, spun, and kicked with his other foot, landing a hard blow against her ribs. Gasps rippled through the observers, fueling Jouler's momentum. He lunged again, swiping an alabaster fist aside, and jabbing his dagger at her exposed belly.

In a fluid motion, Ishariel caught his wrist, pulled him off balance, and kicked his feet out from under him. Jouler slammed into the frozen ground, air pouring from his lungs. He struggled to pull a breath while the Ascended chuckled and returned to camp.

"You would have stabbed me," Ishariel said, helping him to his feet.

"I guess we'll never know," Jouler said, grinning to hide his hatred of the woman.

Her raised eyebrow said he hadn't hidden it well. "Either Tristian is a better trainer than I thought…" she said, waving for the slender Ascended. "Or there is more to your skill than natural talent."

Jouler sheathed his daggers as an excuse to avoid her gaze. "I've always caught on quick."

"This," Ishariel said, rubbing her side, "didn't happen because you're a quick learner. You truly are Prophecy made flash, aren't you?"

"I'm just a farmer," Jouler said. "Just a plain old, simple Human farmer dragged down Prophecy's rough trail."

"A simple Human farmer who speaks Boordish without a Human accent, and who fights like a Boorde twice his age."

"Twice?" Tristian said, walking up to them. Almost as tall as Ishariel, he held her gaze before tilting his head, recognizing her authority. "I'd put Jouler up against any hundred-year-old Boorde."

"That's precisely my point," Ishariel said. "Whether you admit it, Vidimir, Prophecy guides your hand as time guides the seasons. It doesn't take a Seer to see that much." She turned to Tristian. "Add the sidaiyo to his training."

"He already knows those Basic Forms," Tristian said.

"Is that what he told you?"

"It's what his footwork told me," Tristian replied with a note of scorn. "I would appreciate it if you left the weapon mastering to a weapons master."

Ishariel regarded Jouler with an inquisitive look. "What other Forms has Diou taught you?"

"Diou only taught me the staff," Jouler said.

"Who taught you the sidaiyo?" Tristian asked.

"Grim."

Ishariel's pale, fire-diamond eyes flared with danger. She stepped close to Jouler, and the salient memory of their time in the pool gripped him in fear. "How did you come into his company?"

"It wasn't by choice," Jouler replied.

"He taught you the Forms out of the kindness of his heart?"

"More like a twisted form of torture," he replied

"Just a simple Human farmer," she said in Boordish, dragging her finger along his jawline.

"Prophecy may guide his hand," Tristian said, pulling Jouler away from Ishariel. "But he still has a lot to learn. Will you tell Quirr'Ik to join us?"

Ishariel raised an eyebrow, tapping a finger on her djohai. "Very well, First Blade."

Tristian's glare followed her as she walked away. "I hate her."

"You and me both," Jouler said.

"I imagine you feel that way for all of us," Tristian mused, then looked at Jouler's empty eye socket. "Although, I imagine your hatred for her burns brightest."

"I don't hate you," Jouler replied, getting into position for the first Dual-Daggers Form. He drew his weapons, Wrath held upright, Scorn gripped downward. In an open field, range won far more victories than skill with a blade, but most weapons were too wieldy close up. Slip past a guard or slide through a jab, and the dagger won every time.

Tristian drew his slender sword and dagger, and stood across from him. The tall, lean Boorde accompanied Jouler through the Forms, attacking or blocking to show different ways to utilize each maneuver. Jouler finished the First Form with a spinning flourish, and Tristian's lips curled in amusement.

"You've been practicing in your mind," the tall Boorde said, tapping the side of his head. "Take me through your dance, Vidimir. Let me see what that mind of yours can do."

Jouler tilted his head and slid into a relaxed stance, both daggers held downward. The sidaiyo's Forms felt strong and rigid like a mountain, while the forms for the spear and staff were leaves dancing in the wind. Daggers needed to flow like water, both powerful and fluid, gentle and violent. He assessed Tristian's stance, how he held his sword and dagger, the small twitches of his eyes, and sway of his hips.

Jouler sprung into action, leading with an obvious feint, while he slid his foot to twist through Tristian's jab. Scorn slid down the slender blade, while Wrath clashed against Tristian's dagger. Jouler's gift guided each strike, slice, and sweeping leg, the movements feeling as right as the truth snapping into place.

Tristian parried and riposted, finding a rhythm to Jouler's attacks. Like water adapting to a new trail, Jouler shifted his dance, chopping at Tristian's thin blade, kicking his legs, and stomping at his feet. Tristian leaped back, and Jouler lunged into a slide, tripping Tristian, and stabbing at his shin. Tristian rolled back, and Jouler's dagger slammed into the ground.

Tristian stood in a smooth motion and bowed to Jouler. "That was impressive, Vidimir. Your Form is…"

"Formless?" Jouler offered, and Tristian shook his head.

"More like…"

"Adaptive," Quirr'Ik said, walking toward them, her firedancer dress swirling around her legs. "Like a dance."

"Like water," Jouler said.

Quirr'Ik pondered his words and gave a begrudging nod. "Maybe with a little more practice. Water isn't so clumsy, young Human. Is that why you asked me here, Tristian—to help Vidimir with his atrocious footwork?"

Atrocious?

Jouler knew he'd never be as graceful as a Boorde, but he couldn't be *that* clumsy. After all, he'd landed a blow on Ishariel.

Tristian scanned the horizon, then nodded as if to himself. "Jouler, begin the First Form again. Quirr'Ik, if you would please, show Jouler how a firedancer might react at each step."

Quirr'Ik dipped her head, and loosened her djohai, her gaze catching on Jouler's daggers. "Proceed, young Vidimir."

Jouler bowed at the waist and lunged into the first step.

Quirr'Ik twisted her djohai chain around his wrist, pulling him off balance. "Why did you really bring me here, Tristian?"

Jouler repositioned himself into the second set of the First Form, leading with his dominant foot and striking with both daggers. Quirr'Ik lashed her djohai chain around his ankle and yanked his foot from under him.

"Lyndara approached me this morning," Tristian said, helping

Jouler to his feet.

Knowing better than to openly eavesdrop, Jouler assumed the third stance in the Form.

"She approached me last night," Quirr'ik said.

"What did you tell her?" Tristian asked.

"I told her I'd wait to talk to you." Not waiting for Jouler to move, Quirr'ik twirled her djohai, seeming to tangle it around her body and legs. With a swift jerk, she kicked, and the darted end of her djohai shot toward Jouler.

Jouler flung himself to his back, his instincts snapping his hand out to catch the chain. He twirled on the ground, tangling the chain with his legs, and launching to his feet. The sudden jerk yanked the djohai from Quirr'ik's hands.

She shot him an annoyed look, her gaze once again catching on the daggers. "You were supposed to block with the third step."

"Still," Tristian said. "That was quite impressive."

"For a Human," Quirr'ik said.

"A Human trained by Diou *and* Grim," Tristian replied with a pointed look. Quirr'ik cast a dismissive wave, and he continued. "Jouler doesn't have our heightened senses. He wounds as easily as any Human and heals just as slow. He lacks our battle prescience, and yet, he moves like an Astasi."

Quirr'ik coiled her djohai and strapped it to her waist. "What happened at the creek?" she asked Jouler. "Ishariel's been different since that night."

"Different how?" Jouler asked.

"Don't play coy with me," Quirr'ik said, flames dripping from her fists. "What did you tell her?"

"Me?" Jouler said. "Do you actually believe I could change her?"

"You got to Kherlyn," she growled.

"He did not get to Kherlyn," Tristian said, pain wrinkling his brow.

Quirr'ik breathed a heavy sigh. "Something happened that night."

Tristian bowed his head. "You're right, of course. But we will not learn the truth if we fill him with fear." He turned to Jouler, the

Boorde's face as calm as his voice. "Please, tell us what happened that night at the stream."

"I think she'd gone there to kill me," Jouler said, and the two Ascended shared a silent look. "She'd wanted to, at least, but something changed in her. One moment she was…"

She was drowning me, he thought. *She* had *drowned me*.

For some reason, that moment felt too personal to share with Quirr'Ik and Tristian, even if they'd taken to treating him more like a companion than a prisoner.

"One moment it felt like she wanted to kill me," Jouler said. "The next, she was telling me I'm the Dawn, and that nothing mattered more than me completing this mission. Not her Matron, not her House. Nothing."

"I see," Quirr'ik said, her voice dripping with disappointment.

"Kherlyn believed in Jouler," Tristian said. "So do I. So does Ishariel."

Quirr'ik grumbled through a heavy sigh. "I can't believe you're going to make me do this."

Jouler froze, holding his breath. Whatever quiet conversations fluttered behind Ishariel's back, Jouler knew her life balanced on Quirr'ik's next words.

"We never should have taken this mission," she said, slumping.

"We didn't have a choice," Tristian said.

"How many had the same orders as Lyndara?" Quirr'ik asked.

"All but our team," Tristian said.

"Zhyndor?" Quirr'ik asked, and Tristian shook his head.

"He turned after Kherlyn's death. You and I were the last to be approached."

"*You* were the last," Quirr'ik replied, and he dipped his head. The firedancer cursed under her breath, squeezing her hands into fists. "All of them?"

"I doubt Ishariel's team would turn against her, but the other teams have their orders."

"Sacred Flame preserve us," Quirr'ik said, turning to Jouler. "You'd better be worth this, Vidimir."

"I'd say ushering in the Time of Plenty," Tristian mused, "is worth whatever price we have to pay."

"You really believe he's the Dawn?" she asked, examining Jouler.

"I do," Tristian replied, pulling another grumble from the firedancer.

"I thought I'd live to see my eyes pale," she said, the corner of her lip curling into a half smile.

"Our eyes *are* pale," Tristian said with a pointed look. "Just not as pale as Ishariel's."

Quirr'ik turned to Jouler. "I take it you've surmised what's about to take place?"

"I believe so," Jouler replied. "The other Ascended are planning on killing Ishariel."

"They plan on killing her team *and* you," Quirr'ik said, "and leaving your corpses to crumble to dust on the Blasted Lands."

Jouler shivered, though not from the cold. Assuming none of Ishariel's team turned on her, Quirr'ik and Tristian made six to Lyndara's nine. Not the best odds, but maybe good enough, considering Ishariel's fame. Jouler asked when the others planned to attack, and they both shook their head.

"Which means soon," Jouler surmised. "If Tristan was the last to be approached, we have to assume it's imminent."

As if in response, the clash of steel and roar of fire sounded from camp.

"STAY OUT OF THIS," Tristian said, his long legs pulling him ahead of Jouler.

Quirr'ik raced beside her First Blade, the long tail of her topknot swishing against her back, djohai flickering in her hands with a blue flame.

Jouler pumped his legs up the gentle slope, watching the two Boorde disappear over the crest. Breathless by the time he reached the top of the gentle hillock, Jouler skidded to a stop, his childish thoughts of joining the fray crumbling under a maelstrom of blades and fire.

Ishariel's three il'Spada protected their firedancer, their spears whirring and clacking with melodious harmony. Jouler gaped at their skill, understanding why Quirr'ik had called him clumsy. Vaelithrae, Thalrion, and Nyrr'kas, their eyes almost as faded as Ishariel's, kept the seven il'Spada at bay, maneuvering with a grace that belied centuries of practice.

Lyndara and the other seditious firedancer spun and flowed like black-and-alabaster flames behind the wall of il'Spada, djohais whipping globs of fire and molten darts.

Ishariel danced behind her il'Spada, a goddess among mortals, her djohai slithering and coiling around her in rhythm to her mesmerizing grace. Thirteen serpents made of liquid fire slithered around her, striking at il'Spada and intercepting firedancer attacks.

Glowing blades and spearheads sliced through fiery whips, jets of flame, and molten darts. Ishariel's il'Spada Thalrion cried in pain, his right arm missing below the elbow, the spurting wound steaming in the cold. A glowing Boorde spear burst through his chest, and he toppled to the ground.

Ishariel's dance shifted, and three of her serpents darted, slamming into a Boorde wielding twin hooked swords. The serpents swarmed over the Ascended, melting his head, and silencing his screams.

Tristian raced toward Lyndara, his slender blade lancing through her dress, dagger deflecting the dart of her djohai. The thin il'Spada leaped and twisted around her snaking djohai, his dagger and sword licking the firedancer's alabaster skin.

Quirr'ik slid into a violent dance, and engaged the seditious il'Spada, blue flames rippling down her djohai. After a looping sequence, she stomped her foot, her dart slamming into the ground, releasing a line of blue fire at the seditious il'Spada.

Three peeled away from Ishariel's team and darted at Quirr'ik. The firedancer twirled, her djohai whirling around her, its darted end slicing deep into an il'Spada's thigh.

Ignoring the wound, the il'Spada stabbed his glowing spearhead into her side and lifted her off the ground.

Tristian bellowed, rolling through Lyndara's djohai and slamming his dagger into her heart. Steaming tears dripped from his pale eyes, his rictus snarl exposing his elongated canines. In a fluid motion, he spun, yanking his dagger free, and slamming a foot into a il'Spada's face. Diverting a spear meant for his belly, he slipped past the Ascended's guard, snaking his slender blade up through his chin and out the top of his skull. With a rage-filled shout, he yanked the blade free, spraying blood and brains. His dagger turned a sidaiyo meant for his neck, his knee catching the il'Spada's chin.

Ishariel's il'Spada Nyrr'kas crumpled to the ground, his neck steaming with blood. Only her First Blade, Vaelithrae, stood between her, three other il'Spada, and one firedancer.

The firedancer's movements shifted into a powerful dance, her feet stomping, hands fluttering upward. The ground rumbled and cracked, spewing a fountain of lava. Molten rocks clumped together, forming a legless body with thick arms, a smoldering head, and viscous mouth. Cracks formed and merged across its body, leaking rivulets of lava that steamed in the cold air.

Tristian spun and twisted around Zhyndor's spear, maneuvering to keep his once-companion between him and the second il'Spada's sidaiyo. Like a pale-eyed master disciplining unruly disciples, Tristian flowed with their attacks, forcing missteps and deflecting Zhyndor's spear into sidaiyo chops.

The sidaiyo-wielding il'Spada cries out in pain, his hands bleeding on the ground still clutching his sword. The Boorde stumbled back, and Tristian's slender blade sliced his throat.

"I knew you'd never sway," Zhyndor said. "Even after she killed your Bonded."

"Do not presume to know Kherlyn's heart," Tristian said.

"I'll not grant you Myr'koth."

"Such an honor cannot be given," Tristian said, raising his slender blade, "by those who have no honor to give."

Zhyndor's lip curled, and he leaped forward with a jab.

Tristian rolled past the spear, stabbing his dagger through the back of Zhyndor's neck, the tip spurting from his mouth.

Zhyndor crumbled without a sound.

The three remaining il'Spada split their attack on Vaelithrae, while the molten creature the firedancer had summoned lurched for Ishariel's First Blade. The nimble il'Spada rolled under a molten fist and into a waiting spearhead, the glowing blade stabbing through his chest.

Ishariel's scream shattered the air. Her thirteen fiery serpents struck at the il'Spada and firedancer. She snapped her fingers, and the serpents exploded in a violent shower of liquid fire. Countless molten needles pierced the seditious Ascended, killing them, and the molten beast melted to the ground.

Ishariel slouched to her knees, her gaze locked on Vaelithrae's corpse, the emerald heron on his polished onyx eye sparkling under the bright sun.

Silence permeated the still air.

Jouler gaped at the inexorable end of the Ascendeds' deadly dance. *A dance of masters,* he thought, his mind replaying the performance.

Tristian knelt beside Quirr'ik, steaming tears dripping on her alabaster skin.

Without knowing why, Jouler made his way down the slope and began dragging the corpses away from Ishariel and Tristian. He imagined they'd still want pyres for the fallen, but sending the traitors to the Sacred Flame next to Quirr'ik and Ishariel's il'Spada seemed wrong.

By the time he finished his macabre task, the sun dipped well past its zenith, slipping behind long, languid clouds. Quirr'ik, Vaelithrae, Thalrion, and Nyrr'kas lay on their own pile of sticks, grass, and moss. The other corpses rotted in a pile on the other side of the hillock.

"Thank you," Tristian said, climbing up the slope to stand beside Jouler. "You truly are tilandari."

Jouler shivered into his thick coat, letting the unfamiliar word roll on his tongue, tasting its meaning. "Made of honor?"

"Close enough," the slender Boorde mumbled, his somber gaze

resting on the pile of traitors. "Their souls don't deserve to join the Sacred Flame."

Ishariel joined them at the top of the hillock, her pale fire-diamond eyes devoid of emotion. "Let them freeze for eternity. Them and our Matron."

"Once Matron," Tristian corrected, and expounded upon seeing Jouler's confusion. "Apparently, *three* orders had been given—bring back the Heiress Apparent, bring you back once you receive whatever power awaits you in the Codoine Ruins, and leave Ishariel's team in the Blasted Lands to rot."

Ishariel stood tall and statuesque, her streaked hair fluttering in the breeze, eyes flaring with rage.

"Why would she do that?" Jouler asked, pulling his coat closed against the cold. "You obviously had the strongest team."

Tristian sucked an elongated canine. "Because she's about to do something Ishariel wouldn't condone. Something that would have demanded Myr'koth."

Ishariel's brow tightened, her jaw clenching. The burn on the side of her face glared at Jouler, drumming up images of her naked form and myriad scars. How many centuries had she served her House? How many awful deeds had she committed for her Matron? How many lives had she taken, only to be discarded in the Blasted Lands, and refused the honor of returning to the Sacred Flame?

"I'll find more moss and grass for the others," Jouler said, warring with the rage in his heart for the woman who had taken his eye, and the pride he felt standing between her and Tristian.

"Thank you," Ishariel said, looking down at him, her pale eyes shaking with uncertainty. She rested a hand on his shoulder, and Tristian did the same.

In that moment, something changed in their relationship. Where unwavering confidence had once reigned, the two Ascended now regarded him with the wanting hope of the lost. Jouler realized they both waited for him to say something. To give them direction. To do something.

The masters no longer lead the servant.

"I think I saw some small trees back that way," he said, pointing east. "It's not too far. Maybe we should all fetch wood together."

Tristian regarded Jouler, his soft pale eyes brimming with gratitude.

"Then," Jouler continued with a pointed look to Ishariel, "we wait for my friends."

Ishariel gave a curt nod, a sparkling tear steaming down her cheek. Without a word, she walked to Vaelithrae's corpse and retrieved his spear. Composed once more, she returned with her confident grace. Tristian met her, and they shared a blank look before tilting their head to each other in a bow. Together, they strode in step up to Jouler, and knelt before him.

Ishariel presented him with Vaelithrae's spear. "He wanted you to have this."

Jouler blinked in surprise.

"He believed in you," she explained. "I believe in you."

Not wanting to ruin the somber moment with clumsy words, Jouler took the spear.

Tristian unsheathed his dagger and sliced off his topknot, then he handed the blade to Ishariel to cut off her tail. Next, she passed a hand over their head, singeing the rest of their hair from their scalps.

"We are Anlidari. Houseless," Ishariel said, and the two bald Ascended bowed, pressing their forehead to the ground. "We pledge our flames to you, Jouler Davinin, Vidimir, Dawn of Prophecy."

BLAILON'S cruel tundra bit through L'Veyna's coat and wrap, her toes as numb as her fingers and nose. After suffering a week of the frozen landscape, she realized a surprising amount of life endured this harsh climate. It lacked Onatah's tall, luscious trees and soft beds of moss, but lichens, grasses, and shrubs slept beneath the carpet of snow. To the west, a smattering of pines stood tall and proud in their white dresses.

Well…tall for the tundra.

They would have been sticks in Onatah. Her chest tightened as usual when her thoughts meandered toward home, and the war that plagued its boundaries. Had her people repelled the empire? Did a ring of Vrath and Sotouri surround the Sacred Forests, or had the empire rolled over Onatah like it had everything else?

No, she mused, shaking the thoughts from her mind. Hundreds of saplings likely still dangled high above the forest floor, waiting for her and Jouler to fulfill Prophecy.

How long would they dangle—weeks, months, years? She doubted the man who'd sent Breya to hunt and kill saplings would wait too long before cages started to mysteriously fall to the ground.

She'd never understood how saplings could turn against their parents. Now it seemed obvious. For the thousandth time since she fled Onatah, she wondered what her parents would have done had Keeper Orenda not ordered her to heal Jouler, and instead, L'Veyna had joined the rest of the saplings for the Blossoming festivities. L'Veyna wanted to believe her parents would have helped her escape, but they weren't hardened warriors like Prack or powerful keepers like herself. Gentle and studious, they'd feared Prophecy as much as any other scholar.

A dark realization tainted her fond memories. If not for her brother and Keeper Orenda, she would be dangling from a cage with the rest of the saplings, assuming Marun didn't kill her outright. After all, what good was a wooden cage against a Keeper?

Her gaze drifted ahead toward Pegrans, and her heart fluttered at the thought of finding Jouler within the destitute town. Unlike the other towns she'd visited, no dark haze drifted over Pegrans, the air seeming as clear as the open tundra.

Horgar whistled in amazement. "Never thought I'd see a clean town."

"Just because the air looks clean," Prack said, "doesn't mean the town is." He clicked his tongue and shook his head. "Something's not right."

"You always say that," L'Veyna said.

"And I'm always right. Let's find information about our wayward friend and leave. I don't want to spend any more time in that town than I have to."

"Ain't nothing in Pegrans to be scared of," Horgar said, puffing out his chest.

Humans were so weird, particularly the men. Although, from what she'd seen in Onti and Urna, the women weren't any better. Other than Dilna, of course. L'Veyna's heart twisted at the memory of her friend's enviable hair kissed with the shade of night, the mischief behind her not-so-innocent eyes, and the fun-trouble they always found.

"What about you?" Horgar asked, his confidence wavering.

"Sure?" she replied, wondering what she'd just agreed with.

"Yeah," Horgar said, shifting the hempen pack she'd asked for him. "Just a plain old town like any other."

"Have you ever been to Pegrans?" Prack asked.

"Why would I?" Horgar replied. "It's too far inland, and besides, everyone knows there's nothing in Pegrans."

"One of these days," Prack said, his light tone belying the somber strain around his emerald eyes, "you'll have to introduce me to this Everyone fellow. He seems to know a lot."

"Sounds more like a she, to me," Horgar said, cackling.

L'Veyna fixed him with a pensive look. "How so?"

Horgar's laughter fizzled. "Huh?"

"How does Everyone," L'Veyna said, her voice a placid mountain lake, "sound like a she?"

Horgar sought help from Prack, but her brother's gaze was fixed on the town.

"You know how women are," Horgar mumbled. "Not you, of course. Just, you know…"

"I don't," L'Veyna replied. "Please…explain."

Horgar shrugged, his gaze dragging on the ground. "It's just something the crew would have said."

"A crew full of boys who wouldn't know a woman if she slapped them across the face. You mean that crew?"

The young pirate wilted from her gaze.

"Well, Horgar," she said, lacing her fingers like Jouler mid lecture. "As a soon-to-be woman, I can assure you, it's the men who believe they know everything."

"That's because we do," her brother joked.

"Prack…" Horgar whined with a pleading look.

"You got yourself into that one," Prack said, using his fingers and hand to imitate a man running off a cliff. "Charged right off it."

Horgar draped an uneasy smile, trying to hide the obvious hurt on his face. He was like an awkward stranger, trying to find his place among someone else's family.

A twinge of guilt wormed into L'Veyna's irritation. Even in the Alliance's unforgiving cold, her brother had been with her. Horgar had no one. Even after they rescued Jouler, Horgar would still be the stranger in a group of friends.

"I'm just teasing you," she said, giving him a playful bump. "Men really do know everything." Horgar offered a half-hearted chuckled, and L'Veyna bumped him again. "Come on. That was funny."

Horgar offered her a distracted nod, and L'Veyna followed his gaze to the town. No farmers wagoned their goods into Pegrans. No town guards manned the dilapidated gate. No loud din greeted them when they entered the frozen streets. The town languished in misery, a lame foal of the empire left to wither in the harsh tundra.

L'Veyna pulled her thick coat against a sudden chill knocking at her heart. Without the thick throng of Phaerians she'd seen in the other towns, a hushed despondency draped over Pegrans. What few people skulked the town, ducked into alleys and abandoned buildings. A loud crash startled a yelp from L'Veyna, and she huddled closer to her brother and Horgar.

"It was a sign," Prack said, pointing to a pile of broken boards. High above the pile, two frayed ropes twisted in a breeze. "Get it? A sign."

"You're not helping," L'Veyna said.

"I told you this place felt wrong." Prack peered down the wide avenue, and up the tall stacks of buildings, where empty clothes lines stretched from dark windows.

Horgar stared upward, his mouth agape. "I can see the sky. The blue sky."

"And it doesn't stink," L'Veyna said, breathing in the town's decaying aroma. "It doesn't smell good, but it's a lot better than every other town."

"Stay close," Prack said, his talons drumming his tsah.

"Maybe the Boorde killed everyone," Horgar said. "Cook them all for their meat."

"Boorde rarely eat people," Prack said. "Only when there's nothing else to eat. We don't taste that good. Not compared to cows, pigs, and cottlewomp."

Horgar's face skewed in confusion. "How would you know? Everyone knows Prytha only eat fruits and greens."

"He's bonded to a Boorde," L'Veyna explained.

"Bonded how?" Horgar asked.

"Life," Prack replied.

"More like mischief," L'Veyna said.

"Which is a part of life," Prack noted. "A necessary part, I might add."

"I still don't get what he sees in you," L'Veyna teased.

"I can't see inside him, he'd say." Prack chuckled, his emerald eyes drifting along a fond memory. He'd spent most of his life with Diou, exploring the empire, always together in pain and in joy. Prack laughed and joked, but he couldn't hide his heartsick—not from her.

Horgar spurted, hopping and pointing. "People! They aren't running away and hiding."

Down the wide, frozen avenue, a small crowd of townsborn gathered around a tall statue of a young Human girl. Carved from stone, her thick curled locks draped down her back, her stern face promising revenge for whatever wrongs those intense eyes had witnessed. The Humans knelt, bowing to the statue, and murmuring.

"I bet that's Makayla," Horgar whispered, gawking at the statue.

"It is," an old man said, approaching from the crowd. Dressed in drab, patch-worked clothes, he spread his arms in welcome. "May her light shine upon you."

"And guide your path," the crowd intoned.

"She's so pretty," Horgar said, still gawking.

"The Light blessed her with many gifts," the old man said.

"But, isn't *she* the Light?" L'Veyna asked.

"She is," the old man said. "Just as the sun lights the day, and the moon the night, so too does the Light encompass creation and Prophecy. The Light created the universe, and everything therein. Its power created the gods and Prophecy." The old man gestured to the tall statue of Makayla. "She is the embodiment of that power. The Light is the Light, and she is also the Light."

"That makes no sense," L'Veyna clacked.

Prack peered at the old man. "You don't seem surprised to see Prytha."

"Are you not from…oh, what's that name?" The old man tapped his lips. "Whamee…whantee…"

"Whawee," Prack said, and the old man snapped his finger.

"That's it. A group of them passed through here not three weeks ago. Headed to join the Voice in the north."

"Who made this?" Horgar asked, still enthralled by the statue.

"Why, I did," the old man replied, chuckling at Horgar's wide-eyed amazement.

"But…but how?" Horgar asked.

The old man held out a hand. L'Veyna's stomach churned, and a blue light popped to life over his palm.

Horgar yelped and scurried back a step, his eyes darting about.

"You can shape," Prack said.

"Lots of us can," the old man replied, banishing the light. "Well, a lot of us could before they all left."

"To join the Voice?" Prack asked, and the old man nodded.

"These bones are too old to take me that far. They barely get me out of bed." The old Phaerian knuckled the small of his back and gave a hearty chuckle. "No, I'll stay here, and leave all that fighting to the youngins."

"Forgive me," Prack said, "but you don't act like a townsborn."

"Know a lot of townsborn, do you?"

"Yes," Prack replied. "I do."

The old man's mirth faded, and he measured Prack with a calculating look. "Yes, I suppose you do." He gestured to the statue. "She Awakened us. All of us. The whole town. That's what we call it—the Awakening—because that's how it feels. Like, one moment you're you, and then you're waking up as the person you were always meant to be. For me..." L'Veyna's stomach churned again, and small flames danced at the tips of his fingers. "I was always meant to be a shaper."

L'Veyna's stomach churned once more, and the flames shot up and popped into small sparkling showers.

"Are you all right, my dear?" the old man said, reaching toward her with wormy fingers.

L'Veyna scooted back a step. "I'm fine. Just something I ate."

The old man's lifted brow said he knew better, but he didn't press.

"Did everyone leave to join this Voice person?" Prack asked.

"No," the old man said. "The few that didn't join Makayla or the Voice left town to live a skirter's life."

"But not you," L'Veyna said.

"Someone has to stay here," he said. "This place is sacred. It's where Makayla was born. It's where Prophecy broke its chains, and started us down the Path of Light."

"Did any Boorde pass through recently?" Prack asked, and the old man peered at the three of them.

"They have a friend of ours," L'Veyna said, keeping her voice calm despite her racing heart.

"A friend, you say..." The old man pointed west. "You're close. Less than half a day ahead. But, your *friend* didn't look in any trouble. More like..." The old man's gaze settled on Horgar, who still gaped at the statue. "More like a young Human among dangerous strangers." The old man tapped Horgar's shoulder. "I take it you like the statue?"

"I just..." Horgar tore his gaze away and beamed at the old man. "I just never thought I'd see her."

"You could stay here, you know?" the old man said. "Let your companions find their friend."

What? No! L'Veyna thought, her skin prickling around the thought of losing Horgar.

"Companions?" Horgar's head jerked back, and he stepped away from the old man. "They're my friends. And when their friend is in trouble, my friend is in trouble."

L'Veyna's chest warmed, her cheeks cramping with affection. She fought an urge to wrap Horgar in a tight hug, though she couldn't keep the smile from her face. The young Human swelled with pride, and L'Veyna swatted at him with a giggle.

"Please forgive me," the old man said, bowing. "I misjudged."

"Your heart was in the right place," Prack said, clapping the old man's shoulder. "You're a good man. It's a shame Makayla wasn't born somewhere warmer."

"That it is," the old man said with a chuckle. "I hope you find your friend before they reach the Blasted Lands."

Suspicion narrowed Horgar's eyes. "What makes you think they're headed there?"

"That's the only thing out there," the old man said with a flippant wave to the west. "It gets closer every year, you know."

"The Basted Lands?" L'Veyna asked, and the old man nodded.

"Maybe you can do something about it," he said. "Don't Prytha bear the power of life? Makes sense you'd be able to renew dead land."

Prack's eyes narrowed. "Forgive me for sounding suspicious, but, for a townsborn from Pegrans, you know a lot about my people."

"Praise be to Makayla for that," the old man said, and the zealots behind him intoned once more. The old man stepped back with a bow. "Good luck to you."

"And you," Prack replied, lead L'Veyna and Horgar down the wide avenue.

L'Veyna's thoughts danced around the young pirate. Even if Pegrans had little to offer, he could have stayed here among his own people. He knew the danger that awaited them, even if he couldn't comprehend that danger. How could he? He'd never seen a Boorde, much less an Ascended. She shivered at the memory of her failed attempt to rescue Jouler, when the firedancers had her pinned to a boulder, toying with the pesky leafeater the way cats toyed with their prey.

Horgar couldn't shape. He had no Power of Prophecy, or gift to empower him. He was a normal Human, like Pendric and Dilna, and he still trudged into danger.

All because we're his friends.

L'Veyna mulled over the thought, testing it against the friendships she'd made in Onatah. L'Veyna doubted any of her friends would have followed her to the edge of the forest, much less across the Blasted Lands.

Not even my parents.

Prack stopped them at the edge of town, pointing toward the wide horizon.

Ahead in the distance, four pillars of flame twisted into the sky, two pillars yellow, the other two blue.

NIGHT TWINKLED THE SKY, the half moon blinking behind rolling clouds. Breaking the darkness, four pillars of fire, two yellow and the others blue, coiled high into the air.

"Wait here," Prack said before disappearing in a blur of motion. He returned a few breaths later with a quizzical frown pulling his face.

"What is it?" L'Veyna asked. "What's wrong? Is Jouler okay?"

Prack shook his head, then he nodded. "He is, but…"

"But what?" L'Veyna said, rising to her feet.

Horgar stood beside her, mesmerized by the pillars. "Those aren't for Jouler, are they?"

"He's fine," Prack said. "More than fine. He's…" Prack shook his head. "Just…just come look."

Her brother led them down a lazy descent, keeping the fire to their right, just over the rise. When the ground leveled, he paused, a smile curling through his confusion. "He truly is M'Ljot."

Horgar shivered, and mumbled, "Harbinger of Death."

L'Veyna's heart skipped, her stomach fluttering with anticipation. "What about the Ascended?"

Prack's smile faded. He gestured for her to lead them down a game trail that headed toward the coiling pillars of fire. "You'll see."

L'Veyna headed down the trail, the chill night air defying the raging inferno. The half moon drifted high above, hanging over the blue and yellow pillars. Three people stood away from the conflagration, their figures silhouetted by the twisting flames. L'Veyna's heart recognized the smaller figure, even if the fire still hid him from her eyes.

That ancient familiarity swelled within her, cramping her cheeks in a smile, and pulling his name from her lips.

"Jouler."

37

A BURRIED PATH

Clouds drifted past Jouler, obscuring his view of the desecrated land far below. Only a sliver of the Astrakane Queendom remained. Where Codoine's glorious tiers had once challenged the sky, flat bone-white plains fell into a raging sea. Gone were the queendom's famed mountain ranges and lush pine forests. The causeway connecting Astrakane to Blailon faded into lifeless plains the empire eventually called the Blasted Lands.

A blasted lie, Jouler thought.

Far below, the ground shook in rhythm to the anger rising in his heart.

Boom…boom.

The so-called Sacrifice hadn't stopped some grand iniquity. Astrakane had never posed a threat to the empire.

Boom…boom.

The queen hadn't lost control of her queendom when she renounced the Paradigm and Three Laws. It resulted in raging prosperity, strengthening her rule, as it would have done for the rest of the empire.

Boom, boom, boom.

As it will *do for the empire, once I topple it.*

How many people drown when Astrakane sunk into the sea? Millions of souls, Human, Prytha, and Boorde, all lost to hide the truth Queen Laceyl uncovered. Without the empire pitting the kingdoms and races against each other, Prytha, Boorde, and Human communities would trade and flourish together. Without the Paradigm and the Three Laws demanding oppression, Phaerians would thrive and bring a new era of prosperity to the land.

Boom, boom, boom, BOOM!

The ground erupted where Codoine had once stood, and an impossibly black beam streaked toward Jouler, engulfing him in a void.

JOULER JOLTED AWAKE, bumping into L'Veyna, who'd insisted they sleep back to back. She hadn't left his side since last night, insisting he stay within earshot.

More like whispershot, Jouler mused.

"Huh?" L'Veyna mumbled, rolling over, her autumnal braids warmed by the soft campfire. "What did you say?"

"Must have been a dream," Jouler said, keeping his voice low to not arouse the others.

L'Veyna yawned and rubbed her eyes, then sat up into a stretch. "You were telling me how stars eat yellow trees..." Her face scrunched with confusion. "That makes as much sense as the old man in Pegrans."

"Who?" Jouler asked.

"Just some old Human who made no sense at all, talking about how Makayla is the Light, but also the Light is the Light. Did you see the statue?"

Jouler nodded. "She looked so...angry."

"That's what I said." Sleep still heavy in her emerald eyes, her gaze flitted to the eyepatch she'd asked for him, and a flash of anger marred her light-brown complexion. "Is it uncomfortable?"

Jouler ran his fingers over the black eyepatch, feeling the uncut emerald fixed to the center of the shield. "It feels fine."

"*Just fine?*" she clacked.

"*It feels good,*" Jouler tapped, and she smiled.

"I hate her," L'Veyna said, glaring at Ishariel's empty bedroll.

"No more than I." Jouler ran his fingers along Scorn and Wrath, inciting fond memories of Kherlyn's kindness and their deep conversations. Vaelithrae's long-bladed spear rested next to the daggers, a morbid reminder of the Ascended's unwavering loyalty to his team.

And to me, it seemed.

"Then why is she still here?" L'Veyna asked, holding her hands to the fire Ishariel had danced. Jouler gestured to the flickering flames, and L'Veyna rolled her eyes. "I can ask wood. We don't need her, or the skinny one."

"Tristian," Jouler said. "They pledged themselves to me."

"But she took your eye."

Jouler touched his eyepatch again, quelling his kindled anger. "I trust her. I trust them both."

"How can you say that?"

Horgar stirred on his bedroll, and Jouler put a finger to his lips.

"*How can you trust them?*" L'Veyna clacked, with a pointed look. "*They took you.*"

"She was betrayed by the person she trusted most."

"*So?*" she clacked, shouting with hard clacks.

"*Hold on. Let me finish,*" Jouler tapped, and she grumbled under her breath. "All the other Ascended turned on them. This whole time, Matron Nith'Iil, the person Ishariel trusted most, had planned to have her and her team killed and then leave their corpses in the Blasted Lands. She and Tristian are as homeless as you and I."

"*What's stopping them,*" L'Veyna clacked, "*from taking us to beg for their Matron's forgiveness? How can you just…be their friend—especially with her?*"

"I'm not," he said. "I'm not excusing what she did. I'll always hate her, but you know what it means for a Boorde to remove their hair."

L'Veyna's mouth quirked to the side, and she offered a begrudging nod. "Doesn't mean I'll ever forgive her."

"Nor do you have to," Jouler said, satiating a spike of anger. "Some things don't deserve our forgiveness, but that doesn't mean we can't trust them."

"If you say so." L'Veyna leaned against him, and he draped his arm and blanket over her shoulders. "The eyepatch does make you look… tough. Less like a farmer, and more like a Harbinger."

Jouler chuckled. "I guess there's that."

L'Veyna shot him a teasing smile. "Did you miss me?"

Same old L'Veyna, Jouler thought with a chuckle. "I already told you a thousand times I did."

L'Veyna rolled her eyes and nuzzled against him. "Barely a dozen."

Jouler stared into the fire, mesmerized by its flickering dance. His mind drifted to Horgar and Prack, sleeping across from them, their soft rumbles drifting on the gentle breeze. The young man reminded Jouler of Pendric. Mostly the braggadocios part, especially around L'Veyna. Not that Jouler blamed Horgar. Her beauty made sunsets seem dull, her smile like a warm blanket around the soul.

"What did you dream?" she asked, interrupting his thoughts.

"Just now?" he said, her aroma, the scent of dew on a golden meadow, sparking memories of Headwater in the late summer, just before fall, when the mornings turned brisk.

She nodded against his shoulder. "What woke you up?"

"One of those dreams I've been having," he said. "The ones about the Blasted Lands."

"That's nice," she replied, her voice thick with sleep. She yawned and snuggled against him. "What else?"

"This time," he said, as much to help her fall back asleep as to help him understand his dream, "I saw the aftermath of the Sacrifice, right after it happened."

"Mhmm," she mumbled, nodding again.

"It was wild," he said. "Astrakane was so beautiful. You would have loved it."

"Who's Astrakane?" she asked, poking his side with her elbow.

"Not a who," Jouler said. "A what. Astrakane was the queendom the empire sunk into the ocean."

Her head jerked up, and she peered at him. "You saw that?"

"I think I used to live there," he said.

Her brow wrinkled over her sparkling emerald eyes. She yawned again and returned her head to his shoulder. "I think being stuck with those Boorde has muddled your brain." Her gaze wandered to the Ascended's empty bedrolls. "Where are they?"

"Out there," he said, with a flippant wave. "Making sure we're safe."

"Or planning a trap," L'Veyna said. "Are you sure we can trust them?"

"I am," Jouler replied, her blissful aroma stirring thoughts of a wagon ride to Alduos. Remembering that first day of that miserable trek stirred a chuckle.

"What's so funny?"

"I was thinking about a trip Kael and I took. We'd drank a little too much ale the night before, so we were sick the whole first day. Kael more than me, but gods curse me if I wasn't miserable. See, Kael, he'd been having these…"

Jouler's mouth went dry.

"He'd been having what?" L'Veyna asked, nudging him.

"Dreams," he whispered.

Kael had always said they felt so real. His dreams that were not dreams. The ones about the alabaster-skinned girl.

Of Makayla.

"Have you been having strange dreams?" he asked.

"No," L'Veyna said. "Why?"

"Kael had the same types of dreams I'm having," he said, trying to keep up with his racing mind. "His were about a Phaerian village. Maybe Headwater, but we were never sure. It could have been anywhere, honestly. Well, not *anywhere*—"

"Focus, Jo," L'Veyna said, jabbing his side.

"Right," he said, sprinting down his train of thought. "Kael dreamed of Makayla, and—"

"Are *you* dreaming of her?"

"No, let me finish. Kael's dreams were about Makayla. Mine are about Codoine."

L'Veyna yawned again and rubbed her eyes. "Can you explain it to me like I'm still half asleep?"

"Sorry," Jouler said, struggling against his jumbled thoughts. "I'm not making sense to myself, either. Let me start over. Kael said he had dreams that felt too real to be dreams. Those dreams were of Makayla."

"Who had alabaster skin."

"In his dreams," Jouler noted. "From what I've gathered, her skin is as brown as mine. Anyway, Kael had these dreams, and after we arrived in Onatah…" His voice trailed, realizing he'd charged right into the worst day in L'Veyna's life—the day her god Tálise had died. "I'm sorry. I didn't mean to bring that up."

"It's okay," she said, though Jouler heard the pain in her voice. "What—" She cracked another yawn. "What does it all mean?"

"I don't know," Jouler replied. "It could mean we're on the right path. It could be a warning we're not. If Kael was here, I could compare our dreams and maybe figure something out. As it is, we might as well be floundering in a void."

Or a beam of darkness.

Jouler wondered about the meaning behind the black beam. Had the dream been real, a window into the past like his other dreams, or had Prophecy injected a dose of symbolism?

"Speaking of which," L'Veyna said, yawning again. "I think I need to find my own void." She patted his arm and crawled onto her bedroll. "Jouler?" she said, wiggling on her bedroll. "Will you lay down?"

He settled on his bedroll, and L'Veyna scooted to press her back against his. The scent of dew on a late summer meadow caressed his senses, easing his troubled mind, and carrying him to sleep.

L'Veyna followed Horgar's gaze back toward the four pillars of fire, still twisting into the distant morning sky.

"Beautiful, isn't it?" Ishariel said, the scar covering the side of her head tugging at L'Veyna's attention as much as her bald scalp. Hers and Tristian's, their head as smooth and white as Katima's.

"It's fire," L'Veyna grumbled, refusing to acknowledge anything the foul woman did as beautiful. No matter how majestic and captivating the blue and yellow pillars were, she'd never praise that woman.

Horgar turned back around, his gaze catching on L'Veyna before resting on Jouler and his eyepatch. The young Human hadn't spoken much since they caught up with Jouler, especially not when Ishariel and Tristian were near. The young pirate still gawked at the tall Boorde, like now, his mouth agape, thoughts roiling behind his dark eyes.

"We should reach the Blasted Lands by tomorrow," Tristian told Jouler. "Do you really believe your plan to wheel in a cart full of dirt is going to work?" The tall, skinny Ascended measured Prack and Horgar. "Ishariel and I can carry one each." Ishariel lifted an eyebrow, and he dipped his head. "If we had to."

"Was that your plan for Jouler?" Prack asked, clicking his tongue. "To carry him?"

"Precisely," she replied.

"What about sleep?" L'Veyna asked.

"Boorde can go a few days without it," Ishariel replied. "Enough to get us to Codoine."

"The handcart should work," Jouler said. "In theory, L'Veyna should still be able to ask if she has Currents-rich soil. Which means she should be able to repair whatever damage the Blasted Lands cause to the wheels."

"Should," Tristian said. "Do you not think someone has already tried that approach?"

"Not to my knowledge," Prack said. "Keepers rarely, if ever, leave their forest. Even when they do, none come here."

"Until now," Tristian said, gracing L'Veyna with a sympathetic look. "Vidimir told us about your home and the Curse."

"We will not let that happen," Ishariel said, her pale fire-diamond eyes flashing.

"You can't stop Prophecy," L'Veyna said, their passion chipping at her distrust. Yesterday, they'd bowed to her, pressing their forehead to the ground to pledge themselves to her and Jouler, but she'd never trust them like she did Diou and Katima. They couldn't just abduct Jouler, take his eye, and expect to be friends.

"Unlike the lower races," Ishariel said, earning a sneer from L'Veyna, "Boorde view the Prophecies more like fire." She held out her hand, and a dancing flame flickered over her palm. "The flame is hot, regardless of its shape. Likewise, Prophecy will be fulfilled, no matter which path It takes. We will free your people, young L'Veyna. How we free them is not up to Prophecy, just like the shape of a flame is not determined by its heat."

"So, Jouler," Prack said, his voice bouncing with mischief. "You should ask Horgar what he did before we stole him."

"They didn't steal me," Horgar said, turning to Jouler. "I was a sailor."

"He was a pirate," Prack said.

Jouler's brow climbed with excitement, the uncut emerald in his eyepatch catching the morning light. "You were a pirate?"

"No," Horgar said with a pleading look to L'Veyna.

"That's incredible," Jouler said, moving to walk beside the young Human. "I wish Pendric was here. He's always wanted to meet a pirate. I bet you have some amazing stories."

Horgar puffed his chest, shedding his bashful slouch.

"*He's going to say it,*" L'Veyna clacked to her brother.

"*Of course he is,*" Prack replied.

"*Say what?*" Jouler tapped.

Horgar beamed at Jouler. "Everyone knows pirates have the best stories."

THE EVENING SUN settled over the west Blailonian tundra. A long, narrow mound stretched westward to the flat horizon, awakening old memories of Jouler's travels along the once glorious causeway when Queen Laceyl Granivin reigned over Astrakane. He cast his gazed over jagged creeks that had once burst with life, cared for by Keepers and shapers alike. L'Veyna assured him the land still thrived, but she hadn't seen it before the Sacrifice.

Before the empire destroyed my home.

He let his rising anger drift to the biting winter chill, the soft smell of dried grass, and the sound of footsteps crunching in the snow. A heavy blanket would soon cover this barren land, dragging life to a frozen halt. Even terrentors, native to the Sunken Queendom, huddled in caves during Blailon's coldest weeks.

Jouler cradled his spear in his arm and flipped up the collar of his thick Boorde coat, the tail whipping at his ankles. He wondered how long the garment would keep him alive in a blizzard. With his stout Boorde boots, a thick wool cap, and enough food…

He chuckled at his hubris. Terrentors, the largest predator in Torgeir, hid away in caves during Blailon's coldest season, but Jouler, the farmer from Headwater, could tough it out in a coat and boots.

"What's so amusing?" Tristian asked, walking beside him.

"My pride," Jouler said, earning a confused frown from the slender Boorde. "I was wondering how difficult it would be to survive one of Blailonian's infamous blizzards."

"For a Boorde," Tristian said, and shrugged. "With a decent slab of meat, I suppose it would be no more difficult than any other day."

"What about a Human?" Jouler asked, the black-steel cap of his spear clinking on rocks hidden beneath the snow.

"I'd say about as difficult as digging to the center of Yrsa." Tristian frowned in consideration. "With a teaspoon."

"Then let's hope we don't run into a blizzard."

"I think the blizzard would run into us," Tristian said.

"Do blizzards run?" Prack mused, joining the conversation.. "I think they float."

"Or drift," Jouler offered.

Ishariel fixed them with an unamused stare. "Are you really debating the movement of blizzards?"

"Actually," Prack said, raising a taloned finger, "blizzards touch the ground, so they could walk, or run."

"Or charge," Tristian said.

"What do you think?" Jouler asked Ishariel.

"I think incinerating you would be a kindness to the world."

L'Veyna's long, emerald-jeweled ears perked, and she squeezed between Jouler and Ishariel. "Handing Dra'Nahl victory would be a kindness?"

"I spoke in jest," Ishariel said. "But you bring up a good point. You assume Jouler's death wouldn't serve the Light."

"Okay," Jouler said. "You've piqued my curiosity."

Ishariel looked down at him, amusement quirking her lips. She held out her palm, and thin lines of fire raced above her hand, warming her scarred face. The flame darted and swirled into a small depiction of Mh t'Pralab, the Wall of Prophecy. "There is no denying the Prytha Prophecy shows what will happen if you lead the saplings to war. It's quite literally carved into stone." The fiery image of the wall swirled into a glowing book. "Similarly, the Human Prophecy is written on paper." The fiery book burst into a sparkling shower, and she let her alabaster-white hand fall to her side. "But not the Boorde Prophecy, which is a compilation of nebulous, dream-like visions."

"What's your point?" L'Veyna asked.

"Why is the Boorde Prophecy different?" Ishariel replied. "Why did we get nebulous visions, while the other Prophecies are set in stone and paper?"

Prack clicked his tongue. "Our Prophecy was given directly from Alnazet."

"So says your Prophecy," Ishariel retorted, sucking her teeth. "I would deign to assume the gods suddenly lifted their voice from the world, leaving Prytha and Humans to squabble over poorly worded lines. Doesn't it seem more likely they were *all* interpreted from visions?"

"Or dreams." Jouler shared a look with L'Veyna.

"If the Dawn is truly composed of five Facets," Ishariel continued, "maybe slaying the Harbinger of Death is precisely how we usher in the Time of Plenty."

"That can't be true," Jouler said. "Every Facet is needed to ensure the Light's victory over the Dark. Incinerating me would destroy Yrsa."

The silence of his gift settled over him, suffocating his thoughts.

"That could very well be true," Ishariel conceded, dipping her head in a bow. "But on the other hand, my ears wouldn't bleed from mind-numbing ramblings about the movement of blizzards...which obviously storm across the land. Sacred Flame, I can't believe I had to point that out."

Jouler, Prack, and Tristian burst into laughter, while L'Veyna sneered.

Horgar chuckled and rolled his eyes at them. His foot caught a rock, and he stumbled, almost tripping to the ground. Warbling his arms, he recovered his balance, and rolled his eyes again, reigniting the laughter.

"What if," Tristian said, once their mirth faded, "the Human and Prytha Prophecies only tell of death and destruction because they're incomplete?"

The question hung in the air, tickling Jouler's curiosity.

"Incomplete?" L'Veyna asked with a bite to her voice.

"Exactly," Tristian replied. "Boorde Prophecy gets more refined with each vision. The other Prophecies are stagnant. As Ishariel said, literally chiseled into rock and written in millennia-old books. What if those Prophecies are stagnant because Humans and Prytha don't have Seers?"

"What if..." Jouler wrestled over a cloud of implications roused by his silent gift. "What if those Prophecies aren't about the choices we should make? What if they're warnings of paths we were never supposed to take?"

His gift stirred with the words.

38

THE BLASTED LANDS

Horgar's "Everyone knows" stories rolled off Jouler's mind, skittering around his troubled thoughts.

Maybe the Prophecies were warnings of paths not *to take…*

He hadn't been completely wrong. His gift had stirred as if not enough of what he said was true, just like the book Emril had given him.

Jouler scanned the flat horizon for Tristian and Ishariel, his arms and legs still aching from his morning lesson. He touched the uncut emerald in his eyepatch, its rough edges dulling his anger. He'd sent them to measure the distance to the Blasted Lands, more to get Ishariel out of his sight than a need to know. He eyed his shadow, guessing four blessed hours had passed without having to endure her scarred presence.

"…easily as long as the hull," Horgar said, his incredulous claim snagging Jouler's attention. "I'll wager you never caught a fish that big."

"How could I?" Jouler said. "The ocean is over a hundred miles away from my hometown."

"Everyone knows a hundred miles isn't nothing to sailor."

"That's very true," Jouler pointed out, clearing his throat to hide his smile. Maybe it was Horgar's innocent worldview, his problems easily solved with a sturdy line and a sail full of wind. Maybe it was the way he fawned over L'Veyna and floundered for her attention. It didn't matter, but the boy had grown on Jouler.

"Nothing better than being a sailor," he said, sneaking a peek at L'Veyna, who walked beside her brother.

"She's beautiful, isn't she?" Jouler said.

"Yeah…" Horgar mumbled, then sputtered, seeming to realize what he'd said. "No, I don't—I mean, yes, she is, but I don't…I mean I'm not…" He breathed a heavy sigh. "I don't think of her like that. I know she's your girl and all."

Jouler chuckled, shaking his head. "She's not my girl."

"But I see you holding hands and cuddling."

"That's just her culture," Jouler said. "Prytha are an affectionate people. That's why everyone—well, Humans anyway—believe they're…shall we say, promiscuous?"

"Sure?" Horgar said, with a shrug. "But the way she looks at you. I don't know, I just thought…"

"Ah, that," Jouler said. "We share a special bond. All Facets do. You know that feeling when you come home after a long voyage—that familiarity that satiates your homesickness?"

"The sea was always my home," Horgar boasted.

"Okay," Jouler said, swallowing his impatience. "Do you miss the sea?"

"Of course."

"How do you imagine it will feel when you finally get back on a ship?"

"Like coming home," he said.

"And familiar," Jouler offered, and Horgar nodded. "Imagine that same familiarity, except it feels like it's been there for thousands and thousands of years. That's why she looks at me like that."

"So you don't, you know…like her that way?"

"Gods no," Jouler said with a chuckle. "She's still a little girl. She's only thirteen."

"Yeah," Horgar said with an uneasy chuckle.

"You're what, sixteen?" Jouler guessed.

"Fifteen," Horgar corrected.

"That's only two years' difference," Jouler said. "I'm nineteen."

"So? The Captain was older than you, and he—"

"I'm *not* your captain," Jouler said, and Horgar winced. "Where I'm from, girls aren't considered women until they're old enough to be a proper mother. Same with men, except with being a father, obviously."

"What's this I hear?" Prack said, skipping into the conversation. "Men aren't men until they're old enough to be mothers?"

"Whose mother?" L'Veyna chimed, squeezing between Jouler and Horgar. "What are you two rambling about?"

"Men becoming mothers," Prack said. "Or something like that."

"Something like that," Jouler said with a chuckle. "What brings you to our lonely neck of the tundra?"

"You," she said, and Horgar's puffed chest deflated.

"And to what do I owe this honor?" Jouler asked, his sweeping bow pulling a chuckle from her lips.

Horgar jerked his thumb over his shoulder. "I'll just go over—"

"No!" L'Veyna snaked her arm around his, and he gave a contented sigh. "You stay," she said, and turned to Jouler. "How do you feel?"

Jouler raised a hand to his eyepatch. "Fine, I guess. Why?"

"You notice nothing different?"

"I take it you're not talking about the landscape?" he said with a sweeping gesture to the spatter of lichen-covered rocks and bushes poking across the flat snowscape.

"I mean with your gift," she said. "Is it acting strange?"

"I don't know. I haven't tested it lately."

"You have a gift?" Horgar asked.

"Of course he does," L'Veyna replied, taking Horgar's hand. "He *is* M'Ljot."

"The..." Horgar swallowed. "The Harbinger of Death?"

"Exactly," L'Veyna said, swinging the young pirate's arm.

Jouler's gift stirred, slow to snap into place.

"What was that?" L'Veyna asked, peering into his eyes. "Something just happened. It was your gift, wasn't it?"

Jouler nodded. "It was slow."

"Slow?" L'Veyna said, confusion wrinkling her brow.

"Yeah, like it doesn't want to snap into place. Why?"

"What exactly *is* your gift?" Horgar asked.

"I can tell when words of Prophecy are true," he replied.

Horgar's head jerked in confusion. "But…aren't you the Harbinger of Death?"

"He can also learn dead languages," L'Veyna said. "And any other language." She rolled her eyes. "And anything, apparently."

"It just seems odd," Horgar said. "I thought it would have something to do with, well, death."

"I think my gift has more to do with the Harbinger part," Jouler said, refraining from commenting on the Death portion of his title. No need to bring up the Sapling's Curse.

"What about you, L'Veyna? What's your gift?"

"I don't know. Maybe I don't have one. Or maybe," she said, wiggling her taloned fingers, "*I'm* the one with the power of death."

"Why the curiosity about my gift?" Jouler asked.

L'Veyna looked to Prack, and he nodded. She held out her palm, and a tea sphere splashed into existence, steaming over her hand.

"That's so amazing," Horgar said. "I'll never get over it."

"I asked without asking," L'Veyna said, handing the sphere to the young pirate.

"What do you mean?" Jouler said.

"It's like the asking already knows what I want. Like it's just waiting for me to tap into my ever-blossoming power."

"I take it that's not normal?" Jouler asked, his mind raging with implications. His gift waned while hers seemed to wax. Was this her Gift of Prophecy? Did it siphon the gift of others, or was it all coincidental?

"Asking takes effort," L'Veyna said. "Nothing just locks into place on its own. At least, not that I've heard."

"Could it be," Jouler offered, "that you're transitioning to the next phase of Keeper? To whatever is after Bud?"

"Trunk," L'Veyna said. "And no. That's not how it works. We don't gain special powers. It gets easier to ask, but I've never heard of them locking into place on their own."

"Neither have I," Prack said. "Something like that would be common knowledge, especially among Keepers."

"Maybe your gift is finally manifesting," Jouler said.

"Sounds better than yours, Jo," Horgar said, sipping the last of his tea.

"I agree," L'Veyna said with a playful sneer for Jouler.

The sun dipped past its zenith by the time Ishariel and Tristian returned. Packs bouncing on their backs, they ran toward them, bald scalps fading against the snow.

About six hours there and back, Jouler thought, guessing it would take as long for everyone to reach the Blasted Lands from here.

Ishariel and Tristian bowed to Jouler and L'Veyna, no more out of breath when they stopped than if they'd jogged the whole way.

"To say there is nothing in this land," Ishariel said, "is an insult to nothing."

"There's still life here," L'Veyna said. Her gaze went distant, and she shivered. "Not a lot, but it's..." She shivered again, and gagged as if tasting something vile. "Ack. Never mind, I take it back. It's not right here. Not right at all."

"It's the Blasted Lands," Ishariel said. "They're spreading."

"They've always been spreading," Prack said.

"Not like this," Tristian replied, slipping his pack from his shoulders and weighing it in his hands. "I hope we have enough meat." Tight-lipped, he slipped on his pack again. "Not that this cursed land has anything to offer, if we don't."

"We'll be fine," Ishariel said with a sharp tone of finality. She ran a hand over her bald scalp, her too-black firedancer dress whipping in the sharp wind. "We'll ration."

"Then let us not delay," Tristian said, and bowed to Jouler. "I am afraid I must cease our lessons."

"My aching muscles thank you," Jouler said, returning the bow.

They walked in contemplative silence, the weight of their inexorable task lightened by a round of ha'ath tea. At least L'veyna's power seemed to improve as they neared the Blasted Lands. Strange that his would weaken, but then, she was the Warden of Preservation. Her gift could be reacting to the needs of the land, a desire to be whole again, and who better to do it than the Prytha Facet?

When Ishariel stopped them, the languid sun dipped toward an endless sea of white, pulling its twinkling blanket of darkness. A few hundred paces ahead of them, the Blasted Lands cut a sinuous line across the tundra. No snow or lichen touched the flat landscape, only bone-white powder.

"We're here," Ishariel said, pressing a hand to her stomach.

Jouler clenched the hilt of his daggers, enduring a wave of fear. The few people who'd ventured into the Blasted Lands never returned. Authentic accounts, not like the legends enshrouding the Kralnach Hills.

Horgar shielded his eyes against the setting sun. "Is that a line of steam?"

"That's the Blasted Lands spreading," Tristian said, pointing to what looked like a thin line of steam running north and south across the land. "It's actually blasted powder, lifting as it eats the land." He made a gesture like puffing smoke. "There and gone."

Jouler's fear rolled up his back, and he raised his fingers to his eyepatch, finding a strange comfort in the uncut emerald. "We'll rest here for the night."

L'Veyna doubled over and vomited. Prack rushed to her side, but she waved him away. "I'm fine," she said, her stomach clenching again. "It's the land. Even this close, it makes me sick."

"Let's head back a league or so," Tristian said, also holding his stomach. "We'll find no rest here."

L'Veyna and the Boorde, all three sickened by the Blasted Lands, while Jouler, Horgar, and Prack seemed unaffected.

Lands bereft of the Currents of Power.

The connection seemed obvious, but not how. Ishariel and L'Veyna both wielded magic, but not Tristian. No special powers coursed through the slender Boorde's veins. Why was he sick and not Prack?

Or me?

Other than his waning gift, nothing had changed. No weakness or confusion. No urge to vomit.

"Prack, can you shift?" he asked.

"I…" He clicked his tongue. "Maybe?"

"It's our connection to the Currents," Ishariel said, reading Jouler's face. "Meat staves our sickness."

"Hence Tristian's concern about having enough," Jouler said. "But why does it make L'Veyna sick too? Why is my gift fading, while hers grows stronger? It has to be connected to the Currents, but how?"

"Come," Prack said, helping his sister away from the Blasted Lands. "Let's discuss it over a warm fire."

"And tea," L'Veyna mumbled. "Lots and lots of tea."

L'Veyna quirked her mouth at the diagram Jouler had sketched into the ground. The handcart seemed simple enough, but did the wheels have to be so large? It made the thing look…well, awkward.

"What about water?" she asked, and he stared at her as if she'd spoken some strange language. "Water. You know, the thing that makes my askings stronger, unlike soil. I'd have to make the cart a little bigger to hold enough, maybe twice the size…"

"Too heavy," Jouler said. "What about a couple barrels? Would that work?"

"That'll barely do anything for my askings," she mumbled. "The cart is already too small to make much of a difference. Lakes, rivers, or even a nice-sized stream or pond, that's what I really need."

"What about three barrels?" Jouler asked, frowning at the sketch, his chin cupped in his hand. "Every little bit helps, right?"

L'Veyna sighed over a sharp retort, unamused by his enthusiasm.

It's far too early for happy, she thought, sipping her hot tea. No jumping around or exuberant chatter before she finished her first sphere. At least he and Tristian hadn't startled her awake with their incessant training.

"Why not make the cart smaller?" she asked, grasping for things to vent her annoyance. "It seems a little big for some dirt."

"Hence the oversized wheels," Jouler said, beaming with a dumb smile. "Makes it easier to push larger loads. I want to make sure we have plenty of soil. We don't know what's going to happen once we get deep into the Blasted Lands."

"Fine," she mumbled. "Can I at least finish my sphere?"

"I guess so," he replied, noticing her glare. "I mean, yes, of course."

"Alone…"

"Ah, yes." Jouler jerked his thumb over his shoulder. "I'll go check on Horgar."

L'Veyna put her tea to her lips before she barked some hurtful insult, letting sweet currents of ha'ath sweep her irritation away.

If only it was that easy, she thought, pulling her thick coat against the crisp morning air, and mumbling a curse to the frozen climate.

She sipped the last of her tea, wishing she'd asked a larger sphere, and settled into her miserable work. Sitting in the Posture of Root, legs folded, hands resting on her knees, she examined Jouler's diagram. The handcart seemed simple enough. She still didn't think it needed to be so big, but she wouldn't be pushing the rotten thing. Besides, she'd much rather say she'd told him so than have to listen to him whine about the cart being too small.

She conjured an image of the plagued thing—two enormous wheels on an open box filled with healthy soil, an arm bar, and four rods to keep it from tilting too far. Without asking, her power flared within her, ripping the image from her mind, and forcing it into reality.

She stumbled, clutching her head, and her brother rushed to her side.

"What happened?" Prack asked, peering into her eyes. "What was that?"

"I'm fine," she said, pushing him back. "It's nothing."

"That wasn't nothing," her brother said.

"It's like when I asked in the Alliance," she said, rubbing the back of her head and neck. "But worse." She leaned away from her brother's searching gaze. "I'm fine. Just a little headache."

"No more asking until done with this place," Prack said, and L'Veyna rolled her eyes.

"And I guess we're supposed to grow leaves and eat sunlight?"

Seeming oblivious of everything but the handcart, Jouler examined L'Veyna's work, rubbing his chin, the uncut emerald in his eyepatch glimmering in the morning sunlight. He moved behind the hand bar and lifted it with ease, then he dug in his heels and pushed. After some effort, the cart creaked forward.

"Ha!" he shouted in triumph. "It works!"

"It's a handcart," Ishariel said, folding her arms. "Not a water clock."

"A perfectly balanced handcart," Jouler said, holding it level with one hand.

"Cute." Ishariel sucked an elongated canine. "If everyone is quite done stalling, we have Blasted Lands to conquer."

Horgar ducked under the hand bar to help Jouler. "Everyone knows it's easier with two people."

Jouler gave the young pirate a playful nudge, and they set the cart into motion behind the two Ascended.

"Are you sure you're all right?" Prack asked, walking beside L'Veyna. "Maybe you should ask a bunch of food now, before we get into the Blasted Lands. I don't imagine it will get easier once we get there."

"Prack's right," Jouler said, halting the cart. "Maybe we should head back where it won't hurt to ask."

"It's not that bad, honest." L'Veyna looked back at the snow-laden tundra and its windy promises of frozen limbs. Here at least the pain passed quickly, unlike warming icy skin.

"I'll just do it here," she said, crouching into the Posture of Root. Rubbing the dull ache in the back of her head, she gritted her teeth, bracing herself against the wave of pain, and asked.

"You want me to take a turn?" Horgar asked amid an endless sea of white.

"Save your strength for later," Jouler said, blowing sweat from his lips. The drops beaded on the blasted ground, evaporating in moments. Arms cupping the crossbar, he pushed the handcart with his torso, each muffled footstep landing with a soft puff. Behind them, thin trails of powder lifted from the wheels and fell without dusting the air, the cart's path smoothing over almost as quickly as it formed.

His concern drifted to L'Veyna and the two Ascended, who seemed to grow worse with each passing mile. Especially L'Veyna, face contorted in misery, her coat crusted with vomit.

Horgar kicked the ground, and clumps of lifeless white powder rose a few feet in the air before plummeting back to the ground with lazy puffs.

"We need to stop," Prack mumbled, clutching his head with a grimace of pain.

"No," Jouler said, despite the ache festering his body. Stopping meant death. "We tried that and your sister had to fix the wheel."

Ishariel halted, leaning on Tristian for support. "You might be ready to march straight to Codoine, Vidimir. But us mere mortals need rest."

"Little Sprout," Prack called when L'Veyna kept walking forward. "Sprout… L'Veyna!"

She startled and turned, her brow wrinkled in confusion. "Brother?"

Jouler lowered the handcart stands and released the crossbar with a heavy sigh. The stands hit the ground with a dull thud, dumping a handful of apples and oranges. The fruit melted into lifeless white powder, portending a morbid fate if they stopped for too long.

"Just a little rest," Prack said, clutching his head.

Jouler stretched and kneaded his sore muscles. "Not too long. I don't want your sister to ask if she doesn't have to."

"Is she all right?" Horgar said, handing Jouler a waterskin.

L'Veyna winced, pressing a hand to the side of her head. She looked around as if confused, not seeming to notice Jouler's approach.

"Are you okay?" He rested his hand on her shoulder and she jumped.

"Jouler?" she asked, peering at him. She crouched, clutching her head. "Why is my head so tight? It's so hard to think."

"It's this place," Jouler said, but she didn't seem to hear.

"Everyone is sick but us," Horgar said.

"It has to do with magic and the Currents," Jouler said. "It explains why it took longer for the Blasted Lands to affect Prack, and why Ishariel is worse off than Tristian."

"But you have magic." Horgar swallowed. "You're, you know, the Harbinger of You-Know-What."

"You mean my gift?" Jouler asked, and the young pirate nodded. "It's gone as far as I can tell."

"But you're not sick like them," Horgar said, gesturing to the others.

"Maybe it's because we're Human," Jouler offered.

Horgar shrugged and gave a worried look to L'Veyna. "What are we going to do?"

"Horgar?" L'Veyna said, as if recalling the name. She looked up at Jouler. "What...what are we doing here? Where are we?"

Horgar yelped, hopping. "My soles—they're gone!"

Jouler lifted his boot and swore. "Mine are almost gone too." He cursed again and raced to the handcart. Lifting the crossbar off the stands, he pushed and felt the flat spot on the wheels.

Thump...thump...thump.

"Damn this godsforsaken place!" Jouler cursed, making sure their packs and weapons wouldn't fall out of the wagon. "Get up, everyone. We have to keep moving."

"What about our feet?" Horgar said, no longer hopping.

"Looks like they'll be fine," Jouler replied. "Does it hurt?"

Horgar shook his head, stomping a foot, and L'Veyna winced. The young pirate unlaced his boots and kicked them off. "Feels kind of good, actually. Weird, but not in a bad way."

Jouler did the same, setting his boots in the handcart, and letting his bare feet touch the blasted ground. The soft powder tingled his bottom of his feet, similar to the way the metallic tubes of Prophecy had felt in his hands.

"Feels weird, don't it?" Horgar said, wiggling his toes in the lifeless powder.

"Help me get everyone else into the cart," Jouler said. "Hopefully, the Currents-rich soil will help them feel better."

"But if they're all in there…" Horgar's brow wrinkled with doubt. "We can't carry them all, can we?"

"We don't have a choice," Jouler replied, pushing the cart toward the falling sun.

THUMP…THUMP…THUMP…

Jouler pushed through the ache radiating throughout his body, cursing the moon for taking so long to cross the night sky. The bottoms of his feet burned, the skin raw from the inexorable decay of the Blasted Lands.

A cramp balled his calf, and he cursed, stretching out his leg and hobbling until the cramp released.

"How…much…longer?" Horgar panted, pushing from the back of the handcart.

Thump…thump…thump…

"If…we stop," Jouler said between breaths, "the cart…will turn… to powder."

He looked over his shoulder, noting how much smaller the wheels had gotten. L'Veyna sat on the edge of the cart, hands buried in the dirt, her head on her brother's shoulder. Lying on her back, Ishariel winced in rhythm with the imperfect wheels, while Tristian slouched with his eyes closed.

Thump…thump…thump…

Something about the rhythmic noise worried Jouler. Something important, but his exhaustion ripped it from his mind. He slapped his face, focusing on his pain to help keep him awake. His head throbbed, his chest raw from the crossbar, while his throat begged for water. His calf cramped again, then the other. He halted, unable to walk, and bent over to pull up his toes. His thighs cramped, and he fell with a cry of pain.

Prack's head bobbed, and he jerked awake. Stretching, he groaned, "Are we there?"

"Come here, Jo, so—" L'Veyna yawned, infecting everyone around her. "Come here so I can heal you. You too, Horgar."

Knowing better than to argue, he worked his way to his feet, and waddled to the side of the handcart. She folded her legs in the Posture of Root, and placed a hand on their head. She cried in agony, and a shiver coursed through Jouler, loosening his knotted muscles, softening his aches, and mending his raw feet. Relieved of pain, exhaustion poured through him, and his knees almost buckled. Horgar shivered beside him, cracking a yawn.

"You need water too." Gritting her teeth, she grunted in pain, and two orbs materialized over her hands.

"Thank you," Jouler said, deciding he'd wait to tell her she needed to repair the wagon wheels too. He sipped his sphere, cool fresh water soothing his parched throat.

"And the wagon," she said with a deep sigh.

"I wasn't going to say anything."

"I could see it in your eyes." Tears streamed down her cheeks, her brother mirroring her anguish. She drew a deep breath, closed her eyes, and screamed.

Prack pulled her into his arms, and the handcart rose a few inches, the wheels returning to their normal size.

Burdened with guilt, Jouler returned to the crossbar, not daring to get too comfortable. His legs throbbed, eyelids heavy with the exhaustion that soaked his body.

"Jo, you can't keep going on like this," L'Veyna mumbled, sounding just as tired as he.

Jouler's eye shut, and his head bobbed.

No!

If he stopped, the cart would disintegrate, the soil would blast, and everyone would die.

"Jouler..." L'Veyna's voice trailed as she slumped into oblivion beside her brother, the emerald jewels in their long pointed ears sparkling in the moonlight.

Horgar slumped against the cart and sank to his knees.

"Get up," Jouler said, nudging him with his foot. "Get in the cart." Horgar shook his head, and Jouler kicked him. "Get in the blasted cart before I leave you here."

Horgar scowled, but obeyed, crawling onto the dirt, and lying with a heavy sigh.

Jouler settled behind the crossbar, shaking the sleep from his head.

Now, bend and lift, he told himself.

His eyelids closed, and he wavered on his feet.

"No!" he said, slapping his face. Reaching through his fatigue, he summoned his will, bent to pick up the crossbar, and fell into darkness.

THE SAPLINGS TRAIL

Alerix startled awake in his hammock, a hand pressed over his mouth, vines binding his arms and legs. Chest pounding, he focused on his breathing to calm his racing mind and clear his weary vision. Moonlight beamed through his window, twinkling in a pair of apatite-colored eyes.

Tai'Enth?

He relaxed, and she pulled her hand away, the vines writing back into his floorboards. Shouts from his fading dreams seemed to seep into the waking world. Dreams of battle and raging fire. Of Onatah, ravaged by d'Tormena.

Rubbing his eyes, he slid off his hammock, his bare feet slapping on the cold wood floor. The distant clash of battle still rang clear in the air, and a dark realization draped over Alerix.

That's no dream. The empire had broken through.

His gaze settled on Tai'Enth, and he noticed her combat shirt and pants, colored to blend in with the forest.

"Get dressed," she clacked against her beltboard. *"It's time."*

THE FAMILIAR SCENT of Alerix's well-worn barkarmor—wood, moss, and the gentle musk of sweat—eased his troubled mind. Killing imperials was one thing. Killing his own forest kin…

He flipped the long, woven tail of his braided hair over his shoulder and squeezed the haft of his chk'da, wishing it would temper the sickness plaguing his heart.

Tai'Enth placed her palm against the only section of wall in his office not covered by book-lined shelves, and a portal rippled in the wood.

"What about Orenda and the others?" Alerix asked, running their plan through his mind. Free the saplings, and get them out of the forest. Seemed simple enough, if not for the army of imperials digging at their garden, or Marun's sycophants plaguing Onatah's ranks.

"Don't worry about the Chosen," Tai'Enth said. "She is more than capable of taking care of herself *and* the others."

"But where'd she take them?" Alerix asked. "V'Nahuu can ask, but he's still a sapling."

Tai'Enth slid her arms around him and squeezed him in a hug. Her fragrance, moss on an autumn breeze, teased his senses, stirring memories of the innumerable perils they'd survived. Perils that made sneaking a handful of saplings out of the forest seem as easy as growing ha'ath.

Alnazet preserve us, he prayed, knowing it would take the power of a god to save his home.

"We," Tai'Enth said, stepping back and holding his hands, "need to worry about our role."

"Free the saplings," Alerix replied.

"The rest," Tai'Enth replied, cutting off his protest, "will be dealt with when we get there."

He took a slow, calming breath, letting the importance of their mission settle onto his back. Knowing he'd never be ready to kill his forest kin, he nodded to Tai'Enth, and followed her through the portal and onto the Sun Branch.

From the top of ta'Ajiilee's branches, the empire's devastating advance spread out below him. Ashen scars gouged into the Sacred

Forest, belching thick plumes of black smoke. Distant shouts floated up ta'Ajiilee from senseless ny'tein still scrambling on their community platforms. With the empire's front line almost within arrow shot of ta'Ajiilee, Alerix doubted any of them would live to see tomorrow.

Tai'Enth pressed a finger to her lips and pointed to the Cage Branch below, where the forest's saplings huddled in terror.

Alerix filtered through the distant sounds of battle and picked up muffled coughing and laughter from the Branch. It didn't seem that long ago he'd thrown Kael into the same cages that held the saplings. Kael and the other Human who could hardly breathe, who seemed to catch everyone's heart.

Even mine, I suppose.

Alerix crept down the ramp, the whispering breeze carrying his whispered steps away into the dark of night. He stopped when the Cage Branch came into view and crouched against ta'Ajiilee's trunk. Fourteen Keepers sat on the platform around the pulley system, sharing ha'ath while saplings sat in dangling cages. Alerix knew all fourteen Keepers, they all called him friend, but how many now followed Marun?

Alerix tightened his grip on his chk'da, and was about to shift onto the platform when the Keepers stood as one.

"We've been waiting for you," O'Nahaa said, looking at Alerix through the darkness. Moonlight cast her winter-green braids in a faint glow, her soft, ruby-colored eyes welcoming him down the ramp. "The Chosen of Alnazet sends her regards."

Relief flooded Alerix, his grip on his chk'da softening as the other Keepers set to raising the cages. He followed Tai'Enth down the ramp to greet her fellow Keepers. Talons clacked against beltboards, and ha'ath pipes exchanged hands as frightened saplings poured onto the platform.

O'Nahaa frowned at Alerix and waved him over for a hug. "You look...relieved."

Alerix returned the hug and accepted her ha'ath pipe. "I wasn't sure if Marun's people had snuck into your ranks."

"They did," O'Nahaa said, while the other Keepers gathered the saplings onto ta'Ajiilee's ramp. "We've known about them for weeks. Which is why they're not here."

"I hate to end our joyful reunion," Tai'Enth said, and Alerix returned O'Nahaa's pipe. "But we have a future to preserve."

O'Nahaa made the sign of the Sacred Tree. "The Chosen of Alnazet will meet you on the forest floor. We will provide the distraction. Godspeed, High Rose."

"May Alnazet preserve you," Alerix replied.

Tai'Enth waded through the frightened saplings, and pressed her palm to ta'Ajiilee's trunk, opening a large treewalk portal. "Shall we save our future?"

ALERIX STEPPED from the treewalk portal and into the deafening clamor of battle. Burning housetrees cast the night in a deadly glow, flames dancing along the empire's inexorable advance. A thick line of Prytha warriors and Keepers struggled against the overwhelming force, their flanks protected by a pair of towering Sentinels. The massive detritus golems slammed Humans unfortunate enough to slip too close to their clubbed fists.

A small round void opened near Onatah's left flank, sucking in debris, bending small trees, snapping branches, and devouring anything unfortunate to get too close. Prytha warriors and Keepers scrambled to flee, but the black sphere proved stronger, yanking them from the ground, their bodies shredded by the void's pull. One Sentinel leaped to save a screaming warrior, its arm ripped off and devoured alongside the Prytha. A moment later, the void burst with a violent explosion, obliterating the Sentinel and knocking half the surviving Prytha off their feet.

Alnazet's mercy. How could anything withstand such a force?

Terrified saplings poured past him from the treewalk portal, followed by Tai'Enth. "Where's Keeper Orenda?" he asked, herding the saplings toward the dark forest, away from the battle.

"We'll find her once we're safe," Tai'Enth said, helping him gather the younglings. "This way."

The saplings followed in silence, faces wide with terror. They didn't stop until the sounds of battle faded behind them, the warm light of the enemy's flames fading to the dark of night.

"Everyone, listen to me," Alerix whispered. "We're heading to the Saplings Trail. No talking, just walking. Is that clear?" They nodded. "You've been doing well so far. I'm proud of you." Whispered mumbles floated through the saplings, his praise turning a few smiles. Alerix scanned the darkness for Tai'Enth. "Where's the Keeper?"

A thick wall of brambles shot from the ground, surrounding them. The saplings' screams filled the air. Vines wrapped around Alerix's ankles and wrists, thorns digging into his skin, holding him fast. The wall of brambles parted, revealing Marun, moonlight washing his autumnal braids and smug face.

Marun's wicked smile dripped with satisfaction. "Tai'Enth is… permanently indisposed."

"You filthy rot!" Alerix shouted, consumed by rage. He fought against the vines, pulling and yanking. Thorns ripped his flesh, blood seeping from wounds. A vine snapped from his wrist, and three more replaced it.

"Impressive," Marun mumbled. "You didn't really think *none* of the Keepers guarding these plagued saplings were mine, did you?"

The wall of brambles shook, and Marun grunted, confusion twisting his face. His arms fell to the ground, cut above the elbows as if from an impossibly sharp blade. He crumbled into a sloshing heap, his torso sliced in half, blood steaming the frozen night.

More invisible blades chopped down the bramble wall, and sudden hot pain seared through Alerix's gut. Warmth spilled from his belly and splashed onto the ground. Falling into darkness, he watched the saplings float to a group of Humans with colorful cords wrapped around their shoulder.

40

AMBASSADOR

Frozen in place, sweat beaded down Dilna's face, dripping from her nose and chin, and soaking her ry'ku.

"Again," il'Diou said, his voice bouncing against the tall marble walls of the spacious, empty room.

She stood upright, her feet slapping on the cool marble floor, and she bowed at the waist. Daggers clenched in her hands, she entered the Second Basic Form, Tezrel, swirling her blade backward and slicing in a fluid motion. She swung her feet, gathering strength from her core, drawing upon her hatred for every last imperial bastard she'd had the misfortune of crossing in this blasted city—especially the self-important nobles and their stupid festivities. She jabbed her daggers, releasing a sharp yell.

"Tsuh!"

She twisted, jabbing to either side with another yell to help channel her strength. Flowing through Tezrel, she sliced and stabbed with both daggers—always with both—ending the Form with a powerful thrust.

"Tsuh!" Lungs screaming for air, she froze in place again, or as best she could, with quivering arms and legs.

That had to be the last set, she thought, doubting she could muster the strength for another round. She'd stopped counting after the thirtieth set, which seemed days ago.

Il'Diou's unreadable gaze drained her hopes of respite. "Again."

"But—"

His raised eyebrow silenced her with the memory of her Shai'jan's intolerance for disobedience. A hundred more sets of Tezrel sounded better than subjecting herself to il'Diou's creative punishments—making her sit against a wall, holding a ribbon with her arms held straight out, balancing a bucket of water on the end of a staff, or digging holes just to fill them.

She hid her irritation behind another sharp bow and flowed through the Form once more. Drawing on her anger to fuel her limbs, she imagined one of Eio's so-called nobles who'd slapped her for whatever offense they'd imagined. Every time she left the Ambassador's Wing, some Shield-baring bastard got their britches in a bunch over a Phaerian who dared stalk their "sacred" halls without the appropriate drab livery. The joy in their eyes over the prospect of getting to beat and maim her almost reach the same level of disappointment when they realized who they'd almost beaten—the now notorious Phlem Astasi.

"Again," il'Diou said.

Dilna slumped, gasping for breath, her cold daggers like mountains in her hands. "I…can't."

"You will," her Shai'jan said, his voice as hard as the lean muscles hidden beneath his too-black ry-ku. He looked odd in his pristine garments, her memories of him filled with his faded, worn out blouse, tattered belt, and frayed trousers. "And you'll keep doing it until you learn to purge your emotions."

"What if…" she said between breaths, "I…pass out?"

"Then you will have cheated in accomplishing your task," he said, fetching the water bucket. "Your blades will never glow until you learn to harmonize your inner flame. You must turn it from a chaotic inferno to a controlled blaze."

Dilna sheathed her blades and plunged her hands into the bucket, splashing the sweat from her face with the cool water. A wonderful idea crossed her mind, and she lifted the bucket to guzzle the crisp water, not caring how much soaked into her ry'ku and onto the marble floor.

Damn, that's good, she thought, wishing she could find something wrong with the water. *Never too cold, always pristine, and best of all…*

The bucket refilled, and she ladled a scoop of delicious water.

"No more strength, huh?" il'Diou said with a wry grin.

"Now I do," she said, dumping more water from the bucket to watch it refill.

"It's fascinating, isn't it?" he asked.

"And infuriating," she said. "Everyone should have one of these, not just lords and ladies. Do you know how useful this would have been on the farm? Especially the sinks that fill with warm water. I never would have complained about washing up for supper."

Her Shai'jan raised an eyebrow. "I doubt that."

"It's just…why?" Dilna asked. "Why can't everyone have clean water? It's not like I'm asking for everyone to live on floating islands. I just…" She fought for the right words to express how deep these nobles got under her skin. Or any noble, for that matter. "It just makes me angry. And when I'm angry…" She drew her daggers and jabbed with a sharp cry. "I'm stronger."

"But, are you?" il'Diou said, standing in front of her. "Stab at me with your daggers."

She thrust, and he stepped back, pulling her off balance. She swung her back foot around, but he caught it with his, and she toppled to the ground.

"Whether it's a duel or an argument," il'Diou said, helping her to stand, "control will always make you stronger. Now…" He patted his belly. "Use your anger to push me over."

She gave him a dubious look, but didn't hesitate to obey. Placing her hands on his iron stomach, she summoned an image of the yellow-haired idiot who'd sneered at her this morning, and she pushed with all the might her weary muscles could muster. As suspected, her steel-muscled Shai'jan didn't budge.

"Why couldn't you push me over?" he asked.

"You're a lot bigger and stronger," she said, stating the obvious.

"Exactly. Why would you ever believe you could muster enough anger to push me over?"

In a flash, he tipped her over and held her by the ankle. Dangling upside down, she crossed her arms and glared at him.

"Point taken."

He let her down, and she rolled to a stand.

"I get it," she said, sheathing her daggers. "I'll never be as strong as you. Or any other Boorde, for that matter."

"Not to mention most Human and Prytha men. At least, not the type you'll face in battle. To you, we might as well be mountains."

"So, how do I push over a mountain?" she asked.

"You don't *push*," he said. "You make the mountain crumble. Stand behind me. Now, kick me behind the knee. Make sure you—"

"Use my heel," she finished, and he dipped his head. She closed her eyes, focusing on her core—her inner flame. Anger, joy, sorrow, the annoying lordling who'd slapped her for wearing all black—they all went right into the flame, over, and over, and over until her inner flame blazed like the sun.

Opening her eyes, she kicked the back of il'Diou's knee. His leg buckled, and in quick succession, she drove her other heel into the back of his other knee.

He crumbled to the ground with a chuckle. "Very good," he said, getting back to his feet. "Had your heels been daggers, I would have been more helpless than a Phaerian in the Founders District."

"You're never helpless," she said.

"Even I have to sleep."

"Still not helpless," Dilna said, and the corner of his lips curled.

"Why did you follow with your other heel?" il'Diou asked, and Dilna shrugged.

"It just seemed right," she said. "Like the way water flows."

"And as water, you must be," il'Diou said, in his deep, rolling accent, "both gentle and powerful, conforming and forceful. Toss a pebble into the mighty Lake Skjold, and there it will sit, unchanged by the crushing depths. And yet, water can carve gorges through the tallest mountains, and drip holes through the hardest granite. Strength is far more than big muscles, ed'Dilna. It can be found in the mother and father who go without food, so their children can eat and be healthy. In the old man who gives his own life-saving medicine to save a baby." Il'Diou knelt and sat back on his heels, his eyes still level with hers. "And in the child who lost everyone she knew, and who keeps moving forward despite everything life throws in her path."

Dilna's cheeks warmed and cramped with a smile. She *had* been through a lot in her short life. Well, mostly in the past year, but she'd hadn't done anything strong.

"I'd call it survival," she said. "I just did what I had to. Everyone else did all the work. That's not strength. That's…" She shrugged and sat across from her Shai'jan. "Like I said, that's survival."

"Was it easy?" il'Diou asked.

"Yes and no," Dilna said, her legs and arms throbbing in relief. "Walking up and down those blastedly steep hills—the Kralnach Hills —that was hard. And almost being trampled in Iaroca was scary, but I just ran between everyone's legs. There's a lot more room than you'd think, for someone as small as me. Then, Reylan snatched me up, and all I did was read this, and read that, then read some more, and when I was finished…"

"Read some more," il'Diou said, in a surprisingly accurate imitation of the old Phaerian.

"It never ended," Dilna said. "I read a *lot*, but I don't know if I'd say it was hard. And, to be honest, I liked learning all those things about plants and medicine."

"And how do you feel about your current training?" il'Diou asked.

"Being your Astasi is more fun than work."

"Even after a hundred sets?"

"Is that how many I did?" she asked, impressed with herself. She'd like to see Jouler do that many.

"No," Diou replied. "Almost half."

"Fifty?" she said, slumping in defeat.

"*Almost* fifty," il'Diou said. "Does it still feel like fun or work?"

Her mischievous grin rumbled a chuckle in his chest, and she ladled another scoop of water. "I mean, it *is* work," she said, sipping from the ladle, "or I wouldn't be soaked with sweat."

"A lot of that is water," il'Diou said.

"But it's *fun* work," she said.

"Not challenging?"

"Maybe in the beginning," she admitted, dropping the ladle so more water would spill over.

I could watch that all day, she thought, but her joy fizzled under her Shai'jan's raised eyebrow. *Did he want me to do another set, or…? Oh, right, my training!*

"Tezrel was hard at first," she said. "But that's only because I'd never done it before."

"And now?" il'Diou asked.

"Now it's as natural as walking."

"Do you know how many eleven-year-old Boorde wish they could say the same?"

"Does it really take that long for Boorde to walk?" she asked with a sidelong look.

Il'Diou ruffled her hair and motioned for her to follow. "At your age," he said, leading her from the spacious room he'd cleared for their training, "Boorde children are on their last year of learning the staff. After that, they graduate to the spear. A few years after that, they learn the bow. Then, as part of their rite of passage into adulthood, Boorde receive their sidaiyo or djohai." He gestured to the daggers stuck through her belt. "Most Boorde only learn the double daggers after they've learned half a dozen other weapons."

"Maybe they all just needed to start with daggers," Dilna said. "Like me."

"Possibly," il'Diou said, amusement flickering in his fire-diamond eyes. "But there's an advantage to learning those other weapons first. The spear, sword, staff, and bow are the most common weapons you will encounter. Learning them not only teaches you how to attack and defend an opponent; they teach you how your opponent might attack and defend against you."

"Yeah, but can't they just figure that out themselves? Like…" Dilna struggled for the right words. "I can tell how you're going to block my swipes and jabs with whichever weapon you use. It's just...obvious."

"Interesting," il'Diou said, leading her into the tea room.

Dilna skipped to the pastry table, her belly begging her to devour every last treat on the ornate silver tray. Sweet lemon tarts—Katima's favorite—savory meat pies, gooey cheese breads, and Dilna's favorite, the tubs of frozen fruit cream.

"Battle prescience is a Boorde trait," il'Diou said, smacking her hand away from the tub of frozen peach cream. He handed her a fried pastry stuffed with seasoned beef.

She stuffed the pastry into her mouth, and her tastebuds cheered the flaky dough and well-seasoned meat. She snatched three more pastries and sat at a small round table.

"It's what makes us superior fighters," il'Diou said, pressing a hand to his belly. "Our inner flame tells us what to do in battle, and those with a keen mind hear best."

His words stirred Dilna's memory of her talk with Katima, high in the mountains overlooking Lake Skjold. Would Dilna's name truly fill imperials with fear? The more she trained with il'Diou, the more she believed those words.

"And...do you think I have a keen mind?" she asked, biting into another meat pastry, this one stuffed with sweet pork.

"In all my years and studies," il'Diou said, "I've only known of one other Human who spoke about the Forms like you—like a Boorde."

"Who's that?" she asked, saving her favorite savory treat for last. Breaded, and deep-fried, the soft, teardrop-shaped potato dough hid shredded chicken seasoned to perfection. Tears of the Gods, she called them, savoring its shredded succulence.

"Jouler spoke of fighting like you," il'Diou said. "He put the weapon where it wanted to be, as he said. Where it felt right. But he has something you do not."

"Yeah," Dilna said, grabbing another Tear of the Gods. "He's a Facet."

"Something else," il'Diou said, sitting across from her at the table.

"What's that?" she asked.

"Control," il'Diou said. "That is a warrior's true strength."

"Oh yeah?" Holding his gaze, Dilna pushed the Tear of the Gods away, and rested her hands on her lap. "No control, huh?"

THE LOUD DIN of Upper Tier Nobles filled the massive Great Hall of the Archon's Manor. In the Boorde Alliance, the shining white bastion would have been seen as a giant mortuary, or a museum dedicated to the dead. To Humans, all the pristine white symbolized superiority and purity. Hence all the shaped, Boorde-white faces gracing the Founders. Unlike Katima's people, vibrant colors shouted from the Citizens. Hair in blue, green, orange, and every color imaginable bobbed above equally offensive clothes.

Spine tingling from all the pattern-forging, Katima ripped off a strip of jerked beef, and chewed on the tough morsel. Humans butchered meat, never adding the right spices—too much of this, too little of that, or, in the case of Blailonians, adding no spice at all. Just plain, overcooked meat. Meru'utians were especially terrible, which made sense. Theirs was the only kingdom that favored the Prytha's ridiculous vegetable diet. When they did add meat, it was usually fish, which never sat right with Katima. Not like beef, pork, and chicken.

Especially chicken.

Spicy, savory, sweet, fruity—what couldn't be done to chicken?

Whatever the blazes Humans do to it, she thought. *That's what.*

"You look positively excited to be here," Diou said, scanning the massive crowd.

Dilna stood beside him, her tiny ry'ku still wrinkled from their afternoon session. The empire-red ribbons wrapped around her daggers looked ridiculous against the all-black garments. No other Astasi would have been required to bind their weapons, but Dilna was far from a traditional Astasi.

"We've been here a month," Katima mumbled, "and we're no closer to finding Kael than we were the day we arrived. All we've done is subject your Astasi to pointless abuse."

Dilna kept her gaze on the floor, playing her part in their subterfuge. Her ry'ku could use a wash, but Katima supposed the smell kept most Citizens from getting close enough to slap her. Not that any but a Founder would dare touch the girl with her Shai'jan nearby.

A short Founder with silver hair waved at Katima, her vibrant dress changing colors as she moved. "So good of you to join us, Heiress," the Founders said, her thick, singsong accent betraying her Meru'utian upbringing. "How are you enjoying our fine city?"

Fine is an overstatement, Katima thought, maintaining her placid mask. *More like a sty full of overdressed swine.*

"It's quite lively," Katima said, understanding why her people kept to their peaks. The extreme altitude kept these colorful leeches away. No matter what her brother said, she'd never understand how such inept people ruled the empire. Humans, it seemed, favored buying the appearance of power over acquiring the real thing.

The lords, anyway.

"Hildara Eiryksdir," the Founder said, extending a gloved hand.

Katima frowned at the much shorter Human. "I am unaware of your house. Are you Eiocian?"

"Silrinian," Hildara said, dropping her proffered hand. She swallowed, and offered a furtive glance at Diou. "My, your people really are tall...aren't they?"

"Have you never met a Boorde?" Katima asked, and the short Founder shook her head.

"I only leave Silrin for the Ceremonies," Hildara said.

"Silrin," Katima mumbled, recalling what little she knew of the city. "Known for its rum, stunning seascapes, and pirates."

"Privateers," Hildara corrected.

"What side of the city do you face?" Katima asked, remembering a note about the strange hierarchy of class within the city.

"The south, of course," Hildara said, pride curling a smile.

"Ah, yes," Katima said. "The side with the sights."

"I can assure you," Hildara replied with a note of challenge in her voice, "this isn't a more majestic view in the empire."

"I'd love to see them, one day," Katima said.

"You will have to come visit," Hildara measured Diou with lascivious intent. "You and your…"

"Brother," Katima said.

"Perfect," Hildara said, biting her lip.

"You might be able to help me," Katima told her, germinating an idea. "Well…you might be able to help my brother."

"Oh?" Hildara replied.

"You see, we," Katima said, ignoring her brother's sneer, "or, rather, *he* has been studying the mind of the empire's darkest enemies."

Hildara's head jerked in surprise. "That's…that's so macabre. I like it."

Katima swallowed her disgust for the simpleminded Founder. "Might you know where to find such a specimen?"

"Why, the dungeons, of course."

"No," Katima said. "The *worst* people."

"Well, if it is not the dungeons, I can assure you, I do not know where such rabble might be." Hildara feigned being called to, and dismissed herself, swishing away in her ridiculous color-changing dress.

"That was subtle," Diou said.

"I'm tired of dealing with idiots," Katima mumbled, the incessant festivities burning her patience. Fortunately, the Archon's Ball would end the superfluous carousing. Unfortunately, it would also last a week. How else was everyone to know the Archon was better than everyone else? It wasn't like he had a massive, glowing white manor at the top of a city the size of a mountain.

"You'd think," she said, sucking her teeth, "that such short-lived creatures would endeavor to spend what little time they had on something more productive."

"Humans live as much by their emotions," her brother said, "as they are by reason."

"It's what makes them so inept at battle," Katima said.

"Inept in battle, but not in here," Diou said, gesturing to the opulent decorations. Glimmering showers of light tumbled from the vaulted ceiling, where illusions of tiny dragons, fairies, and other fanciful creatures pranced through the air. Below the illusions, tables brimmed with enough untouched food to feed a thousand families. "In court, emotions rule. A slighted lord might break a generations-long alliance, throwing houses into a bloody feud. A stunning young man or lady might earn a contract with a lascivious merchant, where a stoic prude would be turned away."

"An infuriating weakness."

"And yet," Diou said, "They've ruled Torgeir for over two thousand years."

"Because we let them," Katima said. "At least your Astasi has learned a semblance of self control. If only the rest of her kind were so disciplined."

"I don't know if I'd call her disciplined," Diou said, winking at Dilna.

"Compared to these peacocks..." Katima gestured to a Silver Lord in a purple suit and plumed hat, chugging a bottle of the emperor's favorite peach-rose liqueur. "I'd say Dilna is the model of discipline."

Unlike the other parties, closed to all but Upper Tier nobles, all the city's tiers were invited to the Archon's Ball. Of course, no Districter could afford passage up the Petitioners Penance, while the makers of the Makers District were too busy with work to attend such frivolities. The only soldiers from the Steel District were high-ranking officers, or the guards stuck on duty. Obviously "open to all" meant something far different within the Alliance than it did with these disgustingly dishonorable Humans. Especially all the Founders in their fake Boorde-white skin, feeding off the attention of their lessers. It seemed every lord and lady in Eio filled the enormous hall except for the one she'd hoped to find.

Everyone but Rodak.

"Maybe we can't find any information," Diou said, "because everyone's afraid you'll burn them to ash."

"Flames, if only I could." Katima sighed, and forced herself to relax, in posture, at least. "Where the blazes is Rodak? You'd think a Founder with Boorde black hair would stick out among all this color."

"You can't find him," her brother said, "because you're looking for a Human, instead of a Boorde."

"But he is a—"

"Trust me."

Katima scanned the crowd again, ignoring the Humans in their vibrant attire, and focused on finding one of her own kind. Looking over the crowd, she finally saw the archon sitting in a high-backed, purple velvet chair.

Rodak stared back at her.

I know why you're here, his smile said. *And you'll never find him.*

41

CODOINE RUINS

Wrong...

The soft voice teased L'Veyna awake to a dull, perpetual pain that swelled in her head and radiated down her neck and arms. Sharp light pierced through her eyelids, prying them open, and she groaned through the ache and sat up. White powder sloughed from her head and left arm, while a blanket of white and blue dominated her vision.

Not a blanket, she thought, her mind sluggish from the pain in the back of her head. *Sky and...land?* Maybe a land made of ground up bones, or...

She put the back of her hand to her forehead, a gentle breeze chilling her scalp. She ran her hand over the smooth skin, a bubble of sorrow drifting through her confusion. Sharp needles of pain stabbed up the tips of her fingers. Fingers as bald as her scalp.

I should have talons...right?

Five other people awoke beside her, all of them as bald as her, their faces tingling her memories. Two had skin so white, it made the powdered land seem dull. Two of the other people had light-brown skin, not quite as dark as her own. One had an angry scar around his missing eye. The fifth person had long pointed ears like her's, his emerald-green eyes and face so familiar his name floated from her lips.

"Prack."

He looked at her, blinking in confusion. "Who…L'Veyna?"

Understanding stirred within her addled mind, whispering names, and stirring faint memories.

The older Human, handsome despite his missing eye, sat up, lifeless white powder running off his naked skin, exposing hard, lean muscles.

"What happened?" he asked, running a hand over his scalp.

"I'd say we all fell asleep," the tall, white-skinned woman said, sitting upright, her brow drawn in pain. A burn scar melted one side of her head, while myriad scars decorated her otherwise smooth skin.

Her slender companion lacked the burns, but his lean body bore far more scars. He stood, grimacing, and exposing elongated canines.

They're so tall and beautiful, L'Veyna thought, noting their corded muscles, and captivating fire-diamond eyes.

Even the younger Human bore a physique suited for hard labor. He sat upright, seeming as confused as Prack and the other Human.

L'Veyna stood and stumbled back a few steps, clarity seeping into her mind, clearing her shroud of confusion. She looked down, and her face heated.

I'm naked!

Blossoming warmth radiated in her head, and hot pain seared her mind. She screamed, falling in agony, her head threatening to explode and implode at the same time.

Wrong…

The soft voice seemed to ease the pain, though the back of her head still thrummed with a dull ache.

A comforting hand rested on her back, and she looked to see the one-eyed Human squatted beside her.

"Are you all right?" he asked, seeming oblivious to his nudity. He tugged at L'Veyna's skin, his face drawn in confusion. "How?"

Not my skin, L'Veyna realized, her body wrapped in a bright-green strip of cloth. She shook her head, feeling as confused as the man looked. "I don't know."

He stood, still oblivious to his—

L'Veyna squeaked, and pulled her gaze from his naked body, her cheeks burning.

Oh, Alnazet's mercy! she thought in a sudden moment of clarity. *Jouler!*

She covered her face with her hands, trying to shake the embarrassing image from her mind. Maybe if she asked Jouler some clothes, she could think of anything other than his corded muscles and smooth brown skin.

At least he won't remember.

Her gaze flitted to her brother and Horgar, still huddled together in the cold while Ishariel and Tristian stood, unfazed by their nakedness or the freezing wind. Everyone needed clothes, but Jouler first.

Closing her eyes, she forced those mortifying images from her mind, and focused on an image of Jouler in the same Boorde attire he'd worn the day before, with his black eyepatch with its uncut emerald.

Nothing.

No shaking. No resistance to reality. Just a simple image in her mind, like every other fleeting thought. Confused, she sat in the Posture of Root, legs folded, hands rested on her knees. Again she formed the image of Jouler in his thick coat, layers of shirts, trousers, belt, sturdy boots, and eyepatch…

Nothing but that ache thrumming the back of her head.

She tried again, and again, pleading to her Goddess.

Nothing.

Alnazet had truly forsaken her.

Then how did I ask this wrap?

Thankfully, the cold sent Jouler to huddle with Prack and Horgar.

Still naked, Ishariel pressed a hand to her stomach, looking like she might be sick. "How did you ask your wrap?"

"I don't know," L'Veyna said, looking away from the striking woman.

"Would you please figure it out soon?" Ishariel said. "I'd rather not stare at naked men this whole trip."

"I'm trying," L'Veyna said, a dull ache growing in her head.

"Interesting," Tristian said, holding his stomach. "Your brother and the Humans still seem out of it. Whatever hold the Blasted Lands have on them seems to have passed for the three of us. It's almost as if it's eating their mind."

"Why not us?" L'Veyna said, pushing through her incessant ache. "And why can't I ask now?"

"You obviously can," Ishariel said, plucking L'Veyna's Wrap. "Focus. Unless you figure out how you asked, there will be three new mounds of blasted powder."

"Meat," Tristian mused.

Ishariel scowled at him. "We'll deal with food once we figure out—"

"Not that," Tristian said with a grimace of pain. "Feel your inner flame, Ishariel."

The firedancer's eyes widened. "It burns like I just ate a small morsel."

"We should be famished," Tristian said. "We should all be blasted, for that matter."

L'Veyna winced through a thrumming wave of dull pain, forming a simple image of a lily—Jouler's favorite flower.

Nothing.

"Can you do any magic?" she asked Ishariel.

"No," the firedancer replied. "But my insides no longer feel like they're being shredded apart. It feels more like I ate spoiled meat."

"We must be feeding off her," Tristian said, gesturing to L'Veyna. "That, or her power is sustaining us somehow."

Jouler, Prack, and Horgar still huddled together, shivering, skin paling, their gaze distant. If L'Veyna didn't figure something out quick, they'd die from exposure long before the Blasted Lands took them.

"They're going to die," Ishariel said, rubbing Jouler's arms and legs, while Tristian worked on Horgar.

L'Veyna did the same for her brother, his lips purple, olive skin frozen.

No, no, no…

"Fires curse you, child, do something!" Ishariel shouted.

L'Veyna startled into action, forming an image of everyone clothed —Prack, Jouler, Horgar, Ishariel, Tristian, all clothed, their skin healthy, eyes gleaming with life…

Nothing.

"I will *not* let them die," L'Veyna said and her voice caught. She continued rubbing her brother's arms and back, his gaze empty, breathing shallow. His shivering body slackened and her vision watered. "Please, brother…I need you."

Wrong…

The soft voice echoed through her thoughts, and power burgeoned with in her. Hot pain pierced her mind and her vision went white. Each agonizing second stretched into minutes, into hours, into days. After a lifetime of torment, whimpers trickled through her sharp suffering.

My whimpers, she realized, the world rocking around her.

"Shhh." The familiar voice wavered in her ringing ears.

"Brother?" She cracked open an eye, and Prack smiled down at her. Relief flooded through her pain, joy pouring down her cheeks and blubbering her cries. She buried her face in his chest, the familiar aroma of his cactus leathers wrapping her in a soft blanket.

Leather?

She bolted upright, his wide grin filling her vision. Unbraided autumnal hair fell in a long tail and his long pointed ears sparkled with emeralds. He helped her to her feet, and he spun, displaying his long coat and thick leathers.

"It worked," she said, the thrumming ache radiating from the back of her head.

"What happened?" Prack asked.

"I couldn't ask," she said. "It was like…like I lost my connection with Alnazet."

"Your power's gone?" Jouler asked, still bald like Ishariel and Tristian, while Horgar sported his mess of dark, curly hair. Jouler looked good bald, draped in his long black coat, his black eyepatch with its uncut emerald adding to his dark image. Dark and sinister, like the Harbinger of Death should be. A dark, sinister, and very much embarrassed Harbinger.

"My power is still ever-blossoming inside me," she said, rubbing her bald scalp and neck. "But it's different now. Like a piece of my soul was ripped out when I asked."

"That can't be good," Jouler said, averting his gaze from hers.

So he remembers being naked, L'Veyna mused.

Dressed in thick sturdy clothes, Horgar also avoided her gaze, ducking behind Jouler whenever she looked at him.

He remembers too.

"Thank you for restoring our dignity," Ishariel said, bowing with Tristian, their attire dark, but not quite Boorde black. "And for saving the Harbinger's life."

Jouler took a deep breath as though working up the courage to meet L'Veyna's gaze. "Yes. Thank you."

She winked, offering him a teasing smile, and he lifted an eyebrow, his embarrassment replaced by a somber look that melted her confidence.

"What?" she asked, faltering under her brother's mischievous grin.

Prack leaned close and whispered, "We, uh...we remember everything."

"What do you mean everything?" she asked, and her mouth went dry.

They saw me naked!

Alnazet's mercy, Jouler remembered standing in front of her. She ducked behind her brother with a squeak, her thin Wrap doing nothing to assuage her humiliation. "Give me your coat."

"Since when did you get shy?" Prack teased, handing her his coat. "Don't you want to bask under the sun?"

She slipped the coat on, flipping up the collar, wishing she could hide from her memory of Jouler standing naked in front of her... Her face warmed again, and she pulled the coat over her face.

"How did you ask?" Ishariel said.

"I don't know," L'Veyna replied, her voice muffled under the coat.

"We can't hear you," Prack said, pulling the coat down.

Face still hot, she winced from the ache thrumming down the back of her head.

"It's my power," she said, though she couldn't explain why it hurt, like claws shredding her soul.

"But it's never hurt you like that before," Prack said, shivering without his coat.

Great, L'Veyna thought, dreading another bought of pain. *I'll have to ask more clothes for myself.*

"It also hurt in the Boorde Alliance," she said.

"Not like this," her brother replied.

"Soil," Jouler said, raising a hand to the uncut emerald on his eyepatch. "Specifically Currents-rich soil. For now, it's the only connection I can think of, but it makes sense."

"Interesting," Prack said, his voice thick with sarcasm. "Now, would *you* mind making sense?"

"Your power," Jouler said to L'Veyna. "It never hurt like this until after we lost the soil."

"But why does it hurt?" she asked, rubbing the back of her neck. "It's so much worse than before."

"It must be connected to the Currents," Tristian replied.

"Our powers aren't tied to the Currents," she said. "It's connected to life. That's why water makes us stronger."

"Too bad we're not on a ship," Horgar said. "You could probably unblast the Blasted Lands."

"Actually," Jouler said, "I have a theory about water and the Currents."

L'Veyna squeezed the brim of her nose, the perpetual ache gnawing at her patience. "Is there a short version?"

"Water embodies creation," he said. "It doesn't need the Currents. Alnazet also embodies creation, so it makes sense that water would amplify your powers." Tristian told him something in Boordish, and Jouler bowed. "You honor me, friend."

L'Veyna rolled her eyes, running talonless fingers over her bald scalp. Not that long ago the Boorde had been Jouler's captor, and now he called him friend. At least he'd only said it to Tristian.

"You're not going to die, are you, El?" Horgar asked, wringing his hands.

"I'll be fine," L'Veyna said, her eyes tight with pain. She ran her hand over her bald scalp again, finding a grim fascination in her smooth skin. "And, Horgar?"

"Yes?" the young pirate said, hope lifting his voice.

"Don't ever call me El again. My name is L'Veyna."

FLAT, endless, lifeless white. Dull like the perpetual ache thrumming the back of L'Veyna's head. It couldn't be too soon for her talons to regrow, but for now, the smooth skin kept her mind distracted. She pressed on a fingertip, sending sharp needles of pain into her sensitive fingertips, chasing away her exhaustion and hiding the ache in her head, if for only a moment.

The sun crept toward the horizon, threatening an end to their fourth day. Only a few more hours until Alnazet finished pulling her twinkling blanket across the clear sky, and L'Veyna's true nightmare began.

She pressed on her fingertip again, drowning those unpleasant thoughts.

Tristian and Ishariel walked on either side of her, their iron face cast in perpetual concern. At least they'd stopped pestering her every time she winced, asking if she was all right.

Do I look all right? She mused, her face, her jaw, her entire body tight with pain.

Jouler led the destitute group, using the stars and his strange dreams as his guide. As usual, Horgar walked beside him, filling Jouler's days with stories of heroic pirates, bountiful treasures, and, of course, his favorite person Everyone.

Exhaustion dragged her feet along the endless white powder, her body begging for rest that would never come.

"We should stop," Prack said from behind her.

The fear of stopping shocked life back into her limbs. She shook her head, trying to clear the webs clogging her mind. Forcing her feet to obey, she pressed forward.

Wrong...

The soft, mysterious voice teased her weary mind, adding its foreboding weight to her steps.

What's wrong? she thought, knowing the voice wouldn't respond. It hadn't said anything else these past four days—why start now?

"How much farther?" Tristian asked from her side.

"We should reach Codoine by noon tomorrow," Jouler replied, gazing at the twinkling sky.

"Don't stop," L'Veyna said, her voice betraying her exhaustion.

"At this point," Ishariel said, adjusting her grip under L'Veyna's arm, "we're just dragging you."

"Please, not yet," L'Veyna pleaded through the radiating pain in the back of her head and neck.

"I'm sorry," Ishariel said, pity softening her stoic gaze. "Tristian and I can carry you, but your brother and the Humans need sleep."

Fighting back tears, L'Veyna nodded, and they helped her to sit on the ground. Her ache thrummed down the back of her head.

"I don't need to eat," Horgar said, yawning. "If that helps?"

"I think we can all skip tonight's meal," Jouler said, his concerned gaze laden with exhaustion.

"Thank you," L'Veyna mumbled, body begging for sleep, while Alnazet's setting glory promised another agonizing night.

"The sooner we sleep," Prack said, crouching to press the back of his hand to L'Veyna's forehead. Concern pressed his lips into a tight line. "The sooner we can get back up on our feet."

As L'Veyna had done for the past three nights, she gritted her teeth, watching them lay on the lifeless white powder. Power ripped from her soul and leeched into her companions, protecting them from the deadly effects of the Blasted Lands.

The thrumming ache swelled into sharp, pulsating pain, consuming her dreams of sleep, tears freezing in the merciless night.

L'Veyna startled, her eyelids too heavy to open, her ache an ignorable presence now that everyone had risen to their feet. She felt them walking around her, their footsteps thrumming down the back of her head.

"Come on, Sprout," Prack said, shaking her awake. "Only a few more hours left."

"I'll ask breakfast," she said, still unable to open her eyes.

"We can skip," Jouler said. "We're almost there."

Bracing herself, she formed an image of a mound of nuts, breads, and succulent fruits, then she asked, tearing off a piece from her ever-blossoming power.

A scream ripped from her throat, searing pain lancing through her head and down her back. Leaning on her brother for support, she endured the agony, focusing on her breathing until it faded to bearable.

"That was stupid," Jouler said, though he looked hungrily at the pile of food already blasting from the bottom up.

"That was me waking up," L'Veyna replied, though she still couldn't fully open her eyes. "Besides, we'll get there faster on a full belly."

She ignored Jouler's disappointed look, and grabbed a cluster of grapes and a soft roll, while her brother stuffed his pockets with nuts and flatbread, a banana sticking from his mouth.

"You look ridiculous," she said, her soft chuckled pounding through her head.

"Sorry," Prack said over the banana.

"Shall we?" Jouler asked, adjusting his eyepatch, his pockets stuffed, oranges clutched in his arm.

Not waiting for a reply, Tristian scooped L'Veyna into his arms. "You're not walking."

"Thank you," she mumbled, patting him. "Sorry I can't ask meat."

"You honor us with life," the tall, slender Boorde said, munching on a handful of almonds. "That is the greatest honor anyone can receive."

Jouler set another grueling pace, seeming determined to reach Codoine well before the sun peaked. This morning, Horgar filled Jouler's time with questions about Headwater. Jouler endured the innocent interrogation, nodding and shaking his head with a smile.

Like a big brother, L'Veyna mused.

She curled in Tristian's arms, drifting asleep despite the ache thrumming down the back of her head. Every time she jolted awake, the sun skipped a step across the sky.

"It's past noon," Prack called from behind the pack. "Shouldn't we be there?"

Jouler spun, his eye searching the flat, lifeless landscape. "We should be there. Or close enough to see it."

"What are we looking for?" Horgar asked.

"A big hole in the ground," Jouler said. Horgar's face skewed in confusion, and Jouler motioned for the young pirate to follow. "Everyone stay here, while Horgar and I see what we can find.

"Fine with me," L'Veyna mumbled. The blissful sun warmed her face and easing her aching head. Snuggling into Tristian's arms, she gave in to her exhaustion.

GENTLE SNOWFLAKES DRIFTED from a cloud formation, evaporating in small puffs before the flakes touched the ground. Pines once lined the causeway leading to Codoine's south gate, the roads cramped with Phaerians and Citizens alike.

"How big was your farm?" Horgar asked, his gaze flitting to Jouler's eyepatch.

"Oh, I don't know…small, I guess," Jouler said, half-listening to the young pirate's barrage of questions. Codoine's Shining Wall should have filled their vision. Or they would have if the empire hadn't blasted his beloved home.

"Did you grow fruit?" Horgar asked, and Jouler nodded. "What kind?"

"Mostly oranges and stone fruit," he replied, letting his memories guide him toward the city. "Peaches, plums, apricots…"

"What if a terrentor tore up all your trees?" Horgar asked.

"A terrentor did tear through my farm," Jouler said, painful memories of that day scurrying through his thoughts.

"You're walking quick," Horgar said, skipping to keep up. "I never had to walk this much on the ship. Even when we made port, I never walked this much. Not like you. Did you really walk all the way from Glaedia to the Boorde Alliance?"

"All the way to Urna," Jouler replied. "If you think I'm fast, wait until you meet Pendric."

"That's your friend with no breath, right?"

"He still has his breath," Jouler said. They stood where Codoine's southern gate had loomed, or as near as he could tell with no stars. Guided by his memories, he led Horgar through the ghost of Codoine's Workers District. Unlike the rest of the empire, Districters had flourished in Astrakane, their streets clean, the air crisp, their trades thriving.

"But," Horgar said, chewing on a thought, "you said Pendric's breath was stolen."

"It's complicated," Jouler said, continuing toward the center of the once vast city.

"But you're going to fix it with the Black Breath." Horgar's eyes widened. "Is Pendric going to breathe the Black Breath?"

Jouler rubbed his eyes and looked at the land. A few hundred paces ahead, the lifeless, flat ground bulged with a small mound.

"Huh?" Jouler turned Horgar toward the mound, and he pointed. "Do you see that?"

Horgar squinted, rubbed his eyes, and looked again. "Is that a hill?"

"A hillock at best," Jouler said, haunted by the memory of the terrible black beam. "I'll bet it's what we're looking for."

"What do you think we'll find?" Horgar asked, jogging beside him. "What if it's a cave with a pod of terrentors?"

"Then…I guess we'd all get eaten?"

"Yeah. But what if they're hibernating?"

"Do terrentors hibernate?"

Horgar shrugged. "But what if they do? Then what?"

"Then I suppose we'll have to be extra quiet."

Jouler rounded the mound and stopped, his heart pounding in his chest. Before him was a circular tunnel with black glassy sides, its gentle slope consumed by darkness. He turned, following the tunnel's angle into the clear sky where'd he'd floated in his dream.

Horgar edged away from the tunnel. "I don't think there's any terrentors in there. Jo? What's wrong?"

Crazed voices tangled through Jouler's mind, their madness caressing his reawakened gift.

Here, you're here, the Harbinger is come, Death's embrace, M'Ljot, Qi'k'sadra, take me, take me, take me…

Not terrentors, Jouler thought, fear turning his limbs to mush. *Something far worse.*

42

A WELCOMED ENEMY

Rodak Torren waved for his son Lokir to wait until their honored guest left the room. As much as he respected Grim, a Soutori's heart only bore room for the empire. Rodak admired their devout loyalty, but it made them far too predictable.

"Say nothing around a Sotouri," he told Lokir as the door clicked shut, "that you wouldn't tell the emperor to his face."

"Not even Grim?" Lokir asked, picking at the arm of his wooden chair, his silky black hair spilling over his shoulders and chest.

"Family," Rodak said, leaning back in his obsidian throne. "Family is the only thing you can trust. It's the only thing worth living for."

Lokir continued picking at his chair, his thoughts undoubtedly wrapped around Aglia. One day, his son's skills at torture would rival his own, but not until Lokir learned to control his lust for his victim's final breath—the kohlithee, as the Boorde called it. No amount of romance or shared dreams rivaled such intimacy. No drug or pair of legs compared to that intoxicating rush, especially when coupled with the nuances of pleasure and pain. Both could be the same, in the right frame of mind. Intense pleasure could tumble into pain, just as the right type of pain could ripple into ecstasy. That nuance eluded Lokir, for now, at least.

Had you been any different at his age? he thought in his wife's voice.

Blinded by youth, and stubborn as a bollard, he'd eschewed the yellow-and-green cord for a black-and-orange. After all, men entered combat while women tended the wounded. Oh, how ninety-some-odd years changed a man's perspective. Joining the tii'Vrath would have given him access to patterns deemed too dangerous to the likes of those who wielded the Currents like a weapon. After all, those who knew how best to assuage pain, knew how best to induce it, and none save Sotouri Masks could maintain a life as well as a tii'Vrath.

Oh, the wonders he could have wrought with a yellow-and-green cord. The pain he could have explored. The pleasure he could have discovered, if only he hadn't been so headstrong in being a 'man'.

In two years, Lokir would choose his own cord. He yearned to don the black-and-orange, no matter how much Rodak said otherwise. No amount of wisdom seemed to penetrate that boy's skull.

Look at him, his wife's voice teased in his mind. *The two of you couldn't be any more alike.*

Rodak's chest tightened with her memory, and he cleared the lump forming in his throat.

"Father, how'd Grim know where Kael—" Lokir clamped his mouth shut, his hands darting to his lap. Dressed in Toren black-and-gold, he could have been Rodak's much younger twin, with just as much fear for his father, it seemed.

Oh, Nesaea, Rodak thought, conjuring images of his beautiful wife, before the sickness had taken her. *How I've failed you.*

"I know that name bothers..." Lokir cleared his throat and stiffened his back, ready to face his punishment like a proper man. Or what he *thought* a proper man would do. "I'm sorry, Father."

"It's fine," Rodak lied with a casual wave of dismissal. "With these blasted festivities done with, it won't be long before I hear his screams.

"Why don't you come down with me?" Lokir said, his golden eyes wide with excitement. "You can have a bit of fun before we leave."

Rodak scowled, hiding his pang of fear for the man who had become Prophecy made flesh.

"If only I had time," he lied.

You had plenty of time, his wife chided in his head, drumming up memories of a blinding figure of light.

"Ah," Lokir said with a flippant wave. "You won't miss much. Those dungeons really aren't made for fun."

Rodak pushed down a wave of fear and dismissed his son with a wave. "You heard Grim. The Boorde know where we're holding our two guests. Go fetch them. I want to be away from Eio as soon as possible."

"Three guests," Lokir corrected.

"No, two," Rodak said, hiding his mirth from his wilted son. "I'll not have you drag that filth with us."

"Back to Imutia, I guess," Lokir mumbled, drooping deeper into his chair.

Rodak's only surviving child had glowed on the trail, his zeal for life revived on their travels. Maybe it would do the boy good to follow Rodak across the empire, instead of returning to the Citadel. Founders didn't *need* a cord. Their alabaster-white skin carried far more influence than a Vrath ever could, and Rodak could mold Lokir into the man he should be. A man who lusted after more than throes of death.

"Not Imutia," Rodak said, and Lokir straightened in his chair. "You're coming with me."

Lokir blinked. "But... But you're..."

"Leading the emperor's forces against the Voice."

Lokir fell back in his chair, mouthing the words.

"You're going to start fresh," Rodak said, soaking in Lokir's astonishment. "A new life with a Phlem of your own, to mold, and to learn the nuances of pain and pleasure. Subtleties *I* will teach you. Maybe a Phlem a few years younger than you, with dark ruddy hair, and a terrible disposition for rebellions?"

"Makayla?" Lokir said, his excitement tugging at Rodak's heart. "What about King Ashtur? Won't he want Makayla for himself?"

"Very astute," Rodak said, swelling with the same pride that puffed his son's chest. "He can have Makayla when you're finished."

Lokir's excitement twisted into confusion. "But...she'll be dead."

"That, my dear son," Rodak said, "is a habit I aim to break. There's a finer side to pain. A whole new world for you to explore. I can't wait to show you."

"What about Aglia?" Lokir asked.

"Do with her as you will," Rodak replied, his mind skimming around thoughts of which techniques to teach Lokir first. "Just make sure *he* watches her die. Now go. I'll meet you at the staging yard by the west gate. I mean to be away from here before the other lords clog up the causeways."

Lokir strode from the room, on his way to make the long trek to the Sotouri's dungeons, reserved for the empire's worst criminals—traitorous Sotouri and Founders. People whose very existence threatened the natural order. What would Districters do if they learned Sotouri had turned to the Cabal? Masks, mostly, but Blades had also been known to sway from time to time. It made sense. Spending so much time with any people inexorably chipped away at a person's sensibilities.

Why didn't you go with Lokir? his wife's voice sounded through his thoughts.

Haunting memories of a broken Shining Wall flashed in his mind. He stumbled back and fell into his chair, his heart slamming against his chest, his lungs crying for air.

You've had plenty of time to go down there. Plenty of time to look our son's killer in the eyes.

"Stop." Rodak pressed his palms against his eyes, but terrifying images of the blinding figure of light still filled his vision.

You didn't go, his wife's voice whispered over the raging memories. *Because you're terrified of him. You know what he is.*

"No..."

Say it.

"No..." Rodak whispered, chest sucking in air, fear coursing his veins.

Say it!

His wife's booming voice echoed in his mind, yanking the words out with a sob.

"Crier of Change."

Rodak curled in his chair and wept.

"THE BLASTED MAN is playing with us," Katima said, and Dilna spared a quick glance at her Shai'jan's sister.

No one else occupied the speeding lift, but after over a month in this soulless city, Dilna had learned alone wasn't so alone. Even now, speeding up the city to confront Rodak, she only dared lift her gaze for a breath.

Katima stared into the distance, waves of heat emanating from her clenched fists.

Gods, how is she even prettier when she's furious?

"*Ex*-Archon Rodak Toren," Katima said. "At least there's that tiny joy, even if it means that water-soaked man leads the emperor's armies."

"Maybe he's secretly hunting Facets," Dilna said.

"The empire does not believe in the Prophecies," Katima replied. "It's widely known that the empire uses the Prophecies to oppress your people."

"That's what they say," Dilna said. "But what if they actually believe in them?"

"It's highly unlikely," Katima said. "Imperial schools and the Citadel teach that the Prophecies are tools. Nothing more. Interestingly, Districters are the most vociferous with their disbelief. It's like they resent the Prophecies."

"Maybe only the emperor knows the truth," Dilna said.

"There have been too many emperors," Katima said, shaking her head. "Too many defectors, too many people who want to destroy the empire... There are simply too many moving parts to keep such a thing secret. We're not talking about a triviality like the emperor's true hair color, or which concubines he bedded before breakfast. We're talking about something that would rock the foundation of the empire. If Citizens believed in the Prophecies, someone would have exposed that truth long ago. But such has never been the case."

"What about Queen Granivin?" Dilna said. "There isn't a Phaerian on Torgeir that hasn't heard of her. Maybe she uncovered the truth about the Prophecies, and *that* is why the empire sunk her queendom."

"Now that is a decent line of inquiry." Katima gave her a nod of praise. "You're starting to sound like you've spent too much time with Reylan and my brother."

"Thank you," Dilna said, bowing at the waist.

The lift continued upward, through the lower half of the Bronze District. Citizens could say all they wanted about Phaerian towns. Life below the parapet of the Shining Wall was far worse. Towns might reek of the same waste, vomit, and misery, but they didn't have a gigantic wall trapping all that humid, oily air.

The lift broke the heights of the Shining Wall, and Dilna breathed in the fresh, brisk air. Up here, overlooking Haldr's Bowl, with the lake shimmering beneath the afternoon sun, it was easy to see why Upper Tiersmen carried themselves with such superiority.

Of course, reality couldn't be farther from the truth. Sure, all the lords and ladies spoke...well, like lords and ladies—all proper, with long words that sounded made up—but for all their talk and self-importance, she'd never seen a more worthless people. Dilna had endured countless hours of boring conversations about mines and trade routes and contracts, but they never actually *did* anything. They just came up with dumb ideas for other people to carry out.

I could do that, except I'd have good ideas. I'd like to watch any of them practice Vis'mar all day.

The lift stopped at the Silver District port, and a lone noble walked onto the wide platform. The man moved to the other side of the lift, his dark-skinned face shadowed by the hood of his black fur-lined cloak.

Dark skin? Dilna wondered, trying to get a better look at the man without lifting her head. Only Phaerians had dark skin. Them and...

Sotouri!

Dilna's heart slammed in her chest, her clammy hands quivering by her side.

"Gods, girl," the Sotouri said, lifting a gloved hand to his crooked nose. "Your ry'ku reeks of Reylan's patterns."

He lowered his hood, and fear doused Dilna's attempts at igniting her core. Less than a dozen paces away stood the man who'd kidnapped Jouler, Pen, and Kael. The man who vowed to kill Diou's Astasi.

"Grim," Katima hissed, pulling Dilna behind her.

"Katima Nith'Iil," the dark-skinned man said. "Shall I still call you Heiress? We are alone, after all. And this must be the famous Phlem Astasi I've heard so much about." Grim's gaze fell to the daggers at Dilna's waist, and he lifted an eyebrow. "Impressive. A shame we can't cross blades. I'd love to see what Diou has taught you."

"I bet you would," Katima said, her hand dropping to her djohai.

"I'm afraid you're going in the wrong direction, My Lady." Grim pulled a simple iron ring from his finger. "It won't work for a Boorde," he said, gesturing to Dilna. "But it will for her."

"What is it?" Katima asked.

"A map to the Sotouri's dungeon," he said. Katima took a step forward, and Grim shook his head. "Not you, My Lady. I'm not that stupid. Not yet."

Dilna breathed in through her nose, gathering her fear into her chest, then released it into the crisp air.

"She'll have to hold the ring to keep from falling off," Grim said, waiting with the ring on his palm.

Dilna told herself he hardly needed her to cross the lift if he wanted to kill her. He could rip her to shreds with a single thought, which meant he really did just want to give her the ring. He just wanted to scare her.

Dilna breathed in and released her fear again, then strode across the lift, and stood before Grim. She met his eyes, letting a wave of terror wash through her body and into the lift. Feeding her fear into her inner flame, she took the ring from Grim's dark hand and returned to Katima's side. Heart pounding with relief, Dilna turned the heavy iron ring in her hand. Only a stamped Imperial Shield decorated its scratched surface.

"Slide it on any finger," Grim said, amusement fluttering in his dark eyes, "and tap the Shield. Not here, of course. Too many eyes." The lift stopped at the Gold Port, and Grim gestured toward the crowd of nobles. "This is your stop. Kael is at the base of the city, in a cell close to the nodestone. Just follow the ring, and when you see him, tell him I said hi. Good luck, My Lady." He turned his dark gaze to Dilna. "Train hard, little one. We'll meet again."

Before Katima could tell the man to suck on ice, he disappeared behind the crowd of boarding nobles.

Dilna hid the ring in her fist, careful not to raise her gaze from the floor as she followed Katima onto the lift going down.

"Do you think Grim's lying?" she asked.

Katima sucked her teeth again. "Sacred Flame burn me, but I don't think he is."

43

THE BLACK BREATH

Jouler led his ragged team deeper into the replete darkness of the tunnel, the shuffling footsteps of his companions as hesitant as his own. Eye closed or open made no difference in the pervasive darkness. No wind caressed his skin, the tasteless air neither hot nor cold. Nothing but the smooth floor under his feet, one in front of the other.

That and the blasted voice, he thought, focusing on his echoing footsteps to help tune out its pleas.

The Harbinger is come…Qi'k'sadra…take me, take me, take me…

"Are you *sure* we don't need light?" Horgar whispered.

"Just keep your hand on my back," Jouler replied, wishing he sounded more confident.

Horgar's grip tightened on Jouler's coat. "But what if there's a spider?"

"A what?" Prack said.

"A spider," L'Veyna said through a yawn. "What if there's a spider?"

"Then we step on it," Ishariel said, her voice charging down the tunnel.

"Not that kind of spider," Horgar said. "A *big* spider. Like, a terrentor spider."

"Spiders don't get that big," Jouler said.

"That's what they say about fish," Horgar mumbled. "But everyone knows they get as big as a ship. Bigger, even. Why not spiders?"

"They just don't," Jouler said.

"Besides," Ishariel said. "We're likely the first living things to roam this tunnel."

"A bird could have flown here," Prack said.

"Possibly," Ishariel admitted. "But when was the last time you saw a bird?"

Prack clicked his tongue. "The day we entered the blasted Blasted Lands."

"Precisely my point," Ishariel said. "The only thing we have to worry about is falling into a deep crack."

"A crack?" Horgar chirped.

"From a quake," Ishariel said.

"Or the ground settling," Tristian mused.

"Can we be afraid of shallow cracks too?" Prack mused. "I might not die from the fall, but a twisted ankle would really put a damper on this joyful day."

"Don't listen to them," Jouler said, squeezing Horgar's hand. "The tunnel isn't cracked."

"But how do you know?" Horgar asked.

"I can ask glowshrooms," L'Veyna said, the hesitation loud in her weary voice.

"No," Jouler and Prack said in unison.

"I was just offering."

"We don't need light," Jouler said. "The tunnel isn't going to drop into a crack. We'll be fine." He stomped his foot, the heavy clomp bouncing down the tunnel. "There isn't a power on Yrsa that could crack these walls. I saw what created the tunnel."

"The Black Breath," Tristian said.

"Presumably," Jouler replied. "That or whatever placed the Black Breath beneath Codoine."

They continued down the gentle slope, the echoes of their shuffling feet leading them onward. They had to be getting close to the nodestone chamber. He'd never been there, but every Upper Tiersman knew…

No, he thought, shoving away those false memories. *That wasn't me. I'm Phaerian, not an Upper Tier noble.* Headwater was his home, not a long-lost imperial city, and yet, he couldn't deny the comfort resting in his soul—the weary traveler returning home after a lifelong long sojourn.

"L'Veyna," Jouler said, surprised by his loud voice.

"Alnazet's mercy, Jo!" she grumbled. "You scared the roots out of me."

"How does this place feel to you?"

"Wrong," she said, her voice heavy with exhaustion. "This place feels wrong. We should turn back."

"I feel it too," Ishariel murmured as though distracted. "Resonating with my inner flame."

"We can't go back," Prack said. "We'll all die."

"We don't know that," L'Veyna said, but the exhaustion in her voice said otherwise.

"Do you need to rest?" Jouler asked.

"I'm fine," she insisted. "I'm not the one walking."

"Don't stop on my account," Tristian said, shifting L'Veyna in his arms.

"How about you, Ishariel?" Jouler asked.

"Worried about me, dear?" the Boorde replied.

"Just hoping you'd fallen in the crack you talked about."

Ishariel's barked laugh skipped down the tunnel. "Now that was good Boorde humor."

"It was the truth," Jouler tapped in Talontongue against his belt.

Prack chuckled and tapped, *"If only we were that lucky."*

Jouler continued down the scentless tunnel, the slope taking them deep below the city. A flicker of motion teased his vision. He rubbed his eyes, and looked again—nothing but flat, boring darkness.

Great! Now I'm hallucinating.

The flicker caught his vision again. A pinpoint of darker darkness, like a star in reverse. He held his hand in front of his eye, and the pinpoint disappeared.

"The Black Breath," he breathed, and his gift stirred as if from a deep slumber.

Horgar leaned around him. "All I see is black."

"I see it too," Prack said.

"See what?" L'Veyna murmured.

"Hush now, little one," Tristian said, his shuffling feet stirring images of the slender Ascended rocking L'Veyna in his arms. "It's nothing you need to see."

"I don't like this," L'Veyna said, tight with pain. "My gift doesn't like this."

"I agree," Ishariel said.

"Your gift tell you that?" Prack teased.

"Hardly." Ishariel sucked her teeth. "I don't need special powers to know this place is wrong. This tunnel, these walls, everything about it, is wrong."

"You think we should turn around too?" Jouler asked, his gift sputtering with truth. His mind tumbled in confusion. How could that be true? His Seer vision had shown him his Path of Prophecy. It had shown him this entire journey.

"Pendric will die without the Black Breath."

Again, the truth sputtered within him.

"We can't stop," L'Veyna said, muttering with pain. "This place feels wrong, but no more than turning around."

"I'll carry my sister," Prack said, and Tristian thanked him. "I don't *want* to carry her. I just figured, in case we *do* encounter something, you'll be better in a fight than a Chi'indi who can't shift."

"Wow, thanks," L'Veyna mumbled.

The pinpoint of darkness grew with each step, from a tiny black star to a raging beacon. Painful to look at, Jouler dropped his gaze.

Not a star in reverse, Jouler thought. *A black sun.*

"Besides," Prack said in his typical jovial tone, "if we *do* encounter someone, my sister won't fall as far when I drop her to run away."

Jouler's foot fell on a rough ground, and he halted. "We're here," he said, shielding his eyes from the painful darkness.

L'Veyna's sharp cry pierced the tunnel, and waves of glowshrooms sprouted over the ground, up tall cavern walls, and across a cragged ceiling high above, exposing a vast chamber. A stalagmite as thick as a rustwood rose from the center of the cavern, its top flat as if hewn by a giant blade. Carved steps twisted up the stalagmite, leading to the painful darkness swirling atop a pedestal.

The Black Breath called to Jouler, urging him forward, caressing his will with a lover's seduction. He walked toward the darkness, pebbles crunching beneath his feet. Distant shouts floated through the alluring calls, but the voices sounded so far away, and the darkness was so close…so very dark.

So pure.

It needed him. He was the key, the vessel to fill the darkness, to free it from its prison. He climbed the spiraling stairs, ignoring the distant shouts of his friends. Didn't they understand? It needed to be whole.

Something clutched at him, but he yanked his hand free and made his way to the top of the stalagmite. The painful darkness swirled in front of him, pulsing with heavy waves of silence. Something pulled at his coat, so he let the garment slide off. A cry whispered between the pulses of silence. The pleading voice sounded so familiar, like a friend calling to him from ages past.

Jouler held up a hand against the painful darkness, his eye burning and watering. A bald young Prytha crouched behind him, clinging to his hand, her eyes squeezed shut, tears streaming down her cheeks.

"L'Veyna?" he said, the name caught by a pulse of silence. He yanked his hand free and reached for the swirling darkness. "It needs to be whole."

L'VEYNA'S stomach churned with a putrid sense of wrongness. She stirred in her brother's arms, shielding her eyes from the pulsating darkness ahead of them. At least the incessant ache in her head had lessened.

"We're here," Jouler said, his words echoing into what had to be a massive cavern.

In the middle of the replete void was a ball of darkness so black it pained her eyes.

The Black Breath.

Before anyone could tell her otherwise, she formed an image in her mind and reached into her power. Pain ignited inside her head, countless fiery talons raking her soul. Her drowning agony ebbed to a dull ache, and soft light teased her eyelids open.

"You shouldn't have done that," Prack said.

"We needed light," L'Veyna replied, taking in the enormous cavern.

Carpets of glowshrooms covered the uneven ground, looming walls, and jagged ceiling. The Black Breath swirled at the top of a tall stalagmite, the painful darkness seeming to suck in the surrounding light.

Like the sun in reverse.

She bade her brother to put her down, her boots crunching on the rocky ground.

"What is that thing?" Horgar asked, shielding his eyes with his hand. "I don't like it."

"It's foul," Ishariel hissed. "Antithesis to the Sacred Flame. We should grab Jouler and leave this place."

"I won't argue about that," Prack said, turning his back to the Black Breath. "It's like staring at the sun, but…"

"But wrong," Tristian said, peering at the swirling darkness.

Jouler stepped forward, pebbles crackling beneath his boots.

"Jo, stop," L'Veyna said through her ache, but he continued forward. "Jouler wait. Something's wrong."

Prack stepped into the cavern to grab Jouler and her brother grunted in pain, collapsing to the ground.

"Prack!" L'Veyna shouted, but he waved her away.

"Stay back," Prack said, vomiting.

"It's the Black Breath," Ishariel said, clutching her belly.

"Jouler!" Horgar shouted, retreating a few steps into the tunnel. "Come back! Why isn't he in pain?"

L'Veyna watched Jouler shambled toward the pillar, urgency coursing her veins. She had to stop him before he reached that foul darkness. An idea wormed through the putrescence plaguing her body and mind. Swallowing back a surge of wrongness, she stepped forward, bracing herself for an onslaught of misery. The ache still wracked the back of her head, the wrongness still churned her stomach, but no extraordinary pain pulled her to her knees like it had her brother.

"We're Facets," she said, glad, at least, to be right about that.

"Well, don't just stand there," Tristian said, dragging Prack to the safety of the tunnel. "Go bring Jouler back, and let's be done with this place."

L'Veyna trudged forward, her ache growing with each step. She shouted for Jouler, but he didn't seem to hear. Almost to the stairs, she reached for him, grabbing his hand. "Stop!"

Without looking back, he shook his hand free and headed up the spiraling stairs.

Squeezing her fists against the pain in the back of her head, she followed him up the pillar. Her stomach twisted with every step, emptying four times before she reached the cursed top.

This is wrong, she thought, spitting out sour bile. The tunnel, the cavern, the swirling darkness, it was all wrong the way the sun was right. This couldn't be Jouler's path.

In the center of the hewn column, the Black Breath raged atop a nondescript pedestal. The swirling darkness pulsed, buffeting her with thick waves of silence. She covered her eyes with one hand, waving her other hand before her, searching for Jouler. Her hand hit his arm, and she yanked him by the coat, sharp needles lancing up her talonless fingers. The coat slid from his back, and she fell back with a cry, almost toppling from the ledge.

"Jouler!" she shouted, the Black Breath sucking her tears dry as they formed. Her power swelled and pain clawed down her back and into her legs. She reached for his hand. "Jouler…please."

His head turned, and a flash of recognition sparkled in his dark eye. "L'Veyna?"

Her heart leaped with a surge of encouragement. "Please, Jo, you don't have to do this."

He shook his head and reached for the Black Breath. "It…to be… ole," he said, the words popping between waves of silence.

With a surge of strength, L'Veyna jumped onto his back, and darkness enveloped her once more, sensation fleeing with her sight. She tried to speak, but felt no mouth to form the words. She tried to move her arms, her legs, her toes…nothing. Not a single clenching muscle, no brush of skin, no weight of existence.

I'm dead.

"Hardly," a voice sounded, seeming to come from everywhere and nowhere.

A speck of light formed in the darkness. Unable to look away, or move, or do anything but watch, the light grew into a tiny blue orb.

Not growing, she thought, as more colors and details emerged on the orb. *I'm getting closer.*

Now the size of her thumb, the orb shone with streaks of white over brilliant blues, browns, and greens.

Yrsa! she realized, making out Torgeir, the continent seeming a lot smaller than she'd imagined. On the other side of the planet, separated by a vast ocean, was another continent far larger than Torgeir. The foreign land disappeared over the planet's horizon as her vision settled over Onatah. A vast army of plague-riddled Citizens surrounded the forest. Vibrant banners in ochre, slate, yellow, silver, white, or shimmering purple flapped at the head of each column of soldiers. Purple for the empire, which made the others the Five Kingdoms.

Between the armies and the forest, a thin ring of Prytha blended with the colors of the land, chk'da, spears, and bows in hand. A paltry defense against such an enormous foe.

Why am I here? Please, don't make me watch this.

A familiar figure strode from her people to challenge the empire, a black spear in her hand, her emerald eyes sparkling with pride.

That's me!

She looked down and found the cursed spear in her own hands. Startled, she tried to let the foul weapon go, but her body wouldn't listen.

I'm in the vision body, she realized.

She thrust the spear before her, releasing a wave of corruption. Grass withered as the putrid wave roiled over the land. Gaining power and momentum, the wave crashed into the soldiers who bore the ochre banners. Rust ate holes in metal, leather rotted, and soldiers aged, crumbling to lifeless husks.

With such power, she could save her people and bring an end to the empire's cruel reign. She could stop the Saplings Curse.

But at what cost?

Sickened by the rot left by the black spear's wake, she strained to let go of the weapon, but her hand remained gripped on the haft.

Not my hand, she thought. *This isn't me.*

It couldn't be. She would never defile Alnazet's glory or desecrate her blessed land.

A sudden drain weighed on her soul. Her hand opened, and the wicked spear puffed into a painful black cloud.

JOULER FLOATED ABOVE A WAR-RAVAGED LAND. Below, an army of Prytha fought against a sea of Phaerians, countless blue orbs streaking over the battlefield.

Headless?

A flash of alarm rippled his consciousness, and he willed himself to a group of Keepers and three massive Sentinels. The isolated group struggled against the mob of the mythical undead, the Keepers' war cries met by shrieks of metal over ice. One detritus golem snatched a headless in a large fist. In a blur of motion, the undead stabbed its swirling blue spear through the Sentinel's chest, blasting a hole through the golem. Thick vines and twisting branches grew from the Sentinel's arm, writhing through the headless and tearing the undead to pieces. The headless' blue orb burst, releasing its energy and restoring the Sentinel's blasted wounds.

So much effort to defeat a single headless, only for a dozen more to take its place, blasting the Sentinels and shattering the Keepers' flesh.

What is this? he asked, knowing the Black Breath would respond.

"Clever," the artifact said, its voice seeming to sound from everywhere and nowhere. "The other one took longer."

Jouler's consciousness sped to a familiar Phaerian girl, her olive skin and wavy black hair darker than he'd imagined from her statue. Vibrant blue tentacles, the same color as the headless, writhed from Makayla's back, shredding any Prytha or Sentinel who ventured too close. Rancid power poured through her and into the land, and more blue-orbed monstrosities rose from the ground.

This is Kael's dream, Jouler thought, recognizing his friend's description of the ravaged land.

"The Crier failed," the Black Breath replied, its ancient voice rumbling in his head. "This is your truth. Your chance to end the suffering."

Jouler's perspective shifted again, this time to another familiar figure dressed in all black, his eyepatch sparkling with an uncut emerald. Piles of ancient armor strewn about him from headless he'd slain. Jouler saw himself, holding a peculiar black sword, the end half shaped like a sickle, with a spike jutting from the base of its curve. He streaked across the battlefield like a headless, trailing a line of inky black with wisps of cerulean. Ancient armor collapsed in his wake.

"You have the power to stop it all," the Black Breath said.

Where Jouler's darkness trailed, blue orbs burst.

An unfamiliar sapling approached his vision self, her face far too young for the murderous intent in her aquamarine-colored eyes.

"M'Ljot?" she asked, her dark bark-like armor similar to what he remembered on Alerix.

Jouler willed himself into his vision self, letting his consciousness spread throughout his form.

"You must choose," the sapling said, her gaze lowering to his hands.

In his right hand, Jouler held the peculiar black sword, faint blue mist lifting from its wicked blade. Power filled his empty eye socket, hinting at hidden gifts bestowed by the strange weapon. In his other hand was a nondescript wooden staff, the familiar grain of the wood comforting his soul.

"What are you waiting for?" the sapling asked, her chk'da dripping with blood. Growling, she turned and charged into a group of Phaerians, their left temple shimmering with a warm-yellow symbol of a rising sun.

"Wait!" Jouler shouted, but his cry fell on dead ears, the Prytha's chest shattering from a swirling-blue spear.

"No!" Jouler cried. The Black Breath amplified his voice, his command halting the battle, undead and living alike.

Let go… The Black Breath's voice echoed in his mind, drawing his gaze back to the sword. *Release the darkness within.*

Prytha and Phaerians shook their head, awakening from their sudden stupor. One crazed sapling scooped up a chk'da, and charged the immobile headless. She swung with a shout and the weapon blasted as it passed through its swirling blue orb. The Prytha's back shattered from a blue sword, and she crumbled to the ground.

More Prytha awakened from their daze and charged the headless, littering the ground with shattered flesh and puddles of blood. Vines and roots slithered from the soil, entwining the headless and crumbling to lifeless white powder.

"You can save them," the Black Breath cooed.

The plain wooden staff was heavy in his hand, while the peculiar sword begged to exact vengeance.

"You must choose…"

Jouler dropped the staff, and a surge of power filled him.

L'Veyna looked across a wasteland, her consciousness still heavy and drained from the last vision. Charred trees poked from a sea of gray, their burned corpses standing like blackened spears, crackling embers the only sound. Ashen vortices swirled through the smoky desolation, while an angry fire raged in the distance, painting a dark streak through the smoky sky.

Still a helpless passerby in her body, she wiped a sleeve across her eyes, her chin quivering. Her vision-self stumbled forward, bones crunching and snapping beneath her feet. Her tattered green wrap fluttered in an unfelt breeze.

What is this?

"An avoidable fate," the deep voice rumbled in her mind.

A horn shrieked from behind her, and her vision-self slumped to her knees. "It's over," she said, defeat heavy on her breath.

No, get up! L'Veyna tried to shout.

Behind her, a low rumble rolled through the ground. Her shoulders shook, and she cried.

Get up!

She'd done it before, taken control of her vision-self enough to drop the plagued spear. The rumbling grew louder, the sound of charging horses drawing closer with every breath.

Get…up…now!

Her vision self breathed a heavy sigh and lifted her leg to stand.

Yes! Yes, hurry!

Keepers could regrow the Forests, but death lasted forever. Chin quivering, she turned to face the charging horses, and L'Veyna's hope tumbled with her tears. Behind the charging wedge of cavalry, ta'Aji-ilee's charred remains poured smoke into the sky.

"Stop the suffering," the ancient familiar voice said.

Do something! she screamed, helplessly grasping for control. She scrolled through her memories of the previous vision, searching for a clue to help her regain control. She'd denied the rotten black spear, but this vision had no darkness to forsake.

A sob tumbled from her lips.

Don't cry! she thought, straining for control. *Ask, plague you!*

The cavalry's lances lowered, the rumble of hooves shaking the ground.

"Accept my power," the Black Breath cooed. "Free your people."

Never, L'Veyna thought, the denial seeming to drain her consciousness even more.

A lance pierced her chest.

JOULER STOOD at the helm of a ship, sails furled and secured because of the raging seas ahead. Atop three tall masts, his banner, a black silhouette of his spiked sickle-sword over a field of sky blue, whipped and snapped in the harsh wind.

In full control of his vision body, Jouler took in the large vessel brimming with Prytha saplings and a smattering of Boorde. Brown- and green-skinned children huddled on the deck in misery, while a portion of saplings clung to the railings, emptying their stomach.

Behind their ship, dozens of clunky warships followed, their wide flat decks bristling with catapults and scorpions.

"The fleet is ready, M'Ljot." A sapling saluted him, slapping palm to chest. Her fluorite-colored eyes drew in concern.

"Speak your mind, N'Aara," he said, the name floating from his mouth.

"Shouldn't we go *around* the Sea of Storms?"

"Not if we want to get to where we're headed," he replied.

Leaned against the quarterdeck rail was the familiar nondescript staff. As usual, its comforting grain called to him, almost sparking a memory. Someone had given it to him. Someone important, but the memory dissipated from his mind.

The young Prytha quirked her mouth to the side. "But, Horgar said—"

"Horgar doesn't know where the Cabal is headquartered." Jouler spotted the young sailor on the deck, securing a loose barrel. Horgar waved and gave Jouler a thumb up. "Get everyone inside!" Jouler shouted above the screaming wind. "That means you too, N'Aara."

The young Prytha started to protest, then gave a curt nod. "Yes, M'Ljot."

Horgar loped to the quarterdeck, slapping palm to heart in salute. "Everything's secure, Captain."

"How many times to I have to tell you?" Jouler said. "I'm not a captain."

Horgar jerked his thumb at the armada. "I beg to differ."

"Would a captain drag his fleet through the Sea of Storms?"

"Not a sane one," Horgar replied, his eyes full of wonder, like a boy staring at his hero.

"Have I ever told you," Jouler said, ruffling Horgar's hair, "you remind me of my brother?"

Horgar swiped at Jouler's arm. "Yes."

"You'd better get inside," Jouler told him, rain pelting their face.

Instead of listening, Horgar handed Jouler his safety line, and tied a line for himself.

Jouler situated the flat strap of leather against his back, the ends tied to thick metal loops at the base of the wheel. Horgar imitated him, peering at Jouler from the corner of his eyes to get the leather strap in the same spot on his back. Harnesses would have been better, at least for keeping them from tumbling into the sea. A large enough wave could still pull their legs from under them, or even flip them out of their safety lines. A design for a harness materialized in his mind, which he stored away for later thought.

The ship's bow crashed through a giant capping wave, seawater pouring over the deck and splashing across the quarterdeck. Lightning broke the air with thunderous cracks, bathing the dark sky purple. Soaked through, Jouler leaned back against the safety line, his breath catching as the ship plummeted down the back of the wave, only to swoop into another.

Jouler gripped the wheel, the rudder protesting their given course. Horgar shouted to him, but the biting wind swallowed his words. Another capping wave coursed over the ship, and again Jouler's breath caught from the plunge, his stomach climbing into his throat.

Horgar shouted again, pointing to their rear.

Jouler turned in time to see three large warships twist and break in the raging sea. His heart sank at the thought of so many saplings and Boorde, drowning because of him.

Stop the suffering.

The Black Breath's call pierced through the wind and crashing waves. Another weaker call pleaded to Jouler, drawing his attention to the nondescript staff, which still leaned against the quarterdeck rail, unmoving despite the rolling ship. The staff begged him to choose it, but what could a piece of wood do against a storm? He'd witnessed the power of the Black Breath. He'd felt it course through him, its power sweet and seductive. With that weapon, he could do anything. He could be the person Horgar saw when he looked at him.

Jouler grabbed the staff, comforting familiarity spreading up his arm to his chest. The staff...loved him. Another flash of lightning cracked the air, and an explosion rocked the sea. Smoke billowed from a ruined warship.

Gritting his teeth, he tossed the staff into the sea, and drew the Black Breath. Dark power surged within him, filling his eye socket, and chomping at his will to be set free. He pointed the spiked sickle-like blade at the calm heart of the storm, and released a black beam so dark it pained his eye. The beam met the swirling storm with a silent boom, and the raging clouds dissipated as a ripple of calm spread across the sea.

Horgar gawked at him. "That was..." The safety line slipped from his hands, and thudded on the quarterdeck, the sound loud amid the sudden calm.

The below-deck hatch popped open, issuing dozens of saplings. Wide eyed, they flocked onto the deck, staring at the flat water in silence.

A faint noise bobbed within the calm sea. Almost too quiet to hear, the staff's pain-filled cry tore at Jouler's heart.

"What did I do?" he asked, dropping the Black Breath. It clattered on the deck and disappeared in a puff of shadow, only to reform at his waist.

Horgar frowned, and cast a sweeping gesture to the colorful young

Prytha, just now beginning to murmur about M'Ljot and the conquered storm. "You saved them. You saved us all."

The Black Breath's power swelled within him, whispering at hints of more hidden powers.

"But at what cost?"

44

SAYING PLEASE

Pattern-forged alarms peeled and rang throughout Eio, and for once, Katima wished humanity moved a little faster.

The lift, at least.

She shielded Dilna from the Upper Tier lords and ladies packing the platform. Katima turned away from the loud dresses, suits, and hair, longing for the black-on-black palette of the Alliance.

A palette I'll never see again, she thought, a pang of loss burning through her anxiety. *At least, not while Mother lives.*

The lift stopped at the Lower Bronze Port, inciting a loud scuffle between the Upper and Lower Tiersmen. Katima's shaping sense rippled down her spine, and a force barrier pushed the Lower Bronzmen back from the lift, allowing the gate to close. Angry shouts followed them into the city's bowels.

Katima pretended not to hear the pathetic drivel spilling from the Upper Tiersmen's lips about making room for Humans and Citizens. She patted Dilna's tiny shoulders and told her to ignore them. "Cowards hide behind words, Dilna."

A prickling wall of shields and spears met them at the Steel District. Tight-knit formations of soldiers filled the port, waiting to file onto designated military lifts. The Makers District came and went, the vacant port unsettling Katima with a festering unease.

"What's going on?" Dilna asked. "Where is everyone?"

"Probably another drill, " a short, plump woman said, holding a black velvet snuff pouch to her nose. Smooth pink hair fell past her shoulders, her green silk shirt exposing the pale skin of a Silver lady. "Unsurprising with all the attacks. At least that little Phlem whore is dead. What was her name…Mikenna…Melinda…"

"Makayla," Katima said, biting off a surge of impatience.

"No…that's not it." The Silver lady shook her head. "It doesn't matter. She's dead. I heard she slept with half her army. It's the only thing those Phlem are good for." She cast a plump smirk at Dilna. "It's bad enough they infest our lovely city."

"Oh, I don't know…" Katima mused. "I think Phaerians bring a certain honor to this place." She reached for the woman's pink hair, and the lady flinched back. "They compensate for people like you. Self-important Upper Tiersman, sitting in your tiny estates, lording from on 'high'."

Dilna dared a smirk at the lady, and mumbled, "Pathetic."

"I will admit," Katima said, sucking on an elongated canine. "As pampered as Upper Tier lords and ladies are, I imagine your meat would be nice and juicy. Well marbled."

The Silver Lady shrunk back, bumping into another lord in vibrant clothes. He scowled and pushed her back with his hip.

Katima tapped her djohai, bumping the spike against her hip, no closer to understanding how such weak creatures ruled the empire. These pretentious lords and ladies had dominated Torgeir for over twenty-five hundred years, and not once had the Lower Tiers risen in protest. At least three quarters of the imperial population lived below the heights of the Shining Wall, suffering the humid stench permeating the air, toiling every day so their so-called betters could live in luxury. At least Phaerians have stood up to the empire, even if it ended up with an entire queendom blasted into the sea. In the end, Astrakane had stood alone, while Boorde and Prytha had hidden in their mountains and forests.

Those Humans, Phaerian and Citizen alike, had shown more honor than the whole of the Alliance. Them and Makayla, whose war still ravaged Blailon without her. It was a shame she'd died in the Battle of Serolle. Such emblems of honor seldom graced history, their lives burning bright and short.

The stench of the Workers District singed Katima's wandering thoughts, reigniting her urgency. If they didn't rescue Kael, there would be no world for heroes to grace. The lift stopped, the rails slid open, and the Upper Tiersmen poured into the Workers District port, presumably heading for the staging area.

"Use your ring," she told Dilna once the platform cleared.

Dilna slid the large ring over her thumb and pressed the engraved Shield. A hollow, imperial-red image of the city sprung to life above the ring. "Gods! That scared me."

"We must be the flashing red dot," Katima said, tracing her finger along a line that connected the dot to a group of cells near the node-stone cavern at the center of the city. "That must be where Kael is…"

Her voice trailed at the sight of Diou waving at them from the port exit.

"Il'Diou!" Dilna chirped, activating her ring to show him. "I know where Kael is!"

He frowned at the imperial-red image of the city. "Who gave that to you, ed'Dilna?"

"Grim," Katima said, and his eyes flashed with anger.

Diou held out his hand, and Dilna gave him the ring. He dropped it, and in a fluid motion, drew a glowing dagger and rammed it into the cobbled ground, splitting the ring.

Dilna's eyes went wide with shock. "But…we needed that to find Kael."

"I already know where he is," Diou said, waving for them to follow into the bustling Workers District. He plunged into the thick crowd, ignoring shouts and curses as he forced his way through the droning throng.

"What's going on?" Katima asked, shoving any Citizens who got too close to Dilna.

"The city is being evacuated," Diou replied. "It's a distraction. The Sotouri are transporting Kael and Makayla."

"She survived the explosion?" Katima asked, swarming in a confluence of relief, excitement, and unease.

"Who?" Dilna asked.

"Makayla," Diou replied, knocking over a stubborn lady who refused to move. "And yes, she's alive."

"Who? What explosion?"

"Makayla," Katima replied, her mind focused on the young Phaerian who'd reignited her people's long-lost desire for freedom.

"You both keep repeating that name," Dilna said, "like it's supposed to mean something. Do you realize how many Makaylas there are in…" Shock stole her voice, her eyes widening. "Makayla? As in, *the* Makayla?"

"The same," Diou said, turning down an empty, mud-laden alley to a nondescript door. "She's in a cell next to Kael's."

Katima halted at the door, overcome by a sudden realization.

"What's wrong?" Diou asked, his eyes darting up and down the alley.

Heroes seldom graced history—Laceyl Granivin, the queen who'd dared to consider Phaerians as Human, Kestrad Corgan, the il'Spada who saved Emperor Hrothmund during the Ormgeirr Rebellion, and Brynhildr Gudrund, the Meru'utian Weaver who'd developed waterboxes. They'd all lived centuries apart, and now a handful of such emblems of honor lived at the same time. Makayla Penfrost, the Light of the West who'd dared challenge the empire. The Facets of Prophecy—L'Veyna Elmhand, the Warden of Preservation, Kael Aelastair, the Crier of Change, and Jouler Davinin, Vidimir, the Harbinger of Death. Her brother Diou, an il'Spada whose fame would endure millennia, and his Astasi ed'Dilna Freeman, the first magicless Human to don the sacred prefix. Pendric Loyalton, who embodied his surname, and Reylan, who sacrificed a life of wealth, power, and prestige to pursue Prophecy.

"This truly is the dawn of a new age."

"The Dawn of Prophecy," Diou said, handing her a thick strip of jerked meat. He unsheathed a pair of daggers and their blades glowed like embers. "I don't think the Sotouri are going to let us walk into their secret dungeon."

Dilna imitated her Shai'jan, unsheathing her daggers. "What if we say please?"

Katima swelled with pride at the Astasi's courage.

Sacred Flame, I love that little girl.

She devoured the strip of meat and her inner flame flared with life. Harmonizing her core, she danced a gentle flame over her hand and burned the hair from her scalp.

Diou bowed his head. "Sister, if you would be so kind."

Katima's heart burned with love for her older brother, and she pulled him into a tight hug. "Thank you."

Hair singed, Diou wiped his bald scalp. "Feels…interesting."

"I think I'll keep my hair," Dilna said.

"Now we're ready," Katima said, dancing flames around her fists. "Let's go say please."

DILNA POURED her fear into her core, hoping to ignite her inner flame, but frozen claws of doubt chilled her will. Still, she followed her bald Shai'jan down narrow hallways, forcing her stiff limbs into action. Katima's light steps pattered behind her, heat emanating from her fists.

"Shaping," Katima warned, and Dilna's heart sunk.

Gods, what am I doing? she thought, hands trembling around the hilt of her cold daggers. *This isn't the training yard. It's real life, and real death, and real Sotouri. I can't shape. I'm just a stupid little girl with a stupid little mind.*

Katima's warm hand rested on Dilna's back, her confident, fire-diamond gaze wavering in Dilna's watering vision. "Remember, young Astasi. Prophecy is hardly done with you. Stick to your Shai'jan's side, and you'll be fine."

Stay with him? Dilna wondered, her throat too tight to speak. *Won't I get in the way?*

Il'Diou tapped his left side, and Dilna's training melted through her terror. She moved beside him, her too-black ry'ku turning her into a shadow down the dim, twisted hallways.

My Shai'jan's shadow.

Il'Diou halted before a door, the blades of his daggers glowing like hot embers.

Again Dilna fed her fear into her core, hoping to control her raging firestorm. Still, her daggers remained cold and dark.

Il'Diou moved away from the door and nodded to his sister.

Katima's hand undulated, the wave riding up her arm, and back down. She thrust her hand out, and a thick stream of liquid fire burst through the door and into another hallway. Katima twisted in a whirling dance, and the stream exploded. Fire poured down the hall, filling the air with screams and desperate cries.

Il'Diou dashed through the singed doorway, his glowing daggers shattering patterns, and a pair of Sotouri flopped to the ground, mouths agape in silent screams.

Two more Sotouri ran into the hall, their long daggers crackling with power. Il'Diou dashed at them, his ry'ku whipping. His daggers shattered the Sotouri's patterns and snaked past their defense. One glowing blade sliced through a neck, while the other drank a Sotouri's heart.

"Keep up, Astasi," il'Diou said. "I can't protect you if you fall behind."

Dilna scurried to her Shai'jan's side, his confidence and skill melting her fear. She followed him down the hall, brick walls still crackling with heat.

Just keep up, she thought, sneering at the back of her Shai'jan's bald head. *Well, don't move so fast.*

"More shaping," Katima warned, sucking a long canine. "A lot more."

Il'Diou threw a thoughtful gaze down the hall. "Darts?"

Katima considered the question and shook her head. "Serpents."

Diou lifted an eyebrow, his lips whispering a name Dilna didn't quite catch—Ish-something.

Katima entered a seductive dance, her hips twisting and shaking. One arm slithered upward, the other held before her, hand upraised before her chest. Fire swirled around her feet, scorching the brick floor. The flames grew, flickering into three snakes, glowing fangs dripping with liquid fire.

"Firedancer!" someone shouted from behind a nearby wall.

Katima twitched a finger, and a fiery serpent pierced through the brick, igniting a flurry of muffled screams.

More shouts trickled down the hall, lancing Dilna's focus with frozen spikes of fear.

Katima's remaining serpents slithered down the hall, and Il'Diou followed. Dilna trailed close behind, trying not to think about the type of people they faced.

"Shaping!" Katima shouted, flinging her serpents through the wall beside them.

The wall shifted, and a rough hand threw Dilna forward, into a large room. The wall fell with a heavy thud, spilling dust into the room, choking Dilna. Coughing, she pushed herself to her feet, muffled shouts calling her name. A sudden breeze cleared the dust, revealing three dark figures with her in the room.

Sotouri, she thought, terror loosening tears from her watering gaze.

Invisible bands snaked around her, lifting her off the floor. Dilna gripped her daggers, refusing to let them go, scrambling to ignite her inner flame.

"If it isn't the famed Phlem Astasi," one of the Sotouri said, her scratchy voice as ugly as her wide face and drooping lips.

Dilna closed her eyes and focused on her breathing. Diou's voice rumbled into her mind, trickling into her limbs, and comforting her pounding heart.

Emotions trick the mind into believing what it wants, not what is.

Her inner flame sparkled, igniting a flicker of hope.

An Astasi's power comes from control.

Dilna fed her emotions into the flame—joy, sorrow, doubt, fear—

letting her feelings flow through her, until only her inner flame remained.

Control leads to harmony.

She gripped her daggers, breathing calm.

Harmony reveals our true self.

"My name," she said, her heart as tranquil as her voice, "is Dilna."

She opened her eyes, and her calm crumbled under a wave of terror. Her daggers rested cold in her fists.

"Cute," the ugly Sotouri said.

Invisible hands wrapped around her neck and plucked the daggers away. The hands tightened and sparkles flitted through her vision, darkness encroaching around her. Desperation shocked her into motion. Tears streaming down her cheeks, she struggled against her bonds, shaking and squirming, straining to breathe.

Please! Gods, no! Please! I don't want to die.

Her thoughts fluttered with every unrealized dream, smothering her with regret. She'd never see Kael, or Jouler, or Pendric, or L'Veyna! Gods, she'd never see her Prytha half again. She'd never know love.

I guess it doesn't matter anymore…

Darkness enveloped her, and she let go, slumping against her bonds.

Wind ruffled her hair, stirring her consciousness. The sound of shattered glass sounded in her ears, and the rush of life poured into her wanting lungs, scattering the darkness with an explosion of light.

Life.

Sweet, clean, pure life filled her, coursing into her veins. Her vision focused around il'Diou, standing over the ugly Sotouri's corpse. Dust coated his snow-white skin and ry'ku, relief burning in his fire-diamond eyes.

Dilna breathed in sweet life, and climbed to her feet, sparkles dancing in her vision again. Two charred corpses smoldered on the floor, while the ugly Sotouri stared with empty eyes, bright blood pooling around her from a deep gash in her neck.

"Dilna, are you hurt?" Katima asked, flowing into the room.

Dilna considered the question. She'd seen the void that awaited at the end of life, that unfeeling bliss of nonexistence, and she realized a sobering truth—fearing death was pointless. Life, it turned out, truly was the sweetest gift of all.

A gift Sotouri don't deserve.

"My throat hurts a little," Dilna said, her voice hoarse. She retrieved her daggers off the floor, finding a strange calm amid her newfound rush of life. "But I know just the thing to cheer me up."

45

FREEDOM

*T*hey *all deserve to die.*

The unbidden thought floated through Kael's mind, stirring images of Baelorin, Maelly, and Rodak. In a flash, Kael stood on a familiar dirt road tunneled by trees.

No...

Olan stood before him, drowning Kael's anger in a fresh wave of misery. Soft whimpers replaced Olan's image with an image of Makayla, shaking from another nightmare, her battered body curled on a cold stone floor.

Kael called out to wake her, but no sound came out of his mouth. He tried to reach for her, to shake her awake, but his limbs wouldn't work.

Because you're asleep, you fool.

He jolted awake and stretched, careful to not kick over his waste bucket. Sliding back his mind-trap shackles, he rubbed his chaffed wrists, savoring the sharp pain. Faint singing whispered into his ears, pulling him upright. He tilted his head and held his breath. It wasn't really a song, and more like a melodic urge. A symphony of sorrow, calling to him for help, begging for freedom.

A heavy sigh washed out the sad song.

Gods, how long has it been?

Despite Lokir's promises to visit his dear Aglia, he'd only come to feed her a handful of times. Maybe they'd only been here a handful of days. It didn't seem right, but nothing seemed right in the replete darkness. Awake...asleep—it grew harder and harder to distinguish the two apart.

"Makayla!" Aglia snapped.

Kael startled with a kick and groaned from the stench of excrement sloshing over his feet and ankles. He kicked his waste bucket off his ankles, sat up, and leaned against the wall.

"I'm awake," Makayla said, moaning as if through a stretch. "Although I'm not sure this is any better. Kael?"

"I agree," he replied.

"That's not what I...never mind," Makayla said.

"Kael," Aglia said. "Who deserves to die?"

Kael wracked his mind, trying to remember from the long list of people who deserved such a fate.

"You said they all deserved to die," Aglia said, sparking his memory.

"Oh, that was a dream," he said. "Half dream, maybe. Right on the cusp."

"Who is it?" Makayla asked.

"You know who," Kael replied. "Both of you know better than I."

"Founders," Makayla said.

"Not just them," Kael said. "Sotouri, Vrath, Pattern Weavers, and every other person who bears that blasted Shield."

"Kael, that's not..." Makayla's voice trailed with uncertainty. "I understand how you feel, but—"

"Do you?" Kael asked. "You lived under the empire's thumb, but do you really know how I feel? Do you really know what they did to me?"

"Kael..." Aglia's voice cracked with sorrow, tempering Kael's rising anger.

"They did far worse to you," Kael said.

"But you wore that same Shield," Aglia replied. "You carried that same curse."

"Exactly," Makayla said. "I understand your anger, Kael. I do. But I was wrong, and so are you."

"I'm not," Kael said. "Prophecy doesn't foretell an end to the empire's oppression. It foretells Torgeir's destruction, because it's the only way to cleanse the world of its filth."

"You changed," Aglia said.

"I'm a Facet," Kael said. "Change is in my title."

"So then change," Makayla said. "If you did it for me, you can do it for anyone."

Kael thought to mention Rodak, draping a long stretch of silence over their cells.

"Kael?" Aglia asked, prodding the silence. "Did you really meet... what was His name?"

"His?"

"The tree god," she replied. "The one you said you met. Did that actually happen?"

"Tálise," he replied. "He looked a lot like Reylan, but only because he knew that appearance would comfort me. To you, Tálise may have resembled your mother or father, I suppose."

"Then the Prophecies *are* real," Aglia mumbled.

"Were you hoping otherwise?" Makayla asked.

"At least then," Aglia said, "the gods would have had an excuse for not doing a damn thing to stop the empire. All the power in the universe, and they just sit there, doing what—being gods?"

"They can't do anything," Kael said. "The war between the Dark and the Light would have destroyed the universe. Planets, stars, every-thing. So, Prophecy bound them and gave us a path to end the war."

"What about Tolrik?" Aglia asked. "Laa, Surar, Meldun—what about *our* gods?"

"What gods?" Kael retorted. "From what little Tálise told me, they were all adopted from the Prytha pantheon."

"Figures," Aglia said with a sniff. "An empire ruled by men, with laws written by men, can't possibly have a pantheon ruled by a woman."

"That would be tragic," Makayla said, her voice oozing with sarcasm.

"So, gods just sit there?" Aglia asked. "Wherever there is. It really is pointless to ask them for…well, anything, isn't it?"

A dozen platitudes floated through Kael's mind, each as empty as his fetid waste bucket. Even if the gods heard their prayers, they couldn't act on them…could they?

Does it matter?

If bound gods couldn't answer prayers, what was the point of asking them for help?

"When have gods ever intervened?" Kael asked. "Why would they start now?"

"What about my power?" Makayla said. "It came from the Dark. I can still feel his blight on my soul."

"I don't know," Kael said, mulling over the question. "Maybe the Dark isn't as bound as the Light. Maybe he found a way to free himself."

"Wouldn't the world be dead?" Makayla asked. "If the Dark were free, I mean."

"Maybe he's only partially free," Kael offered.

"It's so strange," Aglia said, "hearing you talk about gods like this." She laughed, as if to herself. "Remember when you used to scowl whenever anyone mentioned Prophecy or Tolrik?"

Kael knew the pain that awaited him at the end of those happy memories, but his yearning heart didn't care. He remembered every second he'd spent with Livia, from the blundering moment he first saw her, to the agonizing moment she'd left him at the edge of Headwater. He remembered every detail about her, how the sun kissed her wavy hair into cascading waterfalls of honey. The way she enjoyed an extra dollop of strawberry or peach jam on her biscuits. How she always tapped her lip whenever stuck in a thought, how she preferred sunrises over sunsets, and picnics over candlelight dinners. Most of all, he remembered her smell—orange blossoms and jasmine.

"Kael?" Aglia said, sounding so much like *her*. "Remember that day at the lake?"

His heart broke, and he sobbed her name. Her true name. "Livia..."

"I'm so sorry," she cried

"Livia, it's okay," Kael blubbered, his gut churning with sorrow, loss, rage... He cleared his throat, and took a deep breath.

"Please, don't call me that," Aglia said. "It hurts too much. I'm not that person anymore. I wish I was, but..."

"I understand," Kael said, wishing more than anything to have Livia back again. To hear her voice—her *real* voice, not the tortured sounds that escaped Aglia's lips.

"Liar," she said with a chuckle, igniting more happy memories.

The Ul'Kral had shown him the life they could have had with Livia —two beautiful children, and a quaint little house—but his cowardice at Headwater had robbed him of that happiness. Instead of staying to protect the village and rid the world of Rodak's filth, he'd let his friends carry him away with the belief of a doing greater good. He, the strongest shaper in history, the Crier of Change, the mistaken Light of Prophecy, able to embody the Currents of Power, had run away.

"Do you..." Aglia mumbled. "Do you think the gods, the *real* gods, will forgive me?"

"Of course," Kael said at the same time Makayla said, "If not, then there's no hope for me."

"What do you think they'll call me?" Aglia asked.

"What are you getting at?" Makayla asked. "You're scaring me."

"When I meet them," Aglia said. "The Gods. Do you think they'll call me Aglia, or..."

Her words faded with the sharp slam of a bolt, and the metallic squeak of hinges.

"Oh, Aglia," Lokir sang, his voice echoing in the darkness. "Aglia, dear Aglia... We're leaving. Isn't that great?"

Fear lanced Kael's heart, the playful tease in Lokir's voice stirring with familiarity like an older version of a voice from Kael's past.

I wasn't going to keep it.

Kael sank under the memory of Olan, reaching for his cowardly hero.

You could have saved him.

The truth slammed inside Kael's chest.

You could have saved them all.

Pain cracked inside his skull, his shoulders hitting the cold stone floor.

Just as you could save them now.

Kael gripped his head, his mind trap shackles warm around his wrists.

But you won't. You'll let them die. You'll let her *die.*

"No!"

The footsteps and clanging metal halted. "Well," Lokir said, sarcasm sharp in his chipper voice. "Sounds like someone isn't so excited. You should be happy for Aglia. She's going to a better place, which is more than I can say for you, Kael."

The bolt locking Aglia's cell slid open, and the door shrieked open.

"Ah," Lokir cooed, "there you are, my dear. Oof, the smell." He gagged. "Ah, better. Now, where were we? We're leaving for a better and far brighter future. No, oh, no, don't cry, my dear. This is a happy day. Come...come, let's share with the others. It's all right, come on. That's it...there, that wasn't so bad, now was it?"

Makayla's door unlocked and creaked open.

"I'll even let you feed your friends," Lokir said.

"Aglia," Makayla said.

"It's all right," Aglia said, calm despite the morbid truth steeled in her voice. She knew Lokir was going to kill her, and she refused to cower. In the shadow of her final moments, Aglia stood unwavering, facing her end with a quiet defiance, an emblem of true strength.

"Y-Yes," Lokir stammered. "Of course it is. Give the filthy Phlem her food. Kael is waiting."

The latch on Kael's cell door slid open.

"Guess who?" Lokir sang, pulling the door open. The soft light of a glowglobe warmed the lordling's alabaster skin. Clothed in black to match his long silky hair, he tugged on leather gloves stamped with House Toren's golden moon and stars.

Three Vrath stood behind him, one from each branch, according to the cords looped around the shoulder.

Lokir pulled Aglia into the doorway and shoved her inside Kael's cell. Wispy hair matted against her scalp, her clothes tattered and filthy, she raised her chin, her uneven eyes filled with the same acceptance he'd seen the day he fled Headwater. The day she thought she'd die.

Guilt drew his eyes to the floor, but his whispered name drew his gaze to hers. A familiar coy smile cracked her lips, and his heart swelled with memories of the times she'd given him that look. The slight raise of her eyebrow, the hinted dimple in her cheek, and the confidence in her eyes that had always dared him to pursue her.

Livia.

Kael's heart saw past the tortured soul Rodak had created to the person who still held his love. He stood and took her hands. Lokir, his Vrath, and the cell all faded to cascading locks of honey, warm skin brushed with a golden shade of brown, and the comforting aroma of orange blossoms and jasmine. She reminded him so much of the day they'd met and his fumbled words—the day she'd stolen his heart. The warmth in her smile spoke of dreams whispered in a moonlit meadow. Of a tender kiss shared on a lake shore. Of two souls promising eternal love.

"It's not your fault," she said, squeezing his hands. "It never was."

His throat tightened, guilt pouring down his cheeks.

"Goodbye, Kael," she said, pride blazing in her eyes.

"Goodbye, Livia."

Her chin quivered, and she mouthed, *Thank you*, tears dripping from her chin.

She grunted and crumbled into his arms, her eyes empty. Warm blood poured over his hands, the hilt of Lokir's dagger sticking from her back. The pain of shattered dreams and stolen love tore at Kael's heart, and the pressure in his head burst with waves of blissful power. His skin blazed with the Currents, his pattern-forged shackles melting from his wrists. Power poured into him from the nodestone deep beneath the city, its haunting melody calling to him, begging him for release.

The three Vrath attempted to shape, but the Currents severed their gift. Their patterns unraveled as they fell to the ground, screaming.

"You were right," Kael said, the power in his voice shaking the cells. He laid Livia on the floor, peace finally resting over her tortured face. "She *is* in a better place. Which is more than I can say for you, and everyone else in this gods-forsaken city."

MAKAYLA CURSED Lokir's echoing boot falls, wishing he would trip and smash his smug face on the floor.

"Aglia, dear Aglia," he sang, tapping something metallic against cell doors as he passed.

Tink-tink-tink…

"We're leaving."

Tink-tink-tink…

"Isn't that great?"

Tink-tink-tink…

"No!" Kael shouted, startling Makayla.

"Well," Lokir said, in his annoyingly sarcastic tone. "Sounds like someone isn't so excited. You should be happy for Aglia. She's going to a better place, which is more than I can say for you, Kael."

He's going to kill her, Makayla thought, her chest tightening.

The bolt locking Aglia's cell slid, and the door creaked open.

Panic tumbled through Makayla's mind, shaking her limbs. She pressed her hands to her ears and hummed, blocking out the lordling's teasing voice.

A moment later, her door creaked open.

A glowglobe hovered in the doorframe, casting Lokir's tall, skinny frame in a soft light. Draped in black clothes trimmed in gold, the lordling snickered at Makayla, and pulled Aglia into the doorway. He motioned for his Vrath to hand her a plate of food. "I'll even let you feed your friends."

Aglia stared at the plate, frozen in a thought. After three…four…five breaths, she stood up straight and squared her shoulders.

"Aglia," Makayla said, helpless to prevent her morbid fate. Not against Lokir and three Vrath, their disgusting Shields shimmering on their temple. Not unless her power magically reappeared.

"It's all right," Aglia said, standing tall and commanding, as though Lokir had come down here at her behest. Gods, what a woman she must have been before Rodak got his claws in her. Strong, confident, proud—everything Makayla wished she could be.

"Y-Yes," Lokir stammered, tapping a narrow dagger stuck through his belt. "Of course it is. Give the filthy Phlem her food. Kael is waiting."

Aglia knelt to set the plate down, then she wrapped Makayla in a tight hug, and whispered, "Stay strong, sister. Keep Kael safe."

Makayla's throat clenched, her vision watering as Lokir pulled Aglia away and shut the cell door.

"Guess who?" Lokir sang, rapping something metallic against Kael's door.

A long stretch of silence passed before Aglia said, "It's not your fault. It never was."

"Goodbye, Kael."

Thick silence weighed over the cells.

"Goodbye, Livia."

Makayla wanted to scream, to pound on her door and plead with Aglia—with *Livia,* to run. To fight, and scratch, and claw…anything! The soft thuds of her crumpling corpse sounded loud in the silence.

Pristine white light burst under Makayla's cell door, flooding her cell. Screams erupted, followed by whimpering cries.

"You were right." Kael's voice shook the walls. "Livia *is* in a better place. Which is more than I can say for you, or everyone else in this gods-forsaken city."

Another scream, shrill with pain and desperation, reverberated through the dungeon.

Makayla pressed her hands to her ears, telling herself Lokir deserved whatever Kael did to him, but the Founder's cries stretched on and on, breath after breath, and then it was gone.

Silence reigned over the dungeon once again.

A moment later, Makayla's door flung open, and blinding light stormed into her cell. Gasping, she covered her eyes, and Kael mumbled an apology.

Warm, joyful power enveloped her, seeping into her aches and pains, and comforting her troubled mind. The anguish she'd endured in Maelly's caravan, Lokir's kicks and punches, weeks of mind-shattering darkness…it all evaporated under the loving warmth of Kael's power.

Her shackles fell from around her wrists, clattering to the ground, and she dared to peek between her fingers. She dropped her hand, Kael's blazing light no longer burning her eyes.

"I can feel it," he said. "The nodestone. It's so pure. It…it's calling to me. It wants me to…" He shook his head, spraying sparkles of power. "It wants to die." His light-filled gaze turned to her. "They all want to die."

THE PURE POWER of the Currents poured into Kael, infusing his body, burning away his pain and sorry until even the memory of his torment seemed wrong. Those things Maelly and Rodak had done, the torture and suffering, had happened to some other Kael from a different reality.

He balanced his will on the delicate line between submission and domination, careful to keep his emotions from sparking an unbidden pattern. Like a loyal dog waiting for its master's commands, the Currents sprung at his slightest whim, eager to protect and carry out his will. Even now, they reacted to a gentle bubble of annoyance at the wall between him and the nodestone chamber. A simple geometric pattern, symmetric and angular, formed around his annoyance, and the wall crumbled into a tunnel.

Makayla startled behind him, and the Currents reacted to his warm concern, wrapping her in a force bubble. The void in her soul glared at him, reeking of the Dark's influence, challenging him to mend the wound he'd made on that fateful day. Unbidden, his power flowed it into the void and disappear in its insatiable depths.

Makayla gasped, her eyes rolling back, hands tight. "Kael...stop."

"Sorry," he said, staving off the power and banishing the bubble of force. "The Currents seem a little anxious."

"*They're* anxious?" she said. "What was that?"

"It seemed like the Currents were trying to heal your power."

Makayla hugged herself and shook her head. "It didn't feel like it."

The shrill call of the nodestone begged Kael to destroy it. The empire didn't deserve such a precious gift. He'd seen what they'd done to this land when the inhabitants welcomed the empire onto its shores. He'd studied at the Citadel and lived the lie that kept the empire in power. He knew of its corruption. He knew, like the filth infesting Makayla's soul, no amount of goodness could save the empire.

Holding her hand, Kael led her into the cavernous nodestone chamber. All around him, tainted power from countless spent patterns flowed toward the center of the cavern, to a thick column that stretched up from the floor. Spiraling stairs climbed the column, reaching a flat summit where the nodestone hovered above a pedestal. Rough and teardrop-shaped, the nodestone burned with radiant, shifting colors.

Filtered Power, Kael realized, watching spent Currents pass through the stone. In all the empire's brilliance and genius, it seemed no one had thought to question how much the nodestones could take, perpetually filtering spent patterns and pattern-forgings.

That, or no one had cared to ask.

The nodestone's shrill call begged him for release, caressing him toward the tall pillar.

"Kael, no." Makayla pulled on his hand, but gentle sparkles of power loosened her grip.

"I must destroy it," Kael said. "Can't you hear it? It can't take it anymore. It wants to die." The nodestone's sad wail echoed his concerns, begging him for release. "They all want to die."

"Think about what will happen," Makayla said, shaking sparkles off her hand. "You'll blast the entire city right on top of us."

Images flashed in his mind of Eio crumbling into lifeless white powder. His vision from Tálise, of an empire ravaged by war, morphed into a land spotted white where proud imperial cities had once stood. New Torgeir, the Island City, shining beacon of the empire, swallowed by the sea, like Astrakane before it.

"This is how I fulfill Prophecy," he said, walking toward the column. "This is how I destroy the empire."

"Kael!" Makayla rushed toward him and gasped, doubling over and falling to the ground in pain. Her stomach heaved, and she vomited from the nodestone's influence. "Kael…help me."

Waves of power reacted to Kael's concern, carrying her back from the stone's effect.

"Please!" Makayla shouted, rising to her knee, and wiping her mouth. "Don't do this!"

"After all the empire's done," Kael said, his voice shaking dust from the jagged ceiling. "You would still protect them?"

"I want to do what's right," she replied. "And this doesn't feel right. There has to be another way."

"They *want* to die," Kael said, climbing the stairs that wound up the column. "Don't you see? This is how I take down the empire. This is how I fulfill Prophecy."

"Then why does it feel wrong?" Makayla said. "Don't do this."

"You don't hear it," Kael said, reaching the top of the glorious column.

The nodestone glimmered above its cradle, suspended by the very Currents it filtered. As tall as he, the rough, teardrop-shaped gemstone blazed with brilliant colors.

Kael suddenly floated in a vision, drifting above a healthy, vibrant land teaming with placid Currents. No turbulent waves of power crashed against each other, only gentle streams coursing through the land, spilling into vast lakes of power. Lush forests and grasslands covered the blasted spots where imperial cities had once stood, Phaerian towns rebuilt and thriving, the Boorde Alliance expanded across Haldr's Bowl, and the Sacred Forests open to all. Without the empire, without shaping, peace would reign across the land.

Shaping really is the problem.

Pressing his hands to the stone, Kael drained its power and absorbed it into himself. The cavern walls shook, dust tumbling in the air. A loud crack snapped through the nodestone, spilling colorful sparkles onto the pedestal and column. Encouraged by the fissure, Kael bore into the multihued stone, stealing its power.

"Kael, stop!" Makayla pleaded.

She doesn't understand, a voice mumbled in Kael's head. *This is how you fulfill Prophecy. This is how you defeat the Dark.*

"I know," Kael replied, sucking more power from the stone. "Soon enough, they'll all understand."

Power siphoned into him, spreading more cracks across the nodestone. Multihued sparkles poured down the column, lighting the massive cavern.

"Kael!"

That's not Makayla's voice, Kael thought.

"Kael!"

He turned from the nodestone, and saw a familiar figure standing by the tunnel he'd opened. "Dilna?"

Dressed in peculiar black clothes, she stood beside two tall Boorde, a male and a female, both bald, their too-black clothes disappearing in the darkness.

"Dilna!" A sob ripped from Kael's chest, tears of power sparkling down his cheeks.

"Kael?" Her excitement twisted with confusion. "Is…is that really you?"

Kael stepped to the edge of the column, power still pouring from the cracks in the nodestone. Dilna shied behind the male Boorde, the fear in her dark eyes shaking Kael's excitement at seeing her.

She doesn't understand, the voice whispered in his mind. *None of them do.*

The Boorde woman stopped at the edge of the nodestone's influence, her firedancer dress rippling in an unfelt breeze. She took in the scene, and her eyes went wide with shock.

"You fool!" she shouted. "You'll kill us all."

Free them, the voice whispered to Kael. *Free them all.*

Kael turned away from Dilna, Makayla, and the two Boorde, and he pressed his hands to the nodestone, siphoning its power into himself. A deep crack snapped in the stone, issuing waves of multihued sparkles. Power gushed from the stone, pouring around him, consuming the column, and splashing across the floor.

A flash of alarm rippled through Kael, and the Currents wrapped Dilna, Makayla, and the two Boorde in a bubble of force ten paces thick.

Free them…

Another crack popped, and a large shard of the nodestone fell to the ground, shattering in a burst of vibrant sparkles. Deep, reverberating laughter filled his mind, and the nodestone exploded in a violent shower, releasing a wave of destructive power.

The cavern blasted in an instant, and Kael plummeted through lifeless white powder as the power he'd stolen from the nodestone wrapped him in a cocoon of light.

MAKAYLA'S HEART leaped to her throat as the sphere Kael had shaped plummeted through fine white powder. A loud, deep rumble shook the air, and the tall male Boorde wrapped his arms around Makayla and the young girl named Dilna. Makayla struggled against his grip, but the man could have been a mountain for all he budged.

"Relax," he said, his voice deep and commanding.

The other Boorde shouted, her words eaten by the deafening rumble.

Something slammed into their sphere, and Makayla echoed Dilna's cry. Water rushed around them, pulling them down the charging current, slamming the sphere into jagged rocks.

Fear ripped from Makayla's throat, her screams loud in her ears.

"Stop screaming!" the Boorde said, curling around her and Dilna.

Sudden blinding sunlight washed the sphere, the sky bright and glorious. Behind them, a torrential stream raged down the mountainside, ripping trees and boulders from their purchase.

Makayla's stomach leaped to her throat as the sphere plummeted once more, her gaze wrenched to the ground so far below.

"Now you can scream," the Boorde said.

46

SACRIFICE

Over a hundred times, the Black Breath had showed Jouler the fates of his different Paths of Prophecy. As had happened in every other vision, he ignored the pleading staff and accepted the black, spiked sickle-sword. Power swelled within him, churning his stomach with its foul taint. He pushed away the deep sense of loss that always accompanied the discarded staff, as though he'd somehow betrayed the thing. His heart always yearned for him to choose the staff, but he needed something stronger than a glorified stick.

Especially for this mission, he mused, standing before a towering Shining Wall. A long, rocky coastline hugged the wall, perfect for the gulls squawking in the air, and the seals vying for purchase on the jagged rocks. Only one city boasted such a grand wall.

New Torgeir.

Power flared in his eye socket, leaking cerulean mist, and lending him a Boorde's battle prescience. He rammed the sickle-sword into the wall, and black cracks snaked up its smooth surface, splintering into a dark web. Jouler flexed his will, the dark web constricted, and New Torgeir's Shining Wall exploded. Protected by the relic's dark powers, pieces of stone passed through him, his body wavering in an incorporeal blur.

He summoned a burst of wind to clear the rising dust, revealing a wide staging area edged by stables and pristine white buildings. An army of Vrath in tight, organized units waited for him on the open grounds. Thousands of do'Vrath in black-and-orange mail filled the front lines, with hundreds of tii'Vrath sprinkled throughout. Behind them, Weavers and ra'Vrath operated massive pattern-forged scorpions and catapults designed to launch gravity balls or rain shards of force.

Jouler stabbed the sword into the ground, commanding the Black Breath's power. Liquid shadow bubbled from the rent ground and poured into the staging area. Jouler's stomach soured from the relic warning of the Vrath's patterns. Giant slabs of granite shot up beside him from the ground, threatening to crush him, while fire and lightning splashed against tentacles of liquid darkness.

The Black Breath reacted to his pang of fear, and the liquid darkness swarmed over the looming slabs of rock, dissolving them. The dark liquid whipped at the Vrath, boring through their pathetic barriers of force and swallowing their attacks, their patterns bursting with cerulean power. Catapults and scorpions thrummed, and tentacles shot from the dark liquid to snatch their pattern-forged projectiles.

The power in Jouler's eye socket flared again, unveiling light shields at his left flank moments before they dropped. He turned to meet the hidden formation of Sotouri—Marks, Blades, and Spades, by the looks of them.

Finally, some fun.

Jouler's stomach churned from their useless patterns. He tapped into the power swarming in his eye socket and shifted like a Chi'indi, darting between Sotouri. The Black Breath sang in his hand, trailing wisps of inky black and cerulean. Crimson misted the air.

Hot pain ignited in his leg, his thigh leaking blood from a Sotouri's blade. Jouler rammed the spike on his sword into the woman's chest. The Black Breath drained her life force, leaving a dried out husk, and healing Jouler's wound. With all the Sotouri dead, he turned his attention back to the pain-filled shrieks soaking the staging area. Jouler directed the liquid, forming a tall wave, and sending it into the remaining Vrath.

Silence dripped over New Torgeir.

A soft hand rested on his shoulder, and he spun, slicing empty air. At his feet was the nondescript staff. Over a hundred times he'd seen it, and over a hundred times he'd denied it. Curious, he picked it up, its familiar grain calling to him with that ancient familiarity, as though he'd owned the thing his entire life. Or, somehow, even longer. It tugged at his heart, begging him to toss away the foul sword. An image flashed in his mind of a beautiful Prytha face with autumnal braids and emerald eyes. It was a face he knew even better than he knew the staff, but the name teetered on the edge of his tongue.

The Black Breath flashed at his side with annoyance, and the image faded.

A small figure appeared in the staging area, her alabaster skin a stark contrast to her wavy black hair. Tentacles the same blue as a headless orb whipped around her and slithered on the ground. The same blue misting from the wicked blade and leaking beneath Jouler's eyepatch.

Unlike the Prytha's name, the young Phaerian's came clear to his mind, drifting from his lips. "Makayla."

"That belongs to me," she said, pointing to his sword, as she had in all of his visions. Her slithering blue tentacles pierced the ground, and dozens of headless arose from the staging area.

Please, the staff seemed to beg at Jouler's feet, its plea tugging at his heart, begging him to throw down the Black Breath. His grip around the black sword loosened, and the weapon dangled in his hand.

The staff sang with hope, its warmth encouraging Jouler, urging him to let go.

The air filled with shrieks like metal scraping over ice, and Jouler's heart dropped once more. Guilt tore at his chest, duty weighing like a mountain on his soul.

"I'm so sorry," Jouler cried. Heart shattered, he dropped the staff, and the Black Breath's vile power swelled within him. Cheek wet, he gripped his cursed weapon, enduring its filth in order to save the world.

A HUNDRED TIMES L'Veyna had escaped the Black Breath's influence, maybe more. Each vision seemed to drain her strength, her power waning every time she denied the dark relic's temptations. She'd long stopped counting the times it had offered its seductive power, torturing her with visions of bloody wars, burned forests, and frozen tropics. She'd watched countless loved ones perish again and again—Prack, Jouler, Dilna, Horgar, and every other person she'd cared about, all tortured and killed, and she'd done nothing to stop it.

L'Veyna breathed in the acrid smoke, choking the air, reminding herself this was just one more vision. The scorching heat and blood-soaked mud squished through her toes were all a figment of her imagination.

If only it were that easy.

No matter how many times she told herself this was all a dream, that her loved ones were just figments of her imagination, flames still burned her skin, blades still sliced her flesh, and her heart still broke each time her loved ones died, the pain as fresh and agonizing as any she'd felt in the real world.

"Because it's real," the Black Breath said, filling her mind with its ancient, rumbling voice.

She ignored the foul relic, letting its voice float through her consciousness. As soon as she acknowledged it, the plagued relic would demand she choose its power or let the world burn.

"Stop the suffering," the Black Breath said, its ancient voice resonating from everywhere and nowhere.

She squeezed her eyes shut and hugged herself against the relic's sickening call. The same words had echoed in every vision. They were lies, of course. She'd seen the relic's so-called end of suffering. No people, no trees, no shrubs, no water, just a barren land devoid of life.

"It doesn't have to end that way," the Black Breath said. "Take my power. End the suffering."

L'Veyna's stomach curled at the thought of that revolting power licking her soul again. Nothing good could ever come from the Black Breath. How could it when it came from Dra'Nahl, a literal puff of the god's foul breath?

Ash and smoke burned her lungs, forcing a cough.

Nothing is real, she thought, despite the ash and smoke burning her lungs.

"But it is," the Black Breath said. "Each Path you've walked has been as real as your own, for they are all yours. Every battle you've lost, every burned forest, every death you've witnessed. Even your own. It has all been real. Or, it will be, unless you take my power."

With a weary sigh, she opened her eyes, and her resolve drained into the bloody ground.

Death covered the land. Body parts strewn about, entrails spilled from mangled torsos, and empty eyes staring from crushed heads. Prytha, Boorde, Human, and the strange reptilian-like species who summoned the dead—they all littered the ground.

Her gaze caught on familiar faces. She'd never seen the people, but her vision-self knew who they were. Their names teased the back of L'Veyna's mind, but she shoved them away.

It's not real.

"Oh," the Black Breath crooned, "but it is. You know it is. You cannot deny it."

The words reverberated through her soul, as undeniable as her waning power. The names she'd shoved away crashed through her mind—*M'Kasi, Halna, Shynoa, Anoky…*

She screamed, drowned by painful memories.

The relic's voice rang clear in her mind. "Take my power before he takes yours."

He who?

Annoyance rippled across her consciousness. "He will take it all, if you let him."

"All what?"

"He'll take it all…"

"He who? Take what?"

"Your life."

"Who's taking…" L'Veyna squeezed tears under a rush of under-standing. "Jouler." He drained her life force, not the Black Breath, likely to keep him strong against the foul relic's temptations.

But then, why would it want me to take its power?

The answer blossomed as soon as the thought came to her mind. Without taking her life force, the Black Breath would have killed them both.

This must be my role, she thought, finding a grain of strength nestled within that insight. It all made sense that the Warden of Preservation should do just that—preserve life. Even at the cost of her own, she supposed, and what better life to preserve than M'Ljot's?

Her ever-blossoming power waned, and she fell to her knees, mud sloshing around her calves.

"He'll take it all if you don't accept my power."

"Never!" she shouted, and what little strength she had drained into the muddy ground. Her eyes closed, and she fell forward, carried into darkness by rumbling laughter.

TINY MOTES of dust danced through thin rays of sunshine, the light piercing through tiny gaps in familiar wooden walls. Darkness clung to the room, defying the intrusive rays. Jouler took in the simple desk and shuttered windows, the small round table with a muted oil lamp and a small pitcher filled with Reylan's tonic. Almost two years ago, Jouler had visited Kael in this very room. Instead of a sick bed waiting for its patient, Pendric sat across from him in a wooden chair.

"Pen!" Jouler leaped from his chair and froze from Pendric's raised hand and somber face. Jouler returned to seat, reminding himself his childhood friend was somewhere far away. "You're just another vision."

"A wha—" Pendric's head jerked back, and then he leaned forward and poked Jouler's forehead. "Did that feel like a vision?"

"As real as any other," Jouler replied, noting the soft aroma of spring grass wafting from Pen. "Who are you?"

Pendric leaned back in his chair, mischief tugging a smile.

"You're not Pen," Jouler said, looking past the brown skin and disheveled hair. Even the food stains in his shirt and fidgeting fingers reminded Jouler of his friend, but ancient wisdom had never coursed through Pendric's eyes. "I wish more than anything that you were, but you're not." Jouler squeezed his eyes against the pain of seeing his friend after so long. "You're just another figment I'll have to watch die like the rest. Kael, Livia, L'Veyna, Dilna... All of them, and more times than I care to count."

"All but me."

"Which you wouldn't know unless you were part of the vision."

Pendric dipped his head.

"But why now?" Jouler asked. "What changed?"

"You."

The word hung in the room.

"What are you doing?" Pendric asked. "The Jouler I know would never choose that foul thing."

Jouler followed Pendric's gaze to the wicked sword leaning against a dark corner of the room. When Jouler turned back to explain himself, Pendric held the familiar wooden staff. As always, the staff begged him to choose it, its once powerful calls now whispered pleas from a dying loved one.

"You don't understand," he said, wishing Pendric didn't look so much like himself. "You'll die if I don't bring back that weapon. Not you. The person you're imitating. The real Pendric Loyalton. My friend."

"You're wrong," Pendric said.

"I'm not," Jouler growled over the pain in his throat. "This...whatever you are. You weren't there when the Ul'Kral took his breath. You haven't seen him struggle to breathe after a short walk. You don't know what he was like before those blasted creatures cursed him."

"No," Pendric said with a pointed look. "You are wrong"

"I wish I was." Jouler slouched with a sigh, his gaze falling on the simple wooden staff dying in the crook of Pendric's arm. Hints of a name drifted alongside the staff's familiarity, skirting the edge of Jouler's mind. "Who is that?"

"You know who it is," Pendric said.

"Not you," Jouler replied, grasping for the name that wouldn't form. "Not Pen, I mean. It's familiar, but in a different way. Older, like...like the wisdom in your eyes."

Pendric's brow lifted, and he leaned forward in his chair. "Oh?"

"Yeah," Jouler said, searching the feelings that emanated from the staff. "Like I've known it for ages and ages. Like it loves me."

"And..."

Jouler took a slow breath to clear his mind. "And it's all trick."

Pendric deflated in his seat.

"A trick," Jouler repeated. "No different from all the other visions." He turned from Pendric's hurt gaze, catching the aroma of sweet wildflowers and soil after a light sprinkle. "Who are you, really?"

"Pendric," he said with a voice that stirred Jouler's memories of simpler times in Headwater, when chores were their hated foe, and taking a trip to Alduos was the talk of the village.

"You are not Pendric," Jouler said, wishing so much that it was him. "You look like Pen, and you even carry his mannerisms. I'll give you that. But you don't smell like him."

"Oh?"

"You smell like..." Jouler sniffed the air, and a memory of the field behind the sick house blossomed his mind. "You smell like a spring breeze. Like grass, wildflowers, and healthy soil."

"So I do," Pendric said, working the hem of his sleeve. "Why did you choose it?"

Jouler regarded the spiked sword. The foul relic pulsed with the power of the Dark, promising an end to the empire and freedom for his people. More importantly, it promised freedom for his friend. "I have to."

"You don't."

"I do!" Jouler shouted, snatching the staff from Pendric. Renewed pleas saturated him with loving warmth. His chest swelled with heartache for the times he'd cast the staff away. His vision wavered, his throat thick with pain.

But what could a staff do? What would he tell the Ul'Kral? How would he face Pendric? The real Pendric, not whatever being posed as him. How would Jouler tell him he'd abandoned the key to Pen's salvation over a broken heart?

"You don't have to do this," Pendric said.

Loving staff in hand, Jouler lumbered to the window. Without the Black Breath, he was a Facet with no power, no better than a snapped shaper. A simple farmer from a backwoods village.

"Please," Pendric pleaded, working the hem of his sleeve.

The familiarity of the staff caressed Jouler's soul, urging him to remember. A name drifted just out of reach. If he but stretch his mind, just a little... But that meant abandoning Pendric, and facing Prophecy with nothing but his bare hands. It meant risking the fate of everyone that is and ever would be to the Dark's corruptive power. It's hatred for life itself.

With a heavy sigh, Jouler opened the shutter, flooding the room in bright sunlight.

"Jouler...please," Pendric said, the defeat in his voice mirrored on his face.

The staff added its cries, begging Jouler to stop. Its desperation clawed at his soul. It's pain laced with betrayal.

"Jo..."

Jouler clung to his dark truths, while his heart echoed the staff's cries. Prying his hand open, he dropped the staff out the window, feeling as though he'd let his little brothers fall from a cliff, or...or the name he refused to remember. Heart shattered, he closed the shutters and shambled to his dark fate.

Jouler hefted the sword, the weight of the world resting in its foul blade.

"This is my burden alone to bear," he said, cerulean mist swirling from the Black Breath. "I am the Harbinger of Death."

L'Veyna's power sputtered, its energy bolstering Jouler's, helping him rebuke the Black Breath's temptations. Her exhausted consciousness floated in that space between visions, struggling to keep the darkness from consuming her. She doubted she had the energy to endure another vision. It would be so easy to let go, and give in to that eternal slumber, but Jouler needed her. She had to resist a little longer. Just a little more pain, and it would all end—the terrible visions, the unending heartbreak from watching her loved ones die... all of it gone, swallowed by that blissful peace.

"Stop the suffering..." the foul relic droned, its deep, ancient voice reverberating through her soul.

Never, L'Veyna thought.

The Black Breath's laughter rippled over her consciousness, and the relic's presence vanished.

Alone, she...what—floated? Existed? Was that what this was—the life of a lonely soul cursed to an eternity of solitude?

Jouler must have resisted all the Black Breath's trials, and not a moment too soon.

At least Jouler had succeeded.

Her thoughts drifted amid the crushing silence. Time passed, she supposed. It had to, didn't it? Did it matter to the dead? She thought of Jouler, awaking triumphant, only to find her corpse at his feet, having to carry her to her brother.

"Such savory thoughts."

The familiar, ancient voice froze her consciousness.

It's back. But, how?

"I never left," the Black Breath cooed.

Hot, vile pain consumed her, tearing at the last sparkle of her power. Threads of her consciousness unraveled from her soul, each a lost part of her self.

At least Jouler defeated you.

A heavy pang twisted through her. She'd never see him again. Or her brother, or Pendric, or Dilna.

Deep laughter rumbled the void as more threads of her consciousness unraveled from her soul. The rumbling halted, and the Black Breath rippled with waves of frustration.

"Don't go…"

The voice sounded distant, stirring her torn memories.

"Come back…"

A new, youthful light blossomed within the void, its soft glow soaking into L'Veyna. Her power sputtered to life, drawing strength from the light. The Black Breath raged against her, clawing at her soul, but all that mattered was the new power growing within her.

The Black Breath stabbed at her, and a brilliant flash of light filled the void. A sound like metal scraping over ice pierced her, the noise as revolting as the relic.

"Take me instead," the distant voice pleaded as the familiar, youthful light continued to pour into L'Veyna.

Young…

"What? No!" she shouted into the void, finally understanding the source of the light. "Horgar, no!"

L'Veyna pushed against the power, but she may as well have tried stopping the tides. Helpless, she watched the last of Horgar's life drain into her.

Her soul flared anew, breath flooded her lungs, and light filled the void, burning her eyes. Needles pierced her skin as sensation ignited throughout her body. She blinked, color draining into her vision, her mind working to make sense of the scene before her.

Four people were with her on top of a tall stone column. A slender Boorde helped a ruggedly handsome Human to his feet. Faint blue light glowed beneath the human's eyepatch, a foul black sword at his waist. His eye met hers, and guilt twisted his face. A younger Human stood next to a seated Boorde. Beautiful despite the burn scaring half her bald head, the Boorde held a familiar young man in her arms, his brilliant autumnal locks bright against her white skin.

Prack!

L'Veyna's screams shook the cavern, dust tumbling from the ceiling. The light had been his, not Horgar's. She formed an image of her brother with his confident smirk and infectious laugh. She recalled the way he always made her feel safe and loved—always loved. The image shook, her power flared, and the asking shattered.

Desperation clouded her mind and ripped at her broken heart. She asked again, holding a simpler image this time, her brother's untraditional hair held back in a tail, his emerald-colored eyes glimmering with mischief.

The image shattered.

Again and again she tried, altering the image just so, all to the same effect. An alabaster hand touched her shoulder, and she brushed it away. Ignoring Tristian's pleas, L'Veyna held her brother's cold hand.

"L'Veyna," Jouler said, his chin trembling, cheek wet with tears. Blue light, like a clear sky, leaked from beneath his eyepatch, and sparkled in the uncut emerald.

Horgar stood beside him, his eyes wide with shock, his hands trembling at his sides.

L'Veyna pleaded with her ever-blossoming power—*Prack's* power—to return to him, but it wouldn't budge.

No, please don't leave me…

She formed a new image, envisioning her power as a seed planted within him, her power helping it to grow from seed to sprout, and budding with life. The image locked into place, the asking accepted by her Goddess. Within the span of a thought, L'Veyna's power grew and expanded to fill her soul, her power blossoming into what it was always meant to be. Not the morsel she and the other Keepers toyed with. This was true connectedness with Alnazet. This was the power of a Facet, the power of Prophecy.

Life, pure and sweet, coursed through her, chasing away her exhaustion. It poured into her brother, soaking the hewn column, and onto the ground below. The column shook, shedding slabs of rock for fresh loamy skin. Cracks snaked across the cavern, bubbling healthy soil, and filling the cavern with the pleasant aroma of a freshly plowed field. Loud deep snaps resounded from above, and large sections of ceiling crashed to the ground, leaking rays of sunlight into the cavern.

The rumbling stopped, and the power coursing through L'Veyna eased. Exhaustion flooded her, and she slumped, barely noticing the blasted powder falling from the ceiling and churning into soil when it touched the ground, or the grass sprouting where the sun beamed through the ceiling.

She didn't care. How could she? Her brother was gone.

47

A FINE WHITE POWDER

Utterly consumed by boredom, Pendric sputtered his lips. He sucked in a wheezing breath, his lungs too weak to fill. The iron ring Reylan had pattern-forged helped a lot, but he still couldn't wait for Jouler to make the Ul'Kral return Pendric's breath. Maybe he'd replace it with the Black Breath, and then those blasted creatures could feed off that for the rest of time.

"How long are we going to be here?" Pendric bemoaned.

Reylan hung a wet shirt over the clothesline he'd stretched between a tall rock and a poor excuse for a tree. L'Veyna would have called it a glorified bush, but Pendric supposed it held the line well enough. Reylan's curved pipe dangled from his mouth, trails of smoke leaking from between his lips.

"Is the adventurer's life not as entertaining as you imagined, Pen?"

"This is hardly adventuring," Pendric said, waving at the brown, rocky landscape—and not even a nice, rich brown. More like darker sand, and completely barren of any interest. Sure, the rocks had been fun to explore on the first day, but it seemed Dilna and the Boorde had been gone for years. He looked to Eio, tucked into the north rim of Haldr's Bowl, and he wondered if they'd already rescued Kael. He imagined them fighting off a horde of Sotouri and Vrath, fire and patterns flinging through the air.

"I had more fun with Kael and Jouler," Pendric said, wondering if he'd be able to see such a fight from here. "And that wasn't any fun at all."

"Don't you have a book to read?" Reylan asked, grabbing one of Pendric's shirts from the washbasin.

"I already read them."

"All of them?" Reylan asked, and Pendric nodded. "Read them again."

"But I *just* finished them."

"Practice with the staff L'Veyna asked for you."

"It makes me too tired," Pendric replied. One more reason to move closer to the Kralnach Hills, but the old man refused to budge a pace. At least, not since Reylan found the stream a few weeks ago.

More like a few years ago.

"Be thankful this is all we're doing," Reylan mumbled, hanging Pendric's extra shirt on the clothesline.

Thankful? Pendric thought, sputtering a sigh. Doing nothing but gathering plants, and washing clothes, and sleeping, and gathering *more* plants… All that might be fine and chipper for the old man, but Pendric needed something more than rocks and dead shrubs. At least the west side of Haldr's Bowl had proper trees to climb, and sticks, and all sorts of hidden little places with secret stories to tell.

Maybe he'd climb the desolate mountain range again, where he'd definitely be able to watch Kael and Katima fling their magic. From up there, the Bowl looked like Tolrik had punched the ground. Pendric's imagination flourished with an image of a giant, bearded god slamming a fist into the ground.

But why would Tolrik do that? Pendric shrugged. Maybe there was an evil monster, like a dark dragon, or a huge terrentor, like the king terrentor. Maybe Tolrik saw Dra'Nahl's face, and He couldn't bear the sight. Whatever the reason, the punch had to have made some cracks or caves, right? Mountains had caves, and Haldr's Bowl was just a big, round mountain range. There had to be something more than brown rocks to explore.

Not that Reylan would let him venture out far enough to find anything fun. Not even after Pendric showed him the first Basic Staff Form, which he'd modified, of course. After all, every famous il'Spada had their own style. Kestrad Corgan, Gaut Vandil, Diou Nith'Iil, and Grim, the only Human on the list.

For now, Pendric thought, grinning over an image of him with his staff in hand, imperial soldiers groaning in pain around him. Even Diou had recognized his skills before he'd trotted off with Dilna and Katima.

I've never seen anyone swing a staff like you, he'd said, but Pen knew what he meant.

"What's rattling in that head of yours?" Reylan asked, draping his spare robe over the clothesline.

"Nothing," Pendric said. "I'm bored."

"Being bored is good for your mind," Reylan said. "Helps germinate creativity and innovation."

"But we've been here for years," Pendric moaned.

"It's only been a few weeks," Reylan said.

"Yeah, like a hundred."

"Like four…maybe five."

Pendric huffed, leaning on his staff. "And we've done nothing but sit here in the cold and freeze."

"You read all your books," Reylan said.

"Which I did, sitting down and freezing."

Barefoot, Reylan slapped his socks over the line, the cuffs of his coat soaked and dripping.

"You won't let me fish…" Pendric said.

"You have nothing to fish with."

"You won't let me venture out…"

"Ascended are still hunting us."

"You won't let me do anything," Pendric grumbled.

"It sounds like you need…" Reylan turned toward Eio, fear splashed across his face. "Dear gods…"

Pendric followed his gaze north, and his mouth went dry. The horizon shifted, sinking as a creeping white pallor spread from Eio, devouring the land's color in its wake. Trees collapsed, boulders crumbled, and the city, once nestled against the mountainside, disintegrated into a cascade of white dust. The mountains groaned behind the city, their dying echoes reaching Pendric's ears, before the once proud peaks crumbled into a formless white void.

The northern shore of Lake Skjold collapsed with a deafening roar, and water surged with devastating force, ripping through Haldr's Bowl. Ships, piers, and docks crashed through the tumultuous current, splintering hulls and sending jagged timbers down the back side of the mountain. Faint screams carried on the wind, fractured by the cacophony of destruction. The lake drained, pulling its stolen waters down the massive rent in Haldr's Bowl, leaving a muddy scar where life had once thrived.

Pendric stood frozen, his heart a stone in his chest. "What happened?"

"The nodestone," Reylan replied. "They must have…but how?"

"Where's Eio?" Pendric asked, his mind tumbling with fear. "Where's Dilna, and Kael, and Diou, and…" A sharp pang tightened his throat, and tears streamed down his face. Reylan wrapped his arms around him, and Pendric cried into his chest.

Reylan patted his back, telling him everything would be all right, but he didn't know that. How could he? Reylan saw the city turn into white powder. He watched the lake drain, same as Pen.

"The others are fine," Reylan said, his strong, confident tone soothing Pendric's worried mind.

"They are?" Pendric asked, sniffling. "But…how do you know?"

"I just know."

Pendric marveled at him. Reylan must have some secret shaper power that let him know, well, everything, it seemed. Pendric's da knew a lot too, but not like Reylan.

"What do we do now?" Pendric mumbled, still worried about his friends, despite Reylan's reassurances.

Reylan stood by the clothes line, his gaze distant, wet shirt forgotten in his hands. He drew a deep breath and released a heavy sigh.

"I..." Reylan rubbed his face, and stared at the gash in the mountainside where Eio had been, the lake a whisper of its former glory. "I don't know. I—" Reylan froze, his eyes wide with fear. "Run, Pendric!"

Pendric sputter his lips. "You know I can't run. I mean, not far, but—"

"Gods damn it, Pen. Run!"

Invisible bands snaked around Pendric, pinning his legs together and his arms to his sides.

"Reylan?" he said, fear ripping his heart, filling his mind with images of Grim's evil grin.

A stone's throw away, a group of rocks shifted, their forms changing into a small group of ragtag people. Or maybe they were some sort of rock people that could turn into normal people. He counted three...no four. No...just three. The other one really was a rock. One of the rock people almost looked like a bald Boorde, but not so tall, and with black skin instead of white, like he'd covered himself in charcoal.

Maybe rocks were just bad at replicating people, and it thought Boorde had black skin. It would explain his too-black clothes that almost looked like a ry'ku. The other two rock people looked like Humans, which they did a much better job impersonating. Unlike the dark Boorde, the other two looked like actual Humans. The scruffy male looked worse than Kael before he learned how to shave, but with dark, curly hair, and skin like mud. Time had added its own color pallet to the man's shabby attire. His long faded coat may have been black once, or blue, or dark gray maybe. Same for his ragged shirt with more holes than...well, than whatever has a bunch of holes.

Especially his boots!

The faded part, although the leather looked about ready to show his feet. Only something posing as a Human would look so ridiculous, even if his spear and the sidaiyo dangling from his belt seemed real enough.

He certainly looked better than the woman by his side. Why

would a rock person choose to imitate someone so hideous—and a Citizen to boot? Her strong jaw and pronounced brow made her look manly, like the rock person didn't know what a woman looked like. Still, she seemed as Human as the man. Maybe even more so with the terrible burn scar covering the right half of her head, her Shield melted and disfigured, her right arm missing below the elbow. White and grey hair covered the un-burned side of her scalp, falling in loose waves past her shoulder. Unlike the man, her drab, hardy clothes still had a dozen years on them, as long as she kept her coat and boots well oiled. She also had new soles, by the look of them.

Obviously a tanner, Pendric thought with a soft note of pride.

The thin sword dangling from her belt looked like it would snap from a twig, although the daggers sheathed along her thighs looked deadly, along with the metallic whip looped at her waist. Resting on her good arm was a strange club fashioned out of a hollow metal tube and capped by an oddly shaped chunk of wood. The club seemed especially awkward since she held it backwards, with the wooden clubbed end tucked into her armpit.

How would she even swing it with one arm?

"You're getting old," the scruffy man said, which made no sense to Pen. Sixteen—no, seventeen was hardly old.

Pendric almost told the man as much, but the panicked look on Reylan's face froze his tongue.

"Let the boy go, Thannel," Reylan said, and the scruffy fellow dry washed his face.

"Now, why would I do that?" Thannel asked, his gaze flitting about the campsite.

"Grim isn't here," Reylan said.

Of course he's not, Pendric thought, wondering why Reylan would say such an odd thing.

Thannel reached into Reylan's pack and retrieved four metallic tubes. "Two pairs? My, my, you have been busy."

"Please," Reylan said, jerking his head toward Pendric. "He won't make the trip. Listen to his breath. The Ul'Kral, they—" Reylan grunted, and floated to Thannel. Tears tumbled down Reylan's dark cheeks. "Please. He's just a boy."

"I was far younger when the Cabal recruited me," Thannel replied.

"Reylan?" Pendric said, dangling from his bonds, fear sapping his strength. "W-What's happening? Where are they taking us?"

"To the Tempest's Embrace," Thannel said. "Cabal Headquarters is dying for a chat."

RODAK PULLED himself up the rocky slope, while Lake Skjold dumped down the cliff side behind him. Pain cracked the back of his head, shattering his pattern, and his force barrier fell. Breathless, he pulled himself up the cliff, hatred fueling his weary muscles.

A hand grasped the collar of his coat, pulling him away from the raging waters.

"Are you all right?" a man asked, mud streaking his Founder-white skin.

Rodak sucked in heavy breaths, unable to speak over the exhaustion soaking his muscles. Kael had done this, as sure as the sun rises in the east. He'd destroyed the nodestone, and taken the last good thing from Rodak's life.

And so I will destroy his.

48

A FALLEN TREE

Halsyone Lalsco watched the Vrath platoon gather at the base of the Life Tree.

Or ta'Ajiilee, as Prytha call it, she mused, gazing up the tree's massive trunk and marveling at the large community platforms nestled in its massive branches. Realizing she fiddled with the new knot tied into her blue-and-white cord, she dropped her hand to the hilt of her pattern-forged hammer at her belt.

"Trying to wear a hole in your cord, lieutenant?" Captain Aegle gave her a sidelong glance, her black-and-orange mail still blemished from a recent scuffle with Prytha Keepers.

"Speaking from personal experience, Captain?" Halsyone asked.

"Always," Aegle said, gazing up at the massive Life Tree. "Amazing, isn't it? Who could have guessed that the source of the Currents resided below these trees?"

"Well..." Halsyone extended her will, sensing the formidable Currents churning out of ta'Ajiilee, and the calm pockets of power surrounding the Vrath. "I believe it was Ylva Alfrund who first surmised—"

"Simply marvelous, isn't it?" Aegle interrupted, and Halsyone rolled her eyes. Many ra'Vrath had surmised the Life Tree held the secrets of the Currents of Power, not that Aegle cared. The captain had an inquisitive mind for a do'Vrath, though she loathed Halsyone's droning lectures, as she called them.

"How goes the battle in the forest?" Aegle asked.

"A few pockets of resistance remain," Halsyone said, rummaging through her memories of the report. "Most are aimed at the convoys heading to Ingyatia, although there are still enough in the forest to warrant the reinforcements from Nyatia, which arrived this morning. I don't imagine it will take much longer to purge the forest."

"I don't know why we don't just burn it all. So many lives lost because of greed." Captain Aegle breathed a heavy sigh. "What about the hostages?"

"The last batch should arrive in Ingyatia by the end of the week." Haslyone marveled at the houses, seeming grown from the branches of giant oaks, walnuts, and maples. Their treehouses seemed quaint and homy, their rugs and tapestries woven with a master's skill. "They truly are a beautiful people."

"Were," Aegle corrected. "They *were* a beautiful people." She put two fingers to her mouth and released a shrill whistle. A young ra'Vrath scurried up to her and rendered a salute, slapping palm to shoulder. "Tell Sergeant Temenos to begin."

The young ra'Vrath snapped another salute and ran to relay the message. A moment later, dozens of tugs stippled the back of Haslyone's mind, and white-hot blades of force sliced into the Life Tree. Streams of fire bored into the trunk, and a groan shuddered up the giant tree.

"Emperor's ass," Halsyone mumbled, acutely aware of her proximity to the massive tree and its giant branches. "Maybe we should move back?"

Aegle jerked her chin at the Vrath at the base of the trunk, cutting into the tree. "They'll push it the other way. Just think of the power once the blasted thing is gone. It'll probably be like pulling a massive plug."

The ground rumbled behind them, and a sound like a thousand

giant horses charged toward them. Halsyone turned and looked in time to see a dark wall of water crash over the forest.

POWER SURGED THROUGH KAEL, wrapping him in a bright cocoon, his skin glowing with light. Blinded to the outside world, he waited, wondering about Makayla and Dilna, and the two Boorde. Dilna's friends, obviously sent to rescue him. Ironic, given the destruction he'd caused. A pang of guilt seeped into his thoughts, questioning his decision, begging him to consider all the lives he'd taken.

Kael clung to the memory of the stone's pleas, begging him for release, and his visions of a land free of the empire—a land free of shaping. The empire had defiled the nodestones with their perverse cities and shaped patterns. They'd proven they couldn't be trusted with such a sacred gift. Not them, not the Cabal—no one.

His cocoon of light melted away, and he found himself in a muddy wasteland. The trees of a once grand forest lay twisted and broken around him. Cracking limbs and dripping water trickled through the still air, drawing Kael's gaze up the path of destruction. A muddy scar stretched up the mountainside to the gash in Haldr's Bowl, left by the blasting.

Dilna, Makayla, and the two Boorde gaped at him from inside their force sphere, and Kael's heart dropped. The sphere rested against the charred remains of ta'Ajiilee's massive stump. The base of the tree reeked of shaping residue where Vrath had sliced into it with their foul patterns. Where powerful Currents had once raged with life, a trickle of power now ebbed from the stump.

The Life Trees are the source of the Currents, Kael realized. *The source of life.*

The understanding chilled Kael with an unforgiving hatred for the empire, for Vrath, Sotouri, Weavers, and every other filthy shaper who dared touch the Currents with their foul will.

Especially me.

"Kael!" Dilna called, pounding against the sphere's thick wall.

The pattern released, and the Currents settled them on the muddy ground.

Remembering a promise he'd made in a cold Blailonian cave, he sent the Currents into Makayla to that tainted void in her soul. She gasped as power poured into her, devoured by the insatiable hole. Kael gathered as much of the Currents as he dared without blasting the land. He reached into himself, to the power he'd stolen from the node-stone, sending every bit into Makayla.

"Kael...stop!" she cried, her body stiff.

The last of his power drained into the tainted void in Makayla's soul, and his Gift of Prophecy faded. His skin returned to the pale clammy flesh of a man who hadn't seen the sun in weeks, and he slumped to his knees, burdened by sudden exhaustion.

"Kael!" Makayla cried, running to his side.

"I'm sorry," he said, slumping with his hands on his knees. "I had to try."

Dilna approached him, doubt twisting her face, her fists clenched around the hilt of the daggers at her waist. Her black hair, tied into a topknot, disappeared against her strange, dark clothes.

Dressed like Dilna, though lacking his iconic hair, the tall Boorde male towered before Kael. "Diou Nith'Iil of the House Nith'Iil," he said, then gestured to the other Boorde. "This is my sister, Katima Nith'Iil."

As one, the Boorde knelt before Kael, snow-white scalps bright against their too-black clothes. Dilna gave a begrudging look to the mud before splashing to her knees beside them. Diou drew a dagger while his sister uncoiled the strange weapon at her hip, and they bowed before Kael, offering him their weapons. Dilna presented a dagger of her own, her jaw set in stubborn defiance to the fear welling in her eyes.

"I pledge my flame to the Dawn," Diou and Katima said in unison, and Dilna mumbled the same.

No longer that little girl, Kael thought with a pang of loss, a thousand questions rumbling through his mind.

Makayla edged closer and took his hand, her dark eyes darting about the mangled forest. Given the chance to come in peace, the empire had torn through Onatah, killing everything in its path. They'd chosen death and destruction, and they always would unless someone stopped them. Someone strong enough to destroy nodestones, and bring the empire's way of life to a powdery white halt.

"Kael…" Makayla said, looking up at him.

If not for Vrath, if not for *shaping*, ta'Ajiilee might still be standing. If not for shaping, life could truly thrive throughout the land.

"I'll bring an end to the empire," Kael said. "I'll destroy every last nodestone, and hunt down every last shaper."

"Kael, you're scaring me," Makayla said, squeezing his hand.

"I'm the Dawn," he told the kneeling Boorde and Dilna. "And I accept your pledges. I've seen the end of Prophecy. I've seen the end of the empire and of shaping, and it was beautiful." He held Makayla's gaze. "Shapers really are the problem."

"Then why does it feel so wrong?" she asked, her dark brown eyes brimming with fear.

"Because you've lost your sight," Kael said, placing his hands on her shoulders. "But I'm going to fix that."

"But you just tried."

"Maybe I need more power," he said. "More nodestones."

"What if you're wrong?" she asked.

The Boorde shared a blank look and stood, sheathing their weapons.

"I'm not," he said. "I felt it when I tried to heal you. The Currents want you whole."

"Why?" she asked, her beautiful face swarming with concern.

"Because you're a Facet, and your power holds the key to defeating Dra'Nahl."

49

NEW LIFE

Prack had never been one for somber goodbyes. He'd always found some way to make L'Veyna laugh before he left on one of his harrowing adventures with Diou, contorting their experiences in some funny way that stitched her sides and left her cheeks aching. She clung to the fond memories, refusing to let them fade. Her brother would have hated seeing her like this, her eyes red and puffy, nose raw and cracked.

Little Sprout, he would have said with his feigned sincerity. *You look worse than a wet owl.*

Tears streamed down her cheeks, and she drew a shuddering breath, embraced by the aroma of home. Sunlight poured into the cavern through a massive hole in what remained of the ceiling. No more blasted powder rained from above, the land now dark with healthy soil thanks to her brother's sacrifice. He would have been so proud to see a new Sacred Forest forming in a land that had long since abandoned life. Vibrant grass already covered the ground, while thick beds of moss climbed the cavern's walls.

He'd always be with her. Not in the empty platitudes people would tell her after they learned of Prack's fate. Her brother would actually be with her, fueling every asking. Her heart clung to the bitter truth as she knelt and laid a wreath of flowers at the foot of the sapling growing from her brother's grave. Already taller than she, the new ta'Ajiilee would grow to its full height in a year, or so said the stories. Soon, a thriving Sacred Forest would cover the Blasted Lands, awakened by her Gift of Prophecy.

New Onatah, she thought, returning to her feet, and standing beside Jouler.

Faint light the color of a clear blue sky glowed beneath his eyepatch and shimmered within the uncut emerald. He raised a hand to the eyepatch and scowled, glaring down at the cursed black weapon hanging at his hip.

"I can feel Dra'Nahl's power tainting my soul." He threw the blade with an angry shout, faint blue mist trailing from the sword. L'Veyna's stomach churned, and the wicked sword materialized in his hand from a cloud of darkness. Defeat weighed on his shoulders, pulling a heavy sigh. "I trusted the Seers," he said, his voice hoarse. "I trusted Prophecy to guide me down the right Path, and It brought me here. To this. To an actual piece of the blasted Dark." He threw his foul weapon again, and again it materialized in his hand. "I'm tired of doing what gods and Prophecy say is right. They haven't been right since I left Headwater. They've never been right, for all I'm concerned. I'm tired of being used."

L'Veyna put a hand on his arm, sharing in his rage and burning pang of betrayal.

"What now?" he asked, faint blue mist rising from his sword and leaking from beneath his eyepatch.

"We save my people," she said.

"What about the Saplings Curse?"

"To the void with the Curse," she said. "To the void with Prophecy. Look where it's gotten us."

Jouler's gaze drifted over the lush cavern, a thoughtful frown pulling at his lips. "So we just...what, do nothing?"

"We stop following Prophecy," she said, lacing her wormy fingers with his, "and we forge our own Path."

THE END OF
THE BLACK BREATH
Book Two of
THE CHRONICLES OF TORGEIR

A NOTE FROM THE AUTHOR

Thank you for joining me on this dark adventure. Be sure to sign up at jceyler.com for free digital wallpapers, bonus content, and be the first to hear about the next books.

GLOSSARY

A'a'nxil (aw-aw-n-xil): Species of humanoid who inhabit Sati. The general appearance of an A'anxil is that of a human covered in scales, with a slightly pointed face as thought pulled at the mouth. Their head is a gentle blend of human and reptile of the same coloration as their back, looking neither more human nor more reptilian. Their nose is a short ridge with a slit on each side for nostrils. Near lipless mouths contain human-like teeth with slightly elongated canines. See also Pantheons.

Aandari (On-DAR-ee): Boordish word for Headless. Loosely translates to, "one who steals another's honor, but can never attain it for themself." *See also* Boorde, Headless.

Advanced Forms: Second degree of the Boorde Weapon Forms. *See also* Basic Forms, Boorde, Master Forms, Weapon Forms.

Ages of Torgeir: The different periods throughout Torgeirian history. 1) Age of Arom (AA), known as the First Age, lasted from 1AA to 687AA. 2) Post Sacrifice (PS), known as the Second Age, arose after the Sacrifice that created the Blasted Lands. After the Sacrifice, the emperor declared that the empire had been reborn, and renamed the imperial capital New Torgeir. 3) After Prus (AP), known as the Third Age or Common Age. This Age arose during the Ormgeirr

Rebellion, after Kestrad Corgan saved Emperor Bjarrik who'd been captured and taken to Prus. The emperor declared a new Age on the day he was saved. Years After Landing (YL) is also commonly referenced throughout the empire as the common age.

Alnazet (AL-naw-zet): Also known as the Light, Alnazet is the antithesis of Dra'Nahl, and is worshipped by Prytha. *See also* Pantheons, Prytha.

Alnazet's Wreath: A protective barrier made from living vines, briars, and trees that surrounds every Sacred Forest. The Wreath prevents Citizens, shapers, and anyone with ill intent from entering the Sacred Forests. *See also* Sacred Forest.

archon: Governor of an imperial city.

Army of Light: Army of Phaerians who believed Makayla Penfrost to be the Light from prophecy and is now led by Nilam Fonth, the Voice.

Ascended: Ascended are highly skilled Boorde who travel the empire in search of lost relics and texts. Known for their House loyalties, the unofficial capacity of Ascended is to eliminate House targets. When on official House business, it is common for Ascended teams to consist of four members—three il'Spada led by a firedancer. Because of this, imperials often refer to them as Quads. *See also* Boorde, Quad.

asking: Prytha magic; the name is derived from the manner in which Prytha magic functions—Keepers form an image in their mind of they want to happen, and then they ask permission from Alnazet, who will either grant or deny their request. *See also* Alnazet, Keeper.

Astasi (ah-STAH-zee): Boordish word for 'apprentice'. Title given to il'Spada apprentices. *See also* il'Spada

Awaken: Awakening unlocks an individual's genetic potential. An Awakened person's ability to shape will also amplify; however, it will not give a person the ability to shape.

Basic Forms: First of three levels of the Boorde Weapon Forms; also known as the Basic Sword Styles or Basic Styles: Vis'mar, Tezrel, Chelt, Sodat, and Os'om. They are the first five Forms learned for any given weapon. All Boorde are instructed in the Basic Forms. Traditionally, male Boorde learn the sidaiyo, female Boorde learn the djohai, and eidraael Boorde learn either or both. *See also* Advanced Forms, Boorde, eidraael, djohai, Master Forms, sidaiyo, Weapon Forms.

blademaster: Common misnomer for il'Spada. *See also* il'Spada.

Blailon: 1) One of the Five Kingdoms of Torgeir. 2) Capital of the self-named kingdom.

Blasted Lands: A large portion of land in western Blailon that was blasted during the Sacrifice. *See also* Great Uprising, Sacrifice.

blasting: The complete removal of the Currents of Power from an area, which in turn removes the potential for life and transforms the land into a white powder. Blasting occurs when a shaper syphons too much power for the Currents to replenish. *See also* Shaping.

bone-tek: A'a'nxili machinations created by Mancers, such as auto-carts, curriers, golems, trains, and propellers for ships. *See also* A'a'nxil, Mancing.

Bone Theory: *See* Shaping.

Boorde (BOOrde): Characterized by their silky black hair, pale skin, diamond-shaped pupils, and love for meat. They normally stand taller than a human and are renowned for their skills with weapons and Firedancing. Boorde live in a matriarchal society, which is divided into Houses. Their homeland is called the Boorde Alliance, which is comprised of four large cities, and is lead by the Council of Flame. *See also* Council of Flame.

Cabal: Organization of Phaerian shapers. The official position of the empire is that the Cabal is nothing more than individual groups of Phaerians who learned to shape and who took up the name.

Cadet: Initiate in the Citadel.

Castantor (CAST-an-tor): 1) One of the Five Kingdoms of Torgeir. 2) Capital of the self-named kingdom; known as the River City.

Chelt: 1) In Boordish, 'sodat' is the sound of a burning log in a campfire. 2) Third of the Basic Sword Styles, or Basic Styles. *See also* Basic Sword Styles

Chi'indi (chih-IN-dee): Elite Prytha warriors. During a Prytha's rite of passage into adulthood, some are blessed with the ability to move swiftly over short distances, becoming a blur of motion. Few are blessed with the power of a Chi'indi, and as such, it is one of the greatest honors bestowed upon a Prytha. The traditional weapon of a Chi'indi is the tsah, a slender, needle-like dagger. Originally, Chi'indi were tasked with guarding the Grove and grove members; however, since the formation of the Sotouri, Chi'indi have expanded their role to hunt and kill Sotouri.

chk'da (chk-DAW): Ancient and iconic weapon of the Prytha, traditionally made from ironwood by a woodsmith. A spike protrudes at an angle from a large ball, topping the end of an arm-length haft.

Chosen of Alnazet: Also called Mother's Keeper and Will of Alnazet. Highest ranking Keeper of a Sacred Forest. *See also* Keeper, Prytha, Sacred Forest.

Citadel: Iconic home of the Vrath. Located in the Makers District, Citadels educate Cadets and train them to shape. The Citadel is divided into three branches—do'Vrath, ra'Vrath, and tii'Vrath. *See also* Vrath.

Citizen: Any human born of two Citizens and who bears the Imperial Shield (with exceptions for Sotouri). *See also* Imperial Shield, Sotouri.

comtab: A pattern-forged tablet used to communicate between linked comtabs, or tabs for short. Once established, a link can only be broken by destroying the comtab. Anything written or drawn on one comtab appears on any linked comtabs. *See also* Patter Forging.

Constable: Chosen by archons and kings to enforce imperial law in Phaerian towns. Constables oversee between four and six Phaerian towns. Each town houses a thousand imperial soldiers, led by a do'Vrath officers who report to the Constable through comtabs.

Constable's Gift: Yearly gift Constables give to the soldiers under their command. Traditionally, when the Constables receive the Imperial Allowance, they take a portion for themself, and then disperse to the rest to their officers and soldiers. *See also* Imperial Allowance.

cottlewomp: Herbivore known for its fluffy white fur; native to northern Blailon and Neuheim. Cottlewomp have thick white fur adapted to cold climates, and resemble a cross between a sheep and cow. They live in matriarchies called covens, consisting of 20–30 adults. Docile in nature, their only defense is a pheromone released when a cottlewomp is attacked. The pheromone drives the other cottlewomp in the coven into a desperate flight, which often tramples the youngest calves. Because of this, the expression "as cute as a cottlewomp" is often used to describe people who are far more dangerous than they appear, but with a clumsy undertone, while "sacrificial cottlewomp" is used to describe a person who's always bearing the burden of others.

Currency:

- 1 crown (gold) 10 marks
- 1 mark (silver) 10 pence
- 1 penny (copper) 10 imperials
- 1 imperial (bronze) 10 chips
- 1 chip (steel)

Currents, the: *See* Currents of Power.

Currents of Power: A force of nature that flows over and through the land like the currents of rivers. Ironically; water is the only substance devoid of Currents. Certain humans can use their will to shape a portion of the Currents to perform magical feats. When an area is completely drained of the Currents, matter devolves to a fine white powder and loses its potential for life. *See also* Blasting, Shaping.

Currier: Bone-tech machination. Curriers are boxes that resemble millipedes, used to deliver mail.

Dark, the: *See* Dra'Nahl.

djohai (JOE-high): The traditional weapon of Boorde women and eidraael meant to compliment a firedancer's flow. The djohai is a long cord affixed with a dart at one and, and a small hoop at the other end of the cord.

d'Tormena (d-tor-MEH-nuh): Prytha insult for shapers; translates to "one who drains life."

District, the: *See* imperial cities.

do'Vrath (DOUGH-Vrath): *See* Vrath

Dra'Nahl: Also known as the Dark. *See also* Pantheons.

ed: Boordish prefix given to Astasi. *See also* Astasi, Boorde, il, il'Spada, Shai'jan.

eidraael (AY-dray-el): Nonbinary Boorde. *See also* Boorde.

Ensnarement: Betrayal of the empire to the Prytha. During the Great Uprising, the Prytha refused to support the Emperor Hrafnagud's plan to end the war with the Phaerian rebels by blasting northwest Blailon and sinking the kingdom of Astrakane. Because of the Prytha's perceived betrayal, the emperor designed a trap to ensnare all of the Eldests, grove members, and all but the youngest Keepers. The emperor slaid them all, incinerated their corpses, and dumping their ash into the sea. Much of Prytha culture was lost on that day—all their ancient teachings as well as their ability to understand their ancient texts, including the Mh t'Pralab (the Wall of Prophecy), and the so-called Lost Postures. *See also* Great Uprising, Mh t'Pralab, Lost Postures.

Facets of Prophecy: Chosen by Prophecy, there are five Facets: the Incarnation, Crier of Change, Harbinger of Death, Warden of Preservation, and Emblem of Life. Each Facet plays a unique role in the Prophecies, known as their Path of Prophecy. As the each Facet walks their Path, their actions either strengthen the Light's or the Dark's influence on Yrsa. *See also* Prophecy of Light, Light.

fingertalon: Name for Prytha talons; from 2–3 inches in length. Broken talons regrow over the course of few months, unless regrown by a Keeper. *See also* Prytha, Talontongue.

firedancer: Female Boorde with the innate ability to manipulate fire and heat. Firedancing requires harmonizing the body with the desired effect, which looks like a graceful and sometimes violent dance. Powerful firedancers are able to harmonize their bodies without motion. Unlike other Boorde, a firedancer's dress has a strip of color that shimmers like fire. *See also* Boorde, ra'ku, ry'don, ry'ku.

Founders District: *See* imperial cities.

glowshroom: Mushroom that glows in the dark with a soft blue light. Used by Prytha to illuminate dark spaces, glowshrooms are only found within Prytha forests.

Great Uprising: (AA 675) Revolution of Phaerians against the empire that resulted in the ruination of northwest Blailon and the creation of the Imperial Paradigm. According to imperial records, the Great Uprising began when Archon Laceyl Granivin, the Betrayer, raised a Phaerian army to overthrow the emperor. *See also* Blasted Lands, Ensnarement, Sacrifice.

Guild, the: *See* Pattern-Weavers Guild.

Haldr's Bowl: Mountain range in Meru'ut that cradles Lake Skjold.

harmonize: firedancers harmonize their bodies in order to create feats of magic, resulting in a type of dance. Through centuries of practice, firedancers are able to harmonize their bodies without moving. *See also* Boorde, firedancer.

headless: Mythological undead creatures said to have a sphere of swirling blue energy in place of their head.

Headwater: Hidden Phaerian village in Glaedia.

hogswoggle: Similar to "Nonsense!"; common in Phaerian towns in Glaedia and Neuheim, but has been heard as far as eastern Blailon.

house-tree: Prytha houses which have been grown in the branches of common trees (e.g., oak). *See also* asking.

Hrafnagud, Emperor (HRAF-naw-gūd): Emperor during the Great Uprising, who ordered the Sacrifice and led Prytha Eldests and Keepers to their death.

Hunter: Name townsborn Phaerians give to Citizens disguised as Phaerians.

Hymns of Tolrik: Hymns of the Phaerian pantheon.

Iaroca (EE-uh-row-kuh): Phaerian town in Neuheim.

il: Boordish prefix denoting the title 'master'. *See also* Boorde, ed, il'Spada.

il'Spada (ill-SPA-da): Boorde weapon masters. To acquire the title il'Spada, a Boorde must master all Weapon Forms from five different weapons, one of which being either the sidayo or the djohai. *See also* Astasi, Boorde, djohai, Sho'jan, sidayo.

Imis Plains (IH-mis): A large expanse of plains that stretches from Central to Southern Neuheim.

Imperial Allowance: Yearly allowance of one copper penny, distributed to each Phaerian in the empire by the governing Constable. It is widely known and accepted throughout the empire that Constables keep most of the funds and distribute the rest to the garrison, which is known as the Constable's Gift. The funds for the Allowance are based on an estimation of the Phaerian population in each town and not an official census; *see also* Constable's Gift, Constable.

imperial cities: Tiered, conical shaped, and surrounded by a massive translucent wall called a Shining Wall. Each city is tiered into seven Districts. Special passes are required for lower-tier residents to move to higher tiers, though day passes can be acquired. *See also* Imperial Genealogist, Shining Wall.

- Workers District: Largest and most populated tier. Residents are classified as low-class manual laborers, tradespeople (bakers, smiths, carpenters, etc.).
- Makers District: Second tier and home of the Citadel and the courts. Higher class and quality laborers and tradespeople than in the Workers District, including jewelers, goldsmiths, silks, dyes, and other finer trades and merchants not allowed in the Workers District.
- Steel District: Also known as the Barracks. Houses the military and city guard.
- Bronze District: Lesser gentry, wealthy merchants, traveling merchants. Half of the Bronze District sits above the top of the Shining Wall.
- Silver District: Mid gentry, perfumers, high-class traveling merchants, bankers, highly affluent.

- Gold District: Gentry, merchant lords, bank lords.
- Founders District: The topmost tier, where rulers and the most affluent reside. Climbing to the Founders District is all but impossible, almost all residents inherit their position. To reside in the Founders District, one must prove genealogical connection to one of the original Founders of the empire, or be declared a Founder by imperial decree.

Imperial Genealogist: Second in imperial authority to the emperor. Responsible for maintaining genealogical records of all Founders, including the emperor. Has the authority to declare a person to be a Founder, and also to remove a family from the line of Founders.

Imperial Shield: Also called the Shield, it is the marking that identifies a Citizen. Placed upon the right temple, the Shield is shaped like a triangle capped at each point by a circle. Seals of imperial accomplishments, profession, and District are added to the Shield (Potential, Vrath, Workers District, Founder, etc.). The application of the Shield and Seals are tightly guarded by the Citadel.

Imutia (IH-MYOO-tee-uh): Imperial city in Glaedia, governed by Archon Rodak Toren.

Inaa'sa: Phaerian pantheon; goddess of order, daughter of Tolrik, sister of Meldun. *See also* Pantheons.

Ishariel sa'Nith'Iil (ish-are-REE-el sa-nith-EYE-ill): Legendary Preserver of Knowledge for House Nith'Iil. Ishariel's firedancer techniques are considered necessary techniques in studios throughout the Boorde Alliance. *See also* Boorde, firedancer.

Jouler Davanin (JOE-ler • DA-va-nin): Young Phaerian from Headwater; Facet of Prophecy—the Harbinger of Death.

Jubhax (YOOB-hax): City in the Boorde Alliance.

Kael Aelistair (KALE • AY-leh-stir): Strongest shaper in history; Facet of Prophecy—the Crier of Change. Has the ability to transform into living Currents of Power, making him appear as a being of light, and significantly amplifying his power.

Keeper: Title of Prytha who have the ability to ask, and who are tasked with the welfare of the Sacred Forests and their people. *See also* asking.

Kestrad Corgan: Boorde il'Spada who saved Emperor Bjarrik from the Ormgier Rebellion.

Kings and Castles: Complex game of strategy in which two players maneuver pieces on a board, the goal of which is to capture the opponents King and Castle pieces.

kohlithee (ko-LITH-ee): Boordish word meaning 'final breath', usually used when referencing a foe. *See also* Boorde.

Kortian Massacre (CORE-tee-an): According to Imperial Records, the entire Phaerian population of Kortia was killed by Archon Rodak Toren and his Vrath after a Phaerian threw mud on the archon. After the massacre, King Toren, Rodak's older brother, held a lottery throughout his Phaerian towns to repopulate Kortia. *See also* Rodak Toren.

Kralnach Hills (CRAWL-knock): Hills south of the Kralnach Mountains, bordering Glaedia and Neuheim. As a result of a legends that none return from adventuring into the Kralnach Kills, Upper-Tier Citizens from across the empire take the challenge.

Laa: Phaerian god; mother of the god Tolrik. *See also* Pantheon.

Laceyl Granivin: Queen of Astrakane who betrayed the empire, and is the most despised figure in imperial history. *See also* Great Uprising, Sacrifice.

Life Tree: *See* ta'Ajiilee.

Light, the: 1) *See* Alnazet. 2) Figure from the Prophecies of Light and the Hymns of Tolrik, foretold to liberate Phaerians and destroy the empire.

Longing, the: The result of having one's Shield removed, usually as a penance for treason or induction into the Sotouri; leaves the person with an eternal sense of loss and a longing to be whole. *See also* Imperial Shield, Sotouri.

Lost Postures: A series of Keeper Postures lost during the Ensnarement. The Postures of Growth, Decay, Life, and Death. *See also* Ensnarement, Keepers, Postures.

L'Veyna Elmhand (Luh-VEIN-uh • ELM-hand): Young ny-tein Prytha Keeper from Onatah.

Maelly Bodiou (may-EL-lee • BO-dee-oh): Founder, Phaerian sympathizer, and powerful shaper from Blrododok.

Master Forms: Highest degree of the Weapon Forms. The rank of il'Spada is conferred upon Boorde who learn the Master Forms for five different weapons. *See also* Advanced Forms, Basic Forms, Boorde, il'Spada.

Measurements (units of length):

- Inch...............Length of Emperor Droag's (first emperor) last digit of right thumb
- Hand ....4 inches
- Span ....9 inches
- Foot ....12 inches
- Cubit ....18 inches
- Pace...............30 inches
- Yard ....3 feet
- Furlong ....distance a plow team could furrow without rest (~600 feet)
- Mile ....5280 feet
- League ....one hour of travel by foot (~3 miles)

Meldun (mel-DUNE): Phaerian pantheon; god of mischief (chaos), son of Tolrik, brother of Inaa'sa. *See also* Pantheons.

Meldun's Mischief: Festival held in Phaerian towns and villages across southern Neuheim, Glaedia, and Castantor. Phaerians hold a large festival after harvest in order to trick the God of Mishief into attending the festivities instead of ruining the land for the next crop.

Meru'ut (MARE-root): 1) Officially called a Parliamentary Realm, it is one of the Five Kingdoms of Torgeir, and the only kingdom to allow same-sex rulers. Rather than rule the kingdom, the kings and queens of Meru'ut act as dignitaries and ambassadors. The Quorum of Education governs Meru'ut. 2) Capital of self-named kingdom, home of the Society of Educators and the Valkija. *See* Society of Educators, Valkuja.

New Torgeir: Name of the imperial capital. 'New' was added after the Great Uprising, symbolizing the new era of Torgerian rule.

    Nilam Fronth (NIH-lam • FRONTH): Known as the Voice, Nilam leads Makayla's Army of Light.

    ny'ir (nigh-EAR): *See* Prytha

    ny'tein (nigh-TANE): *See* Prytha

Onatah (OH-nuh-tah): 1) Name of Sacred Forest south of New Torgeir. Home of Orenda, Prack, and L'Veyna. 2) Name of Prytha city in Onatah Forest.

    Orenda (or-REN-da): Chosen of Alnezet for Onatah. *See also* Keeper.

    Ormgeirr Rebellion (ORM-gear): Silver District nobleman Lord Ormgeirr led a small army into the Imperial Compound, kidnapped the emperor, and held him captive in Prus, until Kestrad Corgan led a group of Quads to free them.

    Os'Om (osse-OHM): 1) Boordish for the raging torrent of an inferno. 2) Fifth of the Basic Sword Styles, or Basic Styles. *See also* Basic Sword Styles

paampus (paw-AUM-pus): long, tubular wooden instruments that emit a deep, haunting buzz-like call.

    Paradigm, the: Imperial laws governing the Five Kingdoms. The Paradigm also defines Phaerian characteristics, such as mental and physical competencies, as well as customs for Phaerian interaction with Citizens (e.g., Phaerians must first be given permission to speak, Phaerians must obey Citizens without question, etc.), and punishments for breaking those laws. Every aspect of Phaerian life is covered in detail, from day-to-day activities, to the layout of Phaerian villages and towns, as well as religious beliefs and practices. *See also* Three Laws.

Pantheons: Phaerians, Prytha, and A'anxil worship gods.

- Phaerian: (Note: Gods and religion were designed by the empire to help control Phaerian population.)
  - Tolrik: Father of the gods, the Creator, Lightbringer.
  - Laa: Called the Mother, the Origin, the Dawn of Creation, and the First Light, Laa is the mother of Tolrik.
  - Meldun: God of mischief, son of Tolrik, brother to Inaa'sa.
  - Inaa'sa: Goddess of order, daughter of Tolrik, sister to Meldun
  - Surar: Goddess of chaos, daughter of Dra'Nahl.
  - Dra'Nahl: Brother to Tolrik, the Destroyer, the Dark.

- Prytha:
  - Alnazet: The Light, Mother of All, Creator Divine, Light of Lights. She is the world, sun, moon, and stars, while her counterpart (Dra'Nahl) is the darkness in between. Alnazet created her only child, Tálise, as well as the Prytha.
  - Tálise: Son of Alnazet, represented by a large oak-like tree with a large dark hole in its trunk. There are three Tálise Trees, one in each Prytha forest next to the Mh t'Pralab. The Tálise trees are identical in appearance. They share a single life force and a single fate; whatever happens to one, happens to the others.
  - Dra'Nahl: The Dark.

- A'a'nxil:
  - Qi'k'krasz (Dra'Nahl): The Undying, Betrayer of Death, Savior, Hope of Life. Qi'k'krasz blessed Its people with

power over death (i.e., necromancy), demanding nothing in return, not even worship. Very few religious buildings are dedicated to Qi'k'krasz, as Its teachings eschew wasteful worship, and instead promotes a more socially-oriented agenda.

Paths of Prophecy: The choices each Facet makes as they fulfill Prophecy. Their choices aid in either Alnazet's or Dra'Nahl's victory. *See also* Dark, Facets of Prophecy, Light, Prophecies of Dark, Prophecies of Light.

patterns: Shapers shape the Currents of Power into patterns, which then accomplish feats of magic. Vrath patterns are sharp, angular, and rigid, with a specific design for the desired effect. Cabalist patterns are soft, curvaceous, and fluid, always changing in shape.

pattern-forging: Applying a permanent pattern to an item which imbues the item with a specific effect. It is important to note that patterns used for active shaping are different from patterns used to pattern-forge; some effects can only be attained through pattern-forging (e.g., hardening metal), while some can only be attained through active shaping (e.g., fireballs).

Pattern-Weavers Guild: A guild of imperial shapers who turn down a corded lanyard at the end of training at the Citadel, and instead pursue membership into the Pattern-Weavers Guild. The Guild, as it's commonly know, focuses on discovering new patterns and pattern-forging techniques. The Guild is rumored know more patterns than the Citadel, as well as holding the largest trove of Forgotten Patterns within their Sacred Vault. *See also* Shaping.

Pegrans (PEH-grans): Phaerian village in east Blailon.

Phaerian (FAIR-ian): The Imperial Paradigm describes Phaerians as sub-human, witless, and incapable of coordinating everyday day-to-day activities without imperial guidance. Left to their own devices, Phaerians would lose all civility and revert to their primitive, savage ways. Phaerians work the land under strict imperial oversight, in order to provide the empire with its foodstuffs. Phaerians and Prytha are the original inhabitants of New Torgeir. *See also* Paradigm, Three Laws.

Phlem: Euphemism Citizens use for Phaerians.

Potential: Cadets within the Citadel that show considerable power and aptitude with the Currents, especially in their range of influence and efficiency with shaping. *See also* Citadel.

prophecies, the: Written words from the Prophecies of Light or the Prophecies of Dark. *See also* Prophecies of Light, Prophecies of Dark.

Prophecies of Light: Also known as the Human Prophecies. *See also* Hymns of Tolrik.

Prophecy: 1) The entity who bound Alnazet and Dra'Nahl. 2) Short for Prophecy of Light.

Prytha (PRIH-thuh): One of the five races of Yrsa, Prytha are characterized by their long talons, eyes that shine like gems, and hair that changes color during the seasons, with skin tones that range from light to dark brown or green. Prytha are linked to a tree or plant (elm, spruce, dogwood, rosemarry, etc.), which passes through the father's lineage. The type of tree or plant determines a Prytha's hair color, which can range from deep greens to warm autumnal colors, depending upon the season. From the mother's lineage, Prytha inherit their infamous eye color, which shines like a precious gem (ruby, amethyst, emerald, etc.). Prytha live within the Sacred Forests. Their societies are centered around ta'Ajiilee. Some Prytha live on massive platforms within the tree's branches, while others live in housetrees asked within a common tree. *See also* house-tree.

- **ny'ir (nigh-EAR)**: Prytha who live in house-trees asked within a common tree (e.g., an oak). Most ny'ir are tied to evergreens or non-flowering plants like moss and ferns, which can be seen in their hair—dark green in the summer and light green in the winter. Their garb is generally more modest than that of their tree-dwelling cousins, preferring loose, sleeveless blouses with plunging necklines, and baggy trousers. They see their tree-dwelling cousins as arrogant and pretentious.\

- **ny'tein (nigh-TANE)**: Prytha who live amidst the branches of the lifetree, in communities established on large platforms. Unlike their ground-dwelling cousins, ny'tein wear as little as possible, preferring bright shimmering colors that compliment their skin and eye color. They see their ground-dwelling cousins (ny'ir) as prudish, bland, and uncouth.

Qi'k'krasz: A'a'nxil name for the Dark.

Qi'k'Sadra: A'a'nxilish name for the Harbinger of Death.

Quad: Moniker given to a team of Boorde Preservers, which often consists of four Boorde. *See also* Boorde, Preservers of the Lost.

ra'Vrath: *see* Vrath.

ris'wahri (ris-WAH-ree): Boordish word meaning 'true path'. *See also* Boorde.

Roach: Euphemism Phaerians use for Citizens.

Rodak Toren (ROW-dak • TOR-en): Archon of Immutia and younger brother to King Toren of Glaedia. Known throughout the empire for his power in the Currents, his military stratagem, and his harsh treatment of Phaerians. *See also* Kortian Massacre.

ry'ku (REE'koo): Traditional male Boorde attire; all black. Thick, buttonless shirt that wraps around the torso, held closed by a thick cloth belt, with wide, flowing trousers that fall to the floor, covering the feet.

sa' (saw): prefix given to Boorde who are adopted into a House and bestowed the House name.

Sacred Forest: Also known as the Prytha Forests, there are four Sacred Forests across Torgeir—Onatah, Ehawee, Wichahpi, and Whawee. A Life Tree (ta'Ajiilee) grows at the center of each forest, which is home to the reclusive Prytha. The Currents around the Sacred Forests are notoriously turbulent, making shaping near impossible, and an impenetrable living barrier of vines, brambles, and trees surrounds each forest. *See also* Alnazet's Wreath, Prytha, ta'Ajiilee.

Sacrifice, the: The Great Uprising threatened to destroy the empire. In order to help quell rebellion, the emperor ordered every Citadel to send its Vrath to the front lines of the war in northwest Blailon. The line of Vrath stretched from sea-to-sea along the border of Blailon and Astrakane. The cumulative power of the Citadel blasted land, and sunk the kingdom of Astrakane. *See also* Great Uprising.

Sati (SAH-tee): Name of A'a'nxil continent. *See also* Yrsa.

Scourge: Prytha word for Headless. *See also* Headless.

Sentinel: Powerful Prythan Keepers are able to create golems made of plant life (e.g., vines, roots, branches, etc.). Sentinels are semi-sentient, able to receive simple commands and discern between friend and foe. Sentinels enter a rage when they see a Headless, and attack the undead creature with no regard for its own safety until it or Headless perishes.

Shai'jan (SHY-jan): An il'Spada who has taken upon an Astasi becomes the Astasi's Shai'jan. The Shai'jan trains their mentor, guiding their Astasi through the Weapon Forms they mastered. *See also* Astasi, Boorde, il'Spada

shaping: The manipulation of the Currents of Power to produce magical effects. For reasons unknown, shaping extends the shaper's life, allowing them to reach over two-hundred years of age. *See also* Currents of Power.

- Bone Theory: The philosophical idea that a person's soul resides within their bones. The idea derives from the fact that shaping can repair bones, but not alter their shape, length, or density. Citizens who can afford the fee pay for Vrath and Pattern-Weavers to alter their appearance, turning their skin white, changing their hair (color, length, texture, etc), erasing skin blemishes, etc.; however, shaping can't change a person's height, or regrow a missing limb. Proponents of Bone Theory also point to the fact that even the brain can be altered through shaping (size, density, structure, etc.); however, ever alteration of the brain has also resulted in altered personalities and traits.

Shield: *See* Imperial Shield.

Shield-Day: The day a Citizen is given his/her Shield.

Shining Wall: The massive translucent wall that surrounds each imperial city. The walls are five-hundred feet tall and one-hundred feet wide, and were created to allow filter light. At night, the Shining Walls glow.

sidaiyo: Boordish word for the thin, curved blade known as a Boorde-style sword/blade.

Sigbjorn (SIG-b'yorn): The sword of the emperor, passed down through the line of succession.

skirters: Name given to Phaerians born outside of imperial controlled towns; *see also* townsborn.

snapping: Similar to pushing the body until it collapses from exhaustion, snapping occurs when a shaper uses the Currents until their mind snaps and the ability to shape is lost forever. Most snapped shapers lose their will to live. *See also* Shaping.

Sodat: 1) Boordish word for a wildfire that creeps over mountains. 2) Fourth of the Basic Sword Styles, or Basic Styles. *See also* Basic Sword Styles.

Sotouri: 1) The elite imperial guard charged with protecting the empire and destroying the Cabal. They also act as the emperor's personal guard. Their Shields are stricken from their temples during their induction. 2) An individual who has been inducted into the Sotouri. There are three types of Sotouri: Blades—masters of weapons whose skills rival Boorde il'Spada. Masks—the empire's eyes and ears, spying on Phaerians as much as Citizens. Spades—masters of the Currents of Power, and among the most powerful shapers in the empire.

Steel District: *See* imperial cities.

Surar : God in the Phaerian pantheon. *See also* Pantheons.

ta'Ajiilee (tah-aw-jee-ee-lee): Massive trees worshipped by Prytha as a direct link to Alnazet. *See also* Prytha, Sacred Forests.

ta'Axette (tah-OX-ette): Prythan word for the land of eternal death, where the souls of the damned dwell.

Talontongue: Prytha mode of communication using talons to tap and clack words and phrases. Each Prytha society has its own Talontongue, which is unique to that society, i.e., Prytha from Onatah cannot understand Talontongue from Whawee.

terrentor (tor-RENT-tor): Massive beasts that primarily roam the North and Northwest. Reachign twice the height of a man, Terrentors have four arms; two arms are massive and end in pincers, while the smaller arms (still larger than a human's) protrude from the chest, ending in three fingers and a non-opposable thumb. The skin on terrentors' face is thin and tight, and a mane runs down their back, concealing thick bone-like spikes along the spine. Terrentors are ravenous carnivores that travel in small pods, usually from three to five. Their expansive territory can cover over twenty leagues.

Testing, the: At twelve years old, every Citizen is tested for the gift of shaping. Those with the gift are immediately inducted into the Citadel, where they spend the next eight years in academic studies and learning to shape the Currents of Power. *See also* Shaping, Citadel.

Tezrel: 1) Boordish for flickering flame. 2) Second of the Basic Sword Styles. *See also* Basic Sword Styles.

Three Laws: Founded off of research conducted by the Citadel. The Laws are believed to be fundamentally true for all Phaerians.

- First Law: Phaerians are subhuman, only capable of simple verbal communication.
- Second Law: Phaerians are incapable of self-governance.
- Third Law: Phaerians are incapable of ethics and morality.
  See also Paradigm

tii'Vrath (TEE-Vrath): *See* Vrath.

Tolrik (TOLE-rick): Phaerian pantheon. Father of the gods, the Creator, Lightbringer. *See also* Pantheon.

townsborn: Nickname for a Phaerian born in an imperial controlled town.

Ul'Kral (OOL-crawl): Small, fairy-like beings that inhabit the kralnach Hills. Their wings look like leaves that changes color according to the season; furry brown skin; long thin tails that end in a leaf; small lipless mouths; no ears; grass for hair; voices sound like the wind. They feed on desire, trapping their victims with powerful illusions that cater to each creature's unique desire. The U'Kral's victim eventually dies from starvation. *See also* Kralnach Hills.

vis'mar (vis-MAR): 1) In Boordish, vis'mar is the first flicker of flame. 2) First of the Basic Sword Styles. *See also* Basic Sword Styles.

Vrath: Imperial organization of humans that are trained to shape the Currents of Power. Vrath are organized into three classes and are characterized by the color of cord wrapped around their left shoulder:

- do'Vrath (DOE-Vrath): Cord: black and orange. Officers in the town guard and army. Enforcers of imperial law.
- ra'Vrath (RAH-Vrath): Cord: white and blue. Philosophers and scientists who study the mysteries of shaping, history, culture, etc. Ra'Vrath are the Citadel's counterparts to the Guild's Pattern-Weavers. *See also* Pattern-Weaver's Guild.
- tii'Vrath (TEA-Vrath): Cord: green and yellow. The Citadel's Healers.

Weapon Forms: A collection of Boorde weapon techniques. There are three degrees of Weapon Forms—Basic, Advanced, and Master. *See also* Advanced Forms, Basic Forms, Boorde, Master Forms.

Workers District: *See* imperial cities.

ydu (eedoo): Traditional female Boorde attire; all black. A straight-cut, ankle-length robe with wide sleeves, and fastened by a wide sash. See also Boorde.

Ynipy (ee-NI-pee): The Prytha act of forgetting memories due to the passage of time, which then makes room for new memories. For this reason, ha'ath is an important part of the Prytha culture, helping them to forget superfluous memories.

Yrsa (IR-suh): The name of the world.

Zealots of Laa: Followers of the Phaerian goddess Laa; stereotyped by their unwavering devotion and self immolation. *See also* Pantheon.

ABOUT THE AUTHOR

From rural beginnings in Northern California, J. C. Eyler's adventurous life has taken him to the front lines of combat, across the beautiful beaches of Brazil, and into a philosopher's classroom to study ethics. Now, he sips coffee, and wonders why his characters refuse to take the paths he so clearly laid out for them.

www.ingramcontent.com/pod-product-compliance
Lightning Source LLC
Chambersburg PA
CBHW031148310726
48969CB00001B/14